PENGUIN BOOKS

Tom Clancy's True Faith and Allegiance

Thirty years ago Tom Clancy was a Maryland insurance broker with a passion for naval history. Years before, he had been an English major at Baltimore's Loyola College and had always dreamed of writing a novel. His first effort, *The Hunt for Red October*, sold briskly as a result of rave reviews, then catapulted on to the *New York Times* bestseller list after President Reagan pronounced it 'the perfect yarn'. From that day forward, Clancy established himself as an undisputed master at blending exceptional realism and authenticity, intricate plotting, and razor-sharp suspense. He passed away in October 2013.

Mark Greaney has a degree in international relations and political science. He is the author of *Commander in Chief, Full Force and Effect* and *Support and Defend*. With Tom Clancy he co-authored *Locked On, Threat Vector* and *Command Authority*. He has written five books in his own Gray Man series: *The Gray Man, On Target, Ballistic, Dead Eye* and *Back Blast*. In his research for these novels, he travelled to fifteen countries and trained alongside military and law enforcement in the use of firearms, battlefield medicine and close-range combat tactics.

Tom Clancy's True Faith and Allegiance

MARK GREANEY

PENGUIN BOOKS

PENGUIN BOOKS

UK | USA | Canada | Ireland | Australia
India | New Zealand | South Africa

Penguin Books is part of the Penguin Random House group of companies
whose addresses can be found at global.penguinrandomhouse.com

First published in the USA by G. P. Putnam's Sons 2016
First published in Great Britain by Michael Joseph 2016
Published in Penguin Books 2017

005

Maps by Jeffrey L. Ward

Set in 12.5/14.75 pt Garamond MT Std
Typeset by Jouve (UK), Milton Keynes
Printed in Great Britain by Clays Ltd, St Ives plc

A CIP catalogue record for this book is available from the British Library

PAPERBACK ISBN: 978-1-405-92230-2
OM PAPERBACK ISBN: 978-1-405-92231-9

www.greenpenguin.co.uk

MIX
Paper from
responsible sources
FSC® C018179

Penguin Random House is committed to a
sustainable future for our business, our readers
and our planet. This book is made from Forest
Stewardship Council® certified paper.

Principal Characters

Thomas Russell: Assistant special agent in charge, FBI Chicago Division; director of Joint Terrorism Task Force

David Jeffcoat: Supervisory special agent, Federal Bureau of Investigation

US MILITARY

Carrie Ann Davenport: Captain, United States Army; copilot/gunner of AH-64E Apache

Troy Oakley: Chief warrant officer 3, United States Army; pilot of AH-64E Apache

Scott Hagen: Commander, United States Navy; captain of USS *James Greer* (DDG-102)

Wendell Caldwell: General, United States Army; commanding officer of United States Central Command

THE CAMPUS

Gerry Hendley: Director of The Campus and Hendley Associates

John Clark: Director of operations

Domingo 'Ding' Chavez: Senior operations officer

Dominic 'Dom' Caruso: Operations officer

Jack Ryan, Jr: Operations officer / senior analyst

Gavin Biery: Director of information technology

Adara Sherman: Director of transportation

Helen Reid: Pilot of Campus Gulfstream G550

Chester 'Country' Hicks: Copilot of Campus Gulfstream G550

OTHER CHARACTERS

Dr Cathy Ryan: First Lady of the United States

Dr Olivia 'Sally' Ryan: Daughter of President Jack Ryan

Xozan Barzani: Kurdish Peshmerga commander

Sami bin Rashid: Security official, Gulf Cooperation Council

Abu Musa al-Matari: Yemeni national / Islamic State operative

Vadim Rechkov: Russian citizen in US on a student visa

Dragomir Vasilescu: Director of Advanced Research Technological Designs (ARTD)

Alexandru Dalca: Researcher for ARTD; open-source investigations expert

Luca Gabor: Romanian prison inmate; identity intelligence expert

Bartosz Jankowski: Lieutenant colonel (Ret.) US Army; call sign 'Midas'; ex-Delta Force operator

Edward Laird: Former CIA executive; intelligence community contractor

'Algiers': Algerian ISIS operative

'Tripoli': Libyan ISIS operative

Rahim: Leader of ISIS cell 'Chicago'

Omar: Leader of ISIS cell 'Detroit'

Angela Watson: Leader of ISIS cell 'Atlanta'

Kateb Albaf: Leader of ISIS cell 'Santa Clara'

David Hembrick: Leader of ISIS cell 'Fairfax'

The man sitting in the restaurant with his family had a name familiar to most everyone in America with a television or an Internet connection, but virtually no one recognized him by sight – mainly because he went out of his way to keep a low profile.

And this was why he found it so damn peculiar that the twitchy man on the sidewalk kept staring at him.

Scott Hagen was a commander in the US Navy, which certainly did not make one famous, but he had earned distinction as the captain of the guided missile destroyer that, according to many in the media, almost single-handedly won one of the largest sea battles since the Second World War.

The naval engagement with the United States and Poland on one side and the Russian Federation on the other had taken place just seven months earlier in the Baltic Sea, and while it had garnered the name Commander Scott Hagen significant recognition at the time, Hagen had conducted no media interviews, and the only image used of him in the press featured him standing proudly in his dress blues with his commander-white officer hat on his head.

Right now, in contrast, Hagen wore a T-shirt and flip-flops, cargo shorts, and a couple days' stubble on his face, and no one in the world, *certainly* no one in this outdoor Mexican café in New Jersey, could possibly associate him with that Department of the Navy-distributed photo.

So why, he wondered, was the dude with the creepy eyes and the bowl cut standing in the dark next to the bicycle rack constantly glancing his way?

This was a college town, the guy was college-aged, and he looked like he could have been drunk. He wore a polo shirt and jeans, he held a beer can in one hand and a cell phone in the other, and it seemed to Hagen that about twice a minute he glared across the lighted patio full of diners and over to Hagen's table.

The commander wasn't worried, really – more curious. He was here with his family, and his sister's family, eight in all, and everyone else at the table kept talking and eating chips and guacamole while they waited for their entrées. The kids had soft drinks, while Hagen's wife, his sister, and his brother-in-law downed margaritas. Hagen himself was sticking with soda because it was his night to drive the clan around in the rented van.

They were here in town for a club soccer tournament; Hagen's seventeen-year-old nephew was a star keeper for his high-school team, and the finals were the following afternoon. Tomorrow Scott's wife would drive the rental so her husband could tip back some cold brews at a restaurant after the match.

Hagen ate another chip and told himself the drunk goofball was nothing to worry about, and he looked back to the table full of his family.

There were many costs associated with military service, but none of them were more important than time. The time away from family. None of the birthdays or holidays or weddings or funerals that were missed could ever be replaced in the lives of those who served.

Like many men and women in the military, Commander

Scott Hagen didn't see enough of his family these days. It was part of the job, and the times he could get away, get his own kids someplace with their cousins, were few and far between, so he knew to appreciate this night.

Especially since it had been such a tough year.

After the battle in the Baltic and the slow sail of his crippled vessel back across the Atlantic, he'd put the USS *James Greer* in dry dock in Norfolk, Virginia, to undergo six months of repairs.

Hagen was still the officer in command of the *Greer*, so Norfolk was home, for now. Many in the Navy thought dry dock was the toughest deployment, because there was a lot of work to do on board, ships did not regularly run their air conditioners, and many other creature comforts were missing.

But Scott Hagen would never make that claim. He'd seen war up close, he'd lost men, and while he and his ship had come out the unquestionable victors, the experience of war was nothing to envy, even for the victorious.

Russia was quiet now, more or less. Yes, they still controlled a significant portion of Ukraine, but the Borei-class nuclear sub they'd sent to patrol off the coast of the United States had allowed itself to be seen and photographed north of the coast of Scotland on its return voyage to port in Sayda Inlet, north of the Arctic Circle.

And the Russian troops that had rolled into Lithuania had since rolled back over Russia's border to the west and to the Belarusian border to the east, ending the attack on the tiny Baltic nation.

The Russians had been embarrassed by their defeat in the Baltic, and it would certainly surprise everyone in this outdoor Mexican restaurant in New Jersey to know that the average-looking dad sitting at the big table under the umbrellas had played a big part in that.

Hagen was fine with the anonymity. The forty-four-year-old was a pretty low-profile guy, anyway. He didn't hang out with his family in his uniform and regale them with tales of combat on the high seas. No, right now he goofed off with his kids and his nephews, and he joked with his wife that if he ate any more chips and guacamole before dinner, he'd sleep in tomorrow and miss game time.

He and his wife laughed, and then his brother-in-law, Allen, got his attention. 'Hey, Scotty. Do you know that guy over there on the sidewalk?'

Hagen shook his head. 'No. But he's been eyeing this table for the past few minutes.'

Allen said, 'Any chance he served under you or something?'

Hagen looked back. 'Doesn't look familiar.' He thought it over for a moment and then said, 'This is too weird. I'm going to go talk to him and see what's up.'

Hagen pulled the napkin from his lap, stood up, and began walking toward the man, moving through the busy outdoor café.

The young man turned away before Scott Hagen could make it halfway to him, then he dropped his beer in a garbage can and walked quickly out onto the street.

He crossed the dark street and disappeared into a busy parking lot.

When Hagen got back to the table Allen said, 'That was odd. What do you think he was doing?'

Hagen didn't know what to think, but he did know what he needed to do. 'I didn't like the look of that guy. Let's play it safe and get out of here. Take everybody inside to the restaurant, use the back door, and go to the van. I'll stay behind and pay the bill, then take a cab back to the hotel.'

His sister, Susan, heard all this, but she had no clue what was going on. She hadn't even noticed the young man. 'What's wrong?'

Allen addressed both families now. 'Okay, everybody. No questions till we get to the van, but we have to leave. We'll get room service back at the hotel.'

Susan said, 'My brother gets nervous if he's not sailing around with a bunch of nukes.'

The *James Greer* did not carry nuclear weapons, but Susan was a tax lawyer, and she didn't know any better, and Hagen was too busy to correct her because he was in the process of grabbing a passing waiter to get the bill.

Both families were annoyed to be rushed out of the restaurant with full plates of food on the way, but they realized something serious was going on, so they all complied.

Just as the seven started moving toward the back door, Hagen turned and saw the young man again. He was crossing the two-lane street, heading back toward the outdoor café. He wore a long gray trench coat now, and was obviously hiding something underneath.

Hagen had given up on Allen's ability to manage the family, and Susan wasn't proving to be terribly aware, either. So he turned to his wife. 'Through the restaurant! Run! Go!'

Laura Hagen grabbed her daughter and son, pulled them to the back door. Hagen's sister and brother-in-law followed close behind with their two boys in front of them.

Then Hagen started to follow, but he slowed, watched in horror as the man on the sidewalk hoisted an AK-47 out from under his coat. Others in the outdoor café saw this as well; it was hard to miss.

Screams and shouts filled the air.

With his eyes locked on Commander Scott Hagen, the young man continued walking into the outdoor café, bringing the weapon to his shoulder.

Hagen froze.

This can't be real. This is not happening.

He had no weapon of his own. This was New Jersey, so even though Hagen was licensed to carry a firearm in Virginia and could do so legally in thirty-five other states, he'd go to prison here for carrying a gun.

It was of no solace to him at all that the rifle-wielding maniac ahead was in violation of this law by shouldering a Kalashnikov in the middle of town. He doubted the attacker was troubled that in addition to the attempted murder of the one hundred or so people in the garden café in front of him he'd probably also be cited by the police for unlawful possession of a firearm.

Boom!

Only when the first shot missed and exploded into a decorative masonry fountain just four feet to his left did Scott Hagen snap out of it. He knew his family was right behind him, and this knowledge somehow overpowered his ability to duck. He stayed big and broad, using his body to cover for those behind, but he did not stand still.

He had no choice. He ran toward the gunfire.

The shooter snapped off three rounds in quick succession, but the chaos of the moment caused several diners to knock over tables and umbrellas, to get in his way, even to bump up against him as they tried to flee the café. Hagen lost sight of the man when a red umbrella tipped between the two of them, and this only spurred him on faster, thinking the attacker's obstructed view could give Hagen a chance to tackle the man before getting shot.

And he almost made it.

The attacker kicked the umbrella out of the way, saw his intended victim charging up an open lane in the center of the chaos, and fired the AK. Hagen felt a round slam into his left forearm – it nearly spun him and he stumbled with the alteration to his momentum, but he continued plowing through the tables.

Hagen was no expert in small-arms combat – he was a sailor and not a soldier – but still he could tell this man was no well-trained fighter. The kid could operate his AK, but he was mad-eyed, rushed, frantic about it all.

Whatever this was all about, it was deeply personal to him.

And it was personal to Hagen now. He had no idea if anyone in his family had been hurt, all he knew was this man had to be stopped.

A waiter lunged at the shooter from the right, getting ahold of the man's shoulder and shaking him, willing the weapon to drop free, but the gunman spun and slammed his finger back against the trigger over and over, hitting the brave young man in the abdomen at a distance of two feet.

The waiter was dead before he hit the ground.

And the shooter turned his weapon back toward the charging Hagen.

The second bullet to strike the commander was worse than the first – it tore through the meat above his right hip and jolted him back – but he kept going and the shot after that went high. The man was having trouble controlling the recoil of the gun. Every second and third shot of each string was high as the muzzle rose.

A round raced by Hagen's face as he went airborne, dove headlong into the man, slamming him backward over a metal table.

Hagen went over with him, and both men rolled legs over head and crashed to the hard pavers of the outdoor café. Hagen wrapped the fingers of his right hand around the barrel of the Kalashnikov to keep it pointed away, and the hot metal singed his hand, but he did not dare let go.

He was right-handed, but with his left he pounded his fist over and over into the young man's face. He felt the sweat that stuck there, soaking the man's hair and cheeks, and then he felt the blood as the attacker's nose broke and a gush of red sprayed across his face.

The man's hold on the rifle weakened, Hagen ripped it away, rolled off the man, heaved himself up to his knees, and pointed it at him.

'*Davai!*' The young man shouted. It was Hagen's first indication this shooter was a foreigner.

The attacker rolled up to his knees now, and while Hagen shouted for him to stay where he was, to stop moving, to put his hands up, the man reached into the front pocket of his trench coat.

'I'll *fuckin'* shoot you!' Hagen screamed.

An unsheathed knife with a six-inch blade appeared from the attacker's coat, and he charged with it, a crazed look on his blood-covered face.

The kid was just five feet away when Hagen shot him twice in the chest. The knife fell free, Hagen stepped out of the way, and the young man windmilled forward into the ground, knocking chairs out of the way and face-planting into food spilled off a table.

The attack was over. Hagen could hear moans behind him, screams from the street, the sound of sirens and car alarms and crying children.

He pulled the magazine out of the rifle and dropped it,

cycled the bolt to empty the chamber, and threw the weapon onto the ground. He rolled the wounded man on his back, knelt over him.

The man's eyes were open – he was conscious and aware, but clearly dying, as compliant now as a rag doll.

Hagen got right in his face, adrenaline in control of his actions now. 'Who are you? Why? Why did you do this?'

'For my brother,' the blood-covered man said. Hagen could hear his lungs filling with blood.

'Who the hell is your –'

'You killed him. You murdered him!'

The accent was Russian, and Hagen understood. His ship had helped sink two submarines in the Baltic conflict. He said, 'He was a sailor?'

The young man's voice grew weaker by the second. 'He died . . . a hero of . . . the Russian . . . Federation.'

Something else occurred to Hagen now. 'How did you find me?'

The young man's eyes went glassy.

'How did you know I was here with my family?' Hagen slapped him hard across the face. A customer in the restaurant, a man in his thirties with a smear of blood across his dress shirt, tried to pull Hagen off the dying man. Hagen pushed him away.

'*How*, you son of a bitch?'

The young Russian's eyes rolled back slowly. Hagen balled his fist and raised it high. 'Answer me!'

A booming voice erupted from near the hostess stand at the sidewalk. 'Freeze! Don't move!' The naval officer looked up and saw a New Jersey state trooper with his arms extended, pointing a pistol at Hagen's head. This guy didn't know what the hell was going on, only that, in a mass of dead and wounded lying around the nearly destroyed restaurant, some asshole was beating the shit out of one of the injured.

Hagen raised his hands, and in doing so, he felt the wounds in his side and arm.

His brain went fuzzy, and he rolled onto his back. Stared up at the night.

Behind him now, over the shouts and screams of shock and terror, he was certain he could hear his sister crying loudly. He could not understand this, because he thought he'd given his family the time they needed to run.

2

Unlike his famous father, Jack Ryan, Jr, did not have any fear of flying. In fact, he rather trusted airplanes – certainly he trusted them *much* more than he trusted his own ability to fly through the air without one.

His relative comfort with aviation was at the forefront of his mind now, chiefly because in mere moments he planned on throwing himself out the side door of a perfectly functioning aircraft, into the open blue sky, 1,200 feet above the Chesapeake Bay.

Jack had packed his own parachute, following the instructions and oversight of Domingo Chavez, the senior operative in his clandestine unit, and he felt certain he'd packed it exactly right. But his mind wasn't working in his best interests now. While he needed his brain to reinforce his certainty that everything would go off without a hitch, he couldn't get out of his head the fact that on his last trip out of town, he'd forgotten to throw his favorite pair of running socks into his carry-on.

He thought he'd done a fine job packing *that* day, too.

Not the same thing, Jack. Packing a carry-on has no relationship to packing a damn parachute.

His imagination seemed intent on giving him an ulcer this morning.

Jack was in the middle of skydiving training, not as part of a military or even a normal civilian-based course, but a course developed by the cadre at Jack's employer. Jack worked for The Campus, a small but important off-the-books intelligence organization; it was populated with former military and intelligence types, a few of whom were seasoned free-fall experts.

And it was decided that Jack Ryan, Jr, needed to pick up this critical skill, because although he had begun his work at The Campus in the position of intelligence analyst, in the past few years his job had morphed into an operational role. Now he wore two hats; he might spend weeks or months at a time working in his cubicle unraveling the accounting practices of a corrupt world leader or a terrorist organization, or he might find himself kicking in a door at a target location and engaging in close-quarters combat.

Jack's life did not go wanting for diversity.

But he didn't have time to think about the ironic course of his life right now. No, now he began quietly reciting his checklist once he stepped out of the aircraft in exactly –

Someone at the front of the plane shouted now. 'Ryan! Four minutes!'

In exactly four minutes: 'Step out, head forward, arms away, body flat, knees slightly bent. Arch back, pull the rip cord, ready yourself for the snap, and check for good canopy.'

He mumbled his extraordinarily important to-do list softly as he sat in the side-facing seat that ran along the fuselage of the plane.

This wasn't his first solo jump. He'd started out with ground school two weeks earlier, then moved outside the classroom to begin leaping off a slow-moving pickup with his gear, and tumbling onto a grass strip. After this he jumped tandems for a couple of days, riding through the sky attached to Domingo Chavez or strapped to his cousin and the third member of the Campus operational team, Dominic Caruso.

Chavez and Caruso were both free-fall experts, trained in both HALO (high altitude, low opening) and HAHO (high altitude, high opening), and they put him through his paces in the beginner portion of his training.

Jack did what was asked of him, so he moved quickly on to static line jumps – Ding Chavez referred to these as 'dope on a rope' – where the chute was pulled open automatically as soon as he left the aircraft.

The next stage in his skydiving course involved low-level jumps into water, where he pulled his own rip cord, but did so immediately upon exiting the aircraft – these Chavez called 'hop-and-pops.'

He'd been through five hop-and-pops so far; they all had gone according to plan, as evidenced by the fact Jack was not lying face-first, dead in some field in Maryland. And while he was by no means a natural, nor had he even graduated to his first free fall yet, he'd earned a few attaboys from John Clark, director of operations for the small unit.

This in itself was quite an accomplishment, because John Clark knew his stuff – before The Campus, Clark had been a Navy SEAL, a CIA paramilitary officer, and the leader of a NATO special operations antiterrorism force, and he had performed more covert and combat jumps than all but a few men on earth.

Even though Jack had been doing hop-and-pops for the past two days, this morning's jump would be very different from the others, because as soon as he hit the water he would swim to a nearby anchored yacht and join up with the other two men on the team, already on board. Together they would perform a training assault on the vessel, which was filled with Campus cadre performing the role of an opposition force.

With just a few minutes before his jump, Jack looked across the cabin of the Cessna Grand Caravan at the two other men who would be involved in today's exercise. Dominic Caruso was head to toe in black – even his parachute harness, his goggles, and helmet. His chest rig was filled with thirty-round nine-millimeter magazines, and he wore a SIG Sauer MPX submachine gun with a silencer strapped behind his right shoulder.

Jack knew that the mags for Dom's sub gun and for the Glock pistol on his hip were filled with Simunitions – bullets that fired a capsule full of paint instead of lead, but bullets nonetheless, which meant they still hurt like hell.

Clark and Chavez's mantra was 'The more you sweat in training, the less you bleed in battle.' Jack understood the saying, but the truth was he'd bled in training many times, and he'd bled in real fights as well.

Jack was decked out in much the same gear that Caruso and Chavez wore, with a couple of notable exceptions. First, Jack wore swim fins strapped tight on his chest. He would put them on his feet when he hit the water. And second, the two men sitting across from Jack wore MC-6 parachute systems, special rigs outfitted with the SF-10A canopy designed for US Special Forces that would allow them to fly great distances and land with precision, even giving them the ability to back up in the air.

Jack's parachute, on the other hand, was a much more basic T-11 model, giving him very limited mobility. He'd fall at nineteen feet per second and land pretty much where the aircraft's velocity, the wind, and gravity sent him.

The other two guys were going to hit right on the deck of the boat, while Jack simply had to hop and pop and make sure he didn't miss the vast waters of the Chesapeake Bay directly below the aircraft. Jack was still in the 'training wheels' stage, so he'd have to swim to meet up with the other men to take down the boat. It was a little embarrassing having to swim to the target, but he knew exactly *zero* other beginners to the world of skydiving ever incorporated mock combat assaults into their jumps on their second week of training, so he didn't feel too much like a lightweight.

Ding Chavez sat next to Caruso, facing Jack, and right now he wore a cabin headset so he could communicate with the flight crew, the regular pilot and copilot of The Campus's Gulfstream G550 jet. Helen Reid and Chester Hicks were slumming, flying the much less powerful and much less high-tech Cessna Caravan, but they both enjoyed today's change of pace.

Dom Caruso noticed that Chavez was in communication with the cockpit via the headset, so he leaned over to talk confidentially with Jack, speaking into his ear. 'You good, cuz?'

'Hell, yeah, man.' They pumped gloved fists, Jack doing his best not to show his unease.

Jack felt he pulled it off, because Caruso said nothing about Jack having a pasty white face or jittering hands. Instead, Caruso double-checked to make sure Chavez had his headphones on and couldn't hear any conversation between Jack and Dom. Then he leaned forward again.

'Ding says we are facing an unknown number of opposition at the target, but between you, me, and the lamppost, there are going to be five bad guys on that yacht.'

Jack cocked his head. 'How do you know that?'

'Process of elimination. Look at the people we have in The Campus who could possibly be drafted into shooting it out against us. Adara will play the role of the kidnap victim, she let that slip yesterday. Clark, obviously, will lead the OPFOR.

He'll be down there with a gun. That leaves our four security guys: Gomez, Fleming, Gibson, and Henson.' The Campus contracted well-vetted former military and intelligence assets to serve as facility security personnel. They were all ex-Green Berets or ex-SEALs. Additionally, Gibson and Henson had served with the CIA's Global Response Staff, a tier-one security service that protected Agency installations around the world. All four men were in their fifties but as fit as Olympic athletes and tough as nails, and they had been friends of Chavez's and Clark's going back many years.

In addition to site security, the four also helped out with training from time to time, as they were all experts with firearms, edged weapons, and even unarmed combat.

Jack said, 'You could be right, but Clark has thrown curveballs at us in the past. A couple guys from the Campus analytics shop who used to be shooters might be down there helping out. Mike and Rudy, for example? They were both Army infantry.'

Caruso smiled. 'They were Rangers, I'll grant you that. But Rudy called me first thing this morning from the office. He's thinking about buying my truck, and he asked me to leave the keys under the seat so he could go by my place and take it for a spin on his lunch break. He said Mike would come along with him.'

Jack tried to think of others involved in their organization who might have driven the two and a half hours from the office in Alexandria, Virginia, to play the role of bad guys this morning. 'Donna Lee was FBI. She knows her way around a submachine gun.'

Dom said, 'Adara told me Donna tweaked her knee at CrossFit on Wednesday. She's on crutches for the next couple weeks.'

Jack smiled now. 'You've really thought this through, haven't you?'

'You and I run into enough assholes who want to shoot us out there in the real world. I'm not looking to take a Sim burst to the junk today. I've got plans this weekend. I'll game the system if I have to.'

Jack laughed now, glad for the diversion that kept him from thinking about his parachute-packing skills and the jump to come. 'What do you have planned for the weekend?'

Dom looked like he was considering whether or not to answer the question, but just then Ding pulled off his headset and Dominic leaned back away from Ryan.

'What are you two knuckleheads conspiring about over here?'

Both men smiled but made no reply.

Chavez raised an eyebrow. 'Two minutes out, Jack. You'll be dropped three hundred yards or so from the boat, at the stern, to avoid detection. Obviously it's daytime, and any sentry in the real world looking aft would see you, but this is training. The OPFOR on deck knows to keep their eyes in the boat. You get a free pass to swim up, as long as you don't make it too obvious.'

Dominic said, 'Yeah, don't dog-paddle up in a big yellow rubber ducky.'

Jack gave Chavez a thumbs-up.

'Once you're out the hatch, Helen will take us up to six thousand and we'll jump from there, sail right onto the deck. We'll spot targets on the way down and try to take them out on landing. By the time we hit the deck and strip away our harnesses, I want you climbing up the sea stairs ready to stack up with us.'

'You got it,' Jack said. This was going to be an arduous

swim. The waters of the bay looked choppy from the window behind him.

Just then, Chester 'Country' Hicks climbed out of the copilot's seat and moved back to the cabin door. He flipped the lever and slid the big hatch open, filling the already noisy cabin with the locomotive-like drone that came along with the air rushing by the aircraft moving at ninety knots.

Hicks held up a single finger, indicating one minute till jump, and Jack pulled himself to his feet, along with Chavez. Jack and Dom pounded fists again, and then Jack walked closer to the open hatch.

Chavez leaned close into Jack's ear as he moved up the cabin with him. 'Remember . . . Don't forget.'

Now Jack cocked his head, leaned into Chavez's ear. 'Don't forget what?'

'Don't forget anything.' Chavez smiled, slapped the younger man on the back, and pointed toward the open door. 'You're up, Jack. Time to fly like a piano!'

Jack fought a bout of queasiness, waited for the signal from Country, and then leapt out.

3

Seven minutes later Jack bobbed in the water at the sea stairs at the stern of the *Hail Caesar*, a seventy-five-foot Nordhavn yacht owned by a friend of Gerry Hendley's, director of The Campus. The yacht was anchored off Carpenter Point, at the northern aspects of the Chesapeake Bay, a few miles east of the mouth of the Susquehanna River.

Jack was tired from the swim, and he blamed the Susquehanna, as well as the North East River, which flowed south into the deeper water here, for messing with his stroke. He hadn't been wearing diving gear, just the fins and a snorkel/dive mask rig, so he'd done the majority of his swim on the surface. The waves forced him to work for every yard, and they also caused him to drink a substantial amount of seawater down his snorkel, and now while he stowed his excess gear on the sea stairs and readied his silenced submachine gun, he gagged a little.

He checked his watch and saw he'd made it just in time. And then, as if on cue, his waterproof headset came alive with Ding Chavez's whispering voice. 'One is in position.'

Caruso then came over the net. 'Two. On time. On target.'

Jack's transmission wasn't as macho as his cousin's. 'Three. I'm here. Headin' up.'

'Roger that,' Chavez said. 'We're right above you.'

Jack climbed the sea stairs and saw Ding and Dom in their black gear. Their chutes had been rolled and stowed under a thick spool of line on the main aft deck, and just a few feet in front of them, Dale Henson, one of their security men and a member of the OPFOR, sat with his back against the starboard-side gunwale. A pair of red splotches adorned the breast of his khaki jumpsuit, and a submachine gun lay on the teak deck next to him.

Henson had taken a candy bar out of his pocket and was now eating it, looking up at the three assaulters with no pretense of playing dead for the duration of the exercise.

He winked at Jack, then rolled his eyes back, jokingly feigning taking two gunshots to the chest.

'Cute,' whispered Chavez. Then he said, 'Fleming is on the flybridge. Dom stitched him in the back before he knew we were overhead.'

Jack nodded. Two OPFOR were down with minimal noise, and neither had had time to broadcast a warning on their radios.

Silently the three Campus operatives formed in a tactical train and moved up the starboard-side deck toward the door to the main saloon.

Ding was in front, Dominic right behind him, and while Jack brought up the rear, he saw Dom hold up his right hand and extend three fingers. It was Dom's covert way of letting his cousin know there were only three more to deal with in the opposition, based on the theory he put forth in the Cessna.

At the hatch to the main saloon Ding stopped and waved Jack forward. He ducked below the little portal, pulled an HHIT2 – a handheld inspection tool. It was a mini-video camera with thermal capability and a long, flexible neck that ran between the lens and the device itself. Jack bent the neck, then slowly raised the eye up to the portal while looking at the cell-phone-sized monitor. The half-inch-wide camera showed Jack the scene just inside. There, the other two training cadre, Pablo Gomez and Jason Gibson, sat on chairs, watching TV. Both men had eye protection on, pistols on their hips, and sub guns positioned within reach.

Jack held two fingers up for Chavez and Caruso.

While he watched, Gomez reached for the radio on the table next to him, spoke into it, and then adopted a look of concern. Jack assumed he hadn't received a reply from Henson or Fleming on deck.

Gomez dropped the walkie-talkie, launched from his chair, and went for his SMG, and Gibson took the hint, doing the same just an instant behind.

Jack took his eye out of the device, stowed it in a drop bag hooked to his belt in the small of his back, and hefted his MPX. As he did this he turned to Chavez, and in an urgent whisper he said, 'Compromised!'

Ding reached for the latch, Jack readied his SIG, flipping the selector lever to fully automatic fire, and then Ding turned the latch and pushed the door open with his foot.

Jack fired quick, controlled bursts at the two men, dropping Gibson first with three rounds to his well-padded chest rig, then taking Gomez in the same area just as his MP5 began to rise at the threat. Both men fell back into their chairs, put their guns in their laps, and raised their hands.

Jack moved quickly into the room, swung his weapon to cover the blind spots, and was immediately passed by Chavez and Caruso, both of whom began rushing for the ladder that led down to the lower deck.

Jack caught up to the others. They all hurried now, because while Jack's weapon was suppressed, it still made significant noise, and there was a hostage on board this yacht who would be imperiled by the sounds of the thumping full-auto fire.

They cleared staterooms quickly and efficiently; all three men worked together for each room instead of splitting up. Then, at the third of the four rooms, Dom pushed down the latch silently and shoved open the door. Inside, Adara Sherman sat on a bed with a mug of coffee in her hand and a magazine in her lap.

She didn't even look up from her magazine. 'Yay, I'm saved.' The comment was said with playful sarcasm.

Adara was the transportation manager for The Campus, among other duties, but today Dom knew that she was here to play the role of the hostage. Still, no one knew if she'd been booby-trapped or armed with a pistol and ordered to fire on her rescuers in a mock Stockholm-syndrome scenario, so Dom approached her with his weapon shouldered and pointed at her chest. He did this with an apologetic look on his face, and it took him out of his game for a moment, just long enough to miss clearing the head off to Adara's right.

His mistake came to him suddenly, but just as it did he heard his cousin's voice from behind, back in the passageway. 'Contact!'

The door to the remaining stateroom flew open, and John Clark stood there with an MP5 submachine gun at his shoulder and goggles over his eyes. He opened fire, but managed to squeeze off only a single round before Domingo Chavez shot him with a three-round burst to the chest. Ding knew his rounds would strike in the thick old canvas coat Clark wore over his three layers of thermal henleys, minimizing the pain from the impact of the Simunitions.

Clark had been shot by Sims many times before, and Chavez knew he was no fan.

In the stateroom with the hostage, Dom heard Chavez

call out that he'd ended the threat in the passageway, and he lowered his weapon a little, feeling certain he and his team had eliminated all the shooters in the opposition force. Then he turned back to Adara to search her, just as he would any recovered hostage.

While he did this, Jack covered him from the doorway between the stateroom and the passageway, but Jack didn't know the tiny head with the toilet, sink, and shower on the left had not yet been cleared by his cousin.

With his back to the head, Caruso did not see the pistol that emerged from behind the shower curtain there, and the shower was just out of Jack's sightline, so he couldn't see the threat.

Only when the crack of a pistol filled the room did both Dom and Jack know they'd screwed up. Dom took the shot straight between the shoulder blades, pitched forward onto Adara, and then caught a second round before he could raise his hands, signifying he was down.

Jack Ryan, Jr, burst into the little stateroom, dove past Dom and Adara on the bed, and fired a long, fully automatic burst into the head, desperate to end the threat before the hostage was also hit.

His rounds slammed into the shower curtain, shredding it just like they were real metal-jacketed bullets.

'Owww! Okay! Ya got me!' The voice had a distinctive Kentucky drawl, and instantly Jack's blood went cold.

Gerry Hendley, former *senator* Gerry Hendley, director of The Campus Gerry Hendley, stepped out of the shower now, covered in red splotches and rubbing a vicious purple welt growing by the second on the side of his neck. 'Holy hell, Clark was right. Those little bastards *hurt*!'

'Gerry?' Jack croaked. Hendley was in his late sixties, and other than maybe some quail hunting, he was *not* a shooter.

He'd never even been present for any of the Campus training exercises, much less taken part in one.

Jack could not fathom why the hell he was here. 'I am so sorry! I didn't know –'

John Clark called out from the passageway, 'Cease fire! Exercise complete! Make your weapons safe!'

Jack thumbed the fire selector switch down to safe, and let his weapon hang free on his chest.

Adara launched from the bed now, ripped off her safety glasses, and rushed over to Gerry. 'Mr Hendley, let me get you topside to my med kit. I'll get the worst of those cleaned and bandaged.'

Jack tried to apologize again. 'I'm sorry, Gerry. If I had any idea you were –'

Hendley was in obvious pain, but he waved the comment away. 'If you had any idea I was in the OPFOR, this wouldn't have been good training for you, would it? You were *supposed* to shoot me.'

'Uh . . . Yes, sir.'

Gerry added, 'Of course I would have appreciated a little better marksmanship. I wore a padded vest because John assured me I'd catch a round or two right in the chest, and that would be that.'

Jack had tagged Gerry in both arms, his neck, chest, stomach, and right hand. The hand and the neck bled openly, and Gerry's shirt was torn at the arm.

As Adara led him out of the stateroom and back to the ladder up to the main deck, Gerry Hendley looked at Clark in the small passageway. He said, 'You certainly made your point in one *hell* of a dramatic fashion, John.'

Jack looked up at Clark now and saw the always unflappable sixty-seven-year-old looking utterly embarrassed.

'Sorry, Gerry. It shouldn't have gone down like that, no matter what the circumstances.'

Jack sat next to Dom on the bed. Both young men looked like students in the principal's office just after getting caught skipping class.

Chavez leaned against the wall in the stateroom. 'Damn, Jack. You just sprayed your employer at close range with a dozen rounds of Sims traveling five hundred feet per second. He's going to feel like he tripped into a hornets' nest for the next week.'

'What the hell was he doing here in the first place?' Dom asked.

John Clark entered the master stateroom and stood by the door. 'Gerry was here because I wanted him to see for himself. The Campus cannot operate safely in the field with only three men. We've been lucky lately, and that luck is not going to last. Either we get some new blood in the operational ranks to help us out or we severely curtail the types of missions we take on.'

Chavez nodded. 'I'd say we illustrated the point. Dom's dead, two in the back. You didn't clear the head?'

Dom said, 'I came into this expecting five bad guys. When the fifth went down, I dropped my guard.'

'Which means?' Chavez asked.

Dom looked at him. He didn't try to excuse his error at all. 'Which means I fucked up.'

Clark wasn't happy about how things went today, and he didn't hide his feelings. 'That started well enough. Jack's jump was good, I watched it with my binos. You all three hit the boat with authority, got down to the hostage quickly, and used your speed, surprise, and violence of action to take down five opposition. But the only thing that matters in combat is how you finish, and you lost one-third of your number in that drill. That's a fail in anybody's book.'

No one replied to this.

Clark added, 'Clean all your gear, return it to the lockers at The Campus, then all three of you have the weekend off. But you have homework. I want to bring two new members into The Campus's operational staff, and it's your job to each come up with one candidate. Monday morning we'll meet and discuss. I'll vet the prospects, talk to Gerry, and make my recommendations.'

Caruso said, 'One of the security staff might work.'

Clark shook his head. 'All men with young families. All men who have served decades already. Ops is a twenty-four-seven, three-sixty-five job, and the guys up on deck aren't the right fit.'

Jack agreed with Clark's assessment – they needed new blood, and they had to look outside The Campus to find it. Clark had retired from operational status a couple years back, and Dominic Caruso's brother, Brian, had been on the team before that, but he was killed on an op in Libya. He'd been replaced by Sam Driscoll, who then died in Mexico. Since then, it had been just the three operators.

Jack decided he'd think long and hard this weekend about who he would like to bring into the unit to help out, because the hot spots of the world weren't getting any cooler, and it was clear that with the depleted numbers, The Campus wasn't as strong as it needed to be.

Ten minutes later Jack was back on deck. He'd apologized to Gerry again, and again Gerry waved off the young man's concern, except now he did it covered in bandages with a cold bottle of Heineken in his hand.

Jack wanted to throw up. Gerry Hendley had just recently

allowed Jack to return to The Campus after spending six months on probation for disobeying orders.

And now this.

Jack knew this wasn't exactly the best way to thank Gerry for showing his trust in him.

4

It should come as no great surprise to anyone that Tehran Imam Khomeini International isn't the most welcoming airport in the world for foreigners, but after nearly five hours in the air, the passengers of Alitalia flight 756 were happy to deplane and stretch their legs. Sure, this wasn't such a long hop for many of the business travelers walking down the jet bridge, but most of these people had been through the international arrivals terminal here before, and they knew the lengthy customs and immigration process ahead would ensure they weren't getting out of this airport and to their hotels anytime soon.

With one exception. One man ambling out of the jet bridge and into the terminal was a regular guest of the Iranian government, and he knew his way through immigration would be easier than those of the other poor unfortunate travelers around him. He was a businessman working directly with various federal agencies of the Iranian government, and for this reason he was given his own minder the second he walked off the plane. His minder would be at his side the entire three days he was in the country, serving as his translator and liaison with government agencies. In addition to this, the traveler knew a private driver would already be outside, parked in the tow-away zone in a government-flagged Mercedes, waiting to ferry the traveler and his minder wherever they wanted to go in the sprawling city for the length of his stay.

At the end of the jetway an Iranian man in his forties stood against the wall. The wide grin on the Iranian's face grew when he recognized the tall, fair-haired man in his thirties stepping out of the line of passengers from Rome and waving to him.

The fair-haired man pulled along a roll-aboard and carried a briefcase. In English he said, 'Faraj! Always great to see you, my friend.'

Faraj Ahmadi wore a bushy mustache, a head of thick black hair, and a dark blue suit with no tie. He touched his hand to his heart and bowed a little, then extended his hand for a strong handshake from the new arrival to his country. 'Welcome back, Mr Brooks. It is a pleasure to see you.'

The smile on the Westerner's face turned into a mock frown. 'Really? Are we gonna go through this again? Mr Brooks was my dad. I've begged you to call me Ron.'

Faraj Ahmadi bowed politely again. The Iranian said, 'Of course, Ron. I always forget. Your flights went smoothly?'

'Slept most of the way from Toronto to Rome. Worked all the way from Rome to here. Productive on both flights, as far as I'm concerned.'

'Excellent.' Faraj took the handle of the roll-aboard and motioned toward the immigration controls area. 'By now you are well aware of our routine here at the airport.'

Brooks said, 'I could do this in my sleep. In fact, I probably have, once or twice.'

Faraj grinned even wider. 'You *have* been coming here quite regularly, haven't you?'

Brooks walked along with his briefcase while Ahmadi pulled his luggage. He said, 'I was just looking at my calendar the other day. This is my sixteenth visit in the past three years. Works out to more than five trips a year.'

Again the wide smile grew under the thick mustache of the Iranian. Ahmadi was Iranian government, but he had one of the brightest, most pleasant faces Brooks had ever seen. 'We are always happy to see you. I know my colleagues are hopeful you will always be able to travel here from Canada so easily.'

'No kidding. All that talk about a travel ban on the news has got me worried.'

They made a turn to the left, and the massive lines in front of the immigration booths came into view. There were easily three hundred people waiting to have their documents checked. But the two men walked on, veering to the left of the crowd and continuing on down an empty lane.

Faraj said, 'We are all hopeful businessmen like yourself will be allowed by the United Nations to continue operating as always.'

'Couldn't agree more,' Brooks said. And then, 'At least we know who to blame for the new bad blood between certain countries of the West and your nation.'

Faraj's grin remained constant, but he nodded. 'Too true. I'm just a liaison, not a politician or a diplomat, but I watch the news. Clearly the American President is once again shaking his fist at my peaceful country.'

Brooks said, 'You don't want to say his name in public. I get it. Well, I'll say it. It's all the fault of that son of a bitch Jack *freakin'* Ryan.'

Faraj laughed now. 'I think, when you say it like that, nobody around here minds.'

They passed a restroom, and Faraj, always the empathetic host, said, 'Immigration will only take a few seconds, but traffic is bad on the Tehran–Saveh Road this morning.' He motioned to the men's room. 'If you would like to –'

'Not necessary, Faraj. I took care of business before we

landed.' Brooks winked at his friend. 'That's why I'm called a businessman.'

Seconds later they stood at the immigration booth. Even the officer seated at the VIP immigration lane recognized the tall man with the light hair and blue eyes. In good English, but English not nearly as good as that of Ahmadi, the white-haired officer said, 'Good morning, Mr Brooks. Welcome back to the Islamic Republic of Iran.'

'Pleasure is mine, sir,' Brooks replied. He didn't even set his briefcase down. He knew he'd be walking again to the car within seconds.

He handed over his Canadian passport with his visa inside, and he stood in front of the camera and smiled while his picture was taken. A green light glowed on the fingerprint reader on the ledge in front of him and he placed his thumb there, just as he'd done fifteen times before.

'How long are you visiting, Mr Brooks?' the officer asked.

'Only three days, unfortunately. Just a short drop-in for some meetings.'

'Very good, sir.' The seated immigration officer clicked some buttons on his keyboard.

As he did this Ron Brooks looked to his chaperone. 'What's first on the agenda today, Faraj?'

Faraj Ahmadi had moved behind the immigration desk, familiar like an employee of the airport, so many times had he been here collecting businessmen working with his government. He placed his own paperwork down, and he glanced at the computer monitor as he prepared to shepherd the Canadian beyond the immigration bay. He said, 'I thought we might grab a quick lunch at that restaurant you like on Malek-e-Ashtar Street before going to the hotel so you can relax. Dinner tonight will be with –'

Ahmadi stopped speaking, and his ever-present smile faltered a bit as he looked at the computer monitor with mild confusion. He turned to the immigration officer and said something in Farsi.

The uniformed officer replied in Farsi, tapped a few more keys on his keyboard; his own expression morphed to one of puzzlement.

The men spoke back and forth softly, but Brooks didn't understand Farsi, so he just checked his watch with a smile. He glanced back to his minder after a few more seconds of conversation, and he thought he detected some annoyance in Faraj Ahmadi's expression now.

The Canadian businessman placed his briefcase on the floor. Clearly this was going to take a moment. 'There a problem, Faraj?'

The wide smile returned instantly. 'No, no. It's nothing.' Faraj spoke again to the seated immigration officer, squeezed the man on the shoulder playfully, and made some sort of a joke. Both men smiled, but Brooks noticed the immigration officer was typing in his computer faster now, cocking his head, still looking at something on the screen.

Fifteen times through immigration here, and Brooks had never seen this before.

After another exchange between the two Iranians, the Canadian said, 'What is it, Faraj? Did my ex-wife put out an all-points bulletin on me?'

Faraj scratched his head. 'Just a problem with the fingerprint reader, I think. Would you mind trying again?'

Ron Brooks blew on his thumb dramatically and placed it back on the reader. 'Tell me who sells you your scanners, and I'll get you a better model from abroad, *and* undercut what you're paying now.'

Faraj smiled, but his eyes remained locked on the computer monitor.

The immigration officer wasn't laughing at all. His hand slipped under his desk, and Ahmadi snapped angrily at him. The reply came in an apologetic tone, but even though Ron couldn't understand the language, he realized the seated officer had hit some sort of a button. Three more customs officers, one out of uniform and wearing a badge on the lapel of his suit, walked over immediately and looked at the monitor.

Brooks made a joke. 'I knew I should have claimed that pocketful of pistachios I took out of Iran when I was here in May.'

Faraj wore no smile now, and he wasn't even listening to the Canadian. Instead, the senior customs officer spoke calmly and professionally to the government minder, and Faraj responded in Farsi with more fervor than Brooks had ever seen from the normally calm and happy man.

The exchange ended with Faraj Ahmadi turning to Brooks. 'I beg your pardon, Ron. There is some sort of a system issue with our computer today. Honestly this has never happened before. We will get everything in order, but your visa cannot be processed until we do. Will you come with me, please, to a waiting room? We can have some coffee while they sort everything out.'

Ron Brooks heaved his shoulders a bit and gave a little smile. 'Sure, Faraj. Whatever.'

'I do apologize.'

'Don't stress about it, my friend. You should see what I have to put up with when I visit the United States. Bunch of assholes.'

*

This didn't look like a waiting room to Ron Brooks. He'd been led into a room no more than fifteen by fifteen feet, the windowless space adorned with just a simple table with three chairs around it, and on the wall an unframed poster of the Imam Khomeini airport and another of the current president of the nation.

A large mirror ran across one wall, and a camera was pointed down at the table from a high corner.

He knew what this was. It was a reconciliation room, a place where smugglers were taken to have their bags checked over carefully.

Three armed police officers in tactical gear and with automatic rifles across their chests stood in the doorway. They looked at Brooks with some curiosity, but they didn't seem nervous or agitated. When Brooks turned to Faraj and pointed out the presence of the three men, the chaperone went pale with embarrassment. 'It's just the damn rules. They will all owe us a big apology in moments, Ron. In the meantime I will bring you a coffee. Just the way you like it. One sugar only.'

Brooks smiled at his friend, but his smile was getting harder to muster. 'Look, I know this isn't your fault, but I'm really tired, really hungry, and I'm not too crazy about this little reception committee watching over me like I've done something wrong. Perhaps you can call General Rastani and he can put some pressure on these guys. He is the one that insisted I come to Tehran this week for a meeting. He'll be interested to know about what's going on here.'

On the Iranian's face came a glimmer of hope. 'Yes, of course! I will do this right now. Coffee first, then I will call –'

'I had coffee on the plane. How about we just call the general's office?'

Faraj bowed. 'Certainly. We will be on our way in no time.'

Two hours and twenty minutes after his chaperone raced out of the small reconciliation room with a promise to resolve the matter and return in short order, Ron Brooks sat alone at the table. He'd not seen a hint of Faraj, nor a hint of any coffee, and even though the door to the hallway was not locked, the three armed guards outside had turned to eight armed guards, and every time Ron opened the door and asked for someone who spoke English, a stern young man in tactical gear with a gun on his chest merely waved him back inside the room and shut the door in his face.

Ron had stood, he had paced, and now he sat, looking at his watch. Furious, he even looked up at the camera high in the corner and pointed down to his crotch, making plain the fact he had to take a leak.

Seconds after doing this he was about to put his head down on the table when the door opened and three men in black suits entered. None of the men wore smiles, and they offered no greetings or introductions.

One by one, Brooks returned their steely gaze. He'd had enough of this, and he did not mask his irritation. 'Where is Ahmadi? I need my translator.'

The oldest of the three men sat down; he wore a gray beard and a suit with a collarless shirt. Brooks knew neckties were considered Western and liberal here in conservative Iran, and there were regulations prohibiting them, although these rules were flouted by many.

But not by this guy or his colleagues.

The man with the gray beard said, 'You will not need a translator. We all speak English.'

'Good. So that means you will be able to tell me what the *hell* is going on.'

'Certainly, I can do this. There is a serious problem with your documentation.'

Brooks shook his head now. 'No, buddy, there's not. I'm not some dopey tourist. It's not my first trip here.'

'It's your sixteenth, in fact,' Gray Beard said, momentarily confusing Brooks.

'Yeah . . . that's right. And it's the same damn documentation I've used the last fifteen times I've visited Iran without a single problem.'

Gray Beard said, 'Yes, I agree. But in contrast to this visit, sir, the last fifteen times, we were unaware that there were errors on several lines on your passport.'

Brooks recoiled at the accusation. 'Errors on *which* lines?'

Gray Beard leaned forward a little. 'To begin . . . the line with your name on it.'

'I . . . I don't understand.'

Gray Beard turned his hands over, held them up apologetically. 'Your name is not Ron Brooks.'

'The hell it's not! You contact General Hossein Rastani and ask for –'

'Your name' – Gray Beard spoke right over the loud Westerner – 'is Stuart Raymond Collier.'

Brooks cocked his head. '*Who?* Pal, I can promise you . . . I've never heard that name in my life.'

'And there is an error on your occupation. You are not the owner of your own international purchasing and exportation firm. You are, in fact, employed by the CIA.'

'The C.I. – are you for *fucking* real?' Brooks launched to his feet, startling the three men, but he turned away from them, began pacing the floor by the mirror. 'What's the game here? Are you guys shaking me down for money?'

The three men just looked at one another.

'Get me someone in charge. I work very closely with some extremely important men in your government.'

The man with the gray beard gave a heavy shrug. 'And that is of great concern to us, obviously. Trust me when I say everyone you've come in contact with on your visits here will be collected, detained, and questioned at great length about their affiliation to you. General Rastani included.'

Ron pointed an accusatory finger at the seated man. 'This is complete and utter bullshit. You have to show me proof. You can't just –'

Gray Beard was shaking his head before Brooks finished speaking. 'We don't have to do anything, Mr Collier. You, on the other hand, have to do exactly what we ask of you. And now I ask you to remain very still, for your own safety, of course.'

'Huh?'

One of the standing men opened the door to the hall. All eight of the men in tactical gear moved into the room now, converging on the man the Iranians called Stuart Collier, and they turned him around, pushed him against the mirrored wall. He didn't resist, but he shouted loudly while they removed his suit coat, his belt, and his shoes, and they frisked him thoroughly.

'I'm not Stuart Collier! Hey! Listen to me, you sons of bitches! I'm not Stuart Collier! I've never even heard that name. And I'm not in the CIA!

'Faraj! Where is Faraj Ahmadi? Somebody talk to Dr Isfahani! And General Rastani. Tell them to let these guys know I'm not Stuart Collier, and I'm not CIA.'

He was surrounded by the tactical team as they moved through back hallways of the airport, no one speaking but him, though eight sets of polished black boots on the tile flooring made considerable noise.

The Westerner shouted over the footfalls: 'This is a big mistake! Somebody call the Canadian embassy! I'm Ron Brooks! I'm Ronald Charles Brooks, of Toronto. I'm not Stuart Collier!'

He found himself in a parking garage, the door to an SUV was opened, and dozens of men stood around, all of them clearly police or security officials. Ron saw Faraj now, but he was being led into the backseat of another unmarked vehicle.

'Faraj! Tell them! *Fucking* tell them!' Once more before his head was pushed down and he was virtually body-checked into the side door of the SUV, he looked back and screamed, 'My name is *not* Stuart Collier, and I'm *not* CIA!'

5

In the Oval Office, the director of the Central Intelligence Agency looked across the oaken desk into the worried eyes of the President of the United States and said, 'His name is Stuart Collier. He's CIA.'

Director Jay Canfield did not mask his frustration as he told President Jack Ryan about the arrest of a CIA officer in Tehran. 'We have no clear answer on how he was blown.'

'He's a NOC?' Ryan asked. Non-official cover operatives were the most secret of the CIA's National Clandestine Service. They operated as private citizens abroad while serving as spies, and received none of the diplomatic immunity offered to 'covered' diplomats.

Canfield nodded. 'Yep. A damn fine one, too. He was operating under the name Ronald Brooks, a Canadian. He'd been working this cover for nearly four years. Been traipsing around inside Iranian tech firms for over three.'

The rain outside the thick windows of the Oval Office beat down in sheets, and the midafternoon skies were as dark as dusk. Ryan noted the bad weather matched the news from the CIA director.

The President took his glasses off and rubbed the bridge of his nose. 'How long ago?'

'Eight to ten hours. We just heard from the Canadians, who heard directly from the Iranians.'

'The Canadians knew we were running a NOC using a Canadian alias?'

'They did. They issued him a real passport, so there was no chance at all that the Iranians found forged documents on him and discovered his alias.'

'The work Brooks – I mean Collier – was doing. What kind of access did he have?'

'Not going to say he was the tip of the spear on what we know about Iran. His role to the Iranians was that of a procurer of dual-use equipment that was legal under current sanctions. Their military procurement people would give him a shopping list of tech items, and he'd go out into the West and secure suppliers, negotiate terms, arrange transport and paperwork. Nothing illegal, but we were expecting the Iranians to ask him to help them with more nefarious equipment sooner rather than later.'

Ryan reacted with surprise. 'So the Agency was helping Iran's military get what it needed from the West?'

'They were going to get it anyway and, like I said, it wasn't equipment subject to sanctions. We put Collier in the mix because this way we'd know what they had, where they were procuring it, and how it was getting into the nation, in case we managed to get tougher sanctions in place. And when they started asking him to get sanctioned items, we'd know about it first, we'd be in a position to stop it, and we'd be able to provide evidence to the UN.'

Canfield rubbed his own face now. 'But none of that matters anymore. That op is dead. The only issue is . . .'

'The only issue is,' President Jack Ryan said, 'how the *hell* was Collier compromised?'

'Exactly, Mr President. The total number of people who know about his operation is fewer than two dozen, myself included, and we are as vetted as anyone can be in the intelligence community. Electronic systems are stable, no compromise there. So far, this is a complete mystery. Obviously we are shaking the trees, trying to find out what happened.'

'What will they do to him?'

'He's a NOC, so they can do whatever the hell they want. Still ... With your permission we can quietly go to a third-party nation, the Swedes, for example, and let it be known Canadian businessman Ronald Brooks has value to us. Humanitarian concerns, something like that. They'll know that's a bunch of baloney, but they'll keep him secure, something to trade down the road. Obviously it's tacit admission by us that he's Agency, but otherwise they might hang him from a construction crane.'

Ryan nodded. 'Approved. I want him out of there.'

'Yes, sir. But you know how this works. They'll hold on to him for a while and turn the screws, on him *and* on us. The more precarious and miserable his situation is, the more the Iranians will get from us to let him out. If they agreed to go light on Collier at the outset, he'd become a weaker bargaining chip.

'Mr President, be under no illusions. Stu Collier is going through hell right now, and he will continue to do so for the foreseeable future. Not a damn thing we can do about it.'

Ryan leaned back in his chair, looked off at the wall across the room with a gaze that made it appear as though he were searching a point a thousand yards distant. After a moment he turned back to Canfield. 'Use back channels to test the waters. See what getting Collier back is going to cost us.'

'Yes, sir.'

'Do we expect the Iranians to bring him in front of the media?'

'You can bet on it, sir.'

Ryan sniffed. 'Disavow publicly. We'll get him home as quietly as we can.'

'Of course, sir.'

Ryan asked, 'Why isn't Mary Pat here?'

Mary Pat Foley, director of national intelligence, made a point of coming to the Oval whenever an intelligence community crisis anything like the magnitude of this had to be delivered to the President. Ryan and Foley had a long, tight bond, both professionally and personally.

Canfield said, 'She's on her way to Iraq, actually. She's personally involved with an operation.'

'*Personally?* Why?'

'Apparently she didn't want to lose touch with the HUMINT side of things. Said she was spending too many years in conference rooms and too much time staring at computer monitors.'

Ryan wasn't happy about this. While he understood and appreciated the sentiment behind Mary Pat's actions, the fact she wasn't here during a debacle like the arrest of a CIA NOC in Tehran meant Ryan missed out on the immediate input of the most senior member of the US intelligence community.

'When is she due back?'

'I sent word through her second-in-command. I assume this news out of Iran will cut her trip short. I can get her on the phone for you.'

'No, I'll let her do what she needs to do. She can call me if she has anything on this. I sure as hell hope whatever she's got going on over there is worth it.' Ryan waved the thought away. 'Just keep me posted, especially on your investigation into how his legend was burned.'

The intercom on Ryan's desk beeped, and his secretary

came over the speaker. 'Mr President. Attorney General Murray is here, he would like five minutes of your time.'

Ryan looked to Canfield, and Canfield stood.

'Send him on in.'

Canfield greeted Dan Murray as he entered, and started passing him for the door.

Murray said, 'This might prove interesting for you, too, Jay. I'd like you to stick around, if it's okay with the President.'

Ryan motioned both men to the sofa across from him, and he sat back down himself.

Murray said, 'That thing in New Jersey last weekend. It was definitely *not* a random act.'

Ryan raised his eyebrows. 'The fact you are bringing this to my attention, and Jay's attention, tells me there is some sort of a national-security implication in a shooting at a Mexican restaurant in New Jersey.'

'Afraid so. This will hit the news in an hour or two, but you need to know about it first. It turns out the shooter was a twenty-three-year-old Russian named Vadim Rechkov. He was in the US on a student visa. He'd been studying computer science at a tech school in Oregon, but dropped out. Local cops picked him up for drunk and disorderly several months ago, and he was given an order to appear. He would have been deported after his hearing, but he didn't show up.'

Ryan just said, 'Do criminals facing deportation *ever* show up?'

'Not very often, so that's not a surprise. But here comes the real surprise. The shooter had a brother who was a machinist's mate on the *Kazan*, one of the Russian subs sunk by the USS *James Greer*. And they've kept it quiet until now, but one of the victims in the Mexican restaurant was Commander Scott Hagen, captain of the *James Greer*.'

'Oh my God,' Ryan said. He'd gone to meet Hagen and his crew personally when they returned to Virginia with his damaged Arleigh Burke-class destroyer.

Murray hastened to add, 'Hagen is going to survive. Shot twice with an AK-47. But his brother-in-law took a round to the back of the head. Dead, along with a waiter and another patron. Six injured, including the commander.'

Neither Canfield nor Ryan asked if there was any chance this was a coincidence. Both men had been around too long to even wonder.

Murray added, 'Scott Hagen told the police after the fact that he'd caught the shooter eyeing him before the incident. Got so creepy that he and his family were just leaving when the guy came back in with guns blazing.'

'Didn't Hagen have security?'

'When he got back to the States, DoD arranged to keep a car with a couple agents in front of his house for a few weeks. Local police upped patrols in his neighborhood, and of course there is a lot of security at the shipyard where the *James Greer* was in dry dock. But no threats materialized, and this trip to New Jersey Hagen took wasn't anything official, so he wasn't looked after. Honestly, since there'd been zero direct threats on the commander, DoD went above and beyond the call of duty giving him any security at all.'

Ryan said, 'The assumption is that this Russian just read the newspaper and saw that Commander Hagen was captain of the *James Greer*, he blamed him for his brother's death, so he tracked him down and tried to kill him?'

'Seems like what happened. It's weird, honestly. FBI investigators haven't discovered how Rechkov knew Hagen was going to be at *that* restaurant at *that* time. The Russian rented a car in Portland six days earlier, drove cross-country, bought the AK and ammo just outside of Salt Lake City, then bought more ammo and a knife in Lincoln, Nebraska. If he ever shot the weapon at all it would have been by the side of the road somewhere. We can't find any evidence he even visited a gun range.'

Canfield said, 'So this probably wasn't a terribly sophisticated plan if this clown just got a tip about Hagen from the far side of the country, and then acted spontaneously.'

Murray nodded. 'We have a lot to learn about this, but that is what we think happened.'

Jay Canfield thought a moment. 'I don't see any chance in hell Moscow had anything to do with this. Not because they're above it, but because this would-be assassin sounds like such a screw-up.'

'Right,' agreed Ryan.

Murray said, 'DoD is ordering up personal protection for all the Marine and Navy commanders involved in the Baltic, on the off chance this is part of a wider scheme.'

The President then told the attorney general about the arrest of the CIA's officer in Iran.

Murray looked to Canfield. 'No idea how your guy was compromised?'

Canfield shook his head. 'None.'

Ryan said, 'The same week a NOC in Iran is exposed through unclear means, a military officer is exposed through unclear means. Does that seem weird to anybody but me?'

Canfield said, 'Hagen wasn't in a covert position like my NOC was. Still . . . I take your meaning. Somehow his travel plans made their way to some flunky with a grudge.'

Ryan blew out a sigh. 'What a damn mess.'

6

If Dominic Caruso had not joined the FBI and then joined The Campus, he probably would have opened a restaurant.

He loved to cook. He'd learned from his mom, had spent countless hours in the kitchen as a child, and even as a teenager he could make authentic Italian dishes from scratch, while his twin brother, Brian, rarely assembled anything more sophisticated than a bologna sandwich with mayonnaise and American cheese.

Dom had gotten away from the kitchen when he was in the FBI, and during his first couple of years in The Campus he was on the go all the time and had no one to cook for anyway, but now, as a single male in his thirties, he relished the opportunity to prepare meals for company.

Especially attractive female company.

Tonight the entrée was eggplant parmigiana; his dish was in its last stages now as he browned the cheese in the broiler. And to offset this vegetarian entrée, he'd prepared an impressive-looking charcuterie platter that now took up half a shelf in his refrigerator.

The Fontanella Mt. Veeder chardonnay was chilled and waiting in the ice bucket on the small table just inside the door of his balcony, which provided a nice view of DC's Logan Circle below without the warm air and street noise he would have had to deal with if he actually set up the table on the balcony.

The doorbell to his condo chimed at seven sharp, and

Dom pulled off the towel tucked into his belt that he'd been using as an apron, checked the eggplant in the oven quickly, and then went to answer.

Adara Sherman stood at the door. She wore a simple black dress, wedge heels, and stylish glasses. Her blond hair was shoulder length these days, and Dom could see the muscles in her neck and shoulders from her near-daily workouts at the CrossFit gym near her condo in Tysons Corner.

Dom couldn't figure out why, but he still hadn't gotten used to seeing Adara away from work. As the transportation logistics coordinator for Hendley Associates, and The Campus, she worked in two distinctly different settings. When she worked in the Alexandria office she wore business attire. But as the flight attendant for the Hendley Associates Gulfstream G550, she wore a generic-looking flight attendant uniform; navy skirt, navy jacket, and white blouse.

And there had been times, multiple times in the past couple years, when Adara Sherman the flight attendant had become someone else right in the middle of a trip. She would step into the galley of the G550, take off her skirt and blouse, and don 5.11 tactical pants and a dark tunic. She'd then heave an H&K UMP .45-caliber submachine gun from a hidden compartment behind an access panel in the galley, and she'd slide an H&K semiautomatic pistol in a paddle holster under her waistband.

Adara provided security for the aircraft, as well as serving as the medic for the operators in The Campus.

This job did not fall into her lap; she'd had years of training. She'd been a Navy corpsman in Afghanistan, she'd saved the lives of Marines in combat, and she'd carried an M4 herself and used it on more than one occasion.

No, she wasn't the typical flight attendant one might find

on a high-end corporate jet, and no, Dom still could not get over seeing her in a sexy outfit at night, because it was so far removed from her appearance throughout the day, no matter what role she found herself in.

Dom and Adara had been dating for a year now, but they had not made their relationship public to the others at Hendley Associates. Dom had a suspicion that his cousin knew. Adara agreed, and she insisted her 'woman's intuition' was infallible on such matters.

Still, if Jack *did* know, he'd not said anything, and Dominic appreciated his cousin keeping the relationship on the down low.

There was no specific prohibition against employees dating at The Campus, but they both assumed it would be frowned upon, so they didn't make a big deal about it. Both Adara and Dom led busy lives anyway, so it wasn't like they were living together, spending each evening watching TV till bedtime. No, this had been a relationship primarily of dinners and movies when they were both in town and had some free time, which was a rare enough occurrence.

Yes, things had gotten physical. That began in Italy, back at the beginning of their relationship, and although things were still physical, their careers had gotten in the way even though they both worked for the same employer.

Dom and Adara had an interesting relationship. They might go weeks without talking shop at all when they were alone together away from the office, or they just as easily might slip into work talk.

This was a night full of the latter. While they ate their eggplant parmigiana and drank their perfectly chilled chardonnay, they discussed the events of the previous morning on the boat in the Chesapeake. Dom was still angry at himself for letting Gerry Hendley shoot him in the back, and even more for creating a scenario that forced Jack to save the hostage by applying 'overkill' to the situation.

Adara had been right there with a front-row seat to the debacle, and she listened to Dom now, before putting in her two cents.

Adara said, 'Don't blame yourself. You guys *are* short-staffed. You are doing your best, but you need a larger force.'

Dom realized Adara had been upstairs with Gerry on the yacht when John Clark proposed exactly that to the men.

'We're getting two new operators.'

'Really? Who?'

'I'm sure Clark has ideas of his own, but he wants each of us to propose one candidate.'

Adara cut into her eggplant, ate slowly, drank slowly, all the while waiting for Dominic to say something else.

When he did not she asked, 'Who are you going to suggest for the position?'

Dom shrugged. 'Not sure. I know a lot of guys in the FBI still, and through the training cadre at The Campus I know some guys who used to be in military special mission units, but they all have families now, and working at The Campus is a tough job for a dad with young kids.'

He added, 'I think I know who Ding is going to suggest, and I know who Jack will nominate, and either of those guys would make excellent officers. I might just second one of their choices. Clark might think I'm taking the easy way out, but I've got to go with my gut.'

'That's true.' Adara could be calculating when the situation called for it, but at other times, she could be quite direct. She put her fork and knife down and looked across the table at Dom. 'I have an idea on who you could suggest.'

Dom raised his eyebrows and stopped his fork right before it went in his mouth. 'You do? Who?'

'Me.'

Dom froze, the fork still in midair, his eyes on his girlfriend.

Then he looked down and away.

Adara said, 'I know the job. I'm vetted; I've been in the field with you guys, more or less, on many occasions. I'm jump qualified, I've got my Master SCUBA diver rating, I can shoot. I earned the Navy Expert Pistol Medal and the Navy Expert Rifle Medal with a bronze S.'

Dom said nothing, so Adara said, 'Since you asked, the bronze S stands for "sharpshooter." Also, unlike the rest of you, I have a twin-engine IFR pilot's license, I can operate boats, and I have more medical training than anyone at The Campus.'

She smiled. 'And I do more CrossFit than you do.'

Dom reached for his wine, finished it, then pulled the bottle out of the ice and refilled his glass.

Adara said, 'And, of course, there was Panama and Switzerland.'

He put the wine back in the bucket, looked up at Adara, and said, 'No.'

Dom knew she'd bring up Panama and Switzerland. In the Panamanian jungle Dom and Adara had fought alongside each other, and in Geneva they had worked together as a team on a surveillance op that turned into something much more . . . kinetic. She'd done remarkably well on both occasions, as good as any other operator on the team. Dom knew this to be true, but that didn't mean he wanted her working as a Campus asset.

He saw Adara's cheeks redden a little, and he knew he was in trouble. He said, 'I'm sorry I said it like that. It's just that . . .'

'What?'

'I don't want you on the team.'

Adara nodded a little as she looked off to the distance, out over Logan Circle. Dom had been dating her long enough to read the signals. She was angry, her defenses were going up, and she just might go on offense. Quickly he tried to clarify himself.

'Of course you *can* do it. It has nothing to do with ability. It's me. I don't *want* you to do it.'

'Why? Because it's too dangerous?'

'Yes. That's *exactly* why. Look, that job you're asking me to nominate you to fill . . . I lost my brother in that same position, I was right there with him and I watched him die. Then another guy came in. He became a good friend. And he died, too. Again, I was there when it happened. I don't want to lose you.' He paused. 'I care about you, and that job isn't a place to send people you care about.'

'I understand how you feel, but your brother's death and Sam Driscoll's death had nothing to do with the fact they were in the same position. It was the job. The job all of you have. The exact same fate could be waiting for any one of you.'

'And I accept that,' Dom said. 'I just don't want it for you.'

'What about what *I* want?' she asked.

Dom said, 'The training op on Friday went bad because I wasn't looking at you as a hostage. I was looking at you as my girlfriend. I felt weird about holding a gun on you and checking you for traps in front of the guys, I got distracted, and it kept me from checking the dead space on my left. How do I know that working a real-world op with you won't have me acting the same way, in ways that will compromise lives?'

Adara simply said, 'You make decisions about your life, and you get to do the same to my life? What if I told you to leave The Campus? Would you do it?'

'No.'

'Exactly. Who put you in charge of me?'

'It's not that. It's just —'

'It *is* that. I realize you care. I realize your heart is in the right place. You don't want to see me get hurt. But if you care about me, you will let me pursue something that's important to me.'

Angrily, Dom said, 'You don't need me to recommend you to Clark. You can just tell him yourself.'

'I want your blessing.'

'Why?'

'Because I care about you. And I care about what you think.'

Dom looked down at the street below. 'Don't make me do this.'

'I'm not making you. I'm asking you.'

He stood now.

'Where are you going?' Dom could hear anger welling in her voice.

'To the refrigerator. We're out of wine.'

'Oh . . . well. That's okay.'

The discussion moved to the sofa, and it also moved away from an argument, and into a conversation. Adara and Dom both began to put themselves in the other's place and understand the reasons behind the other's entrenched viewpoint.

After a half-hour of back-and-forth Adara said, 'I understand the position I'm putting you in, I'm just asking you to help me. Look, even if you say no, I'll go to Gerry and talk to him. If you will feel better about yourself, I'll do that. But I just want to know you believe in me, and that you want me there with you, when you need someone you trust.'

He said, 'I do believe in you. I think you would be great in the job.'

'Do you know someone who would be better?'

There and then, he knew she'd won. Dom realized he didn't feel any different from the way he did when they began discussing this more than a half-hour ago, but he had no other arguments to employ. He could be obstinate, or he could be reasonable, even if reason went against his wishes. He said, 'No. I don't know anyone more qualified. I'll put your name in the hat. It's up to Gerry and John.'

'Of course.' She kissed him. 'I know that wasn't easy for you. None of this will be.'

He noticed Adara looking at him expectantly. Like there was something more. 'What?' he asked.

'Are we finished talking about this?'

'I really hope so. Why?'

She smiled. 'Please tell me you made your tiramisu.'

Despite his dark mood, Dom smiled as well. 'I did.'

Adara pumped her fists in the air. '*Hell*, yes!'

Dom smiled. 'Do you come over here because of me, or because of my tiramisu?'

'Mostly you, but you're not the only sweet, good-looking guy in DC. There are one or two others. You *are*, however, the only sweet, good-looking guy in DC who makes unbelievable scratch tiramisu.'

Dom raised his eyebrows. 'You've tried all the others, have you?'

Adara laughed and climbed over onto his lap to kiss him.

7

The narrow, hilly street was full of women and children, all of whom had to move into alleyways and open doorways to let the convoy of big SUVs through. When the vehicles parked by the building at the top of the hill, dozens of women and girls converged around them and stared at the spectacle. Women on rooftops looked on, eyes wide, softly chattering to one another in amazement.

Six black SUVs were parked here on this narrow street in suburban Sulaymaniyah, in eastern Iraqi Kurdistan. Some dozen or more Westerners poured out of the vehicles, big men with guns, tactical wear, and expensive-looking sunglasses and watches, followed by another dozen Westerners in business attire. There were females in the group, all wearing chadors, even though these were clearly American women.

But that wasn't the part that had all the Yazidi women and girls here utterly transfixed.

No, they were amazed that the person who seemed to be the one in charge of this entire entourage was herself a woman.

Mary Pat Foley climbed out of a Land Rover and a group of attendants and protectors coalesced around her. She was the director of national intelligence, head of the sixteen-member US intelligence community, and she warranted the high security and the large number of assistants.

There was no mistaking that the American woman was, indeed, in charge.

Following her out of the vehicle was her chief of staff, an active-duty Air Force colonel, who straightened his blue service dress uniform upon standing. A young assistant stepped up to her from another vehicle, clipboard in hand, and Mary Pat's interpreter for the day, a forty-five-year-old Kurdish woman who worked for the United Nations, motioned toward a whitewashed stone building close by.

This part of Sulaymaniyah had taken the name 'Little Sinjar' because it served as an encampment for many of the Yazidi internally displaced persons who had fled their community on and around Mount Sinjar in the west. The Islamic State had overtaken Sinjar three years earlier, and since then the IDP camps in various parts of Iraq housed virtually all of the world's Yazidi population.

Yazidis were an ethnically Kurdish people, but their different belief system had separated them from the Kurdish population. Still, they spoke Kurmanji, the language of the Kurds here in Iraq, so Kurdistan was the logical location for the IDP camps.

The front door to the whitewashed building stood open, and Kurdish and Yazidi officials stood around it, waiting for Foley and her entourage. Quick introductions were made. Mary Pat had met some of these men this morning at the US consulate in Erbil before helicoptering east here to Sulaymaniyah, so the meet and greet took little time.

She then stepped inside, into the cooler, dark room. Here a young woman stood alone, wearing a chador and clean, simple robes. She looked nervous, completely bemused by all the attention that had been directed toward her since first thing this morning when she was awoken from her sleeping rug on the floor by a relief worker, asked her name, and shown a handwritten document she had signed a month earlier when she came to the camp. She swore everything on the page was true, and then she was taken from the room full of girls, moved to this building, and told some people from America were on their way in a helicopter to speak with her.

Mary Pat and most every one of the intelligence organizations under the umbrella of the DNI had been hunting for one man above all others in their never-ending quest to keep America safe from Islamic radical terrorism, and the hunt had led her and her people here to Kurdistan. The Kurds were good friends to America and they were helpful in the manhunt, but to say they had a full plate at the moment would have been a dramatic understatement. The Kurds were at war, fighting for their lives against the Islamic State, so it took a personal visit by the US director of national intelligence this week to get their political leadership's full attention.

And this morning their help had borne fruit. A Yazidi girl named Manal had made a report to Kurdish officials a month earlier, before she was put into a UN-run IDP camp and promptly lost by UN officials; but overnight she'd been identified and located in a camp far to the east of the battle lines.

Mary Pat Foley would be the first American to speak with her. There were tens of thousands of displaced Yazidis, and hundreds of thousands of refugees and IDPs here in Iraq. But seventeen-year-old Manal warranted this level of personal attention, as far as Mary Pat Foley was concerned, for one very important reason.

She had been forced to marry an ISIS operative in Raqqa named Abu Musa al-Matari.

And the most wanted man on planet Earth to US

intelligence was an ISIS operative known to be living in Raqqa with that very name.

The young lady extended her hand to Mary Pat, offering a handshake and a smile with a shy bow. In memorized English taught to her by a UN aid worker minutes before Foley's arrival she said, 'Very pleasure to meet. My name Manal.'

Foley smiled and bowed, genuinely appreciative of the effort. The interpreter stood close. 'My name is Mary Pat and I come from the USA. I have heard some of your story, and I am so honored to meet such a brave woman.' The DNI knew Manal had recently managed to escape her captors, and that in itself was enough to earn her respect.

The interpreter translated softly between the two women, and the young girl blushed.

In moments all three were sitting on rugs on the floor. The colonel waited outside – he and Mary Pat agreed Yazidi girl might be more comfortable that way – but one of Foley's young female assistants remained in the room to record and take notes. She stood against the wall, just close enough to listen in.

Manal told Mary Pat about her capture, the brutal murder of the rest of her family, and then of being taken away with a group of girls as young as ten. Manal herself had been just fifteen at the time.

'They called us *sabya*,' Manal said through the interpreter.

The interpreter added, 'It means "slaves captured in wartime."'

Mary Pat could see in the nervous eyes of Manal that she had lived through unspeakable horrors.

The young girl said, 'I was told I would be given as a gift to a special man. I waited days in a small apartment. I was not raped at this time, like all the other girls were. I was very lucky. Finally, a man arrived, dressed like a Westerner, a very short beard, short hair. Not like most men in DAESH.'

DAESH was an acronym for al-Dawla al-Islamiya fil Iraq wa al-Sham, the Islamic State of Iraq and al-Sham. Al-Sham was also known as Greater Syria or the Levant.

'Did he tell you his name?'

'Of course. He was proud of who he was. He was Musa. Abu Musa al-Matari.'

'Did that mean something to you?'

'No. But he was important. People were always coming to see him. He had many phones and computers. He was given much respect.'

'I need to know if this is the Musa al-Matari I am looking for, but I do not have any pictures of him. Do you know where he was born?'

'He said he was from Yemen, close to the border with Oman. In a place on the ocean.'

Foley knew the Abu Musa al-Matari she was looking for was from Jadib, located *exactly* where Manal had just described.

'And his age?'

'I . . . I do not know. Much older.'

Mary Pat frowned. '*Much* older . . . like me?'

'No. Not so old,' Manal said quickly. Mary Pat was in her sixties. She wasn't offended, but she smiled at the interpreter's discomfort relaying the young girl's words.

The CIA had pinned al-Matari's age at between thirty-five and forty. Mary Pat asked Manal how old her father had been when he died.

'He was forty-one.' Manal nodded. 'Yes, maybe he was close to my father's age.'

'You were with al-Matari for how long?'

'One year. I was a slave, but he married me. I think maybe he had other wives, because he was not at the apartment all the time.'

'And when did he force you to marry him?'

The young woman listened to the interpreter, then she looked at the older American lady for a long time. There was confusion on her face. Finally, she spoke, and the interpreter said, 'The first time I ever saw him . . . we were married in five minutes.'

'I see. Did he spend a lot of time on the computer?'

'Yes,' Manal said. 'Every day he was on his computer or on one of his phones.'

Mary Pat knew Abu Musa al-Matari was a top lieutenant in the Emni, a branch of the Islamic State's Foreign Intelligence Bureau in charge of finding fighters willing and able to operate abroad. Al-Matari ran the North American section, and it was his job to recruit and train Americans and Europeans to conduct terrorist acts for ISIS in the United States. Nine months earlier he had managed to get sixteen US passport holders into Syria for training, but all sixteen were either killed there in a US drone strike or detained upon their return to the West. The destruction of the cell had been hidden from the press, mostly, to preserve the tactics, techniques, and procedures that led to the intelligence coup, but Mary Pat knew her nation had dodged a huge bullet with the operation. She also knew al-Matari had the skill, the motivation, and the backing in the Islamic State's Foreign Intelligence Bureau that made it a certainty he would try again.

And she most worried that he had already begun.

She asked, 'What else did you learn from him?'

'He told me he fought in many countries before I was

captured. After I was made his wife, he was gone more than he was here. I don't think he was off fighting. He wasn't a soldier . . . He was something else. I don't know.

'One day he came back to the apartment in Raqqa, and he told me he had to take a trip abroad.'

'Did he say where he was going?'

'To me? No, he did not confide in me. I was only there to clean his home, to cook for his brothers and other family and friends, and to give him pleasure. But I heard him talking on the phone. He was going to Kosovo to meet with someone.'

Mary Pat nodded. 'When was this?'

The interpreter relayed the young girl's answer. 'Three months before I escaped. I escaped last month. So . . . four months ago.'

'And did he return from Kosovo?'

'Yes, and he worked harder after this. Met with more men, foreigners. I mean . . . not Iraqis. Different accents. Then . . . maybe four weeks ago, he told me to pack his clothes. He told me he was going on a long journey, and *inshallah*, he would return.'

'Did he say anything about where he was going?'

'Not to me, but I heard him on the phone again. He talked about going to school.'

'To *school?*'

'Yes. A language school.'

Mary Pat cocked her head. 'Where is this language school?'

'I do not know, but I am sure it was far away. He had books. Books in English. I don't know what kind of books, I do not understand English, but he took them, along with Western clothing. He left his robes. This just four days before I escaped.'

'How were you able to escape?'

'When he left, he said his uncle would be watching over

60

me. But his uncle did not come. The American bombs became heavy in the city. Maybe he was killed, or just too scared to leave the house. I did not have any food. Of course I could not go out into the streets myself in Raqqa. As a woman alone, I would be stopped by the ISIS religious police. If they caught me a second time, I would be arrested. A third time and I would have been stoned to death.'

'I understand,' Mary Pat said.

'But I got so hungry, finally I decided I had to try to leave if I wanted to live. I had heard that some people who go toward the sounds of the fighting make it through the lines and survive. I did not know if that was true, but I had no choice. I waited for late at night. I watched the sky to see where the flashes were coming from, and I walked toward the fighting.

'On the second day I met with more women. Some had children. They were doing the same as me. We lived in the ruins until we crossed the lines into Kurdish territory. The Peshmerga found us and helped us.'

The director of national intelligence looked back to her assistant, to make sure she had everything written down and the recorder was on. Then Mary Pat said, 'And now we will help you. Some Americans will come and talk to you tomorrow. They would like you to tell them exactly what Abu Musa al-Matari looks like, so they can try to draw a picture of him. Will you do that?'

'Yes,' Manal said, but she looked down and began playing with the frayed edge of a rug.

Mary Pat knew this girl was doing everything in her power *not* to think about this man, and the last thing she wanted to do was purposely try to remember his face.

'I am sorry, Manal. But it is very important. You can save many lives with your help.'

'I will do it,' she said softly.

'Thank you. We can make arrangements for you to come to America if you would like that. Just until the war is over, then you can return to Sinjar Mountain if that is what you wish. We need help from you, but we would like to give you whatever it is you want.'

Manal continued looking down to the rug in front of her. She thought for a moment, and said, 'I would like to stay here, with my people. But I will help you catch him. He was a monster.'

'Okay. Is there anything you need here?'

'I am fine, but can I get some extra blankets for the older ladies at the camp? The floors are very hard, and some women complain of cold and pain in their backs at night.'

Foley bit the inside of her lip, then said, 'I'll see to it before I leave Sulaymaniyah.'

Outside the house, Mary Pat Foley walked toward the convoy of waiting SUVs. Stonefaced security officers stood all around with M4 rifles, watching the buildings around them as well as the distant hills. They were 120 miles from ISIS territory to the west, but CIA protective agents didn't need to be in a war zone to maintain vigilance.

Foley turned to her assistant. 'Carla, rugs and blankets. Anything else they can get to make it a bit more livable for as many as possible.'

'I'll take care of it. CIA will be back here tomorrow to get an artist rendering from the girl and ask her some more questions. I'll send them with a truckload of creature comforts to give to the UN to pass out.'

Foley said, 'No. Get the officers to deliver the items directly to the Yazidis. The UN might sell them in the market.'

After a look from the young assistant, Mary Pat Foley said, 'Carla, I've been around. Trust me, it's happened.'

'Yes, ma'am.'

The colonel grinned. 'The Agency folks are gonna love handing out home accessories to old ladies.' Then, to Mary Pat, he said, 'That's definitely our boy, and it sounds like he's back in play.'

'Yes, but something doesn't add up.'

The colonel said, 'No kidding. Musa al-Matari already speaks perfect English. If he was planning another attack, what other language would he possibly be studying?'

Mary Pat said, 'My guess is the "Language School" is a code name. A code name for what, I don't have a clue. Get the analysts looking into it. Push them hard. I get the sense Abu Musa al-Matari is at the center of something that is about to happen. It's somewhere in the West. And it's sometime soon. And the son of a bitch has got a month head start on us.' She stopped herself at the door to the SUV, turned around, and waved to all the women and kids looking down on her from the rooftops and out the windows. Some hid around corners, tucked themselves into the buildings, but others waved back.

Every last one was transfixed by the power this lady commanded.

8

Mary Pat Foley thought she was hunting for the man who was orchestrating the next great attack on American soil.

But she was wrong. Abu Musa al-Matari was, in fact, the operational leader of an attack in the last stages before execution, and it was the right thing to do to put the entire force of the US intelligence community into the hunt to stop him before the attack began, but the truth was he had done little of the strategic planning.

The US intelligence community knew about Abu Musa al-Matari's previous attempt to enter the US with terror cells, and they knew he was in the wind again, so it was taken as fact by them that al-Matari would be the architect of any impending plot. He was the senior ISIS operator of the mission, yes; he was the on-scene commander, and he would be the middleman distributing intelligence to the individual cells on their way back to their homes and lives in the United States.

But the *actual* mastermind, the man who conceived the operation, forwarded his plan to those able to approve it, provided it with money and leadership and weaponry, was one of the last people anyone who knew him would ever suspect of being involved in international terrorism.

Fifty-one-year-old Sami bin Rashid was a Saudi Arabian technocrat. He wasn't particularly religious; in fact, he drank when he could get away with it and visited the mosque less than most Muslims did.

Indeed, Sami bin Rashid was a *damn* peculiar choice to orchestrate an ISIS operation to attack the American homeland. For starters, he wasn't a member of ISIS, and he hated all jihadis with a white-hot passion. He had a plum position in Dubai working for the Gulf Cooperation Council, a regional intergovernmental political and economic organization made up to further the interests of the Arabic states of the Persian Gulf.

He was hardly the type that turns to Islamic terror.

But the act al-Matari was preparing at the moment was one hundred percent out of the brain of Sami bin Rashid, and though it had begun for al-Matari only right after the two men met in an ISIS safe house in Kosovo, the plot came to bin Rashid after he lucked into access to a treasure trove of intelligence several months prior.

Sami bin Rashid had never killed anyone in his life. He had done some time in the Saudi military as a young man, but during the first Gulf War he had been a low-ranking intelligence officer, hundreds of kilometers removed from any battle lines.

After his military duty he remained in the Saudi government but moved into the Ministry of Energy, Industry, and Mineral Resources, working in a secret department that collated intelligence from Saudi intelligence and incorporated it into Saudi energy policy.

And then, after twenty years in quasi-corporate intelligence, bin Rashid left the Saudi government with the blessing of the House of Saud, the monarchy that ruled the nation. They placed him in a consultancy position at the Gulf Cooperation Council, located in Saudi Arabia's capital, Riyadh. Here, he worked as a de facto intelligence chief, toiling behind the scenes developing initiatives to better integrate all the intelligence agencies of the GCC member states – a difficult task, considering that some of these nations had gone to war with one another at various times in the past.

As his purview changed over the years, bin Rashid had become something of a fixer for the GCC. A problem solver. A quiet man in a quiet office staffed with analysts and operatives who made problems disappear and dirty wars flare if they served the interests of his homeland. He became so good at what he did, in fact, that he was moved out of Riyadh and over to Dubai, set up in a private office that was, in fact, a shell for his real work, all to add another layer of deniability to the House of Saud that any of his actions were done in their name.

He funneled money, intelligence, and equipment to corporate interests, revolutionaries, and enemies of the Saudis, and he did it without drawing attention to himself or his benefactors. He had friends in the American oil sector and in the Middle Eastern intelligence agencies, and contacts in the terror groups that would kill his friends in America – kill Sami himself if they knew the extent of his associations with infidels or his desires to manipulate jihadists to serve the King in Riyadh.

He'd conspired with Nigerian revolutionaries to bomb oil-processing plants, paid off Russian gangsters to enforce strikes at ports to slow crude shipments, and concocted a hundred other ops to help Saudis' fortunes on the global market.

But as much as he accomplished, he was just one man, and the problems were bigger than he could combat because, to put it simply, Saudi Arabia was failing as a nation.

The Kingdom of Saudi Arabia was a wealthy country, of

course, but its fortunes, both in real dollars and in future prospects, had been plummeting in recent years. When oil was trading around US$100 a barrel, Saudi Arabia earned $240 billion a year in oil revenue. Now oil was less than half that and the nation was running a budget deficit of $150 billion a year.

This was a country that could not rein in its spending because there was so much discord in the kingdom that massive subsidies for the poor were the only way to ensure the survival of the rich. The nation would devolve into a riotous civil war in months if the House of Saud ever pulled the plug on the largesse it gave the masses living outside the palaces.

It was clear to people like bin Rashid that the kingdom could not live on oil alone for much longer. US reserves were reported to be larger than Saudi reserves for the first time, and this sent a shock wave through the House of Saud, with reverberations that were felt in Sami bin Rashid's hidden but pivotal office. He was their miracle man, and the House of Saud made itself clear that they expected a miracle from him.

And their problems were not limited to money.

Regionally, the Saudis were fearful of Iran's growth, and the spread of Shia fundamentalism, much more than the spread of Sunni fundamentalism. They took it as given that any new Shia-controlled land would simply become a puppet for Iran.

Iran's increased oil output was a problem, too, and it was expanding its extraction at the same time Iran was expanding its influence in the Middle East.

Bin Rashid's days and nights were filled with worries about falling oil prices, and about Iran becoming the hegemon of the Middle East.

He had a solution to both worries, if only he could come up with a way to make it happen.

War.

Not a war between Saudi Arabia and Iran. That would be a disaster. The Saudis could not stop Iran alone, and all the Sunni nations' militaries put together were no match for the Shia nations, if the Shia nations were formed in a tight coalition. And bin Rashid knew that a Shia coalition brought into a war with the Sunnis, run by the Saudis, would do just that.

No, if there was going to be war around here, it could not be fought by the Saudis. It had to be fought on *behalf* of the Saudis . . . by the West.

As a Saudi, Sami bin Rashid knew his role in the Gulf Co-operation Council was not to further the aims of all the Arab Gulf countries. No, it was to further the aims of the Saudi Arabian kingdom, and the operation he'd conceived of months ago, the operation that was now under way and only days from making headlines worldwide, would do just exactly that.

Sami bin Rashid would never have come up with his grand plan, his Hail Mary to save his nation by using the insane jihadi death cult of ISIS to draw the West back into a massive land war in the Middle East, if one of his analysts had not sent him an e-mail seven months earlier.

Mr Director, I've run across something I would like to show you at your convenience. I could come to your office, or please feel free to come to mine.

Bin Rashid called the young man, a Qatari who had been put on employment probation for his penchant for using his computer for non-work-related ventures.

Moments later Faisal entered bin Rashid's office with a bow and a touch of his hand on his breast. *'Sabaah al-khair, sayidi.'* Good morning, sir.

'What is it?' The Saudi director had no time for pleasantries.

'I have learned about a company on the Internet selling intelligence on the dark web, and I thought you should know about it.'

'The dark web?'

'Yes, sir. There are markets hidden on the Internet, places where one can purchase certain illegal, illicit items.'

'And what were you doing perusing this dark web, Faisal?'

The young man seemed nervous. 'Of course I knew you would ask me this. But I was directed there by a message on a bulletin board we monitor out of Lebanon. It's internal communication between Hezbollah operatives and Iranian citizens, mostly low-level, but still worth keeping an eye on. There is a way for an outsider to post in an open forum, and I followed a post there as the entity posting was given access behind a firewall by the board moderator so the conversation could continue.'

'You've hacked this Hezbollah bulletin board?'

'We did. Some time ago.'

'What did the outside messenger tell the Hezbollah operatives?'

'The outside messenger goes by the code name INFORMER, and spoke English. He offered to sell Hezbollah intelligence on American government agents. And members of the American military.'

'What sort of intelligence?'

'Full targeting packages.'

'Targeting? Like physical targeting?'

'Yes, sir. INFORMER claimed that he could obtain information about any current or retired American spy or special operative, and give that information to Hezbollah.'

To Sami bin Rashid, this all sounded like foolish kids who bought Western action DVDs in the marketplace and fantasized about conducting themselves like spies, so they talked about it on Internet bulletin boards. But he pressed on, hoping Faisal would get to the point. 'How were these transactions supposed to take place?'

'On the dark web. Hezbollah – although I imagine INFORMER has contacted other groups as well – was told they could purchase information via Bitcoin. They would simply place an order for targeting info by the American government employee's name, position, or other criteria.'

'Like picking fruit at the market.'

Faisal nodded with a smile. 'I've honestly never seen anything like it. Of course, illegal markets on the dark web have been around for a long time. Guns for sale, drugs for sale, images and videos that go against the teaching of the Prophet.' The young man looked to the floor, and bin Rashid knew he was talking about pornography.

The Saudi said, 'This seems ridiculous. I am in no way interested in this conversation, Faisal. Interest me or get out of my office.'

'Well, sir, INFORMER provided samples of his wares.'

'Samples?'

'Yes, sir. For instance, he provided credible information about a man flying drones in the United States against targets over Syria. This is intelligence Hezbollah might be interested in, due to their associations with the Alawites in Damascus.'

'How do you know the information was credible?'

'Because we have the same information. The Saudi Army has had contacts with this man's unit, and he does, in fact, exist and hold the position claimed by this source.'

'How do you know this source – INFORMER – doesn't just have assets in Saudi Arabia who stole the information there?'

'Because he has much more than we have on this man, a major in the Air Force. He has a list of all his friends, family, where he went to school. What kind of car he drives, where he lives, shops, eats. Where his children go to school, even his fingerprint. This is something we – I'm speaking of the GCC, and the Saudis – do not have.'

Bin Rashid said, 'If we know this drone pilot, why do we give a damn where he went to school?'

'We don't, sir, but INFORMER claims to have this information on every single man and woman who works for the American government.' Faisal made eye contact with his boss. '*Everyone.* He gives other samples, where the names are redacted but the forms appear authentic. I believe this man, or this entity, selling this information actually does have information we do not have.'

'And who knows about this?'

'That I do not know. The market on the dark web is accessed by invitation only. The security is very good, but one of the Hezbollah fools gave the address to a colleague over a poorly encrypted e-mail. That's how I was able to secure the address and password information to see for myself.'

Bin Rashid was still skeptical. He had access to virtually all the intelligence product of all the intel shops of all the GCC nations, and he had seen nothing like what this mystery private seller seemed to be offering. He asked, 'What is INFORMER's interest in helping Hezbollah?'

Faisal said, 'Financial. Nothing more. He sent this message thinking Hezbollah or Iran might buy intelligence from him.'

Bin Rashid shook his head. 'Then he is a fool for thinking this group actually spoke for Hezbollah's Foreign Intelligence Bureau and could buy and utilize that type of intelligence.'

Faisal stood his ground, something he rarely did with bin Rashid. 'Sir, with apologies. I believe this branch of Hezbollah running this website *are* fools, but INFORMER just does not know that. I've looked long and hard into the way INFORMER hides himself on the Internet. This is quality work. He is no fool. I cannot vouch for authenticity of all the material he is offering, but I believe we should reach out to him and tell him we are interested in a transaction, just to see what he can do.'

'How do we do that?'

'We cannot track his location or identity on the Internet, he is using virtual private networks that no one, not even the Americans, can get into. But what I can do is lock up the Hezbollah bulletin board, keep everyone out of it except for myself and this INFORMER, and communicate with him directly.'

Now bin Rashid was thinking. He could feel this potential source out with no comebacks on himself. 'All right. Do this. The conversation will just be with you and the source. Just to set up your own private means of communication.'

'Of course, sir. And then I will remove our conversation from the bulletin board and open it back up. Hezbollah will never know we were there. They will think there was some sort of a glitch with their servers.'

Faisal then asked, 'When I enter into communications

with this potential source, what do I tell them about my identity?'

'Tell them they have chosen poorly in going to a group of idiots with no money and poor security. You, however, represent a non-government actor who can provide discretion and a lucrative arrangement if and only if the source proves himself to both have the information he purports to have, and has the means to communicate it securely.'

'Very well, sir.'

Faisal seemed a little confused, and Sami bin Rashid noticed this.

'What's the matter?'

'I brought this to your attention so you would know Hezbollah might be about to come into contact with intelligence on America that they did not have before. Of course that could lead to Iran having leverage over America, and that relates to our mission here. I thought perhaps we could test out this INFORMER's access to intelligence to see what new threat this brings. I honestly did not think *we* would be in the market to buy the information on American intelligence sources ourselves. May I ask why we would do that?'

Bin Rashid was a man who always thought several moves ahead on the chessboard. He simply said, 'Let's feel them out. See what they have. Then we can decide if there is something we can do with it.'

Faisal bowed, touched his breast, and promised to keep bin Rashid informed. He left the office.

Sami bin Rashid was skeptical, very skeptical, but if this panned out, he knew exactly what he would do with this intelligence about covert American assets.

He would feed it to ISIS.

ISIS, as far as bin Rashid was concerned, could never

defeat the West, and the genocide that was at the heart of their mission statement therefore built in its own self-destruct button. These fools would make gains and gains until they pushed the West too far. They would never accept their state at any defined border, so they would fight until that moment when the West put all their resources into fighting back.

But Saudi Arabia didn't want to wait for the West to do it on its own time. President of the United States Jack Ryan was using his airpower, intelligence apparatus, and small units of special operations forces to assist the Kurds and, to a lesser extent, the Iraqi Army, into defeating ISIS in Iraq and Syria. The coalition led by America was gaining ground in this endeavor, but this low-intensity conflict would not keep the oil fields occupied in Iraq, and it would not keep Shia influence out of the nations bordering Saudi Arabia.

But if ISIS suddenly began targeting American military and intelligence forces directly, it might bring the American armed forces back into the region, and a total war would create havoc in the oil fields. Iran had been developing major oil projects in the Shia-held south of Iraq, and Saudi Arabia's financial future was directly affected by this. War would push them out of the oil fields and out of both Iraq and Syria, which would increase the price of Saudi oil and reduce the threat of Shia hegemony in the region.

Yes, Saudi Arabia would win in every conceivable way if the Americans invaded the Middle East.

And eventually ISIS would be ground out of existence, and that suited Sami bin Rashid just fine.

INFORMER began communications with Sami bin Rashid almost immediately, and he proved his worth by providing tidbits of intelligence, intelligence bin Rashid already had, so that he could be assured INFORMER was legitimate.

It took a while for bin Rashid's plan to move to the stage where he could involve others, but eventually he went to his leadership, leaving out the other GCC members, and he was given official Saudi blessing to enter into discussions with senior Islamic State leadership.

In his talks with ISIS, he had been told about an operation in the works to bring the fight to America. It involved remote radicalized operatives, men and women in America driven by the slick and powerful propaganda arm of the Islamic State. There were some forty different groups involved in spreading the word of ISIS. It could be argued ISIS wielded the weapon of propaganda better than any other armament in their arsenal. One of the most potent ISIS media organizations was the Global Islamic Media Front. Via websites, social media outreach, well-produced YouTube videos, and an online magazine, GIMF worked to radicalize American Muslims so they would go out into their streets and conduct indiscriminate acts of terrorism. ISIS thought this would force Jack Ryan back to the Middle East, and ISIS wanted this just as much as bin Rashid did.

But Sami bin Rashid was highly skeptical of the Islamic State's plan. Jack Ryan was a wily opponent in possession of cold logic; he would not overreact to a threat. Bin Rashid knew Ryan wanted to wipe out ISIS, but shooting up shopping malls or blowing up a car in Times Square wouldn't force his hand internationally; instead, it would simply lead him to improve his security domestically.

No, bin Rashid's plan was the only way to force the hand of the American President.

He told ISIS leaders that wealthy Gulf patrons would

plan, fund, oversee, and help carry out an attack against the United States of America. The Islamic State officials were skeptical, of course, but bin Rashid convinced them through his intermediaries that he had abilities at both the tactical and strategic levels that they did not have. He needed only some of their best recruits, their blessing, and, it went without saying, their cover.

ISIS was floundering at the moment. They had not achieved a major battlefield success in a year and a half, much of the oil revenue they'd been generating by smuggling Iraqi oil into Turkey and Jordan had been cut off by Western-coalition air strikes, and more air strikes had helped Iraqi Army and Kurdish forces take back territory. There was nothing ISIS needed more than a huge win against the West, and this shadowy group of Gulf benefactors looked like they had the right plan to make that happen.

Islamic State leadership arranged a meeting between bin Rashid and one of their top operatives.

The location of the face-to-face meeting was set up for Podujevo, Kosovo, a town of over 90,000 in the northeastern portion of the nation. Both the Saudis and ISIS had a foothold in the town, and it was seen as a safe location for both a Saudi operative – even though bin Rashid was actually an employee of a regional organization – and an ISIS operative, one Abu Musa al-Matari.

Sami bin Rashid's intelligence contacts told him all about al-Matari. The Yemeni had recently worked his own plan to train American ISIS devotees in Syria, and then send them home to America to wreak havoc on the nation.

Bin Rashid found this plan bold, more or less intelligently crafted, and certainly the right idea, but it was lacking in many respects.

Not the least of which was that it had failed miserably.

The United States detected the training ground in Syria, the CIA and the FBI determined who was there, and then, by a cynical and arguably illegal order of President of the United States Jack Ryan, wave after wave of unmanned aerial vehicles turned the training camp to smoldering ash.

Al-Matari had already left the camp when it was hit, as had several of his US passport holders. But when al-Matari returned to Raqqa, the surviving would-be ISIS jihadists were rounded up at airports in Europe and the United States, and al-Matari's plan came to naught.

Then Sami bin Rashid met Abu Musa al-Matari in Kosovo, and months after that, al-Matari found himself in Central America, days away from beginning the operation against the West that he was certain would uproot the world order and bring forth a ten-thousand-year caliphate.

9

From El Salvador's crowded capital of San Salvador, it is a straight shot south down the highway to the Pacific coast. It's a good road by El Salvador standards, and the beaches at La Libertad are among the most desirable in Central America for surfers, who come from all over the world.

But no surfers end up in the village of San Rafael in La Libertad state, because it's several miles north of the coast and a few miles west of the highway. And certainly few, if any, foreign travelers have ever ventured higher in the hills northeast of the village, following a rocky and winding track that is wholly inaccessible during the rainy season.

But if they did go there, they would see, right in the middle of the jungle, a locked iron gate at the front of a large parcel of private land.

The ownership of the property is confusing to the locals, since no one in the area lays claim to it. Most here assume a drug cartel from Mexico or Guatemala owns the property. It is fenced everywhere the thick foliage, sheer rock walls, or deep gullies don't provide natural barriers, and no one in the town of San Rafael has ever been inside. There are no permanent caretakers, but it is said the municipal police keep an eye out to ensure nobody travels close enough to get a look.

The property had been abandoned for more than a generation, until one strange day six weeks ago.

That Sunday afternoon three large rental SUVs with no plates rumbled through San Rafael and continued up the hill without stopping. The locals who witnessed the unusual event confirmed the drivers and passengers were all Latinos, but they wore hats and shades and beards. The police didn't harass them, but this just indicated to the locals that the police knew they were coming and had been paid to leave them alone.

Over the next few days half a dozen Latino men – those who heard them speak said they were Guatemalan – came into the village and bought enough supplies to sustain dozens of people for a month or more. The villagers of San Rafael knew better than to ask questions, they just wondered how long these narcos would stay, and if they would spend a lot more money in the town while they were here.

Two weeks later small convoys of four-wheel-drive SUVs, all clearly rentals from San Salvador, rolled through San Rafael, and soon after that, the sounds of soft and distant gunfire, sporadic and uncoordinated at first, and then tighter, faster, more organized, rolled down the hills and into the village.

Small explosions could be heard as well.

This went on for weeks and the locals figured the narcos couldn't possibly be fighting each other for so long, so they must have been conducting some sort of training.

Beyond the gate to the property no one in San Rafael ever visited, a row of rusty corrugated metal buildings stood under the hot sun. They had been erected by the Salvadoran Army during the civil war of the 1980s, barracks with a small airstrip used by the American CIA, but the airstrip was invisible in the jungle now, and the current occupants of the property had nothing to do with America, the eighties, or that war.

The villagers had been wrong about the new visitors; the

Guatemalans were not narcos, they were instructors. The six men had come to this disused property in the El Salvador back country to set up a temporary school and train a force in small-arms combat.

The six were former members of the Kaibiles, the Guatemalan military's infamous Special Forces unit. They were all in their fifties, and during the 1980s they had been young men fighting a brutal war just north of here in Guatemala. Since then they'd worked as mercenaries, fighting or training others throughout Latin America.

The six men had taken two weeks readying the property: setting up generators, establishing the Internet, checking over their guns and ammunition, and even building a rainwater-collection station to augment the water they'd trucked in.

The company that hired them was a shell out of Panama. None of the Guatemalans looked into the shell, but still they were curious as to whom they would be training. All six of the former Kaibiles spoke English, a tip-off to them about their students, but English was a common international language, so when a Middle Eastern man who spoke fluent English arrived at the property, no one was terribly surprised. He called himself Mohammed and explained that he was training a unit to learn the combat arts so they could go into Yemen and fight the government there.

The Guatemalans did not know much about Yemen, and they cared even less. The pay was good, the work would be easy, and the Middle Easterner promised that if this contract went well this could turn into a recurring gig.

The students arrived over a two-day period. Twenty-seven in all. The Guatemalans were surprised to see among the expected Middle Easterners, there were gringos, blacks, and other Latinos as well. They also had not expected women, yet four in the class were female. One was black, one was Hispanic, the other two were olive-complexioned women of Middle Eastern heritage.

Whatever, the Guatemalans decided. They didn't care where the men and women came from. If some *bruja mexicana* or some *gringo pendejo* wanted to go get his or her ass shot off in the Middle East, that was their problem.

While the Kaibiles trained the men and women, Mohammed watched over the entire operation, but he spent most of the daylight hours on his satellite phone and on his laptop. The trainers decided he either already knew how to fight or didn't need to know.

The Guatemalans never asked.

At night the Guatemalans retired to their tents next to a stream a few hundred meters from the barracks, but sometimes they could hear the students and Mohammed talking well past midnight. They had the impression he was indoctrinating them on their mission, perhaps teaching them specific knowledge they would need over there in Yemen, but again, they did not really care.

Though the Guatemalans would never know it, Mohammed's real name was Musa al-Matari. He was thirty-nine years old, born to a Yemeni Army officer father and a British aid-worker mother who had converted to Islam. He'd lived both in Yemen and in London growing up.

Al-Matari had served as a lieutenant in the Yemeni Army, an infantry officer, but he left his country to fight with the jihadists in Iraq, because helping to build a true Islamic State was a realization of the dream he didn't dare express to anyone until the day the black flags began moving across the land.

He'd fought for Al-Qaeda, and then in Syria and Iraq for ISIS, and his specialty became recruiting and training cells of martyrs to operate behind enemy lines. He grew so skilled, his fighters so successful, that he was sent to Libya to train operatives there when the caliphate grew into Northern Africa.

His trainees in Libya did well, and soon it was decided by the Foreign Intelligence Bureau that al-Matari could do more outside the war zone than he could inside. He proposed recruiting and training foreigners in tactics that they could take back to their home countries, to move the fight to the enemy's doorstep. His plan was approved, and soon he had a group of recruiters working for him at an office in Mosul. They used the Internet to seek out men and women living in the West, finding them on message boards and in responses to Facebook and Twitter posts.

Those selected would be brought to Syria for training, and then sent back out to the West to kill on behalf of the Islamic State.

His recruits conducted operations in Turkey and Egypt, then in Tunisia and Algeria. Then Belgium and France and Austria.

Al-Matari's successes were rewarded by his leadership. His plans became more adventurous, more ambitious. He had no time for those who wanted to come to Syria and fight. He had time only for men and women with the intelligence, fervency, and documentation that would make them good raw materials for operatives of ISIS serving abroad.

Soon he decided to reach for the golden ring. He wanted to import American-based recruits, train them in operations, and then export ISIS fighters to America.

He did this, trained up his force right to the moment to

release them back into America, and then his plan was thwarted.

After his first operation ended in disaster with the air strikes on his training camp and the arrest of those few fighters he did manage to get on planes back to the United States, he found himself without a force, and without a plan.

But not for long.

It was the leadership of the Foreign Intelligence Bureau who told him to go to Kosovo, where he was to meet with a man in a safe house there. His orders were to take his time and listen to the man's ideas, and then to return and tell ISIS leadership what he thought of it all.

Al-Matari was a skeptic. It kept him alive in his work, but he also followed orders, because this had even more to do with his survival.

He was smuggled into Turkey, and from there he flew to Kosovo.

The meeting in Kosovo took place in a green and lush court-yard, completely surrounded by a three-story building that itself was surrounded by ISIS fighters.

Al-Matari did not know the identity of his contact, but when he stepped into the courtyard, he saw a man in robes sitting alone at a simple table with a tea service in front of him.

As soon as al-Matari sat down, the other man poured tea for his guest, and he said, 'This will be the only time we meet face-to-face.'

Al-Matari reached for his tea. He had learned to be suspicious of everyone, Muslim robes and good hospitality notwithstanding. 'I do not even know what this meeting is about. I was ordered here.'

The man nodded slowly. He was older – fifty, perhaps – and seemed extremely confident. 'I know what happened in your last operation.'

'I am not revealing anything to you. If you think you know something, maybe you heard it from important people. Maybe you heard it from fools. I don't know. Nevertheless, I am not going to say anything that –'

'I applaud what you did; I respect the tactical thinking that went into it. You are brave, smart, and you have big ideas.' The man smiled. 'I am no tactician, but I am a strategist. And that is where you need help. I can assist you on your next effort, increase the chances it is successful, and increase the chances that it has a larger impact than you can imagine.'

Al-Matari looked up at the architecture of the old building surrounding him while he sipped his tea. 'Your accent. You are Saudi.'

'That's right.'

'I don't like Saudis.'

The man shrugged. 'I don't blame you. Saudi Arabia has oil and wealth. Yemen has camels and camel shit.'

Al-Matari squeezed his teacup almost to the point of breaking it.

The Saudi continued. 'I don't really care. Unlike you, I do not believe in bigotry against other Sunnis. I think we all should be united against infidels and Shiites. But I *do* believe in first impressions, and I do not like you so much. Let's agree we are not here to make friends, and get on with this conversation.'

Al-Matari gave a little sarcastic bow.

The older man was all business. 'If you can assemble another group of American mujahideen, and do it quickly, I can provide you with a safe place to train them, and top-level instructors. I can provide you with weapons, ammunition, explosives. I can provide you with the security of keeping these Americans out of lands known to be involved with the jihad, so there will be no alarm by the American intelligence community.

'Most importantly, when you get your well-trained soldiers back into the United States, I can give you targets you cannot possibly dream of getting on your own.'

Al-Matari sniffed. '*Targets?* Targets are not my problem. All of the USA is a target. My fighters can drive down the street and shoot people at random and I will achieve my objectives.'

The Saudi shook his head vehemently. 'This is where strategy is important, not just tactics. Killing American civilians is a waste of time. A futile act. Your soldiers would be hunted down and destroyed, for what? Garbagemen, bus drivers, grocers? I am talking about giving you targets that will hurt America's ability to fight.'

'In what way?'

'I have access to the addresses of men and women in the CIA. I know the schools where Air Force pilots who fly over your head in Raqqa send their children. A bar where, on any night, you can find American commandos, on leave, without weapons, drunk and helpless. I can tell you the license plate numbers of the cars they drive, where the wives of spies and soldiers work.'

Al-Matari was at once skeptical and stunned. 'How is it you have access to such information?'

'*How* doesn't matter. It will be difficult for me, and it will be difficult for you. But ask yourself this, brother. Do you want to work so hard to shoot kids in a mall, or do you want to work so hard to destroy a large segment of America's ability to wage war on us from afar? I say we fight them there, so we force them to come here, in our land, where we destroy them.'

Al-Matari said, 'What do you mean, *our land*? If America comes, the fighting will not be in Saudi Arabia. Your country has a cozy relationship with the infidels.'

But it was clear the Saudi didn't care about what the Yemeni said, because bin Rashid saw the gleam in al-Matari's eye. What bin Rashid was selling was exactly what al-Matari was buying. Al-Matari recognized the value of destroying military and intelligence targets in America every bit as much as the man across the table did.

The Saudi said, 'Everyone in the Islamic State wants one reaction out of the West.'

Al-Matari nodded. 'Of course. We want the Americans to invade in numbers. We are fighting the Kurds and the Iraqis and the Syrians when we could be fighting the West. Yes, the West flies high overhead, scared to stand and battle us on the ground. But if America puts troops in the cities of Iraq, like they did ten years ago, then the uprisings would grow larger, the brothers from as far away as Morocco and Indonesia will flood back in, America will be destroyed and sent home in disgrace.' Al-Matari couldn't hide a little smile. 'The caliphate would then grow into these other countries when they take the fight to their own homelands throughout the Middle East, North Africa, and Southeast Asia.'

The Saudi nodded vehemently. 'Exactly, brother! President Jack Ryan was himself a spy and a soldier. How do you think he will react when one of your operatives shoots and kills his spies in their bathrobes in front of their homes? How do you think he will react when we kill his soldiers while they eat their lunch? He *will* react. America will react. They will *all* react by coming here to fight.'

The older man smiled now. 'And just think of the remote radicals who will grow like flowers in America once you and your instruments of justice begin the real fight inside America. Right now you have many young men and women who would join your struggle, if your struggle were showing some real signs of success. Remember the first two years of the existence of the Islamic State? Foreign brothers and even sisters flooded into the new caliphate. It could be that, again, but not foolish boys running into the meat grinder in Syria. But men and women right there in America, in the heart of the enemy, given good instruction and direction and sent out into their neighborhoods, the lands they know and understand, understand better than you and me, my brother. They can make a difference in our fight in the Middle East. These men and women could be our foreign legion for the caliphate.'

Before the Yemeni could speak, the Saudi added one more thing. 'And you, you my brother. *You* can start this off. In the next few years you can be the one to turn it all around.'

Al-Matari clearly thought this all too good to be true. 'I can get operatives into America. I have developed another group of contacts already in the US. They will die for the jihad. But I need them to know how to *kill* for the jihad. This training location. Where is it?'

The Saudi sipped tea and grinned. 'When the time is right, that will be revealed. You show me you have the operatives, men and women with US passports, student visas for the US, or work visas. I will make sure they are trained.'

Al-Matari said, 'I know of some refugees from Syria who have been sent to America.'

'No,' the Saudi said with authority. 'They will be watched carefully. I only want men and women in your forces who can move freely and without undue scrutiny. Once the first wave of attacks is successful, when the world sees we are not terrorists, but we are Islamic soldiers fighting infidel soldiers, then the follow-on waves of self-motivated will come, they will align themselves with our noble cause, and they will multiply your good work by ten times, by one hundred times.'

Musa al-Matari's heart filled with a purpose and a power he had not felt since the day before the Americans wiped out his last operation before it even began.

'*Inshallah*,' al-Matari said. If God wills it.

'*Inshallah*,' the Saudi echoed.

The war inside America against the military and intelligence community began right there, with two men over tea in a courtyard garden.

10

Abu Musa al-Matari left Kosovo with a new direction. While he did not even know the name of his new benefactor, he did know the man had been vetted by ISIS leadership and met with their approval. He couldn't imagine how the Saudi could possibly obtain the information he promised to pass along, and he didn't understand or even trust the Saudi's motivations. But even though al-Matari had gone to Kosovo with great skepticism, he returned to Syria more excited than ever, and ready to embark on a new mission.

After more consultations with his leadership, he knew this plan would go forward.

Finding potential jihadi recruits in the United States of America was not difficult. Finding potential jihadi recruits in the United States of America who were not on any US government watch list, not already under surveillance, and who had documentation that would allow them to drive, travel, survive a passing encounter with American law enforcement, while simultaneously possessing the intelligence, language, and social skills necessary to serve in an operational role for the Islamic State's Emni branch . . . now, *that* was tricky. Still, Musa al-Matari knew that for this operation he needed cleanskins – operatives with no ties whatsoever to his organization or any history of radical behavior.

Cleanskins were hard to find, but al-Matari had the infrastructure in place to find them.

The average American has no clue who the American

government has caught pledging allegiance to and even planning attacks on behalf of ISIS in America. Musa al-Matari knew. He could recite the latest stats from the FBI, stats reporting that of all the cases of people inside the United States being charged for illegal activities on behalf of ISIS, seventy-eight were United States citizens, eight were lawful permanent residents. Five were refugees, and of those with no US residency, most were on student visas.

Almost a third had at least some college, eighty-seven percent were male, and the average age was only twenty-one.

Seventy-two percent of those caught by the FBI for working with ISIS had absolutely no prior criminal history.

Most cases involved material support, and al-Matari couldn't easily draw from this large group of ideological supporters for a cell of direct-action operators, but there existed a sizable portion of men and in a few cases women who actively sought to travel to the Middle East to wage armed jihad on behalf of the Islamic State.

And there were so many more out there. The FBI had found only the tip of the iceberg.

Dearborn, Michigan, for example, had a significant Muslim population. While ninety-nine percent or more would have nothing to do with al-Matari's aims, it was certain the town nevertheless possessed hundreds of disaffected young men who would take up arms against the infidels. Still, al-Matari couldn't just grab an unemployed man off the street and send him to DC to kill a Pentagon official. No, the integrity of the entire operation would be jeopardized by using recruits more suited for armed conflict in Iraq, Syria, and Libya than political assassination in the United States.

No, he had to choose extremely carefully.

After weeks of searching and consulting with his team of online recruiters, he chose seventy names, men and women located across the United States who had both expressed the will and been found by the recruiters to possess the right raw materials to make a potential operative.

Al-Matari whittled this number down to thirty-nine by sending four two-man teams of recruiters across the US for individual meetings and evaluations. These potential recruits did not know what they were being asked to do at this point, only that they were being considered by Islamic State leadership for a role in the organization. Some clearly thought they would be going into Syria to fight in the jihad; others pieced together on their own from the questions asked by the recruiters that their work would be inside America.

Abu Musa al-Matari spent considerable time looking carefully into the remaining thirty-nine. He found a couple of the possible recruits who, while apparently not on any terrorist watch lists or known to the government as potential radicals, nevertheless had relatives who had expressed jihadist views or had spent time under FBI surveillance.

That would not do. This operation needed the purest of the pure, because this operation was not designed with an end date in mind. He didn't want the FBI to have any interest in these individuals, even after the attacks began.

He eliminated a few more who did not have the physical characteristics he required. One man was too heavy; another had a knee injury that had not healed.

Finally, Musa al-Matari narrowed his choice down to thirty-one potential recruits. His recruiters in the US met with each man and woman again and offered them the chance to serve.

Twenty-seven agreed. Of the four who did not, three

demanded to fight on the front lines in the Middle East, and they were told they would be contacted soon.

One more man, a thirty-three-year-old convenience store owner from Hallandale Beach, Florida, had told his wife, a recently converted Muslim, about his conversations with ISIS recruiters, and she demanded that he report the recruiters to the police. The man refused, but warned the recruiter that his wife might make trouble.

Three days later another ISIS team drove into town, donned ski masks, and shot both the clerk and his wife to death while they worked behind the counter of their store.

And now Musa al-Matari was here in the hills of western El Salvador, looking over his twenty-seven recruits, all of whom had just passed their monthlong training.

The Guatemalan trainers had left earlier in the day, and now, in the evening before the last of the day's light had left the jungle, al-Matari had assembled his operatives in a dry streambed within sight of the rusty barracks. He stood in front of them while they all sat on rocks or on the hilly creekside.

Al-Matari was proud of his students. The trainers had put the class through small-arms training, small-unit tactics, taught them how to fight hand to hand and with edged weapons. They taught them how to build bombs and booby traps and, more than anything, they hardened this class – only a few even knew how to hold a gun on day one, but by the end they could all confidently and rapidly hit targets with an AK-47 at more than a hundred meters, an Uzi submachine gun at fifty meters, and a pistol at fifteen meters. They could reload quickly, transition from shoulder weapon to handgun with economy of movement, and move in groups of twos and fours, covering for one another, keeping up the fire during reloads.

They shot from rusted-out cars and threw dummy grenades and built simple booby traps and explosives.

These weren't Special Forces by any stretch; but after thirty days of training, they were a competent unit of operatives. They had spent much more time firing weapons than a soldier in the US Army's ten-week basic-training course, and their drills were one hundred percent based on killing their targets, and getting away to do it again.

Looking at them now, al-Matari could barely recognize some of his cleanskins. They'd all lost weight in these austere conditions, but they were stronger, more confident, more steely-eyed, and ready for the war to come.

To be certain, some were better than others, but none had washed out utterly. He'd keep his eye on a couple of them, and he'd modulate the missions to play to the strengths of his force, but overall he was more than pleased with the students here at the facility he called the Language School.

Except for those who were related, the men and women here did not know one another's names. Al-Matari assigned them numbers as they arrived. It had nothing to do with seniority or pecking order. Those who arrived first had lower numbers, and the woman who arrived last took the number twenty-seven.

He had separated them into cells, five in all, and though al-Matari had names for each of the cells, he did not share them with the group. He just called them one through five.

But Matari had divided them geographically, based on the city in the geographic center of the homes of the cell members. There was Chicago, five men and one woman. They were members of two families, both second generation, and he had identified them early on as one of his best and most competent teams.

There was Santa Clara, his California cell. Again, five men and one woman. Two with Pakistani passports and two Pakistanis with British passports, and two Turks with German passports. The Turks were husband and wife. All six were students in the San Francisco area and, besides the Turks, they did not know one another. Now they lived and trained together, perspired and bled together.

Fairfax was five men. Four were US citizens of Arab descent, from Algeria, Egypt, Lebanon, and Iraq. And the fifth was an African American named David Hembrick. While Hembrick was a star pupil at the Language School, the rest had had trouble with some decision-making, and they argued among themselves regularly. But they could shoot, and Fairfax was as committed to this cause as any of the other cells.

Al-Matari would have liked a better-integrated cell to position near the nation's capital, but he would make do with the recruits at his disposal, and send other cells into DC to help when necessary.

Atlanta was five – four men and one woman. All but one were American citizens, one a blond-haired, blue-eyed twenty-three-year-old from Alabama who had converted to Islam and reached out online three years earlier to a group in Somalia, where he went over to fight. He made it back to the States without the government picking up on his actions, so al-Matari felt it was worth the risk adding him to the team, because he was the only one of the group who had any sort of combat training. There was also a black woman from Mississippi named Angela Watson, an extremely intelligent college student who'd secretly married a Tunisian student who joined ISIS to fight in the Middle East. She planned on accompanying him over, initially wanting to 'make cubs for the jihad,' but when the opportunity arose to serve ISIS in America, she knew no one would ever think of her as a Muslim jihadi, so she and her husband flew to the Language School, where Angela exceeded her husband's skills in every way.

Detroit was another strong unit. Five in number, four men and one woman. All of them were US citizens or permanent residents, and al-Matari knew they, as well as Chicago, would be the teams he gave the toughest missions to.

Al-Matari addressed them now in English, because it was the one language everyone here at the camp understood. He spoke perfect English, with a decidedly British accent, so the twenty-seven men and women in front of him all assumed he came from the UK.

'It is time to tell you more about your mission. First, know this. You are now soldiers. Warriors. Mujahideen. You will hear the word "terrorist" from the American media, but your targets are not the targets of terrorists. You will soon see that your targets are handpicked to hurt America's ability to fight against Islam, against the Islamic State. You will be proud of your fight, and you have every right to be. You are lions of the caliphate. Vanguards of the jihad.'

The group cheered in unison.

One of the young men from Santa Clara said, 'Mohammed, we trained with the Guatemalans using the weapons they brought. But how are we getting back home with weapons?'

Al-Matari said, 'Remember, you all came here telling your loved ones you would attend language school. You all have return flights. You will all go home on your return flights, and you will not take your weapons. I will bring everything you need to America, and I will deliver it to you before you begin operations.'

As al-Matari talked operational details, the headlights of a pickup truck appeared in the distance, near the corrugated metal buildings. The truck parked, and a man climbed out and then looked around. Al-Matari shined a flashlight toward the man that would be easily visible in the dusk, letting him know his position.

Three hundred meters away, the man began walking toward the group in the dry streambed.

Al-Matari turned back to the students of the Language School. 'You will all leave tonight, but before you go, I have one final exercise. The man coming this way owns the shell company that purchased this property, and I asked him to come here to collect the last of his money this evening.' He paused a moment. 'He is an infidel. He can identify me, and he has shown suspicion about what we are doing.'

The African American woman from Mississippi raised her hand. 'The trainers . . . They are infidels, they sure as hell knew what we were up to.'

Al-Matari nodded and smiled. 'This morning your trainers from Guatemala boarded a helicopter they had stored in a hangar near Playa El Zonte, an hour-and-a-half drive southwest of here. They planned on returning home by flying below radar into Guatemala. Two associates of mine prepared a surprise for them on their helicopter. When they were off the coast and within sight of the Guatemalan border, their helicopter exploded at an altitude of two hundred feet. There were no survivors.'

No one said anything, but some eyes widened.

He pointed to the man approaching, now two hundred yards away.

'Each of the five cells will speak quietly to one another, and you will, together, elect one member of your unit to kill this man who is approaching us now. Pick the one you believe will be the best representative of you to draw blood in front of me. Your most sure killer. When I have my five selectees, I will make the final choice. You have one minute to decide.'

The man was fifty meters away by the time the choices were made. Al-Matari was proud in his abilities as a leader of warriors. He'd correctly predicted the chosen killer in four of the five units. The fifth group, Atlanta, had selected the twenty-two-year-old female college student from Mississippi to do the deed. A mild surprise; he thought she would be their logistics expert, the brains of the unit. That still might well be the case, but the fact she was also the one designated as the first to draw blood for the unit impressed him.

The man arrived at the group now, sweating in the night's heat. He was well into his sixties and seemed uncomfortable and agitated to be here. He looked around at the students, then up to al-Matari.

Al-Matari smiled at him and then, without saying a word, he drew his knife, and stabbed the man through the throat. The man had made no reaction to the movement at all before the blade plunged down, slicing into his airway.

Blood spewed, the Latin man gurgled and wheezed as he crumpled to the rocks of the streambed, then he lay there still.

Al-Matari turned to the others. He saw the shock and

confusion on their faces. 'Very well,' he said, still trying to get his pulse back to normal. 'Your assignment was not, in fact, as I had described. If I am present, I need no help in killing an infidel.'

He wiped the knife off on a handkerchief and returned it to the scabbard hidden under his shirt.

'Each cell has just chosen its leader. Your killers are your leaders. I want killers in charge because *that*, first, foremost, and fully, is your job. Do you all understand?'

One of the Atlanta team, the Jordanian American with the student visa, switched into Arabic to address Musa al-Matari. 'No! I will not serve under a woman! We put her forward to test her dedication, not because she was a leader!'

Al-Matari glared at the young man. 'Then you disobeyed my order. Maybe I'll have her kill you to prove her leadership ability.'

Al-Matari looked at the woman, who had no idea what was being discussed. In English, he said, 'Number twenty-seven, are you ready to lead these men into war?'

Twenty-two-year-old Angela Watson replied, 'Oh, yes, sir. I will not fail.'

Al-Matari nodded. The Jordanian American fell silent.

'Now you will all return to America. Not to your mosque, not to your friends, not to your Muslim way of life. No. You will go to safe houses we have arranged, you will live quietly, establish your peaceful, nonthreatening routines, give all those around you no reason at all to be suspicious of you.

'And then, as soon as I arrive and deliver your weapons, I will assign targets. When these targets are destroyed, *inshallah*, I will assign more, and more, and more. As new recruits beg to join the jihad you, my brothers and sisters, will arm them and send them on their way, directly into the soft targets. But your main mission will always be direct action against the military and intelligence arms of America.'

He smiled. 'A month from now . . . chaos. Three months from now . . . the armies of the West will be leaving to fight in the caliphate. One year from now, *inshallah* . . . the permanent retreat of the West, devastated and demoralized, the bodies of their dead left behind to fertilize our fields. They will run and they will never return. Within five years the caliphate will vanquish the Shiites, including Iran, and we will control their oil. The caliphate will destroy the tyrants in Mecca, the Saudis, the King's severed head at the foot of the Ka'ba, and we will control the oil to the south.

'The West will not be able to burn us in the nuclear fires, because our oil fields will last a thousand years, and without this fuel the West will die.'

He squeezed his hand in front of his face. 'We will own them.'

Now he lowered his hand and his head. 'The twenty-eight of us will not live to see that day. We will surely die in the jihad, and we will achieve paradise for ourselves and for our loved ones. We will make this journey on earth good for all future Muslims . . . imagine the rewards that will be bestowed upon us for our valuable sacrifices.'

The audience was at one with him in his reverence for their fight to come.

'You are the swords against the oppressors, and the shields of the oppressed. There are only two paths forward. Victory or martyrdom.'

The twenty-seven students of the Language School shouted, *'Allahu Akbar!'*

*

At one o'clock in the morning the SUVs that were seen a month earlier going up the hillside out of San Rafael rumbled back down into San Rafael, on their way to the highway. The villagers took note, and they wondered if this meant the sounds of gunfire would cease and the damn dogs of the village would stop barking so much.

11

The three operators of The Campus converged in John Clark's office at nine on Monday morning, each with a steaming cup of coffee in his hand. They were dressed informally; it was hot as hell in DC this summer, so Jack and Dom wore polo shirts and linen dress pants, while Clark wore a collared short-sleeved button-down shirt and Chavez wore a dress shirt with the sleeves rolled halfway up his muscular forearms.

Normally there would be a little lighthearted chatter before getting down to business, but the two younger men were both still painfully aware of their errors on the exercise up in Maryland on Friday. They'd follow cues from the two older men. If there was to be any joking during this meeting, Dom and Jack knew better than to start it themselves.

As they both halfway expected, John Clark made zero small talk before getting down to business. 'I've been planning this expansion ever since I left the operational ranks and Sam died. I wanted Gerry to see how difficult a job you had performing complicated direct-action missions as short-staffed as you are. Frankly, I expected you to succeed, but for Gerry to listen in on the after-action report as you discussed how hamstrung you were with only three guns in the fight. Instead, you two fucked it up. I guess I should be glad that my point was made so well, but it's never a good day when a training evolution informs you that you would have died in an identical real-world scenario.'

No one spoke.

Clark looked around the table slowly. Finally he said, 'Good. I didn't want to hear any lame excuses. It takes character to own your mistakes. Now it's my job to get you the help you obviously need.

'You three have had the weekend to think it over. Ding, let's start with you. Who do you recommend for an operational billet?'

Chavez said, 'I nominate Bartosz Jankowski.'

Clark cocked his head; he didn't recognize the name. 'Who the hell is that?'

Chavez smiled now. He clearly knew he'd be getting that reaction. 'You know him by his call sign, Midas.'

It had been well over a year since The Campus had worked with a small unit of Delta Force operators in Ukraine, during Russia's initial invasion of the eastern portion of the nation. Midas had been the officer in charge of the Delta Force unit, and Clark remembered he'd been one impressive individual.

'Interesting. What do you know about him?'

Chavez said, 'I asked around. I have some buddies behind the fence at Fort Bragg.'

Clark knew 'behind the fence' was a euphemism for working at Delta, who were based at Fort Bragg near Fayetteville, North Carolina, and were, indeed, separated by a fence from other forces there, at least nominally.

'And?'

'Luckily for us, Midas just got out of the military, retired after twenty years, but he's only thirty-eight. A lieutenant colonel.'

Clark did the math. 'If he's been in the full twenty at that age, and an O, then he must have been a Mustang.'

'He was,' Ding confirmed.

Jack said, 'You guys are speaking military again. What's an O, and what's a mustang?'

'An O is an officer, and a guy who enlists in the military, then turns into an officer, is called a Mustang officer. They have to go to college at some point, then leave the enlisted ranks to become an officer. They usually make great O's, because they've seen military from the perspective of the men they lead.'

Chavez said, 'Anyway, I didn't hear anything but good stuff about Barry. His real name is Bartosz, he's first-generation Polish, but he goes by Barry in the civilian world. His men loved him, the other O's respected him, and Delta was damn sorry to lose him.'

Clark said, 'What's he doing now?'

Ding smiled again. 'Fishing.'

'What?'

'He's applied at CIA, but that's a slow process, even for a former Delta dude. Some hangup with all the foreigners in his family, I suspect, although the military didn't seem to care when he got into Delta.'

Clark wasn't surprised by this. 'CIA can be a confounding organization. How long till they get that straightened out?'

Chavez said, 'I called Jimmy Hardesty to see what the scoop was on that. He said that if we wanted Midas, we better snatch him up, and quick. In the meantime, though, a guy who knows him says he's pitching a tent on the grounds of Fort Bragg, fishing the lakes and rivers. Kind of an extended vacation before things get rough again.'

Clark made some notes. 'Good selection, Ding. Okay, on to Jack. Who do you nominate?'

Jack said, 'Adam Yao. CIA officer. We worked with him in

Hong Kong a couple years back, and I ran into him again in California working that North Korea deal last year. He's a very good man, smart as hell, unquestionably brave, and as dedicated as he can be. He speaks Mandarin, which could be handy.'

Clark said, 'Young guy, from what I remember.'

'No, he's getting up there in years. Probably thirty-four or so.' There was a glint in Jack's eyes as he said this. Jack himself was just younger than this, while Clark was twice Yao's age.

Clark's eyes narrowed. 'I can reach you from here, Jack. You want to get smacked?'

'Sorry, boss. Anyway, I checked him out a little bit and found out he's not in the field at the moment. He's working a desk at Langley.'

Clark thought it over. 'Gerry will have to check with Mary Pat. We're not stealing anybody out from under her or Canfield. Good nomination, though.'

Clark turned to Caruso. 'Okay, Dom. Who's your guy?'

Caruso hesitated.

The other three men in the room looked to him. Finally, Clark said, 'Dom. You okay?'

'Yeah. Um . . . Well, my recommendation is that we promote Adara Sherman to an operational role.'

Jack Ryan just muttered softly, 'Oh, boy.'

Dom found himself quickly defending his suggestion, even though he had reservations that were obvious on his face. 'Look, we know what she's done in the field, we know her background in the Navy. She's a terrific employee here, she's as vetted as we can possibly vet anyone, and she has a ton of training, even training we don't have.'

Clark went silent for half a minute. Finally he looked to Chavez with a raised eyebrow. 'Thoughts?'

Chavez said, 'The one worry that keeps running through

my mind is how we will be able to replace her on the aircraft. She's doing such a kick-ass job now.'

Clark nodded. 'If our main concern about promoting her is that she is terrific at her current position, I guess that means Dom has made one hell of a good recommendation.'

Caruso had been afraid someone would say that.

Clark turned to Jack now. 'You said, "Oh, boy." You have a problem working with a woman in general, or with Adara in particular?'

Jack's face reddened, and he looked around the room awkwardly. He said, 'Neither. I think she's awesome. I just . . .'

'You just what?'

Ryan looked to Dom Caruso for an instant, then looked away. 'I think she'd be great. I really do.'

And he left it there.

But Dom knew what Jack was thinking. He was thinking about Dom, knowing that Adara was his girlfriend. And he was thinking about the prospect of Dom losing someone else close to him.

The President had his national security staff in for a morning briefing, and all the principals were in attendance. Surprisingly, the ongoing US air and special ops campaign against ISIS in the Middle East ended up being dropped down to third place today on the list of critical areas that needed to be brought to Ryan's attention. This wasn't because nothing was going on in the fighting; rather, it was just the opposite. The United States, allied with Iraqi and Kurdish forces, and the Shiite forces allied with Iran, were making headway against the Islamic State on multiple fronts.

But other international hot spots competed every day as the primary concern of the Commander in Chief, and it was up to the men and women who wrote the presidential daily brief to decide what took top billing.

This morning, the first issue was China landing long-range bombers on islands it had constructed in the China Sea, and after the conference room discussed this for fifteen minutes, the topic turned to Russia's ongoing attempt to move into parts of eastern Ukraine that the Ukrainian Army was having trouble holding.

Both of these events might have seemed, on the surface, at least, to be less important to American national interests than ongoing military operations involving American troops, but the United States' unique position and responsibility in the world meant the Commander in Chief needed to be up to date on *all* crises, everywhere.

There was a never-ending hydra of challenges around the globe, but Ryan knew the worst possible course of action for the President would be to retreat from the world stage and stick his head in the sand. No, the hydra couldn't be defeated, but with constant diplomacy, and with military and intelligence resources brought to bear, it could be battled back, just enough to keep America and its allies reasonably safe.

Ryan looked down to the third item on the day's briefing. 'Okay, Mary Pat, tell us about your trip to Iraq.'

'As you know,' she said, 'we've been hunting top ISIS personality Abu Musa al-Matari. Since his failed attempt late last year to train and infiltrate sixteen well-trained jihadists with American passports or visas into the US, we've taken it as a given that he would try again.'

Ryan said, 'He made it to within a hair's breadth of getting killers on US soil that we didn't know anything about. And a guy like him is going to be very aware how close he came. Damn right he'll try again. What did you learn?'

'I learned that he left Syria six and a half weeks ago to go to a place he referred to as the "Language School." We are working to find it.'

Ryan looked around at the other members of his NSC. 'How do you know it's not just a place where you learn to speak another language?'

Mary Pat smiled a little. 'We can't rule that out yet, but I doubt it. The intel came from one of al-Matari's teen wives, a kidnapped Yazidi I spoke to. From the context of his other actions and travels, we think there's more to this than an actual language school. We think it's code for a location.'

The NSA director said, 'We've done a broad spectrum data mine on the code phrase "Language School" among Islamic State actors and suspected actors, suspected actors of affiliated organizations, et cetera, et cetera.'

'Any luck?'

'We found the haystack, not the needles. People talk about language schools in their conversations all the time, obviously. But we, I should say NSA and CIA analysts, are combing through the data by hand, and so far they have found nothing that sticks out. Not one suspicious reference in e-mails, recorded phone calls, interviews, international communications between suspects. Not yet, anyway.'

Dan Murray said, 'I ordered the same search to be done in the USA for people currently under surveillance by federal authorities who aren't part of the NSA's purview, because the communications are CONUS to CONUS conversations. So far, same as NSA, nothing, but we're still digging.'

Mary Pat said, 'Al-Matari might have used this as code just between himself and one other person. The Yazidi girl might have heard something that wasn't as wide in scope as we had hoped.'

Jay Canfield spoke up now. 'We did, however, learn something interesting in Central America. Is it related? That we do not know. The day before last a helicopter crashed off the Pacific coast of Guatemala. There were six fatalities, all former Guatemalan Special Forces commandos. The helo had been rented by one of them from a company in Guatemala City, eight weeks prior to the crash. The last time anyone knew where the helicopter was it had landed at a property in Monterrico on the Guatemalan coast.'

Ryan cocked his head. 'There's more, I take it?'

Canfield nodded. 'My local station looked into the men who were killed, and Dan's people down there interviewed their wives and such yesterday. A couple had been told by their husbands they were going to El Salvador to teach a thirty-day guerrilla tactics course.'

Ryan asked the next question slowly. 'To whom?'

'The wives didn't know. Dan gave Mary Pat the info, and I had my station in El Salvador look into it. We came up empty, so I went to DEA on the off chance they'd have heard chatter. DEA has a good ground game in Central America, lots of HUMINT assets. It turns out DEA agents working on the Pacific coast spotted the helo when it was on the ground there. It was at an airstrip near Playa El Zonte, kind of a hippie surfer town. Frankly, it's a *really* weird place to teach terrorist tactics.'

'Surfing terrorists,' Ryan said, and groaned. 'Add that to the threat matrix.' This was a joke, but Arnie Van Damm mumbled from the end of the table.

'If the press heard a word of that, their heads would explode from excitement.'

Canfield said, 'The DEA guys jotted down the tail number. It matches with the helo that crashed off Guatemala.'

Ryan summarized. 'So a guerrilla-warfare school was set up by Guatemalan ex-commandos somewhere in the west of El Salvador. Do I need to run down the list of groups that may have been in that school?'

Canfield answered, 'Local insurgents, other Central American revolutionaries, South American revolutionaries.'

Murray took over. 'Zetas, Gulf cartel, Sinaloa cartel, MS-13 –'

Mary Pat reined in the speculation. 'Could be any of those things. But this looks like an ad hoc project, and the timing is right to match up with what we know about al-Matari's movements. For now we have no idea if al-Matari is in our hemisphere and involved with this. But we're all looking, Mr President.'

The meeting wrapped a few minutes later, and Mary Pat went out into the President's secretary's office and retrieved her phone, which she always left in a basket there before going into the Oval. It was a West Wing rule. In offices, conference rooms, pretty much everywhere other than hallways, mobile phones in the West Wing were verboten.

As soon as she stepped into the hall, however, her phone started to ring. She answered without looking.

'Foley.'

'Hi, Mary Pat. It's Gerry.'

'Funny you should call, Gerry. I was just thinking about you. Well, I should say I was thinking about your excellent private equity management firm.'

Hendley Associates was the front company for The Campus. It was, in fact, a working private equity firm, and it even funded Campus operations by the trades it made.

Gerry, however, would be quite certain that Mary Pat wasn't looking to invest some money. No, she employed The

Campus regularly on operations unsuited for any of the agencies under the purview of the Office of the Director of National Intelligence. If she was thinking of Hendley's organization, then she was thinking about espionage.

Gerry said, 'Something we can do for you?'

'Not just yet, but I'd wager that pretty soon I'll be making the drive over to Alexandria for a little chitchat.'

'We're always ready and waiting. Actually, though, that's sort of the reason I called. We aren't as ready as we used to be. As you know, we've lost some operational abilities.'

After a pause Mary Pat said, 'I think of Sam every day.'

'Yes. So do I. We've decided to bring some new blood into the organization, and we're in the processes of narrowing down some candidates.'

'I'm glad to hear that. How can I be of assistance?'

'There is a name that came forward. Some of my guys have worked with him in the past. He's currently employed by Jay. Of course I wouldn't think of making any sort of an approach without your blessing.'

'What's the name? If I know him I'll tell you how I feel about him leaving. If I don't know him, I'll check him out.'

'His name is Adam Yao.'

Mary Pat's pause was brief. 'Gerry, you know I'd do anything to help your operation out over there. You have become an important part of the IC in the last several years.'

'But?'

'But if you take Adam Yao away from me, I'll drive over there personally and punch you in the nose.'

Gerry laughed. 'He's that good, huh?'

'He's one of Jay's superstars. He's done things I can't talk about, not even to you.'

Gerry knew Yao had been involved with operations in

Hong Kong and in North Korea, but he didn't say anything about them. Instead, he said, 'You keep Mr Yao. Sounds like he's already in a position that is getting the best out of him. Plus, I'm not looking to get a punch in the nose. I've had a rough week.'

'Really? What happened?'

'I helped out on an exercise with the assets. Opposition force, they call it. It didn't go so well for anyone involved.'

'You aren't hurt, are you?'

'Nothing that can't be rectified by regular bandage changes and a steady supply of small-batch bourbon from my home state of Kentucky. I was shot eight times with simulated bullets that weren't as simulated as I would have liked them to be. The President's boy did the deed, in fact.'

'My God. I guess if they are drafting you to play OPFOR, they really *are* short of manpower over there.'

'I *thought* that would help you see the problem at hand.'

Mary Pat said, 'I can't let you have Adam, but I'll find ten other suitable recruits for you if you want me to do that. I'm a little busy right now, but as soon as –'

Gerry said, 'Don't worry about it. We have two other good candidates we're looking at, and they don't work in the IC at the moment. Let me see how they develop. If I need more names, I'll circle back to you.'

'Okay,' Mary Pat replied. 'But as I said, something is brewing out there, so you can expect me to reach out sooner rather than later.'

'And we'll always be ready to do our best.'

12

The wild-eyed young man sprinted across the flat ground, his chest heaving from the exertion of the run, the fear, and the weight of the rifle in his hands – and then he jolted back with a slap of metal on bone and whirled dead onto the dirt.

Four meters from the tumbling corpse, Xozan Barzani kept going, racing headlong into danger, over brown hardscrabble land, through the supersonic snaps of close-passing gunfire. Men dropped to his left and to his right, while he and others like him continued on to their target. Two hundred meters ahead of him a ceramics factory served as an enemy stronghold. His orders were to take it; his orders were foolish, and it appeared he'd soon pay the price of obeying them, just like the dead man on his left, and the others falling all around.

In Kurdish, the word *peshmerga* means 'one who faces death.' Barzani was a Peshmerga captain, the leader of a company of troops that had numbered 120 three days earlier, but now was down to sixty-six men still able to hold a rifle and press a trigger. His company's heavy machine gunners were dead, their weapons captured by the enemy, and his single recoilless rifle had run out of ammunition in the first hours of the battle.

He and his men had no cover other than a few rills in the dirt, some low earthen berms at various angles – none of which were very helpful in concealing them from the enemy – and a couple burned-out hulks of fighting vehicles.

The only real cover was the ceramics factory, and it was now 185 meters away and in the hands of well-entrenched Islamic State fighters.

As a young boy Xozan had learned to distinguish the difference between incoming and outgoing rounds, and it sounded to him now like the enemy had vastly superior numbers of guns and seemingly limitless ammo.

He estimated the enemy's remaining strength at well over one hundred fighters, all with cover and concealment, and helped out by heavy weapons and vehicles. He'd seen two Russian-built BRDM-2 armored scout vehicles with coaxial machine guns, and at least four technicals, pickup trucks with mounted machine guns.

Things had been going well for the Peshmerga for the past few months, strategically speaking, but as is often the case in war, the situation on the ground appeared a lot more dire than when looking at the map. While the Kurds, along with help from NATO airpower, had been advancing on multiple fronts toward the ISIS-held city of Mosul, the Islamic State had conducted a surprise counterattack east up the road toward Kalak, with their eyes on a strategically important bridge there.

Barzani's battalion, just off the front lines of the fighting to the northwest, was rushed into the line of advance.

The Kalak bridge was secured by the Peshmerga, and all was good, till someone far above Barzani decided to press the initiative and commit his battalion to an advance. This might have looked good on paper, but Barzani's company as well as the three others in the battalion were exhausted and woefully short on supplies. With not enough vehicles and heavy weapons, the battalion was ordered to the west, into ISIS-held lands, with orders to take Karemlash.

Now, two days later, Barzani figured his dead body would be found as close to Karemlash as he would ever get, and he was still kilometers away.

As soon as the Peshmerga attack began, armored civilian trucks loaded with improvised explosive devices had rumbled up the Mosul highway from Islamic State-held territory, and detonated in or near the Peshmerga lines, and slowing this slaughter had cost Barzani's forces all their remaining RPGs, most of which had been ineffective against these suicide tanks.

After that it was close-in fighting on the open ground. ISIS finally pulled back to the ceramics factory, but Barzani's company had no indirect-fire weapons to dislodge them, and the order to take the factory with AK-47s and boot leather was absolute madness.

Barzani stumbled over a low berm now, and found himself in the middle of an ISIS forward scouting position. Two black-clad men seemed as surprised to see the Kurd as he was to see them. He fired his wire-stocked AK-47 from his hip, dropped a bearded man at a distance of five meters, and when one of Barzani's sergeants shot the other man through the jaw, they both softly chanted *'Allahu Akbar,'* their words indecipherable because of their heavy breathing.

Just then the dirt and stone around them kicked up, bits of rock pelted the captain in the face and hands, as a heavy machine gun, probably on the roof of the ceramics factory, opened up on his position.

Barzani dove headfirst into the foxhole with the bodies for cover, then he looked around for his sergeant. The man was dead three meters from the hole, his head missing.

Barzani had told himself he would keep running all the way to the factory, but despite this, his training took over, and he remained there under cover as the machine gun tilled the ground inches from his head.

Three men lay dead nearby, but looking down the pocked desert landscape, he saw a few dozen of his men still in the fight. They had all found their own little holes to crawl into. It filled him with pride that he would die today with such brave warriors, but he could not stop thinking about Kalak, the Kurdish town ten kilometers behind him, and the Kurdish civilians there. Women. Children. The aged. The wounded.

He'd never take the factory, and when Barzani and his men were all dead, ISIS would have no one to stop them from heading right into Kalak, driving straight up the main street and taking whatever they wanted, including the lives of every last living thing.

Just then, the machine-gun fire stopped, and he could hear the rumble of heavy equipment. He peered over the edge of the foxhole; saw both of the BRDM-2s rumbling out of the ceramics factory, fifty meters apart, and heading in his direction.

The scout cars were armored with up to fourteen millimeters of steel; the Peshmerga Kalashnikovs would do nothing more than annoy the occupants of the cars with the sound of bullets pinging off the hulls.

And the machine guns on the roof of the factory had Barzani's company pinned down in little holes like rats, so the armored cars could come and methodically clean them out.

Three unarmored technicals came out behind the scout cars, hauling more weapons and fighters his way. They were led by a white Toyota Hilux with a fifty-caliber machine gun mounted in the bed.

Barzani spoke as calmly as he could into his radio. He

knew if he ordered a retreat now, whoever was left would be shot in the back, because there was nearly a kilometer of open ground behind them. 'Brothers, do not waste your fire on the armored vehicles. Kill the technicals. Shoot the drivers, the gunners. We will martyr ourselves today, and we will do it fighting, not hiding!'

The chattering of AKs from the dirt to his left and right lifted his spirits, emboldened him, but only until the two BRDM-2s opened up with their KPV 14.5s and their coaxial 7.62s, raking back and forth, keeping heads down, increasing the carnage.

Barzani knew he and his men would all die in the dirt, and then Kalak would fall by dawn.

The closest BRDM-2 was just one hundred meters away from him now, churning up the hard earth to Barzani's left with its machine guns. He tried to put it out of his mind so he could focus the blade sight of his rifle on the front windshield of the white Hilux barreling right down toward his foxhole, its own machine gun thumping loud in the air as the truck bounced across on the brown and barren landscape.

But just as Barzani readied to fire on the truck, an ungodly sound ripped through the sky over his head. He turned to look, and his eyes blinked hard at the sight of the nearest BRDM-2 disappearing in a cloud of dust.

It stopped rolling forward, stopped firing. The dust settled while the Peshmerga captain looked on, confused by whatever the hell had just happened.

And then it happened again.

The sound of ripping metal, the strikes of high-powered cannon rounds, sparks and flames erupting out of the armored car, and then, out of the dustup from the dirt around the vehicle, an explosion and a fireball.

Barzani looked left and right at his men, but there was no reason to do so. He knew better than anyone in the company that there existed no weapon in his arsenal that could have done what he'd just witnessed.

A private far to his left pointed to the blue sky to the north. It took Barzani a second to focus on a speck there, but the speck grew quickly. It was a helicopter gunship, American, and within seconds, the sparkle of light from its nose told him it was firing its chain gun.

Barzani shifted his eyes to the second BRDM-2 just as it, too, was enveloped by the brown dust of these flat lands.

High above and just behind the first helicopter, a second helo dotted the sky.

They were American Apaches from the US Army, and they'd just thrown Barzani and his men a lifeline.

Peshmerga captain Xozan Barzani couldn't hear the radio broadcast coming from the helicopter racing over the landscape a thousand meters to his north, but if he could, he might have been surprised by the sound of a calm female voice on the net. 'Pyro One-Two, Pyro One-One. Target bravo is toast. That's all the light armor. I'm goin' after the soft-skinned vehicles.'

A male voice responded instantly. This was the helo far above and just behind the helo firing. 'Pyro One-Two, roger. Smoke those technicals.'

'Pyro One-One is engaging.'

Captain Carrie Ann Davenport was the copilot-gunner of an AH-64E Apache attack helicopter, call sign Pyro 1-1, hovering north 1,500 yards from the ceramics factory, barely outside effective range of the ISIS machine guns, but well within range of her M230 chain gun.

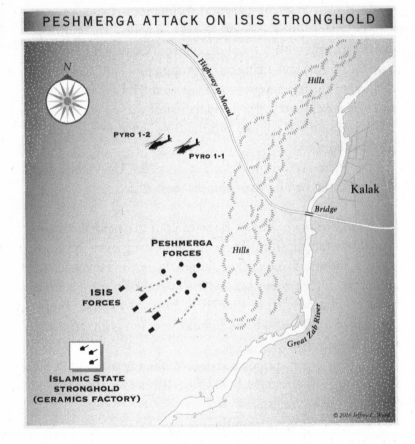

PESHMERGA ATTACK ON ISIS STRONGHOLD

N

Highway to Mosul

Hills

PYRO 1-2

PYRO 1-1

Kalak

Bridge

PESHMERGA
FORCES

Hills

ISIS
FORCES

Great Zab River

ISLAMIC STATE
STRONGHOLD
(CERAMICS FACTORY)

© 2016 Jeffrey L. Ward

Behind and just above Davenport in the cockpit of the helo was her pilot, Chief Warrant Officer 3 Troy Oakley. Oakley spoke into his headset now. 'Nail that bastard!'

Carrie Ann squeezed off a ten-round burst, watched the camera image of the technical on the multifunction display on her console, and realized her rounds had missed, striking the ground just behind the moving Hilux.

'Damn, adjusting.'

'You got 'em,' Oak encouraged from the pilot's seat.

Davenport led the technical and pressed the trigger again. As the chain gun fired, it belched puffs of gray smoke fifty feet down in angles off the port and starboard sides of the nose of the aircraft. Thirty-millimeter rounds sprayed out of the M230, and the Hilux 1,500 yards away flipped over at speed, skidded on its roof, and immediately burst into flames.

'Oh, shit!' Oakley exclaimed. 'There's one for the highlight reel.'

Davenport was already looking for her next target. 'Seventy rounds remaining. Wish we had a few Hydras left. I could use them on the techs and the thirty mike-mike on these troops in the open.'

The Hydra-70 were 2.75-inch FFAR, or folding-fin aerial rockets. Both Pyro 1-1 and Pyro 1-2 had left their forward operating base near Erbil with a full close-support role complement of thirty-eight of the unguided rockets, but they had used them all in an attack on an ISIS armory and fuel depot just north of Mosul.

'Just do what you can. We're bingo in five.'

Davenport said, 'Roger. I'll deal with the trucks and then we're outta here. The Pesh will have to clean up the squirters.'

This flight of two AH-64Es had been heading back to base after annihilating their primary targets when they were notified of the heavy fighting west of Kalak. In the scheme of things, with engagements up and down a semicircular front line a hundred miles in length, the fighting at Kalak wasn't seen as strategically important. Yes, ISIS threatened to take control of the bridge there, but the Kurdish and Iraqi attack westward wasn't planning on using this road, and the strategic objective had been all along to encircle and cut off these ISIS troops.

Still, when the Pyro flight heard reports of multiple technicals and light armor approaching a company of Peshmerga caught in open ground, they checked their moving map displays, their fuel levels, and their weapons loadouts, and decided they had enough gas and guns to divert and make a couple passes on their way back to their base.

Pyro 1-2 wasn't involved in this fight, because they were down to zero rockets, and had only fifty rounds left in their M230. They flew high-cover, ready to provide support in an emergency and to help with target acquisition, while Pyro 1-1, Davenport and Oakley's aircraft, took on the targets of opportunity below.

The last of the technicals turned around and began racing back to the ceramics factory, but Pyro 1-1 didn't care that the Islamic State fighters were disengaging. The men in the truck were still alive, and their equipment was still operational.

Oakley said, 'You gonna frag that last one?'

Davenport's answer was given with a rumble of the M230 below the cockpit. Sixteen hundred yards away the ground behind the technical turned to dust and fire, and then the vehicle itself exploded.

Oakley came over the radio now. 'Pyro Two, Pyro One-One, that's all the big stuff we see from here. You have eyes on anything else before we RTB?'

Pyro 1-2 was piloted by a CWO-4 named Wheaton, and his authoritative voice came over Davenport and Oakley's headsets. 'Pyro One-One. I'm, uh ... I'm seeing emplacements on the roof of that rectangular building ... Uh, one-point-five klicks southeast of you. The taller structure. You see 'em?'

Davenport looked at the FLIR camera view on her multifunction display. Oakley increased altitude a little, and Davenport panned the camera across the top of the building. The sandbagged positions came into view, and the one in the middle flashed, causing black-hot blooms on the infrared screen.

Davenport said, 'Roger that, One-Two. Looks like three gun positions. A couple PKs and ... uh ... That's a twelve-point-seven in the middle there.'

Wheaton said, 'You wanna rake those guys before we exfil?'

'That's affirm. I've got them. We're bingo fuel, but we can put thirty rounds on them before exfil.'

'Yeah, go ahead and light 'em up, One-One.'

Davenport took a moment to direct Oakley to a position where she could get a good angle for her rounds onto the machine gun emplacements, then she fired three short bursts, one at each weapon.

The carnage was immediate, but a few men crawled across the roof through the bodies and wreckage.

CWO-3 Oakley said, 'Nail that Kord again, just to be sure.' The Kord was the Russian-made 12.7-millimeter machine gun in the center. It had the power to, among other things, take down an attack helicopter at great range, and no Apache pilot liked seeing one of those left operational in the hands of the enemy.

Davenport unleashed twenty more rounds of 30-millimeter shells onto the roof of the ceramics factory, destroying all equipment and virtually all of the ISIS fighters positioned there.

After speaking again with 1-2, Oakley turned his aircraft to the northeast, flying behind Wheaton and leaving the battle behind.

Carrie Ann Davenport knew she had taken out the biggest threats to the Peshmerga in the open. She didn't have a feeling of victory, or even of great satisfaction, just a feeling that she wished they had the fuel and the ordnance to do more for the brave Peshmerga below. If she and Oakley had had more gas and guns, they could have virtually cut a swath of safety all the way through the ISIS stronghold in the factory.

One hour later Captain Xozan Barzani clicked his last loaded magazine in his AK, racked the slide to charge the weapon, and thumbed the fire select lever up to the safe position.

He stood in the center of the ceramics factory.

The fight was over.

The tide had turned instantly with the arrival of the American helicopters, and now the last of the ISIS troops had disappeared back to the west. They were all on foot, which gave Barzani great pleasure, because he'd seen with his own eyes as bearded men in black robes had climbed out of operational pickup trucks and run from them as if they were ticking time bombs, so sure were they that the helos were targeting anything with four wheels to the west of the Peshmerga line.

Barzani walked up to a brown truck on the road through the factory complex, put his hand on the roof, and stroked it in admiration. He looked inside the cab and saw the keys in the ignition. This was not a technical – there was no heavy weapon mounted in the back – but it was a good solid vehicle, and in the front passenger side he saw an RPK light machine gun with a cylindrical seventy-five-round magazine and, on the floor of the vehicle, a canvas satchel with three more loaded mags.

This was one truck he was glad the Americans had left alone.

After his squad leaders reported in, he learned he had only fifty-one troops left in his company from the 120 he had when he arrived at Kalak three days earlier, and he would mourn those martyred this afternoon when he had time to do so. But for now he gave the order to collect every weapon, every bullet, every knife, and every scrap of intelligence that could be found on the bodies. When this was done they would go back to Kalak to their sandbagged positions, and they would hope that ISIS would need some time to regroup before attacking again.

He would have liked to have held the ceramics factory, but it was too isolated a position to defend with fifty men and no heavy weapons. He knew better than to depend on the luck of an arrival of American Army helicopters over the battlefield the next time.

13

Adara Sherman sat at the conference table in Gerry Hendley's office, across from both Gerry and John Clark. This was her big interview, and she was nervous, though the two men had gone out of their way to convey informality and friendliness. This was a serious meeting about a serious job, but they treated her the same as they would on any other day.

Adara told herself she was ready for this. She *wanted* this. She could ace any testing or training they had in store for her. Although well into her thirties, she was in better physical shape now than she had been when she climbed high in the Afghan Kush providing combat aid for Marines, and she knew it.

She also knew she just had to make it through this conversation, and she'd get the job she'd wanted ever since she first understood what was going on here at the mysterious Campus.

Clark switched from idle chitchat to the interview by saying, 'We know you, obviously. We know how capable you are, what an intelligent young woman you are. You are brave, honest, a complete self-starter who requires absolutely no oversight.'

Gerry said, 'Hell . . . we could all go home and you'd have this place running better than it is now.'

Adara smiled. 'Kind, but untrue.'

Gerry said, 'We do have one concern, actually.'

She found a way to sit up even straighter. 'And what is that, Gerry?'

The two older men looked at each other. Their awkwardness suddenly made her uncomfortable. Finally Hendley said, 'It's Dominic.'

Adara's stomach fell through the floor of the room. She blinked a little slower, and a little harder than she would have liked. 'What . . . specifically . . . about Dominic?'

Clark spoke up now. 'Obviously, your relationship with Dom presents a special challenge to our operation. It's just something we haven't had to deal with before.'

Adara Sherman looked down toward the floor. 'So you know about that.'

Clark said, 'We do. It's obvious in the way you two act around each other.'

Her shoulders pulled back now. 'I'm sorry, but I have to disagree. I am *certain* I act in an appropriate manner at all times around all the employees of the organization, Dom Caruso included.'

Gerry put his hands out. 'Of course you do. But when Dom is in the room, you go out of your way not to look at him, not to engage with him in the same relaxed way as you do the others. He is the same way with you. You two are stiff and formal around each other. You have been hiding a relationship for a while.' Gerry added, 'Even I could see it, and I'm the one guy around here who isn't a spook.'

Adara nodded slowly. She wasn't as confident as she had been one minute earlier, but she knew she owed her employers an explanation. 'We were only keeping it to ourselves because we knew it would not get in the way of work, and we felt it would be unprofessional to act differently toward one another. Here, Dom is just another of the operations staff, and I'm just a member of the flight crew and the transportation and logistics coordinator for The Campus. We weren't trying to be deceitful, just discreet.'

Clark said, 'You aren't in trouble. There is no rulebook here. Gerry did tell the boys to keep away from you when you joined the team, but that was more of a word of warning and less of an official conduct policy.'

Gerry smiled, 'Thank God only one of the single guys made a move on you.'

Adara frowned playfully. 'Who said *Dom* made the move on *me*?'

Gerry's eyes widened, then he cleared his throat nervously.

Clark fought a smile. 'Anyway, I have a great team in Ding, Dominic, and Jack, and unit cohesion is critically important. I have no doubts you will fit in with the boys, I've seen it ever since you started here. Honestly, I only wonder if Dominic will act differently if you are put in more danger as an operative. I would very much like to add you to the team. But not at the expense of losing Dom as an effective asset.'

'We have discussed this,' Adara said, 'and he is fully on board with my application to the operational ranks.'

Clark shook his head. 'No . . . he's not. I could see it in his eyes when he nominated you. He's scared about you getting hurt. And you shouldn't blame him after what's happened here.'

'I don't blame him. Of course I know about his brother, though that was before my time. I *was* Sam's friend, and I know he and Dom were close. But I want the opportunity to show him, to show all of you, that I will fit right in.'

Clark continued, 'Having the four of you to call on would

be a boon to our operation. Not all at the same time, though. I want you to know that if we bring you aboard, we will not have you and Dom working together. I think it's better for everyone that way.'

Gerry said, 'We make allowances for the fact Jack's dad is the President. There are places we just won't send Jack. With you it will be the same way. Some ops won't be right for you.'

'Of course.' She nodded eagerly. She could feel the tide turning back her way.

Clark said, 'And then there is the training. There is a lot you do know, but a lot you do not know. Are you prepared to undergo months of rigorous training?'

'Actually, I look forward to it.'

'Surveillance training will begin just as soon as we pull in a second new recruit.'

Adara blinked. 'Wait . . . Somewhere in there, did you just offer me the job?'

Clark and Gerry looked at each other. Gerry said, 'You damn well deserve a promotion around here, and since we don't have a bigger plane to put you on . . . yes. You pass your training phase, and you'll be an operative of The Campus.'

Adara reached out to shake the men's hands. As Clark took it, he said, 'You might regret this decision. I owe it to you to make the training ultrarealistic and tough.'

'I will give one hundred percent, every day.'

She stood to leave, but as she got to the door, Gerry said, 'Adara, we're going to bring Dom in right now and tell him. He's going to act tough and unconcerned, but this will eat him up inside. I'm not going to tell you how to live your life, but I hope you understand he just feels that way because he cares.'

She nodded. 'I do. Thanks, Gerry and John, for your understanding to both Dom and me. And I'll keep everything transparent from now on.'

Mary Pat Foley had worked late at the office, then spent only one hour talking to her husband before they both went to bed, and now she woke suddenly to the sound of her ringing mobile phone by her head on the nightstand. Her husband, Ed, himself a former top American intelligence official, had enjoyed a forty-year career of late-night phone calls, but Mary Pat was the one still in government service, so Ed just sat up next to his wife while she fumbled with the phone.

'Foley.' She looked at the clock and saw it was four-fifty a.m. She'd miss out on her last forty minutes of sleep today.

The line was encrypted, she knew, because the director of the CIA was the man on the other end of the line.

Jay Canfield said, 'Good morning, Mary Pat.'

'Morning, Jay.'

She'd just wait for it; there was no need to ask him to get to the point.

'You know I like to provide solutions to your problems, but I'm afraid I have a brand-new problem for you that is completely out of left field.'

'What now?'

'We picked up some SIGINT out of Indonesia. A US consular affairs officer is preparing to pass some sort of classified material to North Korean officers in Jakarta.'

Mary Pat rubbed her eyes. 'God Almighty. What an idiot. The North Koreans don't even pay.'

Of course Canfield knew what she meant. Why would any American spy for North Korea? They had an ideology nobody but *nobody* outside the DPRK's borders ascribed to, and they were notoriously cheap when it came to purchasing intelligence product.

'Yeah, this is a weird one, that's for sure,' Canfield said.

'Who is he?'

'We don't have his name. We picked up the North Korean side of a phone conversation. By context we can tell they are talking to a US official at the embassy, not terribly well connected. Their previous interactions must have been done either in person or via some other method of comms. E-mail, perhaps. They told the American where to meet them with the information they demanded. We don't know what information he is being asked to pass. From what we heard the American doesn't sound like he wants any part of this, but he *does* sound like he's ready for the transaction to be over and done with. I think he's going to go through with it.'

Mary Pat said, 'Sounds like a compromise of some sort. They have pictures of him that would ruin his life. Something along those lines.'

'I agree. I've already contacted Dan. This is FBI jurisdiction.'

'When does the pass take place?'

'Forty-eight hours from now. They are giving the mole time to retrieve the intel they are demanding. Dan Murray is flying a team into Indonesia to have them set up on the pass location and take it down, but they have to go in under cover. Working with the Indonesians on something this in extremis is just about impossible, and we need to roll this guy up quickly and quietly. Dan's boys are flying in from Hong Kong. They should be on the ground around eleven a.m., East Coast time, today, so that will give them a day and a half to prep for the snatch. We'll be close by in an advisory role.'

'Okay,' Mary Pat said. 'Keep me posted.'

She hung up the phone, looked over at Ed. He was looking back at her in the dark. 'Is it bad?'

'It's unrelated to the Musa al-Matari hunt. Some State Department guy is about to pass intel to North Korea.'

Ed nodded. 'Definitely a compromised individual.'

'Exactly. Dan Murray has a special team racing in to handle it. I'll go in early to clear some other items off my desk, because I'm sure there will be a meeting about this at some point today.'

'I'll start the coffee,' Ed said with a tired smile.

Both of them climbed out of bed.

'Poor baby,' Mary Pat said with genuine sympathy as she headed to the bathroom. 'You thought you would get to sleep in when you retired.'

'Not at all, dear. I'm a pretty smart guy, so I knew I wouldn't get to sleep in till *you* retired.'

14

John Clark looked out over the one-man campsite, and wished he could stay here a couple days, because this was his kind of place. Yes, it was a simple affair: a pup tent, a fire burned down to coals, a cooler to sit on, and some fishing gear leaning against a tree. But it was just twenty-five yards or so from a beautiful lake, the pines surrounding it gave off a great smell, and the air was still a little cool this morning, even though it was summer.

While Clark eyed the camp with his binoculars from a hill a hundred yards away, he assumed the resident of the campsite must have been out fishing now.

It was just eleven in the morning on an overcast day, and he heard a rumble in the sky to his left. At first he thought it was thunder, but when he looked in that direction he saw a pair of C-17 Globemasters, massive US Air Force transport aircraft, flying just a thousand feet or so above the terrain. While he watched, men began jumping out of both planes simultaneously. Round parachutes popped open instantly.

Clark mumbled to himself. 'Eighty-second Airborne.' This was Fort Bragg, after all, their home. It was no surprise to witness a drop here.

He wanted to sit and watch the entire spectacle from the hill, it was an amazing sight to see, but he had work to do, so he began walking down to the little campsite. The last thing he wanted to do was surprise anyone down there, so he called out when he was still forty yards away, on the off chance the owner of the tent was still zipped up inside.

'Hello? Anybody home?'

But when he got to the campsite he found it empty and quiet.

He walked through the pine trees down to Mott Lake, peered out over the water looking for any sign of a fishing boat in the distance, but the lake was still and empty.

There wasn't a soul in sight.

Just then, a voice right behind him, not twenty-five feet away. 'Last time I saw you, we were on the other side of the world.'

Clark did not spin around at the voice. He didn't know this man very well, and this man barely knew him at all. Clark didn't want to do anything to put him at unease.

Clark smiled and turned slowly, his hands away from his body. 'Ukraine. A bit more urban, a lot more noisy than it is here.'

The bearded man with the ball cap said nothing.

Clark asked, 'How've you been?'

The man answered flatly. 'Fair.' And then, 'You're going to have a tough time trying to sell me on the fact this is some sort of a chance encounter.'

Former Delta Force officer Barry Jankowski stood in the foliage, leaning against a tree. He wore a US Army T-shirt and cargo shorts, but Clark could see the imprint of a pistol under the T-shirt in an appendix holster. The man's right hand was close enough to grab the gun in a flash if he had call to do so.

Clark said, 'No, Barry. I came here to talk to you. Wanted to do it face-to-face, and this area seemed like we might have a little privacy.'

'Oh, it's sure private here. No tourists, no fishermen. No fish, as a matter of fact.'

'They aren't biting?'

'I blame it on the C-17s over there at the Luzon Drop Zone. Fish can feel that rumble and it freaks them out.'

Clark cocked his head.

'Just a theory,' Jankowski said. 'Some might even call it an excuse.'

Clark said, 'You've got the drop on me, so I am in complete agreement with you.'

Barry smiled. 'I'm not as skittish as you take me for.'

'I hate to disturb a man enjoying all this peace.'

'You can feel free to call me Midas. I'm not Army anymore, but nobody at Bragg has called me Barry since . . . since pretty much ever.'

'What about Bartosz?' Clark asked.

'Well, now. You really *have* been looking into me, haven't you?'

'I'd appreciate a few minutes of your time. Maybe after we talk, the fishing will be better.'

'I got a heads-up the other day that your buddy Chavez was asking around about me. Should I be worried or flattered?'

'You have a beer in that cooler up there?'

'I've got a few, yeah. I guess it's five o'clock *somewhere*. C'mon.'

A few minutes later the two men, one in his late thirties, the other in his late sixties, sat on low tree stumps and sipped cans of Miller High Life. They swatted the occasional mosquito, talked a bit about Fort Bragg, and finally Midas grew bored with the conversational dance between the two.

He said, 'So . . . ?'

Clark nested his beer can in some pine needles on the ground. 'You've applied at the Agency.'

'From what I remember, you aren't with the Agency anymore. In fact, right after that whole thing in Ukraine, I had some serious-looking dudes show up and tell me you and the rest of your gang don't exist.'

'Where would this country be without the serious-looking dudes skulking around telling people that what they just saw didn't happen?'

'Debatable,' Midas said, sipped his beer. 'Yeah, I applied. I guess it takes longer when your name is Bartosz Jankowski than if your name is Jack Ryan.' Midas raised an eyebrow. 'Of course, Jack Ryan, Jr, isn't Agency, either.'

'Just another guy who doesn't exist,' Clark said.

'So I am told.'

'Look, Midas. My group . . . the guys you met, minus one who is no longer with us . . . we are an outfit that gets to do some interesting things. Important things. It is possible that you might rather work for us than for Langley. I can give you a list of men and women who know who we are, what we do. You will recognize some of the names.'

Midas did not hide his disappointment. 'Is this because I didn't get in CIA?'

'Not at all,' Clark said. 'I won't lie, I hear you are going to be offered the job in the National Clandestine Service, sooner or later. I'm not here because you didn't get in. My organization is not the booby prize. We're the unit that you don't apply to. We're the group that comes to *you* if we see something we like.'

Midas nodded thoughtfully, grabbed a mosquito out of the air in front of him with a hand fast enough to impress Clark. He asked, 'This unit of yours. How big is it?'

'A small information technology and analytics section, a small admin section. In the operational ranks? Three.'

'Three hundred?'

Clark shook his head.

Midas's eyes widened. 'Three *thousand?*'

Another shake of the head. Clark held up his right hand and extended three fingers.

Midas looked at the hand. 'Oh. Three, as in one, two, three.'

'Yeah, that three. We're looking to expand to five. We are small, but we punch above our weight. We really do have a robust analytical side, and a logistics and information technology component that is absolutely second to none.'

'Fair enough. You don't have to sell me on that. I saw what you boys can do. We damn sure would have been overrun without your help in Sevastopol, and we would have lost a lot of boys in Kiev if you weren't there fighting alongside us on that hit there.'

Clark said, 'I can promise you action. I can promise you ops that are crucial to the security of the United States, and I can promise you a great group of committed individuals you would work with every day. You will be a strategic-level asset. Oh . . . and we pay better than the government.'

Midas said, 'That's not hard to do, but all those government bennies add up if you live long enough to use them.' 'Bennies' was slang for benefits; military folks revered their significant retirement and health insurance perks, because their monthly take-home wasn't much to get thrilled about.

Clark said, 'I can't go into too much detail until I know if you want in, but you will be making probably two and a half times what you'd start at with a GS-9 rating. There are other options and benefits that greatly outpace government service. And you'd get the satisfaction of serving the interests of the US without all the bureaucratic mumbo jumbo to deal with.'

'Like walking out of the Army as an officer in Delta and having to wait six months to a year to know if you got in at CIA?'

'Yeah, exactly like that. You say yes today, you can start tomorrow.' Clark shrugged. 'You said the fish weren't biting.'

Midas smiled again. 'You mentioned one of the guys I met over there in Ukraine is no longer with your group. Did he get his benefits when he left?'

Clark looked out over the lake for a second. 'No . . . but his mom did.'

'Damn. It wasn't little Jack, because I'd have heard about that.'

'Sam passed away.'

Midas nodded. 'I remember him. Good dude. In the field?'

Clark was still gazing out through the pines and over the water. He nodded. 'Doing his job. Making a difference.' Clark looked at Midas now. 'You'd be his replacement. We're looking at another in-house promotion, too.'

Midas asked, 'How deep did you look into me? You know all my secrets?'

Clark said, 'For a group like us, the secret stuff is the easiest to find out. But we never found out how you got your call sign. Wasn't Midas the guy who turned everything he touched into gold?'

'Yeah. Back in the initial invasion into Iraq, I was a sergeant in 5th Group. I ended up staying a couple nights in the palace of Uday, one of Saddam's kids. It was a big gilded room. A couple nights later I was in Al-Faw at one of

Saddam's palaces. Again, me and my A-team ended up in a room with all this gold-leaf shit everywhere. Then, up in Tikrit, we were billeted in Saddam's mom's palace. I don't even remember if the room had gold in it, but I'm told it did. A few years later, after I made officer I went through selection and assessment at Delta. One of the cadre remembered running into me and my A-team in all these golden rooms. He said I must have had the Midas touch because he and the other D-boys always had to stay in some cinder-block shit house.'

Clark laughed. 'Let me guess, you haven't been in another golden room since you got the name Midas.'

Midas said, 'Yeah, it's been pretty much cinder-block shit houses ever since.' He looked at Clark. 'You were a SEAL, right?'

'In another life.'

'What did they call you back on the teams?'

Clark answered flatly, 'They called me Kelly.'

'Why?'

'Because that was my name back then.' There was a tone that told Midas he'd asked one question too many, so he left it right there.

Clark said, 'I've seen your DoD photo. With the possible exception of Jack Junior, I've never seen anybody in my life who looks more different when he wears a beard as compared to when he doesn't.'

Midas cracked a little smile. 'I kind of look like a banker or something.'

'I was going to say computer repair.'

Midas nodded. 'Yeah, that works. I see my brother and his family once a year or so. If I wear my beard my little niece bawls her eyes out.'

Both men sipped beers in silence, then Clark said, 'There would be a training workup, but nothing like what you went through to get into Delta.'

Midas said, 'That's good. I left the bottoms of both feet somewhere on a hill up in West Virginia.'

Clark said, 'SEAL training was damn tough, but Delta Selection and Assessment just sounds cruel.'

Midas shrugged. 'They try to weed out the sane guys by making it to where only crazy folks would stick it out, and then they take what's left and weed out the ultracrazy. There is an acceptable level of freak that works best in Delta.' Midas shrugged. 'I served ten years in the Unit, so make of that what you will.'

'I'll make an offer. I want you to come work for us. You interested?'

Midas said, 'Let's say I agree. Let's say I get in and it doesn't work out. I don't know why, maybe I spend a year twiddling my thumbs, don't feel like I'm making an impact. Is my working with you going to damage my chances at getting in the Agency?'

'Not at all. If you come to me and say you want out, I'll put in a good word for you wherever you want to go.'

Midas shrugged. 'All right, Mr Clark. You've just caught yourself a fish. Let's see what this is all about.'

Both men climbed off their stumps and shook hands.

15

The Office of the Director of National Intelligence is located in Tysons Corner, Virginia, a ten-minute drive south from CIA headquarters, and a half-hour west of the White House in good traffic, which pretty much exists only in the middle of the night.

The government complex that houses the organization is called Liberty Crossing, abbreviated in the government to LX, with the property split into two main sections. The National Counterterrorism Center fills up LX1, and the ODNI is at LX2.

On the top floor of LX2, in the office of the director, Mary Pat Foley returned from a meeting at noon. A cranberry chicken salad and an iced tea had been placed on her desk for her so she could work through lunch, and she'd just sat down when her secretary's voice came over the intercom.

'Madam Director, I have Directors Canfield and Murray on a conference call for you.'

Mary Pat's shoulders slumped a little. The salad looked good, and now she'd have to just stare at it through the phone call.

The call was put through, and Dan Murray spoke first. 'My snatch team, the guys who flew from HK to Indonesia to pick up the Department of State guy spying for the North Koreans. They were just detained at the airport in Jakarta.'

Instantly, Mary Pat realized this had a familiar ring to it. *'Detained?* Why?'

Jay Canfield said, 'Same as in Iran. We don't know, but the word is it had something to do with the fingerprint scanner.'

Murray added, 'Their covers were solid. *Rock* solid. The biometric data of those men matches their passports. Somehow the Indonesians knew the men's actual identities.'

'How is that possible?' Foley asked, and then she answered her own question. 'Somehow, in some way, there has been a breach of data, and it has been exploited by multiple parties.'

'But that doesn't make sense,' Canfield said. 'Iran was my guy. CIA. New Jersey was a Navy officer. And this . . . these guys are FBI. How the hell could Russians, Indonesians, and Iranians simultaneously find out the identities of all these different assets across all these different divisions of the US government?'

Mary Pat said, 'I have no idea, but we have to find the commonality between these three incidents. We also have to figure out how large this is. We have a lot of assets out in the field, obviously, and no idea who might be compromised.'

Dan Murray said, 'Look, all this is true, but putting that crisis aside for the moment, I have to get somebody into Jakarta, now.'

Canfield asked, 'Don't you have anybody at the embassy there who could take care of it?'

'Not really. I have special agents there, but they aren't trained in counterintel to the point they could be relied on to tag and bag this unknown traitor right in front of the North Koreans without it turning into a big mess.'

Mary Pat had an answer. 'We need somebody who is not part of the US government, and we need them to be discreet and skilled.'

Dan Murray said, 'You're talking about Gerry Hendley's

boys.' Murray had recently been read in on The Campus and its work with the US intelligence community abroad.

'Yes, I am,' Mary Pat said.

There was a short pause, then Director Murray sighed. 'Yeah, okay. I don't know what other options we have. I'll send everything I have on the case directly to you. I assume you can pass it on.'

'I'll take care of it personally.'

Two minutes later Foley's salad remained untouched, and she was on the phone with Gerry Hendley. 'We've got an emergent situation in Jakarta. Is your team in a position where they can get moving quickly and help us out?'

'How soon do you need us there?'

'Now, frankly.'

Gerry spoke quickly. 'The Gulfstream is at Reagan, a ten-minute drive from the office. The flight crew is at the airport now, and all three of my operatives are here in the building. I can get them in a van fifteen minutes from now. I imagine they'll have to refuel en route, and I don't know the flight time.'

Mary Pat said, 'The flight time is twenty-two hours from Andrews, including a refueling stop. DCA will be virtually the same.'

Gerry said, 'Then I can have Chavez, Caruso, and Ryan there by roughly this time tomorrow. Will that do you any good?'

Mary Pat said, 'That's within my time window, but barely. Please get them moving, I'll give you specifics when everything is in motion.'

'Of course. Any special equipment they need to bring with them?'

Mary Pat thought for a moment. She said, 'Basic surveillance gear. And some weapons for their own defense. This might involve a hostile party willing to put up a fight.'

'Understood.'

Gerry ended the call, then started to call Clark's office, but he remembered Clark was in North Carolina tracking down Barry Jankowski. So he called Chavez, gave him the news of the in extremis op, and asked him to notify the others. This done, he contacted Helen Reid and Chester Hicks.

Twenty-five minutes later, the three operators of The Campus carried their go bags up the stairs of the Gulfstream G550, parked on the tarmac just west of Runway 1 at Ronald Reagan National Airport. The cockpit crew was already on board, and the two Rolls-Royce turbofan engines were already spinning. The Campus operators knew only where they were going, not why, or what they would be called upon to do once there.

Nobody liked spending twenty-two hours in the air, but at least they would be traveling in style. The G550's interior was as plush and luxurious as any aircraft in corporate aviation. There were multifunction monitors around that could display their route in the air, the Internet, or the latest films, and there were cabin chairs that reclined fully, along with a sofa in the back that turned into a bed.

It was nice, but it would be less nice on this trip, and all the boys knew it the second that copilot Chester 'Country' Hicks met them just inside the cabin. They had always been met by Adara Sherman, who would take their luggage and their coats, talk to them about the flight, and bring them drinks or help them in any possible way.

But Adara had been given the day off to prepare for the start of Clark's training program. This meant no warm greeting, no update on flying time, the itinerary, no handling of the hotels and vehicle rentals while en route, no meal choices, and no offers to take their bags for them.

Nope, Country just gave the three a quick nod, told them to stow their shit and to strap their asses down for takeoff.

The trip in the Hendley Associates Gulfstream from Washington, DC, to Jakarta, Indonesia, was 8,833 nautical miles, and the moment the three men entered the aircraft this fact was noted with looks of resignation when they saw the distance yet to travel on their monitors. They treated the news with slumped shoulders and depressed sighs; they'd be in this luxurious but tiny space together for the entire next day.

Once in the cabin, Dom said, 'Hey, Country. I'll have a Sapphire and tonic, extra lime. And can I get one of those really fluffy pillows?'

Dom was joking, and Jack stifled a smile.

Country gnashed his teeth before saying, 'If Clark was here I'd say it to his face. Adara might turn into a fine member of your little outfit, but we are not happy we lost her. She made every part of our jobs better.'

Chavez said, 'Gerry knows he needs to bring in a replacement for her. He's probably working on it already, but this thing in Indonesia has cropped up in the meantime. Don't worry, we'll take care of ourselves back here, and we can work out the logistics of our stay in Jakarta while en route.'

Country seemed to calm a little. He nodded to Chavez and Ryan, gave Caruso a half eye-roll, and started back to the cockpit. 'There are plenty of frozen meals on board, but I don't even know how to work the microwave. There's drinks or whatever you guys want in the front galley. If you make some calls I'm sure you can arrange to have fresh food delivered to the plane when we stop in Van Nuys to refuel.'

He added, 'Buckle up. We'll get through customs and start taxiing in a couple minutes.'

Dom said, 'No drink? Really?' He was still joking, already on his way to the galley to make a round for himself, Chavez, and Jack.

They'd been in the air for only twenty minutes when the three operators sat at a table in the middle of the cabin, upon which a speakerphone broadcast the voice of Mary Pat Foley. She gave them everything she knew about the situation in Jakarta, and she sent along several files from Dan Murray, all of which were available on a monitor in the wall by the table.

When she told them she needed to rush them over to Indonesia to stop an unknown man from passing over intelligence material, Chavez asked, 'Isn't there someone at the embassy . . . Marine security, deputy chief of mission, *anybody*, who you can just call? They could just get in this guy's face and say, "We know what's up."'

'It's not that simple. We don't know who the traitor is, and the SIGINT source that we used to intercept the communication isn't something we want broadcast to embassy personnel.

'We considered just blanketing the pass-off location with Marines, calling in a bomb threat, all sorts of things, but we don't know the North Koreans won't communicate with the traitor some way we don't know about and make other arrangements. The only way we can be sure to stop this from happening is to have someone there able to visually identify the person who shows up to make the transaction.'

Chavez said, 'Makes sense. I don't like the thought of leaping off an airplane after a day of travel and going into an unknown situation, but I recognize the predicament you're in.'

Mary Pat said, 'Dan Murray is having his local agent go to

the meeting place and take some video for you; it should help you get an idea of the layout. I'll send it along in a few hours. That might help.'

'It would help a lot,' Chavez said. 'Okay, you know where to find us for the next day. Right here. Please feel free to contact us at any time with updates.'

'Will do,' Mary Pat said. 'By the way, where are you with bringing new blood into your team?'

Chavez said, 'We're looking to bring in two new operators. They should fit in nicely with the team once we get them trained up.'

'Former military?'

'Yes, both of them. A lieutenant colonel from the Army, ex-Delta Force, named Bartosz Jankowski. And a former Navy corpsman who deployed with Marine infantry in Afghanistan. Her name is Adara Sherman. She's been with us for years as the transportation coordinator and flight attendant on our Gulfstream. She's served alongside us as a quasi-operative on more than one occasion.'

'Excellent,' Mary Pat said. 'I'm glad The Campus is growing. Whatever this breach of intelligence is that we're dealing with, I can see the need for some people outside of the conventional system stepping up and helping out.'

Chavez replied, 'We're at your service. We just ask that we get as much information as you have just as fast as you can get it to us. As this stands now, the bad guys have all the advantages.'

16

Abu Musa al-Matari stood in the rainy evening, looked out over the flat jungle of western Guyana as the lights of the approaching aircraft shone through the darkness.

The plane itself came into view over the trees and under the clouds seconds later, and it touched down perfectly on the runway, a spray of rainwater and loose gravel behind its wheels.

Al-Matari was no expert on aviation, but he had been told the plane was the right tool for the job at hand. The mysterious Saudi had arranged it all, and he explained that this thirty-year-old Antonov An-32 had been purchased by a Bolivian charter airline from a freight company in Lima. The aircraft was larger than what he needed, but its range would get it from this location to his destination, well over 2,000 miles away, with only a single stop for fuel.

Al-Matari turned and looked back over his shoulder. Two of his top lieutenants were here with him, and they'd be going along on the mission to the USA. Both men were named Mohammed, but one was from Libya and the other Algeria, so al-Matari called them Tripoli and Algiers, respectively.

They would serve as al-Matari's bodyguards, and they had decades of military and insurgency experience that would make them assets to the other cells in the United States. They were both expert bomb makers as well, and their forged driver's licenses and other papers were good enough to pass scrutiny with American law enforcement, as long as they weren't challenged too hard.

And if they were challenged too hard, Algiers and Tripoli were cutthroat killers.

Behind the three Middle Easterners, a semi-trailer sat in the rain, its doors still shut. Inside, all the equipment they'd be taking into the US had been split into locked plastic cases weighing fifty pounds each. A dozen boxes for each cell, roughly six hundred pounds of weaponry per group.

The cab had been uncoupled from the trailer minutes earlier, hitched to an empty trailer waiting here, and then it left the abandoned airport, heading back to the west.

The white, nearly featureless An-32 rolled to a stop in front of the three men and their cargo, the stairs came down and splashed in a deep puddle. The copilot descended the stairs, then chocked his own wheels while the pilot shut the aircraft's engines off.

The pilot and copilot walked up to the three men standing in the rain and they all shook hands. The pilot spoke in accented English; al-Matari assumed he was Bolivian. 'It's raining very hard, *señores.*'

This was Guyana during the rainy season, so al-Matari knew the rain should come as no surprise to anyone, certainly not a South American cargo pilot.

The runway was one thousand meters, which, as far as al-Matari was concerned, was more than long enough, because he'd been told the fully laden aircraft would need nine hundred meters for the takeoff roll.

But the white-haired pilot fixed his eyes on the semi-trailer. It was clear there was a problem. 'What is the final weight of the cargo?'

'One thousand eight hundred fifty kilos.'

The man shook his head. 'No way we can take off in this rain.'

Al-Matari all but lunged at the pilot now. 'What are you talking about? Planes fly in the rain all the time.'

The man shook his head, pointed to the airstrip behind him. 'That, my friend, is a gravel runway. Gravel! If there is a rejected takeoff, with the amount of weight we will be carrying, my brakes will be worthless. I won't be able to stop before the end of the runway. There is simply not enough room.'

Al-Matari wasn't having it. 'Then I suggest you *don't* reject the takeoff.'

The pilot rolled his eyes, but al-Matari stayed firm. 'We are not waiting on the weather. We take off now, or you do not get paid.'

'Yes, well, I want more money.' He jerked a thumb to his copilot. 'We both do. Five thousand more US. Each.'

Al-Matari had anticipated something like this. He thought about just killing the men when they landed in the USA, but that would compromise their mission.

He swallowed his anger and said, 'I pay five thousand more. Total. You two can split it or fight over it. I don't care. But we load up now, and we fly now. Do you understand?'

The captain looked at al-Matari angrily for a moment, then motioned for the men to begin loading the plane.

Al-Matari's two men, the pilots, and al-Matari himself all worked together to place the sixty hard plastic containers inside the aircraft. The boxes were numbered on the top, one through five, so al-Matari wouldn't have to open them to determine which container went to which cell.

The copilot secured the load while the three rain-soaked Middle Easterners grabbed their own luggage, then climbed aboard with rolling duffels and large backpacks.

The An-32 took off to the north in the rain – there was no rejected takeoff to worry about, and by the time they'd climbed over the clouds they were leaving Guyana airspace and heading out over the Caribbean Sea.

Musa al-Matari had nothing to do for the next several hours but sit and wait for the next phase of the operation to begin, so as soon as the plane reached a cruising altitude, he strode back to his containers and looked them over, running a hand over the rough plastic crates inside the netting holding them in place in the cargo bay.

Most, if not all, attacks done in the name of ISIS by so-called remote radicalized attackers in the United States had employed weapons purchased in America. The United States was rife with small arms, after all. It was a nation where one could walk into a store and walk out with a fire-arm twenty minutes later. A thousand dollars would buy you a quality carbine rifle, although special features like holo-graphic optics, enhanced grips to better control the recoil, flashlights that attach to the front of the weapon, and extra magazines, could easily double this price. And with $500 to $800 you could purchase the exact same handgun used by most American law enforcement agencies, as well as many of America's best special operations units.

But these purchases, despite what many who know noth-ing about guns think, require paperwork, a show of identification, and a near instantaneous but nevertheless effective check of a national database of those legally pro-hibited from purchasing a firearm.

There were ways around this: one could buy a gun from a private seller in his or her home state without jumping through the same hoops one would have to jump through when dealing with a federal firearms licensee, meaning someone in the business of selling guns. But these private purchases were still subject to laws and required making contact with unknown parties who might or might not be with the government or might or might not find themselves curious enough about the purchaser to contact the Bureau of Alcohol, Tobacco, Firearms and Explosives.

Even though none of al-Matari's cell members had criminal records with felonies or domestic battery charges, had been adjudicated mentally ill or, as far as he knew, were under investigation by law enforcement or intelligence agencies, he decided it was still too dangerous for his Language School operatives able to buy weapons in America legally to do so. Every time one of his cell members stepped into a gun shop and asked to look at an AR-15, an AK-47, a pump-action shotgun, or even a handgun, it would invite scrutiny on the cell member, and scrutiny was one thing al-Matari was trying to avoid.

Two-thirds of his cell members looked Arab, whether they were born in the USA or not, and the Yemeni assumed all Americans were suspicious of all Arabs, and would send the FBI after anyone making a gun purchase.

Plus, one simply could not purchase fully automatic weapons in the US without lengthy wait times, paperwork, and additional scrutiny, and the same went for short-barreled rifles, which were much easier to conceal than a full-sized AR-15 or AK-47 pattern rifle.

He and his two subordinates had instead decided to bring the guns in from out of the country and distribute them to the twenty-seven cell members.

The Saudi had acquired all the gear, and the Yemeni had to admit the man had done an admirable job. Originally, the

Saudi had planned on purchasing weapons from Mexican drug cartels, but an easier and better option presented itself. He explained to al-Matari that he managed to arrange a shipment of military small arms from Venezuela to be driven over the border to an airport nearby in Guyana, where a few thousand US dollars ensured the airport would be closed for the night and the security officer working there would accidentally leave the gate open.

Venezuela did not have much in the way of food or democracy, but what it did have in abundance were crime and weapons. They were ranked the eighteenth top purchaser of weapons in the world, and the Venezuelan military's controls on these arms had grown lax in the past few years.

A colonel in the Bolivarian Armed Forces, desperate for money in the economic disaster that was Venezuela these days, agreed to sell whatever small arms and explosives the mysterious man who contacted him via e-mail wanted. Money was placed in an offshore numbered account and the number was given to the colonel, along with assurances more money would be transferred in as soon as the weapons were delivered.

The weapons arrived in the trailer, then al-Matari and his two men personally inspected and separated the equipment right there in a warehouse next to the airfield in Guyana.

Now as al-Matari walked through the cargo section of the An-32, he could look at each crate and know what was inside. There were twenty-five Uzi nine-millimeter submachine guns and twenty-five AK-103 rifles. The Avtomat Kalashnikova model 103 fired a much more powerful round than the Uzi, but the weapon was twice the length and therefore much harder to conceal. The Kaibiles from Guatemala had brought similar versions of both guns to the

Language School, so all the students were capable operators of both.

There was a crate of hand grenades for each cell, along with C-4 explosives, military-grade detonators, and other bomb-making equipment.

The Saudi had also purchased four AT4s, American-made antitank rocket launchers, and eight RPG-7 rocket launchers with thirty-six rockets, along with four Russian-made Igla-S man-portable air-defense systems, or MANPADS. These were shoulder-fired antiair missiles, capable of downing a jumbo jet.

Unfortunately for al-Matari and his students, the Kaibiles had never used an Igla-S and there wasn't even a mockup at the school to train on, but fortunately for the Islamic State operatives' plans, there were YouTube videos instructing one how to properly prepare, aim, and fire the weapons.

It wasn't as good as real training, but the YouTube vids would be a treasure trove for the terrorists employing MANPADS for the first time.

Instead of separating his four shoulder-fired missiles among four different teams, al-Matari had decided to keep them all with him, and distribute them when the time was right. Tripoli and Algiers would fire the weapons, or even al-Matari himself.

There was a Glock 17 pistol on board the aircraft for each and every language student. It was the principal sidearm of the Venezuelan military, and while large for a handgun, it was still very concealable and could fire eighteen rounds of nine-millimeter ammo before the operator needed to reload. This meant to al-Matari that a five-man cell could, if operating together and in unison, dump ninety bullets at a single target in ten seconds or so – at a guard shack, a table full of

Navy pilots, a stage where an American intelligence official was making a speech.

Ninety bullets! His operators did not need to be snipers; they just had to be brave and committed.

He knew the Glocks and Uzis would be the principal weapons of close-in assassinations, while the rifles would be more for distance work and large clusters of targets, and the explosives, rockets, and missiles used more to take out vehicles or other large targets.

There were thirty Kevlar vests on the aircraft, too. These could stop handgun rounds, but would be useless against anyone shooting a rifle at one of his cell members.

There were another thirty vests in the cases. These had not come from Venezuela, but had been flown into Guyana directly. These were suicide vests. They could be detonated via remote signal, or via a pressure switch on the end of a cable that could be slid down the sleeve of a shirt and held in the hand.

He would send his men and women out with the Kevlar under their S-vests. He would do what he could to protect them, until that moment he would do what he needed to do to martyr them to achieve his objectives.

Al-Matari had arranged for each team's full complement of equipment to fit into a single van or large SUV and still provide room for the driver and a passenger. Of course the cells would not travel with all their equipment at all times, but he wanted to minimize the chance they would be detected by hauling around large amounts of ordnance in multiple vehicles.

Finally, Abu Musa al-Matari returned to his seat and looked over at Algiers and Tripoli. Both men were brimming with excitement but aware that this journey of theirs would be a one-way trip. They would stay in America until they were martyred. They prayed their martyrdom happened at the moment they fired the last bullet, threw the last grenade, or launched the last missile now stowed in the cargo hold behind them.

17

As one aircraft approached the United States from the south, another flew across the country, then landed at Van Nuys airport near L.A. for a quick refueling stop. A half-hour later it was back in the air, this time for the longest leg of the journey. The men of The Campus had worked on the trip across the US, and they'd work some more on the last leg, but from California to Seoul, Korea, the men tried to get some sleep. The three men and one woman on board did deplane in Seoul during their fifty-minute refueling stop there, but they weren't going through customs here in Korea so they didn't walk more than fifty feet from the aircraft. They did stretches, ran in place, but mostly they just wandered around bleary-eyed and bored, just like they'd been on the aircraft.

After taking back to the skies the three operators used the last segment of their flight to come up with a specific plan on arrival. They had more intelligence from CIA and FBI about what they'd encounter at the scene, which was a damn good thing, considering they'd arrive close to five a.m. and have to race off the aircraft into a waiting rental car, then proceed directly to a hotel for a final comms and gear check before the nine a.m. meeting between the North Korean agents and the unknown US Department of State employee.

They landed in Jakarta on schedule and went through customs, where they had their luggage checked thoroughly.

Helen and Country taxied into a hangar, taking their time to do so, because the three operatives were busy revealing hidden access compartments in the galley, pulling out their Smith & Wesson M&P Shield nine-millimeter pistols, inside-the-waistband appendix holsters, extra magazines, state-of-the-art covert earpieces, emergency medical equipment, and other items they would need on their operation.

Domingo, Dominic, and Jack took their hand luggage and hurried down to the waiting rental car, while Country and Helen headed to the fixed-base operator's office to fill out some paperwork. They would immediately refuel and restock the aircraft for the flight out of here, and then they would both find a comfortable cabin chair or sofa in the back of the aircraft and try to get some sleep, while remaining at the ready for a quick getaway.

They didn't expect to be leaving for at least five hours, but they knew when the call came that the team was en route to the airport, they would very likely have to preflight and clear customs quickly, so a little sleep in the meantime would be helpful.

At six a.m. the three American men drove their rental to a twenty-four-hour pharmacy and loaded a handbasket up with items. Water, snacks, and other odds and ends, mostly, and Ding bought a box of fifty paper surgical masks, worn regularly here because of the potential for disease transmission and the high pollution in the air.

Back in the car, Ding passed out a fistful of masks to the other two.

Dom quipped, 'We're gonna be here for a week?'

'You start sweating, running, breathing hard, these things will get soggy fast and melt off your face.'

'Right,' he said. 'Maybe I'll wear two at a time.'

'Not if you want to breathe freely.'

Jack said, 'The location of the meet is a pedestrian zone that allows bicycles and motorized scooters but not cars. Do we want to get a scooter just to have at the ready?'

Chavez pulled back onto the road, heading in the direction of downtown, where they had secured a hotel just a few blocks from the location of the North Koreans' meeting with the unknown American State Department worker. 'I think we want to get two scooters. That, and this car. It will give us more options. Like we talked about on the plane, we're going to be winging it on this one. The more flexibility we have, the better.'

They checked into their hotel at seven a.m., and through the clerk they arranged for a pair of rental scooters to be parked next to their rental car. Then they went upstairs, where they double-checked their equipment and changed clothes. All the men wore outfits that could make them look like either joggers or very casual tourists, as most tourists usually were.

The meeting was to take place in Merdeka Square, in central Jakarta, at the foot of the National Monument, a white 433-foot tower built to commemorate Indonesia's independence. Their hotel was just a few blocks west of the square, so they had a few minutes to drink some bottled water, eat some protein bars, and stow their binoculars around their necks and tuck them inside their shirts.

As they prepped they talked over the plan one more time, reexamined a map of the area, and tried to shake off the onset of jet lag so they could concentrate on the action to come.

*

The men arrived at three different corners of the square at eight a.m. Chavez parked the car to the northwest, Dom parked his scooter at the southeast, and Jack kept his helmet on and drove his scooter straight toward the location.

It was a massive space, with flat open grass fields, fountains and statues, wide cobblestone thoroughfares with scooter traffic racing by, and a significant number of pedestrians passing through the area on their way to work. The tower itself was in the dead center of the huge square, on top of a large grassy hill, and sightseers milled about, even at eight in the morning. Stone steps, some fifty yards wide, ran up ten yards or so to the base of the tower.

It made sense for the North Koreans to do the pass here, because the US embassy was on the southeast corner of the square. But there were many reasons this didn't seem like a good spot at all for a clandestine transaction, as both the Indonesian Ministry of Internal Affairs and the headquarters of the Army were both right here on the edge of the square as well.

'Damn, this is a big space,' Jack mumbled.

Chavez said, 'Dom, I guess you and me are joggers. We'll cover more territory.'

Dom groaned. 'We're gonna run for an hour before going up against DPRK agents?'

Chavez replied, 'If we ID the agents in time, maybe we can avoid them. Run a few minutes, take breaks to look around, then run a little more. We're each going off on our own here, but stay in comms.'

Jack putted down the cobblestone road through the enclosed square. 'If you pull a quad, cuz, I can run down to the store and pick you up some Bengay.'

'Kiss my ass,' Dom grumbled.

As each operator moved through a different section of the square, all closing in on the National Monument and the steps there, the men talked over their comms at length about just why, in this day and age, this meeting to transfer classified material would be done in public, by hand. These things usually happened electronically these days, so this felt like the makings of an eighties spy thriller.

Dominic was the first to come up with a plausible answer. 'You know what I think? If this dip e-mails documents there is the deniability factor. He can say he didn't do it, his password got hacked, it's a damn setup. Hard to catch someone red-handed clicking the send button.'

Chavez followed up on this line of thinking. 'The North Koreans want photos of a handover.'

'Right,' agreed Jack. 'And they want to do this so they can own this guy. Use that against him for further intel handoffs.'

Chavez immediately said, 'All right, boys, let's proceed on that assumption and hunt for the photographer of today's event. We're now looking for a standoff position, at least two hundred yards away, where a guy can use a long-range lens to get shots of the transaction. This is an outdoor pass, so it's going to be tough to pin down the photog, but he is every bit as important as ID'ing the other DPRK guys involved. We don't want them getting glamour shots of us, even if we do have these paper masks on.'

Immediately Dominic and Jack began scanning the area.

Jack said, 'Hey, Ding. Did you read the info on this location? It's five times the size of freaking Tiananmen Square.'

Chavez replied, 'Yeah, I read it. Got eyes, too. This is too big for three of us to cover the entire square.'

Dom said, 'I wish Gavin was here with a drone.'

Chavez said, 'We can handle it. Just use process of

elimination. The pass is supposed to be on the north side steps of the National Monument. Even though the photographer might be able to get shots of the State Department dip from most any direction, he'll probably be following the guideline of sticking to the north. That cuts our hunt in half. He won't be far back in the trees, and half of this place is trees, so cut it in half again.'

Jack said, 'There is an observation deck on top of the monument.'

Chavez replied, 'Wouldn't make for a good picture, and it would be damn hard to exfiltrate in a rush. I wouldn't put my overwatch there, and doubt the DPRK would, either.'

The three men moved around on the north side of the monument. After a few minutes Jack said, 'We don't know where on the steps the meet will take place, and it's a big monument. But if you think about it, the US embassy is to the southeast, so they might want to meet the American to the northwest, just in case there was any long-range monitoring from the roof of the embassy that could see over the trees. They'd have to at least account for the possibility that this guy tipped off American authorities.'

Chavez said, 'Makes sense to me, Jack. Also makes me think they will put the monument between the embassy and the photographer. You've got the wheels, so why don't you head to northwest and see if your theory holds water.'

Ryan began driving along the long straight road to the exit of the enclosed square to the northwest. He'd made it two-thirds of the way there when he looked to his right, just inside the line of manicured trees running along the road. There, two men who looked like they could be North Korean stood with a camera on a tripod. The camera had at least a 500-millimeter telephoto lens. At the moment it was pointing due south, not in the direction of the monument, but the camera and the men were far back enough in the trees to where it didn't make sense to have the camera positioned there in the first place.

Jack said, 'I think I've got eyes on the overwatch. Two subjects, say three hundred yards, maybe a little more, from the monument. They've got the lens to get great shots if they move it out to the road.'

Chavez said, 'Good. Remember, we aren't here for the DPRK guys. We want to ID the diplomat, bag him before he makes contact, and get him out of here, if there is any way that's possible.'

Dom was up closer to the steps to the monument now, just fifty yards or so from the northwest corner where the men suspected the pass would go down. He said, 'I'm in position where I can close down on the guy right up until the moment of the handoff. But if he gets this close, it's up to the North Koreans how much noise this whole thing is going to make today.'

Chavez was near a fountain one hundred yards to the west of the monument. He slowed his jog, stopped and sat on a bench, and pretended to lean over as if from exertion. While he did this he pulled his small binos from inside his shirt, then brought them up to his eyes, hidden in his hands. 'I've got six, repeat, six men moving together, approaching the fountain. They could be Korean, hard to say. They are all wearing civilian clothing, nothing uniform about their appearance, but they are all carrying either backpacks or briefcases.' After a few seconds he said, 'They entered the park together, but now they are splitting up into three groups of two.'

Ryan said, 'Are these guys dumbasses, showing up together like that?'

Dom answered this. 'Makes me think there are others around here with eyes on. We haven't been made, so these guys have been waved onto the X with an all clear.'

Chavez agreed. 'It's still twenty-five minutes till. With these six, Jack's two, and the unknown other ones who gave the all clear, this is a *lot* of oppo.'

Jack said, 'Do we want to think about doing something crazy to get this pass shut down? We'll lose our chance at grabbing the American, but at least we'll prevent a handoff of classified intel. One of us can flag down a cop and report a bomb.'

Dom came over the net. 'Not it!'

Chavez thought it over for a second. 'For now, we hang tight. We try to ID the American. If we can grab him before the pass, we do it, but if it looks like he's going to make it to the North Koreans, one of us will pull his piece and fire off a full mag dump into the dirt. That should break up the party.'

There were a couple local cops around on motorcycles, but as this was a huge area, Chavez thought he could avoid a direct confrontation with the police.

At least he really, *really* hoped so.

He said, 'Stay low pro, but keep your eyes peeled. This whole thing rests on getting this guy before he gets close to the North Koreans, and then getting out of here before the Indonesians get involved.'

18

Dominic Caruso had jogged a mile and a half in the past twenty minutes, which was nothing to brag about, but he wanted to be fresh if things got crazy at nine a.m. He was taking lots of breaks along the way to walk, tie his shoes, stretch, and otherwise try to fit into his surroundings here at Merdeka Square. Plus he was on his second paper surgical mask over his face, as the first one had torn due to his sweat and heavy breathing.

He stretched against the western steps of the tower, and he spoke softly after checking his watch. 'It's straight-up nine, guys. I've got nothing on my side.'

Jack was to the northwest, still riding around on his scooter through the increasing number of other two-wheeled vehicles and pedestrian traffic. 'I've got eyes on some of the DPRK guys. The camera crew is remaining in the trees for now, so I don't think the Koreans have ID'd their target, either.'

Chavez was on the far northwestern side of the square on the opposite side from where today's target worked at the US embassy.

He saw a tall man walking alone on the sidewalk toward the National Monument, fifty yards ahead of him. He wore a black trench coat and had a black backpack slung over his shoulder.

'I've got a possible. Northwest side of the square. Still two hundred yards from the monument, moving south down the eastern side of the road.'

MERDEKA SQUARE, JAKARTA

N

NATIONAL
MONUMENT

GAMBIR
RAILWAY
STATION

U.S.
EMBASSY

© 2016 Jeffrey L. Ward

Dom had moved around to the south side of the monument, so he had no view, but Jack turned his scooter around and approached from the northeast with his binos out and up against his eyes.

He saw the tallish man walking with his hands shoved into his pockets, his body slumped forward and his eyes fixed on the ground in front of him. As he watched, the man scanned all around, even turning to walk backward for a second.

'Yeah . . .' Jack said. 'That could be him.'

Chavez quipped, 'And I'm gonna go out on a limb and say he's a first-timer at this spy shit.'

'First time for everything,' Dom replied.

Chavez stepped out of the trees and began following behind the man, jogging along slowly enough to where he wouldn't overtake him at this speed before he arrived at the monument.

He said, 'Okay, our target is ID'd, let's get another check of all the oppo we can see.'

Among the three of them, Jack, Dom, and Chavez counted ten men in the square who might have been DPRK operatives. 'Christ,' Chavez said when the number was confirmed by the others, and he did some quick thinking. If Clark were around he'd defer to him, but Chavez was the senior operative now, and it was his call. He looked over the North Koreans in sight, and he took them for serious men. The fact there were at least ten involved with this also told him this pass was damn important to them. Chavez knew if he just grabbed the American diplomat and started ushering him back to the car, these ten men would intercede, probably with weapons.

Chavez wanted the traitor, he wanted the intelligence the

man brought with him, and he wanted to get himself and his men out of this alive.

The scope of this operation had just increased before his eyes.

He said, 'Jack, here's how we're playing it. Haul ass to the car. It's behind me. Pass close to me and I'll toss you the keys as you drive by. Bring the car here to get us all off the X.'

Ryan went full throttle on the scooter, began racing toward Ding, which meant he'd race right by the tower on his left with the North Koreans standing around and the American diplomat walking south toward them on his right.

But while complying with Ding's orders, he said, 'You *do* know there are no cars allowed here on the square. Local po-po is going to get interested if I get in the car and then plow over the wooden barricade to come back in here.'

Ding said, 'I know. Be ready to do some Fast and Furious shit, because this isn't going to be pretty.'

Caruso muttered, '*That's* not gonna stand out.'

Chavez replied, 'Five minutes from now, the first thing on everyone's mind around here is not going to be the car driving in the pedestrian-only zone, I can promise you that.'

Jack passed the target, who by now had his eyes locked on the northwest corner of the steps to the monument. He was standing more erect, looking directly at his destination, still 150 yards away.

Five seconds later, Jack rolled past Chavez, who jogged along at a relaxed clip in his black warm-up pants and black zip-up hoodie. Jack reached a hand out and Chavez tossed a set of car keys through the air. Jack caught them deftly and headed for the exit at the northwest.

Chavez was closing on the subject slowly. He was just a hundred feet behind him now, and he knew he still had time to draw his gun and grab the man, then pull him back away from the monument where the North Koreans were waiting for him. He decided to do just that, but before he did so, he called for some backup.

'Dom, I'm going to take him in one minute, give Ryan a little time to grab the car. We'll be just across the wide street north of the monument, and in the open. The DPRK guys are going to see us, plain as day, and they aren't going to like it.'

Dom said, 'Roger that. I'm behind the action on the south side, and I've got the bad guys in sight. Nobody's got eyes on me, so I can get the drop on them if they pull weapons.' He added, 'There *are* a whole bunch of them so I'd rather not.'

'Don't draw, just keep reporting what they're doing.'

'Understood.'

Ding said, 'When I grab the target I'm running for these trees to the north. That should give me some cover. I'll link up with Ryan when he gets the wheels. This might turn into a foot chase.'

Dom groaned. 'Why does everybody have to run all over the place this morning?'

Jack Ryan, Jr, raced his scooter past the red plastic and wooden partitions keeping cars off the street that went into the square, heading for the parking lot where Chavez had left his rental. He heard Chavez's transmissions to Dom, and knew the grab was going to take place in just a minute, but while he was listening to this he noticed a black Mitsubishi Pajero minivan idling in a no-parking zone right next to the entrance to the square. The vehicle was empty aside from the driver, an Asian man wearing sunglasses.

There were other vehicles around, but not in this area. To Ryan this guy looked like he could have been North Korean, perhaps the driver that just dropped the six guys off at this entrance, and now he was just waiting to pick them up after the exchange.

Jack said, 'Ding, what if I was able to get us some wheels that the local police couldn't trace back to a rental company we used?'

'We rent cars through shell companies. You know that.' Then Ding said, 'Goin' radio silent, grabbing this asshole in thirty seconds.'

Ryan said, 'What if I was able to take a set of wheels away from the North Koreans?'

When Ding said radio silent, he meant it, because he didn't respond to Ryan. He was closing in on the American on the sidewalk, and couldn't let himself be heard chatting while trying to pass himself off as a passing jogger. But Dom Caruso came over Jack's earpiece. 'You have to make that call, cuz. You don't want to be wrong, and you don't want to get into a fight on your own.'

But Jack had already made the call. The man behind the wheel of the minivan put a walkie-talkie to his lips, and Jack was even more certain he was a DPRK agent.

He drove the scooter in a tight U-turn through the morning traffic, parked behind the vehicle, and climbed off his bike.

On his left scooters rolled by, and a green truck that said *polisi* on the side, which obviously meant 'police,' drove on, but continued past the entrance to the park.

Jack realized that, whatever he did, he wasn't going to be invisible while doing it, so he'd have to do it quick.

Domingo Chavez didn't go for his gun. This man ahead of him had his hands out of his raincoat now and they swung with his walk, and Ding knew he would be able to stop the man from reaching for something, in the unlikely event the man even had a weapon. Instead, he picked up the pace of his jog and came up alongside him. They were two hundred feet from the National Monument and the DPRK men standing among the tourists there, split up in groups of two.

Ding put a tight grip around the walking man's shoulders, and spoke to him in a voice that meant business.

The man lurched with surprise.

'You say one word and I kill you.'

Ding spun the man around and began guiding him quickly off the sidewalk and toward the trees that ringed the square.

The man did not speak at first, he seemed utterly panicked, and Ding spoke for benefit of his earpiece now. 'What are they doing?'

Caruso responded. 'Shit, Ding. They are coming your way. Walking. Wait . . . Nope, it's official . . . they're running.'

'How many?'

'All of them. Eight guys.'

'Shit!' Ding said, and grabbed the taller man around his waist and took off for the thick grove of trees.

Dom Caruso sprinted across the road that ringed the National Monument, chasing fifty yards behind the eight North Koreans just now disappearing into the trees. Chavez had a thirty-second head start on them, but Dom knew he had to get closer in case things went loud.

He decided he'd run straight up the road to the northwest that ran to the left of the trees. That way he could move faster, to get ahead of the North Koreans, and be in a better position to help Chavez out when he came out of the trees and into the vehicle Jack was supposedly in the process of securing right now.

Dom sprinted as fast as he could go, arms and legs pumping with the effort. He saw a police car parked across the road and facing away, but he wasn't that worried about stationary Indonesian cops at the moment, so he just ran on.

Chavez had pulled the man in the trench coat a good hundred yards through the trees now, but it had been work to do it. The American traitor obviously knew he was busted, and he tried to pull away more than once. Chavez shouted at him, knowing the enemy was close behind. 'Come on, man. Run!'

The man in the raincoat tried to pull away now. 'No!'

Chavez brandished the Smith & Wesson in his right hand while holding on to the man with the left. Without breaking stride he said, 'Not asking you.'

The man looked terrified, but again he said, 'No! I *can't!* I have to –'

'You can and you will!' Chavez jammed the gun tight in the man's side and ran even faster. 'How long on the wheels?' he asked Jack over the net.

'What?' the American traitor asked.

'Not talking to you, asshole. Just keep running!'

Now the man in the trench coat heard the shouts in the trees behind, as the North Koreans got closer.

To Chavez's astonishment, the man shouted out to them, 'I'm here! Help me!'

Chavez punched the man in the nose as he ran with him, silencing the shouts. 'You do that again and I'll shoot you in the knee and carry you.'

*

170

Jack walked silently and quickly up the driver's side of the Mitsubishi Pajero, knowing he would be visible in the rear-view mirror and visible to passing traffic on the street. He would have much rather come up the far side, but the driver's window was partially down, and Jack needed access to the driver to pull this off.

Jack surprised the man, who had just put his walkie-talkie down. 'Excuse me? Do you know the way to San José?'

The driver reached to the passenger seat quickly. Jack saw a black semiautomatic pistol lying there, and now he was certain he had correctly identified a getaway vehicle for the North Korean agents.

Jack's own gun pressed against the left temple of the driver. 'Don't know if you speak English, but I bet you speak terminal ballistics. Pick up the gun and I paint the dashboard with your brains.'

The man brought his hand back to his lap.

Jack got him out of the minivan, looked left and right quickly to make sure no police had seen him in the commission of his carjacking, and he got in.

Leaving the North Korean agent standing there by the road, Jack fired the vehicle and launched forward. He turned hard to the right and plowed through the plastic and wooden barricades.

'Be advised, the black minivan entering the square and heading your way is me! Check your fire!'

Ding Chavez could hear the North Koreans closing in on him, not more than twenty-five yards back now. The trees were thick but not impenetrable, and it was obvious the opposition was gaining on him as he tried to force the non-compliant man forward.

After Jack's transmission, Ding told him he'd make his way left toward the road and they'd link up somewhere around halfway between the National Monument and the northwest exit of Merdeka Square. He then whirled his prisoner hard to the left and pushed him on, in the direction of the road.

The traitor said, 'You *have* to listen to me! I can't let –'

A gunshot from deep in the trees behind them cracked; it tore through branches five feet over their heads.

'Shit!' Ding shouted.

He heard Dom Caruso's labored voice in his earpiece. 'Yo! Somebody's shooting!'

'No shit,' Ding replied. 'One of the guys on our six missed high.'

Another shot cracked off. Ding heard this round zip by even closer. His prisoner's eyes were showing the effects of shock.

Jack Ryan spoke over the net now. 'I'm here, I'm looking for you guys.'

Ding said, 'Still in the trees. Not sure how much longer till we –'

Just then, Ding and his prisoner broke out of the trees, even with the black minivan, parked on the street just one hundred feet away.

'Got you!' Jack shouted. He slammed on his brakes, put the vehicle in park, and climbed out to open the side door.

A pair of gunshots zinged close to Chavez and his prisoner. A third slammed into the left calf of the man in the black raincoat, and he tumbled into the grass.

Chavez spun around, dropped to his knees, and raised his weapon. While doing this he said, 'Dom! Suppress that fire!'

*

Dom Caruso was running along the sidewalk fifty yards southeast of the minivan, and he could see Chavez raising his gun back in the direction of the trees and the wounded prisoner rolling in the grass.

He dropped to his knees himself, raised his Smith & Wesson, and took aim at the edge of the tree line. It would be a long shot to hit someone with his compact pistol, especially considering he had been at a full sprint for over a minute and his heart was racing, causing his front sight to bob and weave with his heartbeat. But his job was to suppress the enemy, to give them something else to worry about.

He wasn't here to win a sniper competition.

As soon as he saw movement – a man in a T-shirt and shorts with a gun in his hand – he fired. Off to his left Ding Chavez did the same.

Jack scooped up the wounded prisoner in a fireman's carry, while Chavez fired at the men in the trees. Jack lumbered with the traitor back to the minivan as fast as he could, trying his best to ignore the gunfire going on behind him. He literally threw the man off his shoulders and through the open rear door of the vehicle, then he drew his own pistol and aimed at the trees.

'Ding, I'm covering! Move!'

Jack fired three rounds at a flash of gunfire deep in the trees. As he did this he realized the man he'd scooped up didn't have his backpack on him any longer. 'Ding, the pack!'

In front of him on his right Ding raced toward the minivan, not even slowing down while he swept his arm down and scooped up the backpack lying on the grass. He leapt in the back with the wounded man, and Jack emptied his magazine at dark targets in the trees. He wasn't sure if he'd hit anyone, but now it was his job to drive.

As he got behind the wheel he could see Dom Caruso on the sidewalk, fifty yards straight in front of him, changing out his magazine and firing again on the North Koreans. Jack said, 'I'm on you in ten seconds!' And then he floored the Mitsubishi.

He heard bullets tear through the metal of the vehicle as he raced on, and the shattering of glass in the back.

'You okay back there?' he asked, careful not to use any names this close to their prisoner.

Chavez replied, 'You just get us out of this and we're fine. He's got a GSW to his leg, but he'll make it.'

Jack saw Dom Caruso stand from his crouch and begin running toward the minivan that was quickly approaching him. But Jack saw something Caruso did not. Behind him on his left, the *polisi* car was racing across the street, directly toward Caruso from his left side. They were going to try to get in front of this shooter and cut him off.

Jack shouted, 'Hang on back there!' He turned his wheel to the right, raced past a confused Caruso, and slammed the front of his Mitsubishi into the front-left quarter-panel of the police car, spinning it forty-five degrees and smashing the front left tire.

Jack's airbag deployed, smacking him in the face. Cops inside the vehicle would probably be dazed from the impact, and they'd certainly be pissed, but this was a hell of a lot better than the Campus team getting arrested and held in Indonesia on weapons and kidnapping charges.

Dom turned around and ran back to the Mitsubishi and dove into the open back door, on top of Ding and the prisoner, who by now was crushed facedown on the floorboard.

Dom closed the door behind him, Jack waved away the chalky dust from the deployment of his airbag, and he pushed his minivan forward through the damaged police car, while the snaps of handgun rounds continued striking the vehicle.

'Heads down!' Jack yelled.

As he drove past the cop car he looked down at the stunned and dazed police, through their cracked windshield.

'Sorry, guys,' he said, but they couldn't hear him.

He floored it now, charging east, and then he made a hard left and raced northeast to the exit of the square.

In the backseat the prisoner was pulled into a sitting position. He moaned in pain for a moment, then he shouted, 'Listen to me! You have to –'

Chavez put the barrel of his pistol in the man's open mouth. 'Trust me, you'll have plenty of people who want to hear you talk. I'm just not one of them.' Chavez now turned to Dom. 'This guy is a screamer. He tried to lead the DPRK goons to us in the trees.'

Dom Caruso said, 'I'm gettin' the tape!'

'Good deal,' replied Chavez.

Seconds later Dom used electrical tape from his personal medical kit to tape the man's mouth shut. Ding then rolled the man on his stomach and looked over his calf wound more closely, used gauze and tape from his own kit to stop the bleeding. It wasn't bad at all, but it would be messy if he didn't stanch the flow.

From the front Jack said, 'Something just occurred to me. Either I'm the luckiest dude in the world for finding this van at the particular corner of the park I exited, or they have other vehicles around the square. That means they have other guys mobile who can chase us.'

Chavez said, 'And they know what kind of vehicle we're in, seeing how it's theirs and all.'

'Yeah,' Jack conceded. 'Good point. I'm going to go back to the parking lot to the west. We'll transfer into our rental to take back to the airport.'

'Do it, but watch out for trouble.'

'Sure,' Jack quipped. 'We sure wouldn't want anything bad to happen.'

19

The Hendley Associates Gulfstream G550 took off from Soekarno-Hatta International Airport just fifty-one minutes after Jack Ryan crashed into the Jakarta police department patrol car.

Helen and Country were still in the process of climbing out to the northeast, barely a thousand feet off the ground, when Chavez, Ryan, and Caruso moved close around the zip-tied American prisoner. He was bandaged and stable, but his gag remained in place.

They'd searched him on the way to the airport, and he had no identification with him whatsoever. Certainly he'd left his wallet at the embassy or his home to make the pass with the North Koreans in case something went wrong.

In his backpack they had found three binders full of papers, all of which were clearly marked classified, although the ones Jack had thumbed through briefly were all under the classification Confidential, the lowest level.

Jack and the other Campus men were surprised to find that all this was over documents that were less than Top Secret.

The three men took a few minutes to go through the papers, then Chavez ripped the electrical tape off the man's mouth. Before the prisoner could even speak, Chavez asked, 'What's your name?'

The man looked confused. He said, 'Ben. Ben Kincaid. Benjamin Terrance Kincaid. Did you –'

Chavez started to tape the man's mouth back up. 'All I need to know. It's going to be a long flight, so take a nap,' he said, but before he could push the tape tight, Kincaid managed to push it away with his tongue, long enough to say one thing.

'Jennifer! Let me talk to –'

Chavez stopped. More curious than anything else, he lowered the tape.

'Jennifer?'

Kincaid said, 'Please, sir. I just need to know she's safe.'

Chavez looked at Jack and Dom, then back to Kincaid. 'Who the hell is Jennifer?'

Kincaid stared wide-eyed at the three men. 'Who is Jennifer? *Who?* She's my wife!'

Chavez rolled his eyes. 'Dude, nobody even knew who you were until you just told us. We just knew the DPRK was meeting some embassy shithead passing secrets.'

Kincaid's face morphed into a look of abject terror. 'But that means . . . you've . . . you've pulled her out, right? You got Jennifer out of there. Tell me you pulled her out. Tell me she's safe!'

Again the Campus men looked at one another in confusion.

Chavez said, 'Calm down! Out of . . . out of *where*?'

Kincaid screamed, pulled at his bindings like a maniac. '*Fuck!* You don't even know what's going on here! Jennifer is CIA. On nonofficial cover. She's in danger!'

Chavez blinked hard. 'Your wife is CIA?'

'*Damn it!* Damn you all! She's somewhere in Belarus, and they will kill her now that this has happened!'

This didn't make any sense to Jack. 'If your wife is a NOC, how do you even know where she is? She isn't supposed to tell you any of that.'

'Are you guys fucking idiots? She *didn't* tell me! I haven't heard from her in three months. She told me it would be a six-month assignment.'

'Then how –'

'Because those fuckers in Jakarta, the men you said were North Korean, they showed me pictures of her in the field. They said they could make *one* phone call and she'd be killed by the group she infiltrated. According to them, she was working as an accountant for some shady Mafia outfit out of Belarus. If the pass didn't go off as planned this morning, then they would call the Belarusians, and they would –'

Chavez leapt to his feet. 'I'll be right back!'

Up at the front near the galley, he called Mary Pat Foley. She answered in seconds with 'I hear there was a shoot-out in Jakarta. Are you guys okay?'

Chavez spoke quickly, 'Listen carefully. This man is Ben Kincaid. His wife is –'

Mary Pat gasped. 'Jen Kincaid. God Almighty. She's one of Jay Canfield's top officers.'

'Yeah, well, the DPRK guys told Ben they knew her identity and where she's working right now. They said if he didn't play ball today, they'd drop a dime on her to the goons around her and get her killed. Don't know if that's all BS or if it's true.'

Mary Pat said, 'Where did they say she was?'

'Somewhere in Belarus, working for a –'

Mary Pat interrupted hastily. 'I'll put you on hold and check with Jay.' The phone clicked, and Chavez could tell Mary Pat was crystal clear on the gravity of this situation.

Chavez put the phone down, a sick feeling in the pit of his stomach. In the back of the cabin he could hear Kincaid going back and forth between openly weeping and cussing out Jack and Dominic.

The two Campus men just looked up at Chavez, hoping like hell they hadn't just made a bad situation worse.

A minute later Mary Pat was back on the line. 'Canfield confirmed it. Jennifer Kincaid is in Minsk right now, working deep cover in a legitimate company owned by a very dangerous criminal organization.'

'Shit. How the *hell* could the North Koreans know any of that?'

'I have no idea, but we've run into some similar breaches of undefined origin in the past couple weeks. There is a wide-ranging and ongoing compromise we don't understand.'

'What about Jennifer?'

'We aren't going through any normal processes. Canfield has men racing to her right this second to get her out of there. To hell with her cover, her future in clandestine service. We'll get teams around her and pull her out before anyone has time to do anything to her.'

Chavez looked at his watch. 'Damn, Mary Pat. We've had this guy in our hands for over an hour. He was noncompliant, and we were just trying to get out of the country safely without him compromising us. So we gagged him. The North Koreans have an hour head start.'

'You couldn't have known,' she said softly. Then, 'Look, you know how these things go. The operatives you ran into aren't going to be the ones to expose Jen in Minsk. They would call their handlers, who themselves would have to kick it upstairs. The contact with the Belarusian group couldn't possibly take place in under an hour.'

Chavez said, 'I wish you sounded as confident as the words you're saying.'

Mary Pat paused, then said, 'Yeah. Well, all you and I can do right now is pray Jay's men get to her in time.'

Chavez hung up, put on a confident face, and returned to the group.

Kincaid looked at him, tears streaming down his face. 'What's happening?'

'It's getting taken care of.'

'What the *hell* does that mean?'

'It means Langley is in the process of pulling your wife out right now.'

Kincaid nodded slowly, not quite believing, and then he looked out the window for a moment. He said, 'That intelligence that you protected. The stuff I was handing over. Do you even know what it was?'

'It doesn't matter,' Dom said.

'The *hell* it doesn't! I wasn't handing out launch codes. I wasn't passing off the travel routes of the ambassador. No . . . It was a media list. A *fucking* list of the names of the reporters and producers we go to here in Indonesia to speak on background about issues. Most all of those names and organizations in that binder can be assumed by the press that comes out from them. This was nothing. *Nothing!* Plus, the men who contacted me said they were *South* Koreans.'

Dom was incredulous. 'Why would South Koreans threaten to kill your wife?'

'They claimed they had business contacts here in Jakarta who were making a play for political office. I knew they were dangerous men, but I *didn't* know they were from the DPRK.'

Jack said, 'It doesn't matter. You shared classified material.'

'About nothing consequential, and to save my wife's life.'

Jack said, 'They were getting their hooks into you. That's

all. Once you'd passed over intel, *any* intel, doesn't matter what, they could come back to you, hold your previous treason over your head, and turn up the heat on you to get more and more.'

Chavez nodded. 'That's how it works, Ben. Now, just sit there and chill out. As soon as we hear that your wife is safe, I'll let you know.'

They had just taken off from a refueling stop in Tokyo when the secure phone rang at the front of the cabin. Chavez went to it, took a call, and sat down.

In the middle of the cabin Jack, Dom, and Ben all stared at him, searching his body language for any good news.

Instead, they all got a read on the phone call at the same time. Chavez lowered his head, rubbed his eyes slowly. He nodded, hung up the phone, and just sat there at the bulkhead.

All eyes in the back of the aircraft remained locked on him.

Finally Chavez said, 'Dom, will you do me a favor and untie him? Mr Kincaid, can you come up here, please?'

Ben Kincaid's face reddened, his eyes misted, but he said nothing. Dom cut off the zip ties securing him to his chair, and the Department of State employee walked slowly to the front of the plane, like a man walking to the electric chair.

Dom and Jack didn't even look at each other. They sat there quietly, until Jack said, 'Shit.'

Dom nodded. 'Yeah. Hell of a thing.'

Ten minutes later Chavez headed to the rear, leaving Kincaid at the front of the plane, doubled over in a cabin chair and sobbing softly. He sat down with Jack and Dom; the look in his face was as if he'd lost a loved one. 'Jennifer

Kincaid's body was kicked out of a car at the front gate of the US embassy in Minsk. Her throat was slashed so badly her head was barely attached.'

'God rest her soul,' Dominic said softly.

Jack looked out the window at the cloud layer below. 'That's on us. Our fault. They killed her because we got involved.'

Chavez sighed. 'Incomplete intelligence, Jack. We were the tip of the spear, but the shaft of the spear let us down. If we knew more, if we had more time, we could have done something that –'

Jack replied flatly, 'Yeah, but the shaft of the spear didn't get her killed. We did.'

Chavez said, 'Mary Pat said there is some kind of breach they can't wrap their heads around. This looks like part of that. That woman was dead the second the CIA found out the DPRK was going to get documents from the USA.'

'*Fuck!*' Jack said, slamming the table in front of him.

Chavez left the younger men with their thoughts, and went back up to Kincaid. The man was still their prisoner, and he was just distraught enough to try something crazy if a very sympathetic, but also very capable, man was not standing close by for the rest of the long flight back to DC.

They had another thirteen hours of this flight, and he doubted there would be much talk out of any one of them the entire way.

After a refueling stop in Mexico City that turned into a twenty-four-hour delay due to bad weather, the old Antonov carrying Abu Musa al-Matari, his two subordinates, and a massive supply of ordnance landed at Ardmore Downtown Executive Airport, in Ardmore, Oklahoma, at two-twenty a.m. A single customs agent had been waiting for the aircraft, and only a single controller in the tower was working to bring this NAFTA flight in from South America.

The paperwork and forms had been filed in advance, the cargo had been listed as a return of defective farming machinery, and all there was for the customs agent to do was board the aircraft, check over the documentation of the crew, along with their personal passports, and conduct a quick inspection of the cargo.

The controller in the tower, the customs inspector, a refueling team at the fixed-base operator, and a single security guard in a patrol car far on the other side of the tarmac were the only people on airport grounds other than two vehicles here to meet the plane.

The An-32 did not have enough fuel to make it back to South America, but the refuelers were pumping gas before the stairs dropped from the hatch of the aircraft.

A twenty-six-foot U-Haul truck waiting for the arrival of the turboprop pulled forward, just aft of the aircraft. A Ford Explorer stopped right next to the U-Haul. One woman and five men climbed out of the vehicles and headed for the cargo hatch.

The customs inspector climbed aboard and immediately encountered the pilot and copilot standing in the front galley. He shook hands with the men, handed over their signed paperwork, verifying the cargo was indeed as represented on the manifest, and that the documentation of the two pilots was in order.

He never looked at the cargo, so he saw no rocket launchers or rifles or suicide vests, and he never looked inside the rear galley, so he did not see the three Islamic State operatives sitting there fingering Glock 17s on their hips.

An envelope containing $25,000 was handed over to the customs inspector, and he took it before quickly descending the stairs. He did not even look at the half-dozen or so people unloading fifty-pound crates from the cargo hold into a U-Haul truck.

He really did *not* want to know what was going on.

By four a.m. the Russian-built and Bolivian-owned Antonov was on its takeoff roll back into the morning sky; the entire Chicago cell, plus Tripoli, Algiers, and Musa al-Matari, was leaving the city of Ardmore in the two vehicles, and two tons of deadly equipment had made its way safely into the United States.

The vehicles weren't heading for Chicago. No, now they began a long cross-country road trip that would take them several days. They had to distribute equipment to the other four teams, and it was determined this could be most safely done by driving the goods to cities within a few hours' drive of each cell, renting storage units, and simply dropping off the crates. Then the keys would be FedExed to the leaders of the cells.

By midafternoon the truck had dropped a dozen crates in Alpharetta, Georgia, and by noon of the following day, a ten-by-ten-foot storage unit in Richmond, Virginia, had a dozen black plastic crates stacked inside. They delivered more crates to Ann Arbor, dropped their own crates in Naperville, Illinois, and here al-Matari, Algiers, and Tripoli left the group and set off for a safe house rented in the Lincoln Square neighborhood of Chicago.

The Chicago cell continued on to San Francisco to deliver the last of the weaponry to the Santa Clara cell.

Al-Matari had been given a driver's license owned by a

bearded and bespectacled thirty-eight-year-old American citizen of Palestinian descent, and he had to agree that when he grew his facial hair out this man could be his doppelgänger. With this and credit cards in the man's name, he could go where he liked, and his two Islamic State operatives could do the same with their own documentation, not that they actually expected the American police to pull them over.

They had worked behind the lines many times in their careers, and they had lived in Europe long enough to pass themselves off as Westerners, in attitude, if not in looks. They'd do their best to stay away from the authorities, but if they were questioned, their legends were backstopped and there were others here in the country who could vouch for them.

Al-Matari had worked too hard to leave anything to chance. When it became time for his men and women to begin their attacks, he would be prepared, and no random encounter by a cop was going to derail his plan.

20

The meeting in the Oval Office wasn't on the books, but President Jack Ryan received a call at six a.m. from Chief of Staff Arnie Van Damm telling him that Mary Pat Foley, Jay Canfield, Dan Murray, and Secretary of Defense Bob Burgess would like to speak with him as soon as he could be made available. When he got the call he was eating breakfast with Cathy; she had to leave early for a surgery at Johns Hopkins in Baltimore and he was flying out that afternoon to California to survey the ongoing devastation wrought by a series of wildfires.

His two youngest children, Katie and Kyle, were both in high school, which meant they were still sound asleep, and would remain so until well past the time their alarms told them to get up and get ready.

Ryan told Arnie he'd meet with his advisers at seven a.m. if they could all make it. This was basically his entire national security staff, and he hadn't seen anything on CNN that told him for sure what they'd want to talk about, so he was extra-curious.

He was also extra-experienced, and his experience told him the news he'd get in an hour was not going to be good.

Fifteen minutes after the meeting began, Ryan held his head in his hands, his elbows on his desk. Across from him, Mary Pat Foley, Dan Murray, and Jay Canfield had just personally delivered the news about Jakarta and the fallout of the operation.

After a long delay, he looked back up to them. 'Obviously her husband knows she's dead. Any other family?'

Canfield said, 'Both parents are deceased. No children. Ben and Jen were both looking forward to returning to the USA, both getting posted to DC, and starting a family here. We would have pulled Jen out in another ninety days or so, and she would have been done with covert work after that.'

'Why didn't Ben Kincaid come to us from the start? The minute he was threatened with the intel?'

Murray said, 'Haven't spoken with him yet, the private flight that brought him back just landed at Reagan. But I've done enough of these counterintelligence espionage cases to make an educated guess as to why. He was scared. He probably thought the more dangerous course of action was informing on the people threatening him and running the risk the Koreans would go through with their promise to have his wife killed. He knew the Koreans had his wife over the barrel and they passed themselves off, and passed their needs off, as relatively benign. They just wanted some low-level classified material, and he thought he could hand that over and get his wife out of danger in the short term.'

'Naive,' Ryan said, criticizing the man, but his voice wasn't as critical as his words. He felt for the man and his situation.

Murray said, 'This guy wasn't a spook. He'd never had anything like this happen to him. He reacted, and he reacted poorly.'

The President replied, 'I guess we reacted poorly, too.'

Murray nodded. 'When we couldn't get the first team in

without the compromise, maybe we should have spent more time worrying about the source and scope of the compromise, and less time worrying about busting Kincaid.' He shrugged. 'I don't know. These were North Koreans. They would have exploited the situation far beyond those first binders he was to pass over.'

Ryan said, 'Will he be prosecuted?'

Murray replied, 'I'll talk to Adler. He's done at State, that's for sure, but turning this into a big federal prosecution doesn't do anybody any good. Best bet is we all just move on.'

Canfield nodded. He was nearly despondent with the news of Jennifer Kincaid's death. 'Stopping the pass was the right thing to do. Now we have to find out who the fuck is revealing the identities and locations of our covert personnel to the whole world.'

'To that end, what's happening?' Ryan asked.

Canfield's eyes cleared a little. 'NSA is running with that ball right now. We are providing them everything they need.'

Murray nodded, said, 'Ditto.'

Mary Pat said, 'I'm getting daily progress reports. So far, they haven't found commonalities between those exposed that look like they could be relevant. These weren't people who knew each other, or even part of the same organization, other than the two CIA officers involved so far. They didn't go through the same training programs, live in the same town, attend the same universities.'

Ryan said, 'A database where all government employees' records are kept?'

'Sure, that exists, but we've seen no hint of anything being hacked before, and even if it had been, the way the records are stored for certain covert occupations would mean a bad actor would have to go through, literally, millions of records.

An officer working under nonofficial cover with the CIA isn't in IRS records under that name, for example, and that wouldn't explain how the fingerprints were obtained for the scanners in Iran and Indonesia, or how the hell Jen Kincaid was found in Belarus or Commander Hagen was found at a restaurant in New Jersey. No . . . Whatever the hell is going on doesn't seem like some sort of computer hack.'

Ryan nodded distantly. He looked to Canfield. 'I want to be there for the star ceremony.' He was speaking of the ceremony at CIA headquarters to honor a fallen officer.

Canfield said, 'Mr President, since she was a NOC, we can't –'

'I know there won't be an official release of her name. I'll come quietly. No press, no fuss. And I want Ben Kincaid there.'

Murray cocked his head. 'Jack . . . he's still a prisoner.'

'Who will be treated gently. He'll come to CIA, in your custody.'

'But –'

'Dan,' Ryan said, and Murray knew when to stop.

Soon everyone got up quietly to leave the room. The meeting had accomplished nothing other than the delivery of some very bad news, but as they headed for the door, Ryan asked a question out of curiosity.

'The team that pulled Kincaid out. Who were they?'

Mary Pat turned back to the President and blinked hard a few times. Finally she said, 'Do you mind if I stick around for a moment?'

Ryan shook his head; Canfield, Burgess, and Murray left; and Mary Pat walked back over to the President's desk.

Ryan didn't even need her to say anything. From her actions he knew his son had been involved.

'Is he okay?'

'Jack's fine, Mr President. They all are. I'm sure they are taking the fallout from their successful operation hard, but it was a successful operation from the standpoint of what we sent them in to do. Nobody at The Campus did anything wrong.'

Ryan nodded distantly.

She added, 'If we'd known who we were going over there to snatch, it would have been handled very differently, obviously.'

'Right,' he said. 'Thanks, Mary Pat.' He looked at her. 'Find this leak, and find Musa al-Matari. You do those two things, and America will be a lot safer.'

'Yes, Mr President.'

Mary Pat left, and the President of the United States picked up the phone on his desk.

Jack Ryan, Jr, had been sound asleep, flat on his back in his condo in Old Town, Alexandria, Virginia. The flight around the world and back had come to an end just two hours earlier, the prisoner was delivered to a team of Dan Murray's boys at dawn, and Jack said good-bye to his colleagues and took an Uber back to his place overlooking the Potomac.

He'd spent fifteen minutes in the shower, another fifteen minutes staring at ESPN, and then he hit the sack.

Now he woke to the sound of his mobile ringing next to his head. He found it, saw it was not even eight a.m., and realized he'd slept no more than an hour.

Half asleep still, he coughed and said, 'Ryan?'

'Hey, sport.' It was his dad.

Jack rolled to a sitting position on his bed, rubbed his eyes, and wondered what had happened. His dad called on rare occasions, but never first thing in the morning. He was President, after all. Presidents usually had stuff to do as soon as they got to work.

'Something wrong?' Jack said.

'Not on my end. How are you?'

Jack knew better than to talk about his operations at The Campus with his dad. 'Just fine. I'm . . . I've got the day off today, so I was just sleeping in.'

'Sorry to wake you.' There was a pause. 'Long-haul flights like that can be a real pain.'

So . . . his dad knew. Mary Pat had told him, obviously, which meant she'd been asked directly, because she knew better than to introduce that stress into Jack's father's life.

Jack said, 'Yeah. We're all sick about what happened.'

'Son, sometimes things fall apart, despite all our best intentions.'

Jack said, 'Dad, I find it's probably better for both of us if I don't talk about –'

Jack Senior said, 'I don't care about any of that. I care about you. I care about the effect this can have on you, because you somehow hold yourself responsible.'

'I *am* responsible. It's not about denying. It's about accepting it, figuring out how I can do better next time.'

'You were let down by the intelligence you received. An incomplete picture.'

'Everyone keeps saying that. I know that's true, but I also know that I got into this to be a damn analyst in the first place. The guy that would go out and get the best intel product possible, to avoid disasters like this. Somewhere along the way I turned into something else. Maybe I got sucked into the world of operations. I started to see myself as another team guy, when I should be doing what I do best. But right now I blame myself, not because of what I did in Jakarta, but because of what I didn't do back home. Maybe if I'd been analyzing this situation instead of shooting at North Koreans, I might have –'

Ryan Senior interrupted. 'You *shot at* North Koreans?'

Oh, shit, Jack thought. 'I assumed you knew. We had to. It was nothing.'

'That's *not* nothing, son.'

'My point is maybe I should go back to just being an analyst. Maybe I could play a bigger role that way.'

The father would like nothing more in the world than for the son to leave ops behind and go back to being an analyst behind a desk in a DC-area office. But he also knew he was exactly the wrong person to push that on Jack Junior. He himself had been a teacher who turned into an analyst who turned into . . . *what?* A reluctant operative? But had he really been so reluctant? The elder Ryan understood the lure of direct involvement, too. The adrenaline, the single-minded sense of purpose with life-and-death actions.

Yeah, he'd love Jack Junior to turn away from that before something horrible happened to him, but that was a decision for Jack Junior.

He said, 'Your mom and I, Sally, Katie, and Kyle . . . we love you and support you, whatever you do. You know I want you safe, but I also want you happy. Feeling like you are fulfilling your life's mission, whatever you determine that to be. Your mom and I trust you to do the right thing, and what happened yesterday was a terrible outcome. I am just calling to tell you I know how you feel, and you *have* to put it past you.'

Jack asked, 'Who the hell blew his cover to the DPRK?'

Ryan Senior sighed. 'We don't know, but we *do* know it

goes much bigger than the DPRK, the US embassy in Jakarta, and the State Department. This is something we are seeing across the government in the past few weeks. Getting to the bottom of it is everyone's top priority.' Ryan caught himself. 'Well . . . I hope it is. There is something else in extremis brewing, something unrelated, but something that can easily divert resources.'

Jack Junior knew better than to ask his dad too many questions, or to circumvent his own boss by making any promises about what The Campus would or *could* do to help. Instead, he said, 'Well . . . You are doing a damn good job, Dad. Just hang in there. A couple years from now we'll be out on a boat fishing and talking about how cool and important we used to be.'

Jack Senior laughed. It was nice to hear his son joke around a little. 'I look forward to that day.'

'Me, too.'

'Come see us as soon as you can.'

'I will.'

It was a promise Jack made more often than he fulfilled, but he told himself he'd try to do better.

He hung up the phone and lay there, and within a few seconds he told himself he was going to talk to John, talk to Gerry, and see if he could be of some help in finding out who the fuck was at fault for the leak.

He'd find the son of a bitch responsible for Jen Kincaid's death by working as an analyst, and then, if he could, he'd revert to direct-action operator, and he'd kill that son of a bitch himself.

21

Although he could not know it yet, the man Jack Ryan, Jr, very much wanted to kill was a twenty-nine-year-old Romanian named Alexandru Dalca.

People had described Dalca as a con man since long before he was even a man. When he was a very young boy he'd been a thief, a swindler, like a character out of *Oliver Twist*, and now, still in his twenties, he drove a Porsche and lived in a million-dollar condo in Bucharest's posh Sector 1 neighborhood.

A year earlier, Dalca stepped out through the gates of Jilava Prison and into the rain, a free yet completely soulless man. He'd entered the prison's walls six years before that, and though he'd gone in with deep psychological issues and significant abilities that he used for the benefit of himself and the detriment of others, the person who departed prison that wet morning last year was incalculably more dangerous than the one who went in, because prison had given him the last of the tools he needed to become a true criminal mastermind.

At the prison's gates a car had waited for him, as had been promised, and he shook off the rain and climbed into the back, not even taking time to breathe in the fresh air or look at the green fields to the east.

No, his mind was on his future, his plan.

His retribution. Retribution in the form of personal gain earned via injury to America.

Dalca was born in the city of Râmnicu Vâlcea in 1989, the same year Romanian strongman President Nicolae Ceaușescu and his wife and deputy prime minister, Elena, were ousted from power, then seconds later pushed in front of a brick wall and eviscerated with 120 bullets.

Alexandru grew up in the years after the revolution, and it would be a mischaracterization to describe anything that happened to him in his formative years as a real childhood. His father was unknown to him – his mother never even acknowledged the man's existence, and she herself died in a factory fire when Alex was just five. He was put into a horrific orphanage with little food and zero nurturing, so soon enough he found his way onto the streets of his town. Fortunately for him, Râmnicu Vâlcea had a decent amount of tourism, because it was just a few hours from Bucharest by train and in the foothills of the beautiful Southern Carpathian Mountains. Dirt-cheap Westerners looking for a dirt-cheap vacation flocked to Romania in the nineties, and young Alexandru learned a smattering of English begging from Western tourists, offering to shine shoes for a few coins, or selling items he and his street-urchin friends stole from market stalls and gift shops.

A group of British girls all but adopted the handsome boy during their week in his town, and they brought him back to their youth hostel to give him food and his own bed to sleep in.

He was seven years old, and when the girls went back home to England, Alexandru stayed behind at the hostel. The building had a popular Internet café, the only one in Romania outside Bucharest in those early days of the World Wide Web, and young Alexandru had never before seen a computer. He spent hours every day peering over people's shoulders, sat next to them and talked in his bad English, watched them playing games and communicating with loved ones around the world, asking them a million questions about the amazing device. Often he would swipe bills out of their purses and backpacks while he did all this, but just a few, because he did not want to be banished from the establishment.

Dalca became a fixture of the place, working odd jobs at the hostel and café, but while doing so he became adept at conning travelers of their excess food and change. He improved his English talking to the travelers, as well as by watching the movies that played all day long on a VCR in the great room.

After a few years Dalca expanded on his crimes. In his off time he formed up with some older Romanian teens who had started a scam using the new website eBay to post ads for items that Americans would pay for in advance. The Romanian guys would never ship the items; they would pocket the money and then simply open up new accounts and do it again as soon as their old eBay ID took a hit for the rip-offs.

Good English was the most important skill for these types of scammers, and Dalca's was good enough. As soon as Alexandru's voice changed with puberty, he became the telephone man on dozens and dozens of scams at a time. He spent twelve hours a day in a phone room set up next door to the café making deals, then responding to questions from ever more frantic and angry customers wondering why they hadn't yet received their purchases.

He could adopt a chill, relaxed demeanor to convince his marks that everything was all right, because, in fact, everything *was* all right.

For Alexandru and the boys he worked with, everything was great. They just got paid to do nothing more than make empty promises.

By now he was fourteen years old.

After a while eBay purchasers learned to be suspicious of items sold in some Central European countries where this scam was prevalent, so the gang had to adapt. Alex became an 'arrow,' a money mule. The eBay cons were tweaked so that they went through money-transfer offices and PO boxes all around Western Europe, and Alexandru and other kids like him would spend their days on buses or trains, traveling from one country to another, accepting money at wire transfer offices, picking up checks at PO boxes, and immediately sending them back home to his cohorts.

As e-commerce changed, so did Alexandru Dalca's con operations on the Internet. The work ethic he learned as a starving orphan, as well as the English he learned growing up in the hostel, made him the brains of his own operation by age sixteen, and by nineteen he drove a used Porsche 911 through the town.

There was no doubt his life's track would have him running his own major operation by his mid-twenties, if it hadn't been for the Americans.

The FBI kicked in the door to his Bucharest apartment one night, along with a special unit of Romanian cyber-investigators. Since Alex Dalca was a well-known arrow for a high-dollar ring that had ripped off thousands of Americans, he was made an example of by the Romanians, and sent to Jilava Prison near Bucharest for a term of six years.

He'd had no love for anyone before this point, but now he had a *passionate* hatred for Americans.

Jilava Prison had three things that would turn Alexandru

Dalca into something powerful and dangerous over the next six years. A library, dozens and dozens of other con men . . . and a spy.

The spy was Luca Gabor, a former case officer for the Romanian Intelligence Service who'd been recruited into an Internet scamming company because of his ability as a social engineer and the myriad 'dual purpose' skills that made him both a good case officer when 'running' an agent as well as a crook. Gabor was four years into a sixteen-year sentence, and he saw in twenty-one-year-old Dalca a way to pass on his abilities to someone who could go back on the outside and employ them, and in turn give a cut to the convicted spy's teenage daughter.

Gabor built upon Alexandru Dalca's already impressive skills, teaching him how to convince anyone of anything, but more important, he taught Dalca how to use open-source intelligence to discover people's secrets.

At the same time, Dalca read every piece of literature in the prison library about computers, software, applications, and social media.

His intelligence officer mentor gave him a list of books to read and websites to study for the day he left prison, and he promised Dalca he'd set him up with a job at his old company along with a new start.

On that rainy morning Dalca left Jilava and was picked up in a Mercedes sedan and taken to a new apartment in Bucharest's city center by a new employer arranged by Luca Gabor.

Alex Dalca was a new man, fortified with skills that could have been used for good or evil. He would have been an incredible asset to any intelligence agency in the world, including the United States, if not for one fatal flaw.

Alexandru was in it for the money, and he had no concept of the pain he caused others in acquiring that money.

His childhood made him a person socially disinterested in others, despite his incredible ability to influence them. Prison had just compounded all this, and even though Dalca had the raw materials for survival and even success, he never thought about any other person's wants or needs.

It wasn't just that he was not an empathetic or understanding person.

Alexandru Dalca did not even understand that there was something there to understand.

To him, there was no good, and there was no bad. There was only Alexandru Dalca, and everyone else. He was in competition with all other life forms on planet Earth, here to maximize his own gains, unaware of the costs incurred by others.

Dalca was, by any clinical definition, a sociopath.

Success for him was achieving the objective in front of him, and thereby gaining wealth. He was not married, and he was disinterested in sex other than as an occasional biological need.

No, he worked, day in and day out, for the same company his mentor in prison had worked for, a firm called ARTD, Advanced Research Technological Designs.

There exist companies that are built like regular aboveboard operations but are wholly in the business of illegal activity. They couch their operations and practices in benign titles and descriptions.

Advanced Research Technological Designs is such a company. One can spend as much time on the boring corporate website as one wants and one will not learn a thing about just what it is the company does, what goods or services it provides. One might find contact info for it in the form of e-mail addresses, or a Royal Mail post office box address in London, but no information about where, exactly, ARTD's brick-and-mortar building is located.

And though its mail goes to London, there is certainly no photo of ARTD's glass-and-steel London headquarters on their website, because ARTD's glass-and-steel London headquarters does not exist.

ARTD has its own building – but it's a four-story drab gray communist-era poured-concrete structure in Bucharest's city center on Strada Doctor Paleologu.

The dreary structure was full of some of Romania's best hackers, but it was also full of men and women called 'researchers.' These were the ones who made the scams work, who got strangers on the other side of the globe to give over passwords and bank account info, and other details that helped the hacks along.

And within months of leaving prison, the best researcher in the company was Alexandru Dalca.

He was not a computer hacker himself; he understood computers, but he was no coder – he saw all that technical mumbo jumbo as mind-numbingly boring stuff.

What he was good at was convincing people of things, building trust, smiling with his voice, conveying confidence, and getting what he wanted.

And for a company that trolled the Internet looking for victims, arguably the one thing more important than a good computer hacker was a good con man.

And Alex Dalca was the best.

He'd learned more than swindling people out of their money along the way. His job was to obtain passwords through social engineering, and a key component of this work was developing a connection with his target. He would, for example, find himself tasked with getting into the network of a bank in Cyprus. It wasn't enough to know the name of the CFO, he had to know where the man played tennis, who he slept with on the side, where the husband of the secretary he slept with worked, and where that man went to lunch so he could be spoken with quietly.

These types of investigations became his bread and butter, something he recognized early in his career in Internet fraud as being the most important asset.

He was a master at OSINT techniques, the ever-evolving science and art of open-source intelligence. When he wasn't perpetrating cons he was reading books on the subject, or he was pressuring the hackers in his company to get him information he could find no other way.

Alex learned quickly that no matter how carefully a person tries to hide his or her identity online, armed with only a small amount of knowledge of close associates, Alexandru could find them and open them up like a wrapped Christmas present.

Everybody had someone in his life on social media who liked to talk. Joe might be in the CIA and a first-rate practitioner of personal security, but his sister's roommate from college who lived in Reston was all over unencrypted e-mail talking about the cute guy Joe she met through her college roommate and the fact he knew everything about Paris from his time there in the State Department. Looking deeper, Alex could find someone at the embassy in Paris talking about Joe's arrival party as a consular official, and Alex could back up further, find the moment all Joe's college social media accounts were scrubbed, something that didn't happen to State Department employees.

That meant Joe was a spook, and he was now dating a girl in Reston, Virginia, which probably meant he was back at Langley.

In the intelligence field it had a name – IDENTINT, for identity intelligence – and although Dalca wasn't in the intelligence field, he could develop targeting information on virtually anyone, anywhere, with a computer, a phone, and a little time.

This was Dalca's job. He could out a guy like Joe in a morning fishing expedition, even though spies weren't his focus. But everything changed for the young Romanian researcher the day he was taken in to his director's boss and told that a company called the Seychelles Group had hired ARTD to do some specific work for them.

It would be a gross exaggeration to say that the People's Republic of China had begun outsourcing its cyberwarfare capabilities, but the case of Advanced Research Technological Designs was not unique. China had been caught in some high-profile hacking operations in the past few years, and the plausible deniability afforded to them by working via corporate cutouts with highly skilled computer experts made sense to them.

They saw these corporations – some based in India, others in Central or Eastern Europe – as wholly financially motivated, and the price paid to them by the People's Republic of China – again, through intermediaries – was small change for the huge nation when compared to the safety this scheme afforded them.

ARTD had been using its hackers to attempt to break into various American government servers. They targeted civilian firms with access contracts with the US government, to use their data links to try to 'swim upstream' into military, intelligence, and other networks.

They'd been at it for more than a year, and it wasn't something Dalca was working on at all, when he was called into the surprise morning meeting with the director of ARTD himself, Dragomir Vasilescu.

'Dalca,' Vasilescu said, 'I am taking you off your other assignments immediately. I have a job for you.'

'Hope it's something more challenging than that Petrobras account I'm working on. The Brazilians have me digging into the private lives of some of Exxon's senior staff, the most boring wealthy people on earth. I did it with a phone, a finger, and access to Google. Really, sir, this job is getting too easy.'

Dragomir Vasilescu smiled. Alexandru could build rapport with anyone, even the director of his company, but Vasilescu also knew all about Dalca's skills, and he was frankly afraid of the younger man. He imagined Dalca was somehow using social engineering to dig into his innermost thoughts right now.

The director said, 'This might indeed be more challenging. Our technical staff has gained access to a file from the American government.' He looked down at the paper in front of him. 'It's the complete record on a server at the Office of Personnel Management. Employee records of men and women working for the government who are applying for a security clearance.'

Dalca's eyebrows rose. 'How many records?'

'Over twenty million. All raw data. Application forms and fingerprints.'

'That sounds promising. How did we come across that?'

Vasilescu laughed. 'We hacked into an Indian cybersecurity company that had a contract with the US government to do penetration testing on their machines about five years ago. The Indians managed to exfiltrate this data, and apparently they accidentally kept it on one of their servers. They'd never even accessed it. We *borrowed* it from them to see if it was something we could use in phishing or spoofing operations. The best part is the Americans will never know anything has been accessed and exfiltrated by us, because we took it from a cybersecurity firm that didn't even know they had it.'

'Beton,' Dalca said. It was the Romanian word for 'concrete,' but it was also slang for 'cool.' Dalca thought there could, indeed, be some opportunities to make money in these free files. He asked, 'What do you want me to do?'

'Our client has asked us to see if there is some way you can use this raw data to run full investigations of men and women currently working in the US embassy in Beijing.'

Dalca said, 'So this is for China?'

'Of course not. We work for a company registered in the Seychelles. The Seychelles Group is their rather unimaginative name.' Vasilescu chuckled to himself. 'Of course they are obviously a front for Chinese intelligence. So I need you to wade through twenty-some-odd million files and try to associate these records with people working for the US in Beijing. I'm sure the Chinese want to identify spies to throw them out of their country or to use the intel for blackmail purposes. Plus, the data on the US government employees also has records of their foreign contacts. I assume this will help them find their own citizens who are spying against them.'

'I'll need to take a look at these files and see what I have to work with. But it sounds like something I should have no trouble with.'

Vasilescu said, 'I am giving you a month to go over the macro data of the files, just to find out what all is included, and to build a template of how to go over this data and exploit it in keeping with our client's wishes. You can build tables, databases, and such, and you can have access to anyone and any resource we have here at ARTD. Then I want you to choose a team of researchers to work for you on this project. They will follow your orders on how you want them to exploit the data. We've informed the client that we anticipate having a first package of goods to deliver to them in three months.'

Dalca spent the rest of the day clearing other items on his desk, and that evening he took control of all the files exfiltrated from the Indian cybersecurity firm. The raw data was only here, in the hands of ARTD, and kept on a special machine in a room with no Internet or other devices. There was no offsite server, and the client did not even have access to it.

Dalca was given the code for the room and he accessed the data for the first time at eight p.m., and by nine, he was aware of the full scope of what he, and no one else outside the American government, had access to.

Dalca worked through the night and was seated in Dragomir Vasilescu's office the next morning when the director of the company arrived at work.

As he placed his briefcase on his desk, Vasilescu looked over his twenty-nine-year-old researcher. 'Shit, Dalca. You've been here all night, haven't you?'

'Yes.'

'Well . . . What's on your mind?'

'The SF-86.'

'What's that?'

'It's a one-hundred-twenty-seven-page form that the United States government makes everyone fill out if they are applying for a security clearance. It has all the raw data on the applicant at the time the application was made. We have every single application processed by the US government from 1984 until a point about five years ago, when the Indians exfiltrated the data. Do you realize what we can do with all that information?'

The director said, 'Of course I do. You can use it to obtain the information asked of us by our clients.'

'It's bigger than that.'

'No, Alexandru. It's *exactly* that, because that is the wish of the Seychelles Group.'

Dalca said, 'They aren't thinking very big, are they?'

'What do you mean?'

'Using this data to find their own traitors? Small potatoes compared to the information's real worth.'

'I'm sure they'll identify America's spies in China, too.'

'Yeah, but why not identify every American spy, everywhere?'

'One, twenty-five million records. Ninety-nine-point-nine-nine percent won't be spies. Two, clearly the Seychelles Group are Chinese intelligence. Why do they care about a spy in Romania, or Iceland?'

Dalca shrugged. 'Just seems like we've discovered a potential gold mine here. Working this data the right way could be very profitable for us.'

'Yes, well, working it the right way, in this case, means doing exactly what our client asks of us, and nothing more. Alexandru, we have a clear job with this. Let's focus on Chinese contacts of these Americans, and let's get to it. If we start exploiting this in other ways, then we just might open our client up to exposure. They've paid us a lot of money for our abilities and our discretion. And they'll pay us a lot more money to crunch the data to get them what they want. If we do a good job for them, maybe they will want something else. They are China, after all. ARTD can help them in ways that go beyond fishing out some American spies.'

Dalca nodded, and said, 'Sure. Of course.'

Alexandru Dalca left his boss's office, already formulating a plan. What he could do with this information was much bigger than his assignment. Hell, it was bigger than ARTD. Bigger than the Chinese, even.

Dalca went to work, aggregating the data and cross-referencing it with medical records, insurance forms, property records, and the like. Much of this was done by isolating disparate data points, looking for clues through the analysis of the digital data.

Also included in the pulled sweep of the American server was something called clearance adjudication information. Potential negative information such as deviant sexual behavior, risk of foreign exploitation, and even information tied to interviews with the subject by background investigators.

And fingerprints.

Alex knew these files were a *fucking* gold mine.

True, a gold mine surrounded by a lot of thick rock, but Dalca was the best in the world at getting into this data and pulling out the important bits with OSINT.

There were hundreds of actors in the world who would love to find detailed targeting information on American soldiers, spies, politicians, and diplomats.

And Dalca would introduce this data to those seeking the information.

Dalca would process all this information himself, and he would sell intelligence off to the highest bidder.

Of course, this was something he had never done before. Sure, he could build the files on these individuals, out them as spies or other types of holders of classified intelligence. But *then* what? He had no way to reach out to the Russians, the Cubans . . . whoever the hell wanted this stuff, and sell it to them. Not without the wrong people finding out about him.

Well . . . Maybe there *was* a way.

The dark web. After doing some research, he realized he could set up a commercial enterprise on the dark web, and then reach out to those who might be interested in his product on offer.

It took him a few months to study this, and more time to build it, and all the while he was doing the work asked of him by the clients, the Seychelles Group.

But as he did this, he was also finding a way to test his plan to gain financially from the exploitation of the pilfered American files.

In all Dalca's work on social engineering information from people, he found himself spending a lot of time on the news networking website Reddit. This was an aggregation of discussion forums where community members discussed virtually every major topic on earth. Dalca knew the members of the site did not shy away from controversy, so he began looking for a test case to use the OPM data he had stolen. This was just a few months after the American land and naval attack in the Baltic region, and there were hundreds of bulletin boards on Reddit about the fighting. While many were in Russian, there were some English-language anti-American boards, and Dalca found himself drawn to these.

He knew what he was looking for, a low-risk proof of concept. He found this, after weeks of false starts and waiting for the right moment, in the guise of a Reddit user who claimed to be the brother of a mechanic on the *Kazan*, a Russian submarine sunk in the battle. The man was beyond distraught about his brother's murder; he railed against America and let it be known he was actually in the United States on an expiring student visa. Over days and days, in public forums, the man expressed his rage.

Alexandru Dalca watched a linked news piece that mentioned the name of the captain of the American destroyer given credit for sinking one of the subs and helping the Poles sink the other. Dalca heard the name of the ship, the USS *James Greer*, and that the captain was a man named Scott Hagen. He looked online at a Department of the Navy website that listed all the ships and their captains, and confirmed Hagen was a forty-four-year-old US Navy commander. He accessed the Office of Personnel Management files and, sure enough, found a twenty-one-year-old application for classified intelligence from then twenty-three-year-old Lieutenant Junior Grade Scott Robert Hagen, straight out of the US Naval Academy at Annapolis, Maryland.

He checked several real estate and property records, and found Hagen had a home in Virginia Beach, Virginia, and a rental property in North Carolina. Both homes were also in the name of Laura Hagen, who Dalca assumed was Hagen's wife. Dalca made note of the addresses and then, knowing that a naval commander wasn't any sort of a covert position in the United States government, he used Google to look for references to Hagen from before the action in the Baltic. He found articles, images, and videos of the naval officer, going back fifteen years, saw that he coached his son's baseball team and scooped ice cream for his sailors and their families at an event in Italy a year or so earlier.

Dalca looked at a picture of Hagen with his wife at a ball, and studied the wife's face for a moment before checking Facebook.

First, he looked to see if Scott Hagen had an active account. He did not. Hagen's wife, Laura, did have an account, but it had been locked and unused since the battle in the Gulf seven months earlier.

Undeterred, Dalca went back to the OPM files.

While twenty-one-year-old information might not have seemed relevant to locating a man in the present, Dalca looked up the names of Hagen's family, settling on a sister who lived in Indiana. She had been unmarried at the time, but the application contained her Social Security number. Dalca looked into a database he used regularly in his open-source research that showed all US marriage licenses.

Susan Hagen had married a man named Allen Fitzpatrick in Bridgeport, Connecticut, in the 1990s, and there was no record of any divorce on file.

Once he had Hagen's sister's information, Alexandru simply went back to Facebook. He had been ready to do a number of customized searches on all her page traffic to see if there were any mentions of her brother, Scott, but he needed only one. He typed the name 'brother' into a search of all her posts, took just one simple glance at the second post brought up by the search, and he smiled.

Susan Fitzpatrick mentioned how excited she was for the opportunity to go to Princeton, New Jersey, to her son's soccer tournament over the summer, and she was doubly excited that her niece and nephew would be meeting them there with their parents, because she hadn't seen any of them in some time.

A little research showed Dalca that Susan Fitzpatrick had two brothers: Scott, who was his target, and Raymond, who lived in Winter Haven, Florida. A minute's research into Raymond Hagen revealed two children, but they were both teenaged girls.

Case closed. Commander Scott Hagen, captain of the USS *James Greer*, the man who orchestrated the sinking of the *Kazan* off the coast of Poland, would be meeting his sister in Princeton, New Jersey, in six weeks' time.

It took an hour of deep research into Susan Fitzpatrick online to find she stayed at Hampton Inns regularly when she traveled. Dalca called the Hampton closest to where the soccer tournament was scheduled to take place, said his name was Scott Hagen, assuming the family would stay at the same hotel. In his best American accent he inquired about adding Monday to his Friday-to-Sunday stay.

The clerk corrected him immediately; he was booked Friday and Saturday night only, and she asked him if he'd like the rate for Sunday and Monday.

Dalca smiled, told the helpful hotel agent that he needed to speak with his wife first, and then he hung up.

Dalca reached out to the Russian Reddit user, and over the course of a few e-mails told him he could give him the name of the hotel the commander of the *James Greer* was staying at on a specific day, along with pictures of the man, his wife, his sister, and his brother-in-law.

Dalca added that, if something should happen to Hagen, it would serve the bastard right.

The Russian was intrigued, clearly, but claimed to have little money. Dalca told him he'd give him the information for free. The truth was, in this rare instance, Dalca wasn't looking for money. He was looking to see his system in action. He was looking to show that he could use the OPM hack, bringing up classified applications that could be more than twenty years old, to create real-time targeting data in the here and now.

Dalca sent the Reddit user the complete package, then created a Google Alerts search for the name Scott Hagen, which would e-mail him every time the man's name came up in new stories.

And then he promptly forgot about it, because he had other work to do.

Six weeks later Dalca saw a story online about a maniac shooting up a Mexican restaurant in New Jersey. The article came into his inbox because Naval Commander Scott Hagen had been one of the wounded.

Vadim Rechkov, clearly the Reddit user, had been killed in a shoot-out that also took the lives of three other people. Dalca didn't care about the dead or wounded.

By now he had his pay site on the dark web, and he'd already used it to secretly sell specific intelligence to the governments of Indonesia, North Korea, and Iran.

And he also had a new fish on the line. He'd been contacted through the e-mail address of a terror group he'd reached out to in Lebanon, and notified that his messages to them had been monitored by a group with interest in what he could offer.

While Dalca was initially frustrated that his plan to reach out directly to different actors in the market for US targeting information seemed to have backfired due to the poor security of one of his marks, he wasn't concerned himself. He'd used unbreakable security to reach out to the Lebanese group, as evidenced by the fact this shadowy entity coming to him had to do it through the means he'd established, instead of contacting him directly.

No, they didn't know who he was, he could back away and never make contact with them, but their offer was enticing. They clearly wanted to do business, and they were talking about purchasing vast amounts of targeting info regarding US military and intelligence personnel.

Dalca soon began dealing directly with the group via encrypted e-mail and text messages. And within weeks he was in business with the group he now knew as 'the ISIS guys.' He'd given them that title because they were interested in targeting information on Americans involved in Syria and Iraq. Who else could they possibly be? With the wide-ranging targeting requests he began getting from them, the 'good faith' payments they sent to prove the seriousness of their interest, he'd all but forgotten about dealing with other actors out there. He had ignored further requests for intelligence from North Koreans and Iranians in the past few weeks; he could tell they weren't ready to come through with big money and large quantities of targeting packages.

But 'the ISIS guys' had deep pockets and, it was clear to Dalca, they had big plans to kill a lot of American soldiers and spies.

He'd cultivate this relationship, he'd milk these guys for every penny they had, and in return he'd give them a gold mine of targets. Dalca wanted the money, and he also wanted to watch a lot of Americans die on the news.

22

Bartosz 'Midas' Jankowski and Adara Sherman met for the first time at five a.m. in the underground parking garage of the Hendley Associates building, on the corner of North Fairfax Street and Princess Street, in Alexandria, Virginia.

John Clark introduced the two new operational trainees to each other, and when Chavez, Caruso, and Ryan Junior pulled into their respective parking spaces and climbed out, all dressed for a morning run, he introduced Midas to the other members of the team.

Five minutes later, all of them, Clark included, were running along the Mount Vernon Trail, a jogging and bike path that followed the western bank of the Potomac River. They kept an easy pace and did five leisurely miles together, chatting away for the duration, although John Clark grew silent for the last mile, partially because running five miles at his age was some work, but mostly because he wanted to listen in to the others and get some early impressions about how they all jelled.

It was clear to Clark that the conversation was a little stilted, but he knew this had nothing to do with how well Adara and Midas would fit in with the crew. No, early the previous morning the three Campus operatives had returned from Jakarta, and they were all still sickened by the fallout of their mission there.

Jack was the worst of the three. He was quiet today, save for speaking when spoken to, and Clark knew at any other time he would have been the most hospitable and welcoming person in the building on a new employee's first day.

Clark knew he'd have to watch Jack carefully, do what he could to help him process his guilt, and make sure the death of the CIA officer in Minsk didn't hamper Jack's ability to continue to do his job.

Back at the office at sunup, Midas pulled his gear bag out of the back of his pickup and followed the others inside, where he was shown to a locker room to shower and change for the day.

Jack, Dom, and Ding showered as well, then went to breakfast at a nearby coffee shop before heading into work. Adara showered in the women's locker room of the gym, then went straight up to the third-floor conference room, where she knew coffee, fruit, and cereal would be waiting.

When she got there, Midas had already finished his first cup of coffee and was pouring himself a second.

Adara said, 'Uh-oh. Hope the fact it took me longer to get ready than you doesn't make me look too high-maintenance.'

Midas stirred in some milk and laughed. 'Not at all. My ex-wife would have taken exactly five hundred percent the time it took you to get ready for the day after a five-mile run. I'm a drip-dry kinda guy myself, so I don't fault you running a brush through your hair before coming up.'

Adara got her breakfast and then Clark came in the room, himself showered and ready for the day. 'Midas, I've got to explain something about this morning.'

'It's okay, Mr C. I've been places where nobody liked me before. The guys will warm up to me when I prove myself.'

'It's not you. Twenty-four hours ago they returned from an operation. Doubt you'll ever have need-to-know on the specifics, but let's just say that while the guys did everything exactly right, the fallout from their mission had some very, *very* negative second-order effects. No fault of anyone at The Campus, but the operators are going to be a little quiet for a couple of days. Jack, especially.'

Midas nodded. 'Understood. I've had a few days like that myself.'

Adara knew about what had happened, and she was used to Dom getting a little melancholy when things went wrong. Added to that was the fact Adara was now being trained as an operator, and she knew she had to give Dom some extra space and understanding.

She imagined that wasn't going to be too much of a problem, considering the fact she had a full plate for the next several weeks.

Clark spent forty-five minutes going over his plan for six weeks of instruction with his two new trainees, and at eight o'clock sharp, Gerry Hendley came into the conference room to meet Midas. The four of them talked about the history of Hendley Associates and its special relationship with the government for a while, until Gerry excused himself and Clark officially began his training.

In order to work at The Campus, one had to understand how The Campus worked, as well as the operation of Hendley Associates, the cover company that Midas was now an employee of.

Clark spent the morning moving Midas and Adara from meeting to meeting throughout the building, first introducing them to the investing and analytical team on the Hendley 'white side' as well as the analysts, computer hackers, equipment purchasers, logistics experts, et cetera, who worked on the Campus 'black side.' Adara had worked here for years, but she was not on a first-name basis with everyone in the building. Some of this had to do with the fact that fully fifty percent of her work life took place on board the Gulfstream or else at a tiny office they kept at the airport fixed-base operator, formerly at Baltimore BWI Airport, but recently relocated to Reagan National, just ten minutes' drive north of Hendley Associates in Arlington.

There were just over eighty employees working here in the building today, and Clark took Midas and Adara around to meet most all of them.

The next part of the process was as educational to Adara as it was to Midas. Clark went down the somewhat complicated list of just exactly who around the intelligence community was aware of the sub rosa intelligence work done at The Campus. From the director of national intelligence to the attorney general and, of course, the President of the United States, it was a list with some lofty names, although it remained a relatively short list. The off-the-books organization had been employed on more than a dozen special assignments in the past several years, so many people had come in contact with operators of The Campus, but Gerry Hendley and his executive staff had gone to great pains to keep the exposure small and the affiliations murky.

Midas knew this from his own experience a couple of years earlier. He had been an officer in a highly secretive military unit operating in a battle zone who was then introduced to a group of men and told he couldn't be read in on just who, exactly, they worked for. He'd found it odd at the time, but now that he was on the other side of the coin, it was comforting to know there were just enough people around the government who ran interference for The Campus that he knew he could expect some semiofficial cover during his operations.

In the late afternoon Clark took his team down to the two-lane firing range on level B3, just below the parking garage. Over the next few hours they trained on the MP5 submachine gun, the M4 rifle, and the SIG Sauer MPX, the new sub gun the team had been testing to see if it was worthy of replacing the H&K UMP kept hidden as a close-quarters defensive weapon in the Gulfstream.

Adara actually had more time behind the SIG MPX than Midas. Delta used the H&K MP7 PDW (personal defense weapon), as their short-barreled weapon of choice, while The Campus had been testing the new SIG for the past few months.

Still, Midas and Adara shot identical groups.

Adara was never going to be the shooter Midas was, but a small, mobile unit like The Campus was in need of overlapping expertise. She had more medical training, more logistics training, and a wider understanding of worldwide aviation. She was a pilot, where Midas was not, although they both had significant boating experience.

There would be places Adara could go where Midas would stick out, and the inverse was just as true.

Clark was happy to see that Midas didn't have any qualms about training alongside a female. He could think back to a time in his own military career where he would have found it incredibly odd, to the point of distraction, to run and gun with a woman, but that was a long time ago. Adara had become something of a daughter figure to him in the past five years, and he realized he had to keep aware of his own professionalism so he wouldn't take it easy on her during the training program.

After working into evening at the range, they took an hour off for dinner at a local barbecue shop, then they drove to an outdoor range in Springfield for night fire training. They donned night-vision equipment and used rifles equipment with night-vision-capable holographic weapons sights, and they cleared rooms in the four-room shoot house there.

Again, Adara acquitted herself well, and Midas shot, moved, and communicated like he'd been, just months earlier, a high-ranking Delta Force officer.

That is to say, this stuff was ingrained in Midas's DNA by now.

Adara was bone-tired when John Clark called his last cease-fire of the day, shortly after eleven p.m.

Clark said, 'You both did good today. But today was the easy day. Tomorrow things get harder, and harder still the day after.'

Adara imagined this was true, and she imagined John would say the same thing every day for the next six weeks.

23

The opening play of the Islamic State's worldwide operation to draw American soldiers en masse back into the Middle East did not begin with Sami bin Rashid and Musa al-Matari's fighters in the United States. It began in Sicily, and it was carried out by three young Islamic State plants in the flow of war refugees from Syria.

The men had been trained in an underground ISIS camp in Raqqa, then traveled in the mass immigration out of the war zone from Syria into Turkey, then through Bulgaria and Romania, before leaving the refugee flow and slipping illegally over the border into Hungary. When they made their way into Slovenia these three men were met by other ISIS operatives, already living and working in Europe, and here they were outfitted for their operation.

A total of six operatives, including the three newcomers to Europe, crossed into Italy, then spent a full day on the highways heading south. Down at the tip of Italy's boot in Reggio Calabria, they stole an eight-meter fishing boat with a small Zodiac launch tethered to it, and they sailed across the Strait of Messina over to Sicily.

They anchored in a quiet cove through the daylight hours, then sailed back out into the black Mediterranean in the late evening, using their mobile phones to give them precise geo-coordinates and directions to a point off the coast of Fontanarossa, a sleepy Sicilian beach community. Here the three young men from Syria climbed into the rigid-hulled inflatable Zodiac launch and began heading west toward the beach in the pitch-black night.

Naval Air Station Sigonella was a fifteen-minute drive to the west of Fontanarossa. Considered the hub of America's US Naval Air operations in the Mediterranean, Sigonella served as a main support station for America's ongoing attacks against ISIS targets in Syria, Iraq, and Libya, and other US operations against Al-Qaeda and its affiliates all over North Africa. Flying time from Sigonella to Syria was roughly two and a half hours, and it was barely a quarter of that to northern ISIS positions in Libya.

Sigonella base was well protected with guns, gates, and guards, and local police were on the lookout for any disturbances in the area that might indicate a threat to US personnel. But on this early morning, the waters of the Med to the east of the base were perfectly quiet other than the approaching Zodiac. The rubber boat came into the shallows without use of the motor. The three men climbed out into waist-deep water and tossed their paddles back in.

They didn't bother with pulling the little RIB to shore, anchoring it to the ocean floor, or fixing it to a dock with a line.

No, they would not need the small watercraft again.

Each man carried an H&K submachine gun with several extra magazines, and all three carried a suicide vest, double-sealed in plastic garbage bags. The gear had been provided to them by the three ISIS operatives already living in Europe, and they'd guarded it with their lives since picking it up in Slovenia.

Together the three Syrians scanned the shore in front of them, saw no one around, and then waded out of the water, ran up the sand, and dropped down in the deep grasses by the side of the road. On the other side they saw just what they were expecting to see: a quiet community of one- and two-story homes with tiled roofs.

The nominal leader of the three men, so appointed because he carried the mobile phone with Google Maps on it, pulled the device out of a waterproof bag and looked it over. It took him a moment to orient himself, and when he did he realized they'd drifted too far south on their approach in the RIB. Softly he pointed to the right, and to the others he said, 'Two blocks that way.'

They donned their vests and checked one another to make sure everything was set up correctly. And then they stood and set off up the beach road.

On a street called Via Pesce Falco the small kill team turned left, began running along fenced and gated front yards, making an effort to stay out of the streetlights but sacrificing pure stealth for speed. The last in the group was the man with the mobile phone to his face; he searched the map on the device for just the right house.

Halfway up the street he stopped abruptly, and the men ahead of him ran on a dozen meters before realizing their mistake and returning to take a knee next to him on the darkened sidewalk.

There was nothing special-looking about this house on his right; it was one of dozens on Via Pesce Falco. The property next to it was just a sandlot with tall sea grasses, so they used this to make their way around back. Here they jumped the rear fence, and the first gunman arriving at the sliding glass door at the rear of the property waited till his two colleagues caught up to him. He tried the door, found it to be locked, and then he wiped sweat from his brow.

With a nod to his partners, he turned his MP5 around in his hands and used the butt of the weapon to shatter the glass by the door latch.

He unlocked the door, and the three terrorists moved into the darkness of the home.

This house was a four-bedroom rental property. At present it was rented as off-base living quarters for four United States Naval officers, all lieutenants in their twenties. They were all bachelors, and all pilots of the F/A-18 Hornet.

It was against Italian law and Navy regulations for personnel to carry a firearm off base, but twenty-six-year-old Lieutenant Mitch Fountain always snuck his nine-millimeter Beretta M9 home with him. He knew he'd get a serious reprimand if he was ever caught, but he did it anyway. He was from South Dakota, he'd grown up around guns the way many grow up with footballs, and the thought of fighting a war against terrorists without so much as a pistol next to where he laid his head at night rubbed him the wrong way.

Mitch was the only one of the four in the house who did this, and consequently, when he woke at four-thirty a.m. to the sound of breaking glass downstairs, he knew it was up to him to investigate. He grabbed the Beretta from his nightstand, flipped off the safety, and ran out of his little room and toward the stairs.

As he arrived he saw three men coming up the steps, illuminated by a night light plugged into a wall socket there.

When he realized they were carrying shoulder-fired weapons, he did not hesitate.

Fountain fired three rounds at the sight of the ascending attackers, hitting one man squarely in the throat, the chin, and the top of the head.

And then Navy Lieutenant Mitch Fountain was killed by a fully automatic burst of the second gunman's MP5.

The second gunman then stopped on the stairs, turned, and chased after his dead colleague, who was now sliding down the stairs back to the ground floor. He began taking the man's suicide vest off him, while the third terrorist ran into the second-floor hallway.

The three other Americans were still in the process of waking up; the initial crash of broken glass had happened less than twenty seconds earlier, after all, but they grabbed a ball bat, a tennis racket, and a folding combat knife, and they all came running out of their rooms.

The ISIS gunman in the hall saw the three men pour out of their rooms at once, he let go of his sub gun, and he reached for the pressure switch swinging freely from the cuff of his left arm.

A quick toggle of the safety and a press of the plunger, just as the first American swung a baseball bat at the side of his head, and his job was done.

The second floor of the little villa erupted in fire, killing all four men instantly.

Downstairs, the one remaining ISIS operative fell onto his dead comrade, knocked there by the blast above, then he finished retrieving the vest. He held it in his left hand as he darted out the front door of the home, out into the street, where he turned to his right and took off to the west.

Many of the homes on the street were employed as off-base housing for the air station, this he had been told, although he'd been given no specific secondary target. He ran alone through the dark as lights came on in houses all around, car alarms blared from the explosion, and he looked for more US Navy to kill.

Forty-five seconds after leaving the target home he settled on the largest villa on the street, ran up the drive, and arrived at the front door just as it opened. A man in a bathrobe stood there, searching for the origin of the explosion, but he was knocked down by the young terrorist.

Both men fell to the floor, more people came down the stairs next to them, and the terrorist put a thumb on the detonators of both suicide vests, and jammed down on the plungers simultaneously.

The President of the United States sat in the conference room on Air Force One and looked at the four computer monitors on the wall. As Nebraska crept by, 38,000 feet below him, he conferenced with the secretary of defense on one monitor, the secretary of state on another, the attorney general on the third, and the director of national intelligence on the fourth.

And here in the conference room on the 747, Chief of Staff Arnie Van Damm sat off to the side.

SecDef Bob Burgess continued his rundown of events. 'Nine innocents dead in all, including seven Americans. Five junior Navy officers, four of whom were Hornet pilots in a squadron currently flying ground support operations in Libya and Syria. And a lieutenant commander who was killed along with his wife. He was the new chief of air traffic control at the base. He'd just arrived at Sigonella three days earlier and didn't yet have housing set up, so he was staying in a bed-and-breakfast near the beach, a few doors down from the pilots' off-base rental.'

After a pause, Burgess said, 'Two more dead were Austrians on holiday, a husband and wife. Two Italians dead as well. Five wounded, two of these seriously.'

Mary Pat Foley added, 'An Islamic State website we've deemed credible announced the attack five minutes after the first reports, put up testimonial videos of the attackers, even mentioned the name of one of the dead American F-18 pilots. There is no doubt that this was an ISIS operation, and no doubt they had specific targeting information.'

The President asked, 'How the hell did they know the exact address this guy was staying at? And how did they know the lieutenant commander was staying in the B-and-B up the street?'

Foley replied with obvious frustration. 'We still do not know. The DoD and the entire IC are running tests on all networks, looking for any hints of new penetration that might have exposed these men. So far, nothing.'

Ryan said, 'This is like the Commander Hagen incident, another attack on the Navy.'

Burgess said, 'Except this time the attackers are ISIS, not a Russian college dropout. But, yes, their intel is every bit as good and difficult to account for as the Hagen attack in New Jersey.'

Ryan said, 'Okay. That's our immediate threat abroad. Any chance this attack indicates that Abu Musa al-Matari is in Europe, and not, as we've been fearing, on his way here?'

Mary Pat Foley spoke up now. 'Doubtful. The Islamic State's Foreign Intelligence Bureau has its own European operational leadership. They all live there, work there. Hell, most of them were born there. Al-Matari wouldn't be on home turf in Europe the way a dozen other men of his rank would be.'

'Makes sense,' Ryan said.

'Plus,' Mary Pat added, 'we do have some news on Musa al-Matari.'

Ryan said, 'Good news, or bad news?'

Dan Murray said, 'It's not good. We've been trying to identify this "Language School" the Yazidi girl told us al-Matari spoke of. We think we found it in the jungles of El Salvador, close to where the Guatemalan ex-Special Forces men had gone to teach a training class.'

Ryan said, 'A group of jihadists in El Salvador didn't get noticed by the local Feds?'

'No, but this place was way out in the sticks.' Murray frowned. 'FBI agents toured through it yesterday. It had already been abandoned, totally cleared out, but there were enough shell casings around to indicate some serious training had gone on.'

'Small-arms training?'

'We found evidence of pistols, rifles, and small explosives. But just because we didn't see anything else, that doesn't mean they didn't train on other weapons.'

'Size of the encampment?'

'Hard to say, because these were existing structures. They'd been around since the eighties and weren't built for the use of the ISIS group. But from the burn pit, and from the locals who say they heard shooting for something like three to four weeks, we think we could be looking at a force between twenty-five and fifty pax.'

The AG went on. 'If they are coming here, they'll split up, obviously, groups of four to eight, I'd guess, but the good news is it's not a compartmentalized operation. If we take down one of these terrorists, they will have knowledge of members from other cells.'

'Why would they train them together?' Ryan asked.

Mary Pat jumped in now. 'That's a good question. It flies in the face of normal practice. But al-Matari is a smart man.

This *wasn't* a mistake. He had an operational reason for putting everyone in the same place.'

Dan Murray said, 'I widened the scope of my original investigation. Anybody who had been on the terror watch list in the past five years, men and women who were no longer under scrutiny, we checked out again.

'Almost immediately something popped up. A guy we had looked at once before was murdered last month in Hallandale Beach, Florida. He ran a 7-Eleven, was working at the counter with his wife when they were both shot to death. But nothing was stolen. Local police saw it as a robbery gone wrong, but we put men on it, interviewed the other employees. One of them said his boss had been talking about taking some time off to go to a language school in Guatemala. Right before he was murdered, he told his employee that his wife put the kibosh on the trip.'

Ryan's eyebrows furrowed, but not from interest. He was an intelligence man himself, and this wasn't much to go on, at all.

Murray knew Ryan wouldn't be impressed by that alone. 'We found another guy' – he looked down at his iPad – 'named Kateb Albaf, a Turkish national who'd been in school at UC Santa Clara we'd had on the watch list a couple of years ago due to some of his radical statements to a reporter at a rally. We interviewed him, put a soft surveillance package on him for a couple of months two years ago, and determined he was just a student. He never knew we were interested in him.'

'Where is he now?' asked Ryan.

'Up until a month ago, he was back in California right where he was when we last saw him, but we found out he just went on a trip to Honduras.' Murray looked up from his iPad and to the President. 'According to a classmate, he was going to spend six weeks at a language school – claimed a newfound interest in learning Spanish. We looked into his airline travel and they match the dates the Guatemalan commandos were away from home.'

Ryan said, 'Wonder how good his Spanish is now?'

Dan Murray grumbled, 'Probably not as good as his ability to build an S-vest.'

Ryan looked back and forth between Mary Pat and Dan. 'C'mon. Tell me you have more than this.'

Mary Pat said, 'We do. A second man formerly on the watch list, a twenty-six-year-old used-car salesman from Atlanta named Mustafa Harak, also told associates he was going to Central America to a language school. He says to Guatemala. The dates match up very closely to the Turkish national.'

Ryan rolled his head back and forth. He was seeing some distinct lines between all the dots. 'Guatemala and Honduras both border El Sal. They flew into these other nations, bussed over into El Salvador, and learned how to shoot people and blow things up. You're probably right, we should tail these men carefully now.'

Murray said, 'Unfortunately, we cannot tail either Albaf or Harak, because neither of them are home. Their cars are there. But they are not.'

Ryan asked, 'Credit cards?'

'Neither man's cards have been used since before they went to Central America. Kateb, the Turk in California – his wife, Aza, has disappeared, too.'

Ryan said, 'Shit. They've got tradecraft, and they are already pre-positioning.'

Foley nodded. 'That's right.'

Ryan said, 'We managed to stop Abu Musa al-Matari's first attack against the United States when his training camp was discovered on sat photos over Syria. This time he moves the training to El Salvador.'

Mary Pat said, 'We're looking into boats out of La Libertad, the closest port, just fifteen miles away. Of course flights out of San Salvador, too. Charters, cargo, anything that came up to the States in the past ten days.'

Murray added to this. 'They could have flown out of somewhere else, stopped and transferred along the way. But it's all we have to go on.'

Ryan said, 'There have to have been hundreds of planes that fit that description just landing at Miami International. Throw in Houston, L.A., Atlanta . . . Good Lord.'

Mary Pat said, 'Jay and I will keep at it on our end, and Dan will keep the heat up on the domestic side. We've already notified Homeland Security to BOLO these guys.'

Ryan looked down to the artist's rendering made from the recollection of the Yazidi girl. 'It's time to put Musa al-Matari's face out there.'

Murray said, 'I agree. We'll say we think he's here in the US, and he's dangerous, tied to ISIS. It will get the coverage we need, although it's not going to be hard for this guy to alter his appearance.'

Secretary of State Scott Adler had been quiet for the past few minutes, but he spoke up again now. 'Mr President, back to the attack at Sigonella. There is something else you need to know. This might be a bad time to bring this up, but you will be questioned about it in the news conference when you land.'

When Adler said this, SecDef Bob Burgess visibly snarled. The two men could not see each other on the monitors, but

Ryan noted Burgess's reaction to the secretary of state, and this told him Burgess knew about the matter Adler was bringing up, and he wasn't happy about it.

'What is it, Scott?' Ryan asked.

'One of the naval officers murdered apparently had his sidearm with him.' A pause. 'Off base. Which is against Italian regs. Our regs, too.' Another pause. 'It was found at the scene. One of the terrorists was shot by it.'

Ryan shook his head. 'Scott . . .'

'Sir, I'm just the messenger. The Italians are pissed off, but I will tell them, very quietly, to kiss my ass. If they can't protect our military in their country, then our military has to protect itself.'

This relaxed Burgess some, Ryan saw immediately.

The President held up a hand to his secretary of state. 'No, Scott. Thanks for saying what I'm thinking, but no. You have to be the chief diplomat. I'll talk to President Morello, smooth that over. If a reporter asks me about it I'll say I can't comment on the investigation.' He shrugged. 'And then I'll say I'm personally glad our Navy flier shot one of the bastards.'

Ryan looked over to Arnie Van Damm, who said nothing.

Burgess said, 'Obviously, Mr President, our concern now is for other military personnel at off-base housing around Sigonella.'

Ryan said, 'And other locations involved with the actions against ISIS. Bahrain, Frankfurt. Incirlik. Shit . . . We've got bases all over Europe, and in some degree or another, they all have some involvement with our actions in the Middle East.'

Burgess said, 'That's right. And we don't have the space on base to hold everyone and their families. Off-base housing is a necessity.'

Ryan said, 'As far as I'm concerned, pilots are on the front lines. I want them on base. Special operations forces, all senior officers, too. As far as Sigonella goes, I'll get President Morello to allow us to post guards off base, MPs, for the short term, while we try to get all our men and women inside the wire.'

Burgess said, 'Sorry, sir, but that sounds like a capitulation to terrorists.'

Ryan said, 'It's not a capitulation to terrorists. It's a capitulation to this damn intel leak that's causing all this! We don't know how big or wide this goes, and I'm not going to sit around and wait for our servicemen and -women to get nailed again by something we clearly don't understand.'

Burgess nodded on the monitor. 'Yes, sir.'

The videoconference ended a moment later, and immediately Arnie Van Damm slid his chair closer to Ryan's.

'This is going to rekindle a lot of hostility to the policy in the Middle East.'

Ryan nodded. 'A couple years ago nobody wanted another land invasion of Iraq. And *nobody* has ever wanted our troops in Syria. Fighting this war with special operations forces and airpower, along with the Kurds and the Iraqi Army, is getting the job done.'

Arnie said, 'I agree, but if ISIS targets our bases in Europe or, God forbid, in the US, then you'll get hit from the right to do more, and to do it faster. You'll get hit from the left as well, who see it as an opening, although they've got nothing to fill it with.'

Jack nodded. 'I believe in our policy. The price of my belief is taking those hits.' The President took a moment to look out the window down at Iowa as it slipped slowly by. He fought the anger welling inside him, born from the frustration that he could not fight that which he did not understand, and so far no one had been able to make sense of the seemingly random scope of the new threats to his nation. It was as if a cancer had crept in, slowly at first, but metastasizing and growing in speed.

He worried that Sigonella was just the next phase of the sickness, and if he and his people didn't get a handle on this soon, this cancer would spread uncontrollably. Knowing that Musa al-Matari was somewhere out there, in play, made him wonder if Iowa itself could be the next front line in this fight.

24

Jack Ryan, Jr, had arrived to work early this morning for the team run, and like the day before, he was quiet and reserved around the others. His mind was still on Indonesia and everything that had happened there, and what had happened *because* of everything that had happened there.

Midas ran along next to him for a while and tried to get a conversation started. The ex-Delta operator was several years older than Jack, but Jack had no problem seeing the man was obviously in peak physical condition, considering how he could run multiple eight-minute miles back-to-back and still keep up a conversation that made him sound like he was chatting over cocktails in a hotel lounge.

But Jack wasn't in a chatty mood. His mind was on what he saw as his responsibility for the woman he'd never met who died alone and horribly in Minsk.

Jack barely paid attention to Midas, and finally Midas pushed ahead and ran on alone.

After morning PT, Jack showered and went into his office, where he started going through some e-mails while keeping an eye on the news out of Italy this morning. Of course he experienced all the anger and sadness most Americans felt when learning about this attack, but on top of this he couldn't help thinking about what his father had said about the rash of leaks of unknown nature going on at the moment, and the possibility that one of these had led to the death of Jennifer Kincaid. Still, Jack had no inside information about the events at

Sigonella; and though the attack on the US Navy personnel was being reported as a terrorist incident, CNN had not reported that anyone had been specifically targeted. Instead, the reports so far had all framed it as if anti-American terrorists had shot up and blown up some rental property near the base, making the reasonable assumption they might kill some Americans in the process.

At eight-thirty a.m. Jack was called into Gerry Hendley's office, where he found Gerry waiting with a small tray of coffee, pastries, and fresh fruit. Also present and sitting at the table across from Hendley's desk was the IT director for The Campus, Gavin Biery. Gavin was a portly and rumpled man approaching sixty, and he was known around the office for never passing a box of donuts without picking one out, so Jack was surprised to see him with a bottle of water and a half-eaten orange in front of him for today's breakfast-time meeting.

Jack said nothing, he just raised an eyebrow as he poured himself a cup of black coffee.

Gavin, however, was a perceptive guy. 'It's a diet, Ryan. Not all of us have four hours a day to work out.'

It was true Ryan was in great shape, and he worked out regularly, but he'd never worked out four hours in a single day in his life, and he didn't bother to point out to Gavin that he hadn't had time to go to the gym all week. Instead, he replied, 'Good for you, Gav. I want you to live for ever.'

'Only because I'm the guy who solves all your technological problems, of which you have many.'

Jack sat down. 'Actually, it's your great interpersonal skills that I'd miss most.'

Gerry Hendley had the TV on his wall tuned to CNN, and the daytime live feed out of Sigonella showed a smoldering house with a dozen emergency vehicles parked down the street in front of it. The sound was muted, but the chyron at the bottom of the screen read: TWELVE DEAD, FIVE INJURED IN US NAVY ATTACK. Gerry and Gavin had been looking at it while they waited for Jack, but now Gerry turned away, picked up his coffee, and moved over to the table, where he sat down with the two men.

'Gavin, Jack asked me yesterday to reach out to the DNI and offer our help in locating some sort of security breach in the US government. I spoke with Mary Pat Foley last night and offered any assistance with the analytics in the search for whatever leak was responsible for the horrible exposure and murder of Jennifer Kincaid.'

Gavin had been told of the events in Indonesia and the tragic fallout of those events.

'What did Foley say?' Gavin asked, picking at his orange.

'She's agreed to bring us into this informally.'

Jack squeezed his fists in satisfaction. 'That's great, Gerry. Thank you.'

Gavin Biery added, 'It sounds like an interesting puzzle. But what do you mean, informally?'

'There are those at NSA and other places who know what our analysts have pulled off in the past.' When Gavin raised an eyebrow, Gerry clarified quickly, 'Not just our analysts, our tech side as well. That thing that happened with China a few years back, specifically.'

Gavin nodded. 'Yes, I sort of saved the world on that one, didn't I?'

'You did,' Jack said quickly. 'You saved us all. Gerry, you were saying?'

'Dan Murray is having a package of details sent over regarding the widespread intelligence leak that has come to light in the past couple of weeks. It should be on our server by now. You guys can see all the data they have on it. If you happen to find something, we'll let Murray or Foley know.'

Gavin Biery said, 'You told me about the thing involving the poor CIA officer in Minsk. But what's the scope of the breach?'

'From what I heard from Mary Pat, at this point, nobody knows how deep and wide this goes. They are getting burned by new compromises every couple of days.'

Gavin asked, 'Could this, in some way, be related to that thing the Chinese did a couple of years ago? Remember, they got onto JWICS.' Early in President Ryan's latest term, Chinese computer hackers accessed intel from the US intelligence community's Joint Worldwide Intelligence Communications System. It had compromised communications between America's spies and created a brief moment of panic around the IC. Fortunately for all, The Campus, led by MIT-trained genius Gavin Biery, had located the culprit of the hack and ended the crisis.

Gerry said, 'That was the first question I asked. Mary Pat said this situation couldn't possibly be related to that intrusion. This breach has compromised people at DoJ, the State Department, the US Navy, and the CIA. Most of them are men and women with identities that would have no reason to be transmitted in JWICS comms.'

Jack said, 'How could it just be one breach, then? All those branches and services you mentioned. They don't pass classified intel on the same network. On top of that, those different networks have to be viewed in SCIFs.' A SCIF was a Sensitive Compartmented Information Facility, a secure location designated for the storage and processing of classified information.

Gavin said nothing, which was a surprise to Jack, because

he always seemed to be ready with some sort of an answer. The man was brilliant, he was arguably the most important person in the entire Campus, and he'd be the first to let others know.

Gerry noticed Gavin looking off into space. 'Gavin, is something wrong?'

'Just processing Ryan's question. I'd like to look at the specs of this leak, or at least what the DoJ has managed to discern from the compromises you mentioned. Jack and I will put our heads together and try to work out how the intel was obtained. How many cases are we going to be looking at?'

'DoJ isn't even certain of that. There is the Kincaid incident, plus the FBI officers who first responded to Jakarta in response to it, a CIA officer detained in Iran, and a US Navy commander targeted with what looks like specific information, but it might not have been anything classified.'

Jack said, 'So either three or four.'

'That they know of. These are the incidents that have come to light in the past couple of weeks, but there could have been others, or there yet might be more to this.'

As he said this, Gerry's secretary's voice came over his phone's speaker. 'Director Hendley? AG Murray for you.'

The director of The Campus knew the attorney general was one of the busiest people in the world this morning, so he snatched the phone off the cradle quickly. 'Hi, Dan.'

Jack and Gavin looked on while Gerry listened to his caller for a few moments.

He said, 'Yes, I saw it.' Then, 'How certain are you?'

When he hung up the phone a minute later, he looked to the two men in front of him. 'Sigonella, Italy, this morning. The terrorists had access to specific intelligence regarding their targets. Dan says this might be part of the same ongoing and unknown intelligence leak.'

Gavin mumbled, 'The hits just keep on coming.'

'I guess we'd better get started,' Jack said.

Gerry looked at Jack now. 'I know this is very personal to you, because of what happened after Jakarta the other day.'

Jack nodded. 'It *is* personal. And that will help me focus on it. It won't be a distraction to my work.'

Gerry looked him over a few seconds. 'That's all I wanted to hear. Thank you both. Let me know if you need anything at all from me. One call to Dan or Mary Pat or Jay, and I might be able to get you more information or resources.'

Hours later, Jack and Gavin were deeply engrossed in the intel sent over from DoJ on their secure laptops. They were seated on opposite sides of a long table in a third-floor conference room, and did little more than read through what was known about each incident and what had been done to date to find out how the information on the victims might have been obtained by bad actors.

Early on they decided to split their evaluation and analysis. Gavin would focus on the work that had been done in the countercyber realm, digging into the investigation to date on possible hacks or unauthorized data access that might involve all the compromised parties.

Jack, on the other hand, focused his attention on all non-cyber-related investigation avenues. Human spies, insider threats, unauthorized sharing of intelligence through friendly liaison relationships the US intel community had with other nations, anything that might have been either accidental or deliberate that could have put these targeted men and women's names out into the open.

As he read through the incidents again, Jack tried to figure out just what had to be known about each person involved in order to make them a target. He found this the more interesting part of the problem. It seemed to him that someone had worked very hard to tailor the intelligence to the targeting of these specific individuals.

The Scott Hagen incident was the first, and then a CIA NOC officer who had been arrested in Iran after entering the country.

The Iranians had claimed on state-run TV that they had proof the man's name was Collier and that he had been in the American spy service for eleven years. The CIA had discerned, through sources and methods not shared in the files sent to The Campus, that the Iranians had used a fingerprint reader to determine Stuart Collier worked for the CIA.

This was curious to Ryan. He couldn't imagine any accidental scenario where a CIA officer's fingerprint was exposed in a way Iran might get hold of it.

As he and Gavin toiled through the afternoon, Jack sent some queries to analysts in-house, and Gavin reached out to some other personnel in his information technology section.

On Gavin's side of the equation, he learned the work the NSA had done evaluating the chance that some classified network had been breached was preliminary; they'd been looking into this as a potential intelligence breach for only a few days, but so far they'd found no evidence of new, successful cyberattacks on the US government that could have led to this information getting out.

The two men took a lunch break in the midafternoon. Gavin picked at a salad he'd brought from home, while Jack ate a grilled chicken sandwich ordered in from a nearby deli.

While they ate Jack bounced what he'd learned off the older man. 'The US intel community, or at least those members looking into this compromise, seem to think the leak is one person who knew all the people burned by the leak.'

Gavin said, 'Highly unlikely.'

Jack was prepared for the pushback. Gavin was a computer guy, so Jack felt sure from the beginning Gavin would assume this was some sort of a computer leak. 'Mary Pat says NSA has run a security review on all networks run by the agencies involved and they found nothing amiss. Also, the fact that many different groups seem to be benefiting from the breach leads the government to the belief this isn't one nation stealing information. The few nations with the potential know-how to break into US networks aren't the type to share intel across so broad a spectrum. That makes it look, to them anyway, like there is a government mole who is selling off this intel to multiple parties.'

Gavin said, 'NSA did a review and found no hints of a breach, so they have effectively eliminated the possibility this has been done via a hack. They're digging deeper, but their preliminary findings are sending everyone except for a few eggheads at NSA off looking in other directions.' Gavin shook his head. 'I still believe this was cyberespionage of some sort. The fact they haven't detected a data compromise doesn't mean there wasn't a data compromise.'

Jack was worried Gavin was too dug in to his theory, but he didn't press any further. The last thing he needed was to entrench the Campus IT director further to one side of this or another. Good analytical thinking required an open mind, and Jack wasn't at the stage where he could draw any tight conclusions and close his mind off enough to argue.

*

Four hours of nonstop reading and working later, Jack rubbed his eyes and turned away from his laptop, ready to ask Gavin if he wanted to go out to grab dinner together and then come back and work into the evening. But when Jack looked across the table he found the big man looking right back at Ryan with a grin on his face.

'Umm . . . you okay, Gav?'

Gavin answered the question with little hesitation. 'I have a theory.'

'Let's hear it.'

'E-QIP.'

Jack had no idea what the hell that meant. 'What's e-QIP?'

Gavin's excitement was obvious in his voice. 'It's the government database that houses all applications for security clearance. The SF-86. Doesn't matter if you're Army, DNI, NSA, Department of Commerce, FBI . . . a contractor designing a new dump truck for the Air Force. *Anybody* who has applied for a security clearance has filled out the SF-86, a super-long questionnaire, one hundred twenty some-odd pages. All that data is housed in one database. If you are telling me a bunch of different government types from across all agencies and military branches have been compromised, I'll tell you to look right there.'

Jack thought it over. 'You are saying to find the commonality, you have to go back to the first thing these compromised parties did to become part of the classified world? To their original application for classified access?'

Gavin nodded. 'That's it. After the initial application for classified access, their subsequent information would have been moved to the issuing authority. The Department of Defense, DoJ, Department of State, or wherever. But the first file created for anyone entering the classified-access realm is all kept at the same place.'

Jack asked, 'Okay, who manages e-QIP?'

'The Office of Personnel Management.'

The younger Ryan thought it over for a few seconds. 'I like your thought process, Gavin, but you can't seriously think nobody at NSA or DIA or CIA has come up with and tested this theory yet.'

'Sure, they thought of it, then they checked to see if e-QIP got hacked. When they didn't find evidence of it, the investigators moved on.'

'But you're certain they missed something.'

'I'm certain of this. There is no other linkage between those involved, which means, yeah, I'm certain they missed something. It happens.'

'What about the theory that an individual in the government had all this intel on different people, a mole? Just because there are a lot of different agencies and branches represented in this, that doesn't rule out a mole. Take Chavez, for example. He knows everybody. You could bring him in here right now and he could give the name of a CIA NOC, a SEAL Team assaulter, a Department of Commerce investigator, an Air Force fighter pilot, and twenty-five other men and women with classified access.'

Gavin shook his head. 'This is a data breach, I'd bet my reputation on it. This isn't one guy spilling the beans on his buddies working in government.'

Jack said, 'I'm not saying I'm on board with your theory, but let's say you're right. What country has the skills to get into the OPM network?'

Gavin really thought this one over for a long time. 'It's not what we've seen from the Chinese. The Russian government, either. Those would be the ones who could most easily break into OPM unnoticed, but they aren't the ones involved in this attack.'

Jack said, 'I agree with that. Russia could be passing out tidbits of pilfered intel to Iran. China could be passing out tidbits of pilfered info to the North Koreans. But neither of them are going to be handing targeting intel of a US base in Italy over to ISIS. You could almost think that China might do it to screw with us domestically, but the risk versus reward just isn't there. They'd have to know the reaction we'd have if we found out this was going on.'

Gavin said, 'I'm going to try to narrow down the hunt for the culprit by reverse-engineering the problem. Give me some time to try to understand what it would take to get into the OPM's e-QIP database. When I figure out how someone got in, I'll look for the hallmarks of the attack that will give me a better idea of who might be involved. It will give us a smaller subset of villains to look for.'

Jack said, 'Okay . . . but that's your wheelhouse, not mine. What can I do to help?'

Gavin looked back down to his laptop. 'I'm gonna be here awhile. You could go find me something to eat. Nothing too heavy . . .'

Jack laughed a little. 'Two questions: Who are you, and what have you done with Gavin?'

Gavin Biery just raised his eyes from his computer.

Jack said, 'Never mind. One kale salad, coming up.'

'I'm not a vegan, Jack, I'm just trying to cut back a bit. Don't kill me.'

Jack stood and headed for the door. 'You just work. I'll worry about dinner.'

25

Abu Musa al-Matari had spent the early morning watching the news out of Sicily on the television in the living room of his safe house, a brownstone on North Winchester Avenue in the Lincoln Square neighborhood of Chicago. Algiers and Tripoli sat with him, along with Rahim, the thirty-four-year-old leader of the Chicago cell.

The other cell members were all out in the city, buying items such as flashlights, phones, extra food and water, fertilizer and nails to build improvised explosives, and medical gear. It was busywork for the team, but al-Matari had nothing for them to do.

Although the others in the safe house celebrated the attack in Sicily, chanting '*Allahu Akbar*' with each new revelation about the death toll or image of the damage, quietly al-Matari was fuming. He knew this was the type of intelligence the Saudi had promised him, and the Saudi spoke nothing of a similar operation going on in Europe in concordance with the American attacks. This was important information for the operatives on the ground here in the US, and the Saudi seemed to be playing favorites by handing out intelligence to whomever he had operating in Europe before al-Matari had even been given his first target.

The Yemeni then spent the day trying to reach his contact, the man he knew only as the Saudi. Al-Matari and each of his cell members had loaded the application Silent Phone onto their smartphones, and with this app they could communicate via end-to-end encryption, using either instant messaging or voice calls, and they could also send files to one another.

Al-Matari, however, was the only one in America who had access to the Saudi, in theory anyway. And he'd been trying unsuccessfully to reach his shadowy benefactor all day long.

For some reason the Saudi wasn't returning al-Matari's messages or calls. With each passing hour, time where al-Matari learned more and more about the attack in Sicily from the local news while the man who was supposed to send him his attack orders here in America remained non-responsive, the Yemeni's anger grew. He knew the Sicilian attack was an Islamic State action – they'd proven it with social media posts of the attackers setting off from Syria – and even from the small bits of information he could glean from the twenty-four-hour news networks he could tell it had all the hallmarks of a targeted act, using specific intelligence on the whereabouts and histories of the victims, *exactly* as he had been promised.

Finally, at ten p.m. Chicago time, he looked down at his phone and saw he had a new message from the Saudi instructing al-Matari to call. He immediately stepped into his private quarters on the second floor of the safe house and dialed the man's number. After taking a few seconds for the end-to-end encryption to be established, the Saudi answered.

'I received ten calls and messages from you. I am a busy man. What is it that cannot wait?'

'I see you are busy. Busy in Italy. You should have told me there would be attacks in Europe.'

The Saudi showed no contrition at all. 'You have several

cells under you, but you are just one part of the international operations of the caliphate. No one promised you full-scope knowledge of all worldwide operations.'

'Listen to you. You aren't even a member of the Islamic State.'

'Don't doubt my loyalty, or my resolve, brother.'

Al-Matari didn't trust this Saudi one bit. He was about to snap back a retort when the man spoke again.

'Anyway, you should be glad the Americans have other places to focus their attention.'

'Well, I am *not* glad. I am here, my operatives are ready, and each day we wait to begin is a further threat to the security of our operation. You promised me targets!'

'And you shall have them.'

'When?'

The Saudi sighed, then said, 'I understand your concern, but I have been very busy with other important affairs. Give me one more day. I will have something for you then.'

Al-Matari was not going to be led around by the nose by this man. 'Perhaps I should begin choosing alternative targets.'

The Saudi shouted into the phone now. 'One day! Do nothing for one day!'

The Yemeni in the Chicago brownstone replied, 'If I don't hear from you in twenty-four hours, if you don't have operations for my teams, then I will begin without your intelligence.' Musa al-Matari disconnected the cell, his hands shaking. He wasn't sure if it was fury at the Saudi or the passion he felt to start his work.

More than 7,000 miles away, Sami bin Rashid looked at the dead phone in his hand, then out the window to his office at the Dubai skyline.

'*Waa faqri,*' he said. Damn it.

It was obvious al-Matari thought the Saudi was holding out on him, but the truth of the matter was that bin Rashid's contact, the man who had promised to pass him intel on American military and intelligence targets inside America, was holding out on bin Rashid. Yes, he'd passed on the intelligence about Sigonella air base, and a few more European-based targets, and these bin Rashid sent on to ISIS's Foreign Intelligence Bureau. Most all of their operations against the West had been in Europe, and bin Rashid knew enough about their organization to know that the head of ISIS's FIB himself was born in France to Tunisian parents and raised in Paris. Clearly from yesterday's news, active European cells had been called in to execute the Sicilian attack, but Sami bin Rashid had no command and control over this operation at all.

He wasn't Foreign Intelligence Bureau of ISIS – as al-Matari had said, he wasn't even ISIS.

What he was, however, was the guy with the money and the intelligence to craft the American operation. Or, at least, that was how he had sold himself.

But up till now he had failed to come through, and the reason bin Rashid did not have the targets was also the reason he was not forthcoming to al-Matari about the delay.

The bastard who did claim to have the real-time targeting intelligence was putting more money on American-based packages. He'd sold the intel on a Navy pilot in Italy, and on other men and women in and around other bases in Europe involved in the attacks on ISIS, but he'd recently doubled his fee for American intelligence inside America, citing his own security. It was a ridiculous claim. The man had spent the past four months promising to Sami bin Rashid to deliver that which he now refused to deliver, and all the while he knew his security was just as good, or just as lax, as he made it for himself.

Bin Rashid knew this was just a shakedown for more money; the man was an infidel with no god, and this was to be expected. But bin Rashid had worked on the outskirts of the business and intelligence worlds for his whole career, and knew he needed to push back against the greed. He had been in the game long enough to know that acquiescing to a source's demands often only led to more demands, and he'd argued more than once with the unknown man he knew of solely by his code name, INFORMER. But now time was running out. Al-Matari was a strong-willed man, of this bin Rashid had no doubt. If he didn't get targets immediately, the man staged in the Chicago safe house would start attacking sites across America, and he and his cells would be lost without maximizing their impact while alive and operational. Bin Rashid knew the only way America would come to the Middle East in massive numbers would be if the President of the United States had his back to the wall with his own military and intel leaders, and this would happen only with a real military and intelligence threat.

Bin Rashid needed targets, and he needed them right now. He'd ask Riyadh for the approval to pay INFORMER what he wanted, and he'd make it clear to the man with all the information that there would be no more negotiations.

Four hours later Sami bin Rashid finally had his approval from the intelligence director of Saudi Arabia, the money had been moved into covert Dubai accounts, and bin Rashid was ready to purchase quality intelligence.

Now the Saudi in Dubai held his phone to his ear and waited while a secure connection was established between himself and INFORMER. To his relief, the call was answered quickly.

INFORMER, whoever he was, spoke English with some sort of an accent that bin Rashid did not have the ability to discern. He wondered if the man was Russian, but that was one hundred percent conjecture.

INFORMER said, 'Good day, my friend. How may I be of service?'

The Saudi had spoken to INFORMER a few times over the phone, and now, as always, he found the man light-hearted and almost charming, as if everything was calm and going according to plan, no matter the topic at hand.

Bin Rashid's patience had worn through, though, so he did not repay the kind tone with friendliness of his own.

He said, 'I need specifics from you. I need you to provide what you promised, and I need you to do it now.'

INFORMER said, 'I am ready to begin funneling you information. But as I have made clear many times, I can well imagine what you are doing with this information, and this will make me one of the most hunted men in the world.'

'We have had this discussion before. You are safe. I won't be connected to the end users of this information. And I don't know you, how to get to you, or anything about you. Obviously you will be even more removed than I am. I just need information, and I need you to not concern yourself with whatever news you hear, news you might somehow think related to the intelligence you sold me.'

INFORMER replied, 'Again, I am ready to proceed, but as I mentioned in my message to you last week, the price has doubled. You can take it or you can leave it. But as I am certain you have had time to prepare things on your end to exploit the information, I imagine you have already gone to great lengths and great expense to move your assets into place. I think you have to agree that even at my new terms, you have no suitable option but to go forward.'

Bin Rashid wanted to reach through his phone, grab the other man by the throat, and rip it out. This shakedown had been planned from the beginning, he had no doubt. This bastard had bin Rashid on the hook, and now he was reeling him in. Every fiber of Sami bin Rashid's being was telling him to tell this man to take his information and shove it up his ass, but he could not do that. He had to acquiesce.

He controlled his breathing, and said, 'I accept your terms, assuming you can give me the latest updated targeting information today.'

INFORMER did not hesitate. 'Of course I can. You simply place an order on my dark website, just as we discussed.'

Sami bin Rashid opened the page on his computer. While he did this, INFORMER said, 'So to recap, my terms are as follows: packages on field intelligence operatives are $500,000, as are military officers over the rank of major. Officers below the rank of major, or intelligence analysts or support personnel, are $250,000. Any general, admiral, intelligence community executive or the like will cost you one million dollars. Special operations military enlisted personnel are $250,000, unless they belong to Joint Special Operations Command. This is the US Naval Special Warfare Development Group, otherwise known as SEAL Team Six, or the Army's Delta Force. Targeting packages for these elite enlistees will cost $500,000.'

They then spent the next few minutes discussing what sorts of targets were available with the latest updates on their whereabouts, and then Sami bin Rashid, for all intents and purposes, placed an order on the e-commerce webpage on INFORMER's site.

Bin Rashid then transferred Bitcoin to INFORMER's dark web address while the two men were on the phone. Five million dollars, for a total of one dozen targets, many of them lower-tier individuals. The Saudi knew his fight in America would cost him an average of one million dollars a day, at least, plus significant operating expenses from al-Matari's cell, but if the end result meant America came to Iraq with boots on the ground, pushed back the Iranian hordes encroaching toward the south, ended pro-Iranian Alawite rule in Syria, and brought the price of oil back up to a level that would protect Saudi Arabian leadership's domestic security . . . well, then, Sami bin Rashid would have done his job, and the King would reward him for life.

A moment later INFORMER confirmed he received the money, and he told his customer to watch his mailbox in the dark web portal on his computer, and to wait for the files to come through.

True to his word, INFORMER's files began popping up, one by one. While bin Rashid clicked on the attachments, a smile grew inside his trim gray beard.

First, the name, the address, and a photograph of a woman. A map of the area around where the woman lived. A CV of her work with the Defense Intelligence Agency, including foreign and domestic postings that would have her involved in the American campaign in the Middle East. Real-time intel about her daily commute, including the house where she would be watering the plants and checking the mail all week for a friend.

Incredible, bin Rashid thought to himself. *Where the hell is this coming from?*

The next file was all necessary targeting info on a recently retired senior CIA operations officer, who continued to work on a contract basis in the intelligence field. He spoke Arabic, trained others in tradecraft, counterintelligence, and counterterrorism, and consulted on security affairs at a pro-Christian DC think tank.

The file after this was of a former Navy SEAL with a high profile and a record of missions against Al-Qaeda and the Islamic State. At first bin Rashid didn't understand why this man had been selected by INFORMER, but after skimming down through the dossier, a rare smile formed on bin Rashid's lips, and softly, to himself, he said, 'Yes. Perfect.'

One by one bin Rashid went down the list of a dozen targets. These weren't admirals or generals or top operatives of the CIA, but he wanted Musa al-Matari's cells to begin their actions with less well-protected victims. The leaders of America's military and intelligence would be worthy targets, of course, but at the outset bin Rashid wanted victories for al-Matari, lower risk for moderate reward. He wanted . . . he *needed* new recruits to flock to the cause, and he knew this would happen only if the operation registered some early wins.

He called INFORMER back after reading through the last of the dozen files.

The man with the curious accent said, 'Hello, friend. I trust you are satisfied with the products I sent you.'

Bin Rashid replied, 'How certain are you of this . . . this information?'

An audible sigh over the line. 'This is what I do. As you see, all the targeting data is completely up to date. Some of the information I updated this very afternoon.'

'I noted that, yes. When will I get more? More like these?'

'When you pay for more. That's how all this works.'

'I know that. I mean to ask . . . are you prepared with more? Of this quality, or perhaps of higher-quality targets?'

'There are an unlimited number of products I can sell you. They all will be different, some perhaps you will find more . . . *interesting* than others. Some you will unquestionably find more expensive than others. The limit to this is your ability to process your way through the targets and your ability to pay.'

The Saudi understood that by 'process,' INFORMER meant kill. It was clear to bin Rashid that INFORMER knew he was providing targets for assassination. But it was also clear to bin Rashid that INFORMER had already seen what happened in Italy, so the man clearly did not possess a weak stomach.

'Very well,' bin Rashid said. 'I will wire additional funds to the account next week, enough for another dozen files. When I am ready for more, perhaps in another week's time, I will be in touch. You have done good work.'

INFORMER said, 'I am happy that you are happy, my friend. I wish you much success with your endeavors.'

Twelve hours later, and just before the twenty-four-hour deadline he'd given the Saudi to provide him with the intelligence he needed to open with his waves of attacks on America, Abu Musa al-Matari sat in his office in his Chicago safe house and read carefully over a batch of dossiers sent to him via Silent Phone. Intelligence officers, both current and former, men and women employed in the fight against the Islamic State. There was a file on a US Special Forces operator in North Carolina, a bar frequented by a Navy SEAL platoon in Virginia Beach, along with photos of four of the men and their bios.

There was no other way to look at it; this was incredible material. He'd successfully had people killed in foreign lands with one-twentieth of the information he was being provided with here.

He focused on the dossier of a former Navy SEAL who had come to prominence in the past few years due to a book he had written and several television appearances he'd made chronicling his days in the teams.

Looking through the dossiers, and then looking through Google on his laptop, al-Matari realized this man had become an actual American celebrity.

The man was staying for a month at a five-star hotel in Los Angeles, overseeing the shooting of a film about his exploits on a raid in Libya against the ISIS affiliate Ansar al-Sharia.

Al-Matari knew instantly that this would be a perfect target for the Santa Clara cell. They were currently based in San Francisco, but could send a couple of cell members down to L.A. tomorrow, to be ready to act the next day. A retired military man moving between a film set and his hotel sounded like a ridiculously easy mark, and the man's prominence here in America would give al-Matari a large return on the relatively low risk to his mission.

In the next dossier he found an immediate operation for a couple of members of the Fairfax cell and then, a few files into his reading, he found another worthy target located within a day's drive of Detroit.

With a lot of moving his men and women around the map of the United States, there were immediate, attainable targets for every last one of his cells. He decided he would keep Chicago out of the first round of activity. He needed them to serve as his protection force, to keep his safe house secure, and to continue providing Algiers and Tripoli with the raw materials for explosives they were constructing for the teams.

But the other four would go to work now.

He decided, after some time looking at his cleanskins and the locations of the targets on the map, that the biggest move of the first wave of attacks would be the Detroit cell. He'd need a few of them, three or four to be safe, to get on the road to the DC area, because he'd have the Fairfax team working on two other missions in that part of the country.

After al-Matari had decided on his initial victims and those assigned to terminate them, he picked up his mobile and opened Silent Phone, which allowed him to send files to the secure mobile devices held by each of the other cells, and he went to work. He delivered individual targeting packages and orders to Fairfax, to Santa Clara, to Detroit, and to Atlanta, along with orders to each unit leader to choose the right number and mix of cell members for each job. They would act at first opportunity, and they were to communicate with him if they had any questions, concerns, or information he might need.

At the end of each message, he typed in additional orders. Just before beginning each mission, al-Matari ordered the operators on scene to broadcast live video of the action through another app that allowed end-to-end encrypted live streaming. He told his leaders he wasn't expecting Hollywood-level films, but he wanted some record of the events so that the Global Islamic Media Front, the propaganda arm of ISIS, could use the clips to whip up the frenzy of excitement for the operations here in America.

Abu Musa al-Matari did not mention any other reason that he wanted to see a live broadcast of each operation. But there was a second reason, and it was much more important than the first. He'd keep that to himself, for now, and with luck, none of his twenty-seven cell members would ever need to know that the suicide vests they wore could be command-detonated by al-Matari if a cell member was captured and decided against detonating the vest themselves. This would ensure a higher body count when first responders came upon a scene, as well as an additional level of operational security for the mission.

The twenty-seven cleanskins should have had enough fervor for the cause to martyr themselves, but if they hesitated for an instant, al-Matari would do it for them from afar.

His plan in America did not allow for any of his people to be taken alive.

26

Barbara Pineda and her burgundy Toyota Camry were stuck in traffic, par for the course on a workday afternoon.

As a civilian who worked at Joint Base Anacostia-Bolling, in the southeastern part of the District, she knew that every commute at the end of the day involved at least a half-hour of gridlock. If there had been no traffic, the thirty-one-year-old would already be home in Vienna, Virginia, leisurely getting ready to go out on a date with the new man in her life, a firefighter named Steve she had met at church.

Instead, this afternoon would be exactly like all others during the workweek when she had important plans. She'd screech onto her driveway late, dash from her car through her front door, fling off her business attire, and take the stairs three at a time to her bedroom in her underwear. There she would dress, rush into her bathroom to touch up her makeup, and come downstairs only at the last moment, if not a few minutes after, when Steve arrived to pick her up.

And on top of all this, this afternoon she had an extra stop to make on the way home.

Barbara was an employee of the Defense Intelligence Agency, where she served as an all-source intelligence analyst in the Directorate for Analysis. Before this she had served eight years in Army intel, joining up after high school, and earning both her bachelor's and master's degrees online at American Military University while enlisted. She'd done a significant amount of her coursework while serving in war zones, and now that she was out of the Army, working as a civilian at DIA provided her a smooth transition from a decade of near-constant deployments.

During her time in the Army she served in Afghanistan or Iraq, or else she was in training or supporting others deployed in the Middle East. Now she spent her days looking over intelligence matters relating to the US's fight with ISIS, a perfect match for the important but niche skill set she'd learned in the Army.

Barbara was happy enough with her work. She knew she probably wasn't going to change the world, but she sure as hell was doing her part for her nation, even at her relatively young age.

Still fifteen minutes from home, she pulled off the 495 and into the suburb of Falls Church, happy to be on the more open residential roads and out of the bumper-to-bumper traffic. She parked on the small driveway of an attractive zero-lot two-story house, climbed out with her purse, and fumbled for the keys.

An old Army friend of Barbara's who now worked in pharmaceuticals lived here, but she was away on vacation at Disney World with her family, and Barbara had offered to swing by every afternoon after work to water the plants, to feed the kids' hamster, and to flip on and off a couple of lights to make the place look as lived in as possible.

As she headed up the drive she remembered she also needed to check the mail, so she turned around and headed back down the little driveway, still trying to find the right key for the front door.

A neighbor walking her dog on the sidewalk across the street waved to her, and Barbara waved back as she pulled down the door to the mailbox.

And as she did this Barbara Pineda's world erupted in a flash of bright light and earsplitting noise.

The explosion had been command-detonated, meaning Fairfax cell members Ghazi and Husam were parked right up the street, close enough to see Barbara at the mailbox. They'd talked at length about waiting until she took the four-pound package containing the bomb out of the mailbox, or else just pressing send on their phone, activating the detonator's wireless number, the instant she opened the mailbox door. They finally decided on the latter, thinking the force of the blast might be heightened and therefore penetrate deeper into the woman's body from the mailbox, as if shot out of the barrel of a gun.

It was the theory of laymen with no understanding of their powerful weapon. The mailbox utterly disintegrated in the explosion, so there was no barrel for the explosion to travel down. But it didn't matter. The bomb had been constructed by Tripoli in the back of the SUV while traveling from Georgia to Virginia for the dropoff of the weapons, and it contained two and a half pounds of store-bought galvanized two-inch nails. When the plastic explosive detonated, it sent the nails in all directions, along with the shock wave of the explosion, large chunks of shrapnel from the aluminum mailbox, and even bits of the brick post. Much of the shrapnel and shock wave slammed into the chest and face of Barbara Pineda.

The thirty-one-year-old woman staggered two steps back into the street, and then she fell onto her side, dropping her purse and the keys as she collapsed, still enveloped inside the massive cloud of smoke.

The woman walking her dog across the street fell to the ground herself, half propelled back by the detonation and half affected by the incredible sound made by the explosion.

When she looked back in the direction of the noise, she saw the woman by the mailbox rolling onto her back, her chest heaving up and down rapidly, and her face all but gone.

Ghazi had pressed the button on his phone that triggered the bomb, and Husam had held his phone on the scene, his camera zoomed in to provide a distant but clear moving image of the incident. The man they called Mohammed had been watching in real time, and he congratulated the men as they drove out of the neighborhood slowly and carefully, and headed back toward their safe house in Fairfax.

They had placed the bomb here instead of at Pineda's home because the targeting data they received just hours before said she would come here each afternoon to check the mailbox, and Pineda's condo had tiny mail slots, meaning they wouldn't have been able to use the device there.

The two men had no idea who was providing the intelligence they used. They assumed their leader, the man they knew only as Mohammed, had teams of spies working in the area.

The cell had discussed simply shooting the woman the moment she pulled into her driveway, but cell leader David Hembrick and Abu Musa al-Matari agreed that the information about the mailboxes gave them the opportunity to use the relatively low-risk remote-explosive option for their first attack. It was crucial that it worked, that the Fairfax cell remained intact, and although al-Matari didn't say anything to Hembrick on the matter, frankly he was worried Ghazi and Husam would fuck up anything that got too complicated.

The police, fire, and ambulance crews arrived on scene almost simultaneously, but Barbara Pineda had already stopped breathing. She still wore her DIA identification card around her neck, but it was too damaged in the blast to be read. The contents of her purse were retrieved, however, and her name was run through the police system. It took no time at all for homicide detectives to find out that she worked for the Defense Intelligence Agency, but this raised no red flags, because it seemed most likely to detectives in those first hours that the actual homeowners had been the intended recipients of the attack, and not the poor woman who had stopped to pick up mail for her friend.

The bombing made the DC-area news at eleven that night, of course, but Pineda's name and employer were not mentioned. The reporter referred to the victim only as a 'family friend' picking up the mail of the homeowner.

This meant that the first salvo of the Islamic State's attack against the US military and intelligence communities on US soil came and went without any immediate recognition of the importance of the event.

The second salvo came very early the next morning, on the opposite side of the country. This was by design, of course. Al-Matari had spent months discussing his plans with the Islamic State's Foreign Intelligence Bureau, and its crucial public relations division, the Global Islamic Media Front. All his acts were chiefly for the benefit of the GIMF department and their slick propaganda, and both the FIB and the GIMF knew a truly nationwide attack would give them the most impact.

To that end, the team leader of the Santa Clara cell, Kateb, and his wife, Aza, sat in the Starbucks on the corner of Laurel Canyon Boulevard and Riverside Drive in Los Angeles, each with a cup of tea in front of them. They'd arrived in town the night before, and they'd slept in their car in the parking lot of a nearby convenience store, waiting till the coffee shop opened at five-thirty a.m.

At five-forty they entered, ordered their drinks, and sat at a table in the far corner of the room by a glass-door emergency exit. Aza had her back to the entrance and the counter, but Kateb could see everything in the store. She carried a purse and he a small shoulder bag, both of which they put on the floor under the table. Inside both bags, loaded Glock 17 pistols stayed within reach.

The couple said little to each other, but they both checked their phones. Aza just wanted to know the time from minute to minute, but Kateb was connected with the man they knew as Mohammed, on an encrypted link that allowed Mohammed to see real-time through Kateb's camera.

A few men and women on their way to work entered the Starbucks, ordered drinks and food, and left. By six o'clock, however, Aza and Kateb were the only customers in the shop.

At ten after six Kateb saw a large black Cadillac Escalade pull up and park by the front door and a group of five climb out. His dossier from the man he knew as Mohammed told him the Escalade came here every morning, shortly after six, and a man named Todd Braxton would be among the occupants.

Braxton was their target, and while he would not be alone, none of his group should be armed.

Softly he whispered to his young wife. 'They are here. It is almost time.'

Aza began breathing shallowly, a show of stress bordering on panic, but her husband saw in her eyes that she was still in control of her emotions.

She was ready, and he was proud of her.

*

Former US Navy SEAL Todd 'T-Bone' Braxton could have played the lead role in the movie about his life, and this was exactly the point he stressed to his agent every time the two men spoke. It was also a point he had hinted at to the producers of *Blood Canyon*, the actual film being made about his feats of heroism while on operations in Afghanistan, Iraq, and Libya.

But T-Bone's agent didn't have the juice to make it happen, and the producers said the film needed a well-established star.

Braxton knew he could have nailed the role. Hell, he'd *lived* it, minus all the artistic flourishes written into the movie. And he sure looked the part of himself. He possessed the confident attitude, a chiseled jaw, spiked black hair, and tats ringing his muscled biceps.

T-Bone served on SEAL Teams 10 and 3, achieving the rank of petty officer first class before leaving the military to write a book about his exploits. The book had been a best-seller, propelled by his numerous TV appearances and paid speaking engagements, and then a screenwriter friend had turned the book into a screenplay.

The Navy had been supportive of both the book and the film, and Braxton had secured himself an advisory role on the set, which basically meant he went to the studio each day, or on location in the Mojave Desert, where he hung out with the actors and filmmakers, and made sure their gear was squared away before the director yelled 'Action!'

Although he would rather have been the star of the film, Braxton did have to admit that the studio had found a good actor to play him in the lead role. Danny Phillips was relatively well known for a hugely popular cable TV series he'd starred in, and although he was eight years younger than

Todd Braxton, the two men looked like they could have been brothers. Phillips had put on muscle and grown his sideburns into huge muttonchops, just as Braxton normally wore, and Phillips had gone out of his way to wear his ball cap in the same manner Braxton did, even when not shooting.

Braxton and Phillips had become friends over the first two months of filming, but the former SEAL was smart enough to presume that the up-and-coming movie star would move on from this role and they'd probably not be hanging out much after the film wrapped.

The five individuals from the Escalade entered the Starbucks, and immediately Kateb recognized Braxton among the group from his signature sideburns, square jaw, and muscular build. He saw another man, of similar build, in the group, but this man had a clean-shaven face and a short haircut. Along with these two were two women and a big black man with huge muscles.

Four of the five ordered coffee, while the black man stood a few feet away from the others.

Kateb nodded once to Aza and wrote the number 5 on the napkin in front of him with a Bic pen and a shaking hand. She nodded, her back still to the counter and the customers. He then placed his phone on the table, propping it up with the foldout easel attached to the phone's hard plastic case. He positioned it toward the counter and nodded to his wife.

The phone was centered on the group, and it was broadcasting live to Kateb and Aza's ISIS leader, who they only knew was somewhere in America.

Aza reached down between her knees and inside her

purse, wrapped her fingers around the grip of her Glock, while across from her, Kateb reached into his backpack.

T-Bone Braxton drank his coffee black, and he'd done so ever since he was a teenager. Caffeine was a drug that got him going in the morning, nothing more. He didn't want to take the time to dress it up into something pretty before he pumped it into his body.

The twenty-five-year-old actor Danny Phillips, on the other hand, always started his day with a venti soy chai latte, into which he stirred several bags of Sugar In The Raw. Similarly, Danny's two personal assistants, sent everywhere with him by the studio, liked their coffee infused with flavored syrup, sweet and light.

Braxton appreciated that at least Danny's bodyguard, a big man named Paul who always wore a polo shirt that showed off his massive pecs, delts, and arms, arrived at the hotel each morning to pick up Danny and the others with his coffee ready to go in a stainless-steel mug that he kept in the Escalade.

Braxton ordered his simple beverage and stood there while the barista made all the other drinks to order. It had been like this every day for the past couple of weeks while they'd been getting up early for the ninety-minute drive to the set in the Mojave. He didn't know why the hell the lady behind the counter couldn't just draw him a cup of hot coffee and be done with him before she began working on the other concoctions.

He'd almost said something; after a decade of living a life of excellence and effectiveness in the teams, any inefficiency drove T-Bone absolutely ape shit, but today he just stood there with his arms crossed. He had other stuff on his mind to keep him occupied, because this was the day he would make a brief transition from adviser to movie star.

Today was his moment, his close-up. His acting debut. He'd had it written into his contract that he'd get a small action role in the film about him, which he thought seemed kind of dumb, but still, it got him a little shine time and he hoped it would lead to feature roles down the road.

To prepare for his brief time in front of the camera, he'd shaved off his muttonchops the night before; he couldn't very well act in the movie as a Navy SEAL behind the guy playing the Navy SEAL who looked just like him without making at least some obvious cosmetic changes. He worried that the lack of tan where his sideburns normally were would be obvious in the movie, but he'd been assured by the makeup artists that they'd have his face so covered with movie tan and movie battle grit and grime that he needn't worry about his skin tone.

Braxton told himself he'd kick ass on screen today, just as he exceeded all expectations on every challenge he ever faced. That was just who he was, and nothing was more important than his positive mental attitude.

Phillips got his drink first. Braxton figured the barista recognized him from TV, and Phillips had just started stirring sugar into his chai latte when the door opened and another group of four customers entered the coffee shop. One headed toward the restroom, while the others stepped up to the counter.

The former Navy SEAL regarded them for a second; it was second nature for him now to check everyone around him to make sure they weren't a threat, and he'd just told himself there was nothing to see when he heard a sudden shout from the back corner. He'd noted the dark-complexioned couple there when he entered, saw they were fixated on their phones and didn't give them a second thought, so he swiveled around to their table in surprise to see what the commotion was all about.

Before he'd even focused on the couple, he sensed the bodyguard Paul turning to the movement as well.

And then Todd Braxton saw the guns.

The shout he heard was the couple chanting *'Allahu Akbar'* in unison, and now they jerked big black Glocks in the direction of the counter and the eight people standing in front of them.

And then cracks of gunfire filled the room.

The two women who worked for the studio screamed. Danny Phillips stood on wooden legs while Paul ran toward him, and Todd Braxton, who carried only a small folding knife, did the only thing that made sense. He took two steps backward and then hurled himself over the counter, knocking the barista working there to the ground, and he shouted for the others to get to cover.

The gunfire was unrelenting, perhaps no one heard him. All T-Bone knew for sure was that no one followed him over the counter.

Braxton pulled his knife, moved down the counter to the end near the front door, as the pops from the handguns continued to snap off. He told himself he'd jump both of the small attackers from behind as they ran out the door, or if they tried to come around the counter to confront him, he'd be ready to launch at them face-to-face. He knew knife fighting from his training in the teams, though he never really thought he'd employ it in a life-or-death encounter in a Starbucks after he left service.

But then the gunfire stopped as quickly as it started.

The baristas lay cowering behind the counter, and T-Bone could hear the two women from the studio crying out in front of the register. Seconds later an alarm went off.

T-Bone had expected to see the shooters pass near his position when they went out the front door, but the alarm told him they'd pushed out the emergency exit. He rose to his feet, stepped around the counter, and saw that the coast was clear.

He also saw a scene of carnage.

Danny Phillips lay dead, shot six times. Paul wasn't dead, yet, but he'd been shot six times as well, and T-Bone knew enough firsthand about battlefield medicine to know the big man would check out in seconds.

One of the women from the studio had taken a round through the kneecap, and a middle-aged commuter had been shot twice, though he wasn't critically injured.

T-Bone ran to the window and looked out as the two shooters disappeared through a hedge leading to an all-night pharmacy. He thought about giving chase, but decided he needed to stay behind to do his best to keep as many of the injured alive as possible.

Aza and Kateb were both positive they'd succeeded in their mission. Todd Braxton's look was impossible to miss, and both of them targeted him from their first shots. For some reason the former soldier had protection; the big black man had thrown himself between the gunfire and Braxton, but Aza and Kateb just kept shooting, killing both men.

It wouldn't be for another hour that they found out they'd made a mistake. While listening to the radio on their way back to the San Francisco area, they heard that a Hollywood movie star had been killed in Los Angeles, along with his bodyguard, and two others had been injured in the attack.

This news made no sense to them at all, but there was one thing they were sure of immediately: Mohammed would not be pleased.

27

Jack walked into the office at ten after eight in an especially foul mood because he'd missed the team run, scheduled today at five-fifteen. It always was a chore for him to get out of bed in the morning, especially when working late the night before. But he did it almost every day because he knew he always felt better after getting some exercise.

This morning, however, his willpower had completely faltered. He'd stayed up working from home till after midnight, then he'd slept through three alarms, and woke with a start at seven forty-five, with barely time enough to take a quick shower. Then he dressed and walked to work, mad at himself all the way for his show of weakness.

The rest of his morning run group had already exercised, showered, eaten, and begun their workday when Jack passed them on the third floor, gave some tired and gruff greetings, then poured coffee for himself, grabbed a Danish from a box by the pot, and shuffled directly into the conference room.

Clark and his two trainees were on their way out of the building to do some shoot-house work at a private range complex in Leesburg, and Dom and Ding were still writing up after-action reports on Jakarta, putting together as much information for Mary Pat Foley as possible that might help her team identify just who in North Korea had been behind the operation against America.

As soon as Jack passed through the door into the

conference room he was sharing with Gavin, he saw that the older man had beat him to work. This was one last kick in the rear that told him tomorrow he would not sleep through his alarms.

Jack pulled up a chair in front of his work laptop. 'Morning, Gavin.'

Gavin looked at the Danish in Jack's hand. 'You know . . . you should start watching what you eat. You won't be nineteen forever.'

'Not today, Gav. Woke up on the wrong side of the bed.'

'Well . . . I hope that's because a new girl was taking up the right side.'

Jack did not answer for a moment, but finally he just repeated himself. 'Not today, Gav.'

'Okay. Well . . . am I, at least, free to discuss work matters pertaining to this intel leak?'

Jack sipped his coffee, willing the caffeine to take the express route to his bloodstream today. 'Of course you are. Anything new from NSA overnight?'

'Nope, nothing. And that just means they are going to be more sure of themselves that there has been no breach of their data.'

Jack sipped scalding-hot coffee as he looked over his laptop at Gavin Biery. 'But you are not dissuaded by the fact they haven't found anything.'

'Nope.'

'Okay. So . . . how do we find out if the government missed something? How do we know if there was a data breach on the OPM?'

Gavin shrugged. 'We don't. We take it as fact that I'm right, they are wrong, and we go from there.'

Jack almost spit out his coffee. '*What?*'

'It's the old Sherlock Holmes philosophy. Once you eliminate the impossible, whatever remains, no matter how improbable, must be the truth. If the government hasn't found evidence of the intrusion, I won't be able to, either, not from here. Send me over to OPM with carte blanche to tear apart their network, dig through code line by line, and look through every record of every remote access of every transaction that has taken place for the last couple of years. Then, eventually, I'll find you something. But that isn't going to happen, and even if it did, a lot more good people are going to be compromised in the interim. I have no doubt that two weeks from now, two months from now, or two years from now, the federal government will realize they've been breached. But we don't have that kind of time. You have to trust me, and we have to move ahead, fully on board with the theory that some bad actor has access to the full SF-86 data on everyone in the US who has ever applied for classified access.'

'That's nuts, Gavin. *Everyone?* Even if I were to take this giant leap with you that someone got into the OPM without anyone in the government knowing about it, why the leap that *everything* was copied and exfiltrated?'

Gavin replied calmly. 'Because once you are onto the network, once you have admin access and have built yourself a back door, taking all the files is no more complicated than taking a single file. In fact, it's easier to take it all and then sort through it later on. You can't just presume they went to all this trouble and just exfiltrated a small percentage of the data.'

Jack leaned back in his chair. 'How many files are we talking about?'

'The system went online in the early two thousands, but

the OPM went back and put a range of old files online as well. Going back to 1984.' He paused for effect. 'We're talking about well over twenty-five million files.'

Jesus, Gavin.' Jack put his head in his hands. 'Let's hope you're wrong.'

Gavin said, 'Hope all you want. But I'm right.'

Ryan said, 'I've been giving this a lot of thought. Having your old application in the OPM database wouldn't be enough to compromise you, not in the way these events have taken place. Whoever is exploiting this data to make real-time targeting packages has to do a lot more work to connect the dots than just pull names off an application. Just because Joe Blow's name is in e-QIP doesn't mean he works for CIA or FBI. Somebody had to take the raw data from the SF-86 and fill in a thousand blanks.'

Jack pulled up the Commander Scott Hagen incident. 'Take this first guy – Hagen. He's in his mid-forties. His SF-86 has to be twenty years old. You can't tell me there is something in that application that is going to tip off a gunman that Hagen will be eating a burrito at a Mexican restaurant in Princeton on a particular night twenty years later.'

He continued. 'An application for security clearance is a snapshot of that person's life at one point in time. It isn't going to have a tenth of the data on it that the terrorists would need to target these guys. Especially when you are talking about the military and intelligence community. Their application says they want a security clearance, so here is all their info as of the date of the app. It doesn't say they are now a CIA NOC in Minsk undercover with the Russian mob, and they live at a particular address.'

Gavin Biery was already nodding his head. 'Ryan, you are

exactly right, but that only helps us narrow down the culprit. The question we should be asking isn't "Who could steal all this data?" It's "Who could steal all this data *and* also possesses the ability to exploit it?"' He pointed to the monitor on the wall. CNN was playing a story about the attack in Italy the day before. 'This is tier-one targeting information.' Now he pointed to his laptop, with all the cases of intelligence leaks of the past few weeks. 'These, as well. It isn't that somebody knew Scott Hagen and Jennifer Kincaid and Stuart Collier and all the others. It's that they knew Hagen was going to be in New Jersey on this date with his sister at his nephew's soccer tournament, and Kincaid was in Minsk on a CIA op, and a compromise to her husband at State at the embassy in Jakarta. Somebody managed to get fingerprint data to the Iranians and the Indonesians, for Christ sakes! This is high-level shit, Ryan, and it was done through a high-level cyberattack and high-level research and high-level social engineering.'

Jack said, 'Look . . . I'm an analyst. I have to take in all the possibilities. I can't put all my eggs in one basket and work under this unproven assumption of yours that we're dealing with a breach of OPM data. *All* the OPM data.'

Gavin said, 'You can do what you want. But you keep saying that there are a lot of people trying to find who is responsible for all these compromises going on. They are all chasing down leads, testing suppositions, and dissecting each event. I am sure of what I'm doing, and you can work with me. We'll be doing something no one else is doing. If we're wrong . . . well, then, somebody at DoJ or NSA is going to solve this issue. But if we're right, we'll be the only ones with a chance to uncover what is going on, and we can end this disaster before it gets any worse.'

Just then, Jack glanced down at his computer when an instant message from Gerry popped up with an audible ding. He read the message twice, a pain growing in the pit of his stomach.

'It just got worse. Did you hear about that mail bomb yesterday in Falls Church?'

'Yeah. Killed a lady.'

Jack said, 'Gerry says he doesn't know if there is any connection, but the victim was a civilian at the DIA in the Directorate for Analysis. She was working on a task force dealing with Islamic State movements in Iraq.'

'Wait,' Gavin said. 'Nobody thinks ISIS really whacked some DIA working stiff in the burbs of DC, do they?'

Jack looked up at Gavin. 'Who knows? Look at Sigonella. Who saw that coming? If this lady's death is related to that leak we're working, this is probably just the tip of the iceberg.' He clicked on a link to a news article that Gerry included in his message. After he read the name of the street where the attack took place, he said, 'I'm going to go over and take a look.'

The drive to the crime scene was less than twenty minutes from Alexandria, so Jack walked home, climbed in his black BMW 5-Series, and headed off. He pulled up on the scene at ten a.m., meaning he arrived some sixteen hours after the event itself.

While he didn't have the exact address of the bombing, he didn't need it. When he turned onto the street he saw the crime scene tape and a squad car out in front of the house halfway up the block. The mailbox was gone, and the bricks of the post were blackened and chipped. There was some dark charring on the street itself, but the loose debris and blood that he assumed had been there immediately after the incident had been cleaned up.

Jack remained in his BMW. He didn't want the Falls Church police officers recognizing him. With his beard it was a rare occurrence, but it did happen from time to time, and it wasn't worth the risk.

Instead, he pulled to a stop at the end of the block, a hundred yards from the blast site, and he looked on at the two-story home. Using a small pair of binoculars to inspect the area from front to back, he then scanned up and down the now quiet street.

He had just been sent a preliminary FBI report that explained the explosive had been rigged with a detonator wired to a mobile phone. This meant someone had to call and set it off the moment Ms Pineda went to the mailbox. This, of course, indicated that the killer or killers were nearby when it happened.

He wondered if they had parked right here. This was as far back on the street as you could sit on the south side and still have line of sight on the mailbox, so he thought it a safe bet they were either right in this same spot or else parked to the north of where the bomb went off.

Jack had also read in the report that this was not the residence of the woman killed. A friend lived here, and Pineda had simply stopped by to pick up the mail. For this reason the FBI had doubts Pineda was the intended target, but Jack realized anyone going to the trouble to command-detonate a reasonably sophisticated bomb would have some knowledge of what their target looked like, and they would have been looking right at her when making the decision of whether or not to set off the device.

Jack felt near certain the killer or killers had taken out *exactly* the person they'd been after.

But that left one important question. Why not target her up at home? Once he got a good feel for this crime scene, Jack knew he had to drive to where she lived and compare the two locations.

He spent fifteen minutes sitting here, looking around, and in the back of his mind he started to connect this place, this bucolic suburban street, with the events in Jakarta several days earlier, and the event in Minsk, the shooting in Princeton, the arrest of the CIA officer in Iran, and the other horrible scenes he'd spent the last full day studying. It was hard to do. Other than the blackened asphalt and the missing mailbox, this Falls Church street didn't look to be the front line of some sort of secret war being fought by an actor who had managed to pilfer information on the personal lives of America's military and intelligence professionals.

He stepped on the brake pedal and pushed the automatic start on his 535i, firing the near-silent engine. He put his car in gear and rolled quietly out of the neighborhood without the police ever noticing he was there.

He arrived at the Vienna, Virginia, condo building of Barbara Pineda ten minutes later, and it didn't take him long to come up with a theory as to why she wasn't killed at this location. He followed an elderly man through the door to bypass the lock, then stepped into the lobby of the small building, and here he saw the mailboxes. They were small PO box-type affairs, with tiny slits in each to slip the mail in.

And there was his answer. Dead simple. The terrorists

used a small package bomb, roughly half the size of a loaf of bread – and when they went to Pineda's condo they realized they couldn't get it into her mailbox. If they left a package for her at her front door, or at a table here by the mailboxes where packages were left for residents by postal workers, then there would be no way to see her retrieve it without standing here in the lobby.

Jack drove back to Alexandria knowing good and well that the key to discerning how Islamic State terrorists successfully targeted a DIA analyst was to figure out just how they found out about Barbara Pineda's plans to pick up the mail at her friend's house. When he learned how they came across this time-sensitive and particular piece of intel, then he would be a lot closer to understanding how the leak was connected to the attacks.

Thinking it over, he decided he himself would take the SF-86 that Gavin kept insisting was at the heart of the leak, and he would then try to use all the means at his disposal to turn that into targeting data that could have put a killer at the Falls Church mailbox yesterday before the bomb went off. As an analyst at The Campus, Jack had access to all sorts of classified databases that would help him track the path of this DIA worker. Hell, he could even get Gavin to find traffic camera footage of Pineda and her vehicle.

But no. Jack decided he wouldn't use classified intel. He realized his mission here was to find out how the perpetrator targeted Pineda, and the perpetrator did not work at The Campus. He would use Barbara Pineda's SF-86 form, and open-source intel, to see if he could build the picture that was used to send killers after her.

As he drove he thought this could be done. It occurred to him that there is so much out there these days about people

280

in open source that a motivated and intelligent individual could take old SF-86 info and translate it into real-time targeting info. As he thought it over, it made more sense. If you knew a woman like Pineda was trying to get a security clearance ten years ago, then all you would need to do would be to thoroughly track her, her friends, family, and contacts through years of open-source hits, to get an idea of where she is now. From different factors you could figure out if she was in a clandestine position today, and perhaps you could make inferences from OSINT about her specific role in the intelligence or military structure. And then, once you've decided this woman was your enemy and hence your target, you could use other OSINT means to find out where she will be next Tuesday at noon. Jack thought the work would be slow and arduous, but if worked by a motivated person well trained in identity intelligence, even open-source data would give up the secrets that would make targeting possible.

He called Gavin Biery's mobile phone while he drove.

'Biery.'

'Hey, it's Jack. Quick question. Do we have a way to look at these SF-86 files you think are at the heart of this?'

'Sure. I am looking at the e-QIP data right now.'

'Really? You figured out how the attackers got in?'

'No. I have classified administrator access. I'm sure the hackers found a way to get the same thing, but I got it from NSA to do my own poking around.'

Jack said, 'Can you send me the application on Barbara Pineda? I want to use it to see if I can do the same thing the bad guys did. To find my way to this mailbox in Falls Church.'

Gavin whistled softly. 'Good idea, Ryan. Might give you

an idea of the types of brains working on the other side of this fight. I knew there was a reason to keep you around.'

Jack wasn't in the mood, but he joked anyway. 'I thought I was just around to bring you your lunch.'

Gavin didn't miss a beat. 'Speaking of which, can you grab me a turkey on whole wheat on your way back?'

Jack smiled despite his dark disposition. 'Your wish is my command.'

28

When Jack returned to the conference room, he found a note from Gavin saying he had to go to an IT meeting, but would return shortly. Jack put the man's sandwich in front of his workstation, then sat back down in front of his own laptop. Here he found a folder containing the complete 127-page SF-86 application, formally called the Questionnaire for National Security Positions, of Barbara Maria Pineda.

The form was filled out in her handwriting and was nine years old.

He decided he'd read it from cover to cover, and then see if he would be able to discern from this, using any open-source intelligence he could find, that this twenty-two-year-old Army sergeant stationed at Fort Huachuca in Arizona would, nine years later, be opening a specific mailbox in Falls Church, Virginia.

The beginning of the form was boring government-speak. Some nods to the rights of the applicant and the scope of the investigation that would be done.

Soon though, Jack started feeling uncomfortable. This young woman was telling her life story up to this point within the squares, boxes, and lines of the form. Leaving nothing out. Friends, boyfriends, teachers, details on her family history, trips she'd taken, and even mentions of her parents' economic problems.

Her father was from Honduras, a salesman who had

immigrated to the US with the help of relatives who had become citizens. Her mom was from Chelsea, Massachusetts. Barbara had never been out of the USA till she joined the Army.

Jack felt voyeuristic, almost dirty, poring over all the details of this young woman's life.

But he kept going. He told himself no one else was looking at this document to see if it had somehow led to the death of Barbara, and could help him track down whoever was responsible for this widespread attack on America.

When he finished reading, he looked up the address of the crime scene. Typing this address back into his computer, he found the owners were Dwight and Cindy Gregory.

Jack thumbed back through the pages of the SF-86 to section 16, titled 'People Who Know You Well.' The second name on the list was a Cindy Howard. Jack didn't think there was much chance to find a connection, Cindy was a common name, after all, but he went to Facebook and typed in the name Barbara Pineda. It was surprisingly common, but the twelfth choice had a thumbnail picture that looked a little like the image sent along with the preliminary report from the FBI.

Sure enough, when he clicked on the page he saw this Barbara Pineda was one and the same as the deceased.

Jack opened her Facebook page and saw she kept her wall private, but he was able to see her friends list.

He did not find Cindy Howard from the SF-86, but he found Cindy Gregory easily, and she didn't hide any posts on her Facebook wall. He began scrolling down her various postings.

And he saw everything he needed.

This is how the data thief did it. By using open-source

intelligence. *This* intelligence. The SF-86 form to identify a person involved in the US government in a classified role, then open-source methods to find out where that person was working. After the person involved placed the applicant in a specific role, he used more open-source in the form of the social media accounts of the friends and family of the men and women targeted. Friends and family the thief found either directly or tangentially from the OPM data breach. Perhaps not exactly as he had done it, but in a similar fashion.

A chill ran up his spine. Whoever was doing this had done what Jack had just done.

And it had taken Jack less than twenty minutes.

Gavin came back into the conference room from his IT meeting, and Jack said, 'I've got something.'

'You *better* have my turkey sandwich.'

'Over there. But I also think I have the last piece of the puzzle.'

Gavin plopped down in his seat. 'Oh, no you don't. This is *my* puzzle to solve.'

'Then I guess I'll sit on this information till you get it yourself.'

Gavin sighed. With a frustrated tone he said, 'Go ahead, genius. Spit it out. Maybe I can poke holes in it.'

'This woman murdered last night. Barbara Pineda, an analyst at the DIA. She was killed getting the mail at a friend's house.'

'Right,' said Gavin. 'So if she was targeted, somebody knew she was house-sitting this week.'

Jack said, 'In order to get that information, I figured they were tailing Ms Pineda, listening to calls, tapping her e-mail. I decided I needed to find out when she made plans to do the house-sitting. I figured I could establish a time window for when they decided to use that location to hit her.'

'Makes sense,' Gavin allowed.

'But I'm no computer whiz kid like yourself, so that was a problem.'

'You are being a smartass, but since no one has called me a kid in forty years, I'll let it go.'

Jack said, 'So I just started looking at Twitter and Facebook. Barbara Pineda wasn't big on either, but it was the low-hanging fruit, so I started there. I found the homeowner's account where the bombing took place, and after only a minute I saw a post where she publicly thanked her friend in advance for watching over her house while she and her husband went on vacation. Barbara Pineda herself responded saying she'd do her best to keep the plants alive. Just joking around on another woman's page, but this was the woman who lived in Falls Church. I found other pictures of Barbara with the family. It was that easy to find out she would be going by the house all week.'

Gavin said, 'Pretty low-tech spy shit, but enough to get the job done.'

Jack pointed across the table. 'And that, my friend, is the point.'

Now Gavin asked, 'Any idea how the bad guys found out she was DIA?'

Jack shrugged. 'That part took more work. If there are, as you suggest, tens of millions of applications, then the search would have to be automated with handmade databases. You could tell the computer to look in the SF-86s for specific schools, programs, backgrounds, that meant the person was Army intel, as was Pineda, or maybe an Arabic-language major at Georgetown or something that might indicate the person had gone into intelligence. She was stationed at Fort Huachuca, which is where the US Army Intelligence Center is located. An automated application could pull out everyone who went there and then filled out an SF-86. It wouldn't be easy to sort through with limited information, but we're dealing with a person who knew exactly what they were doing.'

Gavin picked up his sandwich. Before taking a bite he said, 'So . . . you know how they did it. Does that help you figure out *who* did it?'

'Not really. But the target selection does. I'd say this was someone working on behalf of the Islamic State. Why they picked her specifically, I have no idea.'

Gavin shook his head. 'But ISIS didn't steal this OPM data. That's so far out of their abilities it's not even a consideration.'

Jack said, 'Well, Vadim Rechkov didn't steal the OPM data, either. But this incident looks like it came from the intel leak Rechkov used. I'm thinking the entity who stole the OPM data and built a targeting package on Scott Hagen did the same thing for Barbara Pineda, only this time he gave his targeting package to ISIS.'

Jack added, 'He's a one-stop shop. He's got the intel *and* the means to exploit it.'

Gavin said, 'These are two very different skill sets involved. Makes me think this isn't one guy. It's a group working in concert.'

Jack considered what Gavin was saying. 'You're right. We've been thinking the hack was some government actor. But social engineering of this type, using open-source intelligence to determine patterns, that's what you see in the criminal sector.'

'What do you mean?' Gavin asked, surprised at the statement.

'Getting passwords, identity theft, stuff like that. Sounds like cybercrime. Not cyberwarfare.'

'Yeah ... you're right. But whoever did this, it wasn't some teenager calling customer service lines to trick call center employees into giving out passwords. Like I said, this targeting data is top-notch investigatory work.'

'Agreed,' Jack said. 'It was someone first-rate. A criminal or a criminal organization able to scoop up this classified intel, and to exploit it. So . . . where would you go to find the best in the world at that?'

Biery shrugged. 'Some places are known for cybercrime. The Russians are great. Central Europeans, too. There's a group in Taiwan stealing identities all over the world, but they haven't gone after secure government databases. North Korea pretty much sucks at it, but they try . . . a lot. Hell, even here in the US there is a robust cybercrime problem. You could find some criminal organization in any one of these places and see the skills to expand the raw intel by social engineering and open-source investigations, but how did they get the data in the first place? And why? Why would a private company do this, when there are banks to hack, credit card records to exploit? Individuals to rip off on a large scale. All the easy money for them.'

Jack said, 'What if one of these private companies was doing the bidding of a nation. An enemy of the US.'

Gavin nodded quickly. 'Yeah, that does happen, but usually on a smaller scale. Some nations' intel agencies contract with existing criminal hacking concerns, often based outside of their own borders, to do the dirty work. The company tries to penetrate our systems on behalf of their client. China does it all the time. They work with private hackers all over the world to try to raid American government networks. Sometimes they even get something out of it.' He took another bite of his turkey sandwich. 'But in this case, since we have different types of targets being compromised, it sure doesn't look like China is involved. I mean, why would China be involved with the Russian kid? Why the hell would Beijing use him as a proxy assassin against a Navy captain?'

Jack said, 'I can't answer that. But the US government is looking for the state actor. What do you say we start digging into the cybercrime aspect of this? We can research organizations, study the criminal groups who have been particularly successful. Is there something more small-scale we can do to look for fingerprints of the criminals?'

Gavin shrugged. 'Like I said, we need to figure out the why to figure out the who.'

'Would the private company sell off the data to the highest bidder?'

Gavin made a face. 'Shit. *I* wouldn't. That would be suicide. Evil Hacking Company Inc. doesn't know who it's working on behalf of, because of all the cutouts between themselves and the state actor, right?'

'Right,' agreed Jack.

'But the state actor is the one who hired Evil Hacking Company Inc., so they know exactly who *they* are.'

'Of course,' Jack said, then connected the dots Gavin placed. 'Which means, if Evil Hacking Company Inc. decided to sell the data it stole on behalf of the Russians, for example, the Russians would be pissed, and they would just fly to Bangalore or Singapore or wherever and start killing off the senior staff of the company.'

Gavin said, 'Or tip off the USA about who just stole all their data.'

'Right,' Jack said. 'The state actor would have put a lot of time, money, and risk into this op, they aren't going to let anyone screw them over and survive.'

Gavin deadpanned, 'We computer hackers are a stalwart bunch, but we aren't the types brave enough to go toe-to-toe with Chinese assassins.'

Jack smiled, even though he felt further from a solution than he did before. Suddenly, though, another thought came to him. 'What if someone stole data from the ones who stole the data?'

'You lost me.'

'What if . . . what if the private enterprise who snatched the OPM data for the state actor got ripped off? Another company stole it out from under them, or a pissed-off employee who works for them decides he wants to make money selling off the exploited files.'

Gavin said, 'Possible.' He thought for a moment more. 'Honestly, you might be onto something. It's as good a theory as any for why so many different types of bad actors are apparently abusing the same data, which looks to be pilfered on behalf of a government.'

Jack rubbed his eyes. His head hurt from thinking this through. 'If somebody *did* swipe the files, how would they go about selling them off to Iran, Indonesia, a private Russian citizen, ISIS, and whoever the hell else? Could they really reach out individually to just the right person in each government without getting exposed for what they were doing?'

Gavin said, 'Sorry, Ryan . . . can't help you there. I'm the computer guy. That's spy shit.' He laughed to himself. 'I'm not aware of an eBay for spies.' He laughed at his own humor, but he did not laugh for long.

'Unless.'

Jack cocked his head. 'Unless?'

'I mean . . . If you want to sell something illicit, you do it on the dark web.'

'That's for like drugs and stuff, right?'

'It's a safe way to conduct business between two parties without knowing who the other party is. If I were a thief who'd ripped off the criminal enterprise I worked for, screwed over a very dangerous state actor in the process, *and* wanted to make money by dealing with terrorist groups, organized crime, and other nasty state actors out there . . . I'm not placing an ad in *The Wall Street Journal* with my office address. I'm going to the dark web. I can open up my own little marketplace there, trade in Bitcoin with a Bitcoin hopper so that there is no way I can possibly be traced.'

Jack felt a tingle in his spine. He was onto something solid, he knew it. 'Awesome, Gavin! Let's go to the dark web and start hunting for this marketplace! Maybe there will be some clues into who is behind this whole thing.'

Now Gavin gave Jack Ryan, Jr, a disappointed look. Jack had received this look from Gavin Biery many times in his years working at The Campus.

Gavin said, 'Some days I think I've trained you well. Then you go and say something so dumb I don't even know why I bother hanging around you.'

Jack was used to Gavin's style of admonishment. He didn't take it personally, because he knew Gavin had spent his life with his head hunched over a keyboard, and social skills had never been his thing. 'What did I say?' Jack asked.

'You don't spend a lot of time on the dark web, do you?'

To that question, Jack asked, 'And you do?'

'Hey, man. I do my job around here; it sends me down some creepy alleys. Anyway, you don't *search* on the dark web. You have to have a specific address to type in to find something, and that's how you get there.'

Jack said, 'I get it. You don't look. You are invited.'

'Exactly.'

'Oh,' said Jack, realizing for the first time that he had no idea how this worked.

Gavin leaned close and whispered to him. 'That's why they call it "dark."' He was being a smartass, but Jack ignored it.

'So . . . If we have to get an invitation, then it's hopeless finding the bad guy this way.'

'Not necessarily. What if we were able to hack into someone who our thief was in communications with? Maybe that way we could get information on how to see what he had to sell.'

'How the hell do we do that?'

Gavin looked down at his computer. 'We don't know who he talked to when he made contact with the Iranians, the Indonesians, the North Koreans, or the Islamic State.'

Jack understood. 'But the Russian guy! Vadim Rechkov. He wasn't aligned with anyone, as near as we can tell. He had his own personal axe to grind with his target.' Jack thought another moment. 'And there is another way he doesn't fit the mold.'

'What's that?' Gavin asked.

'Money. All the other actors presumably could pay for the intel they were given. But Rechkov was a nobody. Not even working.'

Gavin was intrigued by this. 'Very true. Why do you think

he was given the data if he couldn't pay for it like the Iranians and the others?'

Jack said, 'Maybe Vadim Rechkov was someone the actual thief knew, or knew about, at least. For some reason, he gave Rechkov a freebie.'

His shoulders slumped a little now. 'But I'm sure the FBI is looking into this already. They'll have investigators taking apart Rechkov's life and poring over his communications with everyone.'

Gavin brushed this away with a wave of his hand. 'Yeah, but there's something you aren't considering.'

'What's that?'

'Even though Rechkov is a piece of shit, and a murderer, and dead, and a foreigner overstaying his visa, the Feds will have to get court orders and everything signed off on before they even look under his doormat. Every step of the way the FBI will have to deal with the bureaucracy that will slow them down.'

Jack said, 'But we don't.'

'Nope, which means by the end of today we can potentially be further along in knowing who gave Rechkov the intel about Commander Hagen than the Feds who have been working on this the past two weeks.' Gavin smiled a little. 'Unless you too are concerned about protecting the late Vadim Rechkov's privacy by jumping through all the legal hoops the Feds have to go through.'

Jack looked at Gavin like he was insane. 'Screw Rechkov. He's a dead asshole, let's crack open his life and see what falls out. If it can help us find who is behind this leak, and save others, I don't give a damn.'

Gavin said, 'Works for me.' He thought for a moment. 'It's safe to assume the person who passed Rechkov the intel about Hagen was a computer guy. Rechkov himself was a computer guy. I'll see what message boards Rechkov hung out on, stuff like that.'

'Where will you get that info?'

'The FBI forensic team has his computer. I'll get Gerry to ask Dan Murray for their findings. What's the time frame we are working with here on the Rechkov attack?'

Jack thought about this. 'Rechkov's brother was killed, and seven months later he went after Hagen. Somewhere after the first event, and before the second event, the leaker made contact with Rechkov.' Ryan looked over the data he had on the Hagen case on his computer. Then he said, 'Rechkov started moving from Portland to Princeton four days before he acted, so it happened before then.'

Gavin was looking at his own information on the case now. 'Hagen's sister booked the hotel rooms five weeks out from the trip. Before that, how would the leaker know to tell Rechkov that Hagen would be in Princeton, New Jersey?'

Gavin said, 'I'm going to do some research on Rechkov's online and e-mail activity in this roughly four-and-a-half-week time window. Maybe it will be a dry hole, but just maybe we'll strike oil.'

29

Two members of Abu Musa al-Matari's Fairfax cell rolled into the city of Fayetteville, North Carolina, just after eight p.m. Even though cell leader David Hembrick wasn't with them, the men followed instructions he had given them, and they proceeded directly to coordinates programmed into their vehicle's GPS.

Namir drove while Karim sat in the front passenger seat, his Uzi down between his knees in a gym bag.

They obeyed the traffic laws to stay out of any trouble, but as long as they kept their weapons hidden they knew they had little to worry about. Karim was Egyptian by birth, but he'd become a US citizen at the age of eighteen. Now, at twenty-five, he was a college graduate with a degree in international studies, and he worked part-time as a waiter in a restaurant just outside Landover, Maryland. He paid taxes and he kept his documentation in order, and there was no reason for anyone around here to be suspicious of him.

Namir was born in the United States to Lebanese parents, he was a citizen and a high-school graduate, and, like Karim, he'd been radicalized over the past few years by watching ISIS propaganda and slowly moving from mosque to mosque around the DC area, seeking out the most conservative teachings. They'd both found the same mullah in Baltimore, a man who'd directed them to an online ISIS recruiter promising them the peace and eternal bliss they would never find living in the belly of sin that was America.

They'd never met before the Language School in El Salvador, a testament to the mullah's ability to compartmentalize his recruits in case one was ever rolled up by the FBI.

But now they were here, on their first mission. The other three had remained up in Fairfax County; the day before fellow cell members Ghazi and Husam had killed the DIA woman and were now back at the safe house, but Karim and Namir were told by David Hembrick that he had confidence in them, and the two of them could handle the Fayetteville assignment as a team.

The GPS took them down a middle-class residential street called Lemont Drive, lined with small 1960s-era homes set back on flat full-acre properties. There seemed to be at least one pickup truck in every driveway or carport, and US flags adorned flagpoles in many of the front yards.

Namir was driving, and he also had his phone live-broadcasting video from his front breast pocket. He knew Mohammed would be watching the feed right now, so he was extra careful to do everything correctly.

'Very slowly,' said Karim as he scanned for the address he was looking for.

'Not too slowly,' replied Namir, as he kept the speedometer around ten miles per hour. 'We don't want to draw attention.'

'Yes, well, turning around if we miss it will draw attention, too.'

'Yes, yes,' said Namir, but he did not slow down.

The house was on the left, halfway up the street, and they almost did miss it, but they did not slow when they passed. A white Ford F-150 sat parked in the drive just outside the carport, and a bearded man in a dirty gray T-shirt and jeans climbed out of the driver's side. In one hand he carried a bag of fast food and an extra-large soda, and in the other was a mobile phone; he was talking on the phone.

'Is that him?'

'I don't know. He does not have the beard in the photograph.'

'It's him. American commandos wear beards. They think they blend in when fighting in the caliphate.'

By now they had passed the yard, as well as the next property. 'What are you doing?' Karim asked.

'I am turning around. You should shoot him before he gets in the house.'

Karim pulled the Uzi out of the bag.

'No. The AK. Use the AK.' Namir pulled into a driveway to turn back around, speeding up his movements.

'Why not the Uzi?'

'He is big. We are too far away. Use the AK.'

Karim put the Uzi down between his legs, grabbed the black AK-103 from between the seats and hefted it. He switched the selector from semiautomatic to fully automatic, he rolled down his window halfway, and rested the polymer hand guard of the weapon below the barrel on the glass of the partially opened window.

Karim said, 'Hurry, now. Don't let him get inside.'

'Yes, yes!'

Mike Wayne was dog-ass tired after a thirty-six-hour land-nav training evolution, and the smell of his own BO almost made him want to take a shower before he ate his chicken sandwich and fries.

Almost. He hadn't eaten anything since the power bar he'd downed around noon, so he'd shovel some shitty fast food into his mouth as soon as he got inside to his kitchen table.

He hung up from his call with his sister and pocketed his cell phone, and walked to the carport door of his modest home. He fumbled with his dinner and the keys for a second, then put the key in the lock. Just as he turned the knob, out of the corner of his eye he saw a gray SUV pull up in front of his driveway and stop.

But before he even turned to check it out, he heard an unmistakable sound, one he'd last heard two weeks earlier on the Syrian–Turkish border.

An AK firing a full-auto burst.

The door in front of him splintered right in front of his knees, and he felt a blow to his right hip that staggered him but did not knock him down. He wore a .45-caliber semi-automatic pistol at the four-o'clock position under his T-shirt, but now he was only thinking about cover.

He dropped the bag of fast food and his drink, got the door open, fell inside, and crawled forward on his elbows.

He knew he'd taken a round right in the hip joint, he was bleeding like hell, and he could not stand up. With a blood-covered right hand he pulled his .45, rolled onto his back, and aimed at the closed door.

And with a blood-covered left hand he pulled his mobile phone out of the pocket of his jeans and called 911.

And then he looked at the floor around him. Wayne was a medic in Delta Force, and he knew what all this blood meant. There was four times the amount of blood he'd expected to see from a GSW to the hip. He felt sure the AK round had slammed into his hip and either tumbled around inside him or broken into pieces. His femoral artery had been clipped and ruptured, and from the location of the hole Wayne knew it was too high on his body to tourniquet.

Too much blood lost too fast.

An ambulance could roll up his driveway right now with a team of vascular surgeons in the back, and he would probably still bleed out before they could save him.

Mike Wayne realized he was a dead man.

After a few seconds to come to terms with his fate, he looked back down the sights of his pistol, and he willed his door to open. More than anything in the world he wanted to shoot the guy who'd just killed him.

Just then, his phone was answered, 'Nine-one-one, do you need police, fire, or ambulance?'

Mike kept his voice strong. 'Gray GMC Terrain. Two occupants.'

'I'm sorry?'

The phone dropped from Mike's hand. The pistol stayed up for a few seconds more, but his hand would lower and then come to rest at his side in a pool of blood before he was able to get one last target in his sights.

In the training at the Language School in El Salvador, the cell members had practiced firing their weapons while seated inside cars. The cars they used had been old junkers lying around the property, and none of them had had any window glass. Karim had misjudged the recoil of his Kalashnikov, because he'd propped it on the glass of the partially opened window to shoot, but as soon as he opened fire, the glass shattered, and the rifle dropped off target. He'd seen the last few rounds hit the street just twenty feet in front of him.

But by the time he lifted the rifle back up to his shoulder and pointed toward the carport door across the street, he just saw the boots of his target as he crawled through the door.

Karim shouted from the passenger seat. 'Damn it! He got away!'

Namir said, 'Get out and finish him! He is wounded!'

Karim did not move. '*You* do it!'

Musa al-Matari's voice came over the speakerphone now. 'Karim! Brother! You are a brave lion! I saw you shoot him! He's in there bleeding to death. Go! Finish it. But hurry! And take the phone, so everyone in the caliphate can see your bravery.'

Karim took the phone from Namir, opened the car door, stepped out onto Lemont Drive, then raced up the driveway. As he ran he held the weapon at his hip and began sweeping it left and right, ready to engage anyone else out here who might have a weapon.

As he passed the F-150 on his left he saw a huge splatter of blood on the carport and a shining smear on the broken glass of the outer door. He swiveled around in front of the door, brought the rifle to his shoulder, and opened the outer door. He got ready to open the wooden door, but an idea occurred to him. He took two steps back and opened fire, emptying his entire magazine.

This done, he stepped to the side of the door, reloaded, then entered the small house.

The bearded man lay on the floor, ten feet from the door. A pool of blood around him. Bullet holes in his T-shirt. He was clearly dead. A pistol lay inches from his right hand. A cell phone lay next to his left hand.

Karim realized the man had been waiting for him to come through the door so he could shoot him.

He held up the phone's camera on the scene while he muttered '*Allahu Akbar*' a half-dozen times.

Then he spun out of the doorway and sprinted back to the SUV.

Namir met him in the driveway, and Karim climbed back

inside. With screeching tires the SUV sped down Lemont Drive, right past a seventy-five-year-old man wearing a US Army Special Forces baseball cap on his head. He'd come outside once he'd heard what sounded to him like an AK-47 firing what had to have been two fifteen-round bursts, a sound he hadn't heard in person since the jungles of Vietnam.

He walked down his driveway just as a vehicle sped in his direction. He didn't recognize the SUV, so he noted the make and model, as had the victim, Mike Wayne. But the old Green Beret standing in his driveway also noticed that the GMC had Maryland tags.

He turned around to head back inside for his phone.

Namir and Karim were miles from the scene within minutes of the shooting. They headed north on I-95, still careful to stay within the posted speed limits, both men fighting the amped-up effects of the adrenaline in their bodies.

They felt euphoric about their operation, and even more so because Mohammed had watched it all live. He'd signed off so they could concentrate on their escape, but he'd praised the men over and over for their great success.

As they drove north they talked about returning to the safe house and telling David Hembrick about their killing of the infidel, and self-consciously they discussed how the video would look when the Islamic State PR people put it to music and effects and broadcast it out all over social media.

They thought they were home free, because other than the old man they'd passed near the shooting, they'd seen no one who could have possibly known what they had done, and they doubted he'd even noticed at all.

*

But they made it only as far as exit 61, which is to say, they didn't make it far at all.

Four North Carolina State Highway Patrol troopers had been parked in two vehicles at the Lucky Seven Truck Stop when a call came out saying a gray GMC Terrain had been involved in a shooting on Lemont Drive. One of the witnesses reported that the vehicle had Maryland plates, and that gave local law enforcement a hint that the perpetrators might show up somewhere northbound out of the city.

And I-95 was local law enforcement's immediate choice, as it served as the spine that went up and down the eastern seaboard.

The troopers raced their two Dodge Chargers out of the truck stop, down the on-ramp, and then they took up positions in the median facing northbound.

Four minutes and twenty seconds later a gray GMC Terrain drove by with two men inside.

The Dodge Chargers were V8s and they probably would have had no problem catching up to the 185-horsepower, four-cylinder rental SUV while in reverse, but they stayed back for a moment. Only when the troopers in the lead vehicle saw that the car they were tailing did, indeed, have Maryland plates did they turn on their lights and sirens.

The Terrain did not stop, which was just fine with the North Carolina State Highway Patrol troopers. By now dispatch had said there was a soldier from Fort Bragg dead in his own home back on Lemont Drive. These troopers had no problems at all with this felony stop turning a little rough.

Ten minutes later they had a helicopter overhead, six more vehicles in pursuit, and a roadblock across I-95.

The GMC saw the roadblock, slowed quickly, and turned to shoot off into the grassy median to try its luck going back southbound, but a cluster of silver-and-black highway patrol vehicles instantly and professionally boxed it in.

The GMC stopped horizontal to the highway, troopers poured out of their cars and SUVs, and shotguns, AR-15s, and pistols were pointed at the vehicle's two occupants from multiple directions.

Inside the Terrain, Namir used his shaking hands to initiate a Silent Phone call with their handler. When he answered, Namir screamed into the phone. 'We are surrounded by police. By God's will, we killed the infidel, but there are many armed men around us now. What do we do?'

The man they knew as Mohammed had Namir pan the phone around in various directions, confirming they were, in fact, completely surrounded by law enforcement.

Over the phone's speaker the two young men heard Mohammed's calm voice. 'You have done well, my brothers. Now you must surrender without incident. Don't worry. I will dispatch forces to liberate you. I'll send a team down today.'

'Yes, Commander Mohammed. Thank you, sir.'

'But leave your phone on, and place it on the dashboard so I can film your arrest.'

A minute later the AK and the Uzi came flying out the side windows of the GMC Terrain, then Karim raised his hands out of the passenger side, and Namir did the same out of the driver's side. By now there were twenty-two State Highway Patrol vehicles on the scene, and the helicopter continued circling overhead. More than forty men and women kept weapons trained on the two suspects.

Following the orders of law enforcement as broadcast

through the PA of one of the trooper's vehicles, Namir opened his car door slowly, reached out with his hands in the sky, and walked backward to a point in the middle of the highway. There he was told to lower to his knees and lie facedown, with his ankles crossed and arms away from his body.

With Karim still reaching out the window with his empty hands, two officers moved forward to cuff Namir in the street. They knelt down, one put a knee in his back –

And then the entire scene erupted in a flash of light.

The two North Carolina State Highway Patrol troopers flew through the air in the explosion.

In the GMC Terrain, Karim crouched down behind the dash, first thinking someone had opened fire. But as debris rained down on his car and smashed his windshield, he looked out over the dash and through the spiderwebbed glass. Namir had been blown to bits, along with the two troopers. More members of law enforcement lay on the ground, clearly injured.

Karim's ears rang; Namir had not activated his suicide vest, so Karim had no idea what had happened.

And he never would.

His own suicide vest detonated ten seconds after Namir's, and the Terrain exploded in a ball of fire, firing projectiles out in all directions and injuring more of the troopers all around.

Above the highway, the helicopter had to bank to avoid the plume of smoke and debris that shot straight into the sky.

30

Jack Ryan, Jr, had worked till midnight analyzing the private-actor angle of the US intelligence data breach, but he forced himself to roll out of bed the next morning at five, slip on his summer running gear, and stagger down his condo stairs in the Oronoco Waterfront Residences.

It was less than a five-minute jog to the Hendley Associates building, but Jack walked it, using the ten minutes to wake up a little, to allow some heat to build in his muscles, and to give him time to win the little mental fight he was having with himself. Most of him wanted to go back to bed for a couple more hours, but enough of him wanted to get some PT in this morning, knowing that it would make his brain work better during the day, that he kept putting one leg in front of the other until the next thing he knew, he was in the parking garage under his office giving tired but uplifting fist bumps to his cousin and Domingo Chavez.

A minute later Midas and Adara stepped out of the stairwell; from the sweat on their clothing it was clear Clark had already been working the two new recruits out in the gym there in the building. This made Jack smile; he knew Clark would be tough on the two newcomers to the operational team, but he also knew the two newcomers would have no problems making it.

There was a brief delay as Clark stopped to take an early-morning phone call. Jack listened at first to see if it was related to the intelligence compromise, but apparently he was talking to an old friend to help with a role-playing exercise for the two new trainees. He tuned out of Clark's call, and while everyone was standing around the lighted parking garage stretching for this morning's run, Jack walked over to Midas, who was a few feet away from the others.

'Hey, man, how's the training going?'

Midas seemed surprised to be spoken to by Jack, which made Jack feel like shit. He'd been in a bad mood all week, and he'd been so damn focused on this intelligence leak that he'd been distant to pretty much everyone in the building except for Gavin.

Midas said, 'I've learned one thing so far.'

'Yeah? What's that?'

'I want to be Mr C. when I grow up. That guy is a machine. My old man's heart blew up at fifty-five while he was watching a game show. Mr C. looks like he's got another sixty years in him.'

Jack smiled. 'Sorry about your dad, but I bet he wasn't in Delta.'

'Sold carpet during the day and drank cheap scotch all night. He was surprisingly good at doing both.'

Jack glanced to Clark. 'Yeah, Clark keeps us younger guys on our toes, for sure.' Now he turned back to Midas. 'Look. I'm not usually such an asshole. It's been a really hard week, and –'

Midas reached out and slapped Jack on the arm. A show of kindness that nevertheless unsteadied him. 'No worries. I heard about what happened. Well . . . in a general sense, anyway.'

'Really?'

'I heard you and your mates did your jobs and did them well, but still something bad happened.'

Jack said, 'Something bad happened. I don't know that I did my job well.'

Midas said, 'There's an old saying you'd hear around Delta. All skill is in vain when an angel pisses in the flintlock of your musket.'

Jack cracked a smile at this. 'Yeah . . . I guess that's true.'

'I personally know some great dudes spending eternity napping just up the road at Arlington Cemetery. They didn't do a damn thing wrong other than pick a profession that kills the exceptional just the same as it kills the unexceptional. Whatever happened, you did your best on the day, and you survived, which means someday you'll be around to have the opportunity to do even better. I hope you can shake it off.' Midas did a neck roll, then spoke with nonchalance. 'Because you're right, you've been acting like a little bit of a tight-ass.'

It was a weird pep talk, Jack acknowledged, but it was exactly what he needed to hear. He laughed and the two men shook hands, and seconds later Clark sent everyone on a four-mile run.

As Jack Junior ran in the predawn along the Potomac River, his father was getting dressed just a couple miles to the north in the White House. Jack Senior had been woken an hour before usual this morning to take a call from Dan Murray. After their quick conversation, the President asked for his senior national security staff to be contacted and summoned for a seven a.m. meeting in the Situation Room.

The President arrived in the underground conference room at exactly seven to find everyone else already seated. Though they stood at his appearance, he immediately motioned for them to sit back down, and he turned the floor over to Dan.

The attorney general stood and walked to the end of the conference table, where a large screen on the wall displayed the presidential seal. He said, 'It appears Islamic State operatives have been conducting attacks in America for thirty-six hours.'

There was a murmur of confusion at the table, although many of those seated, the President included, knew about some of the incidents already. Murray clicked a button on a remote control and the DIA departmental headshot of Barbara Pineda appeared on one of the screens. 'As I'm sure you all know, a young woman was murdered with a bomb the night before last in Falls Church. She was, in fact, an analyst for the DIA, working against Islamic State as an area officer.'

Everyone knew about the incident, but the fact the police had not immediately identified her as the actual target of the bomb had slowed down associating her with her work against ISIS.

Murray clicked the button again. The picture of Barbara Pineda was replaced by the image of US Navy SEAL Todd Braxton wearing his khaki and black service dress uniform and his black garrison cap. Everyone in the room knew Braxton instantly. There wasn't a bigger American celebrity to come out of the military in a decade. He made the rounds on the news as a talking head, and on adventure reality shows, and his book had been at the top of the bestseller lists. There were gasps of surprise around the table, because no one had heard anything about his death. 'Some of you might be aware that yesterday morning in Los Angeles, the television actor Danny Phillips was shot dead along with his bodyguard. What has not been widely reported is that Phillips was with former Naval Special Warfare Chief Petty Officer Todd Braxton at the time of the assault. The two were making a film version of Braxton's book. Even though Braxton was uninjured in the attack, we are confident he was, in fact, the intended victim. We think the assailants mistook Phillips for Braxton, which would have been easy to do because Phillips was playing Braxton, and Braxton himself had adopted a different appearance to play in the same film.'

The secretary of homeland security said, 'How do we know that –'

Dan Murray held a polite hand up. 'Andy, just a second and I'll answer that.'

Now Murray clicked his remote again, and a Department of the Army image of a clean-shaven man in his twenties appeared. 'Last night, in Fayetteville, North Carolina, US Army Sergeant First Class Michael Robert Wayne was shot dead at the front door to his private residence.'

Some in the room had been up late and seen news of the shooting and police chase on CNN, although neither the victim nor the perpetrators had been identified.

Murray turned to Bob Burgess, the secretary of defense. 'Bob, Staff Sergeant Wayne was . . .'

Burgess spoke with sadness tinged with unmistakable anger as he turned to the President. 'He was Delta, assigned to Charlie Squadron. They just got back from ops in Turkey and Syria eleven days ago.'

No one in the room had ever seen the President's nostrils flare in anger like they did now. Ryan said, 'And the killers?'

Murray answered. 'The assassins were stopped on the highway twenty minutes after the first nine-one-one call described their vehicle. They were heading north, out of Fayetteville. Like they were going to Virginia, up to the DC area, but that's just speculation. Their vehicle was rented in

Baltimore, so it's possible they were heading there. Both of the killers detonated suicide vests, killing two North Carolina State Highway Patrol troopers in the process, and injuring four more.'

'Son of a bitch,' Ryan said.

Now Murray turned back to the secretary of homeland security, Andrew Zilko. 'Three incidents in the three states over twenty-six hours. How do we connect the dots? How do we know this was part of a coordinated ISIS operation?' He nodded to the monitor. 'This was broadcast less than two hours ago on an ISIS Global Islamic Media Front website.' Murray took a chest-filling breath and then let it out. 'I warn you in advance . . . this will be hard to watch.'

Again he tapped the remote operating the audiovisual equipment, and a video began playing on the monitor. The setup was familiar to all in the room. It was an Islamic State-produced video; a recruiting plea dressed up like news. But as ISIS PR devices went, this one wasn't particularly slick, well scored, or cleverly edited. It appeared to be something of a rush job.

But there was no question about it. What it lacked in polish, it more than made up for in raw, authentic content.

There was some music at the beginning, a title card wholly in Arabic, then the footage, clearly taken from a medium-quality camera zoomed in to the point of distortion. Still, anyone watching would be able to identify a woman with dark hair pulled back in a bun wearing business attire. She walked down a short driveway as she dug through her purse. She opened a mailbox, and then the entire conference room recoiled in shock at the sight of her death. Some words were superimposed over the frozen image of the carnage in Arabic, English, and French. In English it said, BARBARA

PINEDA. AMERICAN MILITARY INTELLIGENCE AGENT SUPPORTING THE BOMBING OPERATIONS AGAINST THE MEN, WOMEN, AND CHILDREN OF THE CALIPHATE. NOT ANYMORE.

The image switched to a dimly lit Starbucks counter and a large group of individuals there. The video wasn't well centered, so a circle had been superimposed on one man standing in the group off to the side as he stirred sugar into his coffee.

Suddenly the shouts of *'Allahu Akbar,'* and two figures armed with pistols opened fire, their faces shaded out electronically. The man indicated by the animated circle stood flat-footed, and a large black man tackled him to the ground and began pulling him out of the way, but the two of them were riddled with gunfire.

More men and women cowered in terror, and a white man dove over the counter and out of view.

The video froze over the bodies, and writing, again in French, Arabic, and English, said, AMERICAN ACTOR DANNY PHILLIPS. PORTRAYING IN A MOVIE THE INFIDEL NAVY SEAL TODD BRAXTON WHO KILLED HUNDREDS OF THE FAITHFUL. NOT ANYMORE.

The next video was of a little street at nighttime with small homes at the end of long driveways. An armed man fired a rifle out of the passenger side of an SUV; the camera was right behind his head, so it was impossible to see either his face or what he was shooting at.

The audio cut out for several seconds, then the scene cut to the moving image of a dead man in a pool of blood lying on his back in a tiny kitchen. A voice spoke over the music.

'Allahu Akbar. Allahu Akbar. Allahu Akbar.'

The English caption read, DELTA FORCE OFFICER

MICHAEL WAYNE, MURDERER OF WOMEN AND CHIL-
DREN OF THE CALIPHATE. NOT ANYMORE.

A man with a British accent spoke off screen as the video images showed stock photos of US soldiers, tanks, aircraft carriers, the CIA, the Pentagon, and the White House. 'America. You have been fighting us from afar. But now the war has lost its distance for you. Your soldiers and spies can die at home as easily as they can abroad.

'You think you are strong because you attack women and children in Iraq and Syria and North Africa. You wear your body armor, and your machine guns, and you surround yourself with the protection of your fellow killers. But back home you are weak, vulnerable.

'We know who you are, *where* you are. And now we are here, and we will come for you.

'War, total and complete. Everywhere. At all times. You are too afraid to confront us with numbers on the field of battle, so we will confront you with righteousness, wherever we can find you. And believe me, we do have the power to find you. Where you work, where you train, where you relax, where you play, where you sleep at night.

'We call on all other brave Muslim lions here in America, or those with the ability to travel to America. Now is the time. Now is the opportunity.

'The United States Army. The United States Navy. The United States Air Force. The United States Marine Corps. The FBI, the CIA, the Department of Homeland Security.' More stock photos, following along with the narrator.

'If you cannot find access to any of these forces, we call on you to attack state and local law enforcement. Your efforts, while seemingly small, will inspire others to join with you. If you are martyred, your martyrdom will be remembered. You will be at the vanguard of the war in America that we swear is soon to come.'

Again the images of the three dead. 'The Prophet, peace be unto him, said our caliphate would reach Rome and Constantinople. This is true. But it will also reach Washington. New York. Los Angeles. This is only the beginning. Our soldiers are preparing more attacks against greater targets. Keep watching, and join the fight.'

A series of URLs appeared on the screen, and the screen went to black.

Dan Murray said, 'Despite how they try to justify the killing on here, we feel certain Braxton was the intended victim. They screwed up but are glossing over it. Why would they let him live other than the fact they didn't know he was there?'

Jay Canfield nodded. 'ISIS is a death cult, and they killed *someone*. That's good enough for them.'

Ryan asked, 'How widely has this video been distributed?'

Mary Pat answered. 'We saw it instantly, but twenty minutes ago I was told it's been picked up by media all over the world. Suffice it to say that by the time we walk out of this meeting, this will be the biggest news in America, so there is no getting out in front of this.'

It was quiet for a moment, all eyes on the President. Finally Ryan said, 'If ISIS has the home address of a Delta Force assaulter, then they could have anything.'

'Agreed,' answered Burgess. 'Obviously the word will get out that Wayne was Army, at Fort Bragg. We can hide the fact he was a JSOC operator, maybe, but I'm not sure we want to get caught covering that up.'

Homeland Security Secretary Zilko said, 'Killing America's best paramilitary officers at the front door of their homes is a level of sophistication from ISIS that we did not think they had.'

Ryan shrugged. 'Since we are flying blind on the assumption this is related to al-Matari *and* the ongoing multipronged intel leak of unknown proportions going on right now, I don't think we can make any good judgments about how sophisticated ISIS is. Until someone in this room brings in actionable intel, either in the form of the "whats" and the "hows" of the military and intelligence compromise, or the "wheres" in the case of Abu Musa al-Matari, we are going to sit here every damn morning and just talk about whoever has been murdered the day before.'

Bob Burgess said, 'Mr President, if ISIS is doing this, coming here with a few dozen operatives to kill our employees, I have to ask the question . . . Why? This isn't a viable strategy. Nor is it tactically effective. No offense meant to Ms Pineda, who I am told was doing a fine job, but there are thousands of other analysts of her rank and access or higher around the intelligence community. Why *her*? What makes ISIS think they can have any effect on the war in the Middle East by coming over here and targeting her, a single Delta sergeant, and a former SEAL? It doesn't make a bit of sense.'

Mary Pat Foley spoke up now. 'It's for recruitment. They aren't going to defeat us with mail bombs, but they might get enough copycats to be an important force multiplier.'

Ryan said, 'I think Mary Pat is correct, but I think it's possible something else is going on here.' He drummed his fingers on the desk. 'The Islamic State wants a massive over-reaction from the US. A hundred thousand American troops in Iraq would be the single most effective way for them to grow as an organization. Sure, they'd lose Mosul, and maybe even territory in Syria, but they are losing that anyway, and they know it.'

Mary Pat said, 'Are you suggesting al-Matari is over here trying to drum up your anger?'

Ryan said, 'My anger, the military's anger, the voting public's anger. It's a shrewd move if I'm correct. Think how many in Congress are getting phone calls right now from constituents saying how mad they are about this. How weak America looks. Think how many enemies this administration has in the press who will say ISIS is now beating our government in street battles in America.'

Mary Pat said, 'If I thought for a second al-Matari's operation was complete now after these three incidents, I'd frankly be thrilled. But I don't. Not by a long shot.'

Ryan agreed. 'He's got twenty-five to fifty trained operatives, minus the two who were killed in North Carolina. They are here in America, and they are spread out from one coast to the other. They have guns and bombs and suicide vests that we know of, and they are targeting military and intelligence personnel.'

Ryan looked around the table. 'This is just the beginning, and it will go on until *we* stop it.' He set his gaze on Dan Murray. 'Dan, you and Andy are in charge of protecting the homeland. The enemy is inside the wire, so you are the front lines now.'

31

John Clark arrived at La Madeleine café on King Street in Old Town Alexandria a few minutes before eight a.m. The place served a full breakfast, and he looked at the menu longingly, but for now he just ordered two of the simplest coffees he could find on the menu and took them to a table in the front window.

A minute later a white-haired but healthy and energetic-looking man of around seventy arrived, wearing a white polo shirt and khakis. He smiled when he saw Clark, and marched over to his table with a hand extended.

'Good to see you, John!' he said with a firm handshake.

'Eddie Laird! It's been a while. You're looking good for a retiree.'

The men sat down across from each other. 'You kidding? I've been out of the agency for a year and a half and my blood pressure is down to normal levels for the first time since college. Feel younger now than when I was fifty-five.'

Clark said, 'They've still got you training at The Farm, right?'

'On a contract basis. It gets me out of the house, but just a couple days a week. That's plenty for me, and frankly those hopeful young minds of mush don't need to hear a grumpy old cynic like me every day.'

Clark laughed and said, 'Can't thank you enough for helping me out this morning.'

The white-haired man lifted one of the coffees and took a sip. 'Glad to.'

Laird had been CIA ever since graduating from Yale; he'd first met Clark in Vietnam when they were both part of MACV-SOG, the Military Assistance Command, Vietnam – Studies and Observations Group, a black ops task force that Clark served in as a US Navy SEAL. Laird had been a very young CIA case officer in the program, and while Clark didn't get along with many of the Ivy Leaguers at the Agency as a rule back then, he saw quickly that Laird had a real appreciation of the work the SEALs did and, for a Yalie, he was just a regular Joe out there in a shitty situation doing his best.

The two men ran into each other frequently after Vietnam, which was no great surprise, because Clark joined the CIA himself. In Berlin, in Tokyo, in Moscow, and in Kiev, Laird and Clark worked together here and there, and Clark had only greater respect for the man as the years passed.

In the eighties Laird was in Lebanon, and he was one of only a few CIA officers to survive the bombing of the US embassy. He became an expert on Afghanistan in the nineties by working for two years in-country with the Northern Alliance, so after 9/11 he was on the first CIA Russian helicopter into the nation, tasked with enlisting the support of the fracturing alliance and helping them move south as an American proxy force.

Laird had done a magnificent job in pushing Al-Qaeda out of the nation and rolling Taliban forces south and west, better than anyone's wildest dreams, and he was soon rewarded with a senior position in the National Clandestine Service, where he managed case officers in the Near Eastern Division, including for then CIA Director Ed Foley.

After a decade at Langley he began working as a trainer at Camp Peary, home of the CIA training facility known as The

Farm. By then he had grandchildren and wanted to shower them with the attention he'd never been able to give his own kids because of his life in the field. He tried to retire a handful of times, but his wealth of knowledge was so crucial to the young recruits that Ed Foley, and then his wife, Mary Pat, had always managed to convince Eddie to stay on. Even when he officially retired, he continued as a contract trainer.

Laird had been read in on The Campus since the early days, so he was happy to make the three-block walk up to King Street from his home this morning to help his old friend with some training.

Clark asked after Laird's daughter, herself a CIA officer, and though Eddie couldn't say much, he did say she was at Langley at the moment, and he was seeing plenty of her and his grandkids.

Laird in turn asked Clark about his family, which included Ding Chavez's family, as Ding was married to Clark's daughter Patsy.

'Everybody's doing great,' Clark said. 'Although I've got Ding working like a madman, since we're short on personnel.'

Laird looked out the window at the sunny day. 'Yeah, about that. On the phone you said you needed me for a few hours of role-playing to help you whip a couple of new trainees into shape. What did you have in mind?'

Clark said, 'Just a basic surveillance evolution for my two new operatives. I'd like to send you out into the neighborhood here. Pick up a copy of the *Post*, to keep under your arm, and then I'll call them. They are just up the street at the office now. I'll give them your description, and have them try to acquire and tail you. For the first hour I just want you to take it easy on them. Do some window-shopping, maybe stop for another coffee, walk around. We'll start slow, so make no attempts to ID them. After a while I'll call you and ask you to begin an SDR. At that point I'd like you to do what you can within normal parameters to slip surveillance, but I'd also like you to actively try to figure out who is on your tail.'

'Got it. You want me to take this into the District or stick around here?'

'We'll keep this exercise confined to Alexandria. There's no way anybody on earth could tail a man with your experience unless I make the game table nice and small.'

Laird smiled. 'Thanks, John, but my hair is so damn white now, a cosmonaut could ID me from space with his naked eye.'

John pointed at his own head of silver hair. 'In case you haven't noticed, there are a bunch of us around. You'll fit right in. Anyway, I'll see how long they can tail you, and then, when I call time on the exercise, I'll see if you can describe the two people I have on the foot-follow. Sound good?'

'You kidding? I used to have to do this in Moscow in ten-degree snowstorms. An eighty-degree morning walking around a few blocks from my house trying to ID a couple of eager young guns sounds like my idea of a good time.'

Across the street and half a block north on North Pitt Street, four men sat in a Nissan Pathfinder and watched the two white-haired men in the coffee shop through binoculars.

They'd remained silent for a few minutes, but now Badr, the man behind the wheel, asked the question they were all thinking. 'Who is the other old guy?'

Next to him, Saleh answered. 'It doesn't matter. Laird is our target. That doesn't change.'

In the backseat, Chakir lowered his binoculars. 'Do we do it right now? Just drive by and fire into the window? They are sitting right there. It would be easy.'

Next to him, eighteen-year-old Mehdi, the second-youngest of all the operators from the Language School, nodded eagerly. 'I'll shoot both those *motherfuckers* right now.'

Saleh looked up and down the street. Pedestrian traffic was relatively heavy on the sidewalks already and the streets were active, if not crowded. Saleh knew what had happened to the two men in North Carolina the evening before from watching the news and seeing the new ISIS video just distributed. He didn't know which cell they belonged to, but there was no doubt in his mind that they were mujahideen he'd met at the camp in El Salvador.

It was also clear to him they'd successfully taken out their target, and then had been caught by police during the getaway.

Saleh and the other three were operatives of the Detroit cell. They were right in the middle of Fairfax's turf, but they didn't know that. Al-Matari had known from the beginning that the DC area would be ground zero in targeting the types of prey he was looking for, so he'd always planned on sending various groups into the area.

These four men had arrived early this morning, but they missed Laird when he left his house at seven forty-five, a mistake by Badr, the driver. They'd been parked in a metered space on Duke Street within sight of Laird's house on South Royal, but when a police car drove by slowly, Badr spooked and drove off. Saleh, in charge of this four-man sub-unit of the Detroit cell, had chastised his driver; they had been doing nothing wrong, they all spoke excellent English, and Saleh had a cover story ready. Still, they had to find another place to park with a line of sight on the Laird home, and by the time they'd gotten into position, Mehdi noticed Laird walking on South Royal, halfway up to King Street.

Now Saleh had to decide if they should shoot the old man while he sat in the restaurant and then try to race away through the crowded and touristy part of Old Town, or else wait till he headed back home, and do him on his quiet residential street.

Thinking again of what had happened in North Carolina the evening before, he found his choice easy to make. 'We wait till he goes back home. If he walks around awhile, it's okay. But if he looks like he's going to get on public transportation, we kill him immediately.'

Saleh had been told directly by Omar, the leader of the Detroit cell, that Mohammed had precluded any of them from setting foot in DC because of the high police presence and what he assumed would be heavy racial profiling.

The four men in the Pathfinder continued watching their target, some hundred yards distant through the glass of the restaurant.

A few minutes later John Clark and Eddie Laird shook hands again at the front door of La Madeleine.

Eddie said, 'If we wrap up around lunchtime, what do you think about the four of us heading over to Murphy's for a celebratory beer and some wings?'

Clark said, 'How 'bout this? You and I go for the beer and lunch. If my trainees pass muster, they can tag along. If not, I'm sending their asses back to the office to reread the manuals on foot-follow surveillance. They can eat crow for lunch.'

Clark didn't mention that Adara Sherman had proven

herself capable in the field on Campus ops more than once, and Midas Jankowski was already an incredibly well-trained operative from Delta Force. He imagined they would pass today, but he wouldn't commit to rewarding them until they did.

'Well, now, aren't you a hard-charging bastard?' Eddie joked. 'All right, buddy. I'm your mouse, bring on your two little kitty cats.' Laird walked across the street to a CVS pharmacy, where he took his time buying a bottle of water, a pack of chewing gum, and a copy of *The Washington Post*, giving the trainees time to get into the area.

Adara Sherman and Midas Jankowski had been reading books on surveillance for the past hour and a half. Adara had read the books twice before, back when she was on the aircraft shuttling Campus operatives around the world and dreaming about the opportunity to join their ranks to make a larger contribution to the cause.

Midas had read different books on the subject, back when he was new in G Squadron at Delta. This was the recce group, reconnaissance, and they often worked in small groups and in plainclothes on surveillance missions around the world. He fully expected to do a good job today, and maybe even have some fun while doing it. His first week as part of this tiny group of brilliant and dedicated Americans had been nothing short of a blast. Moreover, just the knowledge that the three-man operational force had spent the previous weekend involved in some sort of direct-action mission overseas made his blood pump faster.

Mr C. clearly hadn't been jerking Midas's chain back when he told him The Campus got into the action with regularity.

Shortly after the two of them closed their books, they

received a group text from Clark instructing them to begin double-timing it toward King Street.

Adara had a Smith & Wesson Shield she carried for personal protection here in Virginia, and she started to reach for it. But she stopped herself and turned to Midas. 'Are you carrying today?'

'We can't carry in the District. It's a felony. I have no idea where this target we're tailing is going to go. I'll just take my knife.'

Jankowski carried a small hawkbill-bladed karambit knife in a sheath inside his waistband. He was well trained on the device, even though the one on his person now was a thirty-dollar off-brand. The blade was only two and a half inches long, meaning it was small enough to carry legally in DC, but he'd never get it through a metal detector if their subject went into any federal buildings, art galleries, or other public places. He went cheap with the blade today because he knew there was a chance he'd have to drop it in a garbage can to keep on mission.

Adara had an even smaller two-inch folding blade and a small can of Sabre Red pepper gel, which could shoot a thick stream of goo twenty feet that was capable of burning mucous membranes with roughly the same heat used in bear-attack sprays.

Pepper gel wasn't nearly as effective as a weapon that fired lead, but like the little knife, it could also be safely discarded in a garbage can if she needed to dump her weapons to get into a restrictive location.

A minute after getting Clark's text they were in Midas's Chevy Silverado heading to King Street, and they found parking a block over and walked the rest of the way.

Clark met with the pair in the middle of Market Square,

a large open space in front of the 150-year-old city hall. A farmers' market was under way, bringing hundreds out on this summer morning.

Clark brought Midas and Adara to the side of the action, stood them by the large fountain in the middle of the square, and said, 'Okay, today's subject is within three hundred yards of you right now. He's seventy years young, five-ten, one hundred sixty pounds. He's wearing a white polo and khaki slacks, and he might or might not have a hat on.'

Midas and Adara exchanged a look. This wouldn't be easy.

Clark added, 'He'll be walking with a copy of *The Washington Post*.'

Midas asked, 'Our orders?'

'Tail, surveil, and prevail. When I call time on the op, I want pictures of anyone he talks to, and good notes of where he went and what he did. Any questions?'

Adara asked, 'Does he know who we are?'

'No, and it's your job to keep it that way. You fail if he describes you to me at the end of the run.'

Both Adara and Midas were clear on their task.

'Good luck.' Clark walked off, heading back to La Madeleine now, eager to eat a real breakfast.

The two trainees put earpieces in their ears and then Adara called Midas. Once they established a constant connection between the two of them, they split up to find their target. Midas headed east toward the Potomac River, and Adara moved west up King Street.

Eddie Laird left the CVS after twenty minutes and headed off to the west, staying with the flow of traffic on the sidewalk running up the northern side of King Street.

A block behind him, Badr pulled the Pathfinder into the

weekend morning traffic and said, 'He isn't going home. Home is the other way.'

In the back, Chakir said, 'Did he see us? Does he know we are following him?'

Saleh shook his head. 'He knows nothing. Calm down, everyone. He can go for a walk if he wants.'

Badr said, 'What do I do?'

Saleh was the right man to lead this quartet from Detroit, because he was by far the most calm of the group. 'Drive on ahead of him, then stop and drop the three of us off. We'll let him pass and then stay behind him. If there is a good opportunity to do it and escape, we will proceed. Otherwise, we wait for him to go home.'

After a second Saleh began taking off his shirt. 'Everyone but Badr needs to remove their body armor. It will show under our clothes if we walk around on the street for long.'

Badr said, 'But Mohammed told us to –'

Saleh snapped back, 'The vests are too big! We can't wear jackets to cover them on a day this warm without being detected!'

All three men removed their vests, passed them to the back of the Pathfinder, and donned their shirts again.

Adara found her target checking his bank balance at an ATM on King Street, then he turned and headed to the west. Even if the white-haired man hadn't had the *Post* under his arm, he just had a look about him that told her he was a contemporary – and likely a friend – of John Clark's.

She didn't follow behind him for long. Instead, she turned left on St Asaph Street, so that if he was looking for a tail he wouldn't see her at all. As soon as she was out of his line of sight she said, 'Midas, I have the target. He's about ten blocks from the river on King and heading west. I'll move parallel to him and try to get ahead.'

'Roger that,' Midas said. 'I'm five blocks away on King Street. You stay out of sight on an intersecting street, then fold in behind him, remaining on the opposite side of the street. You take the eye, and I'll stay back and keep my eyes on you. I'm ready to overlap you and take the eye on your call.'

'Got it.' Adara walked quickly, thankful she wore tennis shoes, lightweight nylon pants, and a short-sleeve shirt because it looked like she was going to do a fair bit of power-walking this morning.

The Nissan Pathfinder from Detroit passed by Eddie Laird as he walked in front of a restaurant with sidewalk café seating; then the vehicle turned off King Street and onto Washington. Here it immediately pulled to the side of the road. The three young men of Middle Eastern heritage climbed out; Mehdi and Chakir had small backpacks slung over their shoulders, each carrying an Uzi and extra magazines, and Saleh had a Glock pistol and two extra magazines rammed into the small of his back between his underwear and his skin, covered by his untucked button-down shirt.

Saleh quickly crossed to the southern side of King Street to stay opposite Laird, while Chakir and Mehdi stayed back on Washington until the old white man passed. They waited another minute before taking up the follow behind him.

They both wanted to shoot him in the back now and be done with it, but Saleh was in charge of this group, and he'd told them he'd text or call when it was time to act.

32

Adara Sherman pulled a baseball cap out of her shoulder bag as she headed north on South Columbus, and it was a good thing, too, because her target passed just fifty feet in front of her. He glanced her way, but she had been purposefully walking along right next to a man about her age pushing a baby stroller with a five-year-old boy in tow, and she turned to the boy just as her target glanced at her.

'How old is your adorable sister?'

The boy looked up at the lady who had just spoken to him, then to his dad. 'How old is Mary, Daddy?'

The father smiled at the good-looking woman in the ball cap. 'Just turned six months.'

'She's a doll.' Adara looked back to the boy. 'I bet you take good care of her, don't you?'

The little boy beamed and assured the nice lady that he did, and the dad made a moment's more conversation.

The target had passed by on King Street by now, and Adara felt confident that the white-haired man with *The Washington Post* had dismissed the family of four from having any part in a surveillance detail.

Midas was still in Adara's earpiece, and he'd heard every word. 'Either you just did all that for OPSEC, or you are using this exercise as an excuse to pick up dudes with baggage.'

Adara fought a smile as she slipped off her ball cap and made a left on King Street, falling in behind her target. 'Which seems more likely?'

Midas joked, 'I guess I won't tell Dominic . . . this time.'

'That's good of you. I'm seventy-five feet behind him and on the south side of the street. He's on the north. Moving slowly. I'll soften up, give him some more room.'

Midas said, 'I'll stay on his side, two hundred feet back but ready to close quick if necessary.'

'Roger.'

Chakir and Mehdi walked shoulder to shoulder through a thick group of tourists standing on the corner, both keeping their eyes on their target, wondering where the hell the man was going. Seconds later he slipped into a coffee shop, and the two men from Detroit stopped walking, then stood at the corner, facing King Street like they were waiting to cross at the light.

The crossing signal turned green, however, and neither man moved.

Across the street and fifty feet ahead of the men, Adara Sherman stopped and began looking through the window of an upscale antiques store that had not yet opened for business. She wanted to check her immediate surroundings for anyone standing close by, using the reflections to do so, before reporting in to Midas that the target had stopped. But before she spoke, Midas's voice came into her ear.

'Uh . . . Adara? I think Mr C. might have thrown us a curveball.'

Adara found herself free of anyone who might overhear her conversation. 'What's going on?'

'Not one hundred percent sure, but I might have a couple dudes tailing *you*.'

The blonde fought the urge to look behind her. 'Interesting. That wasn't the drill today.'

Midas replied, 'Clark told us to keep our heads on a swivel. Maybe he has more going on than he said in the brief. Unsub description to follow: Two males, light-olive complexion, early twenties. Both have backpacks. One has a brown T-shirt and a ball cap, the other a green-collared short-sleeve. They are about fifty feet back from you, but on the opposite side of the street from your poz. I'm too far back to be sure they are looking your way, but the second you stopped, they pulled up at the corner, and now they are just hanging out.'

A man stood next to Adara now, looking in the same antiques store, so Adara did not reply. Midas would know she'd received the message, and if these guys were only fifty feet behind her looking her way now, she didn't want them to see her mouth moving.

Midas said, 'Since this wasn't part of the declared exercise, let's just play this as real world. We don't acknowledge them, but we try to lose them while still keeping eyes on the target. It's going to be tricky. Clear your throat if you acknowledge.'

Adara did so, and she immediately turned left in front of the antiques store on South Fayette Street, breaking off coverage of Laird again, but also forcing the team tailing her to either break off from her or follow her down a quiet residential street.

She made a quick right onto Commerce and continued to the southwest, hoping to catch up with the target. Now that she knew the men on King wouldn't be able to see her, she asked, 'What's my tail doing?'

Midas did not answer for a few seconds. Finally he said, 'They let you go. Didn't even look your way or give it a moment's thought. They are still on King. You know . . . I could be wrong about them.'

'I'm sure you have a good nose about these kinds of things. If your gut tells you to keep an eye on them, don't write them off just yet. Laird stopped into a coffee shop, I'll get a block ahead and double back.'

Midas said, 'These two guys are moving again. Still west on King.' A pause. 'Can't be sure, but I think I see the target leaving the coffee shop and heading west.'

Adara chuckled a little. 'Wait, are they tailing me, or are they tailing our target?'

Midas said, 'I thought it was you because of their movements mirroring yours, but if your movements were mirroring our target's, who knows?'

Adara said, 'But it doesn't make sense that they would be following the same guy we are if they are with Clark.'

Midas asked, 'Unless Clark is training another team, too.'

Adara didn't believe that for a second. 'Maybe they are waiting for me to show back up.'

Midas said, 'Possible. I'll stay behind them, and watch this closely.'

Midas followed the two men, trying to also keep sight of the white-haired target, well over one hundred yards ahead on the sidewalk. But this wasn't all he was doing. He had tailed enough people in his life to know that it could feel like looking through a drinking straw if he wasn't careful. Keeping eyes on one person in a crowd had a tendency to make the follower lose sight of the fact that he or she was also out in the open and subject to potential surveillance or other threats. For this reason he took his time now to, as nonchalantly as possible, scan the entire crowd in view on the street. In front of him, around him, behind him, even in windows of buildings above him.

Everything seemed okay behind him, but he wasn't going

to walk backward and give himself away. For all he knew, Clark was monitoring them right now, making sure he and Adara didn't violate their cover-for-action by making a game out of today's surveillance.

Far across the street and ahead, near where Adara had been standing in front of the antiques store, a young man with curly black hair walked with a gait that caught Midas's eye. He was purposeful, almost storming through the slower moving crowd around him, and his head was fixed on something across the street from him.

Out of the hundred people or more Midas laid eyes on in his sweep while he walked over the next three minutes, only this one man stood out to him.

Midas said, 'Adara, what's your location?'

'South West Street and King Street. I'm making a left onto King, unless you tell me otherwise.'

Midas knew this put Adara a hundred feet or so right in front of the guy in the untucked white button-down.

'I've got a possible third unsub. You mind serving as bait to see if he locks onto you?'

'Not at all. I've got eyes on the target across the street.'

'Okay,' Midas said, 'make a left onto King and stay across and behind the target, and I'll watch the three guys behind you to see what they do.'

Adara did as directed, kept her head down and talked into her mobile phone now, pretending to have a conversation with her mom about her upcoming visit to DC and the different museums they'd visit. This kept her right hand and her phone shielding her face in the event the target looked back over his left shoulder.

Adara lowered her tone to a soft whisper. 'Midas, target is four blocks from the Metro and heading in that direction.'

Midas replied, 'Roger that. The three unsubs are not looking at you at all. I do believe all three are focused on our target.'

'So weird. Could this be unrelated to the exercise?'

'I have no idea,' Midas said. He had purposely narrowed the distance a little between himself and the two in front of him, and this helped him get a better angle on the face of the man across the street. Even from this distance he could see the man's hard, determined countenance as he walked forward, his eyes almost never wavering from the direction of the white-haired man.

Midas said, 'I don't like this. I don't like their attitudes, I don't like their proximity to you and our target, and I don't like the two backpacks the duo in front of me are carrying. I'm going to call Clark. I'll take the hit if I fail today's course.'

Adara said, 'Negative. We are in this together, pass or fail. Plus, my phone is already out. I'll call him. I want you watching these guys. Call me back if anything changes.'

'Copy that.'

She hung up the phone and dialed Clark's number.

Saleh answered his cell phone when it buzzed in his pocket. 'Yeah?'

It was Badr, behind the wheel of the Nissan Pathfinder, which had been circling the neighborhood to the west, hunting for a place to wait before rushing in to pick up Saleh, Chakir, and Mehdi in case they found a good opportunity to kill Eddie Laird.

He said, 'There is a Metro station right here. Three blocks in front of where Laird is walking. What if he is heading there?'

Saleh knew he'd have to improvise. They couldn't lose

this man for an entire day, and they couldn't follow him onto the trains without losing their getaway vehicle. On top of this, Mohammed and Omar forbade them from going into DC.

Saleh said, 'You park there and keep an eye out for us. We will take him at the station if that is his destination.'

He quickly hung up and dialed Chakir across the street.

John Clark was a dozen blocks away, leaving La Madeleine and heading back to his Range Rover, parked near the market. He felt like he'd given his two trainees enough time to identify their target and settle into their coverage. Now he'd make it tougher. He reached for his phone to call Eddie to tell him to begin an SDR as well as to begin actively searching for his surveillance, but his phone chirped as soon as he started to dial.

'Yeah?'

'John, it's Adara. We really hope we're wrong here, but Midas and I think there is someone else tailing our target. Can you confirm you aren't training anybody else or –'

'Just tell me what's going on.'

Clark began hurrying back to his SUV.

'Three males, all in their twenties. I am between them and the white-haired gentleman, and Midas is behind with eyes on all three unknowns. First we thought they were with you, just tailing me, but now we are worried they might be doing a foot-follow on the unsub. That doesn't make a lot of sense to us.'

Clark's tone was as urgent as Adara had ever heard from him. 'Those are most definitely *not* my guys. Where are you?'

'The target is entering the parking lot in front of the King Street Metro. What do you want me to –'

'I'll call nine-one-one, and I'm on the way. Your target's name is Eddie Laird. Get on him, and get him inside the station. There will be armed transit police there.'

Adara was confused. 'Why do you think –'

Clark said, 'He's ex-Agency, senior staff. Get him!'

Adara just gasped into the phone. 'Jesus. I'll grab him now.'

The phone went dead and she picked up the pace, closing on Laird now as she reconnected with Midas.

Midas was only one hundred feet behind the men now, but one of the two stepped into traffic suddenly in front of the Hilton and crossed to the other side, joining up with the man in the untucked shirt. Just as this happened, Midas's earpiece chirped.

He answered to hear Adara's intense but in-control voice. 'John says these three aren't his, and our target, Laird, is now our principal. He's ex-senior staff at Langley. We are to move him to the Metro and get him surrounded by armed transit cops.'

Midas said, 'Roger that. Be advised, you've got two directly behind you now. There is one in front of me, crossing the street into the parking lot. I don't think they like the idea of him getting out of here on a train.'

Adara said, 'The hell with this, I'm running for Laird.'

'Do it!'

Eddie Laird's phone rang and Adara closed even faster on him while he stopped to answer it. She wanted him inside the station, where at least there would be options for cover and likely some sort of police presence, but instead he started to sit down on a bench outside.

She hadn't turned back around to look at the approaching

men, so she was thankful when Midas gave her an update, although the news itself was bad.

'Packs are off their shoulders, they've separated, two have moved wide on your left, one on your right. These boys are gonna *fuckin'* hit. I'm running for the guy on your right. If he has a weapon I'll try to take it to engage the others.'

By now Adara had made it up to Laird, and as he rejected the telemarketing call and stood back up from the bench, she got right in front of him.

'Mr Laird?'

Eddie Laird looked up now. 'Well ... if you're one of Clark's students, then *that's* a definite fail.'

She took him by the arm and started leading him toward the large opening to the King Street Metro, one story below the tracks above.

'John will call when he can, but there are three men trailing you right now. Not with us. He wants you inside the station.'

Laird seemed surprised but not panicked. 'Okay. Do these knuckleheads look like they mean business?'

'My colleague is behind them and in my ear. Midas?'

Midas replied, 'They slowed when you made contact with Laird. They're trying to figure out who you are and what you are doing. Still, they are squaring off for an altercation. Keep moving into the station.'

Adara just picked up the pace with her arm around the older man's waist now. 'This could get ugly,' she said.

'You armed?' he asked.

At the entrance to the station they moved through a thick crowd of tourists, just down the escalator from the tracks above the station concourse. 'No,' she replied. 'We can't carry legally in DC, and we didn't know if you'd head into the District. You?'

Laird lifted the front of his shirt and Adara could see the butt of a small revolver.

'You're my kind of guy, Mr Laird.'

He said, 'Never even drew my piece in Kabul. Would be ironic to get my ass in a shoot-out right here.'

33

Midas was at a full run now, heading toward the single man on the right side of the parking lot. At fifty feet away he pulled out his karambit knife and held it down by his side.

Just then the man's backpack dropped to the ground, and a black Uzi sub gun remained in his hand. As soon as Midas saw the weapon appear, he whispered urgently, 'Guns are out, Adara. Get to cover.'

Chakir never got a shot off. He stopped in the parking lot in front of a parked Metro bus, leveled his weapon toward the white-haired man just entering the station, and he felt a presence on top of him. A hooked knife blade appeared in front of his face, then it was dragged back, plunging into his throat.

At the same time a large man crushed him in a tight grasp from behind, then pushed him down to his knees. Blood shot onto the hot sidewalk in front of him and screams of shock and panic erupted in all directions.

Chakir fell face-first in a splashing pool of his own blood as the big man behind him let go.

Through her earpiece Adara heard Midas grunt with effort as he took out one gunman in the parking lot behind her on her right. She and Eddie broke into a full sprint when the screams erupted in the relative quiet of the morning. Eddie reached under his shirt while he ran, but just as they neared a large support column in the rear of the cavernous station hall, fully automatic gunfire exploded directly behind them. Adara grabbed Eddie by the shirt and tried to pull him around to cover, but lost her grip when the seventy-year-old spun and dropped to one knee, raising his pistol toward the threats.

Two submachine guns tore into the tile flooring in front of Eddie and Adara, and Adara whirled her body behind the heavy column. Still, she reached out for Laird, trying to take hold of her principal to yank him out of the line of fire.

But she couldn't reach Eddie, and as he returned fire on the two men at the entrance to the station, he winced in pain and doubled forward, dropping his pistol and crumpling down beside it.

In the parking lot Midas yanked the Uzi away from the man with the spurting carotid artery, who lay facedown, and tried to spin to engage the other shooters, fifty yards away and just inside the wide entrance to the dark lower level of the station. But dozens of screaming and fleeing civilians blocked his path, and before he could level the weapon, out of the corner of his left eye he saw a huge black form barreling down on him.

Midas tried to leap forward, but he took a glancing blow from the left front quarter-panel of the speeding Nissan Pathfinder and it spun him through the air. He landed hard on the hot pavement, knocking the Uzi out of his hands and the earpiece from his ear.

If the driver slammed on his brakes then and there he could have shot Midas dead before he recovered from the impact, but the Pathfinder sped on across the parking lot, bouncing over a grassy median and into the bus lane, then back up on the sidewalk, racing toward the entrance to the Metro station.

Adara dove out into the line of fire, lifted Eddie's revolver with one hand while she grabbed him by the wrist with the other hand, trying to heave him to cover behind the column near the southwest corner of the big open hall.

As she pulled on the wounded man she aimed in the direction of the gunfire and instantly saw that one of the men was down on his back, writhing in obvious agony. She assumed Laird had hit him, and adjusted her aim to the second shooter. He was firing a pistol blind into the station, missing her by ten yards but sending nine-millimeter rounds just over the heads of terrified Metro passengers lying flat on the floor.

Adara watched while the second attacker's hand reached out and pulled the Uzi away from the wounded man. She tucked tighter behind the column as fully automatic fire rang out again and more dust and debris flew around her on all sides.

Saleh dumped the full magazine of Mehdi's Uzi, then pulled it back around his column, crouched down, and leaned his back against the hard cover. The Language School operatives had been taught to tape magazines together, side by side, separating them by small pieces of wood so they would seat easily in the magazine well of the weapons. By this method they didn't have to fish around in their pockets for a second magazine, and they could carry sixty-one nine-millimeter rounds on their fully loaded weapons, instead of just thirty-one.

While Saleh snapped the second magazine into position

he looked next to him and saw Mehdi rolling around in pain, blood smearing on his clothes and the tile floor.

Saleh now looked to where Chakir had been positioned, wondering why he wasn't hearing any gunfire from over there, but instead he saw Badr racing the Pathfinder across the wide pedestrian zone right toward Saleh and Mehdi's position. *Good.* Saleh had no idea where Chakir had gone, but he was reasonably certain he'd shot Edward Laird, and now all he had to do was get the hell out of here in one piece.

Adara did not have a decent shot at the gunman still in the fight inside the station, especially not while multitasking trying to yank a man to safety, because the gunman was crouched behind a column just inside the wide entrance. But to buy herself some time, she fired at the column, breaking off chunks of concrete and letting the would-be assassin know she was armed and in the fight. The revolver held only five rounds, however, so she clicked on an empty chamber after two shots.

Damn it, she thought. She'd just emptied her only real weapon.

Adara saw the Pathfinder just as she pulled Laird farther behind her column. It screeched to a stop inside the station, and a pair of transit police came running down the escalator, some forty or fifty yards off Adara's left shoulder, and immediately fired at the vehicle. The driver dumped a burst from his full-auto Uzi at Adara's position behind her column, and all she could do was throw herself over the form of Eddie Laird and wait out the fusillade.

She looked over the older man and saw that he'd been shot in the chest, and again in the stomach. She tried to render first aid, but he pushed her hand back, then reached down into his pocket, pulled something out, and folded it into her right hand.

She didn't know what he was trying to give her at first, but when she looked at it, she saw it was a speed loader, a cylindrical disk-shaped device with five .357 Magnum shells in it, used to load a revolver more quickly than one could by using loose bullets. It was covered with Eddie's blood, but she didn't bother wiping it off. As the gunfire on the far side of the column continued, she ejected the spent brass from the stubby Smith & Wesson and slid in the five fresh rounds.

Now she returned her attention to Laird, but she could see from his open, vacant eyes that he was dead.

'*Shit!*' she screamed. 'Principal's down! Midas? Where are you?'

When Badr slammed on his brakes inside the station hall, the Pathfinder skidded to a stop right at the edge of the column Saleh was using for cover. He then lifted his Uzi and, blasting through the closed passenger window by one-handing his Uzi across the front seat, engaged the woman and Laird, who were tucked behind the column closer to the back wall. While he did this Saleh stood up behind the column and focused his fire on the several transit police on the other side of the turnstiles near the escalators. He poured round after round at the cluster of four or five men and women, hoping to get them to go for cover so he could dive into the Nissan and make his escape.

He had no idea if young Mehdi was alive or not, because he could not see over the hood of the Pathfinder to where he'd last seen the eighteen-year-old rolling in pain, but Mehdi would have to save himself. Saleh wasn't going to vault the hood and scoop the kid up, exposing himself to gunfire from two directions. No, Saleh fired the last round of the Uzi and raced past the driver's-side door, then opened the door to the backseat. Just as he tucked his head in, however, glass all around him shattered, and he took a blast from a DC transit officer's SIG Sauer P226, right in the neck.

He fell onto his back on the far side of the Nissan from the cops, and dropped his empty submachine gun, while he held pressure on his bloody wound.

He sat back up, looked up at Badr behind the wheel of the Pathfinder, while Badr looked down at him.

But only for a second. Then Badr put his SUV in reverse.

'*Istanna!*' Saleh yelled – Wait! – then he reached for his Glock tucked in his pants.

Midas knew he had to be careful rushing up into the gunfight, because from the sound of it, there were several unknown shooters, probably cops, banging it out with the two terrorists inside the station and the guy behind the wheel of the Nissan, who'd just driven right up to the scene. But Midas was back on his feet, with the Uzi from the dead man in his hands, and he knew both Adara and Laird were somewhere inside.

He'd lost his earpiece when he'd been hit by the car, and he wondered how badly he'd been hurt, but his arms and legs were moving for now, and right now was all that mattered.

He ran as fast as he could past the row of newspaper stands, dodged some more civilians trying to escape the raging battle around them, and then, when the group in front of him scattered out of the way, he saw an injured man sitting on the ground outside the Nissan, holding a neck wound with his left hand and pulling a Glock out from under his shirt with his right.

At the same time this happened, the Nissan launched backward on screaming and smoking tires, right toward Midas.

Oh, God, not again.

Midas was one hundred feet behind the vehicle, and the Nissan would run him down in less than four seconds. He remained calm, leveled the Uzi, lined the bladed front sight up on the back of the head of the driver of the black SUV, and fired a single nine-millimeter bullet from the ten-inch barrel.

The driver's head lolled forward, and instantly the rear of the vehicle swerved to Midas's right. It crashed into iron gates at the edge of the station entrance at speed, so hard and fast it spun 180 degrees, and then began rolling forward again across the pedestrian zone, with a dead man slumped behind the wheel.

But Midas wasn't looking anymore, because he knew he had to stop the man sitting on the ground before he opened up with the Glock.

He swiveled his sights back to the wounded terrorist just in time to see the man's gun arm extended toward him with the barrel pointing his way.

A shot rang out, then a second, a third, and a fourth.

The terrorist jolted forward as if shot in the back, and Adara Sherman appeared behind him. She came running around the column ten feet away from where the terrorist had been sitting, and Midas saw she had a small revolver extended in her hand, pointed at the now prostrate man with the Glock lying next to him.

The other terrorist was lying facedown in a pool of blood just feet away.

A black Range Rover screeched to a halt in the bus lane,

just to Midas's left. Adara ran past Midas and climbed into the backseat of Clark's vehicle, and Midas himself jumped in the front passenger seat.

As soon as they climbed inside, the Nissan Pathfinder, now seventy or eighty yards behind them, rolling at idle in the bus lane, exploded with an incredible boom. As all three in the Range Rover ducked, bits of debris struck the vehicle and burning shrapnel crashed down all around.

Adara looked back and realized that the only thing that saved them from taking more of the massive detonation was that the Nissan had been behind a parked Metro bus when it blew up.

Clark did not race away instantly. He could see blood running down Midas's forearm, streaks of blood on his T-shirt, and Adara had blood all over her white summer blouse.

'Where's Eddie?' Clark asked.

'Sorry, John,' Adara said. 'He's gone. I tried to save him, but there was nothing I could do.'

Only now did Clark step on the gas. He drove quickly, but in a manner that wouldn't give passersby who didn't know better a hint anyone inside the black Range Rover had been involved in the gun battle at the station.

'How badly are you two injured?'

Midas asked, 'Adara?'

'I'm unhurt. Midas is wounded. Covered in blood. We need to get him to a hospital.'

'Negative,' Midas said. 'Just took a bump from that Pathfinder. Most of this blood is from one of the Crows.'

'One of the *what?*' Adara asked.

'Crows. The bad guys.' It was Delta Force talk, and Adara hadn't heard it before.

Clark made a right onto Prince Street, but he knew he'd need to make fifty turns in the next ten minutes to have any prayer of clearing this scene and being certain they weren't being followed. Plus, they'd have to switch vehicles and, more than anything, avoid returning to the office for the rest of the day, if not the week. He listened to the heavy breathing of the two trainees, then asked, 'Who the hell did this?'

Midas said, 'Four unsubs. I only got a good look at the one I stuck. He was twentyish, small, olive, dark hair, but lighter skin. Could have been Turkish or something. Hard to say.'

Adara added, 'The guy who Laird shot . . . when I ran by him I got a good look. I'd be surprised if he was seventeen years old.'

'Middle Eastern descent?'

'Or North African. Yeah,' she said, distractedly. And then, 'I'm so sorry, John. I tried to get Laird behind some cover, but he pulled his weapon and engaged.'

'What weapons did you see on the hostiles?' Clark asked, desperately looking for any indicator about the identity of the attackers.

Midas said, 'Full-auto Uzis, and I saw a Glock.'

Adara nodded in the backseat. 'I saw the same. Handguns and sub guns. Mr Laird killed one of the men.'

Clark just nodded. 'Good for Eddie.' Then he slammed his hand on the steering wheel. 'Who the hell was after him?'

No one responded, because no one had a clue.

34

John Clark, Adara Sherman, and Barry 'Midas' Jankowski climbed out of Clark's black Range Rover as it rolled to a stop at an employee entrance to Tysons Corner Center, a large shopping mall just twenty minutes from the shoot-out in Alexandria. Clark left the driver's-side door open and a bearded man in his forties climbed behind the wheel without saying a word, and then he drove the SUV out of the parking lot and back onto the interstate.

The man was Dave Fleming, one of the Campus security officers. He would drive the Range Rover west, halfway across Virginia, to get it out of the area. He'd park the vehicle on some land owned by one of The Campus's shell companies and then wait to be picked up by Pablo Gomez, another of the security staff. Together they'd return to the DC area tonight in Gomez's silver '69 Pontiac Firebird.

Clark, Adara, and Midas stepped into the side entrance of the mall and immediately turned into the Eddie Bauer store, just feet away. The adventure-wear location was managed by Dave Fleming's twenty-five-year-old son, Pete. Pete was a former member of the US Army 75th Ranger Regiment, who had returned to the DC area to work on his master's at Georgetown with an eye toward future work with the Agency.

A quick call from Clark to Chavez, and then from Chavez to the young man running the clothing store, ensured that the manager was the only person in the store when three individuals walked in, changed into brand-new clothes, and walked out the back employee door, all within two or three minutes.

Only when the three had departed did Pete Fleming notice small blood droplets on the cheap tile floor of the stockroom.

Chavez was waiting behind the wheel of a Ford Explorer with tinted windows outside the exit to the Eddie Bauer stockroom. When he had all three loaded he drove a couple of miles to a safe house kept by The Campus on Turkey Run Road, just a few hundred yards from CIA headquarters in the unincorporated subdivision of Langley.

Jack Ryan, Jr, and Dom Caruso were already waiting at the safe house, armed with sub guns hanging from their shoulders and a hell of a lot of questions about what had just happened on the fifth day of training the team's new recruits.

Adara came through the garage door holding a bloody compress on Midas's arm, and she had time only to make an instant of intense eye contact with Dom before going into the kitchen and commandeering the table there to use as a treatment area for the ex-Delta officer.

While the others stood around the kitchen, Midas pulled off his shirt and dropped his pants, but only after the insistence from Adara and the gravelly seconding of Adara's request by John Clark.

'*Damn*, brother,' Ding Chavez said when he saw Midas's left hip and thigh. The area was bright purple in the center, fading to a dull gray, and the bruise was over a foot and a half in length. 'How the hell did you just walk in here?'

Midas shrugged. 'Nothing's broken. It might ache a little tomorrow.'

Clark said, 'You aren't in the Unit anymore, son. You're allowed to say ouch.'

Midas cracked a thin smile. 'Well, then . . . ouch.'

Gerry Hendley marched through the front door of the safe house with Gavin Biery, followed by Dale Henson and Jason Gibson, two more security men from The Campus, who entered only after making sure the garage door was secure. The security officers took up positions that gave them a view out the front and back doors of the property, and they pulled short-barreled rifles chambered in the powerful 300 Blackout round from discreet deployment bags. They then slung their rifles over their shoulders and took up watch. Gerry was on the phone, but he found the group in the kitchen converged around Midas, who stood there by the table in his Lycra underwear.

'Hey, boss,' Jankowski said awkwardly.

Gerry lowered the phone for a moment while he surveyed Midas's injury to his hip. 'If I had to guess, I'd say that came from the driver's side of a black Nissan Pathfinder.'

Midas's eyes went wide for an instant, as did Adara's, but almost instantly both recognized where Gerry had gotten his information.

Midas said, 'Shit. Security camera?'

Gerry nodded. 'Yep. Gavin had it pulled up in seconds.'

Biery said, 'Nothing to worry about. The quality isn't good enough to ID anyone from any of the angles. You guys are safe on that front. I've also got guys back at the office monitoring social media tags, different cloud services, and the like. If anybody puts video or stills of the event online, we'll check them instantly to be ready to censor.'

Gavin looked at Midas, a man he'd met only once. 'I've got to say, I'm impressed. I watched that impact about five times. You spun through the air for a second like a Marvel superhero.'

Midas looked down at his purple hip. 'Thanks, but superheroes don't slap face-first into the pavement after a second.'

Gerry stepped away, continuing his call, while the others watched Adara work on a long gash on Midas's forearm. She then strapped a big bag of ice to his hip with an Ace bandage from her orange medic kit, transported from the office to her by Dom.

Gerry hung up the phone and walked over. 'Do you need stitches, Barry?'

'No, sir. Seems Ms Sherman has me squared away like the pro she is.'

Hendley and Clark both looked at Adara. They knew to trust her judgment on emergency medical matters. Adara wouldn't sugarcoat things, nor would she make a bigger deal out of them than necessary.

But the blonde leaning over her patient shook her head. 'He'll be fine. But, like he said, tomorrow won't be a good one for him. That hip is going to swell, even with the ice. He got lucky with the lacerations on his arm. He must have caught the rearview mirror or something on the SUV that hit him, but I was able to fold the skin back into place, and it will heal nicely. He has some road rash and bruising on his chest and knees, but nothing to worry about.'

Midas said, 'I've survived six IEDs, I can survive getting knocked to the pavement by a dickhead in a Nissan.'

Clark asked, 'What about you, Adara? You were right in the middle of all that.'

'I'm fine. Not a scratch.' She stole a quick look at Dom, who didn't hide the relief he felt. She added, 'I just wish I could have done something for Mr Laird.'

Gerry Hendley said, 'That tough son of a bitch survived

349

the Tet Offensive in Vietnam in 1968 and he survived the embassy bombing in Beirut in 1983. But he didn't survive a morning walk in Virginia in 2017.'

Adara said, 'He went down fighting. He killed one of them.'

Gerry nodded. 'Doesn't surprise me at all.'

Now Gerry relayed what he learned on the phone. 'DC police have three dead terrorists at the scene. Another possible body behind the wheel of the SUV that blew up. Two dead civilians, including Eddie Laird, and two dead DC transit officers. Eight other civilians injured, and a transit officer who took some shrapnel through the hand.'

'Christ Almighty,' muttered Adara.

Gerry looked at Gavin and Jack now. 'Any chance Laird could be one of the intelligence professionals caught up in this big leak affecting so many the past few weeks?'

Jack hadn't been there when it happened, but he felt like he had something worth saying. 'I don't think so.'

Chavez asked, 'Why do you say that?'

'We think the leak is coming from SF-86 applications housed on a supposedly secure network at the Office of Personnel Management. The digital records only go back to 1984. If this guy was in the CIA in Nam, I'm going to assume he received his classified access a long time before '84.'

Clark said, 'There's something you don't know. Eddie's daughter, Regina Laird, is also with the CIA. She was Naval Intelligence but joined the Agency five years back. Gina's SF-86 will have her dad's employer listed.'

Jack understood now. 'Well, then, that changes things.'

Chavez said, 'It also means, not only does somebody have to tell Eddie's daughter that her dad's been murdered, but also that her career in covert ops is over.'

Gerry turned to Jack now. 'Are you suggesting that some-body out there has all these records, and they have the ability to take this raw data to find out where that person is now and what they are doing?'

'That's it, exactly.'

Jack saw that his cousin Dom had the same confused look on his face that Jack himself had worn when Gavin had first suggested this.

'ISIS has these skills?' Dom asked.

Gavin chimed in to answer. 'Not a chance in hell. Jack and I are working under the assumption that a private group has exploited this data. They then sold or gave a piece of the intel to a Russian kid whose brother died on a sub sunk in the Baltic. Then, after that, they've been using the material as the foundation of high-level identity intelligence exploit-ation, creating individual targeting packages, probably for money, but perhaps for other motivations. They've passed these packages off to several state actors, and now it seems they've given a large amount of information to Islamic State operatives in Europe and the US.'

Chavez thought over the scope of it all. 'Hell . . . everybody in this room has filled out an SF-86.'

Jack Ryan shook his head. 'Except me.'

Clark considered the irony. 'Right, the famous guy is okay. But those of us who haven't been in *People* magazine are now more famous than we want to be.'

'I was fourteen with braces the last time I was in *People*,' Jack said. 'Still, I wouldn't worry about you guys getting caught up in this breach. There are a lot of files this bad actor has to wade through, and any research he does into the present-day status of you all shows you work for a private equity management firm in Virginia. Your careers in corporate security and logistical operations are supported by all the right documentation. No, these bad guys are focusing on people still in the game or, in the case of Todd Braxton, still touting what they did to Islamic radicals.'

Gerry said, 'But if what you say is true, that means there are tens of thousands of men and women who could be in danger right now. Have you gone to the DNI with this yet?'

Jack said, 'No, sir. We just put this together ourselves yesterday, and wanted to test our assumptions a bit. The NSA doesn't believe the OPM has been hacked, but Gavin has all but ruled out anything else.'

'Well, I'd say it's time to talk to Mary Pat. She can make the decision if Dan Murray should know about your identity intelligence exploitation theory, but from what I'm hearing from my contacts in the IC, nobody else has found anything solid.'

Jack and Gavin looked at each other and nodded. Jack wasn't as sure their theory was ready for prime time as Gavin was, but still he said, 'We'll write something up to present just as soon as we get back to the office, but I think I should stay here to help with security for the time being.'

Gerry turned to Clark. 'I'd like to get him back on the analytical side as soon as possible.'

Clark said, 'I agree. Jack, we're fine with the security we have here. You and Gavin can take off, but do an SDR before returning to the office. We're going to stay here till this evening, monitor the news and investigations. If we're clear, we'll move then. I might take Midas and Adara to my place tonight, just to get them out of town.'

Gerry said, 'I'll talk to Dan Murray as soon as I can get him on the phone, see what he can do to dial down any heat on us about what just happened in Alexandria. Anybody looking at security cameras up and down King Street will see Adara and Midas tailing Eddie before the hit. Dan needs to know you two are on our team and you neutralized the threats this morning.' Gerry then asked, 'John, what about your Range Rover? It was seen at the Metro station.'

Clark shrugged. 'There are five thousand just like it around here. Still . . . I guess it's a good excuse for an upgrade. I'll run that by Sandy.' With a shake of his head he said, 'A good man died today. A man who served his country well. Just like Jennifer Kincaid. I know the government will be doing its best to get some payback for this, but I'd sure as hell like for us to be involved in that, too. Gerry, if Jack and Gavin can get us someone to focus on from their investigation, I hope you'll allow us to prosecute that target.'

Gerry said, 'Considering the obvious fact that covert US government operators are exposed by this, I feel pretty sure Mary Pat would appreciate our assistance right through to the end. And I've got no problem with that, at all. If Jack and Gavin can get us targets, I'll secure Mary Pat's approval and get us involved in the hunt.'

35

Late in the afternoon in a third-floor office occupying a corner of a drab square concrete building on Bucharest's Strada Doctor Paleologu, Alexandru Dalca watched the live news reports from America on his computer.

He did this just after checking his foreign bank accounts and confirming that he had become a rich man in the past week. Two deposits of $5 million for twenty-four American targets.

He smiled. Before these deposits he had about one million in his account, money he'd earned in the past year working on commission for ARTD, and here as a single man in Bucharest he'd been living like a multimillionaire, but finally his bank account actually mirrored his lifestyle.

But as much as he enjoyed looking at his money, he was surprised by the feeling that the actions in America were even more satisfying to him. He enjoyed the payback against America, the nation that sent him to prison years ago. And he was also pleased that he had correctly assumed whom he had been corresponding with all this time. Already connections were being made between the Islamic State and the attacks. Not because the Americans were smart — Dalca didn't think Americans were smart at all. No, the connections among the first three attacks were made only via the propaganda video ISIS had released proving their complicity in them all.

The ISIS guys, as he liked to call them, had taken out Barbara Pineda and Michael Wayne, and though they royally fucked up the Todd Braxton assassination, they lucked out and killed someone arguably more famous to the Americans.

Dalca wasn't the introspective or self-critical type, so he didn't spend much time musing about the fact he deserved some of the blame for the error in the Braxton hit. His research into Braxton's day-to-day activities told him the man was traveling to the movie set every day with Danny Phillips, but Dalca wasn't much of a movie person himself, and he didn't consider the fact that Phillips would have changed his appearance to look like Braxton.

He'd found out details of Braxton's location with more ease than most of the other targets. Specifically, he used Twitter, Facebook, Snapchat, and other social media accounts. Just three days before the hit Braxton had posted a picture of himself on Twitter sitting in the back of a big black SUV, saying his entourage was on the way to the set in the Mojave Desert. In the background of the image Dalca had identified a Starbucks sign, and then by using the location metadata saved onto the digital image itself, he'd ID'd the coffee shop as being located at the corner of Laurel Canyon Boulevard and Riverside Drive in Los Angeles. In his picture Braxton had the big muttonchops that were in all the hundreds of other photos Dalca had found of the man taken within the past three years, and Dalca had included similar photos in the targeting package sent to the ISIS guys.

The next day at 6:18 a.m., a Facebook post from Danny Phillips tagged Braxton and said the two men had had their coffee and were heading to the set. Along with the hashtag '#BloodCanyon,' Phillips added '#coffeefortheroad.'

These foolish Americans had made it easy for him, Dalca thought at the time. The metadata revealed it was the same location as before.

Dalca checked pictures of the Laurel Canyon Starbucks on a dining review website and saw it did have a drive-through, but from the Twitter photo Braxton's vehicle seemed to be in a parking space, indicating they had stopped to go into the café.

Since Braxton seemed to be making a daily ritual out of his coffee run, the Romanian determined this would be a good location for his clients, the ISIS guys, to go after their target.

It was solid data, but he had erred in his failure to search for recent images of Danny Phillips. If he'd taken the time to do so he would have found many; he was a popular actor and every day people stopped him for pictures, pictures that made their way onto social media sites like Flickr or into the cloud or onto any of dozens of other photo streams online. He could have seen that Phillips had grown muttonchops, and noted the general similarity in size and appearance of the two men, and he could have then warned his client of the danger of misidentifying their target.

He wondered if his contact, the man who spoke English with an obvious Middle Eastern accent, was going to try to blame him for the failure of the op.

Probably not, Dalca decided, simply because the Braxton assassination, which turned into the Phillips assassination, had been claimed as a success by the group.

Hell . . . none of the ISIS guys had gotten killed on that outing, unlike on most of the others.

On the live news from America playing on his computer now came early reports about the shooting and bombing in Alexandria, Virginia. Instantly Dalca knew the target would be senior CIA Middle East expert Edward Laird. As soft a target as he'd sent to his client, to be sure, yet the reporter on

CNN was claiming that three or possibly four attackers had been killed in the assassination.

He wondered if these jihadi terrorists were just that bad at their jobs, or if Laird had had some sort of protection that Dalca had missed in his exhaustive research into the man's daily activities.

All in all, Dalca was disappointed in what was going on in America. Not because of the carnage of the innocents – Dalca made no distinction between guilt and innocence – but because of the carnage to his clients.

These four assassinations had cost the ISIS guys six of their killers, a hefty price to pay, and considering the four targets were relatively low on the totem pole as compared to some of the other packages he'd provided, Dalca imagined there could well be a lot more dead terrorists in short order.

If the ISIS guys didn't step up their game, Dalca wasn't going to make as much money as he'd hoped from this enterprise, and that meant he'd eventually have to go out and find new customers.

He watched now while the American news recapped the events of the past two days, showing a blurred-out image of a body lying in a pool of blood on a kitchen floor. The reporter declared Michael Wayne was an Army Green Beret.

'Delta Force,' Dalca corrected aloud with a shake of his head. In Romanian he said, 'Fucking reporters can't get anything right.'

From the door to his office behind him he heard a voice. 'What's that?'

Dalca spun around to see his thirty-five-year-old boss, Dragomir Vasilescu, forearm on the door frame, as if he'd been standing there for some time.

'Oh. Hello, Drago.'

357

Vasilescu entered the small room, pulled a rolling chair out of the corner, and positioned himself next to his lead researcher. He kept his eyes on the screen. 'What was that about reporters getting stuff wrong?'

Nobody could think on their feet faster than Alex Dalca. It came from growing up making a living lying to people on the street and on the phone. 'Oh ... I just had CNN on while I worked. Helps me refine my English. There was a shoot-out near Washington, DC. In the space of a couple minutes they gave out two different ages of one of the victims.' Dalca added, 'Unless I am mistaken. Not paying close attention.'

Vasilescu watched the monitor now while the reporter stood in front of a Metro station somewhere in America. The director of ARTD spoke English, but not well enough to entirely keep up with the reportage. When the images switched back to the video released by the Islamic State taking credit for the earlier incidents, he turned away from the screen and looked at Dalca. 'Fucking ISIS, huh?'

Dalca nodded distractedly. 'Yeah, for sure. Fuckers. Did you need something?'

'Yes. The Seychelles Group. Everything going okay with them?'

Dalca was surprised by the question. This was the front company for Chinese intelligence, the ones who started the ball rolling with the hack of the American personnel records database, giving Alexandru access to twenty-five million applications for classified access. Dalca oversaw the project to find the spies the Chinese were looking for, but the team of young researchers under him did most of the day-to-day work. Dalca was the only one allowed into the room with the air-gapped computer holding the treasure trove of raw data, but he delegated most everything so he could spend his days searching files for targets to sell to the ISIS guys.

That didn't stop him from taking credit for everything. 'Absolutely. Everything is more than fine with the Seychelles Group contract. As a matter of fact, I located an American asset in Guangzhou just yesterday, and I sent Seychelles the complete file, including updates of where the woman is working and her known associates. I added a complete picture of her espionage against China. It took us all week to put together. Why do you ask?'

Vasilescu said, 'Because they are dropping in on Monday morning for a meeting.'

Dalca cocked his head now. The Chinese are coming? *Here?* 'You mean . . . *physically* dropping in?'

'Yes. It's rather odd. Obviously, we know whoever comes from this Seychelles Group will have an affiliation with the Chinese Ministry of State Security – we're not stupid. Hopefully they will give us enough credit to realize we will know who they really are. I see no good reason why we should have to interface in person.'

'But . . . why *are* we going to interface in person?'

'Because they are one of our largest clients, and they were *very* insistent.'

'No, I mean . . . what are they coming to talk about?' Dalca's voice almost cracked with worry.

Vasilescu said, 'I have no idea. They wouldn't say. I hoped you might have thoughts on why they felt the need to fly to Romania. It might help me prep for the meeting. You *have* been sending them the product on schedule, haven't you?'

Dalca glanced back to the computer monitor showing the activity in the USA. *This is not good at all.* 'I . . . uh . . . of course. I mean, we, my team and I, have ID'd several CIA officers in the embassy in Beijing, and the consulate in Shanghai. Others in companies based in Hong Kong. And we've provided them with dozens of men and women with connections to these officers. This female agent in Guangzhou I just mentioned, for example. We've done what they requested. These things take time.' He faked a smile. 'Lots of files to pore over, even with the automation I've designed to streamline the process.'

Vasilescu looked at his employee for a long time. Then he broke the staring contest and patted Dalca on the leg, startling him. 'Oh, well. Maybe they'll want to expand our role, give us some new work. That would suit me just fine.'

'Yeah . . . me, too,' Dalca said, but his brain was racing at full speed, trying to figure out what was going on. He fought through the unease. 'Don't worry about it, Drago. I'll talk with them, deal with any concerns they might have.'

'Excellent. We'll meet in the main conference room. Ten a.m., Monday.'

Dragomir Vasilescu left Dalca alone in his office, the monitor in front of him having now switched to images of fighting in Syria.

'Să mă ia dracul,' he muttered. It was a Romanian version of 'Oh, shit,' but was more precisely translated as 'May the devil take me.'

He tried to think of some benign reason for this short-notice visit by the Chinese, but the only thing that came to mind was not benign at all. The Chinese saw the outbreak of attacks in America, just three days old now, and they already had suspicions that the intel that set them off came from the massive theft of OPM files – a theft that could, theoretically anyway, be traced back to China. While Dalca had not imagined that the Chinese could possibly link his sale of intelligence to the raw product ARTD had stolen on behalf of the Seychelles Group, he did have to acknowledge that the Ministry of State Security was a global intelligence powerhouse, and it was not beyond the realm of possibility that they had inside information involving the North Koreans, the Iranians, the Indonesians – information that helped them realize that high-level identity intel, or IDENTINT, had been handed off by a mysterious party weeks ago.

That, and the timing of the ISIS attacks, Dalca understood now, could possibly be enough to spook the Chinese. And while Dalca had handed them over evidence of American spying in China, the MSS would have every right to be concerned about exploiting this evidence now, lest they be lumped in with the other intelligence leaks going on against the Americans.

If they arrested this woman in Guangzhou, for example, would that tip off the Americans that they were part of the leak ISIS and the other actors were employing against America?

There was a lot of bellicosity between the United States and China, but Dalca didn't imagine the Chinese would want to be associated in any way with the killing of American spies, intel analysts, and military personnel in the USA.

'Să mă ia dracul,' he said again. From that first moment months ago when he decided to cash in by merging the OPM data harvest with his unique ability to turn it into viable targeting information, Dalca had known he might somehow be exposed, and he might need to run. He'd made plans for slipping out of Romania quickly, just him and the numbers of his offshore bank accounts full of millions of dollars, and his millions more in Bitcoin.

Yes, he had an escape route, and a good one, but it was a theoretical escape. He'd need the collusion of an old friend to make it happen, and he really did not want to ask anything of this man.

Dalca thought some more. Was it really time for him to hit the panic button? If the Seychelles Group had called for a meeting, did that necessarily mean the Chinese were coming here to snatch him and kill him? Or were they just concerned, seeking some sort of assurance that the data they had ordered converted into information to help their counterintelligence personnel inside China had not, in fact, been misused and passed off to jihadi terrorists and other bad actors?

Dalca forced himself to look at the evidence dispassionately, and when he did, he convinced himself there was little real danger. Not yet, anyway. Yes . . . these men from Chinese intelligence were coming, they might be worried, but they had no proof that anyone, much less Alex Dalca, had screwed them over.

They would need a good talking-to, a convincing story. And if there was one thing in this world Alexandru was good at, it was bullshitting a customer.

He'd stay in Bucharest, he'd keep coming to work, he'd talk to the men from the Seychelles Group, and he'd keep a bag packed, ready for his run if he thought the walls were closing in on him.

36

It was 8:30 a.m. in Dubai when Sami bin Rashid arrived at his office for a Sunday morning of work. He'd not looked at any news on the way in, but as soon as he took off his coat and sat down he flipped on an English-speaking international news station.

With his elbows on his desk he watched a rundown of the attacks in America. He'd already known about the first three; even though they hadn't immediately been worldwide stories, he'd been hunting specifically for news in cities where targets lived, and he'd learned of each incident almost immediately after it happened.

From this research the day before, he knew that two of al-Matari's men had been killed by law enforcement in North Carolina. Losing two men in the killing of one man infuriated bin Rashid, because this was obviously an unsustainable rate of attrition, and because he had a lot riding on this operation. So this morning when the coverage switched to Alexandria, Virginia, to what was described as a massive shoot-out, bin Rashid all but held his breath.

He knew the target would be Edward Laird, former CIA director of operations for Near East Asia. Laird was an old man who lived alone, probably as soft a target as any bin Rashid had sent to al-Matari, and he presumed the assassination would take place in the man's home. But when bin Rashid saw jerky cell-phone video of the Metro station and heard what sounded to him like a half-dozen firearms all going off at once, he knew something had gone horribly wrong.

'Police say two of the nine dead were a DC transit police officer, and four more were the attackers, one of whom was driving a rented Nissan Pathfinder with Michigan plates.'

Four dead?

He felt sweat form on the rear of his scalp and run down the back of his thick neck.

Four dead!

Sami bin Rashid looked at a monitor on his wall that gave him time in all US time zones. It was evening in the DC area. He didn't know where al-Matari himself was in the United States, or even if he had been among the dead, but he snatched his phone up anyway, his hands shaking with fury.

It took a full minute for the man on the other end of the line to answer.

Musa al-Matari sat alone in his room in the Chicago brown-stone, looking at his phone while it rang in his hand. It was a Silent Phone app call, and he'd changed the default set-tings so that calls wouldn't roll to voice mail until twenty rings, knowing that anyone who had this number had some-thing important to communicate. Al-Matari did not want to miss any calls coming in for the duration of his operation here.

But this was one call he did not want to take.

He was alone up here in his room. Two members of the Chicago cell, as well as Algiers and Tripoli, were downstairs, and four more cell members were out, preparing for an operation that would kick off soon.

Al-Matari blew out a long sigh, and on the fifteenth ring

he answered his phone, already dreading the conversation that was sure to come.

'Yes?'

'You lost four men going after a retiree! Explain that to me.'

Al-Matari wasn't going to be lectured to by the Saudi. 'We don't know what happened. Obviously there was protection for Edward Laird that your *fucking* intelligence did not specify.'

'Ah, yes! Of course. Now you will blame *me* for your failures.'

'And what of Todd Braxton? All the information you sent and you fail to notify us not only that he had changed his appearance, but also that he was traveling with a man who looked *exactly* like him?'

The Saudi said, 'Your people on the ground have to identify your targets. I can't come over and shoot people for your cause, brother. I have to do the hard work here.'

Musa al-Matari snapped back, '*We* are over here in enemy territory. Taking the risks. Operating with only the information you send us to go on. Whatever it was that happened today that got four men killed and whatever caused the misidentification of the target in California are intelligence failures, not operational failures.'

The Saudi replied coolly, 'You haven't even attempted any of the top-flight targets. These were the easy marks. And still, six are dead. One in five of your total strength.' The Saudi had been told that a total of thirty operators would be in America at the beginning of the mission.

'I know this. You think I don't? But we've known from the beginning that there will be losses, and that the numbers of operators will move in both directions. Men will be martyred, and new blood will come in in the form of new recruits.'

'*What* new recruits? Success breeds success. We have to have victories to pull more recruits in.'

Musa al-Matari had planned from the beginning to keep operational details away from the Saudi. But he broke his own rule now. 'We will have multiple actions within a day's time. One of them will be a top-tier target.'

'Which target?'

'I am not revealing operational information to someone who, frankly, has no need to know.'

After a time, bin Rashid said, 'Very well. That is how it should be. We are all on the same side here, my brother. I just remind you, you need a win. A *big* win. You need to show the world that your cause is strong.'

Al-Matari just said, 'Watch your television, Saudi. You will see something great, *inshallah*.' And then he hung up the phone.

Adara and Midas drove to John Clark's Emmitsburg, Maryland, farmhouse just after ten p.m. A determination had been made by all that the coast was clear after this morning's debacle in Alexandria, especially after a confidential conference call among Gerry Hendley, Dan Murray, and Mary Pat Foley. Mary Pat and her husband, Ed, had been friends with Eddie Laird for decades, and she and Dan were pleased that Campus employees had killed the four terrorists before they'd managed to do more harm, even if they admitted they would have much preferred that at least one of the men had been taken alive.

The crime itself had fallen under federal jurisdiction the moment it was clear this was a terrorist incident, so Dan assured Gerry the two surviving shooters whom several witnesses reported leaving the scene in a black Range Rover would be identified as personal security for former CIA officer Edward Laird, and that would be that. Gavin Biery had not found any photos anywhere on the Internet of incriminating quality, so they all agreed that The Campus was in the clear.

John Clark had left for his farm three hours earlier than Midas and Adara, so he was standing on the front porch with his wife, Sandy, as the two entered with their go bags on their shoulders.

For safety's sake, it had been decided that Adara and Midas would stay here at the remote farm for a couple of nights, while covert security cameras were installed in and around their homes to see if they were under any surveillance, either from al-Matari operatives or even from local police after what had happened that morning. Sandy showed both of the trainees to second-floor bedrooms, each with its own bathroom, and then she went to bed.

Adara and Midas made their way back downstairs, and the former Navy corpsman noticed that the former Delta Force officer moved slow and held on to the railing to combat the pain in his hip while he did so, but she said nothing. She knew he was a reluctant patient; throughout the day when she'd check on him and he'd brush off her concerns she would have to first remind him he'd been hit by a speeding SUV just hours earlier. She'd pick her battles with him as far as keeping his injuries dealt with, and let him play tough guy as long as it didn't affect his operational status.

They found Clark in the kitchen with three open bottles of beer, and they chatted here for a moment about the old farmhouse before they all moved out to the back porch, where they sat and listened to the sound of tree frogs in the distance.

Clark said, 'Well . . . this isn't how any of us wanted this to happen, but I talked to Gerry this evening. We are going to be working hard in the upcoming days and weeks, as the intelligence community tries to get a grip on what the hell is going on. Jack and Gavin are working on pinning down who is involved in obtaining the intel to target the victims here in the States, and we fully expect that to lead us to a target of our own. On top of that, Gerry thinks there might be opportunities for us to address the domestic side of this problem as well.'

Adara and Midas just sat silently.

'To that end,' Clark said, 'we are going to suspend further training for you two. We'll bring you into the operational staff immediately, on a sort of probationary period. Hell . . . you both did damn fine jobs today. We lost Eddie, but considering you walked into a shoot-out with no guns and walked out of it with four dead terrorists, I'd say you passed any training we could throw at you with flying colors.'

While Adara and Midas were both pleased to be accepted onto the team, this was no celebration.

Instead, Midas just said, 'Thanks for your faith. I, for one, am ready to get after these guys. We're okay to go back to the office tomorrow?'

Clark shook his head. 'I am, you're not. While we won't be pulled into the investigation about the attack at the Metro, there could always be some local in the neighborhood who got a look at you two shooting it out in the station. That could make trouble for us. You both live outside of Alexandria, so you can return to your places the day after tomorrow, just as soon as we're sure nobody is surveilling them. For tomorrow, you can hang out here. I've got a simple firing range down by the creek, and I might be able to scare up a few weapons so you can get some trigger time in.' He said this with a wink, meaning he would have no problem coming up with a lot of firearms for the two new members of The Campus to shoot.

They then spent the time it took to finish their beers listening to John tell stories about Eddie Laird, and both of the two new operators were impressed by the exploits and the character of the man whom neither had gotten a chance to know personally.

Adara had promised to call Dominic before bed, and Midas just wanted to lie flat to take some of the ache out of his hip, so when John suggested they call it a night, they both agreed.

Midas started to stand. As he did so he winced in pain but did his best to hide it.

Clark saw the expression and said, 'You okay, son?'

'Totally. Good to go.'

Clark looked to Adara. She just raised an eyebrow.

Clark said, 'Have you ever taken an Epsom salt bath?'

'Uh . . . no, sir. I can't say I have.'

'Well, I don't like to give direct orders. We're a pretty easygoing bunch at The Campus, definitely more so than JSOC. But if it takes me ordering you to soak yourself in some Epsom salt to get you moving right again, I will do just that.'

Midas didn't appear convinced, but to placate Clark he said, 'Yes, sir. I'll run out tomorrow and –'

Clark smiled, his first smile since Eddie's death. 'No need. I had Sandy put a five-pound bag of the stuff next to the tub in your bathroom. Twenty minutes, minimum.'

'Roger that. Yes, sir,' Midas said. Then he and Adara headed for the stairs.

As they went up Adara said, 'I'm guessing a direct order to soak in a tub before bed wasn't standard operating procedure at Delta Force.'

Midas laughed. 'Not really, no.'

37

Tampa could be brutally hot in the summer, even in the morning, though heat wasn't unfamiliar to the fifty-eight-year-old man running past the softball field in the predawn light. He'd lived in a lot of hot climates in his life, and he was certain he'd find his way back to someplace even sultrier than South Florida soon enough, so he didn't let it faze him.

Still, while he was accustomed to warm weather and bright sun, he knew enough to avoid exercising in the latter if he didn't have to, so even though it was only six a.m. now, he was taking advantage of the last bit of darkness before the sunrise, using the relative cool to push himself harder than he had in weeks.

And just as he was accustomed to warm climates, so was he used to pushing his mind and body.

General Wendell Caldwell was the head of United States Central Command, one of the US military's theater-level Unified Combatant Commands. A West Point graduate and a thirty-four-year military veteran, Caldwell had recently returned from a monthlong trip to Iraq to meet with his battlefield commanders there, and now he was back in Tampa, working just as hard as he had overseas.

But no matter where he was in the world, Caldwell made himself start his day with a little PT.

Gadsden Park was just north of MacDill Air Force Base, home of USCENTCOM, and Caldwell enjoyed leaving the confines of the base for forty minutes or so to do a couple circuits of this park before heading around the base's fence to the southwest. There he would run south for a few minutes with Tampa Bay on his right shoulder, all the way down Picnic Island Boulevard to the park at the tip of the little peninsula that jutted out into the bay.

He would circle the parking lot, then put the exterior fence of MacDill AFB on his right shoulder and head back to the north, passing back through the front gates of Mac-Dill approximately forty minutes after leaving it.

Caldwell lived on base, he worked on base, and during times of high operational activity like the present, he would go days without leaving the wire of MacDill except for his run through the adjoining neighborhoods.

The big news in the past day was, of course, the ISIS attacks here in the United States, but as far as Caldwell was concerned, the bombings just off the Navy base at Sigonella were even more important. He would be meeting today with base security experts here in Tampa who had a plan to bolster defenses at European bases, because Sigonella had a lot of his people moving through it, so he made this one of his many responsibilities.

Though he was furious about the recent spate of attacks here in America, he wasn't worried personally for a couple important reasons. One, he never, *ever*, saw anyone who looked remotely suspicious on his runs, and the thought that an ISIS member would be out here without Caldwell noticing him from 250 yards away was highly unlikely. Plus, Caldwell didn't run with headphones on and he remained vigilant at all times, and now even more vigilant due to recent events. If he did happen to come across someone along his route who looked in any way out of the ordinary, he'd know it immediately.

And that would initiate the second reason he wasn't concerned. In a Velcro band around his waist, under his US Army T-shirt but within easy reach, was a chrome-plated Walther PPK/S, a .380-caliber pistol.

The gun had been a gift from the German Bundeswehr after Caldwell's two-year stint running US Army forces in Stuttgart.

If he saw trouble, he told himself, he'd be ready.

Caldwell wasn't discounting the threat. He expected he'd need to have some meetings with base security officials here at MacDill to make sure all the forces here were awake and aware of this new danger here in the United States to military personnel. Of course it was possible that some soldier or airman living off base might be attacked, depending, of course, on the still unknown strength of the Islamic State operational cell in America. But Caldwell himself had met danger in Panama, in Iraq, in Kosovo, in Afghanistan, and then in Iraq again. A couple of poorly trained ISIS shitheads trying to head him off on his morning run wouldn't stand a chance.

He finished two circuits of Gadsden Park, jogged the long, straight westerly route of North Boundary Boulevard, then made his way through a few neighborhood backstreets that finally dumped him out on Picnic Island Boulevard.

As he ran south toward the park that jutted out into Tampa Bay, he watched a pair of F-16s coming in on final on runway 04 out in front of him. The sunrise had just broken, and the light glinted off the canopies of the fighters as they passed by.

There were several other runners out this morning, and as he passed them he would get looks of recognition from some of his subordinates, whether he recognized them or not. These were always followed by a quick 'Good day, sir' as the junior man or woman jogged by, and Caldwell would respond with a 'Good day' or even a 'Hoo-ah,' if he was feeling it.

Sometimes he wondered how far he could really run if he didn't have to huff out a greeting twenty or thirty times every time he laced up his running shoes and went for a jog.

Today he had PERSEC on his mind, checking out each jogger from a little more distance, focusing on them a little longer, thinking about how he would deal with them if they became a threat.

But he saw no one who looked like they could be a jihadi tango, and he couldn't help finding laughable the prospect that a jihadi tango would pop up here, just outside the wire of MacDill AFB.

Picnic Island Park was a cluster of succulent trees and manicured lawn around a parking lot with several covered pavilions and picnic tables that afforded good views of the bay. It was filled with MacDill AFB personnel on the weekends, and often personnel brought their lunch here during the weekdays, but this morning at six-twenty it was abandoned except for a small white four-door Honda parked nose-in in a space facing Tampa Bay. Caldwell paid little attention to the car; he'd round the tip of the peninsula and pass back right next to it in a minute and he'd check it out more closely then.

The general passed a copse of trees lining the pavement at the tip of the parking lot, and when he made the turn he was startled by a jogger coming his way, just twenty feet or so off his nose. He quickly sized the other runner up; saw the small, slight frame, the shoulder-length dirty-blond hair, and the typical South Florida running gear of shorts and a

T-shirt. He determined this smallish white person was no threat, even though he or she would be passing close by.

He looked away past the jogger, as the Honda fired its engine.

It was only when the jogger suddenly altered his direction, moving in front of Caldwell's route, that the general looked back quickly, and staggered a step to avoid a collision, angry to be pulled out of his stride by this young fool who was probably drunk or high or –

A knife blade glinted with the pink sunrise as it appeared in the jogger's right hand. General Caldwell snatched his T-shirt with his left hand, got his right hand around the grip of his pistol, and quickly tried to stop fully and leap backward, clear of the blade.

The young white man was on him before he pulled the weapon free. The knife blade stabbed into General Wendell Caldwell's ribs, sank hilt-deep, and only then did the general pull back and away to put a foot of space between himself and his attacker.

The general pulled the trigger of the Walther as soon as it came out from under his shirt, and the round screamed out of the 3.3-inch barrel, struck his attacker in the upper thigh, traveling down. The flash of the shot burned the young man in the crotch, the bullet tore through his leg, and blood splattered onto the parking lot between his feet.

The general fired again as both men fell to the ground. This round took the young man in the lower abdomen, just two inches below his belly button.

Both men ended up on their backs, just feet apart.

General Caldwell lay there with his attacker, lifted his head, and looked down at the hilt of the knife, still sticking out of his chest.

He was a tough man, but he felt weaker by the second.

A glance beyond the knife's hilt showed him the man who stabbed him was also still alive, also on his back, facing up. He was a young man, early to middle twenties, and with his blond hair and light eyes, he looked to be as American as apple pie.

His chest heaving, Caldwell asked, 'Why, boy? *Why?*'

The blond-haired kid's face seemed to grow whiter with each short breath. He made eye contact with Caldwell, though his eyes were misting over quickly. *'Allahu Akbar,'* was all he said before his head lowered to the pavement and his eyes rolled back slowly.

Caldwell looked away and up to the sky. He shouted in frustration, 'You gotta be *shittin'* me!'

The two men, one a general in the US Army, the other an American-born foot soldier of ISIS, died seconds apart on the warm asphalt.

Seconds after the two bodies stilled on the pavement, the white Honda Accord rolled out of its parking space and turned to the north, the two occupants inside never looking back.

Angela Watson, leader of the Atlanta cell, and Mustafa, one of her cell members, left Alabama native Richie Grayson there in Picnic Island Park with his victim. Richie had fought for a short time in Somalia, so despite his blond hair and small frame they knew he was a warrior. Both of them also knew Richie would have wanted to die this way, and they praised his conversion to Islam, because his last act on earth would grant him martyrdom.

38

Jack Ryan, Jr, ran alone around the National Mall while a warm summer rain shower beat down on him. It bugged him only for the first minute or so, but once he was good and wet, he put it out of his mind and went back to thinking about the only thing that had been on his mind for the past week.

He'd spent the previous afternoon and evening studying Internet-related open-source intelligence methods and identity intelligence, and using his newfound knowledge to successfully prepare targeting information on all the victims of the attacks of the past several days. It was difficult work — it was no small task to take ten- or twenty-year-old information and use that to identify the right person, and put him in the right place at a specific time.

But he'd done it. US Special Forces Sergeant Michael Wayne's SF-86, five years old, was followed by a move from Fort Carson, Colorado, to Fayetteville, North Carolina, and a purging of all his social media accounts, a tip-off to anyone looking at his file that he'd made the common leap from SF to Delta Force, which was based at Fort Bragg. Two of his references on the application were Joint Special Operations Command officers, which would have made anyone looking into Wayne's file even more certain they were on the right track.

Property records showed he'd purchased the house on Lemont Drive the year before, so it was no big stretch that anyone who'd I D'd him as Delta could find his home address and then drive by. Ryan assumed the terrorists just got lucky catching him at his front door.

American military forces had never had great reason to prepare for a threat in their homes in America, and Jack wondered how quickly that would change now.

Ryan found details on Edward Laird with some more research. The man's decade-long stint as a terrorist hunter in the Middle East had been chronicled, without his permission or input, in a recent book, and he had lived in the same Alexandria home for decades.

Jack thought about all his research now. He didn't know what kind of person was delivering this intelligence to ISIS operatives on the ground in America, but he did know that person needed only the raw OPM data, a good knowledge of OSINT and IDENTINT, and a heart that was almost unimaginably cruel.

It boiled down to the fact that someone was fusing legal data with an illegal theft of data and then weaponizing the results.

He finished his morning exercise at the parking lot near the Capitol Reflecting Pool, then climbed back into his black BMW and grabbed a towel he had folded on the passenger seat for the purpose of drying off. He sat behind the wheel and rubbed the towel over his hair, and at the same time turned on the radio to NPR. The clock told him it was nine a.m., so he was glad to be catching the opening of the newscast.

'*Police officials in Tampa, Florida, have confirmed the stabbing death of Army General Wendell Caldwell, the commander of US Central Command, early this morning. The attack happened near MacDill Air Force Base just after six a.m. General Caldwell's body was found next to a second, as yet unidentified, body, who authorities speculate might have been Caldwell's killer.'*

Ryan pounded his open hand against the steering wheel of his car and threw the towel out of his way.

And when the next story came over the radio, he slowly dropped his forehead to the steering wheel.

Two bombs had gone off overnight in the United States. In Pittsburgh, a mailbox bomb seemingly identical to the one that killed Barbara Pineda in Falls Church detonated, killing a State Department political affairs officer named Denby Carson. Carson was on vacation from his job at the US embassy in Amman, Jordan, staying with his parents.

Jack immediately suspected that Mr Carson was, in fact, CIA.

The second bomb detonated under a van in Monterey, California, killing six US Army officers, all lieutenants and captains. The three men and three women had been studying Arabic at the Defense Language Institute Foreign Language Center at the Presidio of Monterey. According to the NPR report, they'd rented the van to go out to dinner to celebrate passing the course on Friday, and witnesses reported a man on a motorcycle attaching a device to the outside of the vehicle as it drove along the coast on Del Monte Avenue.

Jack lifted his head and pounded the steering wheel again. Eight dead in the past twelve hours, and here Jack was, enjoying a leisurely morning jog.

He and Gavin had told each other they'd work on Sunday, but they hadn't planned on going in till noon. Their minds were getting frayed after nearly a week at such an intense tempo, and both thought it would benefit them to approach the material with fresh eyes after twelve hours off.

But Jack realized he needed to go in now. This had become

deeply personal to him, and he felt responsible for the loss of life, because he had yet to crack the mystery of the intelligence breach, even though he felt the answer was right in front of him in the form of data.

Jack assumed others would die in this debacle, but he told himself he'd be damned if they died while he was slacking off.

He pushed the button on his steering column to activate his phone, and he called Gavin Biery's cell by saying his name aloud.

A few seconds later he heard, 'Hey, Ryan. What's up?'

'Have you heard the news?'

'Pittsburgh, Monterey, and now Tampa. Yep.'

'This is insane,' Ryan said. 'And all we've got are theories.'

Gavin said, 'I'm trying to get something more than that. I just got to the office. I've got all the transcripts of Vadim Rechkov's Reddit chats, hundreds of pages to go through, just in the hope the guy who gave him intel on Scott Hagen reached out to him this way. Figure it's a haystack that probably doesn't have a needle in it, but I have to eliminate the possibility.'

'Sounds like you could use some help. I need to do something.'

'Sure, kid. I could use you.'

'Be there in ten.'

Even though his condo was just minutes from work, Jack didn't go home to shower or change. He drove straight to the office, wearing a soaked pair of shorts and an even more soaked T-shirt. He had a change of clothes in his go bag, which he kept with him in his car at all times. It was for emergency deployments for the operations side of his job, but today he knew he needed an emergency deployment for the analytical side, because shit going on in America was rapidly spinning out of control.

He passed within a quarter mile of the White House on his way west back over the Potomac River, and he looked to right about where his father would be now, just after returning from Mass with his mom, no doubt preparing to go straight to the West Wing to work the full day.

President Ryan wouldn't take a day off with a crisis like this going on in America, and he had raised a son cut from the same cloth.

39

The President of the United States and the First Lady had begun their Sunday by taking their two youngest children to Mass.

They did this as much as they could when they were both in town, but today was special for them, in that the Ryans' elder daughter met them at the front steps of the cathedral to join them for the service. The President didn't get to see much of Sally these days. She lived north of Baltimore and she didn't like spending time at the White House, with the hassle of the media and the phalanx of security she had to endure, although whenever her parents and siblings could get away to their home on Peregrine Cliff she tried her best to drop in.

While Jack Ryan, Jr, had his father's legacy to live up to and contend with, for his sister, it was all about Mom. Sally was currently in a neurosurgery residency at Johns Hopkins, and there, as was the case around the medical community in general, no one particularly cared that her father was the President of the United States. But there was no getting around it for Sally that her mother was the famous Dr Cathy Ryan, chief of ophthalmology at Johns Hopkins.

Of course Cathy was also First Lady of the United States, but she'd been juggling these two hats for many years, and though she was old enough and comfortable enough to retire, she continued working, performing surgeries, teaching younger doctors, and serving on several hospital boards.

While everyone in the family still called her Sally, the eldest of the four Ryan children had begun using her given name, Olivia, over the past few years. Virtually everyone in the United States over the age of thirty knew the story about what had happened to the firstborn child of future President Jack Ryan, when Sally had been severely wounded by Irish Republican terrorists. The name Sally Ryan and the legacy of that attack followed her everywhere she went after that, so once she became a doctor she all but dropped it and went with Olivia.

Olivia had not yet married, but she was two years into a relationship with a good-looking orthopedic surgeon from Turkey named Davi who made her the happiest she had been in her entire life. She had all but lived for her studies in her twenties, and all but lived for her work so far in her thirties, but for the first time working sixty-hour weeks was becoming tough to manage, because with her boyfriend's similarly arduous schedule of surgeries and on-calls, they rarely got to see each other more than a couple times a week.

Of course the press had gotten hold of the fact she was involved with a Turkish doctor, and they intimated that President Ryan would soon have a Muslim son-in-law, and wondered how that would affect US foreign policy. Davi happened to be a Roman Catholic, something it would take the American media too much work to figure out and too many precious seconds of airtime to explain, so they didn't clarify this point.

The President and his elder daughter's boyfriend had gotten along well when they did sit down with each other, but Olivia was a private person when it came to her personal life, so besides a couple of all-but-mandated visits to the White House and a memorable Thanksgiving at Peregrine

Cliff, Davi had been spared much of the public attention that would come with dating the daughter of the sitting Commander in Chief.

But Davi and Olivia's relationship wasn't conducted in complete privacy. The couple also had the Secret Service detail to contend with. Olivia had become a great friend of the two men and two women who worked her detail, but it had added a complication to her romantic life.

Just a month or so earlier Olivia and Davi had stayed at a cabin her parents had recently purchased in the Blue Ridge Mountains for a weekend of fresh air and grilling out. The Secret Service detail came along in a follow car and moved into two rooms of the five-bedroom luxury cabin on thirty-five wooded acres near Old Rag Mountain, and they walked point and rear security while the couple just seeking a brief time away from the city for some romance strolled the nearby mountain trails with their dogs.

It was a shock to the system for Davi, who still hadn't gotten used to the chaperones accompanying him on his weekend getaways with his girlfriend, but by now Olivia was more than accustomed to always having a couple of extra friends with her wherever she went.

After Mass this morning Olivia, Katie, and Kyle went together to the Hirshhorn Museum on the National Mall – along with the personal protection agents for all three of them – while Cathy and Jack Senior returned to the White House.

Ryan said good-bye to his wife in the private residence and turned for the West Wing without even taking off his jacket from church. He knew he'd have to go straight into the Situation Room to talk about the two bombings that had taken place overnight, but when he got there he learned from a frazzled-looking Bob Burgess that the commander of CENTCOM had been murdered that morning in Tampa.

Although today's homily had been on grace, twenty minutes after the sermon ended, the President wanted to put his fist through the wall of the conference room.

When everyone was present and seated, Ryan saw there was a man he did not recognize in the room, sitting just one seat down from Secretary of Homeland Security Andy Zilko. Ryan knew this newcomer would be some sort of a briefer to add to something the DHS wanted to tell the President, but he wanted to know who the man was before they got started.

Ryan, still reeling from the news of General Caldwell's death, said, 'Andy, will you introduce your guest, please?'

Secretary Zilko said, 'Yes, Mr President. Dr Robert Banks is the director of the National Cybersecurity Protection System. I brought him in to give you a briefing on outside intrusion attempts into federal networks.'

Dan Murray interjected, 'If we could, Mr President, I'd like to start with a rundown of last night's terror attacks in the US before we get into that.'

'Sure. Go ahead, Dan, then we'll give the floor to Dr Banks.'

The AG went into detail about the successful attacks in Pittsburgh and Monterey, and the new attack in Tampa. The President asked questions about the evidence found at the various scenes, video surveillance, DNA, and the methods and equipment used in the attacks. All three crime scenes were still active, so there would be more information to follow, but the attorney general had known Ryan would want a lot of detail, so he came prepared with an iPad loaded with all the preliminary information from each scene.

Bob Burgess added his input on the assassination outside

MacDill Air Force Base. The US Army's Criminal Investigative Service had control of the scene, for now, but they had communicated everything to the FBI, so Burgess had little on the case that Murray did not. The Bureau had a full forensics, investigation, and counterterrorism team en route from DC to Tampa, and a Joint Terrorism Task Force unit from Miami was flying over the Everglades in a Falcon 50 right now, but the SecDef made it clear all these hits on the military meant the Pentagon wanted to be involved in every step of the process.

Murray and Ryan agreed that Homeland Security, Defense, and DoJ all needed to partner on this issue.

When Ryan asked about steps being taken to protect the military, Burgess said, 'We are at the highest base readiness here in the States, we are notifying all our commands to communicate this new danger, but we haven't done much tangible for those outside the wire of our bases.'

'Do you have recommendations?'

Burgess said, 'I have a team coming up with a plan right now. Whether it's more guns in the hands of more men and women off base, more armed MPs and security forces in off-base locations that are frequented by military personnel, better coordination with local law enforcement, or other measures, I'll present everything to you just as soon as I can.'

Jack turned to Dan Murray. 'What have we learned from the dead terrorists?'

'We've identified four of them. One of the two in North Carolina and three of the four in Virginia. All four of these men had indeed flown to Guatemala, Mexico, or Honduras during the time window for what we suspected to be al-Matari's training operation in El Salvador.'

'The Language School.'

'That's right. It looks like this proves the camp was, in fact, a training base for the Islamic State.'

Ryan said, 'And the fact that the training seems to have paid off, and everyone was able to get back into the US, will embolden ISIS to try something like this again.'

He turned to Scott Adler now. 'State needs to be on top of this, Scott. Not just with El Salvador, but with all nations in the hemisphere. Get your ambassadors out there, have them talk to national leaders, and tell them what we think went on in El Sal and how it's affecting us now. Let them know we're watching out for it to happen again, and we will do whatever it is we have to do to stop it. Ask these nations for their help, but make clear to them that a lack of help from them will necessitate action from us.'

Secretary of State Scott Adler understood exactly what his President wanted. The State Department wouldn't make threats to any ambassadors or national leadership, but US ambassadors would convey the gravity of this situation. And it would be made clear to all that the Ryan administration would not take no for an answer. The other nations of the hemisphere would have no problem understanding that a failure to act on their part to prevent terror camps within their borders would, at the very least, hurt their relationship with the United States, and could even lead to the United States' violating their sovereign borders to take matters into their own hands.

Ryan knew it was too early for any conclusions, but he turned to Mary Pat Foley and CIA Director Jay Canfield. 'Any chance this is *not* the work of Musa al-Matari?'

Canfield said, 'I would be very surprised. Astonished, actually. He is ISIS's chief lieutenant for North American affairs, and a leader in their Emni unit, which recruits foreign operators. We also know he's been trying to get assets into the US to commit terrorism. He disappeared, trained a group of Americans to commit terrorism, and we know some of these, if not all of these, Americans are back here in the States. From what we know about al-Matari, he is a hands-on type of leader. I think these are his people, and I think al-Matari is here somewhere himself as well.'

Mary Pat agreed. 'We know of no one else in the Islamic State's Foreign Intelligence Bureau who does what al-Matari has been trying to do over here. This is his work. That said, if you look hard, there is *some* hopeful news in all this. There have been a total of seven attacks in four days, and al-Matari's operators have lost seven of their number in these attacks. Judging by current attrition numbers and our estimates of the size of his force, this operation of his will not last three weeks at this pace, though to be fair we have no way to be certain his ranks won't be replenished somehow. As you know, the Islamic State has a robust recruiting program. It is possible they will recruit from the remote-radicalized here in the US and give them orders. This will give al-Matari new blood to draw from, although they won't have the training that his core cell possesses.'

Ryan addressed Arnie Van Damm. 'I want airtime tonight on the networks to talk to the nation.'

Van Damm made a face of disagreement. 'Mr President, you don't have enough to say at this point. Make a statement in the press briefing room, do it this afternoon, take questions. Dodge what you can't answer, but express the grief and outrage you feel and make it clear to the American people that everyone is laser-focused on this.'

'But –'

'If we sit you down behind your desk with what we have

now you are going to look lost. Even much of what we *do* know about the attacks will need to remain classified. Let's do it in the briefing room this afternoon.' Arnie looked at his watch. 'It's Sunday. Even with these attacks the briefing room will be half empty, so I'll need to get all the media in first.'

Ryan said, 'Okay. Why don't you go and get started on that?'

Van Damm left the room, talking to a pair of his assistants on the way out. All three of them would be on the phone with various White House correspondents within moments, frantically trying to get everyone into the building in the next couple of hours.

Ryan said, 'What about the other piece of this puzzle? Where are we with the investigation into the intelligence breach at the heart of this?'

The secretary of homeland security cleared his throat. Ryan had been around Andy Zilko long enough to see immediately he was uncomfortable with what he was about to convey. 'Men and women from the Cyber Threat Intelligence Integration Center have identified a potential compromise of federal PII.'

'What is PII?'

'Personally identifiable information.'

'Okay. At least we've found something. Whose information has been compromised?'

There was a pause, and Dr Robert Banks from the National Cybersecurity Protection System stood up. 'Mr President, the compromise encompasses those who filled out an SF-86 application for sensitive position questionnaire.'

Ryan knew that everyone in government with classified access – as well as millions of contractors who worked for certain government entities – had *all* filled out an SF-86. 'Who, specifically?'

'Well . . . actually, everyone. Everyone since 1984, and up to a point roughly four years ago, that is.'

Ryan blinked hard. 'You are saying every . . . single . . . person . . . who has applied for classified access in the US government during a thirty-year period has been compromised to some unknown enemy?'

'I am sorry to say . . . but that appears to be the case.'

Ryan's jaw muscles flexed, but his voice remained level. 'Explain, Dr Banks.'

'We are still doing forensic work on our servers with the Office of Personnel Management, and so far we have not found evidence of an intrusion, but we have discovered that an unauthorized administrator access was created, and this unsanctioned administrator logged in through a back door to the e-QIP system about four years back. E-QIP holds all SF-86 applications.'

'Who was given this access?'

'At this point, we don't know, but at the time OPM actually had zero IT security staff of their own. They contracted with one of the biggest cybersecurity firms in the nation, but about a year after this, an investigation discovered that firm had farmed out some of its work to a smaller company.' Banks cleared his throat. 'In Bangalore, India.'

'So,' the President said, 'prior to two years ago, we *outsourced* the safekeeping of the personnel records on every person seeking classified access who ever worked in government service.'

'Yes, Mr President. Again, OPM stopped working with the firm and we fined them for breach of contract.'

'So the barn door has been shut, but the horses have run off to China.'

'Uh . . . I don't know about China. Perhaps it was someone else.'

'Pardon my bias. Last time, it was China.'

'It was, indeed. It was found that the OPM did not even maintain a list of which servers, databases, and devices were in its inventory, so it was impossible to protect the data held there.

'Whoever accessed the OPM files, it was during the time the Indian company was working on internal security at the network. The credentials of a contract employee with the correct access were duplicated and these creds were used to create a new user with full admin access.'

Ryan drummed his fingers on the table. 'This cache of files has information on everyone who has ever sought classified status. Everyone?'

'Well . . . since, as I said, 1984 to four years ago.'

'I'm no computer expert, but I'm pretty sure we didn't have this network in '84.'

'No, Mr President. At that time this was all on microfiche. In a modernization plan in the nineties, all the microfiche from 1984 on was transferred to the computer files.'

'Terrific.' Ryan thought for a second. 'I guess I'm in there.'

The briefer, who was already terrified, went white. 'Ah . . . I don't know. I didn't look to see if any individuals –'

Ryan said, 'It would have been a couple years before, but of course other checks were done on me as I moved up through the ranks at the Agency and then in the executive branch.'

The doctor suddenly seemed slightly more relaxed. 'This is just the SF-86 form, along with fingerprints, so if you filled yours out prior, you would not be in there.'

Ryan shrugged. It didn't really matter, this was one of the largest disasters he'd ever heard of. He looked at the nervous man down the table from him. 'Dr Banks, you aren't on trial here. I'm royally pissed about all this, but I know better than to shoot the messenger.' He leaned forward a little. 'You tend to get less clear messages that way.'

'Yes, Mr President,' Banks said, but he didn't seem any more at ease. He added, 'We have incident-response teams working around the clock to identify who has taken this information, exactly when, and exactly how. We do feel it was a one-time data dump, and we have rescinded all admin access of the system until each person involved can be re-vetted, but clearly damage has been done in this case.'

Ryan turned to Andy Zilko. 'Andy, I've seen the numbers. We've spent five billion on the National Cybersecurity Protection System to avoid just this sort of event. After the Chinese got into our intelligence network a couple of years back, people who are paid to watch these things assured us it would not happen again.'

Zilko's unease was as obvious as Dr Banks's. 'Yes, sir. I can say we have made strides to improve our cyberprotection systems in the past four years.'

'What strides?'

Zilko thought for a moment. 'Well . . . since we're discussing the OPM, for example. The new in-house personnel are in the process of making the security there more robust, but they haven't been moving as fast as we would have liked.'

Ryan closed his eyes in utter frustration. The majority of his life had involved, in one form or another, dealing with government bureaucracies. He always thought he couldn't be fazed, no matter the bureaucratic malfeasance. And he was always finding himself to be wrong on this point.

'How many currently holding clearance have been compromised?'

Zilko turned to Banks, who answered the question. 'Right

now, Mr President, there are just over four and a half million people holding security clearances. The vast majority of these people would have filled out an SF-86 before the system was breached. I think we could be looking at a number of around four million men and women.'

Ryan said, 'More than four million current government employees or contractors could be at risk from this breach. Military officers, elected officials, technical experts, those tasked with guarding our nuclear stockpiles.'

Dr Banks said, 'I'm afraid it is every bit as bad as that, Mr President. The SF-86 won't out someone as a CIA employee directly, in fact the CIA uses their own system for classified applications, but many if not most CIA officers had to fill out an SF-86 for their cover job, like working in an embassy with the State Department, or else they were former military or law enforcement with classified access, in which case they would be in there anyway. A top-flight data miner and ID intelligence specialist can look for certain anomalies to see things that don't add up. You have a guy working in the embassy in Madrid, for example, who is a covered CIA officer. He works as a consular officer, but his SF-86 shows him spending eight years in Naval Intelligence, or serving as an Army Ranger or Green Beret. An interested party is going to determine pretty quickly that this guy is an Agency case officer, and not over in Madrid stamping passports.'

Ryan rubbed his nose under his glasses. 'And now it appears Musa al-Matari has this information, as well as others. This is a complete nightmare. Even if we stop al-Matari and all his cell members, even if this misuse of the OPM data is halted, we can never be sure who has all this information that leaked out.'

'That is unfortunately correct, Mr President.'

Ryan said, 'We need the best in the business telling us how to mitigate this damn disaster. We owe that to the people who work for us or have worked for us in the past. That's for tomorrow. For today . . . today we find the people using the intelligence to target our people, and we stop them.

'Mary Pat, we need to develop a full-spectrum counter-intelligence plan to deal with this. All government employees and contractors are, at this point, potential human targets,' Ryan said. 'It's been made abundantly clear to a few of them. General Caldwell, for example. This needs to be communicated to every last one of those affected. *Now.*'

'Under way as we speak, Mr President. As DNI, I can take the lead on this and integrate everyone we need to integrate to get the word out.'

DHS Secretary Zilko raised his hand. 'Mr President. I do want to stress that the breach happened during the previous administration.'

Ryan felt the boiling heat on his face, but he didn't let his anger overtake him. He pointed at Zilko. 'I don't ever want to hear you say that again about this or any other crisis. We aren't here to cover our asses. We're here to serve the United States of America. For four damn years people in this administration have known that a company in India had access to sensitive material. Just because we didn't know they took it is no reason to pat ourselves on the back. Just because you didn't know personally, people you are responsible for did. And just because I didn't know personally, I am responsible for you.'

Zilko looked away. Softly he said, 'Of course, Mr President.'

Ryan moved his pointed finger around the room. Everyone, even Mary Pat and Dan, got the finger and the intense eyes that came with it. 'Everyone in here needs to take responsibility for finding our way out of this debacle. We need to accept that we bear significant responsibility for these deaths and injuries, because despite any excuses we might think we have, this all happened on our watch. Maybe not the initial breach, but the fallout from it.

'Now . . . let me explain what is going to happen. We *will* find Musa al-Matari, we *will* discover who was responsible for the breach and take them off the game board, and only then, when this is over, I *will* ask for a stack of resignation letters on my desk. Ladies and gentlemen, we owed our bravest citizens better than we gave them. We'll fix it going forward, but I want a full accounting of the past.'

Ryan stood and stormed out of the room, as angry as he'd ever been in his life. America was endangered by innumerable outside threats. He had long ago learned to accept this. But he'd never been able to come to terms with the amount of self-inflicted damage the nation incurred because of poor job performance and those who did not take threats seriously.

40

Gavin Biery had been given access to the complete hard drive of Vadim Rechkov's computer, via a two-party authenticated link sent to him by a DoJ computer forensics investigator, on orders from Attorney General Dan Murray. When Gavin clicked on the link and entered the password proffered by his contact at the National Cybersecurity and Communications Integration Center, he opened a window on one of his laptops that perfectly mirrored Rechkov's own computer. It had been set up this way so various DoJ analysts, FBI agents, the NSA, and other personnel involved with the federal investigation into the Rechkov attack on Naval Commander Scott Hagen could look at the data at the same time from multiple nodes.

A quick look at Rechkov's computer's history had shown Gavin that the young man was a habitual visitor of Reddit, a website of message boards where different links from around the Web were shared and discussed and voted on. A key feature of the site was that thriving niche communities of people with similar interests formed in very specific subreddits, each its own discussion forum with its own discussion topic. The complete website history of Rechkov wasn't available from looking at his hard drive; Gavin could look back only a few weeks into the man's online past, but he saw Rechkov had visited Reddit some 160 times in just that period.

Gavin scanned back to the earliest date in the time

window that fell after Rechkov's history appeared on the computer and before he would have left on his cross-country drive to attempt the assassination of Scott Hagen. He clicked on one of Rechkov's Reddit sessions to find his username, and then he used another laptop to log in to the same subreddit online, using a profile he'd created to navigate around. He then typed in Rechkov's username, TheSlavnyKid.

Simply by typing in this handle and clicking on 'Overview' he could see every subreddit that Vadim Rechkov had contributed to for the eight years he had been a member of the website.

Eight years, Gavin noted. The Russian had been surfing these discussion groups since he was fifteen.

Jack returned to the office, showered, and changed into casual attire. When he entered the conference room he had been sharing with Gavin, the older man showed him what he had been doing. The two men sat together while Gavin navigated around Rechkov's entire Reddit history. The young Russian had visited hundreds of subreddits over the years, involving very specific matters related to obtaining a student visa in the United States, jobs in the technology industry, jobs in computer science, money problems, and then, recently and of particular interest to Gavin and Jack, last year's battle of the Baltic.

Even this one subreddit had nearly 2,900 posts in all, and nearly 500 post interactions from Vadim Rechkov, aka TheSlavnyKid, himself.

Jack said, 'That's a lot for us to go through, but the attack on Hagen was weeks ago. Surely to God the DoJ investigators are all over this by now.'

Gavin said, 'A special court order is needed to go through

a suspect's social media, and it has to be done a certain way so as not to abuse the civil rights of any innocents he was in communication with. I'd say DoJ techs have looked into some of these pages here, but they wouldn't have dug down deep into the other user profiles like you and I are going to do.'

Jack said, 'You think he might have used this vector to make initial contact with whoever offered up the intel on Scott Hagen?'

Gavin said, 'I've spent the past hour looking through his website history, and I can say this: Unless the entity who breached the OPM just happened to be a personal friend of Vadim Rechkov's, which I see as very unlikely, then it's a good bet Rechkov was approached through Reddit, specifically through this five-month-long string of posts about the Baltic. He didn't interact with anyone else on the subject online that I can see. How about you start going through his conversations here, and I'm going to keep looking through his hard drive to see if I can find anything else that might be relevant?'

Jack raised an eyebrow. 'So I read five hundred or so posts, write down the usernames of everyone he came in contact with, and look for clues that someone was offering him intel about killing Hagen. Is that it?'

Gavin shrugged. 'You're an analyst. Analyze.'

'Right.'

Jack started with Rechkov's first offering in the subreddit discussion about the Baltic conflict. Under the username TheSlavnyKid, he wrote a diatribe of more than 2,500 words that claimed his brother Stepan was one of the victims of the illegal American naval attack on the Russian submarine *Kazan*, which had come to the Baltic only to defend Kaliningrad from NATO aggression. The post was an angry screed against America, to be sure, but Jack found the writing itself to be lucid and the young man's conclusions thought-out, even relatively convincing. Not to Jack, he was positive his father had done what needed to be done in the Baltic, but at least to anyone reading it whose mind wasn't already made up on the matter of who was at fault during Russia's attack into Lithuania from Kaliningrad and Belarus.

Rechkov wasn't a native English speaker, but he conveyed his message well. Jack could feel the agony in the words of the twenty-three-year-old Russian studying in America, the very nation he blamed for his brother's death. He talked at length about his relationship with his older brother, their love of fishing in the lakes and streams in their rural home near Slavny, and also his brother's complete lack of interest in politics and international affairs.

Stepan died doing his job. He didn't start the fight and had no personal beef with America at all. Therefore, Vadim Rechkov held America responsible for his brother Stepan's murder.

Jack could have argued back that the thousands of men and women killed by Russian sea, air, and land forces during the Baltic War sure as hell didn't start the fight, either, but arguing with a grieving young man would have been senseless.

And anyway, Vadim had died in a Mexican restaurant in New Jersey.

What Jack did not see in this first lengthy post was any personal vow that Vadim Rechkov would exact retribution for his brother's death on anyone, much less the commander of the USS *James Greer*. No, although Vadim Rechkov was very clearly angry, more than anything, he seemed inconsolably sad.

Jack took the time to glance at the dozens of comments below this initial post by Rechkov; he read expressions of sympathy, expressions of agreement with the sentiments voiced against the USA, as well as posts from a significant number of those who said Stepan Rechkov got what he deserved for fighting for an evil power. There were even a few trolls who hoped Vadim's dead brother suffered mightily before his death.

Jack knew well that people with poor character, when allowed to hide behind a pseudonym and shout in others' faces without showing their own, had a tendency to be jackasses.

Next he moved to TheSlavnyKid's responses to individual threads of the conversation; he continued the discussions, the arguments, and echoed the angry sentiments of others.

But as time went on, in further postings under the same subreddit, Jack noticed a change in the writing, a deepening of the invective, a militancy that wasn't there in posts written just weeks earlier.

Jack realized he was watching someone descend into a state of absolute rage, perhaps even into the early throes of madness, consumed by anger and impotence. He talked about failing out of school, drinking himself to sleep, moving from his nice apartment to a dump when he could no longer make rent, and he placed blame for everything back to an ASROC missile that was fired at 3:23 a.m. local time from the deck of the USS *James Greer*.

The more Jack read, the more weeks that passed in the life of this subreddit, the more obvious it was that the life of Vadim Rechkov was falling apart.

And then it happened. Some three and a half months after his first posting in the subreddit, which itself came just ten days after the sinking of the Russian submarine, Vadim Rechkov declared in a post that he would gladly give his own life for the chance to end the life of the man or woman who pressed the button to fire the weapons that sank his brother's vessel.

Jack presumed the person who fired the missile was likely some junior officer or perhaps an enlisted sailor; surely Commander Hagen wasn't the one who fired the shot itself, but of key importance was that Rechkov had expressed his wish to personally kill someone on board the *Greer*.

Immediately Jack wrote down the date of the post, suspecting that the entity he was looking for, the person or persons who somehow had reached out to Rechkov with the intel that led him across the US to a Mexican restaurant in New Jersey, must have read that post and tuned into Rechkov at that time.

There were dozens of commenters on the post itself, some cheering him on, others warning him off, but Jack couldn't discern any particular importance from any of the commenters. Plus, there was always the chance someone reached out to TheSlavnyKid exclusively via a private message on Reddit that Jack had no way of discovering.

Jack decided to take a break. He stood up from his laptop and headed to the kitchen for some coffee, promising Gavin he'd bring him back a fresh cup as well.

Spending too much time in the online life of a man going mad was depressing as hell.

41

President Jack Ryan stood before a rough room. He gave a lot of press conferences, compared with most other presidents, and was comfortable with even the toughest questions, but today he felt such a visceral anger inside him at the attacks going on in the country that he fought hard to temper his comments, to control his mood, and to craft his answers in ways that would show him in control and serving as a calm, reasonable steward over the investigation to capture Abu Musa al-Matari and his fellow terrorists.

This made him come off more than a little flat in front of the cameras, he could feel it, but he wasn't ready to burst forth with his true emotions.

And the press wasn't going easy on him at all.

After opening with a superficial update on the hunt, little more than a promise that all was being done and no stone would be left unturned, Ryan announced that the Pentagon would be putting proposals on his desk by the end of the day to help protect servicemen and -women at home and abroad. From here he offered a subdued but sincere expression of condolences for the victims and their families, and then he opened the room up to questions, with the caveat that he would not be able to answer questions related directly to the ongoing terrorism investigations.

A White House correspondent from CNN went first after being called on by Ryan. 'Mr President, does the fact that ISIS seems to have matured in their abilities to where they can now attack our military inside the United States indicate that your strategy to destroy them in the Middle East has been a failure?'

Jack wasn't surprised by this question at all, but he took his time thinking over his answer before speaking. Finally he said, 'I don't believe so, Lauren. It is in keeping with the normal actions of rebel groups, going back millennia, that when they lose ground on the battlefield, they try to take back ground in the public forum.

'They will commit more suicide attacks on the battlefield, and we're seeing that. And they will work as hard as they can to attack the West in the West. And we're seeing that as well with what's going on currently at home, and in Europe, which has been an Islamic State battleground for the past two years.'

Another reporter, this one from the AP, asked, 'Do we know the size of the force here in the United States?'

'We have some estimates, yes, and it is a relatively small number. I can't give you that number, unfortunately, because we can't let our enemy know everything we know about them. We have to protect our sources and methods.'

The AP reporter said, 'Five? Ten? One hundred? One thousand?'

Ryan reiterated, 'I can't give you that number, Chuck. Obviously several Islamic State terrorists have been killed in the commission of their attacks so far. We expect more to be killed or captured if they continue, due to the diligence of federal, state, and local law enforcement. Our threat levels are at their highest point, and our intelligence on the subject is good and getting better. We will root them out as quickly as possible, and while that doesn't answer your fair question, that's all I can give you right now.'

An older reporter who worked for McClatchy said, 'What are you asking citizens to do to be safe? Should America just hunker down at home until the threat has passed?'

Ryan frowned for a moment. 'Absolutely not, Richard. Let's keep this in perspective for the average US citizen. It is a sad fact that there were more than fifty shootings in Chicago over the weekend, with seven dead. There exists, quite unfortunately, violence all around us. What is happening with these Islamic State terrorists in our borders is of utmost concern to us, but I would not want the average American citizen to do anything more than report any concerns you may have to your local law enforcement agency.

'People have a reasonable tendency to do one of two things when they listen to someone in the government warn them of a threat. They either *tune* out or they *freak* out. I don't want Americans doing either thing. They need to understand there are real threats, but we are working with skill and diligence to remove these threats.'

Now the ABC chief national security reporter, Susan Hayes, said, 'Americans have watched us fight against the Islamic State for much of your term. We have some Special Forces and some airpower over there, but so far we haven't been able to stop them. Yes, they have shrunk in some areas, but if you look at a map of territory controlled by ISIS, you see it remains larger than many other Middle Eastern nations. Will you consider new steps to ramp up the war against ISIS in light of the fact they are over here now, killing people within our borders?'

Ryan considered this carefully, like a professor wanting to give his student the proper context for his answer. 'When you see on television that ISIS has conquered a new city, it is important for you to understand what that means. The media portrays these events by showing a map with an ever-moving, and often expanding, red blob indicating the so-called borders of the Islamic State. The truth is, ISIS has fought weak enemies, many of whom have run without putting up resistance. We should not think of them as really owning much territory at all. They come in, scare local police and government away, set up roadblocks and send out a couple pickup trucks full of men, which serve as death squads. They aren't governing, they aren't turning these locations into real strongholds. They can roll a few more trucks up a local road, and then the next day someone redraws the map of their "borders" to make it look like they've pushed their front line thirty miles overnight. They didn't advance their front line. They drove a convoy of trucks from one village to the next without being destroyed.

'We have intelligence and special mission units in the area, so those of us privy to classified intelligence know the media reports are not accurate.'

A reporter from *The New York Times* called out, 'Then why haven't we defeated them?'

'Two words, Michael. Civilian casualties. Two more words, related to the first two. Human shields. ISIS lives and operates within cities and congested areas. We find a group of Islamic State fighters out in the open and we do our best to put an A-10 or an Apache on them as quick as our people can task them. But we aren't going to shell cities, no matter who is in there that needs rooting out.'

Susan Hayes spoke again, this time without being called upon. 'So are you saying there will be no new offensive against ISIS despite the fact they are now bringing the war to *our* cities?'

'Susan, nobody on planet Earth wants a massive US

invasion into Iraq and Syria more than ISIS. If we return to the Middle East in large numbers, the Islamic State knows their ranks will be flooded by recruits, extremism in the cities will skyrocket, and support for their heinous aims will go up. The average ISIS fighter, poorly trained, poorly equipped, motivated by nothing other than a vague hope of an Islamic State and a specific belief in exaltation in the afterlife . . . this guy doesn't have a prayer of ever shooting down an F-18, seeing an American Special Forces operator in his rifle sight, or winning a fight with a drone or a smart bomb. But if we flood the zone, if we put a couple hundred thousand American men and women in their area, well . . . some of these guys just might get their sights on what they see as an infidel, and that is the best thing they can hope for in their life.'

Ryan shook his head slowly. 'I have no intention of giving them the opportunity they crave.

'Now, the United States is at the vanguard of fighting this evil group, and we will continue to be there, leading from the front. If we see tactical ways to increase our involvement that make sense, we will do just that.'

Ryan took a few more questions, most along the same lines as the others. He closed with, 'As soon as we have more to report, the attorney general, the secretary of homeland security, and the secretary of defense will be speaking publicly as the need arises.'

After Ryan left the press briefing room, Arnie Van Damm was there by his side.

Ryan said, 'What did you think?'

'Not your best performance, Jack.'

'Tell me why.' Jack did not disagree, but he valued Arnie's input.

'You were talking like a historian in there.'

'In my own defense, I *am* a historian, Arnie.'

'Do you think that's what people want to hear? That what's happening now is simply a long-standing insurgent tactic, and nothing to be alarmed about?'

'I didn't say it like that.'

'That's how it sounded.' Van Damm pointed in the direction of the stairs to the Situation Room. 'Back down there you sounded like you wanted to pick up a machine gun and lead the attack into Mosul yourself. That's what the public needs to hear. Not a poli-sci lecture about Third World madmen and street crime in Chicago.'

Ryan thought Arnie had a point, but he said, 'I wasn't ready to be honest with the way I feel right now. We need more of a plan, less groping in the dark. I'll talk to the public when we are prosecuting this fight against the intelligence leak and the terrorists in some meaningful way.' Together they entered the Oval. 'For now we are on the back foot, and I couldn't let that show in my emotions.'

42

This Iraqi village hadn't been much, probably just a few thousand had lived here before the war, but now it was nothing more than a battle-scarred wound built into the hills. A wasteland of destruction, just a dozen kilometers northeast of Mosul, it had been abandoned by ISIS the day before, and now twenty-two-year-old commander Beritan Nerway led her all-female platoon carefully through the streets on the northern side of the town, their wire- or wooden-stocked Kalashnikovs at their shoulders They slowly picked their way through the broken stones in their boots and tennis shoes.

These women were Kurds from the YPJ, an abbreviation in Kurdish for Women's Protection Unit. They were a rebel force, not part of the Peshmerga, although they fought the same foe.

Beritan was a nom de guerre; her real name was Daria. She gave herself the war name of Beritan in honor of Kurdish female battalion commander Beritan, who led seven hundred male and female troops during the Kurdish civil war in 1992 and threw herself off a cliff when she ran out of ammunition.

Kurdish women had a long history of fighting, but never more so than over the past three years fighting ISIS. They'd helped push them back out of this town the afternoon before: over a wide canal they'd watched from their forward positions as trucks and tanks and technicals escaped, heading back into the suburbs of Mosul, fewer than twenty kilometers south.

But by the time of the enemy pullout it was too dark to cross the canal to move into the town, so the YPJ waited till daylight to send in troops to check through what was left. Now several platoons like Beritan's, male and female alike, were picking through the rubble to make certain ISIS had not booby-trapped the buildings or the roads, or even left forces behind to slow the YPJ's advance in this small section of the war.

Beritan knew there could be danger around any corner, a tank tucked into any alley or a machine gun emplacement hidden in any crater or darkened window.

Her radio chirped where it was attached to her shoulder strap. One of her snipers on the far side of the canal reported possible movement in a window two blocks ahead of the YPJ position.

Beritan and her fighters all tucked behind cover on the broken street, but not before the crack of a rifle echoed in the rubble of the town and the first woman fell dead to a sniper's bullet.

Then the gunfire seemed to come from every nook and cranny of the broken buildings.

Beritan and her unit of forty were cut off from other forces and supported only by mortars and DShK machine guns back at the YPJ lines. Serious firepower, but firepower that needed good targeting information.

Targeting information they weren't getting through their binoculars.

Beritan realized she and her women would have to climb up from their cover and expose themselves to press the fight to the ISIS snipers.

*

Fifteen kilometers to the north and five thousand feet in the air, Pyro 1-1 and Pyro 1-2, two Apache helicopters, circled in a wide racetrack pattern. They were in the area in support of a nearby coordinated attack by Peshmerga forces supported by US Special Forces and a JTAC, a Joint Terminal Attack Controller, a soldier on the ground with the ability to call in support from artillery fires and rotary-wing and fixed-wing assets in the area.

So far the Peshmerga advance had not been met with any resistance; they'd walked into a town picked clean and abandoned by ISIS, so the pair of Apaches circling in the desert had had little to do but listen in on the four radio frequencies in their ears as they flew around.

Both of the Apache AH-64E Guardian aircraft had plenty of fuel today. Right now they circled at endurance speed, seventy knots, giving them more time in the air in case they were needed to the south.

Captain Carrie Ann Davenport mentally tuned out the four radio frequencies broadcasting in her ears and spoke to CWO Troy Oakley through the permanently open intercom between the two of them, negating the need to push any buttons to transmit to each other. He was seated only six feet behind and above her in the cockpit, but out of her view except through a small mirror over her head on the door frame.

She glanced at it and said, 'I remember learning at Fort Rucker that each flight hour of the Apache, even if we're just hanging out like this, costs thirty grand.'

Oakley said, 'Thirty-two thousand, five hundred fifty dollars, ma'am.'

She laughed over her mic. 'Then this is an expensive sightseeing flight.'

'If you see any sights, do let me know. Just looks like undulating dirt as far as the eye can see.'

The captain replied, 'Don't worry. At the rate things are going, the fighting will be in Mosul in another month. My guess is we'll have plenty to see there.'

'Yeah, like SAMs corkscrewing right up at us. I imagine that will be a lively time for us both.'

'And then when we win,' she said, 'we just hand the city over to the Iraqi government.'

'Do *you* want it, ma'am?'

'Ha, no, thanks. I just mean I bet the Iraqis will run it like crooks.'

Oakley chuckled into his mic. 'If history is any guide, yes. But good ol' corruption like you see in the rest of the world, around here anyway, is a major step up from the current conditions.'

Carrie Ann Davenport replied, 'Roger that. Stealing money from the state coffer is a shit thing to do, but the local government is choppin' off people's heads now. We aren't helping to turn the place into a bastion of truth and justice, but we are making it a little better, I guess.'

The young woman had become something of a cynic regarding the fighting here. She had no illusions Iraq would turn into a democratic nation, but she certainly did see the logic in uprooting ISIS as quickly and efficiently as possible.

And there was something else she was feeling today. The excitement of going home. This was her last flight before two weeks' leave, and while she would spend roughly thirty percent of her leave either getting home or traveling back to Iraq, she'd have more than a week of family, friends, and whatever the hell she wanted to do, wear, eat, drink, or say.

After three months of life at a forward operating base, she couldn't wait.

Carrie Ann spoke through the intercom. 'I don't know about you, Oak, I'm kinda looking forward to getting a little break from flying these unfriendly skies.'

'Just thinking the same thing. Seventy-two hours from now I'm going to be in my backyard with a beer, two kids crawling all over me, and a wife who isn't sick of me being home just yet. That's as close to paradise as it gets for an old dude like me. How 'bout you? Any big plans for your leave, ma'am?'

The undulating landscape raced by below at seventy-five knots while Oakley and Davenport both thought about home.

'I'll just hang out in Cleveland most of the time with my folks, but I'm going to DC for the weekend to see some friends and go to a party. Should be fun. And then, just about the time I finally get the smell of JP8 out of my skin, I'll turn around and head back here.'

Oak said, 'I've got to build a swing set. And according to Carla, the kids already took some of the pieces out of the box the thing came in, so you can guaran-damn-tee I'll be scrounging through my junk drawer to find –'

Just then their headsets came alive. It was the JOC, the Joint Operations Center, far behind the action back in Turkey. The call was a TIC alert, which meant troops were in contact, and then a set of coordinates. The tasking officer spoke to Pyro flight directly.

'Pyro One-One, how copy?'

'Solid copy,' said Davenport.

'We are going to hold One-Two where it is and send you to this grid. We got a call from YPJ. It's a small unit of them pinned down by multiple snipers. That's pretty much all we know. There is no JTAC embedded with them, so you'll just have to evaluate the situation from above and see if you can intercede without endangering friendlies.'

Nobody liked flying into an unknown area without contact with friendlies on the ground. Carrie acknowledged the order and Oakley turned toward the location, already saved on his screen.

The captain said, 'Great. Any idea what YPJ look like? I mean, I've seen their flag, but can you tell them apart at one hundred knots and five kilometers away?'

'Not really,' Oak confirmed.

As they approached the town from the north, they raced over the front lines of the YPJ on the north side of a wide culvert, flying at five thousand feet. Carrie Ann knew the sniper positions were somewhere a mile to the south, right inside a very congested-looking conglomeration of broken buildings that had once been a small town. She slaved the thirty-millimeter cannon to her right eye for now. With friendlies down in the area, she probably wouldn't use rockets, and her load-out of six Hellfires meant she'd have to be choosy about using a missile on an individual with a rifle, although she wouldn't hesitate to do so as long as there were TICs, or troops-in-contact.

The cannon was accurate to within three meters, good but not perfect, but she could fire ten or twenty rounds at a burst and nail anything she could see with its dual-purpose shells – armor-piercing for light-armor targets, and high explosive as an area weapon.

There was a five-inch-square multipurpose display screen on each side of the central control bank. On these she could choose the TADS, the target acquisition and designation sight, or she could text message with other helos, bring up comms, fuel, and load-out information, or access any of more than 1,500 pages of info in all. A keyboard on the left side of the control bank allowed her to type messages, and even though she wore gloves, she'd gotten as adept at using it as she was at texting on her own cell phone.

Her hands rested on the two video game-like console handholds on either side of her center console, giving her quick access to all her most important controls. She'd been told there were 443 different positions to all the dials, switches, and knobs, and she knew every one of them.

On top of this, she had all the flight controls Oakley had behind her; the cyclic between her knees, the collective by her left knee.

By slaving the weapon to her right eye and looking at the target, she only had to reach down to the cyclic and squeeze the weapon's release trigger to fire the cannon at whatever she was looking at.

She looked down at the multipurpose screen displaying her target acquisition and designation sight by her right knee, desperately searching for any danger. This gave her access to several cameras in a mobile turret below her. Through the 127-times magnification of the TV camera, she saw an enhanced black-and-white view of whatever she was looking at. Also on the screen she could see crosshairs that showed her where Oakley's right eye was pointed.

She looked through her thermal view, hoping to pick up human forms in the dark recesses of the bombed-out buildings, but the heat of the day on twisted metal made this a futile task. Sure, they could sit there over the town and she could take her time, but Oak wanted to keep them moving at speed to make it difficult to nail them from below with an RPG, so Carrie Ann just had seconds to scan on any one building, street, or bomb crater.

'Ma'am,' Oakley said, 'I've got troops, on the road just off our nose. Tucked into the east and west side of the street.'

Davenport looked on the TADS to see Oakley's cross-hairs. She moved her own eye to it and it showed her the 127-times magnification of the street.

There, at least two dozen figures, all with rifles, were shooting at something in a row of buildings to the south.

Oakley increased the magnification. 'Chicks. Those are chicks. I didn't think the Kurdish female soldiers ever got in the fight.'

Davenport said, 'The Peshmerga don't let their females get on the front lines. But YPJ have female units that see combat.'

Oakley asked, 'Are we supposed to be helping the YPJ?'

The captain in the front seat just shrugged and said, 'We're helping ourselves if we kill an ISIS sniper. If the Kurdish rebels happen to benefit from our fight, then lucky them.'

'That's what I like about you, Captain. You can simplify the unsimplifiable.'

'And I like how you make up words, Oak.'

They flew high over the YPJ fighters, who seemed completely pinned down, but even when Oakley circled the entire engagement below counterclockwise, neither he nor Captain Davenport was able to discern any targets. The broken buildings had too many positions from which a sniper could fire, and the recesses were so deep, it would take incredible luck for the Apache above to see anything, even with its TADS.

Oak said, 'How about we go down to two thousand. We

might get lucky and see somebody popping out to take a shot at us.'

'As low as you need,' came the response.

A minute later they were at 1,200 feet, directly above the YPJ fighters. It appeared even the female rebel unit had stopped receiving fire now, because they just remained hunkered down in groups of three or four along the street.

Oakley said, 'Nobody's shooting at us, or them. Hopefully the YPJ will take the hint and use our presence to back out of here.'

Carrie Ann replied, 'Wish we could scare away the bad guys with our presence, but usually they just shoot –'

Just then, a flash came from the third-floor window of a ruined building up the street. While Carrie Ann couldn't be sure it wasn't a YPJ fighter, the indicators were good that it was not when the YPJ began firing back and dust kicked up around the concrete window frame.

She slaved her crosshairs to the window. 'I'm identifying that as a sniper position. Engaging with cannon.'

A twenty-round burst from the cannon below Carrie Ann's feet ripped into the window and sent high-explosive thirty-millimeter shells into the sniper's hide.

The YPJ below cheered, she could see them on her screen, and then they began engaging another dark recess, this one on a building on the east side of the street. Oakley and Davenport both could see the dust and concrete kicking off the hole in the side of the wall.

Oakley said, 'They are marking targets for you, ma'am.'

'Got it,' she said. 'Engaging.'

She pressed the fire button on her cyclic and sent ten more rounds into the hole. Again the women 1,200 feet below raised their hands and waved at the helo above.

'They've got the idea!' Oakley said.

Carrie Ann had trouble getting her shells into a third target, a wrecked building under a collapsed rooftop parking lot. She could even see flashes of sniper fire coming out through the darkness, but whoever was shooting in there must have been a hundred feet or more back under the building, and from her elevation she hadn't been able to reach the sniper.

She had Oakley descend at the north end of the street, and they set up a rocket run just above rooftop level. He slaved her crosshairs to his, flew a steady heading on her target designation, and picked up speed.

Only five hundred yards from the target, Carrie Ann launched rockets right into the deep, cavelike hide of the sniper. The rockets broke apart a couple hundred yards in front of the Apache, and released 650 flechette rounds, tungsten darts that raced forward into the wreckage and destroyed everything in their path, creating a shock wave that collapsed the rest of the structure.

'Good hit,' Oakley said, and then he pulled the nose of his Apache up and began climbing over the town.

Just on the other side of the buildings to the south of the YPJ, they flew over a medium-sized town-square area, with a mosque at its southern end. Oakley was just about to turn to head back to continue the cover for the YPJ, when Captain Davenport's voice came over the intercom.

'Shit!' Carrie Ann said. 'ZPU!' The ZPU was a 14.5-millimeter Soviet-era antiaircraft weapon that could fire six hundred rounds a minute.

As soon as the words left her mouth, big fast-moving tracer rounds painted the sky in front of them, just over the square.

'Hang on!' Oakley pulled Pyro 1-1 over his right shoulder, lifting it and flipping it, turning the armored belly into the threat. Carrie Ann grabbed the handles above her but still her body was pulled tight in her harness.

While their seats were all but bulletproof from below, anything that hit above shoulder height might get through if it was more powerful than a fifty-caliber round, and both Oakley and Davenport were always aware that a lucky shot on the tail rotor, forty feet behind where Davenport sat over the nose of the aircraft, could send them both spinning to their deaths.

He jinked left and right while he increased speed to 185 knots, and they raced out of the line of sight on the weapon.

They headed north back over the street, and saw the YPJ women were on their feet for the first time since the Apache arrived. They were slowly moving to the south.

Davenport said, 'Holy crap, Oak. That was close.'

Oakley confirmed: 'Yeah, did you see the gun emplacement?'

'Affirmative. The way it was positioned in that square between all those high buildings around means we'd have to get right on top of it again to take it out. Better we call for a fast mover.'

Carrie Ann radioed the JOC and requested an aircraft with Hellfires or bombs be sent to destroy the enemy gun emplacement. An F/A-18 could launch from twenty thousand feet, well above the range of the ZPU, while Pyro 1-1 had to fly a few thousand feet directly overhead to see it in the rubble of the town.

While they waited for an answer, Carrie Ann found another two-man ISIS sniper team in her TADS. It was half a block beyond where the YPJ were moving, and

Oakley set up a run-in on her targeting point. She fired four rockets, launching thousands of flechette rounds at a half-collapsed building with three levels of dark recesses. This time they banked as soon as they fired, keeping themselves far away from the mosque and the square with the Russian antiair weapon.

On their next pass the camera showed the sniper position, and it was obvious that the two men there had been torn into tiny pieces.

'Delta Hotel,' Oakley said. Direct Hit.

Just then the JOC came back over the net. 'Negative on the fast movers, Pyro One-One. No resources available.'

Carrie Ann acknowledged the transmission, then spoke just for the benefit of her cockpit intercom. 'These YPJ below us aren't getting much help.'

'They're getting us. You know we can leave that ZPU, but that weapon can be fired down a street just as easily as it can be fired at us. Those women will walk into that square within twenty minutes from now, and they will get nailed.'

Carrie Ann thought it over. 'Let's do a run-in from the south, circle the whole town at low level so no spotters can figure out what we're doing. We can try to hit that gun from behind.'

'Hellfire?'

'Affirm, but we'll have to get closer than I'd like because I have to laze the weapon.'

'Copy all. It's going to take four mikes to circle the city. Let's just hope the YPJ stay put.'

Carrie Ann said, 'That's why I'm not using rockets. Hitting that square from the south will throw flechettes northward up those streets and through any breaks in the buildings. Too much chance of blue on blue.'

They rounded the small town of rubble at an altitude of just two hundred feet, flying as fast as Oak could get his aircraft to go, and with both sets of eyes scanning the sky and the TADS looking for other dangers.

She set up her fire-control system to choose a Hellfire on her right pylon, and she slaved its camera to her MPD by her right knee. For now she just saw the buildings passing by below, but once they got line of sight on the gun, she'd be able to fly it via the camera, right into the target.

Four minutes later they shot at 185 knots over the town from the south. They'd seen the smoke from a couple of rifles shooting at them on their way, but nothing like the ZPU ahead. While Oakley was focused on flying straight and level and fast, Davenport was flashing her eyes between her Hellfire cam and her TADS, looking ahead through the town for the mosque.

Finally she said, 'Do you see the minaret?'

'Got it,' Oakley replied with confidence. 'Taking you up, then down.'

They climbed quickly, getting more altitude and allowing the Hellfire to fire down into the square, hopefully hitting the ZPU still facing to the north.

Oakley added, 'You are going to have to make this work. We're not going to get another shot at this because they'll figure out what we're trying to do.'

'I need six hundred fifty meters' line of sight to laze the target and put the Hellfire on my tag. Give me six-fifty.'

Oakley climbed to five thousand feet, and then pushed the cyclic forward, sending the nose down. Carrie Ann went weightless, lifting up into her straps, but she kept her finger on her fire button and her eyes on the TADS.

When she saw the square below her she looked to the

point where they'd stumbled onto the ZPU fifteen minutes earlier. It was still there, but in the process of turning around.

Oakley said, 'They've seen us.'

Carrie Ann kept her voice calm. 'Press the attack. I'm lazing.' An invisible beam left Pyro 1-1 and shot forward, striking the Russian 14.5-millimeter gun. She pressed the trigger on the cyclic, and a Hellfire dropped off the pylon and launched forward. 'Missile away.'

Oakley kept his ship aimed at the wrecked town below, and shot lower and lower, flying behind the much faster Hellfire missile. Davenport had to keep the laser locked on the weapon until the moment of impact, lest the missile lose its acquisition of the target.

The problem was the Apache was flying right into the potential blast radius of the explosion. Oakley would have to wrench the helo hard to keep them from hitting debris once the Hellfire struck.

'Three seconds,' Carrie Ann said. And then, 'Impact!'

Oak pulled hard on the collective and banked to the left, all but spinning the fifty-foot-long machine sideways above the square.

The ZPU exploded into thousands of pieces, killing the entire gun crew in the process, Carrie Ann's gun camera footage would later confirm.

For now, however, the two hot, sweaty, and exhausted helicopter crew left the town, heading back to the north, hoping they'd done enough for the group of female fighters climbing over the broken rubble toward the south and, eventually, toward Mosul.

43

Jack finished reading every single posting related to the username TheSlavnyKid under the subreddit Baltic War at eight-twenty p.m. This included the postings of everyone who responded to something Rechkov wrote, which had brought the number of individual posts somewhere close to two thousand. He had also created a database of all the usernames of those who commented, and dug into a few of the more prevalent personalities, the usernames that showed up with regularity on Rechkov's postings.

After nine hours of work Jack had finally finished what he'd set out to do. The only problem was that he didn't feel like he'd accomplished a single thing.

While Vadim Rechkov got deeper and deeper into the threats and declarations of war against the USA, going so far as to reach out to others to find out how he could learn the name of the man or woman who fired the torpedo that killed his brother, Jack never saw anyone in the subsequent discussion offer to help in any way that seemed relevant to his own search. There were no promises of intelligence, no 'friend of a friend' who could get him the info, no sly offers to send him some inside information or speak with him in private. Nothing that looked like someone with the information Rechkov would have needed to target Scott Hagen. While it was true some Reddit users helpfully suggested Rechkov 'aim higher' and go for the commander of the ship, even naming Commander Hagen, nobody provided one iota of the specialized targeting information, or even intimated that they knew what specialized targeting information was.

Jack rested his neck by putting his head down on his arms on the conference table.

Gavin apparently saw this from across the table. 'What's wrong?'

'I've got eighty-eight Reddit usernames to go through now, to search everything they've ever said online, and not one of them looks promising.'

Gavin said, 'Actually, it's worse than that.'

Ryan slowly lifted his head and looked at Biery with red-rimmed eyes. 'What the hell does that mean?'

'You don't even know eighty-eight is the right number. A Reddit user can also remove one of their posts at any time. For all you know, the guy we're looking for reached out to Rechkov, or spurred him on somehow, and then removed his posts after the fact. Like when Rechkov got killed.'

Ryan just said, 'Well, *shit*, Gavin. Are you telling me this was an exercise in futility all along?'

Now Gavin smiled. 'No, it wasn't. Because of this.' He spun his laptop around and pushed it halfway across the table to Jack, who still couldn't tell what he was looking at.

'What's this?'

'This is an archived version of each Reddit page, kept on a special third-party server. Completely open-source, free, and legal. These cached pages of the same subreddit will show us if anyone in the discussion removed their posting or postings after the fact.' Gavin added, 'If I just talked a guy into killing someone, gave him the intel to do it . . . and then he freaking went ahead and tried it, you wouldn't find me leaving a trace of it up on some public message board. I'd pull every bit of my side of it down. But even though you can remove your posts from the website, you can't touch the archived pages.'

Jack smiled. 'The Internet is forever.'

'Whether that's good or bad depends on if you are the one hiding or the one seeking.'

Jack came back to life a little. 'I just need to log all the usernames in the cached subreddit and see if there are any on the original version that are no longer around on the current version. Then look into those people and see if I can figure out why they deleted their post.'

'Exactly.'

'And I'm going to do just that.' Jack stood. 'As soon as I get home, eat something, and take a shower. See you back here in the a.m.?'

Gavin said, 'I'm going to sleep in my office, so . . . yep.'

Jack shook his head. 'No way, Gav. I don't even live two minutes from here. You can crash at my place. I've got a guest room I don't think I've been in since I set up the bed in there.'

Gavin said, 'Thanks, but no, thanks. I've got a buddy at NSA who's working on the OPM hack. He's got some special tools that might come in handy, so I've been helping him, in case we need him to help us. He's going to call me in a bit.'

Jack had slipped his laptop in his backpack, and had already moved halfway out the door. 'Okay. I'll bring you breakfast in the morning. Something light.'

'But not too light,' Gavin said, already looking back down to his work.

Jack sat at his coffee table with his laptop open and several notebooks out in front of him. He had spent the last forty-five minutes writing down every username that corresponded with Vadim Rechkov in the cached version of the subreddit regarding the Baltic conflict. He then looked down at the database and saw there were eighty-nine names.

Jack rubbed his eyes and flipped back to the original list.

Eighty-eight names.

One user had removed his post or posts. It took just a couple minutes' more work to find out the disappearing username was that of someone called 5Megachopper5. Quickly, Jack left his database lists and went back to the page that had the archived discussion on the Baltic conflict, so he could see exactly what this user had contributed to the original subreddit.

But to Jack's frustration, 5Megachopper5 had posted only once. Under one of Rechkov's long diatribes threatening death and destruction to the crew of the *James Greer*, this mystery user had posted the most simple of messages:

PM sent

'Private message sent,' Jack said aloud. It was a notice that 5Megachopper5 had sent a private message to The-SlavnyKid's personal Reddit inbox.

Shit, thought Ryan. That's not much to go on.

He then looked up 5Megachopper5's Reddit overview on the archived site.

The username had been created the day of the posting on the Baltic Conflict subreddit, and the username had been deactivated the same day.

Jack knew for certain there was something nefarious to this Megachopper, but he had no idea how he and Gavin would find out who Megachopper was.

He grabbed his phone off his coffee table and pushed a speed-dial number.

After a few rings Gavin answered, and Jack could tell the man was tired, but still working. 'Biery.'

'Hey, Gav. It's past your bedtime.'

'I'm knocking off here in a second. What about you?'

'Same here. In the meantime, though, I found that one private message was sent from a Reddit user to Rechkov. The next day, the user deleted his one post and closed his account.'

'Suspicious. So you want to know how we can read that PM?'

'Yeah.'

'I can't get to it . . . but I know someone who can.'

'Really? Who?'

'You didn't hear it from me, but NSA's got a back door.'

'How do you know that?'

'Somebody told me, but I didn't hear it from them. I'm going to have to kiss a lot of ass to get him to dig around for us, but like I said earlier, he owes me a favor.'

'Right. Well . . . if we can get an idea if the person with the username 5Megachopper5 is the same person who gave intel to Vadim Rechkov, that sure as hell would push us along in our quest to find out who is responsible for the breach.'

Gavin wrote down the username. 'I'll reach out. Might take a little time to get a response. NSA is up to their eyeballs, as you can imagine.'

'Thanks. Get some sleep.'

'You too, Ryan. See ya in the a.m.'

Jack crawled up onto his couch and soon fell asleep, but only after telling himself that when he woke up in a few hours, he would continue his side project of figuring out just how, exactly, his unknown subject targeted all the victims. And then, when Jack finally did have some direction to look in, he would use his newfound knowledge of identity intelligence to target the man who was responsible for all the death and destruction taking place.

44

The black SUV pulled up in front of the office of Advanced Research Technological Designs in Bucharest at ten a.m. Four men climbed out, and Alexandru Dalca, who was looking down from his office window four stories above, saw exactly what he'd expected. They were all East Asian. They wore black business suits and moved with purpose and confidence.

These were Chinese spooks, Dalca felt sure.

And this was a problem, since Dalca had been pilfering the information the Chinese spooks had hired his company to steal, and then selling the material to various bad actors around the world, including the Islamic State.

Yes, Dalca knew he might very well be in some serious trouble. All he could do was hope they were here for some other objective, and he had to be prepared to talk his way through any problems if his initial concerns about the reason for today's meeting proved accurate.

Five minutes later Dalca was dressed in his best sport coat, and he walked into the conference room with as much confidence as he could muster. His seat was across the table from the Seychelles Group members, down at the end of the row of a half-dozen ARTD senior staff. Dragomir Vasilescu was there, as well as the technology director of ARTD, Albert Cojocaru. As the chief researcher, Dalca was at the far end of the table, even though he was the only one of the three with intimate knowledge of the work that had been done on the files for the Chinese. Still, he was the lowest-ranking ARTD employee in the room, so he wasn't even introduced as he entered.

Dragomir Vasilescu spent a few minutes thanking the guests for coming and for being a valued account here at ARTD, and then he read through some stats Dalca and Cojocaru had prepared for today's meeting: the man-hours that went into the original 'acquisition' of the data from India, and other resources used in the project. There were a lot of euphemisms involved in this type of talk: Just as ARTD was a technology firm and not a hacking concern, and just as the Seychelles Group was a private business and not a front for Chinese spies, so went the discussion of what ARTD had done on behalf of China. They hadn't stolen files, they had 'acquired data' from the United States via an Indian security firm. They had 'exfiltrated targeted documents' instead of digging through the files to root out those who might be involved with China, and they had 'identified key personalities' instead of betraying the doomed men and women to the Ministry of State Security.

Dragomir Vasilescu and Albert Cojocaru were both very proud of the work that their company had provided for the client, and it showed on their faces. Dalca's expression appeared similarly pleased, but he was the one ARTD employee in the room who sensed that a trap was about to be sprung by the four stone-faced men across the table.

When the presentation was finished, Cojocaru offered to take the men on a tour of the location, but the head of the Chinese delegation, Mr Peng, waved a hand in the air like he couldn't possibly care less about ARTD's workspaces and computer server stacks.

Peng said, 'We have come a very long way to speak with

you, for this reason. We want to be assured that the data we have requested, the data we have paid well for you to keep absolutely secure, is being maintained with the strictest integrity.'

Dalca could see that Drago hadn't the faintest idea what the Chinese man was getting at. No realization that the recent attacks against America could possibly be coming out of the very material ARTD took from the OPM files on behalf of the MSS.

Dalca adopted a similar look of confusion at the man's insinuation, but in his mind dark clouds formed. *Shit,* he thought. He was right.

They were here because they suspected.

Dragomir, on the other hand, ignorant of what was going on, had no worries in the world. He said, 'Certainly it is. Our sensitive information is kept on special machines that have no connection whatsoever to the outside world. The material we acquired on your behalf resides here in the building and nowhere else.' He held up a hand. 'Other than in its original location in the United States, I mean.'

Albert Cojocaru added, 'And the initial acquisition took place leaving no ability for the Americans to ever discover anything was amiss.'

Albert beamed with pride. Dalca tried not to roll his eyes. Albert was the chief hacker, a tech who lived in cyberspace, and he had no clue of the shit storm that these thugs would rain down on this building if Dalca himself didn't convince them their concerns were unfounded.

Peng conferred with his men in Mandarin for a moment. The Romanians just sat there.

Peng next looked at Vasilescu. 'The person in charge of obtaining the files?'

Dragomir slapped Albert on the back. 'The best in the business, I can tell you that. Albert Cojocaru here. He and his team created the intrusion system that was used to pull the data off the server in Bangalore, India, where it had been residing untouched for the past four years. He did a great job.'

Albert chimed in. 'If you would like a layman's explanation of the process, just in case you had other needs in the future you might want us to handle, I would be happy to —'

Albert shut up when Peng raised his hand.

The Chinese man said, 'As far as the person here in your office in charge of linking the raw data to the committers of illegal espionage activities in the People's Republic of China. Who is that?'

Dragomir Vasilescu pointed down to the end of the table with a proud nod. 'My other best man. Alexandru Dalca here. The top of the industry, and my number-one secret weapon here at ARTD. I personally placed him as the lead researcher on your project. He took all the raw files, millions and millions, as you know, and used his own handmade software to identify those files that met your criteria. He looked for men and women who had studied Asian languages, focused on particular course work in school, had relevant military or civilian experience in their past, or already had associations with men and women in China. From there he still had thousands to go through by hand before he personally —'

Dalca knew he had to short-circuit Dragomir before he made it look like Dalca was the only guy in the building with the skills to turn the American files into targeting data.

He quickly interrupted his boss. 'Thank you, Mr Vasilescu, for making it look like I alone could possibly do all this.' He smiled sincerely at the four dour men facing him. 'The truth is, gentlemen, I am very fortunate to be in charge of a large team of men and women who work exclusively on your project, and have done so from the start. While I originally created and optimized the software that is used to manage all this data efficiently, I do not personally extract the raw data and convert it to the actionable product distributed to you. Instead, I oversee a team of eager young men and women who do. They work so hard, and are so adept at what they do. I honestly couldn't be more proud of all the work they put into this project.'

The Asians nodded a little.

Good, Dalca thought. He made the right assurances to the Chinese that their data wasn't being exploited for the gain of others, while simultaneously hinting that others were involved in the work on the data, distancing himself from the material they clearly feared might have been compromised.

Through his peripheral vision, Dalca could see Albert and Dragomir looking his way now. Dalca was usually the first to take credit for something, to leverage a success for his own benefit. Of course these two would be confused that he was deferring praise onto his underlings. Both men knew how many hours Dalca worked on the Seychelles Group project, and both men would find it strange that he was minimizing his role.

Still, it was less important to Dalca that his coworkers were confused by his actions and more important that the scary guys on the opposite side of the table didn't suspect him of implicating the People's Republic of China in violent attacks on one of the most powerful nations on earth, the United States.

Those four guys would kill him if they thought for a second he had stolen the files to stuff his own bank account.

For the next ten minutes the Chinese asked more questions about the data, how it was extracted, and how it was turned into intelligence product. They were genuinely impressed with the use of open-source intelligence to derive the identities of America's spies and agents, Dalca saw.

But the focus was no longer on Dalca, and this pleased him. Every time he would explain something about how 'his staff' came to their conclusions about the American spies and agents working in China, the Chinese would listen and then direct their next question to Dragomir.

Dalca understood what was going on. These guys were Chinese intelligence, but they were just like most Chinese corporate types Dalca had dealt with in his career. They would respect titles, authority. While Alex Dalca was the only man in the room who truly knew what the hell was going on with the Seychelles Group's contract, he was a senior researcher, whereas Vasilescu was the CEO of the company. All their attention and respect would go to him.

And that was just fine with Alexandru Dalca.

Finally, Dragomir said what both he and Albert had been wondering for the length of the conversation. 'I am sorry, gentlemen. How can we help you?'

Mr Peng and his men talked a moment, then he said, 'We see the items you have given to us, and we watch with great concern some actions that have taken place of late involving American intelligence. Our concern is that perhaps some of the mass data you extracted for us has, instead, fallen into other hands. This puts our . . . our company, at great risk of being implicated in actions we played no part in.'

Vasilescu said, 'Honestly, I haven't been keeping up with the news in America, I've just seen a little about what's happened. But I can assure you that only people who have been

433

authorized to view the files have done so, and that will continue to be the case.'

Vasilescu held his hands up flat on the table. 'I can guarantee that your data is yours alone. No one else has gained access to it.'

Peng said, 'You misinterpret my concern. I will speak with more clarity. I am not worried that you have been hacked, Mr Vasilescu, I am worried you are double-crossing us and using this material for your own profit.'

Vasilescu sat back in his chair. 'Now . . . wait a moment. That is an outrageous charge.'

Peng asked, 'How did those men on camels in the deserts of Iraq track down these American spies inside of America?'

Dalca butted in again. 'You are talking about the attacks by the Muslim terrorists in America?' After nodding thoughtfully, as if considering the validity of the connection the Seychelles Group men had made, he said, 'I see your concern, although I can assure you the source used by these jihadists is completely different from the source at our disposal. I was watching news of the attacks just the other day, wasn't I, Mr Vasilescu? As a specialist in research and investigations, I have a personal interest in how people obtain and use information, no matter what the reason. From what I have seen of what's going on in America, someone has absolute, up-to-the-minute intelligence they are leveraging against these soldiers.' He smiled. 'The information I have been using is many years old, as you know.'

Peng said, 'But yet your company somehow managed to take this old information and tell us exactly where a person in China is now, and what their position is.'

Dalca made a pained face, as if he hated to argue with a client. 'Well . . . we provide only where they are in general.

We might tell you that Mr X is working in the American consulate in Shanghai as a commerce specialist in the durable-goods sector, and living in an apartment on a specific street. But the intelligence from America that the Islamic State possesses is sending terrorists to particular coffee shops, to specific rented vehicles driving to known locations, at certain times.' Dalca shrugged apologetically now. 'Not in our abilities with the data we are using. Somehow these Muslim terrorists must have people inside the American government.'

Peng and his men conferred again. Finally he said, 'We remain concerned. Were it to come to the attention of the Americans that this breach took place, regardless of whether or not this breach was responsible for the recent actions, the authorities would look carefully at you . . . and at us. *This* we cannot allow to happen.'

Dragomir Vasilescu said, 'How can we prove your information is secure?'

Peng did not answer. Dalca felt himself relax a little. These guys were just here to put terror in the hearts of the Romanians, to warn them to be careful with the data. Sure, if Dalca had incriminated himself they would have upped their measures, but he'd given them nothing but assurances, so they would just threaten a bit more and leave. They might not be convinced the ISIS intel had *not* come from ARTD, but they would have no evidence to support the possibility.

Dalca pressed his luck. 'If I might make a suggestion: The raw files are housed on a single air-gapped computer. As per your original request, there are no copies, and the files have not been uploaded so that they can be pulled by multiple machines. The machine holding the data is here in the building. Once the data was uploaded onto the computer, it was erased from the transferring machine, and that hard drive was destroyed off-site so there would be no evidence of it. The machine holding the records has had all its external ports physically disabled. There is no way to upload or download to the machine. You can't even print off records.

'If it would make you more comfortable, you can take the material with you, keep it safe, until all this in America blows over. Obviously it will mean the end of the work we do for the time being, but you would be sure that the data was not being misused.'

Dragomir Vasilescu was confused by the odd suggestion by Dalca, but in truth it was an empty suggestion. These guys didn't want to touch the material on that computer, and Dalca knew it. Other than the conclusions made by ARTD and then sent on to them, they wouldn't go near it.

Peng just shook his head, as Dalca had suspected he would all along.

Now Peng and his three henchmen looked menacingly at Vasilescu. 'We have people in our technical research division who will study what happened to the Americans. If we find any connection between your breach of their network via India and the new threats taking place in the United States right now, we will be back, and we *will* hold you responsible.'

The men from the Seychelles Group left twenty minutes later.

Dragomir Vasilescu turned to Alexandru Dalca in the lobby as soon as they were gone. 'Those guys are lunatics. They think we are working with fucking terrorists.'

Dalca agreed, then added, 'That stuff happening in America isn't coming from the data Albert stole. That's insane.'

Now Dragomir looked at his lead researcher with a cocked head. 'Hey . . . what was that back in there? You usually aren't so quick to pass off praise to your team. That showed maturity.'

Dalca smiled. 'Just wanted the Seychelles Group guys to know there are others involved.' He winked. 'I think it's only fair.'

Back in his office, Dalca poured himself a cup of coffee and sat down at his desk. He felt a little light-headed, and he wondered if he was coming down with a cold. As he reached for his coffee cup, he knocked the liquid over his table. He leapt up, cursed in surprise and anger, and then headed out to the break room on his floor to get some towels.

Keep it together, everything is great, he told himself. He was as chill as a person could be, he told himself this with finality every day. But now as he rushed to get something to clean up his mess, he looked down at his hands and he saw them shaking.

He could convince anyone of anything, but right now his mind could not convince his body that he was, in any way, safe.

Peng and his men were looking hard for evidence that ARTD had helped ISIS, and Dalca was in the middle. He'd sent them away for now, but they weren't going very far away.

Somewhere behind his calm façade he knew they would come back.

45

At 6:53 a.m., sixty-one law enforcement officers from various local and state authorities surrounded the Fresh Fest supermarket on West Ann Road in Las Vegas, Nevada. Two ambulances had already made the scene and left, their sirens wailing as they raced off to hospitals. But even now two more ambulances sat parked behind the police cars while EMTs and paramedics treated three lightly wounded civilians in the parking lot.

Forty minutes earlier, an Air Force Reaper unmanned aerial vehicle pilot had stopped in to pick up groceries on his way home from a twenty-four-hour shift at Creech AFB, northwest of the city. He'd been walking up to the checkout counter when he noticed a young olive-skinned couple next to him fidgeting nervously, glancing his way. The major was uneasy enough to walk over to a self-checkout lane, and when he looked back up at the couple he realized they were moving his way. The woman reached into her purse, and the man reached under his shirt.

As the guns came out and the major dropped his groceries, he heard a shouted command from up the magazine aisle. There, an older man in a baseball cap had drawn a small stainless steel pistol. He held it on the couple and ordered them to drop their weapons, but both of them instead turned to him and opened fire.

The old man shot the woman once in the chest, and once in the face, and while the first round merely rocked her back on her heels, the second shot killed her instantly. The civilian himself took a round through his shoulder and a second in his right hand. He fell to the ground clutching at his wounds, dropping his gun in the process.

A kid stocking shelves helped drag the wounded senior citizen to cover, and then through the market to escape out a back door.

The Air Force major bolted out the front door of the supermarket, chased by screaming nine-millimeter rounds. A store security guard, armed with a .38 revolver he hadn't fired since qualifying with it, emptied his weapon at the would-be assassin, missing with all six rounds before he was hit in the throat by return fire. He bled to death quickly in front of the ATM just inside the doors.

A police car had been idling in front of the convenience store adjacent to the market while two LVPD officers inside the vehicle drank coffee, and they heard the gunfire even with their windows up and the AC running. They rolled up in front of the market within forty-five seconds, just as the deli and bakery employees passed by, running for their lives.

One officer grabbed his shotgun and the other pulled his Glock 22, and they rushed inside toward the unknown threat.

The surviving terrorist had been trying to revive his female partner, and he was surprised by the quick arrival of the police. He ran back deeper into the large store, but not before he was hit in the back by four pellets of buckshot. He kept his footing, shot and wounded a civilian who stumbled into his path in panic, and emptied his magazine over his shoulder toward the police while he retreated all the way to the stockroom.

He made it to the loading dock, and could have escaped

out into a rear alley, but he saw employees ducked behind cars back there: men and women who could have pointed out his direction to police. Instead, he returned to the storage area of the grocery store, found a darkened corner behind pallets of breakfast cereal boxes, and collapsed in pain, exhaustion, and grief.

Kateb knew that he and his wife, Aza, had failed to kill their target, just as they had failed to kill the Navy SEAL two days earlier in L.A.

And now Aza was dead and Kateb was fucked.

Those first two police officers on the scene did not pursue the armed man into the stockroom, chiefly because when the cop with the shotgun knelt to check the body of the female attacker, he saw something horrifying. Her face was covered in blood from a ragged wound just to the left of her nose, and he found it odd she had a wire hanging out from the cuff of her shirt. At the end of the cord, he saw the detonator with the black swivel safety cap turned to expose the red button below it.

The young cop stumbled back onto the floor, then leapt to his feet and shouted to his partner to get the hell out.

As more law enforcement arrived the entire shopping center was evacuated and sealed off. The injured were hauled out by other civilians while the police held their pistols at the low ready, still coming to the slow realization that a couple minutes after enjoying their morning coffee and talking about their kids' baseball tourney that weekend, they had rolled up on a terrorist attack with international implications.

The Las Vegas Metropolitan Police Department's SWAT team is called Zebra; they are known as one of the best forces in the nation, and they made the scene within twenty-five minutes. No one on scene could tell them whether they were facing a hostage situation or simply a barricaded suspect, so the commander of the Zebras called for a robot.

The Zebra unit was not going through the front entrance of the market until the bomb squad checked the vest on the body fifty feet from the door, so they moved around back. They formed at an open loading dock and an unlocked employee entrance door, and waited for the negotiator on the scene to give the word to breach.

A small tactical robot run by the Zebra unit was sent through the automatic doors of the market. An officer with a controller watched the monitor in front of him and followed a blood trail all the way back into the stockroom.

Kateb sat propped against a pallet of cereal boxes, his blood soaking into the cardboard. His phone was to his ear, and his pistol hung between his knees in his other hand.

'I am sorry, Mohammed. Aza and I have failed you. I am wounded and she is dead. A stupid old man had a gun, like he was a cowboy in a movie. We did not expect trouble from the civilians. After she died and I shot the old fool, I turned back around to kill the major, but he was running out the front door. I tried to hit him, but I failed.'

Mohammed said, 'I know, Kateb. It is on the news. They have you surrounded, my brother.'

The wounded man was not listening. Instead, he said, 'She died right in front of me.'

'She was *martyred* in front of you. She was a warrior, as are you, my brother.'

Kateb looked at the dried blood on the back of his hand. Then he looked up. There was a sound echoing around the warehouse now.

'I can hear something. I don't know what it is.'

'They will be coming now. It is time for you to become a martyr as well.'

'Yes, Mohammed. I did not kill the major. But I will kill these policemen.'

'Good! Very good! Allah be praised.'

Kateb put the phone down, fought his way up to his feet, and raised his pistol out in front of him. With his free hand he took the plunger of the suicide vest, and he held his thumb over it.

The noise became louder and louder, it was an electronic whine of some sort.

Then it stopped abruptly.

Kateb rubbed sweat from his forehead with his shirt-sleeve, then raised the gun again. He could hear his own heartbeat.

Suddenly a voice called out from right around the corner of the row of pallets, just ten feet from where Kateb stood.

'This is the Las Vegas Police Department –'

Kateb screamed, *'Allahu Akbar!'* and spun around the side of the pallet, firing the pistol, and the instant he made the turn, he pushed the plunger down.

Three feet in front of him was the robot, smaller than a push lawn mower. Over its speaker the negotiator was telling the wounded man to throw out his gun as Kateb detonated his vest, destroying the robot and several pallets of cereal boxes.

Abu Musa al-Matari placed his phone back on the table now that the connection was lost, and he cursed.

The drone pilot operation had been a failure. These two from the Santa Clara cell had been a joke. Yes, they spread terror from Los Angeles to Las Vegas, and killed some people along the way, but they'd failed in both of their objectives.

They'd even failed in another sense. The woman, Aza, had been wearing a suicide vest and a camera mounted around the vest with bungee cord inside her open zip-up jacket. Al-Matari had been watching the attack in real time, and when he saw the policeman standing over her, he placed the detonation text on his phone, but the bomb did not go off.

He could only assume that the old man who'd shot her had severed the control wires to the detonator.

Lucky shot for him. Lucky break for the cop.

Good riddance, number fourteen and number fifteen, al-Matari thought, still thinking of the cell members by their Language School designations. He had better operators out there, and they were still bringing the fight to the infidels. Better he spent his time working with the real warriors and not have to waste his days dealing with the fools.

On the previous evening, three more attacks by the men and women of Musa al-Matari's cell had taken place across the country.

The wedding of a Marine Harrier pilot in New Orleans was attacked with a bomb placed in the reception facility. The Marine and his bride were uninjured, but three guests were killed and six more wounded.

A CIA case officer posted in Oslo, home visiting a sick mother in Flint, Michigan, was killed in a drive-by shooting, along with a Good Samaritan passerby who was run down by the getaway vehicle while trying to stop it from leaving the area.

And in St Louis, Missouri, a firebomb destroyed the

SUV of an executive with the National Geospatial-Intelligence Agency. The man was able to escape the flames, but suffered second-degree burns.

Of al-Matari's surviving Language School students, the fifteen men and two women were now working at a fever pitch. They had conducted attacks all over the country, which forced them into hours, and in some cases days, of travel. They were constantly looking over their shoulders, and while the results of the operations were clearly mixed, the Yemeni knew the combined actions were having the desired effect. America was stunned by the abilities of ISIS, the scope and audacity of a dozen acts of terror in less than a five-day period.

On top of this, al-Matari was studying the reactions of the police and the government to each incident, watching everything possible on television, and he was working on a new plan. It would be big and bold, and like nothing done before, it would push the public to demand that their nation send troops into the fight against ISIS.

The killing of the CENTCOM commander had been, by far, the most consequential act to date, but al-Matari's new op would be exponentially larger. Right now Tripoli was with three of the Chicago cell members and Omar, the leader of the Detroit cell. All of them were scoping out locations here in the city for the important mission. Meanwhile, David, Ghazi, and Husam were in Brooklyn, scouting for another operation that would take place in a day or two there. The four survivors from Santa Clara were down in Arizona and action was imminent on their next op, and the four remaining from the Atlanta group had split into two teams of two and were preparing for other missions.

On top of all this, the first copycat attack had taken place just outside Detroit the evening before, where a sergeant in the Michigan Air National Guard was shot dead while sitting in a fast-food restaurant. The local police cornered the assailant minutes later in the public library, and the young man of Somali origin fell to his death as he tried to escape out a third-floor window.

Al-Matari was especially proud that some brave mujahideen had joined in the fight, and he decided he would make sure the Detroit killing was reported in the next ISIS social media blast as having been conducted by someone outside the official cell of warriors under direct Islamic State control. He thought by promoting this unknown man's martyrdom, it would bring out more of the self-radicalized and serve as an important force multiplier in the fight.

The Yemeni had to admit his operation was not without its problems. American law enforcement was already responding to the new threats, getting to the scenes faster and with more force. And American citizens were fighting back with their own personal weapons, something he hadn't seen when he'd orchestrated bombings and shootings in Turkey or India or Malaysia, or when others from his organization executed attacks in Belgium and France and Germany.

But all in all, the men and women of the Language School had caused significant damage and an impressive amount of noise and fear in America. He had only to keep up the carnage to draw in new members, and soon this match he had lit in the past week would turn into a raging fire.

46

Dan Murray had been on the go almost constantly for the past few days. The attorney general moved among meetings at the White House, the Pentagon, and the J. Edgar Hoover Building. His own office was in the Robert F. Kennedy Building, just across the street from FBI, and yes, he did have meetings there throughout the day as well.

Now he walked through the West Wing for his third meeting there in as many days. But for today's get-together he was heading back to the Oval, not to the Situation Room, because the meeting this morning was going to be a smaller affair.

SecDef Burgess had just arrived and was sitting down on the sofa where Mary Pat Foley was already seated. The President of the United States leaned forward from his chair facing the two sofas, and he poured coffee for everyone from the service on the table.

He looked up at Murray. 'Dan is light cream, no sugar. Same as for the last twenty-five years.'

'Thanks, Jack.' Dan took a seat across from Mary Pat and Bob.

There were three people who worked for President Jack Ryan who felt comfortable enough to call him by his first name in private, and Dan and Mary Pat were two of them. Bob Burgess, on the other hand, was a former Army three-star general, he wasn't a friend from way back, and he wouldn't dream of calling the Commander in Chief by his given name, even if Ryan begged him to.

The third person in the 'Jack' club was Arnie Van Damm, and he entered with a notepad, shut the door behind him, and took a seat on the couch next to Murray.

Ryan said, 'Couple of things to get to this morning. The PDB covered the attacks overnight and this morning around the country. As everyone anticipated, it's getting worse by the day. Anything new since the daily brief?'

Murray said, 'The thing in Vegas is the most recent. We're blanketing the scene for evidence, but both the perps are dead, so we won't get anything out of them. Looking at the security cameras of the L.A. attack in Starbucks where the movie star was killed, this appears to be the same couple.'

Ryan replied, 'At least al-Matari is going through his killers rapidly.'

'We can't say yet if his force is shrinking in strength, or growing, at least by proxy, because each day this continues, the risk of copycats increases.'

Jack took that in, then turned to Burgess. 'You've been working on ways to protect servicepeople here in the US. What have you come up with?'

'We are adopting measures to get more security for off-base meetings and conferences.'

'You aren't canceling some of these meetings?'

Burgess shook his head adamantly. 'No way. We will defend against these terrorists, but we won't cave in to them. We start canceling the daily operations of the US military, and ISIS will play that as a victory. We go on as normal, but with increased security.'

'Okay. What else?'

Burgess took a long breath before saying, 'I'd like every serviceman and -woman in the US to have the right to carry a sidearm off base.'

Jack was silent for fifteen seconds. Then he said, 'Why the hell not?'

Murray jumped in. 'I get it of course, but you are going to get a ton of pushback from New York, New Jersey, California, Illinois, and a few other states.'

Burgess said, 'Yeah, states that make millions off of military bases and personnel. Mr President, it's not a perfect solution, but it's the best single option we have. We are also spinning up self-defense and training classes, contracting firearms trainers across the country to give as many classes to servicepeople as they can physically do. The men and women in the military are trained with handguns, but the training isn't what it should be. This will help, and we won't encourage anyone to carry who doesn't want the responsibility.'

'Military weapons?'

'Yes, sir. We aren't going to force some lance corporal who makes seventeen grand a year to go out and buy a six-hundred-dollar pistol, plus a holster and ammo, to protect himself from terrorists. We can issue Beretta M9s, duty holsters, and ball ammo. Standard weapons they are trained on. There are a few other weapons used by other branches, too, so we'll issue those, where warranted. Everybody will go with what they know, so they are more proficient.'

Arnie said, 'Jack, sorry, but the optics are horrible on this. The opposition in Congress and in the media are going to spin this as you admitting America is a war zone.'

'I'll take the hit and explain the situation as best I can.'

Arnie then said, 'The legal age for handgun carry varies from state to state, but it's twenty-one or higher in a lot of places.'

Ryan said, 'If we can send an eighteen-year-old out with a gun to fight overseas, we can give him a gun to protect himself and his family at home.' He turned to Dan. 'I expect you, as AG, to fend off any legal opposition.'

Murray didn't like it, it was clear, but he said, 'Of course. We need to put limits on this, though.'

Ryan said, 'Nobody carries a weapon who is drinking. Zero tolerance, and that has to be stressed at every step along the way during implementation.'

Burgess said, 'Absolutely.'

Jack said, 'I don't know if it will help, but it will let the terrorists know they aren't out there shooting fish in a barrel.'

Dan Murray next gave an update on the investigation. There was some progress to report. The DoJ had been looking into flight manifests from the United States to Central America during the time frame of the Language School training in El Salvador. Through this they had so far identified eleven of Musa al-Matari's potential terrorists. Four of those successfully ID'd were among the dead in Virginia and North Carolina, and all the rest were currently missing from their residences.

Additionally, possible identities of some of the other ISIS assets working in the United States had been discovered by the FBI via the tip lines. A used-car salesman stopped coming to work, a student never dropped out of class but had not attended in the past two months. These and a few other tips were being looked into and they appeared promising, but Murray explained that the FBI was taking these good tips along with thousands of bad ones, and agents and analysts were in the process of working like mad to find out who really was missing and a threat, and who was just playing hooky or happened to be unliked by someone who felt like getting the government to harass them.

Murray said, 'Jack, our tip line is exploding. And yes, it's exploding from jerks who think the Indian who makes their sandwiches at the deli is a Muslim terrorist, that's definitely happening, but it's also exploding from Muslim men and women in this country that want nothing to do with any of this bullshit. ISIS has killed a lot of people, and more of them have been Muslim than anyone else.

'We're hunting two brothers and a sister in Chicago who just fell off the map a few months ago, nobody knows what happened to them. Multiple tips came from Chicago Muslims about these two. A similar thing in Atlanta. A mosque there said one of their more outspoken and radical regulars just stopped coming in and is not answering his phone. Timing is right for this being a Language School student.'

Ryan said, 'That's good to know we are hearing from others inside the Muslim community. It would be a damn ironic thing if all this brought this country a little bit back together.'

Murray said, 'I've directed everyone in the DoJ to reach out to the community and to make sure they tread carefully, so we don't do anything to screw up the goodwill we are getting.'

Ryan said, 'We have identified men and women who are dead or who are not where they are supposed to be. We are putting their pictures out there, but so far we haven't caught anyone. We have thousands of agents looking for the perpetrators, but Musa al-Matari could be in some tiny apartment somewhere running this whole thing from his phone, if he is in the US at all. And even if Bob puts a pistol on the belt of every serviceman and -woman in America, the terrorists have bombs and suicide vests, that somehow manage to go off even after they are dead or incapacitated.

'Long term, Dan, you'll get them, but in the short term they are killing people and creating a lot of propaganda that makes them look powerful and us look weak.'

Murray said, 'I don't disagree with anything you are saying. Look, we could be even more aggressive with some of our tactics, but let's lay our cards on the table. The objective here is to stop these attacks as soon as possible but, as AG, a close secondary objective for me is to prosecute the criminals.'

Ryan said, 'That secondary objective is far less important to me. Putting Musa al-Matari on trial is something I don't anticipate, and it's frankly something I'd happily do without.'

Murray said, 'I understand that. The tools in my toolbox all revolve around the legal system, and I remain beholden to them. Maybe someone with a different set of rules . . .' His voice trailed off.

Mary Pat Foley interjected. 'Dan, if I am not mistaken, there is an employee at Gerry Hendley's shop who retains his FBI credentials.'

Murray nodded instantly. Clearly this is what he had been getting at. 'In a general sense I know the work Hendley and his team have done, both at home and abroad. Since Dominic Caruso remains on loan from us to their outfit, even if just on paper, I would be happy sharing information between myself and their very effective operation. It can only help in our . . . investigation.'

Jack said, 'Let me think that one over, Dan.' Dom Caruso was President Ryan's nephew, and his first thought was to keep The Campus out of domestic operations, even though he was well aware they had operated within America's borders in the past.

AG Murray said, 'Fair enough, Mr President. Just wanted to throw it out there.'

*

The meeting broke up, but Mary Pat stayed behind. 'Any specific concerns you might harbor about bringing The Campus in to help locate Musa al-Matari?'

Ryan looked at her. 'Is that a joke? I will always harbor concerns about The Campus's activities. General and specific.'

Mary Pat said, 'They do good work. Good, honest, confidential work.'

'No argument from me on that.'

'And Dominic can handle himself.' She paused. 'They *all* can.'

She was talking about Jack, the President understood. He didn't like being the one involved in sending his son into harm's way, but, he recognized, that ship had sailed long ago. Since the day Jack joined the organization, against his father's wishes or knowledge, he had been in peril.

Mary Pat said, 'There is no way John Clark would let Jack Junior be involved in the States in something this high-profile.'

'Yeah, well, if he doesn't send my kid, he'll send my nephew, or somebody else's kid. I have no right to balk at the plan because my son is in the mix.'

'If you didn't care that your son might go into harm's way, then you wouldn't be much of a father, Jack.'

Ryan smiled at the floor, but then his face hardened. 'I'll give Dan the go-ahead to brief Dominic.'

'I'll call Gerry and give him the heads-up that this is coming. They'll need time to prepare.'

Ryan nodded. 'Al-Matari is averaging three hits a day now, and it won't be any time at all till the copycats start coming out of the woodwork. Whatever it takes, Mary Pat.'

47

By eight Jack was already sitting in the conference room holding his third cup of coffee of the morning and leaning over a computer, his workspace all but covered with hand-written notes, printed sheets, and books, and his one laptop had turned into three.

Jack had been spending night and day studying the attacks in America, one by one, trying to find out how his unknown adversary put all the pieces of the puzzles together from the Office of Personnel Management records and open-source intelligence.

For Jack it had become nothing less than an obsession. At the office all day with Gavin sitting across from him, then home, a beer on his coffee table as he sat on the floor with his laptop in front of him. He dug through books on OSINT methods, marveling at what was out there, lamenting the fact most average people couldn't imagine how much of their lives was available to anyone who wanted to investigate.

For many of the recent attacks he'd had to look no further than the business networking website LinkedIn to determine how the identity intelligence expert working on behalf of the Islamic State had been able to connect the OPM data to current intelligence community employees. Their names and often their pictures were listed, along with their education and work history, identifying themselves as workers in the intelligence field at CENTCOM or Fort Bragg or for public and private organizations in the DC area. So far three of the victims and one more intended victim had a profile that made it obvious they were involved with human intelligence and targeting operations in the Middle East, and Jack had no doubt in his mind several of America's best and brightest minds in this field were now dead because of their decision to network on LinkedIn.

With a little more work, Jack could see how even clandestine employees of the government, most of whom had no online identities to speak of, were still vulnerable via family and friends letting information slip.

Gavin entered with his own cup of coffee, gave Ryan a nod, and then took his regular seat at the conference table.

As soon as he sat he said, 'I've come bearing gifts.'

Jack didn't even look his way. 'You don't eat donuts anymore, so I doubt that there's anything you have that I'm interested –'

Jack stopped abruptly. He looked up now. 'You talked to your friend at NSA. The guy with the back door to Reddit?'

Gavin corrected him. 'I didn't say he was a friend, and I didn't say he had a back door. But I *did* get into the private message sent by the user you mentioned.'

Ryan snatched a pen off the table and scrambled to find a blank page in a notebook nearly filled with scrawl.

Gavin looked at his computer. '5Megachopper5's message reads as follows: "I've been following your story, my friend, and I think I can help. If you truly want to do that which you claim, I will provide you with all the information you need to make it happen. I am prepared to prove myself to you, and I want nothing in return other than to see that justice is done for Stepan's life."'

Jack just said, 'Wow.'

'He provides an address that can only be accessed by TOR for Rechkov to use to communicate if he is interested. It's a dead link now. And then, the day he sent the PM, the guy we are after shut his Reddit identity down. I assume that means Rechkov *did* make contact with him.'

'So . . . we're screwed,' Jack said. 'Right back where we started.'

'Not at all,' replied Gavin. 'I've been going through the contents of Rechkov's hard drive, just like a dozen other forensics investigators, but unlike them, I am the only one who knows about the URL, and the date of the communication on Reddit. All this information was logged on his hard drive by the date. Remember, Rechkov was a fledgling computer scientist himself, so he has tens of thousands of pages of code saved as text files, all part of his studies, and it's kept haphazardly all over his drive. But it occurred to me Rechkov might have tried to get some info on this person communicating with him, at least just to make sure it wasn't the US government trying to catch him in a sting. I found a few pages of code in a txt format saved on Evernote, a note-taking app, that he'd put there in the days after the Reddit communication, so I went through it, line by line, late last night.'

Gavin waited to be prompted by Jack.

'And?'

'And Rechkov left a clue as to who he was communicating with. In the code was the creator's username, Polygeist999.'

Jack just said, 'You lost me.'

'Rechkov determined this username was affiliated with the person who set up the dark website.'

'I thought 5Megachopper5 did that.'

'Nah, that's a throwaway name he used on Reddit. Poly-geist999 is another name he used.'

Jack scratched his head. 'So . . . Rechkov figured out he was talking to someone online associated with another user-name. How?'

'Maybe something this guy sent him, or by hacking into a service this guy revealed he was a member of. No way to know, but it's nice that that asshole Rechkov left us a clue.'

'How is *that* a clue?'

Gavin said, 'I used link analysis on Polygeist999, to see if it, or a version close to it, shows up in other places online. It's been used hundreds of times in different permutations. "Padding," it's called. It could be 1Polygeist999, or Poly-geist9991 or he might throw an ampersand in there or something else. Computer people often use variations, depending on what they are working on, and they are differ-ent enough that it takes high-level link analysis to figure out that all the different permutations are one and the same per-son. I went to my friend at the NSA, you know, the one who doesn't exist, and had him run some reports for me. The Polygeist username first showed up in March of last year on an apartment service in Romania. After that it was every-where, different types of computer and technical sites, coding, hacking, illegal downloads, et cetera.'

Jack said, 'Romania?'

'Yes,' Gavin confirmed. 'And the link analysis gives us other usernames that show up multiple times along with Polygeist. Dozens and dozens of uses of this name and oth-ers linked to it, all tied to e-mails, computer code, domain registrations, et cetera.'

Together Jack and Gavin began entering the different names into search engines and databases to try to find something that would stick out. Their target inhabited dozens of different online personas, and he was all over different sites, many having to do with obtaining open-source intelligence. But they needed more. They needed to link him to a real identity. Moreover, they were looking to find some way this character had some relationship with the jihadists, a relationship with the intelligence community of any nation in the world, or something that would show them that this person who contacted Rechkov with intel from the Office of Personnel Management and a plan to kill a Navy commander had some motive for doing so.

As they came up with new information, they put it in their shared link-analysis database. This led to more names, all associated with the initial username Polygeist999 and its permutations.

It was slow, arduous, and complicated work, but less than an hour and a half into it, Gavin called across the table. 'Are you seeing what I'm seeing?'

'That no matter what you do, you can't trace back any of these usernames before March of last year?'

'Yeah. It's like he was born that month. I wonder why he just started in March and exploded like he had been doing this sort of thing his whole life.'

Jack looked up slowly from the computer. 'It began with him joining an apartment-hunting website in Romania, right?'

'Yes. Maybe he was trying to hack into it, or he was researching someone who lived in Romania and did business on the website. Maybe he could have been looking up a floor plan of one of his intended identity theft victims. We don't know.'

Jack said, 'I interpret that information more literally. I think he needed a place to stay, so he joined the site.'

Gavin hadn't even considered the fact there might be a straightforward and benign reason for the person's actions. He said, 'Why do you think he needed a place to stay? You think he's actually Romanian?'

Jack said, 'Yes, and he needed an apartment, because he just got out of prison.'

'*Prison?* Where the hell are you getting this?'

'There is no online activity for any accounts, usernames, e-mails, et cetera, et cetera, that take place before March nineteenth of last year. What if he'd been locked up, without computer access? You know a guy like this doesn't just appear out of nowhere online. His skills take years and years to develop, but the link analysis with websites and usernames just begins, as if the man is a fully formed computer and OSINT expert on day one. We have enough data here to cast a wide net, and we aren't finding anything from more than sixteen months ago.'

'It is a possibility,' Gavin allowed.

'Do we have a way to look into Romanian prison records?'

'With some work I can do that, but we don't know when he got out exactly, and it would still be a needle in a haystack.'

Jack said, 'Yeah, but it's a smaller haystack than we had yesterday.'

Gavin chuckled. 'You're right about that. I'll get to work on the Romanian government networks and swim downstream into the prison records. It's going to take me a couple of hours.'

In the end, it took less than four minutes before Gavin shouted in the conference room, startling Jack. 'I've got him!'

'You found Polygeist? How the hell did you do that so fast?'

'Because I didn't have to hack into the Romanian network. Instead, I just ran a search of US government DoJ records of Interpol convictions. I got a list of cases the DoJ was involved with in Romania. There are a hundred thirty-eight of them, but only seventy-one led to conviction. Of those, only twenty-eight have been released. Of those released, only twenty-one were released on or before March nineteenth of last year.'

Jack was impressed, but he was about to be a lot more impressed. 'Message me those names and I'll start to –'

Gavin kept talking. 'Of those twenty-one released on or before March nineteenth, exactly one of them was released *on* March nineteenth.'

Jack stood from his chair. 'You've got a Romanian cyber-crime personality released on the *day* the Polygeist entities started cropping up around the Web?'

'I do indeed. The prisoner's name is Alexandru Dalca. He was held in Jilava Prison for a term of five years, ten months, and sixteen days. Before he went in he had his own online cyberfraud network, bilked customers out of millions.'

Gavin read a portion of the complaint from the US Department of Justice. 'He was an expert in social engineering passwords. A confidence man.'

Jack slowly sat back down behind his laptop. 'That doesn't explain how he got so good at compromising these targets with open-source intel.'

Gavin shrugged. 'Prison, Jack. You can learn all sorts of bad stuff in prison, because that is where all the bad people are.'

'Not *all* the bad people, Gav. We run into a shitload of them out here on the outside.'

'Okay. You got me there.'

'What's he doing now?' Jack asked.

'Beats me.'

Jack typed his name in a Romanian search engine. Seconds later he said, 'I'll be damned. He works at a company in Bucharest called Advanced Research Technological Designs.'

Gavin was typing now, looking the company up in a database he kept on computer hackers. Even before he finished inputting the name he said, 'Wait, I know those guys. Son of a bitch!'

'Who are they?'

'They are damn good hackers, but that's just the start of it.' Now he looked at results in his database, reading through details of the company. 'Yeah ... they started out selling prescription pain pills online for a while, then they branched out into online fraud. They got bigger and bigger, attracted a deeper bench of hacker talent because their social engineers had gotten so damn good at getting passwords and admin access to websites.'

'How do you know about them?'

'They've done some sweet social media scams to get information on bankers, mostly in Europe, but it made the news.'

Jack cocked his head. He'd never heard of this. '*What* news?'

Gavin looked up from his monitor. 'News in *my* world, Ryan. Not on *Entertainment Tonight* or whatever you watch when you leave here.'

Jack just closed his eyes for a moment and let Gavin's snarky comment roll off his back.

'Yeah,' Gavin said as he read some more about ARTD. 'I remember now, three or four years ago at the Black Hat conference. It's a get-together of all the world's hackers.'

'I know what the Black Hat conference is. Must have been on *ET*.'

'Right. Anyway, a guy did a presentation on a hack this company in Romania carried out on the largest cell-phone provider in Holland. Ripped personal ID info from hundreds of thousands. They could never pin it on ARTD but one of their former employees claimed their hackers pulled it off.'

Jack said, 'Are they good enough to do this thing at OPM?'

'Talent-wise, I don't think so. Plus, they've never gone after government networks like this in the past. Still . . . this Dalca guy clearly works for them, and he clearly communicated with Vadim Rechkov, passing the intel about Hagen.'

Jack launched to his feet. 'Good enough for me. See ya.'

'Wait! Where are you going?'

'I'm going to Romania.' He turned and rushed out of the conference room, racing toward the elevators.

Gavin Biery moved slower, but he *did* move. 'Not without me you aren't!'

48

Jack saw an open door to Gerry's office, so he walked right in, only to find Gerry talking to John Clark and Ding Chavez.

'Oh . . . sorry, guys,' Jack said. He noticed the ultraserious expressions on the three men. 'I'm obviously interrupting something.'

Gerry said, 'No, I'm glad you're here. I was about to call you and Dom in. We just got off the phone with Dan Murray. He's asked us to aid in the hunt for Musa al-Matari and his people here in the US. We are considering moving Dominic, along with support, as soon as we can get some place to send him.'

Jack said, 'Because of his FBI credentials?'

'That's right. It will give him freedom of movement around crime scenes, and it's safe to assume the ISIS terrorists will attack again, sooner, rather than later.'

Clark said, 'Sorry, Jack, but you won't be on this trip. The potential you could be recognized on a domestic op like this is too great.'

Jack said, 'That's good news, actually. I came to request that you send me, along with some help, to Bucharest. Trust me, nobody's going to recognize me there.'

Gerry said, 'I'll grant you that, but what's in Bucharest?'

Gavin stepped into the office behind Jack, who was still in the doorway. He answered Gerry Hendley's question. 'A guy named Alexandru Dalca. He is the person, or one of the people, exploiting the Office of Personnel Management files and turning them into targeting packages against American military and intelligence.'

Gerry reacted with surprise. 'I'll be damned! You actually found who is responsible for the breach?'

Jack said, 'We think so, but we don't know exactly what we're dealing with yet. We know where this man works, but that's just about it. Not sure if his whole company is involved, or if he is protected or propped up by some other group. What we do know is that we need to get over there, shadow this man Dalca, and try to figure out what the hell is going on.'

Gerry looked to Clark. 'What do you think?'

Clark said, 'Since we have no idea of the scope of the breach and which government employees have already been exposed to this guy, it makes sense to use our people instead of just notifying Mary Pat and Dan. Dom will need support on his operation here in the States, but in an in extremis situation he can get help from law enforcement. Jack in Romania, on the other hand, will be on his own if we don't send others along with him.'

Gerry said, 'So let's give some extra support to Jack.'

Clark said, 'What do you think, Ding?'

Chavez just shrugged. 'I think I'm heading to Romania.'

Gavin Biery, still standing behind Ryan, cleared his throat.

Jack said, 'We will have a need for tech support. I'll want to run a full surveillance package on this guy, and we don't know what we're up against yet. If Gavin could come along, it would be helpful.'

Clark gave Gavin a hard look. 'Let me make myself perfectly clear. Tech . . . support . . . only.'

463

Gavin said, 'Trust me, I'll stay out of trouble.'

Jack said, 'If tailing Dalca, getting some cams and mics on him, and searching his computers doesn't pan out, maybe we can turn up the heat, confront him, and make him think we have more knowledge than we really do.'

Gerry said, 'Bluff, you mean. John, what do you think?'

Clark said, 'I like it. We've certainly pulled it off before. Gavin and Ryan seem as certain about this call as can be.

'I know a guy in Romania, ex-Army. He was a founding member of their Brigada Antiteroristă, the USLA, back in the late seventies, and he's worked as a fixer for foreign media and business interests traveling in Bucharest. I'll reach out to him and try to hire him to help you guys out with translation and logistics.'

'Sounds perfect,' Ding said.

Gerry called Dominic into the conference room, while Clark called Adara and Midas, both taking a lunch break in his farmhouse kitchen in Maryland, putting them on speakerphone. He then told all three about Jack and Chavez's plan to go to Bucharest to tail a personality implicated in the OPM breach.

Gerry added, 'Ding, I want you to take Midas along. He's new here, obviously, but he's got experience in advanced force operations with Delta's recce squadron, which is all about going in light and covert for recon and such.'

Chavez said, 'Happy to have you on board.'

Midas replied over the phone. 'I appreciate the opportunity.'

Dom was sitting right next to Chavez. 'And me as well, I assume.'

Gerry and Clark exchanged a look, and Dom realized it had to do with him. 'Something wrong?'

'Not exactly,' Gerry said. 'We have another role for you right now.'

Dom stiffened. 'What role?'

'We are going to use you domestically to try to help the FBI run down these terror cells. Dan Murray requested you specifically. If we can get a handhold on a live terrorist, we might be able to get him to talk faster than the DoJ ever could.'

Dom went from defensive to excited in an instant. '*That* is a good idea.'

Clark said, 'Adara, do you remember when I told you, in no uncertain terms, that I'd make sure you and Dom wouldn't be working together, at least at first?'

Adara's voice over the speakerphone was hesitant. 'You mean just last week? Yes, I recall that conversation.'

'Well . . . forget I said that. I need Dom in the USA on this because of his FBI credentials. And I need Midas overseas because of his experience. No offense, but his Delta Force background trumps your Navy background when it comes to covert reconnaissance.'

Adara said, 'I'd be a fool to argue that logic.'

Dom stiffened up again. Coming to terms with the fact he'd be operational with his own girlfriend.

Adara, on the other hand, was already making plans. 'I'll start requisitioning surveillance gear from outfitting. I'm sure we're going to have to bring some tech into this.'

Clark said, 'Good, Adara. As soon as there is another attack, you and Dom will travel to it. You might have to go commercial if the Gulfstream isn't back from Europe yet.'

Adara asked, 'And what about you, John?'

'I'll remain here at the office, but be ready to help in any capacity necessary.'

The meeting ended, and everyone in the office, save for Gerry and Clark, shuffled out seconds later, all focused on their missions. The two older men sat there quietly, until Clark said, 'This means we're just waiting on another military or intelligence officer to get murdered by terrorists somewhere in the country.'

Gerry nodded. 'You better help Dom and Adara get prepped. The way things are going, I doubt they'll have much time at all before they're off.'

49

Walid 'Wally' Hussein left the Ahlul Bayt Mosque in Brooklyn at seven-thirty, following a small group out after morning
prayers. He turned right on Atlantic and headed back for his
car, checking his phone for any missed calls as he strolled.

His Chevy Suburban was parked on the street and he
climbed in, fired the engine, then pulled out into traffic.

Hussein was a thirty-eight-year-old special agent for the
FBI, and he worked in the Counterterrorism Division of the
New York field office in Lower Manhattan. His morning
drive was always something of a pain in the ass, but he was
a lifelong resident of Brooklyn, so a half-hour commute to
go the three miles from his mosque to his office didn't faze
him like it would some FBI transplant from Nebraska.

He listened to his voice mail as he drove north, a message
from a fellow special agent at the field office telling him
they'd received something promising on the tip line, so he
needed to haul ass into work so they could check it out.

Hussein looked at the bumper-to-bumper traffic in front
of him on Adams and he called the other agent back.

'Special Agent Lunetti.'

'Hey, man. Got your message. I'm headed in, but if it's out
this way you might want to come to me. The bridge is backed
up this morning.'

Special Agent Lunetti was a local as well, born and raised
in Queens. 'Hey, Wally. How's it goin'? No . . . this is over
here. A tipster said a guy who looked like one of the BOLOs

467

from the ISIS attacks checked into a two-star joint near the Bowery. The Windsor. You know it?'

'Forsyth and Broome?'

'Yeah. If you want we can meet in front of the Y a couple blocks south of there. Head in on foot. How's that sound?'

'Sounds a lot like the four dry holes we went to yesterday.'

'You're probably right, but whatcha gonna do?'

'This, I guess. Is the subject still at the hotel?'

'Caller says she doesn't know. Said he checked in yesterday, she thought he looked familiar, but didn't know where from till she saw the pictures again this morning on the *Today* show. She works at the hotel, and can meet us outside.'

Wally Hussein looked ahead at the traffic again. He was still half a mile from the Brooklyn Bridge. 'Okay. It's gonna take me another twenty to get –'

Something caught Hussein's attention on the sidewalk on his right. The movement of a long narrow cardboard box falling to the ground behind a man walking into the street. His eyes turned to the motion, and he saw a black man just as he stepped out from behind a donut cart and into the street, some thirty or forty yards away. The man had pulled a long device out of the box before discarding it, and he hefted it on his shoulder. It was a tube with a fat end shaped a little like a football.

Hussein knew he was looking at an RPG-7 grenade launcher, and it was pointed right at him.

'Holy shit!'

The flame and smoke of the launch of the device were the last things to register in Special Agent Wally Hussein's mind before he died.

*

468

David Hembrick was knocked to the ground by the explosion of the FBI agent's big SUV. He dropped the empty rocket launcher and his sunglasses fell from his face but he left the weapon and the shades in the street and crawled back to his feet. He began running to the east through Willoughby Plaza, knocking into a few stunned passersby as he made his escape from the crime scene. A woman sitting on a bench locked eyes with him as he passed, and he wanted to draw his Glock and shoot the bitch, but Mohammed had been clear. His job was not to martyr himself, it was to get away and live to fight another day.

The woman pointed at him and screamed, but Hembrick kept running through Willoughby Plaza, his heart pounding from the terror of the action.

He made a left on Pearl Street, and immediately saw two NYPD officers approaching, responding to the loud noise. Neither of the cops had his weapon out, and at first they let Hembrick rush past, as others were fleeing the area and it didn't look suspicious at all to race away from an explosion.

But Hembrick made it no more than ten yards up Pearl Street before the busybody on the bench said, 'There! *That* man! *That's* him!' and Hembrick heard the order to halt come from the NYPD.

He kept on running. Hembrick was twenty-six, both officers were over forty, and he had a twenty-five-yard head start that turned into a fifty-yard lead by the time he made a right in front of the Marriott. In front of him was Jay Street, and he took off for it.

There was a security camera out in front of the Marriott, *not* the only one in the neighborhood, but this was the only one Hembrick stared directly at as he raced by.

At the curb on Jay Street, a silver Chrysler 200 was waiting for him with the passenger-side door open.

David Hembrick dove into the car, while the back window rolled down. Husam leaned out the window, hefted his Uzi, and centered it on the first of the two cops, now just thirty yards away.

Husam fired short, controlled bursts, slammed rounds into the body armor and extremities of the stunned cops, hitting both of them in their Kevlar, but also tagging one man in the underarm and the other in both legs.

The Chrysler raced north on Jay with Ghazi behind the wheel, following the GPS on his windshield away from the flow of morning traffic into Manhattan. They hit the Brooklyn-Queens Expressway in two minutes, exited at Metropolitan Avenue, and parked in an underground lot near the Graham Avenue subway station.

The three men entered the station and separated at the bottom of the stairs, and then all three entered different cars on the first train heading into Manhattan. They made a connection and arrived at Penn Station shortly after nine a.m. Here they moved separately through the morning crowd, and then each boarded a different car on the first train heading to Newark Liberty Airport.

At the airport train station they separated for the day, following plane tickets they had purchased online from their phones en route, and they all boarded flights within an hour of one another. Hembrick flew direct, both Husam and Ghazi made connections, but all three of them would arrive in Chicago by the midafternoon.

After the chaos that ensued at the FBI New York field office with the murder of one of their special agents, it was past noon before anyone checked out the tip of the man at the Windsor hotel. He was still there, in his room, and he was questioned, but his alibi stood up.

He had nothing to do with ISIS and the attacks here in America.

Musa al-Matari sent the recording of the killing of a Shiite FBI agent on the streets of New York City to the Global Islamic Media Front. The image quality was fair, although the camera attached to David Hembrick's chest with bungee cord moved along with him as he stepped into the street, fired, and fell back on the ground, so the image stabilization was poor.

No matter, the Yemeni sitting in his room in Chicago knew the wizards at the GIMF's headquarters in Raqqa would make the adjustments necessary to create a master-piece as good as an American action film.

Al-Matari had watched the act in real time, and at first he was certain his cell member had been killed in the blast. Hembrick had been instructed to make sure he fired the RPG from a minimum of fifty meters away, but obviously with the thrill of the hunt and impending kill he'd neglected to take his distance into account, and nearly fried himself by launching the grenade at thirty meters.

Still, al-Matari was pleased. A dead FBI agent and two wounded NYPD officers would bring him new recruits, and his three soldiers had all escaped without any injuries.

There had been three more attacks in the past twelve hours, two of them by self-radicalized young men who had pledged allegiance to ISIS on social media while in perpe-tration of their crimes. A man in Connecticut had emptied half a magazine from his AR-15 pistol into a Marine Corps recruiting station before he'd been felled by a Marine who'd carried his own weapon, but not before three other Marines had been wounded. And a thirty-five-year-old man in Kansas City had opened fire with a shotgun on a random city bus, killing six. While this attack had not been directed at the military or intelligence communities, al-Matari was proud to see the wellspring of insurrection building in America, and he knew it would grow exponentially.

The third attack had been carried out by two of the four remaining Santa Clara cell members. They'd thrown four grenades through windows of a home in Scottsdale, Arizona, killing a Department of Homeland Security official.

The Kansas City gunman had been shot to death by police, but the Santa Clara team members had made it out of Scottsdale undetected.

As had the Fairfax team working in New York. Soon the men from both Santa Clara and Fairfax would be here in Chicago. This was more good news, because tomorrow would be the biggest hit in the fight to date, right here in the city. It had been drawn up by al-Matari over several days and nights of work, and Musa al-Matari was especially excited by the prospects of this high-profile hit, because he would play an important part in the operation himself.

50

Dominic Caruso and Adara Sherman arrived in Brooklyn four hours after the death of FBI Special Agent Wally Hussein. They hadn't expected to learn much at the crime scene, and indeed there was not much to learn, other than the fact the terrorists had used an Uzi submachine gun, just like in Alexandria, as well as a rocket launcher, as had been found in El Salvador.

The local Joint Terrorism Task Force set up a large mobile command post near the scene, and here the security tapes from various buildings in the area were available for viewing by FBI and JTTF personnel, so Dom watched them multiple times. The entire attack had been picked up on several cameras in the area, but it was a little hard to make out large parts of the action.

One of the NYPD officers assigned to the JTTF quipped in the command post that they'd all do well to wait around for ISIS to produce its own video so they could watch the attack with music, editing, and better resolution.

But when the feed from the camera in front of the Marriott came up on screens, everyone saw a perfect image of a black male in his twenties running by and looking into the camera as he passed.

Dom was just saying good-bye to the men in the trailer when an urgent call came through. Facial recognition got a hit at Penn Station that matched an image of the man from the attack. The images came through a minute later. It seemed almost assuredly to be the same individual, and they were able to track him via multiple cams all the way till he got on his train to Newark Liberty.

The hit was nearly five hours old by now, but the agents began checking all the security camera footage at Newark, and they sent more agents out in a full-court press at the airport, hoping to find out if the man got on a flight. They promised they'd keep Dominic updated, but as he left the mobile command center with a fist full of business cards, he told himself he'd probably have to pester these men and women for information, because he wasn't a high item on their priority list.

A half-hour after his briefing from JTTF officials, Dom sat at a Starbucks within sight of the attack on Adams Street.

With a coffee in hand, Adara had her iPad out in front of her and was adding thumbtack icons to signify this attack, along with the others from the night before, to a Google Maps page she had created.

Dom spent the time texting Clark details of his conversation with local law enforcement while he sipped an iced coffee, and this made the two of them look like any other thirty-something couple hanging out in a Brooklyn Starbucks on a weekday afternoon.

Until Dominic said, 'Oh, yeah. I forgot to tell you. They've identified two more suspects. They both flew to Mexico City about five days after the Guatemalan mercs arrived at the Language School. Their return flights were from Costa Rica.'

'They flew together?'

'No, but on the same day. O'Hare to Mexico City, direct. San José to O'Hare, via Houston. One lives in Chicago, the other just north of there in Evanston.'

Adara looked down at her map. 'The other day DoJ identified a young Palestinian who flew from Milwaukee to Managua, Nicaragua, then returned, but never went back to his job at a website design firm. If he's one of al-Matari's men, that makes three people identified so far who live in or close to Chicago.'

Dom said, 'Interesting. There haven't been any attacks anywhere around there, have there?'

'Closest was in Michigan, then St Louis. So, not really.' She looked up at Dom now. 'Hey, what if we log the towns all the known subjects resided in? Compare it with the location of the attacks.'

'Good idea, although we're already seeing some copycats, so it's not going to be as simple a picture as just matching al-Matari's terrorists to their crimes.'

Adara shrugged. 'Something to do.'

It took them just ten minutes to add the locations of the known terrorists to Adara's map. When it was done, she said, 'So unless the same big group is traveling all over the country for each hit, then we have different cells positioned here and there around the map. We have a West Coast team, for sure. The two killed in Vegas were students in the San Fran area, but they did the Vegas hit and the L.A. hit.'

'Both of which were botched.'

'Right. There is a third West Coast terrorist ID'd who lived in Marin County, so still near San Fran. And then there is the Detroit-area group. All four guys killed in Virginia lived in and around Detroit. Wonder why they drove all that way.'

'They took a road trip.'

Adara thought about that. 'Maybe because both of the dead from the North Carolina killing were from the DC area. They needed new blood in DC. Of course the Detroit group didn't fare any better than the DC guys.'

'Thanks to you,' Dom said with a smile.

'I had help.'

Dom looked at Adara's map. 'And then there is the guy from Alabama killed in Tampa.'

Adara said, 'Assuming all the groups have begun their attacks, it looks to me like al-Matari had at least five different cells. Michigan, DC, California, somewhere in the South, I guess . . . and Chicago.'

Dom put his coffee down and leaned forward. 'So . . . why hasn't this Chicago group done anything yet?'

'Who says they haven't? Maybe they are traveling the country. The St Louis attack, that could have been them. Same for Michigan, because by then the Detroit guys were all in the morgue in Alexandria.'

Dom rubbed his temples. 'Yeah, but both of those ops were reported as just one attacker. Maybe another for a getaway driver. Still . . . it's obvious there is a group that comes from around Chicago.'

Adara looked down at her map. 'It's a big chunk of the country they haven't attacked yet. There might be a reason for that.'

'Yeah, but maybe they just don't want to shit where they eat.'

Adara had served in the Navy with Marine infantry. There was, *literally*, nothing her boyfriend could say to shock her.

Dom's phone rang, and he was pleased to see it was one of the special agents from the command center, just three blocks from where he now sat. He took the call, listened intently, and thanked the woman for taking the time to keep him in the loop.

'What was that?' Adara asked.

'The killer here has been identified. His name is David Anthony Hembrick. He's from DC. He got on a flight at Newark two hours after the attack.'

'A flight to where?'

Dom smiled. 'Chicago. The flight landed an hour ago, so we've lost him, but at least we know who he is and where he is.'

Adara said, 'I think we should go to Chicago. Something big might be planned there.'

'We don't know *that*. He could have rented a car away from the airport or hopped a bus or a train to his next destination.'

'Or not.' She said, 'Look, if we go to Chicago and don't find anything, it's still the middle of America, and we want to be ready to get to the next hit quickly. What if we relocate there, start digging around deep into the lives of these missing people? If we need to race back to O'Hare to go somewhere else we can do that, but I think we might learn something in Chicago.'

Dom looked out the window at the crime scene a block away. The JTTF mobile command post was a massive affair. Easily seventy-five federal, state, and local law enforcement working, as well as another fifty or so other types of anti-terrorism personnel on hand. He nodded. 'Yeah, you're right. Let's try to make ourselves more useful than just two more people walking around the scene of the last hit. There's plenty of that already.'

Adara pulled out her phone. 'I'll call John and get it approved.'

While Chavez dealt with customs and immigration inside the FBO at Reagan National, Jack, Gavin, and Midas climbed into the G550, waiting just outside a hangar in the afternoon heat. All three men greeted the pilot and copilot, then headed through the cabin, all the way to the back, to slide their gear through the cargo door.

Firearms were already on board, hidden below secure access panels throughout the aircraft. This prevented any customs search of the men's bags here in the US turning up any curious items. Instead, Midas, Chavez, and Jack just packed like regular businessmen, albeit businessmen who packed for a certain amount of comfort in the downtime of their travel.

Gavin wouldn't be carrying a weapon. In fact, Clark had pulled Chavez aside before they left the office and said he didn't want Gavin *touching* a weapon. He'd been in the field before, and he'd done some good things, but he wasn't a shooter.

While Gavin went to claim the long sofa in the back as his own, Midas sat in a cabin chair in the center of the cabin, and he ran his hands slowly back and forth over the chair's arms, confirming they were, in fact, leather. Looking around, the ex-Delta Force operator was impressed with the Gulfstream. He'd flown commercial, military, and government planes through his entire career in the Army, and he'd been on several small jets in that time, but the luxury of the Hendley Associates aircraft put a smile on his face that he worried might get stuck there.

Jack noticed the man's appreciation for the posh trimmings of the jet. 'Not too shabby, huh?'

'I'm more accustomed to sitting on a pallet or in cargo netting when I fly, but I guess I could learn to live with this.'

'What are you drinking?'

Midas raised an eyebrow in surprise. *'Drinking?'*

Jack said, 'Up until recently, Adara took care of us on our flights. Unlucky for you, you're stuck with me. I'm a shitty bartender, so I strongly recommend beer, wine, or something I can pour in a glass without screwing it up.'

Midas said, 'I'm a cheap date. First can of cold beer you can put your hands on would kick ass.'

'An excellent choice, sir.' Jack grabbed Heinekens for himself and Midas, and then a third when he saw Chavez climbing up the air stairs.

Chavez dumped his pack at the door while he moved forward to talk to Country and Helen in the cockpit. Midas grabbed Chavez's pack and took it in the back to push it through the cabin access panel to the cargo hold.

Chavez soon came back toward the galley and took a Heineken handed to him by Jack. 'Six hours in the air, a refuel at Bristol, UK, and then another three and a half in the sky. We'll land in Bucharest tomorrow just after nine local time.'

Jack said, 'I've compiled some info on the area around the target location, Alexandru Dalca's apartment, and his workplace, ARTD. Also I have everything of note from the complaint by the DoJ against Dalca. It's old information, but it will show us the skills he had before he went behind bars. I put everything in a PowerPoint, so we can put it on the wall monitors and go over it together en route.'

'Good,' Chavez said. Midas was back up with the others now. 'We'll carry subcompact pistols off the plane. Deep concealment. Low profile.'

Jack said, 'From the research Gavin and I did on ARTD, they seem to be a big cybercrime concern, no ties to a local mob or anything like that, so I don't think this is going to get anything like as messy as what happened in Jakarta.'

Chavez replied, 'That's what we're hoping. But we've been wrong about that sort of thing before.'

'Point taken. We go in hoping for the best but prepping for the worst.'

Chavez turned to Midas. 'Ever been to Bucharest?'

'Spent about five days there doing advanced force operations for my last job. Three years ago. The AFO work didn't amount to much, but I know my way around the city, more or less.'

Chavez grinned. 'Well, then, that makes the FNG the expert.'

'FNG?' Jack asked.

Midas and Chavez spoke in unison: 'The *fucking new guy*.'

Jack mumbled as he sat down in a captain's chair facing Midas, 'I should have joined the military just to learn all the kick-ass lingo.'

Midas replied, 'I could talk to some people for you, get you right into boot camp.'

Jack said, 'Oh, no. That ship has sailed. I serve my country as one of Gerry Hendley's boys. Gulfstreams all the way.'

The three operators talked about the job ahead. Chavez confirmed their surveillance on Alexandru Dalca would start slow and soft while they determined what sort of countersurveillance capabilities, if any, he had. If he was just a crook stealing data and selling it to bad actors out there, he might be relatively unprotected.

If, on the other hand, he was actually working on behalf of a state actor or even the Islamic State, it stood to reason there would be those with some skills in identifying surveillance with a vested interest in keeping Dalca alive and out of the hands of the Americans.

Either way, Chavez, Ryan, and Jankowski told themselves, they had to be ready for anything.

Country closed the cabin door and within minutes the G550 took off over the Potomac River to the south. It climbed right past Jack's apartment and the Hendley Associates building in Alexandria, then banked to the east to begin its long route to Europe.

Alexandru Dalca woke, covered in sweat. He sat up in bed, listened for any sound that might have startled him, then remembered the dream.

He lowered back into his pillow, amazed, because he *never* dreamed.

He was being chased, someone was close on his heels, and it was his fault. Some miscalculation, some failure to levy the consequences of his actions with the reward, something he had done, somewhere along the line, had led to his imminent demise by an unseen powerful force closing behind him.

In the dream he was a kid on the streets again, alone and afraid, through urban sprawl, then through desert. The dream wasn't focused on the details, but on the reasons for the chase. Dalca was in the wrong, his life's misfortune was his fault, no one else's, and he had nowhere left to hide.

All he could do was run like hell.

And as he looked at the ceiling of his dark penthouse apartment, through the fog of vapor from his steaming, sweaty face, he realized: *That* was no dream. That was his subconscious creating a premonition, and he needed to heed it.

When the Seychelles Group left ARTD, they'd been no more convinced they were in the clear than when they walked in. Mr Peng and his three grim-faced goons weren't buying what Dalca was selling, Dalca could tell by their words and their demeanor.

He'd spent the last two days at work telling himself he was fine, and the night sitting in his apartment working on the next set of targets for the ISIS guys telling himself the same thing. But falling asleep lowered his defenses, and his true thoughts burst through his veneer of forced confidence.

The Chinese were suspicious, and they would act on their suspicions soon.

And that meant . . . Alex Dalca was fucked.

But only if he sat around Bucharest and made himself a stationary target.

He'd checked over his secure offshore bank accounts before going to bed. He had $11 million in the bank, virtually all of it from the ISIS guys, and tomorrow they would be sending another $3 million for the three high-value targets he'd been working on tonight. Dalca didn't have all the targeting information for them, he'd need to return to ARTD to work through the SF-86 files located on the air-gapped computer to get more information. This meant if he made a run for it now, without going in to work for another day, he'd never get that money.

But now he had to ask himself if the three million was worth it.

After a time, he wiped away sweat, and he spoke aloud. 'Three million, for one more day's work? Of course it's worth it.'

Dalca's subconscious thought the jig was up, but his rational, conscious brain was always the one in control, and this told him he retained his mastery of the situation, at least for now. The Seychelles Group had nothing on him, if they came after him it wouldn't be in the next day, and in those precious twenty-four hours he would get all the intelligence he needed from the files to make the three million.

He finally went back to sleep, and immediately returned to his dream.

When he woke up again, less than an hour later, he looked at the ceiling once more in a cold sweat, and he spoke aloud.

'Fuck it.'

Eleven million was good enough, a damn sight better than fourteen million in a bank and his body in some Chinese torture chamber. Yes, it was time to run, *now*, and to hell with the extra three million dollars.

But he could not run now. He had to go talk to a man first, and he could not do this before the workday began tomorrow, so he lay there wide awake, afraid to go back to sleep and return to a dream state that would remind him that, somehow, he had failed to anticipate the Chinese figuring out his game.

He'd stay awake the rest of the night, he'd go see the man in the morning, and he'd get his ticket out of town.

And *then* he would run like hell.

52

The sleek white Hendley Associates Gulfstream G550 landed in Bucharest at nine-twenty a.m. and Captain Helen Reid taxied the aircraft to the customs ramp. Before Country could lower the hatch, however, a customs officer came over the radio and told them the inspector would follow them in his truck to their FBO, where he would do a complete physical inspection of the deplaning passengers' luggage.

Normally when they traveled in the business jet, the men of The Campus could clear customs and immigration upon landing, with a customs official coming on board to visually inspect their luggage and documents. Then they would taxi from the customs ramp to the fixed-based operator that would store the aircraft during its time in country, and here the men on board could gather their belongings and deplane. This afforded the American operatives the opportunity to open hidden compartments on the jet and remove sensitive items like firearms and high-tech surveillance gear.

But things didn't go well in Bucharest. The overly officious customs inspector had the pilot shut down the engine, then the four men in the back of the plane were asked to remove their luggage and come down the stairs. They were led to a table, and here the man took his time as he silently checked each piece of luggage over carefully.

The three operatives kept their cool, because they had nothing to hide. And Gavin kept his cool because he had no real suspicions that anything out of the ordinary was going on. The three operators had left their weapons on board, but they did bring out two large Pelican cases of surveillance gear for the customs inspector to gawk at. He asked them what the goods were for and Jack produced commercial invoices along with a story that they were here in town to bid on a government security contract on behalf of a company Hendley Associates had just purchased in the United States. Satisfied, and somewhat embarrassed by his lack of understanding of some of the explanation of how the items worked, the customs man just pulled a couple cameras and spotting scopes out of their foam storage slots, looked them over to match item numbers up with those on the commercial invoice, and then gave the men a curt nod, letting them know they could seal everything up.

Despite the air of gravity to the situation in the end, the official stamped the men's passports and welcomed them to Romania.

The four Americans were met inside the FBO lounge by Felix Negrescu, a sixty-one-year-old bear of a man with a huge salt-and-pepper beard that made him look like a character from a Harry Potter novel. He welcomed them to Romania much more sincerely than the customs officer, with a wide grin and firm handshakes, and he insisted on taking more than his share of bags out of the FOB to his rented gray minivan in the parking lot.

Once they were all inside the vehicle with Negrescu behind the wheel, Chavez said, 'Well, Felix, we have a problem right off the bat. Our firearms are still on that plane. We didn't see a way to get them past customs. Any way you can help us find some small arms, just for defensive purposes?'

Felix gave a low, gravelly chuckle from behind the wheel. 'Have you tried the local brew?'

Neither Chavez nor Jack knew what Felix was talking about, but Midas said, 'Are you talking about the MD 2000? Yeah, that'll work, if that's what is easiest to get hold of.'

Felix said, 'I can find you others, but those are the most plentiful. We can make one quick stop on the way to the safe house I've arranged and I will pick up one for each of you, along with ammo, magazines, and holsters.'

Chavez said, 'I've never heard of the MD 2000.'

Midas said, 'It's a knock-off of the Baby Eagle. A nine-millimeter double-stack semiauto.'

Chavez nodded now. 'Okay, the Israeli pistol. Does the Romanian version run?'

Midas said, 'It will get the job done. Sidearm of the national army here.' He turned to Jack. 'You know the weapon?'

'No, but if I can figure out which end the bullets come out of, I'll be fine.'

Chavez said, 'Don't worry about Jack, he can shoot, and he can shoot under stress.'

'That's good to know.'

They parked in an alcove near Bucharest North Railway Station at ten a.m. Chavez gave Felix a wad of US dollars, and Felix instructed the Americans to wait in the car. Once he was out of sight Chavez said, 'Mr C. vouches for this guy, but I'm not one to sit around in a car while a dude I just met leaves my sight to talk to dudes I've never met about a weapons deal.'

The door of the van opened and all the men climbed out, taking up positions within view of the car on the street, but not making themselves such an easy target inside.

Their fears proved unfounded fifteen minutes later when Felix appeared at the hood of the van, carrying a backpack and scratching his beard, looking around at the street and wondering where his new friends had gone.

Chavez appeared inches behind him, startling him with his words. 'Everything go okay?'

Felix jumped in surprise, and then laughed as he walked around to the driver's side. 'No problems. They even threw in this shitty backpack for free, although they didn't cut us the best deal on the pistols. They were one thousand each, with all the trimmings.'

Chavez was unfazed. 'Well, beggars can't be choosers, and if it turns out we need them, it will have been money well spent.'

Felix passed out the pistols to Midas, Jack, and Ding. As the van rolled through central Bucharest the three men function-checked their new sidearms, loaded their primary and spare magazines, and stowed the guns in their waist-bands.

While this was all going on, Gavin Biery sat in the very back and pouted.

He wanted a pistol like the other guys.

53

It is extremely rare that a prisoner, once freed, returns to the prison where he served, and to date Alexandru Dalca had proved to be no exception to this rule. He had not been back to Jilava since that day he walked through its gates, and until early this morning, when he woke up panicked that Chinese intelligence officers were circling him, he'd had no immediate plans to do so. But as soon as visiting hours began today he stood waiting at the visitor admittance, signing the book to request a meeting with a current inhabitant of the drab facility.

He'd texted Dragomir Vasilescu and told him he needed some personal time before coming to work because he had to visit a friend in the hospital. Dragomir had replied with 'You have a friend?' and Dalca ignored this. He had no intention of ever returning to ARTD, and that would become clear soon enough to his boss. No sense in continuing with any pretense that he liked or even gave a damn about his boss or his company.

Once through the first set of gates at Jilava, Dalca was thoroughly searched, and his phone, wallet, and car keys were removed. He was handled a bit more roughly than the average visitor, he was certain, because the guards doing the frisking remembered him as a former resident, and they extended him neither courtesy nor respect for now residing outside the prison's walls.

He was escorted into a gymnasium-sized room and told

to wait at a table. This was a familiar place to him. He didn't have family or friends visit him here during his nearly six years of confinement, but his attorneys had sometimes met with him at these tables. Often it had been crowded, standing room only, as all convicts allowed visitors from the outside did so right here.

But this morning, other than a pair of bored guards in the corner and out of earshot, the room was empty.

After five minutes a barred door opened and Luca Gabor strolled in with his hands in the pockets of his prison-issued tracksuit. He seemed mildly surprised to see Dalca, and not particularly pleased about it. Nevertheless, he walked over to the table with a half shrug, though there was no sense of excitement or urgency.

Gabor had been Alexandru's mentor in prison. A former intelligence officer, he'd left government service to work as a con man, a thief, and a fraudster, rising to the ranks of the most wanted nonviolent criminals in Europe. He'd been arrested in France, then deported to his homeland of Romania, where he was charged and convicted of espionage and treason.

And he was now ten years into a sixteen-year sentence.

Gabor and Dalca had been constant companions, if not friends, in prison; the older man had taught the younger everything he knew, with the promise the younger man would look after Gabor's family for the years he was on the outside while Gabor languished in here. But Dalca had done no such thing; he broke his promise as soon as he departed through the prison gates, so he wasn't surprised that Luca Gabor didn't seem happy to see him when the older man sat down in front of him at the small plastic table in the center of the otherwise empty common area.

Dalca knew Gabor was about fifty, but he looked much older, with his thin white hair, the gray skin of a man who saw little natural light, and deep-set wrinkles.

Gabor lit a cigarette. 'I guessed you missed me so bad you came back after sixteen months.'

'And I guess you missed me so bad you've calculated the precise time since I left this shitty place.'

Gabor blew smoke. 'I knew you'd need something from me someday. I had a running bet with myself that it would be inside two years.'

'You win, as usual, Luca.'

The older man motioned to the walls of the prison around him. 'Yeah, I'm a big winner.' He then said, 'I won't ask what you want, at first. I'll ask what you will give me for whatever it is you want.'

Dalca could be an incredibly charismatic smooth talker, but he wouldn't waste his breath on charming Luca Gabor. The man was the one person in the world who knew him inside and out. Instead, he said, 'I have money. Enough for your family.'

'You had money within a week of your release. You're at ARTD, you are their rock star, you drive a new Porsche Panamera Turbo and live in a penthouse apartment in Primăverii.' Primăverii was the most desirable section of Bucharest, overlooking the Dâmbovița River.

Dalca said, 'Yeah, I assumed you had people on the outside keeping an eye on me. Knowledge is power, you used to say.'

'Did I say that?' Gabor smoked in silence a moment. 'Well . . . I was full of shit. I have knowledge now, but no power.' He leaned forward. 'What the hell do you want, you fucking snake?'

'I want to make you a rich man.'

'Go fuck yourself, I'm not some geriatric in America you called to sell a fake land deal. I know you, Dalca. You will screw me over.'

Dalca shook his head. 'I know where your daughter lives.'

Gabor jolted upright, almost lunging forward.

Dalca was not startled. He said, 'That's not a threat, that's an opportunity. I will go visit her today and give her access to a numbered bank account in Cyprus. There will be one million US in the account.' Dalca smiled. 'All for her.'

The older man's eyes narrowed. 'Give me your sales pitch, snake. I'll listen, because I am a prisoner and I don't have anything else to do.'

'I need you to put me in touch with the Macedonians.'

Gabor cocked his head. 'Which Macedonians?'

'Don't play games,' Dalca said. 'You told me there were men who ran a casino in Macedonia. You said they had tried to hire you many times to work for them. You said you were sure they'd take me when I got out, they'd set me up in the casino targeting guests for schemes. You also told me I should only go with the Macedonians if I was desperate, or if someone was after me, because they were crazy and trigger-happy gangsters.'

Gabor tapped his cigarette in the ashtray on the table. Slowly he broke into a raspy laugh.

Dalca was frustrated by Gabor's lack of response. 'Why do you pretend like you don't know what I'm talking about?'

The older man got control of his laugh now. 'I was genuinely confused. You said "Macedonians." The men I told you about *do* own a casino in Macedonia, in Skopje, and they *do* have the ability to employ and protect someone with skills like ours, just like I said. But they aren't Macedonians.

They are . . .' He leaned forward and lowered his voice. 'Albanian.'

Dalca slumped back in his chair. 'Shit. You never told me that.'

'Didn't I?' Gabor asked, enjoying the look of dread on Alex's face. 'Scary fuckers, Alexandru. But if you are in the shit, and let's not kid ourselves, you wouldn't be here if you weren't in the shit, then you want some scary fuckers on your side.'

Dalca considered this. He was afraid of Albanian gangsters. Everyone in this part of the world knew about their danger and reach. Still, Dalca felt like this might be his only way to safety, considering his predicament.

In the end it was an easy calculation for him to make. Treacherous Albanians who would pay him and protect him were vastly preferable to dangerous Chinese who would torture him and kill him.

'All right, Luca. I'll give your daughter one million for you to arrange an introduction between these Albanians and me.'

Gabor puffed on his cigarette and answered through the haze of smoke. 'You already owe me that million for everything I taught you. You owe me another million in penalties for breaking our deal when you got out of prison. The third million you are going to give to my daughter for my introduction to the Albanians.'

A vein throbbed on Dalca's forehead. 'No. No way. You must think I'm insane.'

Gabor smiled. 'Good-bye, Dalca. And good luck, because I get the feeling you're gonna need it.' The raspy laugh came back.

'I'm out of here.' Dalca started to stand from the table,

but then he thought of his dreams, the panic he woke with, and he sat back down. 'A million five.'

'Three million.'

'Don't be a fool, Luca. You can set yourself, your daughter, and your grandkids up for life!'

'Believe me, I intend to. With three million dollars.' When Dalca made no reply, Gabor said, 'I see it in your face. Your terror. Your desperation.'

'I don't have three million.'

'Bullshit. Whatever has got you this scared, it was something you did that got you paid. You wouldn't take such a risk for chicken feed. If you are offering me one million out the gate, that means you have, at least, ten.'

Dalca had eleven, exactly, and he marveled at Gabor's deductive reasoning while simultaneously wanting to rip his heart out.

He said, 'I'll give you two, but no more.'

Now Gabor stood, turned for the barred door. To the guard standing there he shouted, 'I'm ready.'

'Enough with the theatrics, Luca. I know you won't walk away from two million.'

'And I know *you* won't give up your life for one million more.'

Dalca rushed up and grabbed him by the arm. '*Fuck!* All right. Three million. I hate you!'

'You hate everyone. It's coded into your DNA.'

Dalca ignored the comment. It didn't offend him in the least, he was still thinking about the money he'd have to pay, and the logistics of getting everything together. 'Look . . . I have to go into work, but I will visit your daughter this evening.'

Gabor nodded. 'I will be ready with the information. Will you need help getting out of Bucharest?'

'I . . . I don't think so. I don't know.'

'Well, prepare yourself for any eventuality, because I can't get you out till tomorrow. Come back here in the morning and I will have everything set up for you. That is, provided that my daughter contacts me to tell me about her sudden windfall.'

Dalca wanted to leave today, but things were more complicated than he'd anticipated. 'Fine.'

As the older man turned away, Dalca realized something. 'You never asked me what was going on. What I am running from.'

Luca Gabor didn't stop walking, but just shrugged as he continued to the door. 'Why should I? That's your problem, not mine.'

Alexandru Dalca climbed into his Porsche and drove to work. He hadn't planned on going in at all. The Chinese could easily be watching ARTD, so every time he went to the building on Strada Doctor Paleologu he knew he was rolling the dice.

But now he needed to take a chance, because he knew he just had to stay safe for one more day, and he'd earn the three million he owed Gabor by finishing his last targeting packages for the ISIS guys. This would still leave Alexandru with eleven million.

His greed had overpowered his fear, but it had been a very close competition between the two.

54

At eleven a.m. the Campus men and their fixer carried their gear up four flights of stairs to a small, dusty, nearly empty apartment in a gray, communist-era building on Strada Uruguay. They dumped their gear on green military cots Felix had brought in the night before, and then they followed their handler as he stepped into a common hallway and headed down to the opposite side of the building. Here Felix used a key to enter a small, narrow hallway, which was lined with doors on both sides. 'The apartments in this building weren't built with much in the way of closets. Back in the communist days, we didn't have so much extra stuff. Apparently the people who own the building now couldn't get renters because of the lack of closet space, so they sectioned off one of the upstairs corner apartments into storage units.'

The lighting was bad in the hall, but Felix found a key on his keychain and opened up one of the doors. Inside was a four-by-six-foot space, with a table and chair up against the wall in front of a large window that had been covered by wooden planks. Felix reached across the desk and removed one of the planks; clearly he'd loosened it before the Americans arrived, and the hole revealed a triangular intersection.

Felix pointed to a modern-looking four-story apartment building on the opposite side of the quiet street. 'That's your target's apartment, top floor.'

'Which window?'

'All of them, it's a penthouse. The elevator runs up the

right side of the building, and apartments for rent online show the bedrooms in the back, but I can't see into the windows from here without optics, and I didn't bring any.'

He looked up to the men. 'I hope you brought some cool toys in those Pelican cases.'

Jack said, 'Very cool toys.'

Felix smiled. 'There is really not much room here in the closet, but I thought you could position a one-man overwatch here.'

Chavez said, 'This will work great. We have remote cams to set up here and at his place of business.'

Gavin said, 'Let me guess, this is my new home.'

Chavez put his hand on Gavin's shoulder. 'Did you have something even fancier than this closet in mind?'

'I wanted to go to Dracula's castle.' The older man's eyes lit up like a child as he turned to Felix. 'Is that nearby?'

The big bearded man shook his head. 'Several hours from here. Romania is more than Dracula, you know?'

Jack said, 'Sorry, Felix. Gavin is our IT director. He doesn't get to go outside very often.' He turned to the big man. 'Gav, if Dalca tries to hide in Dracula's castle, we'll send you in to flush him out.'

'That would be awesome. I hope he does.'

The team spent the next several hours preparing their operation to come. Gavin and Midas set up a digital camera and a spotting scope in the overwatch, focusing both on the balcony of Dalca's apartment, then attached the camera to a laptop that would record digital video. Next to this they erected a laser listening device on a small tripod on the desk, facing it toward the same window. This would fire an invisible, constant beam of laser light that would strike the window, and then bounce back to a photocell in the device that would record the intensity of the light. The cell was attached through a computer to an amplifier and a headset, which would translate the varying light intensities into audible sound.

Midas and Gavin understood what the others in The Campus knew, that while the laser listening device was ingenious and useful, it did have its limitations. They could point it only at one window in the apartment across the street, the one directly in front of their overwatch, because if the beam hit a window that caused it to reflect at any angle at all it would miss the photocell that needed to receive the light.

Gavin and Midas worked on the problem for a while, trying to come up with a technical solution, but then Midas decided he would just be ready with lock picks to break into the other closets on this side of the storage room in case they needed a straight shot to one of the other windows in Dalca's penthouse.

It was a low-tech solution, but Chavez and Midas agreed it could be implemented effectively and relatively quickly if it turned out Dalca spent time in other rooms when he got home from work.

Once the overwatch was prepped, Ding went down to the street and positioned covert cameras near the entrance to Dalca's building. The neighborhood was nearly empty at this time of the afternoon, and his magnetic-backed wireless cams were small enough to remain undetected when attached to drainpipes or other metal piping running down buildings, even just feet away from where pedestrians passed.

While Midas, Gavin, and Ding worked the area around Dalca's apartment, Felix and Jack drove to the office of ARTD, a couple of miles south. They walked the neighborhood, looking for any security cameras they might be able to patch into, and Jack made notes of addresses and businesses that had cams close by. He looked for places he could position his devices and he almost planted one, but there was a lot of pedestrian traffic in the neighborhood, and the last thing he wanted to do was get compromised outside the building where America's secrets were in the process of being sold off to the Islamic State.

Instead, the two men called an abort and returned to the safe house. As they drove, Jack made a secure call to Gavin, and asked him to work on finding a way into the networks supporting the security cameras already in the neighborhood.

It looked to all in the first couple of hours here in Bucharest like Gavin Biery was going to be the busiest man on the team.

Alexandru Dalca sat in his office and watched a CNN live broadcast from the USA. Four more suspects had been named in the so-called terror attacks, and their faces dominated all the coverage on the news.

To the layman it looked like the ISIS guys might not be around for much longer, but just this morning Dalca had received a request from his Middle Eastern-accented contact for another purchase. An additional $2.5 million for three more high-level targets. These jihadists seemed to be getting bolder after a day with no losses of their own. The three packages he was finalizing today were all tier-one individuals, so it was interesting to him his clients were already ordering up more. It was clear they wanted to up the pace of their attacks, either because they thought they were getting better at what they were doing or because they had new blood in the area to help them along.

Either way, it didn't matter. Alexandru would not be sticking around here to provide them more intelligence. He'd have to settle for the millions he'd made, minus the millions he was forced to pay out to Luca Gabor, to get him out of here.

And to that end he worked hard this afternoon on his targets. He sat at his desk and looked over one of the personalities; he'd already identified him as a top-level American law enforcement officer involved with antiterrorism. Dalca's work today would be the last piece of the puzzle of putting this particular man in a particular place on a particular date.

He'd gotten to where he could build these packages in his sleep by using SOCMINT, social media intelligence, and he lamented the fact all these potential earnings would be lost to him after he walked out the door.

He wished he could steal all the OPM files, take them with him to Macedonia, so he could use them to generate even more income in the future. He could let the Albanians protect him, and make it look like he would be their loyal servant in recompense for what they offered him, but instead he could secretly be waiting for the heat to die down so he could slip away again, somewhere even safer, free of both murderous gangsters and Chinese spies. Once he went back into hiding, either on a Caribbean island or in some other place where those after him could not reach him, he could again go into business selling off the names and locations of America's spies and soldiers on the dark web.

Eleven million would just be the tip of the iceberg.

He knew he could easily access the OPM files today if he wanted to, but stealing the information would be much tougher. He was allowed to go into the air-gapped room that held them to view the OPM data and take handwritten notes from individual files. But as there was no way to download or transfer the information from the computer, the only way to take the intelligence for later would be to write down all the information from the twenty-five million individual files or take pictures of millions of pages off the computer monitor.

And that wasn't happening.

Well ... there *was* another possibility, and it came into Dalca's head as he watched a new terrorist video from ISIS's propaganda service out of Syria showing an attack in America. It was a drive-by assassination of a man in an SUV on a darkened St Louis street. His vehicle was peppered with AK fire; the cameraman ran forward and showed a blond-haired male slumped dead, held in place by his seat belt. The caption said he was a CIA officer. Then the cameraman jumped back into the passenger side of a blue Volvo, just as a man raced from a car parked in an oncoming lane and tried to block the terrorists' escape.

It was the foolish act of someone so jacked up on adrenaline and so in denial as to what he was witnessing before his eyes that he could not conceive he was in any real danger. The Volvo hit the man head-on, he disappeared under the hood of the vehicle in slow motion, and the video showed the entire incident.

Dalca was fascinated by the images, but he was more fascinated by the new idea that popped into his head. He only needed to cause some sort of distraction here in the building, then go into the air-gapped room and physically remove the hard drive containing the American files. It would take him at least five minutes, so he'd need some privacy, but it was the one way he could have his cake and eat it too. The one chance to run and not lose the lifetime meal ticket afforded by the OPM data.

After a moment's deliberation he decided this was worth it. If he was leaving Bucharest tomorrow and never returning, handing himself over to the Albanians for their protection, it would be damn nice to have an ace in the hole.

Thirty minutes later Dalca walked through the basement dry goods storage facility of ARTD, looking for something specific. He found it on top of a shelf. A box of hand sanitizer, used in the restrooms. He knew the material was flammable, because in prison he'd been told they were allowed only bar soap, to reduce the risk of a deliberate fire. He removed the lids from two of the industrial-sized containers, and walked with them to the large paper-products recycling bin. Most all the trash this five-story building generated was paper of some sort, in the form of shredded documents or cardboard boxes, so it was a large container, some two meters high and ten meters long. Now it was only half full, but after Alexandru poured all the flammable hand sanitizer over it, he knew it would make one hell of a distraction.

After checking to make sure no one was anywhere around to see him, he tossed a lit match into the bin, and it went up with a *whoosh* that seemed to suck the air out of the area. The flames shot high as the gases around ignited, and soon black smoke billowed from the massive collection of cardboard boxes and other paper products.

Minutes later, Dalca sat in his office when the fire alarm went off, already waiting with several screwdrivers in the pocket of his slacks and a broom in his hand.

While everyone vacated the fourth floor he walked alone into the air-gapped room, moving along the wall carefully under the security camera centered on the machine in the middle of the five-meter-square space. He used the broom handle to unplug the camera from its power supply high in the corner, then moved quickly to the computer.

In the end it took fewer than five minutes to remove the hard drive and slide the device into his backpack. He didn't bother with screwing the housing of the computer back together, he just propped everything in place and pocketed the tiny screws.

Then he turned off the lights in the room, locked the door, and left for the day without even turning off his monitor back at his desk. He wouldn't leave the country until sometime during the day tomorrow, so he knew he needed to make it appear as if everything was the same as ever, so as not to arouse real suspicion from his coworkers.

After Dalca had climbed into his Porsche, he headed off in the direction of Luca Gabor's daughter's house. After that, he would make some emergency preparations, just in case the walls closed in before he had a chance to make a run for it tomorrow.

He had too much riding on the next few hours to leave anything to chance.

As he left the neighborhood, wailing fire trucks passed him by. He thought nothing of those in the building – ARTD wasn't a concern of his any longer.

Dalca thought of the present, and of the days to come. Even though he was about to give some woman he barely knew the obscene sum of three million dollars, he had to admit it would be money well spent. His original plan to flee Bucharest today a rich man had turned into a plan to flee Bucharest tomorrow a rich man, with the prospect of more riches in his future.

He was more than satisfied with his plan.

55

Adara and Dominic arrived at Chicago's O'Hare Airport on Saturday afternoon, rented a car, and drove east toward downtown. They booked a room at the Chicago Athletic Association hotel just a few blocks from Lake Michigan, and then immediately climbed back into their rental for the fifteen-minute drive to the Roosevelt Road building that housed the Chicago Division of the FBI and the local branch of the Joint Terrorism Task Force.

Adara held no classified access, so she dropped Dom off while he waited to meet with a supervisory special agent named David Jeffcoat who'd agreed to brief him on the situation here on the ground. Dom was taken upstairs to the JTTF floor, where he walked by desks manned by high-ranking representatives of most every government law enforcement, emergency management, and intelligence agency in America.

They stepped into an unused office, and Jeffcoat asked Dom about his interest in the case. It was odd, Jeffcoat explained, that Caruso was just a special agent tasked to the DC Bureau, but had shown up after a call from the director's office asking him to be briefed about anything he wanted to know.

Dom said, 'I understand the question, Special Agent Jeffcoat, but I can't go into a lot of details. Suffice it to say I'm just on a fact-finding mission for interested parties in DC.'

Jeffcoat said, 'I hope this doesn't come off the wrong way,

but some guys were wondering if the fact that your uncle is the President had anything to do with you getting your assignment.'

Dom just shook his head, thinking the man a bit of an ass for his comment. 'No, this isn't a nepotism thing, and I'm not sure there was a right way to suggest that it was.'

The supervisory special agent considered this a moment, then said, 'Well, as you can imagine, we're pretty busy since three of the cell members who went to El Salvador lived around here.'

'Right,' said Dom. 'And the fact the killer from Brooklyn flew straight here.'

Jeffcoat said, 'We think he might have been passing through.'

'Oh?'

Jeffcoat gave a thorough but rather boilerplate briefing about the JTTF's operation and setup here in Chicago. Dom was pleased to see the JTTF locally was keenly aware that at least three of the attendees of the Language School came from the area, and that the man from New York traveled to O'Hare, but it was clear to Dom halfway through the briefing that the local authorities didn't think it likely that any of the ISIS cell members were still in the area.

Dom said, 'Why don't you think Chicago faces any particular threat, especially in light of the fact several cell members have been tied to the area in one respect or another?'

'Look,' the FBI man explained, 'the three locals who went to El Sal just flew back into O'Hare because it made sense for them to book roundtrip tickets. We've canvassed all the known associates of these three, and nobody has seen or heard of them. We think they've gone to ground in some other part of the country. Plus, the guy from the New York attack might be here in the area, but that's unknown. We've spent the past day checking hotels from here to Aurora. We've shown pictures around, and have come up with zip. He could be on the West Coast or in Canada by now.

'Chicago doesn't have any major military bases, it's not exactly a hub of CIA activity, so there is a dearth of good targets for al-Matari's men. The DC area is a better bet for where to find these guys. You should focus your attention there, or maybe around some big military base somewhere.'

Dom couldn't argue with the man, although he thought the lack of activity in this area had a significance of its own.

He asked, 'Is this top-down thinking around here?'

'Absolutely. Special Agent in Charge Thomas Russell runs the entire JTTF in Chicago. He is of the belief O'Hare was just a transit station. These guys had cars nearby and they skipped town.'

Dom asked, 'Is Russell in the office?'

'Yeah. I'd introduce you, but he's a busy man and, again, I am not exactly sure just who or what you are. I was told to take care of you, so that's why we're talking. I wasn't told to pass you on to the boss, so the only guy you get to bug today is me.'

Dom let the snipe roll off his back. He understood this guy was confused as to why his busy day was being taken up talking to some random agent from another part of the map.

Dom shook the man's hand, and Jeffcoat said, 'Hate that you came all the way out here for twenty minutes of spiel I could have delivered over the phone. Call next time and we'll save the government a few bucks.'

Dom said, 'Oh, I'm not just here for the briefing. I'm going to stick around, sniff into the situation a bit more. I'm not as convinced as you there's nothing here ISIS would find worthy of attacking.'

'Not what I said, Caruso. But if you're from DC, I do think an ISIS shithead and his goons will find that to be a more target-rich environment.'

Dom turned for the door. 'You may be right. Good luck to you.'

Once he was out of the building, Adara picked him up. He filled her in on the supervisory special agent's churlishness.

Adara said, 'Do you want me to go beat him up for you, honey?'

Dom just laughed.

'What do you want to do now?' she asked.

'Let's see. A sunny afternoon in Chi-town? I want to take my girl to go see a Cubs game. But I think we'd better keep at it, because the JTTF here doesn't think there is any real threat, and they are concentrating their efforts on digging into the pasts of the three local terrorists. Personally, I'm more concerned about the near future.'

'So . . . what's our plan?'

Dom shrugged. 'Honestly, I think the only thing we *can* do until we get more to go on is work on threat assessments. We'll go through lists of events in town, lists of places where military and senior government LE agencies congregate.'

Adara said, 'Why don't I just make a U-turn and we can go back to the FBI building. If the JTTF is there, then that's where all the bigwigs in LE and intel are in the city.'

Dom conceded the point. 'Very true, but they're well protected. I passed multiple sets of X-rays and scanners, bulletproof glass, and security armed with body armor and rifles. Al-Matari is too smart to hit that building. At best, his people might kill a secretary and a couple of lobby guards before they got slaughtered. We have to think like he does. Try to find exposed targets here in the area. Something akin to what we're seeing in attacks in other parts of the country. Intelligence agency folks, special operations troops, pilots, that kind of stuff, but out in the open. If we can determine where they will hit, we might be able to make ourselves useful.'

Adara said, 'There could be a half-dozen or more cell members in the area, so the scope of their attack could be larger than any of the al-Matari hits we've seen so far. Let's get to work.'

The first news of a fire at the ARTD building reached the Campus detachment working in Bucharest when Gavin called his IT office at Hendley Associates in Virginia and got one of his subordinates to hack into the security camera of a hardware store across the street from the ARTD building.

It took a few minutes for the intrusion to take place, and when the image from the camera showed up on Gavin's computer, he was surprised to see a row of fire trucks.

Felix Negrescu was asked to look into the situation, and he opened an app on his phone that had a local police and fire department scanner. In no time at all he relayed to the rest of the team that a fire had started in some trash in the building's basement, but it had been extinguished by fire-fighters in twenty minutes. There were no injuries, and other than some smoke and water damage, the building was fine.

None of the guys had any indication this small fire had anything to do with their target here in Romania, and they continued on with their plan for the afternoon, which included making entry of Dalca's apartment to plant listening devices and remote-access tools on any computers, phones, pads, or other devices they could find there. Before they could initiate the break-in, however, Chavez decided they would surveil the building for the afternoon and evening to get a baseline for the location. This way they would have some idea of the patterns and habits of Alex Dalca and the men and women who lived around him.

It was a decision that would cost them some time, but Chavez had done this sort of thing for long enough to know this was a worthwhile expense, considering the alternative could have involved one or more of his team being compromised.

The afternoon passed slowly, especially because the men were all suffering the effects of jet lag to one degree or another. Midas made an afternoon coffee run for the team, and around seven p.m. Jack broke off his surveillance, sitting in the van up the street with Felix, so he and the team's local contact could pick up dinner for the group.

Gavin Biery was eating his dinner of chicken paprika at the desk in the little closet in the fading light when a yellow Porsche Panamera pulled into the key code-access parking lot next to Dalca's apartment building. He focused his camera on the sports car when it parked, and recognized his target as soon as he climbed from behind the wheel. The man carried a backpack over his shoulder, and several large bags under his arms.

Gavin touched the transmit key on the wire to his headset. 'Target has arrived. He's alone. His vehicle is a yellow four-door Porsche. Pretty sweet.'

'Roger that,' Chavez replied. He and Midas were in the apartment on the other side of the building. They could see the feed from all the cameras via their iPads, but at the moment they were in the middle of their dinner. 'Report his movements.'

Gavin said, 'I lost him when he went into the lobby. I've got the laser audio transmitter ready if he makes any calls, but if he just sits around and works on his computer, we could be in for a long night.'

Chavez said, 'We already knew we'd have more opportunities bugging his devices than we would hoping he meets with someone face-to-face.'

Jack came over the net next. 'Yeah, computer nerds don't get out much.'

It was directed at Gavin, but Gavin was focused on his work. Through his headphones he could hear the sound of the front door of the apartment opening.

'Subject is in his place. No conversation, still seems to be alone.'

Gavin watched the monitor showing the view of the camera positioned on the desk in front of him. In just seconds, he saw the door to the balcony open and Dalca step outside, a liter bottle of beer in his hand.

'He's on the balcony getting some fresh air. I'm going to tighten on him and get some good pics we can use for the facial-recog software.'

Gavin zoomed in as tight as he could to the young man's face, then adjusted the focus of his cameras. As he did this he saw Dalca peering down into the street, looking carefully in both directions, and then across the street to the building where Gavin now sat.

Chavez came over the net. 'He looks concerned.'

Gavin felt like the man across the street could somehow see him, even though he was invisible in a darkened storage space forty yards away with only a four-inch-wide slit exposing him to the outside. He spoke softly. 'I think he knows I'm here.'

Chavez replied, 'Relax, Gavin. You're fine.' Then he said, 'Hey, Jack. Is it possible he's onto us? Someone tipped him off at the airport maybe?'

Jack replied, 'I don't see how. We don't have any reason to believe he's sniffed out Hendley Associates as being part of the IC, so the Gulfstream's arrival in Bucharest wouldn't have set him off.'

Gavin said, 'Trust me, Ryan. He's definitely worried about *something*.'

'I can't see his face like you guys can, but I trust your judgment. Maybe it's just nerves. He *is* conspiring with terrorists to kill Americans. There's probably a little anxiety that comes along with that.'

Chavez said, 'Hey, I look at it as good news. I came all the way to Central Europe to watch over a guy I didn't personally know was really involved in anything illicit. But just looking at him right now, I'd say he's guilty as hell.'

Gavin panned his optics up and down the street. He switched to the thermal view, trying to pick up anyone loitering in the evening shadows. 'Well, if he thinks someone else is watching him, he's wrong. This street is quiet.'

Jack said, 'I can confirm that. Felix and I are about the only two people around tonight, and we're just hanging out in the van.'

Gavin got his photos; Dalca finished his drink, and then headed back inside. The laser audio transmitter picked up the sounds of television for a while, and then it stopped, and the lights went off.

At ten p.m. Midas took over for Gavin in the closet, so

Gavin could get a few hours' sleep on a cot in the safe house. It seemed clear Dalca wouldn't go anywhere for the evening, so Felix and Jack drove back to the safe house and crashed themselves.

Chavez told Midas he'd relieve him at three a.m., and he went to bed as well, confident it would be a quiet night.

56

Dragomir Vasilescu finished his glass of pinot noir, said good night to his friends, and left Bruno Wine Bar with a slight sway in his walk. He stepped out to Strada Covaci and checked his phone for the time. It was just after ten p.m., but with the amount of wine he'd consumed, he knew he would have a hangover of epic proportions when he woke in the morning.

He looked around hopefully for a taxi, but instead he saw a white Renault Trafic, a light commercial vehicle, pull to a stop in front of him.

The side door was already open, and two sets of hands grabbed him by the shoulders and yanked him in.

'Hey! What the hell?'

He was pushed to an open floor in the minivan, and then a bag was shoved over his head. He tried to push himself up, but he was held facedown. Two sets of zip ties were secured to his wrists, then he was rolled onto his back, yanked up into a seat by impressively strong hands, and shoved upright.

Dragomir was no longer alarmed. Now he was scared.

In Romanian he said, 'What . . . what do you want? I have a wallet. A phone . . .' When he heard no response he said, 'I have a car, a Mercedes at home. It's parked in the garage on –'

A voice interrupted him, speaking English. 'How long have you been working with the Muslims?'

He knew instantly this would be the Chinese from the Seychelles Group, but the voice was not that of Mr Peng.

'We . . . we are *not* working with the Muslims.'

'The data you have in your possession. Data you have been managing on behalf of the Seychelles Group. This data is being used to kill Americans in America. Did you not understand that we would see your scheme for what it was?'

'Scheme? There is no scheme. I can assure you, gentlemen, that –'

'The United States government has identified the location of the breach of their data. It is Office of Personnel Management, the e-QIP data, the exact data that you have in your possession, that you are using to develop product for us. No one else has that product! Only ARTD!'

Dragomir shouted through the bag over his head, 'That's right! No one else has it! And that means we don't hand it out to *fucking* terrorists!'

'Where are the files now?'

'They . . . we house them on an air-gapped server in the office. Your data is completely safe.'

'We will go to your office now.'

'*Now?* It's past business hours. Come back at nine tomorrow and I will give you the entire computer. You will see there is no way anyone could possibly remove the files without –'

The voice leaned in close to Vasilescu's face, silencing him with the threatening tone. 'We will go. Right now.'

The ARTD building had a pair of security officers who worked a desk during the overnight hours, and they were suitably concerned about the fact the director of their company showed up with three unknown Asian men at ten-thirty, but Dragomir Vasilescu simply greeted them without any explanation for his evening visit and made no introductions of his companions.

He had been warned when still in the back of the van that any alert to the guards that he was there under duress would be met with instant and overwhelming violence, and he assured the men he wanted to continue a good working relationship with the Seychelles Group after this misunderstanding was straightened out, so he would do exactly as he'd been told. They cut off his zip ties but remained close enough to reach out and grab him if he tried anything.

Now Vasilescu stood at the front of the elevator, his eyes down, with the Chinese standing behind him. He'd been instructed to keep his eyes to himself since the bag was removed in the back of the van, and he had every intention of carrying out this order. He felt like everything would be okay the moment these psychos saw there was no way to access the computer with the files on it, although he had no real way to prove the material had not been copied earlier and then placed in the air-gapped room with the terminal.

Still, he was hopeful he could satisfy them and they would leave him alone and return to China convinced they were barking up the wrong tree.

The director of ARTD flipped on several lights in the hallway on the fourth floor and walked straight to the door to the air-gapped room, and here he put his hand over the biometric scanner. A green light glowed and he opened the door, then stepped right up to the machine in the center of the otherwise empty space.

'Gentlemen. All the files we have been working from are right here. Perfectly safe, as I have assured you from the outset.'

'Show me,' one of the men behind him said.

Vasilescu turned on the monitor, waited a few seconds,

then clicked the monitor button on and off again. There was only a blank screen.

'Problem?' the man doing the talking asked.

Vasilescu sat at the desk now, tried to restart the computer, but after a few seconds he just said, 'It's . . . that's not right.'

One of the Asian men leaned behind the desk, looked around. As he was doing this Vasilescu said, 'Just a software issue. I'll try to restart the device and –'

The Asian man reached down and lifted the cover off the computer tower. It had not been screwed in place. The man clearly knew something about computers, because he said, 'Hard drive gone.'

'That's ridiculous,' Vasilescu said, then he stood, peered over the monitor, and saw for himself.

Instantly his knees weakened and he slumped back into the chair. His heart began to pound and he felt a sick nausea and light-headedness.

The man who had been doing all the talking stood close behind him now. 'Who has access to this room?'

Dragomir Vasilescu's voice cracked. 'I . . . have my best man working on your case. Dalca. Alexandru Dalca. We can go talk to him now. He will tell you. He is the only one with access to –'

Dragomir Vasilescu put it all together quickly. He remembered that long-ago conversation with Alex Dalca. The one where he said the Chinese were thinking too small and ARTD could exploit the data and sell it to the highest bidder. Clearly, Dalca had been doing just that.

And he thought of the very odd fire this afternoon. Clearly that was Dalca's doing, a diversion to take the hard drive.

The man leaning into Vasilescu's ear from behind noted Vasilescu's hesitation. He said, 'We will talk to this man Dalca. Perhaps he can answer questions that you cannot.'

As Vasilescu came to the realization of what was actually going on, he knew for his own self-preservation he had to somehow convince the men surrounding him now that they were completely off base. He couldn't have Chinese intelligence roughing up one of his people. The information they might uncover could be bad for ARTD, and bad for Vasilescu himself.

The fury that burned inside him was almost enough for him to punch his fist through the monitor in front of him. He said, 'Dalca is my very best employee. And a good man as well. His discretion is beyond reproach.' But while saying this, his inner monologue was singing a very different tune. *I'll fucking kill you myself, you deceitful, betraying sack of shit!*

'Where do we find this Dalca?'

'He . . . he will be at work at nine o'clock tomorrow. Let's all meet again and –'

The man with the strong hands grabbed the back of Vasilescu's neck and yanked him up, turned him for the door.

As they waited for the elevator, two men said something in Chinese, and then one of them stepped in front of Vasilescu, opened his suit coat, and revealed a short-barrelled submachine gun hanging from a sling under his arm.

The English speaker behind him said, 'You communicate danger to your guards, and you will all die. We want security camera files from this building removed.'

Vasilescu stepped behind the front desk in the lobby a minute later, and immediately pulled one of the keyboards to him. He began deleting security camera files. As an explanation to the two very confused guards, he just said, 'My clients here are the shy type. You know how it is.'

The two guards just looked at each other, but they did not respond to their boss.

With a final press of the Enter key, the files were erased and the cams turned off. He stood back up and left with the Asian men and climbed back into the van, and the lights went out when the black bag slipped back over his head.

As they drove through the night, with the interior of the vehicle perfectly silent, Vasilescu realized his only hope for survival at this point was finding Alexandru Dalca and convincing the Chinese that he alone was responsible.

57

Midas was nearly halfway through the ten-p.m.- to-one-a.m. watch, which consisted of little more than gazing bleary-eyed at a few images from low-light security cameras and listening to a mechanical droning sound – the slight vibrations of Dalca's snores from his bedroom, into his living room, picked up by the laser on the sliding glass door, and translated through the headphones Midas had hooked over his right ear and the back of his head, giving him room for the Campus-encrypted earpiece he kept in his left in case he needed to talk to the team.

He sipped water from one of two bottles he had on the floor next to him. The other was empty, for now. He had a standard two-water-bottle system; one full of water and one to use as a receptacle so he wouldn't have to leave the storage room and take the several-minute walk to the apartment to relieve himself in the bathroom there.

He was just about to make use of the empty bottle when he noticed the headlights of a vehicle moving up the street. As it rolled under a street lamp he thought it might be some sort of delivery van on a late-night run, but it slowed even more in the intersection, then backed into the side alley between Dalca's apartment building and the adjacent fenced parking lot. Here it turned off its lights, but Midas could tell the engine was still running.

Midas watched the vehicle in silence for several seconds, thinking it would shut down and the driver would get out, but to his surprise the side door opened. Four men climbed out, all wearing different types of dark clothing: tracksuits, cotton work pants, and hoodies.

Midas snatched his secure mobile off the desk and dialed Chavez. He assumed Ding was sacked out on a cot in the safe house apartment on the other side of the building, but this event across the street warranted waking him up.

Midas's earpiece came alive in his left ear with Chavez's voice, and though he answered quickly, it was clear he'd been sound asleep seconds earlier. 'Yeah?'

'I've got a vehicle in the alleyway alongside the target location, a driver behind the wheel with the engine running, and the nose out to the street. Four pax climbed out and entered through the lobby doors.'

'What's our boy doing?'

'Dalca is snoring. He's coming through loud and clear on the laser mic.'

There was a delay, presumably while Chavez woke himself up. Then he said, 'Okay, I'll be right there.'

'You want me to call the others?'

'How does it feel? Tell me your intuition about the guys you saw. The way they moved.'

Midas thought about it a couple seconds. 'It feels squirrelly, Ding. These guys look like trouble.'

'Shit. Okay, I'll wake everybody up.'

After a long afternoon and evening, and now a late night of static surveillance, suddenly Midas could feel the familiar surge of adrenaline coursing through his body. He had no idea what was going on across the street – but the arrival of this group of men felt significant. The team hadn't been expecting anyone else to show interest in their Romanian target, but whoever these guys were, unless they were up to no good at one of the other apartments in the building, Midas was pretty sure things were about to get interesting for Dalca.

He heard the sound through his headset now. The unmistakable heavy pounding on a door.

Quickly he transmitted to anyone who was up on comms. 'I've got someone banging on the target's door.'

Chavez responded instantly. 'Roger that. Felix and I are on the way to you. Jack is heading downstairs to street level. I've got Gavin coming to relieve you ASAP.'

There was another set of knocks at the door to Dalca's apartment, and Midas focused on the main monitor in front of him, displaying the image from the low-light camera pointed at Dalca's balcony.

Just then Dalca appeared through the drawn curtains, opening the sliding glass door to the balcony the laser audio device was focused on. The opening door made a scratching noise through the headphone so loud Midas had to pull it off his ear and drop it on the desk.

Across the quiet intersection, Dalca had a backpack on his back and he carried a big bag in his arms. Midas had to look closer to the monitor to be certain, but the Romanian also had a black bike helmet on his head.

Midas said, 'The target is on the balcony, looks like he's gonna try to bolt.'

As Midas watched, Dalca knelt down behind the cover of the balcony railing, then returned with the huge bag in his hands. He tossed the bag over the side of the balcony, and it spiraled down, spooling out a long emergency fire ladder behind it. The chain-link ladder spun down, almost all the way to the ground. Dalca attached the hooks at his end to the edge of the balcony.

Chavez and Felix entered the storage room and knelt down next to Midas. Together they looked at the monitor. 'What's he doing?'

'He's got a chain ladder, one of those things you buy to get out of a building on fire. He's climbing down. This guy was ready for a quick getaway.'

Chavez spoke into his headset. 'Jack, be aware, he's going to be at the street when you get around the building to his side. Gavin, we need you in here to relieve Midas, now!'

'Going down,' Jack called over the radio. 'I'll go foot mobile.'

Midas added, 'Target's wearing a bicycle helmet.'

'Then I guess I need to find a bike.'

Dalca was halfway down the ladder, having trouble with it in places where it dangled in the open space between the balconies on each floor, when a man stepped out onto the balcony. Midas, Chavez, and Negrescu looked in silence at the figure, dressed head to toe in black. He looked over the ledge and down to the street, but Dalca was climbing down on his right, and he couldn't see him.

A second man stepped out onto the balcony now, and this man had a silenced pistol in his hand.

Chavez spoke silently. 'Everybody listen up. We want Dalca, but more importantly, our primary objective is keeping these guys away from him. I don't know who they are, but I don't want them getting the intel that he possesses.'

Dalca dropped the last six feet to the sidewalk and collapsed in a heap with a grunt audible all over the intersection. The men on the balcony had started going back inside, but it was clear they heard the noise, even four stories above, because both spun back to the balcony. Looking down, the man on the right saw Dalca as he raced around the corner of the building.

Without hesitation, the man raised his pistol and fired, missing just to the left. The suppressed handgun made plenty of noise in the dark and quiet environment of the street, more than enough to be heard without audio equipment in the Campus overwatch position forty yards away.

Dalca disappeared into the dark alleyway, and the two men ran back inside the apartment.

Chavez said, 'Jack, these guys have no problems going lethal. Subject is heading north on foot through the alley west of his building.'

Gavin came into the storage room now, filling the space. He was panting hard, and still held his shoes in his hands.

'What was that noise?'

Chavez said, 'Gav, take Midas's position. Record everything you can until there's nothing going on, then break everything down as fast as possible. Exfiltration plan, Alpha.'

'Alpha, got it. What about you guys?'

'We're going after the target, but even if we don't get him, he won't be coming back here.'

'Okay,' Gavin said.

Chavez slung his ready bag over his shoulder, and Midas lifted his. Felix had the keys to the van in his hand, and all three men ran for the hallway to take them to the stairwell down to street level.

58

Jack Ryan, Jr, raced across the lighted street to follow after Alexandru Dalca, which meant he worried that the guys chasing Dalca would come outside and see him, and that Dalca himself might be standing there in the dark alley with a weapon, just waiting for some idiot pursuing him to race into his path.

Fortunately for Jack, neither happened, and by the time he made it through the side alley and into a little street running behind Dalca's apartment building, there was enough light for him to see his target riding a bicycle fifty yards to the west. Jack saw a row of bikes parked in a rack right next to him, but as he ran down and checked them out it appeared they were all chained or bolted to the bike rack.

Jack just continued sprinting after Dalca on foot, doing his best to stay out of the streetlights. The American had been awake all of three minutes and now he was running as fast as he could, already dreading the muscle cramps he'd start to feel when the adrenaline left him.

He pressed his transmit key. 'Ding, do I have permission to tackle and zip this guy if I get a chance?'

Chavez said, 'That's affirmative. We don't know who's after him, but we need him more than they do.'

'Just what I wanted to hear.'

Gavin Biery focused his cameras on the white delivery van next to Dalca's apartment as four men piled into the back and the vehicle rolled onto the street, making a right, and then another right to go down the dark alley.

Gavin pressed the PTT button on his headset. 'Jack, be advised. The unknown subjects are heading in your direction in a white Renault van.'

Jack came over the net instantly. It was clear from his transmission that he was running. 'Roger that. I'll find cover. I can still see Dalca but won't for much longer.'

Now Chavez said, 'Felix says he knows a way we can get in front of Dalca and cut him off. You keep tailing him while we try that.'

Alexandru Dalca's leg muscles screamed from the effort of riding a bicycle for the first time in more than a year. He'd pumped up the tires the day the Chinese came to ARTD, and this afternoon he'd purchased the emergency ladder and stocked his backpack with his passport, computer, cash, and the hard drive containing the American files, all to be prepared just in case the Chinese came for him before he had a chance to run to Macedonia.

He hadn't really expected it, but he was glad he'd taken the steps.

Yet he hadn't done a thing to get his body ready to outrun a group of Chinese goons. The banging on his door could mean only one thing, as far as he was concerned. The Seychelles Group had somehow figured out that he had the files, and that he'd been working with ISIS.

The gunshot as he raced around the side of his building had made him doubly sure he'd made the correct decision not to open the door.

He just had to get clear of them now, and his plan to do that was to get himself into the darkness of the massive Herăstrău Park and hide out till morning.

Just then, far behind him, the lights of a large vehicle turned onto Strada Alexandrina. It was way too late in this quiet neighborhood for this to mean anything but trouble. He wasn't sure he could make his way into Herăstrău before they were on him, and there was really nowhere else to hide. He looked back in their direction as they drove under a street lamp, and he saw the vehicle was a white van of some sort.

Dalca jacked his bike to the left onto a wide boulevard. Half a kilometer ahead of Dalca was the Arcul de Triumf, a 1930s-era monument in the center of a large traffic circle. Just to the right of this was the entrance to the park, but that seemed too far, considering how fast the white van was moving.

Dalca knew what he had to do. As he pedaled as fast as his aching thighs would let him, he held on to the handlebars with one hand and pulled out his phone. With his thumb he dialed 112, the emergency number for fire and police.

A woman answered in seconds, and Dalca all but screamed into the phone, 'A group of Chinese men in a white van are shooting!'

'What? Where?'

'Around the Arcul de Triumf! They are crazy. I think they are chasing a man into the park. Hurry!' He hung up the phone, crammed it down the front of his shirt, and pedaled on like mad, wishing like hell he was in his Porsche right now.

The white van raced past Jack on the Strada Alexandrina, but the American remained undetected by leap-vaulting a five-foot-high metal fence and landing in the side yard of a modern two-story home there. He remained crouched on the balls of his feet until the red taillights of the van illuminated the end of the street, then he stood back up.

He saw the dog food and water bowls right in front of him at the exact same time he heard the sound of a large, angry animal rushing at him in the dark. Jack launched back on top of the fence and rolled over, collapsing onto the sidewalk just as a big German shepherd charged forward, its teeth gnashing inches from Jack's face, but on the other side of the fence.

'*Jesus!*'

Jack crawled to his feet and ran on, but as soon as he could catch his breath he spoke to his team. 'Dalca and the white van both made a left onto the road at the end of Alexandrina. I do not have visual.'

Chavez came over the net seconds later. 'We can't pick you up now. We are to the west, trying to get ahead of Dalca. Felix thinks he might try to lose his tail in a park to the north. Suggest you head that way. We'll get you when we can.'

Jack kept running.

Dalca waited till the white van was just meters behind him, then he hopped the curb on his bike and began racing parallel to the chain-link fence lining the southern side of Herăstrău Park. The van tracked alongside him with the front passenger window rolled down, and even though the Romanian on the bike didn't look to confirm it, he felt sure there was a gun pointed his way, so he purposefully laid down the bike, tumbling at high speed just as the crack of a suppressed pistol erupted to his left.

Dalca fell end over end, but he wasn't seriously hurt and

HERĂSTRĂU PARK, BUCHAREST

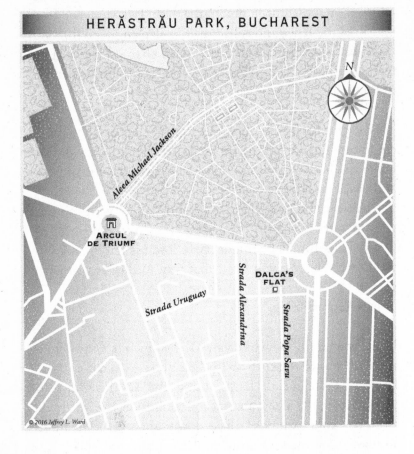

N

Aleea Michael Jackson

ARCUL
DE TRIUMF

Strada Uruguay

Strada Alexandrina

DALCA'S
FLAT

Strada Popa Savu

© 2016 Jeffrey L. Ward

he bought himself a few seconds when the van's driver went another thirty yards before slamming on his brakes and screeching to a halt.

Dalca got to his feet, ran to the metal fence lining the park, and climbed it as fast as he could, ignoring pain in his knee and back from the bike crash.

At two hundred fifty yards' distance Jack could not see the man on the bike in the darkness by the road, but he could certainly see the van, the flash from the gunshot, and then the red brake lights. The sound of screeching tires came next, and Jack realized the action was happening before the traffic circle. This told him Dalca had probably bailed off the bike and climbed the park fence.

Jack had the same fence on his right while he ran, so he immediately shot up to it, heaved himself over, and dropped down into the thick woods of Herăstrău Park.

It was nearly pitch-black here in the trees and he would have killed for some night-vision capability, but all he had was a flashlight in his go bag. He decided against using it, giving up situational awareness for personal security, and he just made his way as fast as he could through the woods, straining his eyes and his ears for some signal as to where Dalca was. He knew the Romanian had to be several hundred yards away still, but if he was coming this way, the two men would meet in under a minute.

He thought it more likely Dalca would continue to the north, because that direction was deeper into the park and the opposite direction of the white van chasing him.

Jack himself turned to the north, drawing his pistol for the first time.

'Jack, what's your location?' It was Chavez.

Softly he answered, 'I'm in this big wooded park. Dalca is in here somewhere, he lost the van on the road. Don't know if hostiles bailed from the van and went in pursuit or not.'

Chavez replied, 'We have the van ahead of us. Be advised, it just turned into the park at speed.' Jack heard Chavez ask Felix for the name of the street the van was now traveling on. Felix answered and Chavez relayed the information. 'Okay . . . the van is now on Michael Jackson.'

'It's *where?*'

Chavez confirmed with Felix, then said, 'It's a big tree-lined street that runs through the park. Aleea Michael Jackson.'

'Cool,' Jack said as he ran on, his pumping legs and arms exhausting more with each yard. He all but stumbled into a clearing, and the light was better here. He looked off to his left and saw someone running across, well ahead of his position.

'I've got him. He's seventy-five yards to my west and back in the trees on the north side of a clearing. Still heading north, but he looks pretty worn-out. I'm going to keep parallel for now and then try to flank him.'

When Chavez came back over the net, he said, '*Shit.* We've got police sirens and flashing lights up ahead. Looks like one patrol car. They will make the turn into the park before we get there, so we'll have to hang back.'

Ryan slowed a little on the far side of the clearing, and he doubled his efforts to stay concealed in the trees and darkness as he advanced, holding his pistol down low by his side as he ran on.

Alexandru Dalca heard the siren as he stumbled exhausted through the trees. His legs had all but seized from the lactic acid buildup, but he pushed on, often pulling himself with branches or shoving off tree trunks, flailing his arms to propel himself to the north, knowing that the main road through this part of the park was just up ahead.

He had no idea if the men had climbed out of the van and were in pursuit of him now, so he couldn't just wait here in the dark and hope for the best.

The headlights of a vehicle began moving through the trees around him, shifting shadows like ghosts chasing from all sides. He broke out into the clearing by Aleea Michael Jackson, and into the glare of the headlights. He knew, without any idea how he knew, that this was the white van. Instantly he saw the police car whip into the tree-lined street a hundred yards behind the van.

Thank God, he said to himself, and with a fresh jolt of adrenaline Alexandru Dalca darted across the road right in front of the van and disappeared into the trees on the other side.

The van raced up to where Dalca had passed and slammed on its brakes, but as the side door opened and men ran around the rear of the vehicle to pursue their target, the red-on-white police car shined a spotlight on the men and skidded to a stop, just thirty meters behind them.

The three men stopped and raised their empty hands.

Felix Negrescu pulled to the side of the road with his headlights off. Just to his right was the entrance to Aleea Michael Jackson. In the front passenger seat Chavez held up a pair of binoculars. Although it was dark, the lights from the police car on the van revealed three men standing there, held at gunpoint by two local police officers, each of whom stood behind his open door.

A second police car approached from the northeast end

of Aleea Michael Jackson, but Chavez could tell this only from the flashing lights in the woods on the far side of the two vehicles.

Midas was in the backseat. 'You see our target?'

'Negative,' Chavez said. 'Ryan, what's your poz?'

Ryan's whispered voice came over the men's earpieces. 'I'm in cover in the trees. One hundred feet to the right of the white van on the south side. A squad car is pulling to a stop right in front of me, and another is holding subjects at gunpoint at the back of the van. I do not see Dalca, but if he got to the other side of the road, I can't get to him now without exposing myself to the local cops.'

Chavez replied, 'Roger that, hold position.'

Midas had scooted over and put his own binoculars to work sizing up the situation. 'If these guys from the van want to shoot it out with the cops, do we get involved?'

Chavez said, 'There are five of them, minimum. There are three of us with guns, and these are untested and unfamiliar pistols.'

Midas didn't take his eyes off the road. The men behind the van were clearly not doing what the cops were telling them to do. They just stood there, as if they were waiting for an opportunity to act.

Midas said, 'You know, in the Unit we used to say, "You piss with the dick you got." These blasters will get the job done.'

Chavez focused his binos to the south side of the road, at the tree line, and he saw movement. At the same time he heard one of the police officers at the rear of the van shouting orders to the men standing there.

Midas saw it, too. 'One pax on foot, south side of the road.'

Chavez snapped into his mic, 'Jack, get back in cover! We see you!'

Jack whispered, 'I *am* in cover. Trust me, you do *not* see me from your poz.'

As Chavez and Midas watched the shadowy figure stepping out of the trees, to the right and just behind the two cops with their guns on the three men at the back of the van, the figure raised a pistol with a suppressor. Quickly he fired off two rounds, flashing in the darkness of the wooded park road.

Both cops behind the van dropped to the ground, dead. The three men who'd been standing there with their hands up now drew their weapons, and turned to move around the van to engage the other cops there.

Chavez barked an order, 'Jack, cleared to engage!' He turned to Felix behind the wheel. 'Go!'

Jack Ryan, Jr, did not respond to Chavez's command, he just spun around the tree and dropped to his knees. He knew he was in view of the man behind the wheel of the white van, plus anyone else inside, plus the three men behind the van. He'd heard the suppressed gunshots coming from the edge of the same tree line he was tucked into, but he hadn't seen the flashes from the shots, so he didn't have this man's location pinned down.

He also had two cops outside their vehicle close to him, but he was shielded from them by the tree on his right shoulder. He hoped the guys he was trying to help wouldn't get an angle on him and shoot him, and he worried about another siren he could hear in the distance approaching from the east.

Jack raised the Romanian pistol as the first man came

around the back of the van, lined the front sight up with his target's center mass, and opened fire. His weapon, in contrast to the one wielded by the armed man in the trees, was not suppressed. It exploded in the night, but he struck home with both shots of his double tap, and the armed man staggered back and fell onto his back in the road.

The second man fired reactively in Jack's direction, but missed wide with both shots. Jack returned fire at the flash, but did so as he was crouching lower, and his shots shattered the windshield of the police car behind the van.

Suddenly cracks of gunfire came from the Romanian police, but Jack could not tell if they were shooting at him or at the bad guys. The situation had to be confusing for them, Jack understood, as they probably didn't even know their colleagues had been killed on the far side of the van.

Jack scrambled back behind the trees, totally covering himself from all angles. 'Ding, I need help!'

The reply came instantly. 'Engaging hostiles now.'

59

As the van raced through the park toward the gunfight, Midas opened the door on the left side of the minivan, just behind Felix. He stood on the floorboard and leaned out, holding on to the back of the driver's seat to steady himself with his left hand.

In the front passenger seat Chavez held his gun out the window, and he leaned out behind it to get his eyes on the weapon's sights. Within a half-second of each other, he and Midas both opened fire. Chavez shot at the figure who had just killed the two cops, now kneeling beside a tree at the edge of the woods. Midas, on the opposite side of the mini-van, engaged the men left standing on the far side of the parked police cruiser.

Chavez struck his target, but another figure revealed himself deeper in the trees with a muzzle flash and the sound of a bullet striking the grille of the minivan. Chavez assumed both these men had climbed out of the van back where Jack had said Dalca had jumped the fence to get into the park.

Another round struck Chavez's vehicle, this time in the windshield. Felix shouted out with pain, and instantly the minivan began to veer sharply to the left.

Chavez kept firing at the second figure, even though he was certain the vehicle he was riding in was seconds from either rear-ending the police car or crashing into the trees.

*

Jack could see no more targets from his position, so he reloaded quickly and looked around toward the second police car on the scene. To his shock the officer near him lay crumpled on his back in the street, his weapon several feet away. When Jack couldn't see the cop on the far side of the vehicle, he worried that the driver of the van might have shot them both. Jack had been so occupied firing at the two men at the back of the van, and trying to get an angle on the men a few dozen yards down the wood line to the west, he'd not engaged the driver, leaving him for the cops to deal with.

He saw no one behind the wheel of the van now, which meant the driver was dead or had debussed during the fight. That he could see no bullet strikes on the windshield worried him the latter was the case.

Just then he saw the lights of his team's vehicle veer off to the left, and he heard the sound of cracking tree branches and breaking glass on the far side of the van.

Jack ran up onto the road and toward the police car nearest him, his weapon sweeping for targets. He dropped to his knees by the driver's-side door to look through the vehicle, hoping to see the cop on the other side. He halfway worried the officer would shoot at him if he saw him, but he was more worried the man was already dead.

He saw no one, so he stayed in a low crouch and began to move around the back of the police car, his pistol still up in front of him.

As he swung around the back, he was surprised to see a man doing the same thing from the far side. Jack realized this man was not in a police uniform, and the man was swinging his gun up to fire. Jack and the dark figure both fired their pistols at the same time from point-blank range.

The men were almost touching, but their extended gun

arms were both off target, so they fired by each other. Jack threw his right elbow up into the man's face, but the instant he struck, the man swept back with his pistol and knocked Jack's gun from his hand.

Both handguns clanked along the darkened park road.

Jack could see his opponent was Asian with a larger-than-average frame, and Jack's elbow had not knocked the man down, so he instinctively tried to tackle the man and put him on his back. But as he threw himself into the figure at the back of the squad car, the man stepped to the side, sending Jack slamming hard against the trunk. The impact hurt, but Jack anticipated a blow from behind, so he spun around with his arm up to parry an attack. A left punch was on the way; Jack took it in the upper arm, then threw his own left jab that struck the man square in the jaw.

This snapped the man's head back, and he reeled on his heels, but *still* he did not drop.

Jack feinted another attempt to tackle, and the Asian man went for it, spinning to his left. Jack went to where he thought the Asian man's movement would take him, and he lowered his right shoulder and put his entire body behind it, slamming hard into the man's chest.

Both Jack and his opponent landed in the middle of Aleea Michael Jackson, fists and knees and elbows thrashing in both directions. Behind the ground fight, the sound of snapping gunfire erupted again.

Jack felt the Asian man trying to reach for something at his waist, so Jack pinned his arms as best he could, and head-butted him mercilessly twice, then three times, before the man dropped back dazed.

Quickly Jack felt around the man's body and found a stiletto clipped into his front right pants pocket.

Jack pulled it away, yanking it from its sheath in the process, and then he rolled off the man and began crawling for his pistol. He got to it just as the man behind him reached down to his ankle and pulled a tiny silver backup gun, so Jack opened fire at close range, stitching him from his pelvis to his face with bullet holes, and ending the fight.

Midas shot the third shooter behind the van, and Chavez pumped four rounds into the last man in the trees, sending him crawling off on his hands and knees, presumably to die, because he'd left his pistol where it fell. Chavez told Midas to look after Felix, and then he climbed out of the minivan and began moving forward carefully but quickly.

He'd called Jack several times over the net but had not received any response. He hated to expose his location, but he also didn't want to walk in front of Jack's gun. 'Ding is comin' to you!' he shouted, then passed the white van on his left.

'It's clear!' came a response from farther back, relieving Chavez instantly. 'All hostiles down!'

Chavez found Jack with a flashlight in his mouth, training it on a wounded Romanian police officer, a young man who couldn't have been older than twenty-three. Jack had found him lying in the grass next to his vehicle. He'd been shot through the forearm and the shoulder, but he would survive.

All in all there were five dead hostiles, and one more who Ding was certain he'd shot multiple times in the torso and was probably bleeding out in the woods. There were also three dead cops. Felix had been grazed in the forehead and had some deep cuts on his cheek from broken windshield glass striking him at high speed, but he was still awake and aware, and apologizing for wrecking the minivan.

Sirens were closing in from both sides of the park by the time everyone started back to the minivan, but Chavez realized there was no way to get the vehicle back up on the road from where it had crashed. They made the decision to pile into the white Renault, although there were several bullet holes in the windows and doors. Chavez climbed behind the wheel, and the other two Campus men helped Felix inside.

As Chavez raced out of the engagement zone with his headlights extinguished, he found a narrow unpaved lane through the trees to avoid the oncoming police vehicles.

It was silent in the vehicle until they got out of the park, turned on the headlights, and began driving normally, despite the holes in the sides.

Chavez said, 'That was nuts, but the only thing I know for sure is that Dalca is gone.'

Jack said, 'We can go north and look for him. He still might be on foot.'

Chavez said, 'Negative. We have to pick up Gavin and get out of Dalca's neighborhood. This whole part of the city is going to be crawling with cops in no time.'

As he drove he called Clark. It was afternoon on the East Coast, and the director of operations of The Campus answered immediately. Chavez spent five minutes filling him in on every detail, and Clark said he'd try to get Mary Pat on the phone and reach out to the Romanian intelligence services. They had a great relationship with the Ryan administration, and although Mary Pat would have some difficulty explaining the fact that several undeclared agents of her government had been at the center of a running gun battle in Bucharest, she also had some cards in her favor for the conversation to come. A Romanian ex-con had been at the center of the ISIS attacks in America, under the nose of the Romanian government, and the Romanian government would have every reason on earth to help America and to keep this out of the news.

While Chavez was still on the phone with Clark, the minivan picked up Gavin and all the team's gear in an alley two blocks from their safe house. The heavyset IT director had lugged everything down five flights of stairs and over a hundred yards, making two trips to do so, and they found him sitting on stacked Pelican cases and North Face backpacks, a sheen of sweat on his face and his chest heaving more than that of any of the three men who'd just fought off a half-dozen armed hostiles and escaped from local police ten minutes earlier.

Gavin loaded gear through the open lift-back, and then recoiled in shock as he realized the big form in the very rear of the minivan was not a duffel bag but, instead, a dead body. He didn't know why the team was hauling a corpse, but he was too winded to say anything at the time.

He just shut the back and climbed into the side door.

They took off again, and by the time Chavez finished his conversation with Clark and was driving farther south, Gavin finally caught his breath.

He said, 'I got a good look at the shooters. Did you see them?'

Chavez said, 'My guess was Chinese.'

Gavin said, 'Yeah. Looked like it to me. I got fair pictures of a couple of faces. We can run them against known Chinese intelligence officers to see if anything turns up.'

Jack said, 'Considering their track record with cyberintel breaches . . . a fair assumption.'

Midas said, 'Why are they after Dalca if they're working together?'

Jack said, 'One of the theories Gavin and I had was that this was some sort of inside job at the cyberfraud company, and one person, Dalca, stole the data from whatever state actor had commissioned the breach. If that's the case – Dalca's the thief, and China's the state actor – then it follows that Dalca would not be thrilled about serious-looking Chinese gents knocking at his door.'

Gavin asked, 'Are we going to the airport?'

Chavez shook his head. 'We don't have Dalca, so we're not going anywhere. We need to find a place to hole up while we figure out our next move.'

Felix spoke from behind a faceful of gauze handed to him by Midas. 'I know a place. My nephew is in the Army, deployed with NATO. He has a little farm in Sinteşti, just fifteen minutes out of the city. It's not much. He's a bachelor and never home, but it's quiet.'

Chavez said, 'Lead the way, Felix. We'll get you patched up when we get there.'

Finally Gavin asked, 'Who is the dead guy in the back?'

The other men in the vehicle all turned to look his way.

'*What* dead guy?' Jack asked.

'See for yourself.'

Jack crawled over some of the luggage and used a penlight to look over the body. The man was clearly dead, with a bullet wound in his forehead. Digging through his pockets, Jack pulled the man's ID and shined a light on it. 'Dragomir Vasilescu.'

Gavin said instantly, 'He's the director of ARTD. Why'd you guys shoot him?'

'We didn't. He came with the car. Either the Chinese

executed him, or else he got hit in the crossfire of the gun-fight. With a hole right between his eyes, my guess is it was the former.'

Chavez said, 'We don't know if he was working for Dalca or not, and we don't know for sure those were Chinese. Either way, whoever was after Dalca decided to hold Vasilescu responsible.'

'Yeah,' Midas said, 'those guys weren't playing around back there.'

Chavez looked at him in the low light of the van. 'Clark said you told him you were looking to make a difference. Does this qualify?'

'We didn't get Dalca, but if we just kept the guy with all the secret intel against our military and spooks from getting picked up by the Chinese, then I guess that is better than nothing.'

'Damn right,' Chavez said. 'Now let's finish the job.'

60

Dominic and Adara spent the afternoon and evening seated at a table in the lobby of the Chicago Athletic Association hotel, their laptops in front of them and their Bluetooth connections to their cell phones wedged in their ears.

They'd been at it for hours, but so far they'd been unable to find any one obvious Islamic State target here in the city.

Adara said again that the single biggest target was the JTTF itself, but again they dismissed it as too hard an objective for al-Matari and his people, since they'd lost a lot of cell members in the past week on attacks that had been utterly unprotected.

At ten-fifteen they'd finished a dinner of pizza in the lobby, and were about to pack up for the night, when Dom's phone rang. He didn't recognize the number, but saw it was local.

'Yeah?'

'SA Caruso? This is Special Agent Jeffcoat.' Dom could hear obvious excitement in the man's voice, which surprised him, because that morning Jeffcoat couldn't have been less interested in talking to him.

'Hey. What's up?'

'Well, either you were holding out intel on me, in which case you and I are going to have words later, or else you are one lucky son of a bitch.'

'How so?'

'Twelve minutes ago we got a facial-recog hit of the New

York shooter, David Hembrick, checking into the Drake hotel, over on Lake Shore Drive. He was with another man. This guy matches the description of Abu Musa al-Matari.'

Dom stood from the table, startling Adara. 'You've got to be kidding me! I'm ten minutes away. They're still there?'

'We're assuming so. We have images of them going together into the elevator with a good amount of luggage, but some of the cams in the building are out of order. Still . . . no images of them leaving, so we think they are both in the same hotel room.'

'What are you guys going to do?'

'We are taking them down now.'

'You think that's a good idea?'

'Chicago PD SWAT is one of the best in the nation, and we'll back them up. We're bringing everyone onto the scene quickly and quietly with a full JTTF mobile unit. We don't have FBI HRT in the area, so Chicago PD's SWAT team is already spinning up. They're top-notch and we liaise with them regularly on counterterror drills. We're moving plain-clothed FBI and CPD into the area to put eyes on all the exits, and when we get set up, SWAT will breach Hembrick's hotel room.' Dom could hear the intensity in the special agent's voice. He was a hunter whose ultimate prey had just walked in front of his gunsight. 'A few hundred hotel guests are going to have themselves a night to remember.'

'Yeah, I guess so.' Even though Adara didn't know what was going on, she was following Dom's lead and quickly packing up their laptops.

Jeffcoat said, 'Your creds will get you under the tape and into our command post, but we won't move into position until the SWAT breach has begun. We don't want anybody around talking about the big black counterterror trailers and a hundred cops bum-rushing the neighborhood, in case al-Matari has confederates out on the street.'

Dom said, 'Jesus, man. I don't know about this.' Dom was thinking how The Campus would do this, and he was sure they would go with a *much* lower-profile operation.

Jeffcoat snapped back. 'No offense, Special Agent, but this call wasn't to consult with you. It was to give you a heads-up.'

'Right. I'm heading that way, and can provide eyes from a distance. What's the room number?'

Jeffcoat said, 'Five-fourteen. Just come to the CP if you want updates, do *not* go to the hotel. When we get set up we will be on East Delaware, a block south of the Drake. I'm serious, don't crowd our scene, Caruso. SWAT and local PD will handle the Drake and do any trigger-pulling, and JTTF and FBI will manage the operation covertly on scene from standoff range via the mobile command. I'm only notifying you because I was ordered by DC to keep you informed. We don't need too many cooks in the kitchen.'

'Right. Good luck.'

Dom and Adara climbed into their rental and headed north on Michigan Avenue. Dom carried a Glock 26 subcompact nine-millimeter pistol in a shoulder holster under his blue sport coat, and a second G26 in his backpack for Adara's use in an emergency. Without comment she pulled it out, along with an extra mag, and slipped the equipment into her purse. She then pulled her hair back into a ponytail with a rubber band.

They were both dressed conservatively, but they knew how to conceal their weapons, no matter what their attire.

'What's our play?' Adara asked.

'We'll go to where the command center is and see who's running the show. Offer any help we can give.'

She asked, 'Does it seem like a good idea to you for SWAT to hit them in their hotel room? There's a ballroom at the Drake, it will be in full swing, and a lobby bar, plus people in their rooms. IED shrapnel or AK rounds are going to go through walls like butter.'

Dom said, 'I'm with you, I'd rather they sat back and put eyes on them, took al-Matari and Hembrick down while they were somewhere else, but this isn't our call to make.'

Adara said, 'Would we be more help if we got inside the hotel, just in case? I mean, sometimes it's better to ask forgiveness than permission.'

Dom looked at her a moment while he drove. 'It's *my* show, Adara. You are subordinate to me on this.'

'I know that.' She went quiet.

Dom thought about what he'd said, and how it sounded. The last thing Dom wanted or needed right now was a fight with his girlfriend. After driving in silence for a minute, Dom said, 'We'll just feel it out when we get there. If we think we can help on the inside, then we'll find a way into that hotel.'

'Okay,' she said, and then added, 'I'll do whatever you think is right.'

Five FBI agents working with the Chicago Division of the JTTF arrived in the lobby of the Drake in ones and twos, sat on benches, walked through the bar and mall on the lower level. They all were in text message comms with each other, as well as with CPD and JTTF officials, who were scrambling to get their big mobile command trailers staffed and moving and patrol cars into the neighborhood to create a cordon around the century-old hotel.

The lobby teams had filtered in covertly in an attempt to identify known al-Matari cell members who might have been going to or coming from the elevators. A lower-level access to the room-floor elevators, one story below the main lobby, was put out of commission by FBI agents dressed as maintenance staff. This led to a brief shouting match with the actual hotel maintenance staff in the lower concourse before uniformed CPD officers intervened and pulled hotel maintenance into an employee-only hallway to explain they'd just threatened to kick the asses of a group of covert FBI agents.

At the same time the altercation was going on downstairs, in the lobby a forty-something couple, both special agents, stepped up to the counter and asked to speak with the hotel manager. They took him into a back room with a flash of their credentials, and told him they needed every unoccupied room on the fifth floor right then. The manager stepped to a terminal with a shaking hand, and with difficulty managed to generate keys for three deluxe king rooms on the fifth floor.

Over the next five minutes, three teams of armed FBI special agents went to the three rooms, posing as guests. All the other guests on the floor were contacted, one by one, by hotel staff inquiring as to their satisfaction with their stay. This identified which rooms were occupied by civilians, and which guests were still out on the town this evening.

There was one exception to the telephone survey – room 514. A decision had also been made not to call David Hembrick's room to avoid the chance the call might make Hembrick and al-Matari suspicious.

Dom and Adara parked in a garage on East Walton, just a block west of the Drake. From the street it looked just like a regular Saturday night in front of the big old hotel, but when the couple turned right on Michigan, then made their way down to East Delaware, it was a different story. A half-dozen obvious government sedans and SUVs covered the road, and motorcycle cops blocked the turn off Michigan onto the one-way street.

As they walked closer to the dozen or so FBI and CPD men standing by one of the SUVs, Adara said, 'Remember how I said I thought the biggest target would be the JTTF itself?'

'Yeah.'

'Well . . . what better way to target them than to draw them all here to one place?'

Dom thought it over. 'That makes a hell of a lot of sense. Jeffcoat said a mobile command vehicle is standing off somewhere, but it will arrive on scene at the same time as the hit on the Drake. This street is going to be a zoo in a minute.'

Adara looked around and said, 'I guess the cops have it under control,' but her voice didn't sound so sure.

There were eleven public or employee ground-floor entrances to the Drake hotel and the small shopping mall attached to it, and this made controlling access to the building a nightmare for police concerned that lookouts at ground level might tip off Hembrick and al-Matari and cause them to barricade themselves, set off an explosive, or try to flee. But as soon as the three groups of agents were in their rooms on the fifth floor, all looking out through peepholes into the hallway, three armored trucks pulled up around the building. One on Lake Shore, and two on East Walton Place. Eighteen men in all, SWAT officers from the Chicago Police Department, leapt from their vehicles and moved on the building. A second unit was parked four blocks to the west as a quick-reaction force to help the first in the case of disaster, and every one of the men on the second team was pissed that he wasn't on the team called on for the hit itself.

One truckload of SWAT leapt out of the back of their vehicle at the south-side main entrance, raced through doors held open by plainclothes cops and Feds, and entered the building. Here the six officers took the stairs up to the main lobby. They shot past shocked hotel guests who watched them with mouths agape, and then they moved to the employee access door, again held open by a special agent who'd been hanging out in the lobby looking for known ISIS personalities. The olive-drab-clad SWAT members moved into a stairwell and began ascending in a tactical train toward the fifth floor.

The second team entered from Lake Shore, ran the full length of the street-level high-end shopping mall, and took the main elevators one flight below the lobby. One floor above, an FBI agent heard the transmission that they were on their way up, so he blocked anyone in the lobby attempting to use the elevators. From now on, the four elevators off the lobby would be only for people trying to escape their hotel rooms above.

The third group entered from the front as well, and they entered the public-access stairwell.

Now a dozen police officers, many wearing uniforms, moved into the lobby. They did not evacuate the hotel completely, and many in the ballroom just a half flight of stairs up from the lobby had no idea anything was amiss.

Two minutes later all eighteen SWAT officers were up on the fifth floor. Three groups of four quietly evacuated the rooms where guests had answered their phones to respond to the survey. The officers did not take the time to check the rooms where no one had answered.

When this was done, a half-dozen officers stacked up a few yards from the door to room 514, and six more men approached slowly, their M4 rifles pointed at the door. The last six took up positions by the stairs but trained their weapons on the entire floor.

The six FBI agents who had checked into the rooms on the floor opened their doors, drew their weapons, and stayed well behind the action, but ready to help, if needed.

A breacher and a security man moved up to the door. The security man kept his weapon up while the breacher gently attached a small water-tamped charge next to the door latch, then stood back with the shock-tube detonator in his hand.

The team leader, back in the stack along the wall, whispered into his mic. 'Bravo One has positive control. Breaching in three, two, one.'

The door to room 514 blasted inward, and the team flooded into the room.

As they did so, the door to room 515, directly across the hall, opened inward, and just as the fourth man in the stack recognized the movement on his right and turned toward it, twenty-year-old Maria Gonzalez, the lone female of the Chicago cell, took one step out into the hall.

Without a word she detonated her suicide vest in the center of the team of SWAT officers.

The door to room 501 opened as well, and Ahmed, another member of the Chicago cell, slung a C-4 bomb the size of a briefcase toward the SWAT officers standing by the stairwell on the south side of the hall. The case landed in the middle of the group, but not before they shot Ahmed to death, riddling his body with bullets.

Even though the would-be bomber was shot, the device exploded in front of the stairwell, killing everyone there and blasting out windows throughout the several floors on the southern side of the building, spraying glass down onto East Walton Place.

Two floors down, three Chicago cell members and two from Santa Clara left their third-floor room armed with grenades and AK-103 rifles. They wore body armor and suicide vests, and together they took the one flight down the main lobby stairs. As soon as they opened the door they saw the police, and while three men fired their AKs, three others hurled grenade after grenade into the lobby.

61

Two massive black mobile command trailers, each with a full array of technical and communications gear, rolled to a stop out of view from the Drake on East Delaware. Instantly the street was reclosed for the block and the entire command post was surrounded by CPD police cars.

Inside and around the vehicles were over forty members of the JTTF, all senior members of the FBI, the Department of Defense, the CIA, the Defense Intelligence Agency, the Department of Homeland Security, the Bureau of Naval Intelligence, Immigration and Customs Enforcement, the US Secret Service, the Illinois State Police, the US Army Criminal Investigations Division, as well as the antiterrorism division of CPD.

Assistant Special Agent in Charge Thomas Russell was not only the local head of the FBI office, but also the director of the JTTF in Chicago. He stepped out of a black Chevy Suburban parked in a fire zone and darted into the trailer labeled on the sides as Mobile Command Unit One the moment the steps had been placed by the side door.

They'd all heard the explosions a block away and five stories above, and now the radios were alive with reports of officers down on the fifth floor. Transmissions squawked into transmissions, the flow of information to the command center deteriorated, but within seconds of the first bit of bad news, the sounds of fully automatic weapons fire crackled up the street.

THE DRAKE HOTEL, CHICAGO

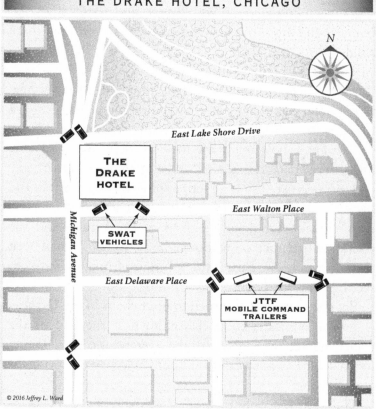

N

East Lake Shore Drive

THE DRAKE HOTEL

East Walton Place

SWAT VEHICLES

Michigan Avenue

East Delaware Place

JTTF MOBILE COMMAND TRAILERS

© 2016 Jeffrey L. Ward

Again the radios screamed. 'We're taking fire in the lobby! Man down! Active shooter!'

'What the *fuck* is going on in there?' Russell demanded.

A CPD communications and dispatch specialist said, 'I'm getting reports of multiple explosions and a gun battle on the fifth floor. Tangos in multiple rooms. And multiple shooters are in the lobby, with S-vests and assault rifles. All our elements from the fifth floor have evacuated, but there are dead and wounded.'

'How many civilians in that hotel?'

'Hotel management said five hundred seventy-three rooms at an eighty percent occupancy. Figure an average of two per room, that's nine hundred sixteen people, but no way to know how many are in there right now, and how many in the bars, restaurants, and conference rooms.'

'Good Christ.' It wasn't supposed to be like this. He and his entire outfit had just performed a full-scale drill on a terrorist attack of Soldier Field six weeks earlier, and the operation had gone off without a hitch, so Russell had been confident in his and the local police department's ability to see this arrest through.

But somehow it had turned to utter chaos in the Drake.

A communications specialist down at the end of the trailer shouted over the din of the operations center. 'Director Russell? I've got a call from room 514, they are asking for you by name!'

Thinking the only possibility was that a SWAT commander on the floor was calling, he answered immediately.

'Russell?'

'Good evening, Special Agent in Charge Thomas Russell.' The caller had a Middle Eastern accent tinged with British vowels.

'Who is this?'

'I am offended you do not recognize my voice. I am certain your drones found ways to listen to my phone calls when I was in Syria. Isn't that how your military found out about my camp there last year?'

Russell grabbed the arm of his second-in-command, a US Army lieutenant colonel. The man had been passing on his way through the command center, and the director yanked so hard he spun him on his heel.

Russell put his finger over the mouthpiece of his phone and whispered, 'Al-Matari.'

The lieutenant colonel raced to alert communications techs to record the call.

Russell asked, 'What's the status of the police officers up there?'

'Up here we have six alive. All under our control. I have more mujahideen on other floors, rounding up civilians. Pull all your forces out of the building and then we will talk again. Unless I hear you have done this in three minutes, I will personally shoot one hostage a minute until you comply.'

'What do you want?'

'For you to follow my instructions. Then . . . we negotiate.' The line went dead.

Russell turned to his second-in-command. 'Get all our people out of there now, and have them bring out the civilians they can grab. They have three minutes. We'll bring in FBI HRT, regroup, and do what we can to defuse this. Stage as many CPD SWAT as you can outside, in case they have to go back in if the shooting starts up again.'

It took Dom Caruso several minutes to find Special Agent Jeffcoat inside the tape on East Delaware, just fifty feet from one of the two mobile command centers. The SA was on his phone, a Benelli shotgun hanging across his chest over his soft body armor.

As soon as he hung up, he looked up to see Caruso. 'Not now.'

'What the hell is going on in there?'

'It was a trap. We have a hostage situation, but we did get a call from inside, so at least they are talking to us. We're backing off, to try to get some people released.'

Dom didn't like that at all. 'No. You've got to hit them right now!'

'You're nuts. They have a half-dozen SWAT officers alive up there on the fifth floor, plus God knows how many civilians. We don't know how many terrorists there are in the building or what weapons they have. We have to get our shit together and wait for HRT.'

Dom couldn't believe what he was hearing. 'All the way from DC?'

'They can be here in three hours. In the meantime, we negotiate.'

'Look,' Dom implored. 'Al-Matari isn't doing what you think he's doing. This is a common tactic jihadist terrorists use all over the world. It's called "negotiation for fortification." These talks are a stall tactic. They are in there right now rigging bombs, making mantraps, prepping for the next stage of their statement. They are waiting for you to get every camera in the country pointed at Chicago, and then they will do what they *really* set out to do.'

Assistant Special Agent in Charge Russell saw the argument from the back of Mobile Command Post One and pushed through the crowd of JTTF responders. 'What's going on? Who are you?'

Dom said, 'Special Agent Caruso, out of DC.'

'Right. You're the guy Murray wanted read in on the situation. Is there something you know that you aren't sharing with me?'

Dom said, 'You are treating this like a hostage situation. You are trying to calm things down and talk. That's the opposite of what you need to do right now. The quicker you get shooters back in there, the fewer innocent lives you'll lose.'

Russell responded by questioning Dom's authority. 'I know you're the President's nephew, but that doesn't give you command of my scene.'

'I'm just trying to help. Look. This mobile command is too close to the Drake. For all you know he has a dirty bomb in there and –'

'Does Washington have intelligence that says he has a dirty bomb, because if you guys do, then I sure as shit wasn't notified.'

'No, sir, but –'

Russell said, 'I don't have time to justify every action I make to an SA out of another division. Stand here with your mouth shut or get on the other side of that tapeline.'

Dom did leave the command post. He found Adara in a growing crowd on Michigan Avenue.

Clearly, she'd seen the entire altercation. 'Did that go as badly as it looked from over here?'

Dom's face was rock-hard and serious. 'I think this hostage-taking thing is a ruse. Their demands, whatever they are, are just stalling tactics. They want as many eyes as possible on them so that when they slaughter all the hostages, they'll get more publicity.'

Adara said, 'What do we do?'

Dom replied, 'We don't sit around and wait. We go in.'

'Do they have any idea how many terrorists are in there?' she asked.

Dom shook his head. 'No. That is a shitty situation in that hotel, and it will only get worse every minute someone waits around to do something about it. If someone can get in there and begin engaging al-Matari's people, get the shooting to start again, then the other SWAT teams will have no choice but to move on the scene.'

Adara said, 'Then what are we standing around talking about it for? Let's get in there and get started.'

Dom hesitated and Adara was about to get angry, because she thought he was going to order her to stay behind.

But before she could say anything he said, 'I need you with me in there.'

'I know. I just had Clark send schematics on the building to my phone. We can go through what looks like an old drainage system under the hotel – it connects to a building on the east side on Lake Shore.'

Dom was already jogging in that direction, pulling a small light out of his backpack. Adara jogged along with him. 'Let's get wet.'

62

Luca Gabor smelled fresh dirt, wet air. He had no idea where the hell he was or what the hell was going on, but he did not ask. The confusion that began when he was taken from his prison cell at four in the morning morphed into fear when he was blindfolded, cuffed, and led out of the prison and into the back of a van, and this fear kept him silent even now.

And while he had spoken little to the people in the vehicle around him, they had said *nothing* back to him.

They'd driven for twenty minutes, then he was transferred to another vehicle. He had the impression he was with a new bunch of captors, but they'd said nothing more than the first group, and they drove him around for another twenty minutes.

Then the vehicle stopped, he was led out, and this is when he smelled nature for the first time.

Now he was pushed onto his knees, and he started to fall forward. As he cried out in surprise he was grabbed from behind and held in a kneeling position.

And then the blindfold was pulled from his eyes, he was released, and he blinked away the sweat of fear. It was dark, but he could tell he was somewhere in the woods, because the headlights of a vehicle behind him lit the scene.

A thick tree line was just twenty meters ahead, but right in front of him, a foot from where he knelt, fresh dirt had been dug, a hole two meters long by a meter and a half wide.

Luca looked inside it.

It was shallow, no more than a foot deep. The body of a man wearing a white shirt and a tie lay faceup. Even though the shadows were thick in the hole, Gabor could see there was a bullet wound in the man's forehead.

In Romanian he screamed, '*Shit! Shit!* What is this? What am I doing here?'

From right behind him he heard a man speak. 'How's your English, Luca? I hear it used to be good, back when you worked for Romanian intelligence.'

'I . . . I speak English. What is going on? Who are you? What do you want? I have done nothing to anyone!'

The person behind him moved even closer now. Just behind his ear. His voice was intimidating in its tone and proximity. 'I heard you're a tough guy. But you whine a lot for a tough guy.'

'I . . . I want to go back to Jilava. Take me back. Now!'

Instead of an answer, Luca Gabor got a boot in the small of his back. He fell face-first into the hole, right next to, and partially on top of, the dead man. His hands cuffed behind him meant he had trouble scooting back off the body.

A flashlight's beam centered on the corpse next to him. Gabor squinted away the light, but he looked at the body, crammed up next to him in the small shallow grave. The dead man and Gabor's face were a foot apart.

'You know this guy?'

'No! No, I swear! I've never seen him.'

'His name is . . . *was*, Dragomir Vasilescu.'

Luca Gabor looked again, then he squinted into the light. 'The director of ARTD. I know the name. I did not know him. But . . . I *swear* I had nothing to do with anything he might have —'

'Alexandru Dalca paid you a visit.'

Gabor began shaking his head violently, but he heard the sound of the slide on a semiautomatic pistol being racked.

'Before you answer, asshole, know this. Ol' Drago there didn't want to talk to me, either. And you see what that got him.'

Luca changed his tune quickly. He wasn't going to risk his life to defend Alexandru *fucking* Dalca. 'Yes, it's true. He wanted me to make a connection for him. To get him out of the country. I didn't know why. I didn't ask. I didn't *want* to know.'

'I know why he wanted to run.' The voice behind the flashlight said. '*I* was why he wanted to run. He's a smart guy, after all. What I don't know is what you told him. You tell me right now, or you end up next to old Drago here for eternity, or until a dog comes by, smells your stench, and drags you off.'

Luca thought about the three million dollars his daughter received this afternoon. He could give up Dalca's secret, but he could not lose out on so much money. He said, 'I didn't help. I refused.'

From his right side, he felt the slap of mud being tossed on top of him. A second later he heard the sound of a spade piercing the pile of loose soil there, and then another load of wet dirt came crashing down. This time it landed on his chest.

He was being buried alive.

'I'll tell you!' he screamed. 'I'll tell you everything!'

Ten minutes later Midas and Jack pulled Luca out of the hole, put the blindfold back over his eyes, and began leading him back to the minivan. They both noted that Luca Gabor had soiled himself somewhere along the process, and they really did not want to drive him anywhere, but a promise had been made. They'd take him back to Romanian intelligence agents waiting in a parking lot in nearby Sinteşti, and the agents would take him back to Jilava Prison. They would probably be pissed that the clean prisoner they'd handed off an hour earlier was being returned to them covered in mud and shit, but the Americans had gotten the intel they needed, and they would apologize for the trouble and the mess.

Mary Pat had moved heaven and earth to make this happen. The moment Clark had called her after the shoot-out with the Chinese, she'd contacted her counterparts at Romanian intelligence and asked them to look into Dalca immediately. She claimed she had proof he was behind the intelligence leaks in the US that had become the biggest story in the world in the last few weeks, and she needed to know everything about the man in minutes, not hours.

She got a call back in under an hour. Dalca's name had shown up in a database as having visited a prisoner in Jilava just that day, and Romanian intel officers knew the prisoner well. They told Mary Pat she could send someone over to interview the prisoner at her convenience, perhaps early the following week.

Mary Pat replied she could have someone ready to interview him ten minutes after she hung up the phone.

This was at two a.m.

Romanian intelligence agents, knowing just how fucked-up their world would be if it turned out the attacks in America had anything to do with a former colleague of theirs and they did *not* make him immediately available to the Americans, went personally to Jilava to cut through any red tape involving the local Bureau of Prisons. Prison officials were rousted out of bed, and at first they tried to send the agents away empty-handed, guards even fingered their guns at one point, but cooler heads prevailed, and promises were made to have Gabor returned before sunup.

No one asked the Americans if they'd had anything to do with the gunfire outside Dalca's apartment earlier in the evening, or the death of three police officers alongside a half-dozen mysterious Asian men in a nearby park.

The answer to this question was clear, but America's involvement in this international incident would be covered up by a Romanian government desperate to not publicize the fact one or more of its citizens had been involved with ISIS attacks in the US.

After Chavez got what he needed out of Luca Gabor, the shot-up white Renault delivered Gabor back to Romanian intelligence, and they left the body of Dragomir Vasilescu in the shallow grave, one more item for the Romanian government to quickly and quietly forget about for its own good.

63

Dominic and Adara entered the Drake Tower, a thirty-floor co-op on Lake Shore next to the Drake hotel, by means of Caruso waving his creds at uniformed police officers on Lake Shore, which had now been closed off. He showed them again, to another officer, standing at the door to the co-op, and Dom could tell from the face of the lone CPD officer that he was well aware he was standing there, basically alone, guarding a door adjacent to an active terror incident.

The cop wasn't happy about it, but he was doing his job.

Once inside the building the two Campus operatives took an elevator down to a lower level, and here they followed the plans on Adara's phone until they found a narrow stairwell. They descended as low as it would go, and this led them to a locked door. Caruso pulled his lock-pick set out of his bag and had the door open in under one minute, then both of them drew their pistols and entered a dark hallway lined with rusty pipes. Dom clicked on his tactical flashlight, and switched to the red filter, because it was harder to detect at a distance, even though it didn't appear anyone had made it down here from the Drake.

This was no drainage pipe, as it appeared to be on the schematic. It looked and smelled like this concrete hallway had flooded recently and it was filthy and disused, but at the moment it was completely dry.

They made a turn and found a set of concrete steps, at the

top of which was another locked door. Adara held the light while Dom knelt and picked the lock.

Adara whispered, 'What other skills do you have that I don't know about?'

Dom said, 'You won't be impressed for much longer. Once Clark gets you back into training, you'll probably be better at this than me.'

The lock clicked and Dom looked up at her. 'But for now, I'm still cool.'

He opened the door carefully and peered in.

When he saw nothing but black, he used his red light again.

A storeroom full of cases of alcohol was as dark as the hallway behind him. He and Adara moved forward to another door, then cracked it open.

Here they were met by blinding light. It was the kitchen of the Coq d'Or, a famous and venerable restaurant on the ground floor of the hotel, directly below the lobby. Adara followed the plans on her phone and realized the elevators were not far from the exit to the bar, but an additional employee-only staircase was just to the right in the hallway below the lobby.

They moved through the dark and empty restaurant, their weapons in front of them, and they could see evidence people had left in a hurry. Drinks on the bar and on the tables still had ice cubes in them, and chairs and barstools were knocked over. There didn't seem to be any victims down here, but it was clear how chaotic it must have been for the patrons when the volleys of gunfire and explosions kicked off in the lobby, right above their heads.

Dom moved carefully into the downstairs hallway, looked to his left, and saw the exit to the hotel. Police had moved back away from the door, but he could see two teams of CPD SWAT officers crouched behind ballistic shields across the street, and using the partial cover of armored trucks that had been moved there.

Adara came out behind Dom and spun right, her gun in her hands in front of her. She found the employee stairs and entered, and Dom moved behind her. They controlled the door so no one in the stairwell could hear it close, and they listened for movement above. There was a slight shuffling. They knelt together while Dom held his weapon up on the stairs, and whispered into Adara's ear. 'There could be civilians trapped all over the place, so make sure of your targets.'

She nodded, pushed back over her ear a wisp of hair that had worked its way out of her ponytail, and began leading the way up. Dom took her by the arm and passed in front of her.

On the landing of the main floor, they found three female hotel clerks crouched in hiding. One of the women sobbed loudly when she saw Dom and Adara with their guns coming up the stairs, but she grabbed her own mouth to stifle a scream. Dom moved up to them and knelt back down, while Adara covered up the stairs.

'You guys came from the lobby?'

'Yes, we were at the counter when it started.'

'How many bad guys?'

They looked between each other. Finally one said, 'We never saw any bad guys. No one but police and guests. There was shooting and explosions. I saw people die. One of the police officers I had just been talking to dropped in front of the counter, I think he's dead.'

She began crying.

Dom showed the women Adara's schematic of the lobby

on her phone and asked them to tell him where they were. According to the women, the other side of the door in front of them led to a back office behind the counter, and no one in the lobby would see them if he went in there.

Dom said, 'Okay, good. Listen, it's clear down these stairs out the front door. Does anybody have a cell phone?'

One of the women said, 'Our phones are at the counter.'

Dom was worried about the women running out onto East Walton with a hundred police with rifles pointing at the door, but he didn't have time to call ahead for them to warn Jeffcoat they were coming out. He said, 'Go into the kitchen of the bar, through the liquor closet, and down the stairs. The long dark hallway leads next door and you'll be safe over there.' He pulled a flashlight out of his backpack and handed it to her.

'Are you . . . are you sure?'

Dom nodded, squeezed Adara on the shoulder, and said, 'I need to see what's going on in the lobby. I want you right here doing what you're doing, covering this stairwell.'

She nodded. 'Be careful.'

Dom slipped into the office, staying low with his pistol in front of him. The door to the lobby was propped open, so he went wide of it and looked out into the large space.

He saw a few bodies on the floor, but looking across into the Palm Court, he could see two men holding Uzis on a group of guests cowering there. Another man was moving several roll-aboard suitcases around the group, and then playing wire out from a backpack. Men and women, mostly over the age of fifty, were seated in chairs and on the floor, and Dom saw panic in many faces, even across the length of the lobby, as the terrorist carefully attached wiring to something inside one of the cases.

Dom was certain the terrorists were prepping a massive bomb, big enough to collapse the higher floors of the building and kill virtually everyone inside.

Looking around, he was surprised he didn't see anyone else in the lobby. Even the stairs down to the main level and the exit appeared to be unprotected by al-Matari's cell members.

Dom took pictures with his camera, zooming in on the Palm Court and what he assumed to be three cases full of explosives, and then he backed into the office. Quickly he texted them to Jeffcoat, then he called him.

Jeffcoat answered, 'You are in the *fucking* lobby?'

Dom whispered, 'Listen to me carefully. I count only three tangos down here, covering two dozen hostages. They are rigging a massive daisy-chain explosive of some kind. In a couple of minutes this whole rig could go up, or they could set it on a dead man's switch and we won't be able to save these people. SWAT needs to breach *now*. I can engage them from here till they come through the front. It's a straight shot to the left for them after that. All the lobby threats are in one place, but you have to act *right* now.'

'We can't! We are missing SWAT officers up on the fifth floor. Al-Matari and Hembrick have them.'

'How do you know that?'

'Because he called and told us! We sent eighteen men up there. Only five retreated down with some FBI agents, and their body cams show at least seven dead in the hallways. There's some dead and missing FBI up there as well.'

Dom thought it over quickly. 'Okay. Here's what you'll have to do. I've got access to employee stairs. I'll go to the fifth floor with my colleague, take down al-Matari and Hembrick, and whoever the hell else is there, and you guys get to the lobby and end the threat here.'

'I don't have the power to make that happen, Caruso.'

Dom thought for a moment. 'Well, notify Russell of my plan. I'm about to start shooting bad guys on the fifth floor. Either SWAT comes through the front and stops these three tangos from setting off that bomb or they don't.'

'No!' Jeffcoat shouted. 'You *will* stand down and get the fuck out –'

'Three minutes and the shooting starts.'

'Wait!'

Caruso hung up the phone. He didn't have a lot of love for his plan, but he saw the consequences of inaction in the next couple of minutes to be even more dangerous than what he and Adara were about to attempt.

64

Back in the stairwell Dom was glad to see that the three women from the counter had left. He began moving up the stairs, covering high, and Adara moved up beside him. He whispered into her ear as he ascended.

'We have less than three minutes to engage on the fifth floor. Unknown number of shooters. They think al-Matari is there with Hembrick, along with hostages.'

Adara nodded and the two of them increased their rate of climb.

On the door out to the fifth floor they paused. Dom brought a hand up and with his fingers he reminded Adara the room number was five-one-four. They opened the door and spun out into the hall, Dom to the left and Adara to the right. In front of them they saw the devastation of the suicide bombing, as well as the explosion that took place at the far end of the hall at the stairwell there. Olive-clad men with black body armor lay all over the place, blood and body parts were strewn on the blue and gold carpet, and the walls were ripped, burned, and bloody.

There were dead men and women in plainclothes as well, and Dom suspected some, perhaps all, were FBI.

But there was no one moving in sight.

Dom led the way to room 514, passing bodies along the way. Each body he saw had a gunshot wound to the head, indicating someone had made sure there were no wounded left out here in the hall.

He saw the door to 514 was propped open before he got there. Adara was just feet behind him, and she noticed 515 also had its door open.

Dom arrived first, spun right in front of the door, and saw a single black man on his knees behind the bed, a submachine gun in his hand. He'd obviously not heard anyone coming up the hallway, and he snapped his gun up in surprise at the movement.

Adara spun left, and she saw two men there, both armed and barricaded behind a desk and a bed, on opposite sides of the room. To their right on the floor were several SWAT officers facedown, with their hands cuffed behind their backs.

The two Campus operators engaged their targets simultaneously.

Dom shot David Hembrick through the forehead before the terrorist managed to fire a single round. He then spun to help Adara when he heard her shooting, and he dropped to his knees and leaned right to try to get a line of sight around her.

Adara fired over and over again, hitting the man behind the desk in the shoulder and hip. He dropped his weapon and fell, so she spun to the second shooter, crouched behind the bed.

Before she could fire she lurched back and fell, tumbling backward over Dom and down to the carpet.

Adara had taken a bullet through her thigh, but as she went down, she continued pumping rounds at the barricaded man's position.

She landed on her back as Dom began engaging the man behind the bed, but as Adara looked forward, she could see under the bed, and she realized she had eyes on the man's knee, shin, and foot.

As pain jolted up from her thigh wound she fought through it, aimed under the bed at thirty feet, and shot the man straight through the kneecap.

Her target lowered behind the bed, stopped firing, and screamed.

Adara saw her pistol locked open, meaning she'd fired eleven rounds at the two targets.

'He's wounded!' she shouted to Dom.

Caruso rose to his feet, raced into the room, leaping onto the bed. He emptied his magazine straight down into the wounded man's back.

Quickly he snatched the Uzi that had fallen on top of the bed when the man went down; then he leapt from the bed and ran back to Adara. She had already begun applying direct pressure on her bloody thigh.

'I'm fine! Secure the scene!' she shouted, knowing that his first thought would be to take care of her.

Dom began checking bathrooms and blind corners, worrying about Adara and hoping like hell everything had gone according to plan downstairs.

Thomas Russell stood at the back of one of the JTTF mobile command centers, listening to the sounds of gunfire just a block away, while simultaneously listening to the SWAT transmissions coming through speakers around him.

There had been ten seconds of sustained shooting, emanating both from the broken windows on the fifth floor of the Drake and from the SWAT team engaging in the lobby. The sounds echoed around the high buildings on all sides of him.

Then the shooting stopped, and a transmission came over the speakers.

'This is Delta One. All targets in the lobby down. Explosives are secure. Moving up to begin room clearing. We'll need CPD blue units to assist with hostage evac.'

The SWAT team commander stood near Russell, and he replied, 'Copy all, send the hostages out the front with their hands up and we'll start moving patrol officers in to frisk them. Get to the fifth floor and assist FBI assets there. Find our men and confirm you have al-Matari's body.'

As the order was acknowledged, Russell's mobile phone vibrated on his hip. He rejected the call, then spent a minute more listening in to police transmissions at the Drake. It sounded like everything was under control, and Russell decided to head over to the Drake himself. He went out onto the portable steps in front of the command center, where his phone buzzed again. This time he snatched it and answered it quickly.

'Yeah?'

It was the same voice he'd heard before on the line in the JTTF command center. 'Did you really think it would be that easy?'

Shit. It was al-Matari. 'Where the hell are you? Your men are dead and your bomb is defused.'

'The bomb was a distraction, nothing more. I doubted my mujahideen would even get as far as they did.'

Russell did not understand. Before he could say anything, Special Agent Jeffcoat met him on the back steps of the command center and said, 'Fifth floor secure. Al-Matari is not, repeat, not there.'

Russell spoke into the phone slowly. 'What do you want?'

'Director Russell . . . what I want is simple. I want a war. My side and your side. We've had skirmishes for weeks, but tonight was the first major battle, and you have lost.'

'You might have slipped out, but you have won nothing.'

'Haven't I? A question for you. Right now, where are all the cameras pointed in America? Where is the attention, and where are over one hundred US government soldiers and spies, infidel enemies of the caliphate?'

A wave of terror washed over Thomas Russell's body, because he understood almost instantly. His eyes rose to the rooftops around him.

At the top of his lungs he screamed, 'Incoming!'

Before anyone, Russell included, could move, sounds of broken glass came over the heavy sustained din of the JTTF command center. And before anyone could identify the source of the noise, flashes of rockets erupted from the windows high in four tall buildings on the south side of East Delaware, and smoke trails streaked down, all converging on the two trailers and the men and women around them.

Algiers and Tripoli had removed panes of glass in their room at the Raffaello Hotel the moment it was confirmed where the mobile command post would deploy in the neighborhood. With their ninth-floor view of East Delaware, they merely had to fire their AT4 launchers down and to their right.

Musa al-Matari himself and Omar, the Detroit cell leader, stood in separate rooms of an unoccupied condominium on the eighth floor of a residential building two doors east of the Raffaello. They had to smash out sections of glass with hammers brought along for the job, then simply heft and point their AT4s down and to the left, a simple shot for both men, even though neither had ever fired the American portable antitank weapon.

Al-Matari and the two North Africans had debated for a

574

day about where they needed to position themselves for the least amount of movement before the main thrust of the evening's attack. They'd reserved and checked into two other hotels within three blocks of here, and had been prepared to move to any number of different buildings, although they knew the JTTF had a limited number of options, and this made al-Matari and his men's jobs easier.

They all agreed the mobile command center wouldn't park on Lake Shore Drive or Michigan Avenue, as both of these streets were too congested to close off without additional chaos to an already chaotic scene. They decided East Delaware would therefore be the most likely choice.

The four men had waited as late in the JTTF operation to retake the Drake as possible, allowing more time for any JTTF officials in the area to arrive on scene, and for more law enforcement to be occupied at or around the Drake, so al-Matari and his men could escape.

And their patience had paid dividends.

When the scene was secure at the Drake and al-Matari made the call to Russell, the four men launched their weapons near simultaneously, sending four eighty-four-millimeter high-explosive dual-purpose rockets down into the JTTF command post below.

After the four launches, the men tossed their spent tubes onto the floors of their respective rooms, then hefted RPG-7 launchers. They fired a second salvo closer to the police vehicles on the perimeter of the command center, creating four smaller explosions than the AT4s, but killing many of those who would have soon been on the way looking for them, keeping other first responders pinned down and terrified, and adding to the real estate of the chaotic scene.

*

Twenty seconds after Director Russell screamed his futile warning, thirty-seven top members of the Chicago JTTF were dead or dying, Russell and Jeffcoat included. Other top local officials from FBI, CIA, DIA, ICE, and Secret Service, along with thirteen CPD officers, were among the dead. Another seventy-one in total, including police and civilians in the surrounding buildings, were wounded, many by falling debris.

After the explosions on East Delaware, confusion on the fifth floor of the Drake hotel reigned for minutes, as the SWAT men called into their radios, but could not get clear answers on whether they should hold or come back down. Transmissions crackled over one another and it seemed as if one hundred sirens wailed outside.

Dom and Adara had worked together to bandage her leg. She fought the pain and the nausea, and he got her up to her feet with her arm around his neck. He then tried to call Jeffcoat back, but the call rolled into voice mail.

The five surviving SWAT officers were unbound and the bodies of their fallen brethren were reluctantly left right where they lay for the investigators, then everyone began moving down the stairs slowly. Dom helped Adara along, still unaware of what had happened outside, but sure as hell certain he needed to get his girlfriend to the hospital.

Other SWAT units and regular police were clearing the other floors, civilians came down from above, and law enforcement, along with other first responders, tried to go up, and it became a chaotic logjam in the stairwell, principally because, for some reason, there didn't seem to be anyone coordinating *anything* from the top down.

*

The four terrorists left their rocket launchers in their rooms and descended quickly. They wore suits and ties and they carried only their Glock pistols under their coats, sacrificing firepower but fitting in with shocked civilians out in the streets.

There was no getaway vehicle close by for the men. By design the four ran and walked individually down streets and back alleys to the south, and hailed taxis seven to ten blocks away.

As al-Matari sat in the back of his taxi twenty minutes after the attack, he thanked Allah for his victory, then thought of the smug Saudi who had conceived the plan to attack in America using special intelligence to target military, espionage, and counterterrorism officials. Yes, his mysterious benefactor had passed on the intelligence about Thomas Russell of the JTTF in Chicago, and this was how the Yemeni had gotten the original idea for the attack as well as the man's phone number. He then spoofed the landline inside room 514 of the Drake with a simple piece of software to solidify to Russell that al-Matari was, indeed, there inside the Drake.

But the rest of this mission al-Matari had planned on his own. He'd done the research of JTTF operations here, he'd watched videos of their mobile command posts outside Soldier Field during their mock exercise weeks ago, and he'd come up with the plan for the ruse to get JTTF deployed to lure the area's top men and women into one small place at the same time, so he could ambush them.

He'd lost ten of his remaining Language School members in this glorious attack, and the loss of life at the Drake ultimately wouldn't be what he'd hoped, but at the moment he was not concerned about this at all. The Islamic State

Foreign Intelligence Bureau would send him a hundred new recruits from abroad, and he'd get a thousand more local self-radicalized recruits here in the US after the video he made of the attack from his mounted phone was cleaned up and distributed by the Global Islamic Media Front.

And more important than anything else, there would be no way President Jack Ryan could avoid a full military deployment to combat the powerful force that had made Middle America look so unsafe, and made this nation of infidels look so impotent.

Al-Matari did not return to the Chicago safe house on North Winchester, nor did the other three men. No, they each took their own cab to the same bar in Pilsen, and then, when their drivers had gone, they walked into the bar, out through the rear exit, and climbed into two vehicles parked there.

Each vehicle contained four Uzis, one thousand rounds of ammunition, and two shoulder-fired surface-to-air missiles.

They were out of the city by two a.m. Chicago had been a success, but Chicago was behind them now.

Now it was time for all four men to converge on Washington, DC, where more infidel victims awaited them.

65

The President of the United States stood in front of a roomful of reporters, like a target in a shooting gallery. It was nine a.m. on a Sunday, all the news shows were covering this live, and the twenty-four-hour networks would run a simultaneous feed of the carnage in Chicago on one half of the screen while the President spoke on the other half.

Ryan started with prepared remarks. He'd long ago banned the use of the cliché 'shocked and saddened' by his speechwriters, but since he'd written the majority of today's opening statement, he'd realized how hard it was to avoid the phrase.

After an expression of grief and horror, and a promise the government would not rest until the attacks in the United States by Abu Musa al-Matari stopped, he opened the floor for questions.

A reporter for CBS raised her hand. When Ryan called on her she said, 'In light of the Islamic State's ability to bring the war to America, do you plan to put boots on the ground in Iraq and Syria to take the war back to them?'

'Shelly, as you know, we have boots on the ground in Iraq and Syria. Special mission units are over there, as well as aircraft of all shapes and sizes and the support elements for them. We are partnering with our coalition, and our strategy is working. The geographical footprint of the Islamic State in the region is shrinking, as is their total number of fighters.

'But as they lose ground, they must gain headlines.

Headlines are far easier to achieve than battlefield victories. The ISIS operatives in America at the moment are few in number, but their effect is well out of proportion to their physical strength. If they are not seen as dangerous and powerful, ISIS will stop pulling in fresh meat, new cannon fodder, and it will not survive as anything other than a bad idea.

'Look at what we've done in the past three years. We've killed and captured top Islamic State leadership. We've committed offensive airpower, and special operations troops, CIA, DIA, and other intel agencies are on the ground there. We've encouraged our NATO partners to be more engaged in that region.

'We've funded some of the Kurdistan militias and the Iraqi Security Force, trained them up, given them state-of-the-art communications equipment.

'We are winning the land war against the Islamic State *without* putting a brigade of Marines in Baghdad and sending them west into ISIS-held territory. This strategy is working better than any other plan out there, and the reason it is working over there is *exactly* the reason they are attacking over here.

'Last night's attack is part of a trap they are trying to lay for us, to get us to move in numbers to their home turf. But we aren't falling for it.'

Shelly followed up. 'So, again, no new call to increase military operations in the Middle East?'

Ryan looked at the woman for a moment. 'Shelly, you and your network have come out against literally every military act I have ever ordered in my time as President. You've been against every CIA initiative that came to light when I ran the CIA. Suddenly it seems as if you are a proponent of a massive land war in the Middle East.'

Shelly did not reply.

'No . . . we will not give them their land war. We will fight them with both resistance and resilience.'

He next called on a reporter for CNN, a woman he knew hated him and everything he stood for. She'd made a name for herself subtly and not so subtly editorializing under the guise of straight news, and all her opinions ran counter to Ryan's policies. 'What do you say to those who simply suggest they hate us for what we do to them? That the very nature of our attacks on them have caused them to finally come over here as a way to defend themselves? As you know, they have been carefully selecting military and intelligence targets. Targets which, you would agree, America itself considers fair game in war. How do you reply to those who say simply that if we just left them alone, *they* would leave *us* alone?'

Ryan said, 'Juliet, you are with CNN, you have spent years working international postings, am I right about that?'

'Many years, Mr President, primarily in the Middle East, which is why my experience in the region indicates to me that –'

'Sorry. You asked me to respond to "those who say." Are you now saying *you* are the one saying that we should leave ISIS alone so we can enjoy peace?'

Undeterred, Juliet Robbins shook her head and answered quickly. 'I'm asking the question, Mr President. Certainly you are aware of the criticism.'

'Of course I am.' He could hear cameras clicking as he organized his thoughts. 'In all your travels over the world, Juliet, have you ever met a group of people who were completely pacifist?'

'I have, Mr President. The Buddhists, for example, and

with all due respect I don't see the Islamic State blowing up hotels and city streets in Nepal.' Ryan could see her sense of superiority with her answer, and her chin rose slightly. If she had been holding a microphone, Ryan imagined she would have dropped it and walked out of the room.

Ryan nodded. 'You're right about that, but that has a lot to do with geographical separation, the secluded nature of Nepal, and the lack of live television cameras.'

'Your opinion, Mr President. My opinion, and that of many learned academics, is that the Buddhists aren't attacked like we are because they don't meddle in other people's affairs like we do.'

Ryan smiled. 'Have you ever heard of the Yazidis?'

Now Juliet Robbins blinked hard. Ryan could see the wheels spinning in her brain as her face changed expression. 'Of course, and I am not –'

'You talked, Juliet. You talked at length to set up your question, to establish your authority, and to make your opinions known. Now you will allow me to answer. Yes, the Yazidis are much like the Buddhists, aren't they, in that they don't have much, if any, real physical defense from the outside world? A passive community. I wonder why you didn't think to mention them in a discussion of the Islamic State. After all, you are an expert, as you mentioned, on the region from which the Yazidis come. Are you also an expert on Nepal?'

'No, Mr President, but your question –'

'*Your* question, Juliet, was, Why don't we just leave the Islamic State alone so they will treat us better? Well, I'll answer you by talking about the Yazidis. They lived on Sinjar Mountain, in a Kurdish-held area, and they've been there for hundreds of years, not bothering anyone. Even when the

Islamic State moved into that territory four years ago, the Yazidis continued to stay for the most part on their mountain, though they were all but unarmed, all but unprotected.

'And then ISIS came up the mountain to root them out. The Yazidis were slaughtered, burned alive, killed ritualistically, sold into slavery. And this increased the flood of membership into the Islamic State. People all over the world joined ISIS when they saw what they did to the Yazidis, as well as others. So the group you think will behave with kindness if only met with kindness is, obviously, a death cult. Nothing more.'

Juliet Robbins started to speak again, but Ryan talked over her.

'So two questions for you, Juliet, and for all of those who agreed with her long preamble about turning the other cheek and simply allowing this scum to increase in size and scope. Do you think the United States of America, with friends and allies in the Middle East, with necessary business to do in the Middle East, should simply lay down all our guns and become pacifist like the Yazidis? And, if so, why do you think the Islamic State would treat us any better?

'I am not here to disrespect anyone's religion. I am here to do my best to protect America and its allies, and if perversions of one particular religion endanger the men, women, children, and ideals I've sworn an oath to protect, then I will use every tool in my toolbox as President of the United States to defeat those responsible, and the ideas that give them strength and perpetuate their evil cause.

'I don't believe, as you clearly do, in appeasing them. I agree with Winston Churchill, who said an appeaser is one who feeds a crocodile, hoping it will eat him last.

'If you want to say we could all be as gentle as a Buddhist to earn a repayment in kindness from those who slaughtered thousands of perfectly gentle Yazidis, then your credibility on the matter is called into question. I will go elsewhere for my advice. I'm sorry, Juliet, you have a worldview that is probably very well-meaning, and surely accurate on many issues, but on this . . . I'm going to think about the Yazidis I have met, and I'm going to think about all the Yazidis I was unable to meet, and I will use them to decide if pacifism is a reasonable response to terror.'

As Juliet Robbins tried to compose a suitable retort, Ryan looked elsewhere in the room. 'Next question?'

After the press conference Ryan returned to the Oval to find Arnie Van Damm waiting for him. Ryan just said, 'I know, Arnie. I was too hard on Robbins.'

Arnie said, 'Screw it, Jack. Glad you gave her hell.'

Ryan said, 'I'm glad you're glad, but if I lose you as the good angel on my shoulder, then I'm in trouble.'

Arnie said, 'We've both been up here too long. I wanted to resign on the spot, grab the mic from you, then tell Juliet she could fly to Raqqa and try turning the other cheek herself.'

Jack Ryan gave half a smile, his first laugh in days. 'You are irreplaceable, but it would almost be worth it just to get a front-row seat to watch that.'

Arnie said, 'You and me, two old guys talking about what we *would* do if given half a chance.'

'Right,' Ryan said. 'Better we focus our time on what we *can* do to make a difference around here.'

66

Alex Dalca sat in the Jeep at the far end of the tarmac in the airport in Craiova, and he watched the Gulfstream land. He was surprised the Albanians had such a nice airplane, and it gave him hope his temporary conditions in Macedonia wouldn't be so bad.

It was afternoon, but the airport wasn't busy. He'd been here an hour and he'd seen only one turboprop domestic commercial flight and a couple smaller cargo jets from other European countries in all that time.

He imagined this luxury jet was orders of magnitude more posh than the average aircraft to land at this back-water airfield.

He climbed out of his vehicle, hefted the backpack onto his shoulder, and walked straight between the two outbuildings, directly up to the runway, as instructed by his Albanian contact that morning. In light of last night's attack by the Chinese, he'd had to cancel meeting Luca Gabor at the prison and call his daughter instead, and he had some concerns Gabor would demand more money for the change in plans. But apparently the man was happy enough to be robbing him for the three million, and just relayed a phone number to call through to the girl.

According to what he'd learned on the phone from the Albanian, it was just as Gabor had promised. They ran a casino in Skopje behind the scenes, and they agreed they could use Dalca to harvest information on guests, either while they were on the premises gambling or before they came to the hotel. The Albanians would use the information to know how much money the guests had, and any valuables, vices, or other tidbits of information that would give the house even greater odds.

Dalca imagined nobody got out of that casino with money, and if they did, they stood odds of getting waylaid and robbed on the street massively disproportionate with crime statistics in the capital.

The Albanians were a tough bunch, it was obvious from the phone call, and Alexandru Dalca would be their newest secret weapon. He figured the work would be easy, and they would pay him fairly. And on top of that he'd be safe, because there were, easily, fifty armed security in the casino at all times.

Just as promised, the plane turned at the end of the runway, then taxied back in his direction. Three minutes later, it stopped, and the air stairs opened. A swarthy-looking short, stocky man in his forties with black hair flecked with gray stood in the doorway, and beckoned him forward.

The man held a bottle of champagne and two flutes.

Dalca smiled. 'Nice.' He was feeling better by the minute.

Alexandru Dalca climbed the stairs into the Hendley Associates G550 with a satisfied smirk on his face, and as he entered the cabin he reached out to shake the hand of the man he presumed to be Albanian.

He spoke slowly and clearly. 'Hello. Do you speak English?'

Ding Chavez took his handshake and clamped down. ''Bout as good as any other East L.A. Chicano, *ese.*'

'I'm sorry?'

Dalca turned now, and he saw three more men in the cabin. One was older and heavy, but he sat in the back. The two men in cabin chairs feet away were bearded, muscular, closer to his age, and armed with handguns.

'Wait. Who are you?'

Chavez put the champagne and glasses in the galley, and then he spun Dalca to his knees, pushed him facedown into the aisle between the armed men.

Behind him, Country came out of the cockpit. 'All cargo loaded?'

Chavez said, 'Loaded. Time to make a trash run.'

Ding handed off the backpack to Jack, who immediately started going through it. As soon as he pulled the black hard drive out of the bag, he waved it at the stunned man with Chavez's knee in the back of his neck.

'What's this?' Jack asked.

With as much insolence as he could muster, Dalca said, 'What does it look like?'

'It looks like something that will get you killed, if your smart mouth doesn't do it first.'

Jack nodded to Country, who immediately closed the hatch and returned to the cockpit.

Chavez frisked the man carefully, zip-tied his arms behind his back, and then blindfolded him tightly and securely. He yanked Dalca into a seat, and then sat down in front of him. 'The good news is, we aren't the Chinese. The bad news is, you didn't fuck over the Chinese as badly as you did the Americans.'

'I don't know what you're talking about.'

'I can help. The US government has had a nice conversation with the ambassador to Macedonia, who grounded the flight that was on its way here to pick you up. On top of that, two of the guys on *that* plane – and I hear it wasn't half as nice a plane as this – had some outstanding warrants, so your Albanian buddies are almost, but not quite, as fucked as you are.'

The Gulfstream took off and began heading to the west. It would be eight hours in the air till DC, which meant to the men of The Campus that they had eight hours to get every last bit of intel out of the bewildered but still smug man tied in the cabin.

The men converged in the back of the plane, leaving Dalca tied in a cabin chair, and they talked about their strategy to get information from him.

They had their man, and they should have all been happy right now, but they'd learned about the attack in Chicago just hours before, so none of them were anything of the sort. Dom himself had called the plane when they were taking off from Bucharest and told them Adara had been shot, but doctors said she'd make a full recovery.

All four of them tried to shake the tragedy in Chicago out of their minds so they could begin the work of extracting information from the man who was, in large part, responsible.

Midas just jerked a thumb at Dalca. 'All this stuff this asshole is responsible for, and he's off by himself. His escape plan was a rope ladder, a bike, and some Albanian dudes in Macedonia he didn't even know. *That's* his nod to PERSEC. No bodyguards, no well-paid goons to shadow him. No affiliation with a state actor, or a nonstate actor, for that matter. Yeah, he's got the deal with the Albanians, but he just worked that out in the past twenty-four hours.'

Chavez asked, 'What are you thinking?'

'Dunno, chief. Like maybe we're missing a piece to the

puzzle. Like there is more to this whole thing than we understand.'

Chavez turned to Jack. 'What do you think?'

'I think this guy started playing in water that turned out to be too deep for him. He didn't think anything could be traced back to him, so he went for the cash.'

Midas next said, 'The question is, how do we get him to talk?'

Chavez answered, 'He obviously doesn't care about others. Let's see if he cares about himself.'

Jack moved up and sat in front of Dalca, Ding and Midas moved nearby, and Gavin remained at the back of the aircraft, working to get into Dalca's laptop computer. The hard drive sat next to it, already attached to a clean computer that Gavin had brought along for just that purpose.

Jack said, 'Time for you to tell us what you know.'

The Romanian replied, 'I want a martini.'

Jack blinked in surprise. 'And I want to shoot you in the face.'

The corners of Dalca's mouth turned upward, disappearing under his blindfold. 'But you can't, can you?'

Jack did not reply.

Dalca added, 'Very dry, up, with a twist.'

Jack thought about the people who had died because of this man. Jennifer Kincaid, a woman he'd never met, but whose husband had sat in the very chair in which Dalca now sat, was at the front of his mind.

Jack said, 'Fuck you *and* your twist,' and he hit the blindfolded Romanian in the face.

Chavez looked to Midas, who was seated closer to Jack, and Midas grabbed Jack's arm right before he delivered an even harder blow.

'Slow down there, Sugar Ray,' Midas said. 'Chill out a minute. This cockbreath's not going anywhere.'

Dalca spit blood down the front of his shirt. 'You need me. I am the only one who knows which targeting folders I sent, and to whom.'

Jack nodded to Midas that he was under control. He took a deep breath and said, 'We know who you sent them to. Musa al-Matari. And we know who you worked for. The Chinese. We don't need you as much as you think. Even without you, the Chinese still have the ability to compromise US government employees, just as you did, because they have copies of the files.'

Dalca sat there without moving for several seconds. 'I am the only one with the files. ARTD got access to them accidentally, by hacking into an Indian security company that had a contract with the American company hired by the OPM to evaluate its network's susceptibility to a hack. The Indians had the data, but it was just sitting on a server, unnoticed and unexploited. When we realized what we had, we pulled it off and air-gapped it to make it safe, then began looking into it.'

Jack was astonished by this. 'You are saying that the Chinese do not have these files?'

Dalca shook his head. 'None of them.'

'Bullshit. You are lying because you think it improves your negotiating ability.'

Dalca shook his head adamantly. 'They didn't want to touch them. We aren't even working with the Chinese directly. We were hired by a front company called the Seychelles Group.'

Jack wrote the name down on a notepad, planning on researching the firm when the interrogation was finished.

To Dalca he said, 'I want a list of everyone you targeted. Everyone.'

Dalca shrugged dramatically. Finally he said, 'I'll talk. But not for free. I want some things in exchange.'

Gavin called Chavez to the back of the aircraft. 'It's going to take me days if not weeks to get past his encryption and get on his machine. If he'd give us the password, it might save a lot of lives in the meantime.'

Jack couldn't hear the conversation in the back, but he could tell by Gavin's gesticulations that he was getting nowhere with Dalca's machine. He balled his fist up again, started to raise it toward Dalca, but Midas put a gentle hand on his shoulder.

Chavez returned from the rear of the aircraft and leaned into Alex Dalca's ear. 'All right, Alex. We're ready to hear your terms.'

And with that, Jack stood up and walked to the galley. He needed a stiff drink.

67

The call was arranged by Mary Pat Foley, and sent to President Jack Ryan's private number. He knew to expect it, but not what would be discussed, so he waited nervously in his private study on the second floor of the White House living quarters.

The phone rang and he snatched it up. 'Clark?'

'Yes, Mr President, sorry to bother you.'

'Mary Pat only told me that this call wasn't about Jack Junior.'

'Correct, sir. Jack's fine. Sorry if this phone call has caused you undue concern.'

Ryan breathed a sigh of relief. 'Not a problem.'

'Right now, the Campus aircraft is flying over Western Europe with a man named Alex Dalca on board as a prisoner. He is the employee of the Romanian computer hacking concern that acquired the files off of the Office of Personnel Management's network. Dalca was hired to find American spies for the Chinese, but he freelanced and uncovered targets in the American government and military, then sold this information off to several countries and concerns, most notably ISIS.'

'Incredible. Where are the files now?'

'On board the aircraft. Dalca says there were no other copies, but we have no way of knowing if that is true.'

Ryan rubbed his eyes. This was all good news, but it had been an incredibly bad month, and it wouldn't end with this man's capture. He said, 'Excellent work, John.'

'Thanks, but I'm not calling to get a pat on the back. We need your help.'

Ryan's eyebrows furrowed, because he feared he knew where this was going. 'Whatever you do, don't say "a pardon."'

Clark sighed into the phone. 'Dalca will help us, but he wants a full pardon and twenty-five million dollars.'

'Oh, for crying out loud.'

'Yes, Mr President. It's up to you, of course, but he is guaranteeing he will reveal every other targeted person in the US and abroad. He sold off the information piecemeal to several actors, apparently.'

Ryan stared at the carpet between his feet. Paying this man off and letting him go made his stomach want to retch. But the more he thought about it, the more he recognized the situation he was in.

Clark prodded him. 'I'm sorry, Mr President, but time is very much of the essence.'

'He wants to talk to me on the phone?'

'Videoconference. He's insisting.'

'Christ. Who *is* this guy?'

'He's a piece of work, for sure, Mr President. No conscience, no code. Just a guy looking for money, trampling over whoever is in his way.'

'A sociopath,' Ryan said.

Clark said, 'I think that's a fair assumption. Anyway, Mary Pat said she could have a videoconference set up in minutes in the Situation Room with her liaison there. You just say the word.'

Ryan said, 'I'll talk to him. Thanks, John.'

'Yes, sir.'

'You know, when I stood up The Campus, I worried about that kind of power falling into the wrong hands. I still worry about it. I put the best man I could in charge in Gerry Hendley, but still . . . you never know. Have to tell you how pleased I am that you're over there, too. The organization is in good hands.'

'I appreciate that. The generation under me is very good, too, sir. I think the organization will be helpful for a long time to come.'

Ryan then blurted out a question he'd been hesitant to ask. 'Is Jack on that plane?'

A pause. 'He is, Mr President. He was instrumental in finding Dalca, *and* he was instrumental in capturing him and securing the files.'

Ryan hesitated for a moment, taking in the information and controlling his emotions. He said, 'He's better than I was at all this, isn't he?'

'Better? No, Mr President. Like you, he is very good at both ends of the intelligence spectrum, but you had quite a few highlights in your own career.'

The President smiled a little into the phone. 'One thing I had going for me was I didn't have to walk around worried people were going to recognize me because of who my dad was.'

'Drives your son crazy sometimes, you're right about that. If his dad had been a cop in Baltimore, instead of his grand-dad, he would have the same freedom of movement you enjoyed.'

Ryan said, 'I know you are up against a timeline. I'll head down to the Situation Room.'

Alexandru Dalca's cabin chair had been turned slightly so he was facing the monitor on the wall next to him. Chavez moved behind him, while Jack, Gavin, and Midas all stepped to the far rear of the aircraft on the sofa, out of view of the camera over the monitor. This way the President would see only Dalca and Chavez, but Dalca would not be able to see anything but the monitor three feet in front of him.

Chavez pulled the man's blindfold off from behind. They both sat there looking at a blank screen for a second, until Gavin adjusted some controls on the remote in his hand.

Suddenly the President's face appeared on the screen. He was sitting at the end of the conference table in the Situation Room, wearing a suit and tie; no one else was on camera.

He adjusted his glasses as he looked at the monitor in front of him. 'You're Dalca?'

'Yes, that's right,' Dalca said. He seemed unimpressed to speak with the leader of the free world. 'As I told the men who kidnapped me, for my liberty and along with a reasonable fee I will give them all the passwords to my computer, and show them who has been targeted by the various parties I sold intelligence to.'

'Well . . . I must say, you are rather up front about it, aren't you?'

'I will play fair with America, if America will only play fair with me. Time is of the essence. I imagine the terrorists are preparing their next attack even as we speak.'

The President said, 'Did you hear about Chicago?'

'Yes. It was on the radio this morning. Thomas Russell was one of the targeting packages I created. Just goes to show you how much damage can be caused by one small identity compromise. There are dozens in the wind now, and only I can stop them from turning into dozens more Chicagos.'

Ryan nodded slowly. Finally he said, 'Who is in charge on that plane?'

Of course Ryan knew Chavez would be the leader of this group, since Clark wasn't on board the aircraft. But for the theater of the moment he had to pretend like he didn't know anyone on the plane personally.

Right behind Dalca, Ding Chavez said, 'That would be me, Mr President.'

'Very well,' Ryan said. 'As your Commander in Chief, I am giving you a direct order with respect to Mr Dalca, which you, and your subordinates, *will* obey.'

'Of course, sir.'

Dalca began to smile.

'You are flying over the Atlantic Ocean right now?'

'That's correct, sir,' said Chavez.

'Good. I want you to open a hatch and throw Dalca out of the plane. Is that clear?'

It was stone-cold silent in the cabin of the Gulfstream for several seconds. Dalca himself spoke first.

'*What?* No! You need me.'

Ryan said, 'I wouldn't say *need*. Your information would be beneficial, yes, but we can live without it. I don't negotiate with terrorists.'

Chavez pushed a button to the cockpit. 'Captain?'

Captain Helen Reid answered immediately over the cabin intercom speakers. 'Can I help you?'

'We need to descend below ten thousand feet. We'll be opening the rear cargo hatch.'

There was only a slight pause. 'Roger. I'll advise when we are depressurized.'

'No!' Dalca screamed.

Almost immediately, the aircraft began to descend.

President Ryan said, 'You had no problem with death when you were facilitating the death of others. Funny that you seem white as a sheet right now.'

Dalca stammered, 'I'll . . . I'll make a deal with you.'

Ryan shrugged, as if he did not care. 'You already made an offer. My counteroffer is your immediate death. Negotiations are complete. Good-bye.' Ryan looked off camera, as if he was telling someone he was done with the feed.

Dalca screamed again. 'Wait! I'll give you everything, *and* I'll help you catch al-Matari.'

Ryan gazed back into the camera. 'How?'

'I . . . I don't know. I'll work with these men. We'll figure something out. I am in communication with someone in ISIS. Maybe it's al-Matari, maybe it's someone else who feeds al-Matari the intelligence. I'll help you. Just don't kill me. Just let me go when this is over.'

Ryan said, 'You mentioned something about twenty-five million. I don't think the taxpayers want to pay the son of a bitch responsible for the death of so many good Americans.'

'Forget about the money! I will help you in any way I can. You just order these men to take me out of the USA and let me go when we are done.'

Ryan looked at the screen for a long time. Then he said, 'Agreed.'

Chavez said, 'Thank you, Mr President.'

'If he gives you any trouble, you boys feel free to go back to my original plan. And if his attempts to help you are not successful, same thing. You have my authorization for extra-judicial termination. No one will question your motives if Dalca dies.'

'Understood, sir. If he is anything less than completely

helpful in this endeavor, he'll go for a high dive and a long swim.'

President Ryan nodded, and the transmission went dead.

In the rear of the plane, Jack Ryan, Jr, grinned from ear to ear.

Soon Chavez called to the cockpit, and the Gulfstream leveled out, and began climbing again.

Dalca was blindfolded yet again, and the Romanian recited the passwords to his computer. Once inside, Gavin entered several other passwords provided by the Romanian, to access all the targeting folders sent.

Jack spent an hour looking them over, but not until after Chavez contacted Clark and read off the names and locations of the targets. Clark would get Dan Murray to grab everyone still in jeopardy, though this would take hours, if not more than a day to happen.

When Chavez was finished with his call, Jack said he wanted to talk to everyone in the rear of the aircraft, out of Dalca's earshot.

Jack said, 'There are forty names on that list, most of them in the DC area, which makes me think al-Matari's got people in DC and they are preparing to act.'

'Sounds reasonable,' Chavez said.

'So . . . I have an idea that will give the government time to get these people out of harm's way, and give us a good shot at taking out al-Matari. It's going to be hard, but I think the risk is worth the reward.'

'Let's hear it,' Gavin said.

'We use the conduit Dalca uses to feed intel to ISIS. We prepare a fake targeting package, giving al-Matari a target that is so perfect for his needs that there is no way he won't jump right on it. We give him a short timeline, like he's got to get his cell members in the area there, *now*, *today*, to take advantage of the opportunity. That way he can't prepare any more than the minimum, and he'll have to pull hitters off of these other targets.'

Chavez cocked his head. 'Great idea. But you will need to feed him a target that you know, without a doubt, he will drop everything to go kill . . . Who are you going to use as bait?'

Jack smiled. 'The son of the President of the United States. The targeting folder will show all the evidence al-Matari needs to see that Jack Ryan, Jr, doesn't have Secret Service protection, and he's all alone at his parents' unguarded log cabin up in the Blue Ridge Mountains. I'll show everything Dalca shows in his other folders, proving that I'm staying up there for a day or two, tops. They'll have to drop what they're doing and come after me.'

Gavin just looked at Jack. 'Are you crazy?'

Jack added, 'We suspect he was in Chicago last night, so it might not be him who comes, but if we can take any of his people alive, we'll have a shot at al-Matari himself.'

Midas chimed in, 'What happens when al-Matari shows up at your cabin with fifty guys?'

'We know he doesn't have fifty guys. Plus the cabin is in a secluded, backwoods area, hard to get a busload of Arab terrorists into without drawing attention, and al-Matari will know this.'

'I don't know, Jack,' Chavez said. 'Using yourself as a lure is a little dicey.'

'Or crazy,' Gavin said.

'It's our best play.' Ryan was confident in his plan.

Jack gave Chavez the precise location of the cabin, then Chavez took the coordinates up to the cockpit to talk to Helen and Country.

He returned a few minutes later, passing a blindfolded Dalca on the way. 'Sorry, Jack. Won't work. The place you are talking about going, there is nowhere for us to land anywhere within fifty miles. Considering flight time back to DC, it will take us most of a day to get there. If we want to make sure al-Matari rushes men there ASAP, we need another location, or another target.'

Jack had been worried about that. 'The location and the target are perfect. There *is* a way to get us there quickly. We have parachutes on board.'

Chavez shook his head. 'Free-fall parachutes, and you aren't qualified.'

'I can make it work.'

Midas said, 'I'm free-fall qualified. I'll go.'

Jack shook his head. 'Sorry, Midas. Al-Matari will send his people after the President's son. I need to be there so they can get positive ID, or they might not move in and reveal themselves. I can't send someone else to do this. I've got to do it myself.'

Ding said, 'These chutes take time to learn, Jack. You don't just strap it on and leap out of a damn jet.'

'What choice do we have? Look at the pace of the attacks. Someone is going to die, today! Maybe many people. Maybe another Chicago! We have to redirect their operation. I'll survive the jump. I might not land gracefully, I might spin a little or get stuck in a tree, but that's better than landing hours away, because we don't have hours to spare.'

Chavez thought it over for a couple minutes, then went to the front of the cabin and called Clark, and they talked quietly for several minutes more. When he returned, he said, 'Green light.'

'Yes!' Jack exclaimed.

Chavez added, 'Clark is going to get some equipment together and get on the road. He'll be there too, out of sight and standing off with a long rifle. He'll spot targets for us if al-Matari's operatives hit.'

'*Us?*' Jack said.

'I'm jumping with you, to keep you alive on the way down. Dom and Adara are still in Chicago. She's recovering in the hospital, and he's with her, as well as helping what's left of the JTTF pick up the pieces, so Dom and Adara are out of this fight. You and I will be alone in the house.'

Midas smiled a little and shook his head. 'I knew it. The FNG has to babysit the asshole with the blindfold.'

'Sorry, Midas. Guard duty is beneath you, but we can't fly him back to DC with only Gavin on board.'

Gavin made a face, but said nothing. It was clear he didn't particularly *want* to fly alone in the cabin with the crazy Romanian.

Jack said, 'Okay, I'll work with Dalca to make the targeting package so we draw al-Matari to the cabin, and we'll send it ASAP. We don't have much time at all to make this happen. But if we *don't* make this happen, somebody in DC is going to get killed today.'

Chavez looked at his watch. 'We've got six hours' flying time remaining. Someone could get killed even if we do everything right.'

68

Sami bin Rashid listened to the phone ring several times, until finally al-Matari answered on the other end.

'Yes?'

'Congratulations, brother. Chicago was a crippling blow. A masterpiece.'

Al-Matari did not share the jubilance of bin Rashid. 'The President spoke at the White House today. He still refuses to put more troops in the Middle East. Even after last night. What kind of fool is he?'

'Patience. It will happen. And I think I know how to make it happen even more quickly.'

'How?'

'I am sending you another folder. This one is the best of them all. It will stick a knife right into the President's heart, and there is no doubt we will have our war after this. He will bring his armies into the quagmire, your leadership will raise a call to arms, the believers will come from all over the world, and the caliphate will grow across the land.'

Abu Musa al-Matari didn't buy into the flowery language of the Saudi. He merely said, 'I'll read what you send me.' And hung up the phone.

Fifteen minutes later he called back. His demeanor had changed completely. 'This is authentic? This is real?'

'Of course it is real, brother,' bin Rashid said. 'It is the truth. The son of Jack Ryan is alone in the woods, a lamb awaiting slaughter.'

'Incredible,' al-Matari said.

'But don't delay. As the file says, he will be in that location for less than a day. By tomorrow morning he will return to Washington, DC. You have to do this now.'

Al-Matari did not discuss operational details with the Saudi, and he was not about to change that now. He just said, 'I will see what can be done.'

But right now Musa al-Matari himself was in a car with Algiers, and just behind them Omar and Tripoli followed. They were in central Pennsylvania, and with a check of the vehicle's GPS, he saw they could be at the location in less than four hours.

He had two more operatives in DC right now, about to begin an operation within an hour, and four more en route from other areas. He could bring them all to meet him near this cabin in the Blue Ridge Mountains, and together they could attack.

If the targeting information was correct – and the Saudi had sent good information thus far – then he and nine others should have no problem assassinating the son of the President.

He gave the order to his vehicle and the vehicle behind them, and then he sent the coordinates to the Atlanta cell.

They would all go after Jack Ryan, Jr.

With a little makeup, civilian dress, and hair blown out, Carrie Ann Davenport didn't much look like the captain of an attack helicopter, and standing here in the sun at a backyard party with a drink in her hand, no one would have guessed that just a few days earlier she had been fighting on the front lines in Iraq.

She drank tonic water with lime and picked at finger food

on a table as she chatted at the party in College Park, Maryland, at the home of a former commanding officer. Though the afternoon temperature was sweltering for most Marylanders, Carrie Ann found it pleasant. At the moment she wore a skirt with a sleeveless blouse, a far cry from the flight helmet, body armor, aircrew battle dress uniform, boots, and gloves that normally kept her roasting in the heat of Iraq.

She forced herself to focus on the now and not on the fact that in exactly one week she'd be wheels-up again, heading back toward the war zone.

Around her at the party were mostly Apache and Chinook pilots, both present and former. She'd served with many of them on deployments, and trained with many others stateside. A couple of senior officers here at the party worked at the Pentagon, as did her former commanding officer, who was now a lieutenant colonel and worked in strategic planning.

Carrie Ann was with the 2nd Battalion, 159th Aviation Regiment (Attack Reconnaissance) of the 12th Combat Aviation Brigade. She was stationed at Katterbach Kaserne Army base in Germany, which meant she was the only person here from her own unit. But she made friends easily, and was having an especially good time talking to a group of nonmilitary in the mix: a half-dozen liberal arts students from the University of Maryland, here at the lieutenant colonel's house because they rented the house next door and her former commanding officer had invited them over for drinks and food.

None of the U of M students believed her at first when she said she was an Army officer. She looked just like another coed to them. When they asked her to prove it with an ID, she instead reached down the front of her blouse and pulled out her dog tags, then spun them around to the laughs of all around her, male and female alike.

A good-looking guy about her age who said he was in grad school working on an MA in history offered to go fetch her another vodka tonic, incorrectly assuming she was drinking alcohol, but she demurred. She wouldn't mind talking to the guy some more, when there wasn't a group of his friends standing around, but instead she went by herself to the picnic table set up with beers, booze, and mixers and fixed herself another tonic and lime.

Carrie liked the fact that, right now anyway, she didn't feel much like the copilot-gunner of Pyro 1-1. She loved the Army but didn't mind stepping away from it once in a while to remind herself of her past life, her other identity. This would all change next week, when she donned her ABDUs, packed her 5.11 backpack, and headed to the airport from her parents' house in Cleveland for her flight to Germany. She'd be at Katterbach less than a day before returning to the battle zone, although she did not yet know where, exactly, she would be sent.

As she stood there alone and sipped her drink she glanced in the direction of the good-looking grad student, hoping to catch his eye, and while she did so it occurred to her that America itself had turned into something of a battle zone in the past few weeks. The same ISIS monsters she'd been fighting over there were now over here – the Chicago massacre the evening before was naturally the main topic of conversation here at the party – and every day on the news there were new stories about a soldier or intelligence officer being targeted somewhere in the country.

It pissed her off, and made her eager to go back to work,

where she might be able to have an effect on the war here at home.

She glanced up from her drink again to see the grad student looking her way, and then he smiled and began walking over, leaving his friends behind. Carrie Ann started to blush, and she hoped like hell the tan she'd picked up in Afghanistan would hide it, while she simultaneously wished like hell she had poured a double shot of gin in her tonic to calm her nerves.

Just as the guy approached he made a peculiar face. It suddenly did not look like he was interested in her at all, but almost immediately she realized he was focused on something behind her. She smiled at his expression and looked back over her shoulder.

And when she did, her own face took on a look of confusion.

An African American woman and a Middle Eastern man, both in their early twenties, walked up the driveway around to the party at the back of the house. There were African Americans and Middle Easterners all around the party, but these were the only two wearing black windbreakers that were clearly covering something attached to their bodies, and as they moved forward they separated, one going to the right along the fence at the far end of the carport, and the other breaking left along the rear of the house.

Their dead-set expressions, their dress, their movements. Instantly Carrie Ann knew something was seriously wrong.

The Middle Eastern man was just twenty-five feet away from Carrie Ann when he reached back over his head with both hands and then flung them forward. From each hand she recognized live grenades launching out, over her head

606

and toward the dozens of men and women behind her. The woman standing on the driveway did the same, and one of her grenades arced through the air in the direction of the picnic table bar and Carrie Ann's own position.

Carrie Ann Davenport turned around, took two steps toward the stunned master's student, and she tackled him across the top of the table, knocking over bottles and cans and ice and stacks of Solo cups along with them. The two rolled off and over, and had just landed on the ground, he on top of her, as the four grenades exploded all over the garden party.

Screams and yells from the wounded and the panicked, and the chants of *'Allahu Akbar'* rang above it all, and then Carrie Ann heard the gunfire. From under the picnic table she could see both the attackers moving forward, pistols in their hands, shooting at men and women scrambling away in front of them.

Carrie Ann rolled off the U of M student, hiked her white sleeveless blouse out of her skirt, and reached to the small of her back. She drew a tiny Smith & Wesson Bodyguard .380 pistol, reached over the top of the table, and aimed it at the body of the man walking toward her. She was just about to press the trigger when she recognized the man might have been wearing body armor under his big jacket, so she activated the Crimson Trace laser on the weapon and put the shaking laser dot on his forehead.

The Middle Eastern man fired at someone behind her running away, then he noticed her there, on her knees behind the table, just twenty feet in front of him.

United States Army Captain Carrie Ann Davenport shot the man through the left eye, dropping him to the ground and sending him writhing in shock and agony. She stood up and put another round in the back of his head, stilling him instantly.

A bullet cracked by her left ear and she looked up, saw the black female aiming at her, and then she saw the woman stumble to her right on the driveway and fall down on her side. She'd been shot by a party guest Carrie Ann had been introduced to earlier, a warrant officer and Chinook copilot. He held a Beretta M9 in his hand, one of the pistols given out to military personnel stateside in the last week, by order of the President, to help protect them from terrorists.

Carrie Ann looked back to the woman lying on the driveway, and saw her pistol out of reach; she also saw a small device in her right hand, hanging from a cable run under the cuff of her jacket.

Carrie Ann spun away, dove to the ground, and again tackled the good-looking grad student, who had just begun to climb to his knees. As she covered him a massive detonation erupted behind her, louder than all four grenades going off at the same time, and shrapnel ripped across the backyard. She felt the wind sucked from her lungs, the bits of debris cutting into her legs, and she heard nothing other than the ringing in her ears.

For a time, everything went still, then, over the ringing, she heard the cries and screams ring out anew.

Carrie Ann looked down at the man – she didn't even know his name – and saw he was alive but out of it, dazed and disoriented.

He looked up at her and blinked. 'Are you . . . okay?'

'I'm fine.'

She rose to her knees, felt blood on her legs, and then pulled herself up to her feet, using the picnic table to do so. There were easily twenty dead or wounded around her, and she staggered into the mass of carnage, hoping to help in some small way.

Somehow, even in the middle of this, she already knew the best way for her to help was to get back into her attack helicopter and wreak some righteous payback for what had happened here just now.

69

Tears streamed down the eyes of Dr Olivia Ryan, older daughter of the President of the United States, and she fought hard the need to sniff, because it was a sound she did not want to make at the moment. She held her hand in front of her mouth, covering a small amount of the shock and surprise on her face.

And then she nodded quickly, blinking away more tears.

For several seconds she couldn't take her eyes off the ring in the little box in front of her, and she pried them away only to look into the eyes of her boyfriend, kneeling before her.

'Yes,' she said. 'Of course I will!'

Davi stood and they kissed for a long moment, promised each other their undying love, and then she put the ring on her finger. Holding each other they turned and looked out over the rolling hills of the Blue Ridge Mountains that played out in a perfect vista behind the big log cabin: the sunset behind them lit the sky in orange and bathed the green hills below them in soft light.

Olivia squeezed Davi hard, and said, 'It's perfect. Everything . . . is . . . perfect.'

As they gazed on at the incredible view through tears of joy, both of their heads swiveled suddenly to the sight of a man in a parachute dropping through the evening air not fifty yards from the rear of the cabin.

The parachutist hit the rolling grassy pasture hard and tumbled head over feet several times, and then his rectangular canopy collapsed on top of him. He crawled up to his knees, tried to control the lines and the chute as it re-formed, and then it pulled taut and started to drag him with it.

Olivia muttered softly, 'Is this ... part ... of your proposal?'

Davi just said, 'Uhh ... I don't know *what* this is.'

A second man appeared in the sky just above the first, and he landed expertly on the struggling man's parachute, collapsing it and arresting the first man's slide across the hill below the cabin. The second pulled out of his harness, helped the man on the ground out of his own rig, and then both men noticed the two standing by the swing on the back porch of the log cabin.

Davi stared back at them. 'What on earth am I looking at?'

As one, the two men down the hillside drew submachine guns from packs harnessed to their bodies.

'Oh my God!' Olivia shouted. 'Back inside! Lock the door!'

Jack Ryan, Jr, recognized his sister as she ran off, and his blood went cold. As Chavez began collecting the chutes he said, 'She's not supposed to be here.'

Ding said, 'Get them in a car and on the road in the next five minutes!'

Jack raced up to the back porch of the cabin and pounded on the door. 'Sally? Sally? It's me! It's Jack! Open up!'

The door opened slowly, and standing in front of him with wide eyes and a baffled expression on his face was Dr Davi Kartal.

His sister's boyfriend.

'J ... Jack?'

Olivia appeared in the doorway behind Davi, saw her brother, the gun in his hand, the gear on his body. 'What the hell is going on?'

Jack looked back out to the trees in the fading light. 'What the hell are you doing here?'

Olivia said, 'Well, I'm not pulling guns on my sibling!'

'Sorry ... I didn't recognize you at first.' He looked around some more. 'Where's the team? Where is your Secret Service detail?'

'We left them in DC. It was a pain in the ass to get them to agree to it, but we wanted to be alone.' There was a note of frustration in Olivia's voice, but it was clear she was astonished that her brother and another man had just dropped from the sky. *Seriously?* You parachute? Since when do you know how to parachute?'

'It's kind of a work in progress. Listen, we have to –'

Olivia held up the ring on her finger. 'Davi just asked me to marry him. We were enjoying the moment, and then you dropped in unannounced.'

Jack took Davi by the shoulder quickly. 'Welcome to the family.'

'Yeah. Thanks.' Davi looked like he needed to sit down. Olivia just looked annoyed. She didn't know what Jack did for a living, only vaguely that he was in corporate intelligence and worked enough with the government that she wasn't supposed to ask any more questions. She was a strong-willed woman, so if she really had been interested she would have peppered Jack with queries – her mom and dad as well, for that matter – but she left it alone. She saw it as her brother trying to live up to her dad's legacy in some small way, and she totally got that part of it.

Before his sister could ask him a third time why he was

here, he said, 'I've got to get you both out of here. I don't know how much time we have. I can't really explain but something bad is about to happen, and you need to get in your car and drive off. Get to a hotel and –'

Davi said, 'My Nissan broke down coming up the mountain. It's in a shop down in Etlan. They gave us a lift up here.'

Jack realized he hadn't noticed a vehicle at the cabin as he parachuted down, but he'd been a little too worried about breaking his legs on landing to pay much attention at the time. 'Shit,' he said.

Olivia grabbed him by the shoulder harness of the chest rig full of ammunition he wore on his body. 'You are going to tell me right now what is happening!'

Jack said, 'There is no other way to say this, so I'm just going to say it. The ISIS attacks going on in America?'

Olivia cocked her head. 'What about them?'

'Well . . . I have a strong suspicion some of those terrorists are on their way here. Now.'

'You mean, here to the *cabin*?' Olivia asked, shock in her voice. 'Why on earth would they –'

Jack shrugged sheepishly. 'Because I invited them. Kind of a long story.'

Just then, Jack's radio chirped. He hadn't put his earpiece in, and he had not answered his buzzing phone in the pack on his chest, so Clark overrode the mute feature on the UHF radio strapped to his chest and his voice blasted. 'Jack, I'm in position on overwatch. How copy?'

Olivia looked at the walkie-talkie. 'Is that Uncle John? He's with you?'

Jack took the handheld unit and pressed the PTT button. 'I read you five by five.'

'Why aren't you up on comms?'

'Uhhh . . . we've got a bit of a . . . complication. My big sister is here.'

Olivia, still standing just behind Davi, pursed her lips and jerked her head toward Davi. Jack saw the expression and knew it well.

'Oh . . . along with her boyfriend . . . I mean, fiancé.'

Clark didn't skip a beat. 'Well, we'll have to toast to their future some other time. For now you need to get them the hell out of there. I've got movement on the road. Three vehicles.'

'Three?' Jack said. He'd hoped that if he made it clear in the targeting information that he would be alone, al-Matari would just send a couple of his soldiers after him. But three vehicles sounded like more than a couple soldiers.

'You have a read of the number of pax involved?'

'Negative. Too far out. But they are pulling off the road, out of my view. I think they are going to debus there and move into the woods to approach. Don't go into the woods, you need to hunker down.'

'Roger that. I'll figure out what we're doing in here.'

Chavez came through the front door now. 'Jack, three doors to this building, lots of ground-floor windows. Say a dozen access points in all. We need to bunker on the second floor and engage them in the bottleneck of the stairs.'

He saw Olivia. 'Hey, kiddo. It's been a while.' He looked to Davi. 'You Secret Service?'

Olivia answered for him. 'He's my fiancé, Davi.'

'Oh. Congratulations. Sorry to ruin your day, Jack didn't tell me this was going to turn into a family affair.'

Jack said, 'Didn't know. She left her Secret Service detail in DC.'

'Too bad,' Ding said. 'We sure as hell could have used a couple more guns.'

Jack shuffled everyone up the staircase off the main room. As he did so, Davi took his new fiancée by the hand.

'Tell me this doesn't happen every day.'

Olivia said, 'I swear it doesn't.'

Jack said, 'Davi, do you know anything about guns?'

The young doctor almost stammered his reply. 'Well . . . uh . . . I did my two years of mandatory service in Turkey. Fifteen years ago. I was a medic, but they gave us some firearms training.'

'On pistols?'

'Yeah, a little, and rifles.'

'Well, I'm not giving you my SMG, so you get my Glock 19.' He held it out for Davi.

'Is it loaded?'

'Yes, no safety, so keep your finger off the fun switch till you're ready to go bang.'

Sally and Davi stepped into the upstairs bathroom. Jack tried to get Sally to get into the tub for her protection, but she refused.

'Sal . . . that's a cast-iron tub. It's the safest place in this whole damn cabin. You *will* get in it.'

'I'm *not* sitting in a damn tub!'

'Mom and Dad will kill me if something happens to you.'

'Well, that doesn't really matter, because I'm going to kill you for screwing up Davi's proposal.'

Jack sighed, and looked to Davi. 'Dude, I'm powerless with her. It's up to you. You need to lock this door behind me, both climb into that tub, and point the gun at the door. Unless you hear me, Clark, or Ding calling your name, don't unlock it, and shoot at anything that kicks or shoots the door.'

Davi nodded; Jack saw he would play ball. He just hoped he had some ability to control his iron-willed sister.

And with that Jack headed out of the bathroom and back down the stairs.

Abu Musa al-Matari parked far enough away from the GPS coordinates programmed into his phone that he knew it would be pitch-black before he and the other teams arrived at the cabin. Including al-Matari himself, there were eight: one from the Atlanta cell and two from the Santa Clara cell, as well as Omar and one more man from Detroit, and long-time ISIS operatives Tripoli and Algiers.

The leader of the Atlanta cell and one of her team had been killed just hours earlier in DC. This left al-Matari with fewer attackers, but he felt confident in pressing on.

They all carried Uzis or AKs, as well as hand grenades, with the exception of Tripoli, who had an RPG-7, along with a Glock pistol shoved into his waistband in the small of his back.

Along the side of the road they turned on their walkie-talkies and put on headsets. They broke into four groups of two, with al-Matari taking Omar along with him.

The woods here were thick, oak and pine mostly, but each team had a phone that gave them their distance to their target pinpointed on a map. From the satellite view it showed the front and rear of the cabin had large open grassy areas, but the north and south sides both had wood lines within twenty-five meters of the walls of the large two-story building.

Al-Matari and Omar, along with the Atlanta man and the

other Detroit operative, went to the north. Algiers took a Pakistani member of Santa Clara and would approach from the southwest to get a view of the cabin. Tripoli took the other Santa Clara member, and they would come up from the woods on the south.

Algiers and a twenty-year-old engineering student from Caltech named Jamal crawled on knees and elbows alongside a hill due west in the fading light. Algiers led the way, because he had one thousand times more combat experience than the young college student who, other than three successful bomb and grenade attacks in the past week and his three weeks at the Language School, had none.

After twenty minutes of advancing, they finally had a view of the front of the property, still across a gravel road and some two hundred meters away. Algiers knew al-Matari and the second team hitting from the north would still be several minutes from their position, and the team approaching from the southeast would be so deep in the thick woods there they wouldn't have a view of the target until they were almost on top of it.

So he decided to set up here on a hill to lead the rest of the teams to the target and provide covering fire if necessary. He peered carefully through binoculars, noticed lights inside the building, but he also noticed something else. 'There is no vehicle. How can someone get here without a car?'

Just then, the front door opened, and a man stepped out with a beer in his hand. He walked along a wooden porch, looking casually out at the wooded hills to the west.

Algiers held his radio to his mouth. 'Yes. It's him. I see him. It's the President's son. Drinking a beer on the front porch. He is not alerted at all.'

Al-Matari replied quickly. 'Can you shoot him from there?'

'Possibly. I . . . have an AK, and I might hit him. But there is no optic on my weapon. If I miss he will flee inside and it will be harder for us to take him by surprise.'

'Wait, then,' al-Matari said. If the American was sitting around with a beer, then they should have no problem getting closer. 'Do you see anyone else?'

'No one. There isn't even a car in the driveway.'

'All other teams keep moving closer.'

70

John Clark *really* wished he could understand the voices on the scanner. He could hear the garbled transmissions of the terrorists through an earpiece in his right ear that searched and locked onto active UHF transmissions nearby. Several of the dead al-Matari men and women in the past weeks had been found with simple walkie-talkies on their bodies, so Clark had brought along the device to capture any comms. Some of the dead so far had been Americans, so he thought there was a good chance they would speak English over their radios.

But not this group, they were speaking quickly, and in various Arabic dialects, and he couldn't understand a damn thing they were saying.

Even so, Clark touched the PTT button on the cord hanging from his ear, transmitting to the men on his encrypted mobile phone, which used a digital band and could not be picked up on the terrorists' walkie-talkies. While he spoke he looked through the scope of his Remington 700 bolt-action rifle and whispered, not knowing where the terrorists were around him. 'Be advised. I've got Arabic radio traffic in the vicinity. Within five hundred yards. Possibly much less. I only hear two voices speaking, and I do not have eyes on anyone at this time.'

He watched Jack Ryan continue to drink his beer on the porch swing, the last of the evening's light fading by the minute. 'That's enough, Jack. Get back in, you're a sitting duck out there.'

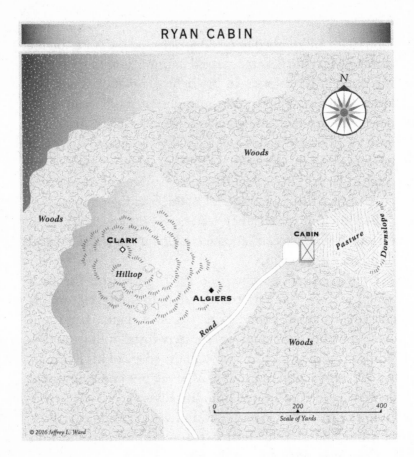

N

Woods

Woods

Downslope

CLARK

CABIN

Pasture

Hilltop

ALGIERS

Road

Woods

0   200   400
Scale of Yards

© 2016 Jeffrey L. Ward

Jack stood up from the porch swing and idly walked back inside the cabin, closing the door behind him.

Clark scanned his weapon's eight-power scope in all directions. The light was bad, but he didn't want to take his eye out of the weapon to use his handheld thermal device, lest he see a target that needed to be immediately dispatched. So far he'd seen no threats, but he knew they were out here somewhere.

He was positioned on the ledge of a rocky hilltop that was only partially covered by trees, four hundred yards from the front of the cabin. Below the man-sized ledge was a steep decline of rolling hill covered in brush. This wasn't an ideal location because he had no cover other than the lip of the ledge in front of him, but it was the only place to get good eyes on the entire scene and still have some standoff distance to use his sniper rifle. If he was sighted during a fight, he'd be a sitting duck, and he'd have no quick way to get off the ledge without standing and climbing higher up the hill.

He just hoped he was deep enough in cover that any of these ISIS terrorists wouldn't see him, or step on him, for that matter, because he had no idea where these guys were right now.

Jack's voice came over the earpiece. 'See anything, John?'

'Nothing so far. But if they're in the woods, I won't see them till they get right up on top of you.'

Jack then said, 'Ding?'

Chavez had positioned himself in a long narrow crawl-space attic, with darkened windows on the north side and the south side of the cabin. He could look out only one side or the other, and now he was facing south. 'I've got nothing but some grazing deer. If the deer spook, then we'll know the bad guys are getting close.'

Chavez turned around and went back up to the north side of the cabin, looked out the window there. It took him thirty seconds of crawling to get there. 'No deer to the north. I don't know if that just means there are no deer or if . . . wait one.'

He saw movement deeper in the trees, something darting through bushes. 'John, get a scope on the north-side woods.'

After several seconds Clark's voice came back over the net. 'Nothing. Nothing on thermal, either, but that's thick brush. I'm scanning south now.'

Chavez kept looking to the north through the window for a few minutes, and finally he saw two figures in the darkness there, moving toward the house. 'I've got two pax. Working together, ten yards inside the tree line on the north. Both carrying weapons. I will engage them from here when they get in the open.'

'Roger that,' Jack said. Chavez knew Jack was at the top of the staircase in the cabin, looking down to the main room and the front door. For now, at least, Jack was completely on his own if anyone made it inside the building.

Clark said, 'Once Ding fires, anyone else in the vicinity is going to go loud, so be ready.'

Chavez acknowledged the transmission, flipped the safety off on his suppressed SIG Sauer MPX nine-millimeter, and then he saw the two figures launch to their feet and begin running out of the trees and toward the house. They were twenty-five yards away and slightly to his left when Chavez said, 'Engaging hostiles, north side.'

He jabbed the tip of the suppressor through the old plate-glass window, shattering one of the small panes, and then he fired burst after burst at the men running there. Flame blasted out of the window, illuminating him and his firing position, and just as both men dropped and rolled onto the grass on the north side of the house, the window frame on his left splintered violently.

Chavez dropped to his right onto the wooden-slat floor of the attic as the window burst in completely, showering him with glass, and he heard a Kalashnikov dumping rounds at his position. There was someone else in the woods he'd not seen, and they were letting him have it.

He shouted over the gunfire. 'Two down, but I'm compromised up here and falling back! Unknown number of hostiles in the trees. Be advised, the north side is now open to the enemy!'

Chavez spun around and moved on his knees and elbows through the black crawl space, trying to get back to the south as fast as he could, hoping to get eyes on any targets there.

Abu Musa al-Matari reloaded his AK-103, after just expending an entire magazine at someone shooting from a window inside the cabin. He'd not expected the President's son to have a weapon, or any security, but it was clear now he had one or both. He'd seen his two men on his right fall into the open ground next to the house, and he cursed the Saudi's intelligence product. The folder had suggested this would be an easy kill. Al-Matari considered pulling back, but he and Omar were just twenty-five meters from the cabin now, and he had four more mujahideen around the property. He stood and ran forward, and Omar followed with his Uzi.

They'd made it only halfway across the grass to the side of the building when al-Matari heard a loud grunt behind him. He kept running but looked back over his shoulder, and saw Omar stumbling forward, his entire forehead had been blown off and away. The man's body skidded in the grass and lay still, the Uzi sliding to a stop next to it.

Al-Matari slammed against the side of the log cabin, looked to his left and right, wondering what the fuck was going on here. He knelt down low, then looked back to Omar. From the direction he'd fallen, it was clear he'd been shot from someone firing from the front of the house, so al-Matari carefully and quietly headed around to the back.

Clark racked a fresh round from his five-round magazine into the chamber of his rifle. He then centered his scope back where the one man had fallen, looking for others. He tapped his transmit button. 'Target eliminated, north side. One hostile made it to the cabin on the north. I do *not* have eyes on. Say again, one squirter made it to the north side of the building.'

Sudden cracks of gunfire below him to his right surprised him. He spun to the source, looked over his ledge and saw the flashes of a fully automatic rifle to the south, lower on the same hill he was on, some two hundred yards away. As the fire continued he heard Jack transmit.

'Taking fire from the west! Tearing up the downstairs windows below me. John?'

Quickly Clark centered his bolt-action rifle's scope on the flashes, and squeezed off a .308 round at the gunfire.

The flashes stopped instantly.

Algiers had been ten feet away from the twenty-year-old Pakistani from Caltech when the man stood on the hillside and opened fire on the windows of the cabin, and then, before he'd gone through his first magazine, Algiers saw the man take a round from a high-powered rifle straight through the upper back.

He lay dead on his face in the dark now, skidding a few meters down through the grass.

Algiers spun around to scan up the hill, brought his binos to bear, but it was too dark for him to see anyone there until they fired again.

He transmitted on the walkie-talkie to the rest of the group. 'Shooter at the top of the hill to the west. Four hundred meters from the cabin. Tripoli, can you see him?'

Tripoli was the only attacker still in the woods. He was on the south side, while his partner, a kid named Parvez who was from Pakistan by way of medical school in California, had made it to the cabin and was now moving around to the front. Once Parvez heard through the walkie-talkie that there was a shooter on the hill with a view to the front of the cabin, the young man dropped flat on the ground, terrified to move.

Tripoli aimed his RPG-7 at the hill, pointed it directly at the top, and waited. He took his hand off the front of the weapon and transmitted through his walkie-talkie's headset. 'Algiers, if you can find cover, I want you to fire at the hilltop to give me a target.'

In seconds the flashes of gunfire lower on the hillside started, along with the echo of an AK firing cyclic. Algiers kept shooting, but Tripoli just looked through the iron sights of his big rocket-propelled-grenade launcher, holding steady on the hilltop.

Finally there was a muzzle flash just below the crest of the hill, and Tripoli pressed the trigger on the RPG-7. As soon as he fired he threw his big weapon into the air away from him, and he ran toward the cabin with empty arms as fast as he could.

He didn't want to be anywhere near the source of the incredible flash his RPG-7 created in case someone saw it.

Chavez had just arrived at the rear window when an RPG launched in the trees below him, lighting up the entire scene.

He saw the rocket-propelled grenade's flaming trail race up toward the hillside to his right, but he had no view of the impact. He then saw the man running from the launch with empty hands, but before Chavez could get his gun through the window to fire, the man disappeared below his position. Chavez shattered out the window and opened fire straight down, holding his sub gun out the window and dumping rounds without looking.

He heard a scream, and thought he might have hit someone there, but his weapon went dry before he could rake the area some more.

He knelt below the window to reload again.

John Clark saw the flash of the grenade launch in the distant trees, and the pinprick of swirling light coming right at him. Instantly he knew he'd been set up. The flashes lower on the hillside were just to get him to fire his weapon and reveal his position, and he'd done as the Islamic State fighters had planned.

The rocketeer's aim was true. Even from this distance John could tell that it was going to make a direct hit on his position.

He knew the incredible impact would come, and there was nothing for him to do but cover his head, open his mouth to minimize the shock wave's effect on his body, and take it.

Unless he threw himself off the ledge. It was the only way to get far away quickly.

John crawled forward on his knees and elbows, tumbled over his rifle on its bipod, and went off the side of the ledge. He thought about Sandy and Patsy, his wife and daughter, and he wished like hell he'd called them today to tell them he loved them.

*

Jack Ryan, Jr, had been completely out of the battle going on around him for the past minute. He just squatted low near the top of the stairs, eyeing the front door and the great room to his right, and listening to his two compatriots fight for their lives. He heard the explosion to the west.

Chavez came through his earpiece. 'Ryan, you've got *at least* one squirter on the south side, as well as the one on the north. They are outside the cabin and I do *not* have eyes. I can hear shooting and explosion to the west, too. Clark, you have eyes on the shooter there?'

There was no response. 'John?'

Jack said, 'Ding, I've got a good position. Go help Clark.'

Chavez did not respond.

Before Jack could speak again, the front door to the cabin began splintering and pocking with incoming gunfire. Seconds later, a baseball-sized object flew through the window, slamming against the flat screen on the far wall. Jack retreated a few feet up the stairs, and the grenade detonated below on his right. It destroyed what was left of the great room, but he was safe from the blast.

He had just taken a step back down to increase his field of view when the door opened below and in front of him and two men reached in from opposite sides, one holding a submachine gun, the other a pistol.

Jack aimed his MPX at the gun on the right and fired, but missed, slamming his rounds into the sturdy walls of the luxury log cabin. The enemy fire all went straight into the main room, which meant they didn't know he was on the stairs.

Shit, Jack thought. *Until I just fired blindly at them. Now they know where I am.*

As he considered leaving the stairs altogether and falling

back to the upstairs hallway, a second grenade came sailing through the front door, right toward the top of the stairwell where Jack crouched. It was a perfect throw, giving him no time to back up the steps and get around the corner or dive down the stairs. He stood up fully, kicked at the spinning grenade, and sent it rocketing back down where it came from.

As soon as it was moving away from him he dropped flat on his back on the stairs.

The grenade bounced once on the hardwood floor and then detonated right in front of the doorway. Jack could hear a scream of agony even over the ringing in his ears.

But a second man spun in now, and fired at Jack with a pistol, holding it in his right hand while his left dangled at his side. Jack returned fire while still lying on his back near the top of the stairs, firing down between his open legs at the wounded man, taking him in the chest before he dropped to his knees, dropped his gun, then fumbled to get his hand onto a detonator swinging on a cable from his right sleeve.

Jack pulled his trigger, but his weapon was empty. He started to reach down to grab his pistol, then remembered he'd passed it to Davi, who was now down at the far end of the hall, hiding in the bathtub with Jack's sister.

'*Fuck,*' Jack said – there was no way the S-vest wasn't going to rip him to shreds from this distance.

Ding Chavez appeared in the hall right over Jack's head, and he shot the wounded man at the bottom of the stairs, then shot him again and again when he realized he held a detonator in his hand.

The man fell onto his face, Ding grabbed Jack by the drag handle of his vest, and then pulled him up the stairs and around the corner.

Two seconds after they made it to cover, the vest detonated below them.

'You hit?' Chavez shouted it over the ringing in his ears.

'No,' Jack shouted back. His own ears were ringing loudly. 'Where's Clark?' Jack asked as he began reloading his SIG.

'He's off comms. Out there somewhere. I tried to get out on the roof but took fire from the west.' Ding said, 'I think John got hit with an RPG.'

Jesus Christ! We have to get to him.'

When Jack had reloaded and aimed his gun back around the corner toward the front door, Ding reloaded his own weapon. 'We didn't figure for so many shooters. Have you seen al-Matari?'

'No.'

Chavez said, 'I shot some guys to the north. He might be one of them.'

They both listened for a moment. There was no more shooting. Chavez said, 'I'm going for Clark. Check on your sister.'

Ding launched to his feet and ran down the stairs to look for Clark. Jack stood up as well, and had made it only a few steps up the hallway before he heard a series of loud noises from the master bedroom.

First, his sister screaming.

This was followed instantly by a pair of gunshots.

Jack ran as fast as he could up the hall.

71

Chavez raced out the front of the house with his SMG on his shoulder, and found himself face-to-face with a dark figure rushing up the driveway in his direction. The figure raised a weapon in surprise, though clearly the last thing this guy had expected to see was one of the defenders of the cabin charging out the front door.

Chavez was faster, and he took the terrorist in the chest with a two-round burst. He charged up to the man as he fell, kicked the man's Kalashnikov away, and knelt over him, rolling him onto his back.

The man was alive, just, and Ding needed at least one survivor, but as soon as he felt the man's back and realized he was wearing a suicide vest, Ding rose up quickly and blasted the man through the skull. He then raced on toward the hill where Clark had been positioned, desperate to find his friend.

Jack ran headlong into the master bedroom as fast as he could, frantic to save his sister. When he got there, however, he saw a man standing in the entrance to the bathroom swiveling a pistol on an outstretched arm right in his direction. Jack dove into a forward roll, a shot rang out, and then Jack rolled back up into a combat crouch and put the red dot sight of his MPX on the shooter's face.

Davi stood there in the doorway, Sally holding on to him from behind and looking out past his shoulder. 'No!' she screamed.

Both Davi and Jack lowered their weapons quickly.

'My God!' Davi shouted. 'I'm sorry, Jack!' He tossed the pistol on the ground, aware he'd almost shot his future brother-in-law.

Jack stood. 'I told you to stay in the bathroom! What the hell were you shooting at back here?'

Sally lifted a shaking hand and pointed a finger to the corner of the bedroom, near the sliding glass door to the balcony that looked to the east. There, a man in a black windbreaker and black pants lay on his side, a pistol inches from his fingertips. He was clean-shaven, forty years old or so, and he blinked over distant eyes, showing Jack he was alive, but barely.

Jack moved to him, knelt down, and secured the pistol. He then felt the man's jacket to see if he was wearing a suicide vest.

'No,' Jack said aloud. 'Of course you aren't wearing an S-vest. The leaders of your band of shitheads get *others* to sacrifice themselves, don't they?'

Abu Musa al-Matari just blinked again; then he looked up at Jack. Blood dripped out of his mouth.

Jack searched him quickly, but as he did so he said, 'Sally. I need this guy alive.'

Davi protested. 'He came up over the balcony, he tried to kill us.'

'I know,' he said. 'Congratulations. You just shot the chief lieutenant for North American affairs for ISIS's Foreign Intelligence Bureau.' He stood back up and turned to al-Matari. 'I'd love to watch him die, but he knows things we need to know.'

Olivia moved to start treating the man, and as she did so, Chavez came through Jack's earpiece. 'I found Clark. He's alive and conscious but he looks like shit.'

'Roger that,' Jack said. 'Is the area clear?'

'Seems to be.'

Jack said, 'Okay, I'm sending you a doctor.' He turned to Davi, and pulled his medical kit off his chest rig. Unzipping it and dumping it on the bed, he said, 'Davi, I need you to help my friend out front. Sally, this asshole is yours.'

The two doctors quickly began grabbing dressings, compresses, tourniquets, and other important items. Davi raced out of the room.

Olivia said, 'Pick him up and put him on the bed. Make him comfortable.'

'He's a terrorist, he doesn't need to be comfortable.'

'Right now, he's my patient,' she said. 'Do what I tell you.'

Jack wanted to tell her that didn't really change the fact the man was a terrorist, but he left it alone, scooped al-Matari up, and dumped him roughly on the bed.

'He's shot through the lung!' Olivia protested. 'Be careful!'

'We just need him alive, Sal. Not happy.' Jack pulled a pair of zip ties off his chest and secured the man's hands on the bedposts. 'This is so he doesn't wring your neck while you're saving his life.'

Olivia ripped away his shirt, felt around his back for an exit wound. It was there; her hand came back bloody. As she began cleaning the wounds to seal them, she looked up at her brother. 'Who *are* you, Jack?'

'We'll talk later, when this guy isn't around.'

Al-Matari coughed. 'Yes . . . who *are* you, Jack?'

Jack knelt over him. 'I'm the end of your road. You don't get to be a hero *or* a martyr today, Musa.'

'You'll never get me to talk.'

'Me? *I'm* not the one asking you anything. Honestly, I don't give a damn what you know. But others do, and they are going to take you somewhere and pump your twisted brain so full of drugs that you won't be able to lie about anything.'

Chavez had found Clark lying in a heap thirty yards down the hill from the ledge. He'd bounced roughly down the darkened hillside, just below the rocket's impact, so although he hadn't taken the effect of the blast into his body, he'd tumbled down in an avalanche of soil and rock. Chavez held a light on Clark and admonished him each time he tried to sit or stand, while Davi checked him for serious injuries. Davi determined the dirt-covered senior citizen likely had a concussion, as well as a broken rib or two, and a sprained or broken wrist. But miraculously he'd suffered no more damage than that.

The two ambulatory men helped Clark back down the hill to the cabin, and by then Jack had called Mary Pat Foley directly to let her know that a wounded but alive Abu Musa al-Matari could be picked up at a log cabin in the Blue Ridge Mountains, and the only charge to the US government for this item would be transport for five to the DC area.

A pair of UH-60 Black Hawk helicopters from the FBI's Tactical Aviation Unit landed behind the cabin forty minutes later. On board were medics prepared to keep al-Matari alive, and to make John Clark a little more comfortable, as the injury to his ribs was making it more painful to breathe by the minute.

The first aircraft took off as soon as it was loaded, but the second wasn't going anywhere for a while. It had deposited a dozen members of the FBI's vaunted Hostage Rescue Team. They spent the entire evening and part of the next morning combing the area with their night-observation devices for other terrorists, but all they found were seven dead bodies and three vehicles, two of which had several rolls of carpet over some cases in the back. They found weapons and ammunition, but when the HRT men pulled out the carpets from the vehicles, they were astonished to find four Igla-7 surface-to-air missiles, each one easily capable of taking down a jumbo jet.

72

Captain Carrie Ann Davenport had been back in theater for a full month, but she still had the garden party in College Park on her mind. The dead and the wounded. The man she'd killed using the pistol that her father had given her, insisting that she carry it on her body at all times, because the President of the United States, Jack Ryan, had said that it was the right of every member of the armed services.

Her dad had been right about her carrying the gun, and she'd never hear the end of it, but she wouldn't complain about his reminding her that he told her so.

Something else had happened the day of the attack. The good-looking guy working on his master's in history had asked her out for coffee that night. They'd both been rattled by the events and they both felt like they needed someone who'd been there to talk to.

Since that night they'd e-mailed each other almost daily, and they'd even Skyped once, which was an ordeal for her because she was at a forward operating base in southern Turkey, on the Syrian border, and it was hard to look her best.

Matt didn't seem to care, he joked that for some reason her loose-fitting desert aircrew battle dress uniform turned him on, and she'd laughed harder at that than she'd laughed at anything in weeks.

As she sat for the briefing for tonight's mission she had Matt on her mind, but only at first. When the major began explaining what was going on this evening, she instantly focused fully on the job at hand.

New intelligence had come out that had pinpointed the physical location of the Islamic State's public relations division, the Global Islamic Media Front. The GIMF was responsible for nearly one hundred percent of all the high-end propaganda coming out of the Islamic State into the US these days, it had its own television stations, radio stations, websites, and social media arm. This meant it was responsible for the remote-radicalized fighters springing up around the world, disaffected young men and women who pledged allegiance to the head of ISIS, then went out and committed atrocities. Since the attack in College Park over a month earlier, al-Matari's attacks in America had diminished greatly, although sporadic attacks continued in America and in Europe. Many suggested the continuing terrorism was all done by copycats, but the United States had said nothing about the capture or killing of the terrorist leader.

Still, shutting down the GIMF, destroying its equipment and infrastructure, would be key in reducing the draw of the organization worldwide. And killing its members would erase the technical know-how that had led to the success of the global outreach of the Islamic State.

Involved in the strike into the heart of ISIS-occupied Syria tonight would be four US Navy F/A-18c Hornets flown off the USS *Harry S. Truman* in the Mediterranean, six Army A-10 Thunderbolts flown out of southern Turkey, as well as an unspecified number of special mission units on the ground near the town of Ratla, just south of Raqqa. These ground forces would be watching Highway 4, the main artery out of Raqqa, because they had intelligence on the make and model of the Islamic State GIMF leadership's vehicles, a remarkably specific piece of intel.

Carrie Ann couldn't help wondering if all this plum intelligence indicated America had the bastard Abu Musa al-Matari in hand, and he was singing like a bird.

Just the possibility of this made her happy.

The special operations units would be extracted by helos from the 160th Special Operations Aviation Regiment, but two Pyro AH-64E gunships from Carrie Ann's regiment would support tonight's attack by flying support for any medevac flights in case one of the aircraft was shot down.

Her job would be dangerous, of course, but she thought it unlikely she and Troy would see any more action than flying a wheel formation with another Apache over the Syrian desert and watching the fireworks from thirty miles away.

It was a shame, Carrie Ann thought.

She was in the mood to kill some of those sons of bitches tonight.

At twenty-two hundred hours, Captain Davenport made one last check to her harness, tightening herself down in the front cockpit, and she scanned the three screens and 240 separate control buttons there. She and Chief Warrant Officer Troy Oakley behind her had spent the last forty-five minutes preflighting, and now they had their aircraft ready and their clearance for takeoff.

Oakley spoke into his intercom. 'You ready, Captain?' Oakley was twenty-one years older than Davenport, but she was still his superior officer.

'Let's do it, Oak.'

They taxied out to the short runway, and Oakley eased up the collective with his left hand. As the Apache rolled forward he pressed down gently on his left pedal, countering the torque of the blades above him by increasing the power to the tail rotor.

As he pulled the collective up, adding power to the main rotor blades, his left foot pushed down farther on the pedal. When he touched the cyclic between his knees forward, the blades changed angle above, and the big attack helicopter began rolling forward faster down the runway. Now he used both pedals to keep the nose of the aircraft steady as it picked up speed.

In the cockpit's front seat, Carrie Ann watched with her hands on her knees. She had all the controls to fly Pyro 1-1 that her backseater did; in fact she did a fair amount of flying. Similarly, Oakley had the power to launch missiles and rockets, and fire the cannon from the backseat.

She almost never let Oakley fire, however, and if they did luck into any targets on this mission, tonight would be no different. Carrie Ann loved Oakley like an older brother, she'd do anything in the world for the man, but *she* fired the weapons in Pyro 1-1.

With the collective at full power and the speed at forty-five knots, Oakley pulled back slightly on the cyclic, and the eight-ton Apache lifted into the air. Just behind it, Pyro 1-2 lifted off seconds later.

They stayed low, left the FOB in an eastwardly heading to fool any ISIS spies nearby with a cell phone and a mission to report helicopter flights into Syria, and then, ten minutes later, they began climbing as they turned to the south for their standoff station thirty miles northeast of Raqqa.

Ninety minutes after takeoff, Davenport and Oakley flew over empty desert in complete darkness, with Pyro 1-2 and Freight Train 1-1, a Chinook CH-47D, both doing the same things at different altitudes. Carrie Ann caught glimpses of the other aircraft through her FLIR monitor from time to time, but mostly her eyes were on the southwest, where a fireworks show of attacking and defending was taking place.

She couldn't hear the Navy radio traffic, but she could listen in on the A-10s following on to the attack in Raqqa firing Hellfire missiles, and it sounded like the mission was going to plan.

All the US aircraft were using Hellfires only, which caused a relatively small amount of damage as compared to JDAMs or big iron bombs, and other ordnance that the F-18s and A-10s could carry. But the target location was in downtown Raqqa, and collateral damage had to be kept to a minimum, so this necessitated several runs from each aircraft to pick the buildings apart, as opposed to a single pass from a couple of Hornets to flatten the area with two-thousand-pound bombs.

The enemy was firing a huge number of ZU-23 antiaircraft cannons, their tracers arced into the sky, but so far the Navy and Army fixed-wing attack had suffered no casualties.

Even the report from an A-10 pilot that a Stinger missile had locked on to his aircraft turned into a non-event, as the weapon apparently lost the lock because of hills or buildings.

Forty-five minutes after the attack began, all the aircraft had egressed the area. The Pyro and Freight Train flights were ordered to reposition to the south while the Black Hawks of the 160th came in to pull their special mission units out of the area, so they set course for another spot of desert, where they would fly another pattern.

Carrie Ann watched while a pair of high-tech Black Hawk helos raced far beneath her, just over the rolling sand, on their way south to pick up their Delta Force or SEAL Team operators.

Seconds after Carrie Ann lost sight of the Black Hawks, the combat controller came over her headset, telling her he was patching her through to the JTAC frequency on the ground in Ratla. This surprised her, as the Joint Terminal Attack Controller was embedded with the special operations troops, and he was in charge of directing aircraft and artillery fire on targets. He might have been used during the attack phase of tonight's mission, although Ratla was far enough away from the target location to where she doubted it. But she couldn't imagine why he wanted to speak with Pyro flight, especially since his extraction helos were on the way.

Seconds later a crackling voice came over her headset. 'Pyro One-One, this is Lethal. How copy?'

'Pyro One-One. Solid copy. Send traffic, Lethal.'

'I am a JTAC embedded with SF.' He read off his grid coordinates to her and she typed them into her computer. 'I have no more air assets in the area, but multiple targets just appeared, my sector. A convoy of eight vehicles, confirmed squirters from target location.' He read off the grid and she tapped this in, saw on her moving map display that the vehicles were on Highway 4 and heading east, between the towns of Ratla and just south of the Euphrates River. JTAC asked, 'Are you available to prosecute these targets at this time? Over.'

Troy could hear the conversation, and he confirmed they had thirty-five minutes of flying time.

Freight Train was armed only with door gunners, so Pyro 1-2 would have to return with the Chinook to Turkey. This left Carrie Ann and Troy alone to fly south, into ISIS territory, to attack the convoy.

She did not hesitate. 'Affirmative, Lethal. We are one Apache with eight Hellfires, seventy-two rockets, and nine hundred dual-use cannon rounds. We are on the way. ETA eleven minutes.'

'Roger that. I'll talk you right to them. We are waving off our extraction until you smoke these guys.'

Carrie Ann's heart began pounding against the steel plate on her chest. Troy came over the intercom, all business, giving her his plan for hitting the highway from the east, so that they could rake the length of the convoy and maximize their effectiveness.

Thirteen minutes later they banked hard to the east at an altitude of only one thousand feet, and Carrie Ann selected a Hellfire missile. When the convoy rolled out of a village, still heading east just south of the Euphrates, she said, 'Firing Hellfire,' and launched at the lead technical. The plan was to destroy the first vehicle and then send wave after wave of Hydra rockets into the convoy.

The Hellfire struck the technical, blowing it apart and whiting out the FLIR screen for an instant, then pilot Troy Oakley went to maximum speed. Through the targeting system over Davenport's right eye, Oakley could see red crosshairs over his own aiming device that told him exactly where his front-seater was aiming. Through this he could line up the rockets directly on her intended target.

'Firing,' she said again, her voice clipped and intense. A dozen Hydras launched in quick succession, and raced across the highway below toward their target two kilometers to the west.

Before the first even struck, Carrie Ann called, 'Cannon!' and switched now to her cannon. This she could aim herself just by moving her head, and she fired burst after burst at the convoy.

On her FLIR she could see multiple explosions down the length of the convoy from the rockets, and then the cannon fire tore through them, eviscerating the soft-skinned vehicles. She could see individuals running off the highway into fields along the Euphrates, but they would have to turn for another pass before taking out any of the ISIS operatives on foot.

Oakley began lining up for a pass from the west, when warning sensors shrieked in the cockpit, announcing a radar lock on Pyro 1-1.

Oakley shouted, 'SAM!' as soon as he knew a shoulder-fired surface-to-air missile was coming their way.

The automatic countermeasures on the Apache began launching flares as Oakley put the aircraft into a steep dive for speed and a corkscrew to outfox the approaching missile. Carrie Ann grabbed on to handles and watched a cultivated field fill up her windscreen and grow larger by the second. She closed her eyes, certain they would auger into the dirt, but Oakley pulled out of the dive and leveled out, sending Carrie Ann pressing deeply into her seat and her stomach retching.

The SAM passed by, but now they were only fifty feet off the ground and racing over the highway, just a couple hundred yards from anyone who survived the onslaught of Hellfire, cannon, and rocket fire. Carrie Ann saw tracer fire from heavy machine guns right over her, dancing by her cockpit from left to right, and then she heard a rapid punching sound below her feet.

Through the intercom she heard Oakley call out to her in a hoarse voice. 'Carrie! Your ship!'

In the front seat Carrie Ann was surprised by Troy's call, but she took her eyes out of her weapons screens and looked instead out the front glass. Simultaneously she grabbed the cyclic with her right hand and the collective with her left.

'My ship!' she said. She was about to ask just why Oakley was handing piloting duties over to her when he spoke again. His voice was weaker this time.

'I'm hit.'

'Where are you hit?'

'Took a . . . took a shot through the canopy. Might have ricocheted, but it's got me in the neck. I'm bleeding pretty good.'

Jesus,' she said. 'We're heading back.'

'Negative,' Oakley said. 'Press the attack!'

Captain Davenport ignored her backseater and raced north away from the highway, low over the Euphrates, as more tracer fire whipped around her from multiple directions.

'Press the attack,' he said again.

'When we get back we can watch the gun cams together. We took out every one of those eight vehicles, and seventy-five percent of the personnel. That's a good night's work.'

Oakley did not respond.

'Oak? Hang in there, Oak, you good?'

'Roger that,' he said, but she could tell he was about to pass out.

And then she looked down at her screen, and saw her oil pressure dropping.

Captain Carrie Ann Davenport landed the wounded Apache in the middle of the open desert ten minutes later, raised the canopy, and unfastened her harness. The 160th Black Hawk helicopters that picked up the special operations forces in Ratla were minutes out from her position and inbound, and there were multiple Special Forces-trained medics on board.

In the meantime, she knew she had to stop Oakley's bleeding and get him unhooked and ready for transport.

She crawled over the backseat, pulling a rag from her cargo pocket as she did so. The blood covering the left side of Oakley's body was incredible, visible in the soft orange light of the controls and displays in front of him. He was unconscious or dead, she did not know which, but she would treat him the best she could, no matter what. She pressed the towel hard against his neck with her right hand, hopefully stanching the blood flow, and with her left she unhooked his harness.

It was twelve feet down from Oakley's seat to the sand, and there was no way in hell any front-seater, much less a five-foot-four, 120-pound female front-seater, could get a wounded pilot down from there without help, so Carrie Ann didn't even try. She just used her med kit to cut away his ABDUs, minimize the blood loss, and get controls, wires, and anything else out of the way that would slow down his movement to a hospital.

A single Black Hawk landed while the second provided top cover, and Carrie climbed back into the front seat to shut down the aircraft, getting herself out of the way while three fit men with beards fought to get the unconscious man out of his seat down to the stubby weapons pylon, and then handed off to four other men on the ground. He was placed on a backboard and rushed over to the waiting UH-64, and Carrie grabbed her rifle, Oakley's rifle, and ran after them.

In the Black Hawk on the way back into Turkey she held Oakley's hand tightly as she knelt down over him. Medics worked frantically on his neck, as well as another wound they'd found above his left knee.

A young man in full battle rattle and a beard seated just

behind her touched her on her back, and she turned around to look at him. He said, 'Our docs are the best. Your dad's gonna be fine.'

She nodded at the joke, started to look back down to Oakley, and the young man said, 'I'm Lethal.' He was the JTAC who had talked her into the target.

'Davenport,' she said.

'Just have to say, Captain, you fucking kicked ass back there. Your ship pretty much single-handedly destroyed any chance that ISIS could get their propaganda machine back up and running after the Navy blew the shit out of their building.'

She thanked him, knelt back down over Oakley, and saw his eyes were open and fixed on hers now. She smiled and tears dripped onto his face. 'Hey!'

He smiled back. 'Hey.'

'JSOC just said you and me kicked ass. That's not so bad, is it?'

He tried to shake his head, but the backboard wouldn't let him. He smiled. 'Not half bad at all, Captain.'

An hour later, an A-10 was launched out of Turkey to destroy Pyro 1-1 with a five-hundred-pound bomb, making certain the enemy didn't have anything to use as a propaganda weapon.

At roughly the same time the Apache blew apart in the desert, Chief Warrant Officer Troy Oakley died on an operating table at Incirlik Air Base.

73

Alexandru Dalca had remained handcuffed on the long flight, and he was pretty sure he'd been given something that made him sleep, because when he woke on touchdown he felt especially groggy. But he shook it off as the plane taxied and finally jolted to a stop.

A man sat down in front of him; in the past few weeks, Dalca had gotten good at telling what was happening on the other side of his blindfold.

The man spoke with derision in his voice. 'Okay, buddy. This is your stop. The President promised you would be released as soon as you gave us everything we asked for. You did your part, so now we are doing ours. You are free to go.'

His blindfold was removed, and he blinked several times to see the inside of the same airplane he'd first seen over a month earlier, the day he'd been shanghaied in Romania by American intelligence, and brought to the United States. Since then he'd been kept locked in safe houses, interviewed and questioned at length, often in marathon eighteen-hour sessions.

But now, to their credit, the Americans were fulfilling their side of the bargain. He checked his pockets and saw he had only some euros, his passport, and a few other things, and he wore the same clothes he wore when he'd been kidnapped, but none of this mattered. He just had to get to a computer or a bank, because he still had $11 million in offshore accounts.

Without a word he stood up from the chair on unsteady legs, walked past the bearded men in the cabin toward the open hatch, and went down the jet stairs to the hot tarmac. He looked around. He had no idea where in the world he was, but he didn't figure it mattered much. He was out of the USA. He was free.

The stairs closed up behind him and the jet began to roll.

Dalca started walking to a terminal a hundred meters away.

Inside the aircraft Midas looked at Dom Caruso. 'How long you give it till he figures out how fucked he is?'

Caruso smiled. 'Not long at all, man. He's a smart cookie. Once he finds out where we dropped him, he'll know he's screwed.'

Captain Helen Reid pushed the throttle forward and the Hendley Associates jet took off from Hong Kong International just fifteen minutes after landing.

At the same time a Gulfstream 550 took off from an airport a few miles to the west, a CIA employee sat in a dim sum restaurant in the Tsim Sha Tsui neighborhood of Hong Kong. Across from him at the little table was a high-ranking member of China's Ministry of State Security. It was an odd meal, but each man knew the identity of the other, so there was no real mystery between the two.

The American's name was Spicer, and he sipped his Tsingtao beer and looked across at his tablemate. 'We wanted to let you know that we are currently hunting very hard for a Romanian national by the name of Alexandru Dalca.'

The name meant nothing to the Chinese intelligence officer, and a cock of his head confirmed it.

Spicer added, 'We're pulling out all the stops. We haven't found him yet, but believe me, Fang, we'll get this guy.'

Fang had been delivered intelligence before by other agencies, and he realized that was going on right now. 'Very well. But . . . why are you telling me this?'

'Because we think your organization might be looking for him, too. We want to be careful we don't accidentally bump into each other and cause an . . . an incident.'

'I see,' said Fang, but he did not.

'What we are prepared to do is back off, for a week, and allow your organization to look for him . . . if that is something you are interested in doing. Purely for the safety and security of both of our nations.'

Fang nodded thoughtfully, though the truth was he couldn't fathom what was going on. But it didn't matter. He had been in the job long enough to know he was being passed something that he was simply supposed to pass on to his higher-ups. The Americans had a hidden agenda here, and if he had to make an educated guess, it had to do with America wanting this guy taken out of action, without America having to do it themselves.

He had no idea why the Ministry of State Security should care about any of this, but he smiled at Spicer and said, 'I will convey your interesting proposal to officials in my organization. I assume you would like some sort of informal reply?'

Spicer said, 'Not necessary. In fact, we request that we know nothing else of your actions on the matter. As I said, we will wait one week, and then we will pursue this man with the full force of our capabilities.'

Fang sipped his own beer. 'Would you have any idea where this man you are looking so hard for might be found?'

Spicer shrugged his shoulders. 'I don't know, but if I just had to take a wild guess, I'd say he's walking through Terminal One of Hong Kong International Airport right now, wearing a white shirt, khaki pants, and a black jacket. He'll probably be sweating heavily, looking for a place to do some banking. After that he'll spend as little time in HK as possible, before booking a flight out of the country.' Spicer downed the rest of his beer and said, 'Only speculation on my part, you understand.'

Fang nodded slowly. 'Of course.'

Spicer walked out of the restaurant a minute later with all the confidence in the world that Alexandru Dalca would be picked up in minutes. Other than the United States, no nation on earth had more against Alex Dalca than China. The danger that he could reveal something to the Americans about their operation to out American agents inside China would be bad for them, for the simple reason the operation was ultimately hijacked by ISIS and led to the death of many Americans.

Yes, China was after Dalca just as the United States had been after Dalca. But China had made no pledge to the man, and had nothing to gain by letting him live.

Spicer hailed a cab. The American CIA officer figured the Romanian would be dead by the end of the day.

74

The light over the camera turned red at exactly eight p.m., and President Jack Ryan, seated behind the Resolute Desk in the Oval Office, addressed his nation.

'Good evening. Tonight I want to tell you about some recent events of national and international importance. Several weeks ago, agents of the United States of America captured Abu Musa al-Matari, alive, here in America. Many details of his capture and subsequent incarceration must be kept secret to protect sources and methods, but I can say some things.

'Through interviews with him, as well as the hard work of our military, intelligence, and diplomatic communities, we have uncovered key details about the terrorist attacks by the so-called Islamic State that have been carried out at home and abroad over the past several weeks.

'An intelligence leak of massive proportions took place here in the US just over four years ago. It involved files of the Office of Personnel Management, and included a treasure trove of information about America's federal employees. This hack was not perpetrated by a state actor, but rather by a company in India that an American firm with security clearances improperly partnered with. The material was copied by the Indian firm and kept on a computer server in India, and for several years this material was not exploited. Recently, however, the Indian company was compromised by a group of Romanian hackers. They obtained the data, realized what it was they had, and one employee of this concern sold some of the material to various foreign actors around the world with aims against the United States.

'We understand how the material was stolen and have made steps to make sure this will never happen again. We do believe we have retrieved all the electronic files, and are reasonably certain there exist no other copies, but we might never be able to know for sure.

'The loss of this material was, by any measure, an egregious failure of the United States government, and for that I am truly, truly sorry.

'Anyone who works in the military, federal law enforcement, or intelligence services in the United States swears an oath to America that states, in part, "I do solemnly swear that I will support and defend the Constitution of the United States against all enemies, foreign and domestic, and I will bear true faith and allegiance to the same."

'Millions of men and women have served this nation with that pledge, with their faith, allegiance, and lives, but their best efforts were not returned to them by their government. Some, sadly, have recently lost their lives due to this fact. We owe all these men and women more than we can ever repay them. I owe them better. This shouldn't have happened, but we *will* take steps to protect those still compromised.

'Upon learning the details of the OPM breach, my first inclination was to go back to the use of typewriters and then destroy the typewriter ribbons, holding all these crucial, sensitive documents in vaults protected by men sworn to preserve them and equipped to do so, no matter what the threat.

'But unfortunately, the world has moved on, and guys, guns, and gates alone can't keep this material safe. We must work harder and put more effort into this, and I pledge to do that with my remaining time as your president.

'We also learned via interviews with Abu Musa al-Matari that the source for the material that exposed the members of the military and intelligence communities was a man al-Matari met in Kosovo some nine months ago. Through the diligent work of CIA director Jay Canfield, and DNI director Mary Pat Foley, along with the efforts of Attorney General Dan Murray, we have identified this man via human intelligence assets, as well as travel and immigration records. The man's name is Sami bin Rashid, and he is not a member of ISIS, but rather a Saudi Arabian national and an employee of the Gulf Cooperation Council, an organization set up to further the political and economic aims of several oil-producing states. Our investigations show us that the objective of this man from the GCC in setting up the attacks in America was *not* to improve ISIS's power and reach in the world. Instead, it was a cynical plot to increase the price of oil and to bring US troops back into the Middle East en masse, to hold back Iran, the sworn enemy of many of these nations.

'Right now, many disaffected Muslims in the world are considering radicalization, joining ISIS, taking up arms against the West. Many have already done so, and they have paid a high price. Each day here in America we are seeing the after-effects of al-Matari's operation in the form of copy-cats. It is important for those considering such a path to understand that all the self-radicalized here in America who followed al-Matari's actions to their death were not doing it in the name of the global caliphate as they had thought, but they were instead doing the bidding of cynical Saudi Arabian business interests.

'I wonder if those seeking martyrdom will actually receive martyrdom while killing and dying for billionaire businessmen. If you pick up a gun today with aims of terrorism in the United States, you aren't working for ISIS, you are working for fat cats in the wealthy Persian Gulf. Reflect on that a moment.'

Jack Ryan then said, 'The question remains: Were the actions of this man bin Rashid sanctioned by his government, or was he a lone wolf? Is Saudi Arabia a problematic partner, or a determined foe?

'As yet we do not have that answer, the Saudis have denied in the strongest terms any involvement, and as President I see it as my job to tell you when we do *not* have proof of something, the same as when we do have proof. We will not punish Saudi Arabia diplomatically or economically for the actions of this man, unless new intelligence comes to light that implicates the Saudi Arabian government.'

President Ryan looked quietly into the camera a moment before saying, 'We were able to derive one more key piece of intelligence from the terrorist we captured. The physical location and key players of the Global Islamic Media Front. This is the very sophisticated public relations and propaganda operation that fuels much of ISIS's lore around the world. Through their television stations, websites, and satellite radio networks they have raised the call for thousands of foreigners to go fight in the Middle East, North Africa, or in other regions where ISIS holds territory, or to stay in their homelands and fight via terrorist acts.

'Destroying the Global Islamic Media Front would be an incredible hit to the international reach of this sick cult known as ISIS.

'And less than three hours ago, we did just that. American

warplanes, helicopters, and special operations troops were involved in an operation in Raqqa, Syria, that severely degraded the GIMF's ability to wage war through propaganda.

'During this operation, US Army Chief Warrant Officer Troy David Oakley of Pawtucket, Rhode Island, was tragically killed in combat. Our hearts and prayers go out to this brave American hero. His sacrifice will not be forgotten by the grateful nation he served.

'Please remember . . . those seeking freedom and peace have no greater friend than the United States of America. At home we have successfully assimilated more disparate groups than any other nation in the history of the world. And abroad we have helped our friends, supported our allies, led coalitions against evil from the front.

'But those who would commit terrorism and other atrocities will find no peace from us. Ever. The capture of al-Matari, and the breakup of the plot to use stolen intelligence files against the United States, should indicate this fact to those in the world who are thinking about doing us harm.'

Ryan looked hard into the camera now. 'Believe me, if your cause involves fighting America, we will find you, and *you* will find no safe haven from American justice.'

After the bright lights turned off in the Oval Office, Jack Ryan waited for his lapel mic to be removed, then stood and walked around the desk. He noticed Mary Pat Foley had made her way into the room, and he was surprised to see her. Arnie was there with her, but Arnie was no surprise at all. He would always be there looming during a media event as big as an Oval Office live broadcast. Jack pictured his chief of staff standing there with a hook in his hand as if Ryan were an old vaudevillian and Arnie the stage manager, ready to yank the act off the stage if he did something wrong.

Mary Pat leaned close to the President as the camera and audio people began breaking down the set. 'I thought you'd want to know immediately. Stuart Collier, the CIA operative held by the Iranians for the past few months, has been released to the Swiss. He's out of Iranian airspace.'

Ryan nodded. 'What was the ultimate price?'

'Time will tell, Mr President. We didn't offer anything other than threats of reprisals against Iran. Ultimately I think they see the fact we revealed the Saudis' tangential involvement in the ISIS attacks as a good thing for them, and they are rewarding us.'

'Christ,' Ryan said. 'That's the Middle East. There are enough enemies there that you can't hurt someone you don't like without helping someone you like even less.'

Mary Pat was about to say something, but Ryan put a hand on her arm. 'Mary Pat. It is terrific Collier is out. Good work, and pass that on to Jay for me, too, please. We need to protect Collier for life, of course.'

'Absolutely. Thanks.'

She left the room along with the network media people, then Jack and Arnie sat alone.

'Did you come to rate my performance?' Ryan asked.

'You were fine, but that's not why I'm here. It's official. Homeland Security Secretary Andy Zilko will hand in his resignation in the morning. He doesn't want you to accept it, but he is making the gesture.'

Ryan shrugged. 'He's not the only fall guy for the mistakes that have happened, but it would show character in Zilko if he left. I'll accept his resignation.'

Arnie nodded. 'I'll let him know. He'll probably run for senator or governor in Indiana next election. I'm sure he'll call on you for your support.'

Ryan thought this over a second, though the last thing he ever wanted to think about again was an election of any kind.

He said, 'I think he should try working in the private sector for a change. Someplace where he's held accountable for his actions. If he makes it back into government in a few years that will give him the perspective he needs. We're here for the country, not the other way around.'

Arnie just laughed. 'We've got to get you out of here quick, Jack. People will think you've gone senile with that kind of talk.'

Ryan chuckled. 'Soon, Arnie. Soon.'

Epilogue

Sami bin Rashid couldn't sleep, not even on the Egyptian cotton sheets, not even with the soft mood lighting, and not even in the cool silk pajamas.

It didn't really make sense to him. Though he normally had trouble sleeping on aircraft, tonight should have been different because he was flying on Etihad Airlines and staying in the Residence, the most opulent commercial airline experience on earth. It wasn't a seat; it was two rooms with an en suite bathroom/shower, private concierge service, and gourmet meals created by the onboard chef.

This flight from Dubai to Sydney, Australia, was fourteen hours long, and for the first three hours he'd dined well and read distractedly, but after that he'd had nothing but time to sit and ponder his predicament.

Overtly, at least, the Kingdom of Saudi Arabia considered bin Rashid a pariah; dangerous, toxic. If Riyadh even admitted they knew his location it would be problematic with the Americans, so he'd used a cover legend and documents and enacted a long-arranged but never seriously considered plan to flee somewhere safe.

He'd chosen Australia. Far away and unknown, the last place anyone would look for him.

Of course members of Saudi intelligence knew he was going; he was doing it with their blessing, in fact. He had been more than pleased to hear through back channels that the kingdom just wanted him to lie low for a time; perhaps a few years, and then they would consider working with him again quietly and at arm's reach.

He didn't know what he'd do in Australia, but he had money to do it with, and now he had nothing but time.

So why couldn't he sleep?

He sat up in the bedroom of the Residence, pulled off his sleep mask, and rubbed his eyes.

Al-Matari. *That's why.* The son of a bitch. Somehow he'd fucked up and failed bin Rashid's American operation. President Jack Ryan had crippled the Islamic State by eviscerating their ability to make slick propaganda pieces to draw in new recruits, and by linking the oil-rich states to the Islamic State, giving off the false impression that the whole fucking caliphate was just part of some evil Saudi oil-business scheme.

Ridiculous.

Sami bin Rashid tossed his eye mask on the bed, stormed out of his little bedroom, through his sitting room, and stepped out of the Residence, still in his silk pajamas.

His personal concierge was on him in an instant, a beautiful woman half a head taller than bin Rashid. She was ready to bring him food or drinks, but bin Rashid waved the woman away, and looked around.

He was glad to see the little bar was open; the bartender stood there with only one patron leaning against the half-moon-shaped surface in the center of the first-class cabin.

Bin Rashid stepped up, still wearing his black silk pajamas. 'Give me a drink.'

'Of course, sir. What would you like?'

Bin Rashid did not drink in Dubai, or in Riyadh, but he'd consumed alcohol working in cover as an intel operator in his younger days. He'd turned down offers of champagne from the concierge when he boarded, but now he wanted a drink more than anything in the world, because he did not want to think about al-Matari, and the failed plan to save Saudi Arabia from domestic rot and international Shiite attack.

He looked to the man leaning next to him. A Westerner in his shirtsleeves, pushing seventy. His white hair was thin, and he had a smile on his face.

The man lifted his glass. In English he said, 'If you want to keep it simple and effective, you can't do much better than a vodka on the rocks.'

Bin Rashid nodded, and the bartender started making the drink.

The American reached out a hand. 'I'm Carl, from Denver, Colorado.'

'Mohammed, from Dubai.'

The older American nodded toward the Residence. 'Hell, pal, I spent a big chunk of my retirement on a seat up here in first class, but you got yourself a condo for the night. What kind of work do you do?'

'Consulting,' bin Rashid said. He wasn't in the mood to talk to anyone, least of all a chatty old American.

'Yeah? I do a bit of consulting myself. Thought I'd come down and look around Australia, see what that's all about.'

The vodka on ice was placed in front of the Saudi, along with a tray of salty snacks. He took the drink and sipped it. It burned going down, and he made a face.

The American smiled. 'Let the ice melt a second, softens the blow.'

Bin Rashid nodded, and he left the drink on the bar. The bartender stepped away to talk to passengers who had just sat at one of the small cocktail tables nearby.

'Is that as nice as they say? The Residence?' The man pointed again to the open door to the space.

Bin Rashid said, 'Yes, it is quite nice.'

'Your concierge sure is a looker.'

Bin Rashid turned to regard the woman as she knelt in his sitting room, straightening the pillows on the sofa.

'Yeah,' Carl from Denver said. 'A little young for me, but a guy like you, why not?'

The Saudi looked at the woman a long time. She was, indeed, beautiful. He wondered if perhaps Australia would have women who looked like that. He was a wealthy man . . . maybe he could make things happen there that hadn't happened for him in Dubai, because of his work.

After a full minute of regarding the concierge while she faced away from him, standing in first class, the American said, 'I bet it's just about perfect.'

Bin Rashid was still looking at the woman's ass. Slowly he turned back around to the American. 'I'm sorry?'

'Your drink. Should be nice and cold by now.'

'Ah, yes.' Bin Rashid drank it down.

The American sipped his own. 'How 'bout another? We can drink to new beginnings.'

The Saudi shook his head. 'No, thank you. I must rest.'

He turned and walked away, back toward the Residence.

'Sleep well, then,' the American called out from behind.

Bin Rashid lay back down a minute later, pulled the sleeping mask over his eyes, and tried to think about something other than his failure in the American operation.

Thirty minutes later he was still trying.

And thirty-one minutes later, his failure in the American operation no longer mattered to him.

The heart attack was sudden, and it was massive. He'd not

even managed to sit up. He just lurched there in the bed, let out a short gasp, then dropped back dead, his hands across his chest.

John Clark still could feel the effects of his two vodkas thirty minutes later, but as he looked at his watch, he doubted his effects were anything like what Sami bin Rashid was feeling right about now. Squirting the eyedropper of advanced neurotoxin into the vodka when the Saudi looked at the woman had taken speed, dexterity, and some luck, but nothing like the luck of having the Saudi step up to the bar when Clark assumed the man was sleeping.

The original plan had involved slipping into the Residence unseen and injecting him with a fast-acting heart-stopper, holding a hand over his mouth while he thrashed for several seconds.

That had been no one's first choice, but it would have been preferable to losing him in Sydney.

To make this work Ding Chavez would have had to do the hit while Clark distracted the concierge and the bartender, and this looked like it would have been a tough op in the small and quiet confines of first class, so both Clark and Chavez were happy that bin Rashid made it easy, and the next eight hours of their flight could be spent in utter relaxation here in the opulence of first class.

Sure, an hour or so before landing there would be a shriek from the Residence, stress from the flight crew, and perhaps some delays in deplaning. But flying to Sydney meant there really was no place for the aircraft to divert to on the way, so no one on the flight would be terribly inconvenienced by Clark's actions.

Except for Sami bin Rashid.

Clark looked away from his watch, confident the job was done, and he looked across the width of the darkened cabin and saw Ding checking his own watch. The two men made eye contact for a moment, Clark winked, and Ding smiled back, and then both men reclined their seats as far as they could and closed their eyes.

He just wanted a decent book to read ...

Not too much to ask, is it? It was in 1935 when Allen Lane, Managing Director of Bodley Head Publishers, stood on a platform at Exeter railway station looking for something good to read on his journey back to London. His choice was limited to popular magazines and poor-quality paperbacks – the same choice faced every day by the vast majority of readers, few of whom could afford hardbacks. Lane's disappointment and subsequent anger at the range of books generally available led him to found a company – and change the world.

'We believed in the existence in this country of a vast reading public for intelligent books at a low price, and staked everything on it'
Sir Allen Lane, 1902–1970, founder of Penguin Books

The quality paperback had arrived – and not just in bookshops. Lane was adamant that his Penguins should appear in chain stores and tobacconists, and should cost no more than a packet of cigarettes.

Reading habits (and cigarette prices) have changed since 1935, but Penguin still believes in publishing the best books for everybody to enjoy. We still believe that good design costs no more than bad design, and we still believe that quality books published passionately and responsibly make the world a better place.

So wherever you see the little bird – whether it's on a piece of prize-winning literary fiction or a celebrity autobiography, political tour de force or historical masterpiece, a serial-killer thriller, reference book, world classic or a piece of pure escapism – you can bet that it represents the very best that the genre has to offer.

Whatever you like to read – trust Penguin.